D0306006

READER'S DIGEST
SELECT EDITIONS

The condensations in this volume
are published with the consent of the authors
and the publishers © 2007 Reader's Digest.

www.readersdigest.co.uk

The Reader's Digest Association Limited
11 Westferry Circus Canary Wharf London E14 4HE

For information as to ownership of
copyright in the material of this book,
and acknowledgments, see last page.

Printed in Germany
ISBN 978 0 276 44284 1

SELECTED AND CONDENSED
BY READER'S DIGEST

THE READER'S DIGEST ASSOCIATION LIMITED, LONDON

CONTENTS

Some books are born to be bestsellers; some achieve bestseller status through glowing recommendations; some have bestsellerdom thrust upon them, thanks to a striking publicity campaign. In other words, you can't always judge a book by its prominence on supermarket shelves.

THUNDER BAY

WILLIAM KENT KRUEGER

453

So, when we're picking four new books for Select Editions we look beyond the bestseller charts, carefully trawling publishers' lists for hidden gems, and staying in close touch with a team of Reader's Digest editors across the Atlantic, who frequently spot American talent before it reaches Britain.

It's thanks to our US colleagues that William Kent Krueger (above and below left) is making his debut in this collection of Select Editions. You won't find his novels in UK bookshops yet, but he's an author with

a devoted following in his home country. We sincerely hope you'll agree that *Thunder Bay*—an unusual mix of mystery, family drama and Native American wisdom—is something special. Set among the glassy lakes and towering pines of northern Minnesota and Canada, it's a wonderful feast for the senses as well as a great read. As always, be sure to let us know *your* opinion by writing to select_editions@readersdigest.co.uk.

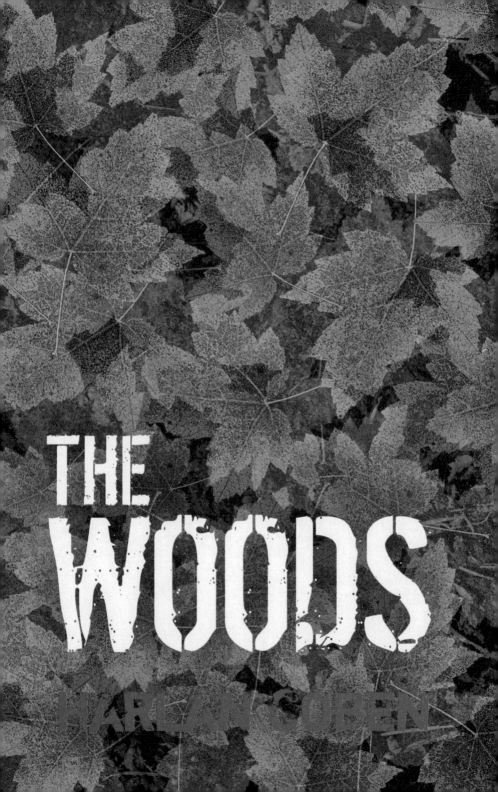

THE
WOODS

HARLAN COBEN

When a man is found dead, and evidence
links him to County Prosecutor Paul
Copeland, the police are intrigued. What
is the link between the respected lawyer
and the victim?
The answers are buried in the past, as
Harlan Coben, master of the unexpected
twist, reveals in his compelling
new bestseller.

PROLOGUE

I see my father with that shovel.

There are tears streaming down his face. An awful, guttural sob forces its way up from deep in his lungs and out through his lips. He raises the shovel up and strikes the ground. The blade rips into the earth like it's wet flesh.

I am eighteen years old, and this is my most vivid memory of my father—him, in the woods, with that shovel. He doesn't know I'm watching. I hide behind a tree while he digs. He does it with a fury, as though the ground has angered him and he is seeking vengeance.

I have never seen my father cry before—not when his own father died, not when my mother ran off and left us, not even when he first heard about my sister, Camille. But he is crying now. He is crying without shame. The tears cascade down his face in a free fall. The sobs echo through the trees.

This is the first time I've spied on him like this. Most Saturdays he would pretend to be going on fishing trips, but I never really believed that. I think I always knew that this place, this horrible place, was his secret destination.

Because, sometimes, it is mine too.

I stand behind the tree and watch him. I will do this eight more times. I never interrupt him. I never reveal myself. He doesn't know that I am there, I am sure of it. Then one day, as he heads to his car, my father looks at me with dry eyes and says, 'Not today, Paul. Today I go alone.'

I watch him drive off. He goes to those woods for the last time.

On his deathbed nearly two decades later, my father takes my hand. He is heavily medicated. He has been in immense pain, but there are no tears. He just closes his eyes and rides it out.

I look at him in the bed. I think about those days in the woods. I think about how he dug, how he finally stopped after my mother left.

Suddenly my father is agitated.

'It's OK, Dad,' I tell him. 'It's all going to be OK.'

He tries to sit up. I want to help him, but he shakes me off. He looks deep into my eyes and I see clarity, or maybe that is one of those things that we make ourselves believe at the end. A final false comfort.

One tear escapes his eye. I watch it slide slowly down his cheek.

'Paul,' my father says to me, his voice still thick with a Russian accent. 'We still need to find her.'

'We will, Dad.'

He checks my face again. I nod, assure him. But I don't think that he is looking for assurance. I think, for the first time, he is looking for guilt.

'Did you know?' he asks, his voice barely audible.

I feel my entire body quake, but I don't blink, don't look away. I wonder what he sees, what he believes. But I will never know.

Because then, right then, my father closes his eyes and dies.

CHAPTER 1
Three Months Later

I was in a school gymnasium, watching my six-year-old daughter, Cara, nervously navigate across a balance beam that hovered maybe four inches off the floor, but in less than an hour I would be looking at the face of a man who'd been viciously murdered.

That should not shock anyone.

I have learned over the years—in the most horrible ways imaginable—that the wall between life and death, between the most innocent setting and a frightening blood bath, is flimsy. It takes a second to tear through it. One moment, life appears idyllic. You are in a place as chaste as a school gymnasium. Your little girl is twirling. Her eyes are closed. You see her mother's face there, the way her mother used to close her eyes and smile, and you remember how flimsy that wall really is.

'Cope?'

It was my sister-in-law, Greta. I turned to her. Greta looked at me with her normal concern. I smiled through it.

'What are you thinking about?' she whispered.

She knew. I lied anyway.

'Handheld video cameras,' I said.

'What?'

The folding chairs had all been taken by the other parents. I stood at the back, arms crossed, leaning against the cement wall.

I gestured at the parents. 'There are more video cameras here than kids. I mean, does anybody really watch this again from beginning to end?'

'You don't?'

'I'd rather give birth.'

She smiled at that. 'No,' she said, 'you wouldn't.'

'OK, yeah, maybe not, but to just film this straight out like this, to subject an unsuspecting friend to that . . .'

The door opened. The moment the two men stepped into the gym I could tell that they were cops. Even if I wasn't the county prosecutor for Essex County—which includes the rather violent city of Newark—I would know. Television does indeed get some stuff right. The way most cops dressed, for example—fathers in the lush suburb of Ridgewood don't dress that way. We wear corduroys or jeans with a V-neck over a T-shirt to watch our kids perform quasi-gymnastics. These two guys wore ill-fitted suits in a brown hue that reminded me of wood chips after a rainstorm.

They were not smiling. Their eyes scanned the room. I know most of the cops in the area, but not these guys. That troubled me. Something felt wrong.

Since this was a daytime event, there were very few fathers here. The mothers adore me. It is not me, of course, but my story. My wife, Jane, died five years ago and I raise my daughter alone. There are other single parents in town, mostly divorced mothers, but I get a ton of slack. If I forget to write a note or pick up my daughter late or leave her lunch on the counter, the other mothers or the staff in the school office chip in and help. They think my male helplessness is cute. When a single mother does any of those things, she is neglectful and on the receiving end of the superior moms' scorn.

Greta and her husband, Bob, have three kids of their own. Their youngest daughter, Madison, is in the same class as my Cara. Greta and Bob have been a tremendous help since Jane—Greta's sister—died. I can't imagine what it would be like without them.

The kids continued to tumble or stumble, depending on how you wanted to look at it. I watched Cara. She was big on concentration and did just fine, but I suspected she had inherited her father's lack of coordination. There were high-school girls from the gymnastics team helping. The girls reminded me of my sister, Camille. She died when she was about their age.

My sister would be in her late thirties now, at least as old as most of these mothers. Weird to think of it that way. I see Camille for ever as a teen. It is hard to imagine her where she would be now—where she *should* be now, sitting in one of those chairs, the doofy-happy-concerned-I'm-a-mom-first smile on her face. I wonder what she would look like today.

It may appear that I'm somewhat obsessed with death, but there is a huge difference between my sister's murder and my wife's premature passing. The first, my sister's, led me to my current job and career projectory. I can fight that injustice in the courtroom. And I do. I try to make the world safer, try to put those who would harm others behind bars, try to bring other families something my family never really had—closure.

With the second death—my wife's—I was helpless and screwed up and no matter what I do now, I will never be able to make amends.

The school principal strapped a smile onto her over-lipsticked mouth and headed in the direction of the two cops. She engaged them in conversation, but neither one of them so much as glanced at her. I watched their eyes. When the taller cop hit my face, he stopped. He gave his head the slightest tilt, beckoning me outside. I made my nod equally slight.

'Where are you going?' Greta asked me.

'I'm not sure,' I said.

'Business?'

'Could be.'

She glanced over at the two probable-cops then back at me. 'Do you want me to pick up Cara after school?'

'Sure, that'd help.'

I headed off. The peals of children's laughter rolled with me. The two policemen followed me into the corridor.

'Are you Paul Copeland?' the taller one asked.

'Yes.'

The shorter guy was meaty with no neck. His head was shaped like a cinder block. His skin was coarse too, adding to the illusion. From round the corner came a class of fourth graders, trailed by their harried teacher.

'Maybe we should talk outside,' the taller one said.

I shrugged. I had no idea what this was about, though I knew it couldn't be about the big, headline-splashing case I was working on. If it had been, they'd have called my office first. I'd have got word on my cell or BlackBerry.

No, they were here for something else—something personal.

We stepped outside. The sun blazed down. The taller one squinted and raised a hand to shade his eyes.

'My name is Detective Tucker York,' he said, taking out his badge. He motioned towards the Cinder Block. 'This is Detective Don Dillon.'

'What can I do for you?' I asked.

'Do you mind telling us where you were last night?' York asked.

Sirens should have gone off at a question like that. I should have right away reminded them that I wouldn't answer any questions without an attorney present. But I am an attorney. A damned good one.

'I was home.'

'Anyone who can verify that?'

'My daughter.'

'Anyone else?'

'I don't think so. What's this about?'

York was the one who was doing all the talking. He ignored my question. 'Do you know a man named Manolo Santiago?'

'No.'

'Are you sure?'

'Pretty sure.'

'Why only pretty sure?'

'Do you know who I am?'

'Yep,' York said. 'You want us to kiss your ring or something?'

'That's not what I meant.' I did not like his attitude, but I let it slide.

'Good. So why are you only "pretty sure" you don't know Manolo Santiago?'

'I mean, the name isn't familiar. I don't think I know him.'

York nodded. 'Do you mind coming with us?' he said.

'Where?'

'It won't take long.'

'Won't take long,' I repeated. 'That doesn't sound like a place.'

The two cops exchanged a glance.

'A man named Manolo Santiago was murdered last night. His body was found in Manhattan. Washington Heights area. We think you might be able to help.'

'Help how? I already told you. I don't know him.'

'Mr Santiago'—York hesitated as though choosing his next words by hand—'had certain items on him that point to you.'

'Point to me as what?'

'Yo, Mr DA?' Dillon—the Cinder Block—had finally spoken.

'It's County Prosecutor,' I said.

'Whatever.' Dillon cracked his neck and pointed at my chest. 'You're really starting to itch my ass.' He stepped into my face. 'Do we look like we are here for a semantics lesson?'

I thought the question was rhetorical but he waited. Finally, I said, 'No.'

'Then listen up. We got a dead body. The guy is linked to you in a big way. Do you want to help clear this up, or do you want to play more word games that make you look suspicious as hell?'

'Who exactly do you think you're talking to, Detective?'

'A guy running for office who wouldn't want us to take this to the press.'

'Are you threatening me?'

York stepped in. 'Nobody is threatening anything.'

But Dillon had hit me where I lived. The truth was, my appointment was still only temporary. My friend, the governor, had made me acting county prosecutor. There was also talk of my running for Congress. I would be lying if I said I didn't have political ambitions. A scandal, even the fake whiff of one, would not play well.

'I can't see how I can help,' I said.

'Maybe you can't, maybe you can.' Dillon rotated the cinder block. 'But you want to help if you can, don't you?'

'Of course,' I said. 'I don't want your ass itching any more than it has to.'

He almost smiled at that one. 'Then get in the car.'

'I have an important meeting this afternoon.'

'We'll have you back by then.'

I expected a beat-up Chevy Caprice, but the car was a clean Ford. I sat in the back. My two new friends sat in the front. We did not speak until we were on the Manhattan side of the George Washington Bridge.

'This must be weird for you,' York said. 'Being on the other side. You're usually the one asking the questions, not answering them.'

He smiled at me in the rearview mirror.

'Hey, York?' I said. 'Do you have a playbill or something?'

'A what?'

'A playbill,' I said. 'So I can see your past credits, you know—before you landed the coveted role of Good Cop.'

York chuckled at that. 'I'm just saying, it's weird is all. I mean, have you ever been questioned by the police before?'

It was a set-up question. They had to know. When I was eighteen years old, I worked as a counsellor at a summer camp. Four campers—Gil Perez and his girlfriend, Margot Green, Doug Billingham and his girlfriend, Camille Copeland (a.k.a. my sister)—sneaked into the woods late one night.

They were never seen again.

Only two of the bodies have ever been found. Margot Green, aged seventeen, was found with her throat slit within a hundred yards of the campsite. Doug Billingham, also seventeen, was found half a mile away. He had several stab wounds, but cause of death was also a slit throat. The bodies of the other two—Gil Perez and my sister, Camille—have never been found.

The case made headlines. Wayne Steubens, a rich-kid counsellor at the camp, was caught two years later—after his third summer of terror—but not until he murdered at least four more teens. He was dubbed the Summer Slasher. His next two victims were found near a Boy Scout camp in Muncie, Indiana. Another victim was at a camp in Vienna, Virginia. His last victim had been at a sports camp in the Poconos. Most had their throats slit. All had been buried out in the woods, some before death. Yes, as in buried alive. Most experts believe that there are others still out there, still underground, deep in the woods. Like my sister.

Wayne has never confessed, and despite being in a maximum-security facility for the past eighteen years, he insists that he had nothing to do with the four murders that started it all.

I don't believe him. The fact that at least two bodies were still out there led to speculation and mystery. It gave Wayne more attention. I think he likes that. But that unknown—that glimmer—still hurts like hell.

I loved my sister. We all did. Most people believe death is the cruellest thing. Not so. After a while, hope is a far more abusive mistress. When you live with it as long as I have, your neck constantly on the chopping block, you long for the axe to fall and lop off your head.

I wished Wayne Steubens would tell us what he did with her. Not to give her a proper burial, though that would be nice. Death is pure, wrecking-ball

destructive. It hits, you're crushed, you start to rebuild. But not knowing—
that doubt, that glimmer—eats away at you. You cannot rebuild because that
doubt just keeps gnawing away.

I was there that night, in those woods. I was questioned by the police.
Under suspicion even. So they had to know.

I chose not to answer. York and Dillon didn't push it.

When we arrived at the morgue, they led me down a long corridor to the
window. You don't go into the room. You stay behind glass. All the gurneys
were empty save one. The body was covered with a sheet.

A woman wearing a mask rolled the gurney to the window. She pulled
back the top of the sheet.

I looked down at the face. All eyes were on me. I knew that. They were
studying my responses. The dead man was about my age, mid-thirties. He
had a beard. His head looked shaved. He wore a shower cap. I knew why
that was there.

'Shot in the head?' I asked.

'Yes.'

'Calibre?'

York cleared his throat, as if trying to remind me that this wasn't my
case. 'Do you know him?'

I took another look. 'No,' I said.

'Are you sure?'

I started to nod. But something made me stop.

'Why am I here?' I asked.

'His driver's licence reads Manolo Santiago. We checked it out. It doesn't
appear to be his real name.'

'Right, but what made you think I would know him?'

York and Dillon exchanged a glance. 'He had your address in his
pocket,' York said. 'And a bunch of clippings about you. About your sister
and what happened in those woods.'

The room dropped ten degrees, but hey, we were in a morgue. I tried to
sound nonchalant. 'Maybe he's a real-crime nut. There are lots of them.'

He hesitated. I saw him exchange another glance with his partner.

'What else did he have on him?' I asked.

A subordinate I hadn't even noticed pulled out a red plastic evidence
bag. They emptied it out onto a table. There was a wallet and a cellphone.

'You check the cellphone?' I asked.

'Yep. It's a throwaway. The phone log is empty.'

I walked over to the table. My legs quaked.

There were folded sheets of paper. I carefully opened one up. The article from *Newsweek*. The picture of the four dead teens was there—the Summer Slasher's first victims. They always started with Margot Green because her body was found right away. It took another day to locate Doug Billingham. But the real interest lay in the other two. Blood had been found and torn clothes belonging to both Gil Perez and my sister—but no bodies. Why not?

Simple. The woods were massive. Wayne Steubens had hidden them well. But some people, those who loved a good conspiracy, didn't buy that. How could Steubens have moved and buried bodies so quickly? Did he have an accomplice?

Even today, eighteen years after Wayne's arrest, people talk about the 'ghosts' in those woods. They say how at night they can still hear Gil Perez and my sister, Camille, howl for vengeance.

I spent a lot of nights in those woods, alone. I never heard anyone howl.

My eyes moved on past Margot Green's picture and Doug Billingham's to the photograph of my sister. I had seen this same shot a million times. The media loved it because she looked so wonderfully ordinary. She was the girl-next-door, the sweet teen who lived down the block. That wasn't Camille at all. She was mischievous, with lively eyes and a sideways devil-may-care grin that knocked the boys back a step. And maybe that had cost her her life.

I was about to head over to the final picture, the one of Gil Perez, but something made me pull up.

My heart stopped.

I know that sounds dramatic, but that was how it felt. I looked at the pile of coins from Manolo Santiago's pocket, and it was as if a hand reached into my chest and squeezed my heart so hard it couldn't beat any more.

My hand went out as if it were acting on its own. I watched my fingers pluck it up and bring it to my eye level. It was a ring. A girl's ring.

I looked at the picture of Gil Perez, the boy who'd been murdered with my sister. I flashed back twenty years. And I remembered the scar.

'Show me his arm,' I said.

'Excuse me?'

I turned back to the window and pointed to the corpse. 'His arm.'

Dillon pressed the intercom button. 'He wants to see the guy's arm.'

'Which one?' the woman in the morgue asked.

'I don't know,' I said. 'Both, I guess.'

They looked puzzled, but the woman obeyed. The sheet was pulled back.

The chest was hairy now. He was at least thirty pounds more than he was then, but that wasn't surprising. We had all changed. But that wasn't what I was looking for. I was looking for the ragged scar.

It was there. On his left arm. I did not gasp or any of that. I was too numb.

'I know him,' I said. 'His name is Gil Perez.'

THERE WAS A TIME when Professor Lucy Gold, PhD in both English and psychology, loved office hours.

It was a chance to sit one-on-one with students and really get to know them. She loved when the quiet ones who sat in the back with their heads down, taking notes as though it were dictation, arrived at her door and raised their eyes and told her what was in their hearts.

But most of the time, like now, the students who showed up were the brown-nosers, the ones who felt that their grade should depend solely on their outward enthusiasm, that the more face time they got, the higher the grade.

'Professor Gold,' the girl named Sylvia Potter said.

'Yes, Sylvia?'

'When you were reading that passage from Yeats in class today, I mean, I was so moved. I loved writing that journal piece too,' she said.

Lucy Gold was tempted to say, 'Do me a favour—just bake me some brownies,' but she kept the smile on and said, 'I'm glad.'

'Mine was about . . . well, my first time, if you know what I mean . . .'

Lucy nodded. 'We're keeping them anonymous, remember?'

'Oh, right.' She glanced down now. Lucy wondered about that. Sylvia never looked down.

'Maybe after I read them all,' Lucy said, 'if you want, we can talk about yours. In private.'

Her head was still down. 'OK,' she said softly.

Office hours were over. Lucy wanted to get home. She tried not to sound halfhearted when she asked, 'Do you want to talk about it now?'

'No.' Sylvia's head was still down.

'OK then,' Lucy said, making a production of looking at her watch. 'I have a staff meeting in ten minutes.'

Sylvia stood. 'Thank you for meeting with me.'

'My pleasure, Sylvia.'

Sylvia looked as if she wanted to say something more. But she didn't.

Five minutes later, Lucy stood at her window and looked down at the quad. Sylvia walked out of the door, wiped her face, set the head high, forced up a smile. Lucy watched her wave at her fellow students and fall in with the group. Lucy turned away. Had that girl been calling out for help?

Probably, Luce, and you didn't answer. Nice work, superstar.

She sat at her desk and opened the bottom drawer. The vodka was there. Vodka was good. You didn't smell vodka.

Her office door opened. The guy who entered had long black hair tucked behind his ears and several earrings. He was unshaven, fashionably so, handsome in an ageing-boy-band way.

'You,' the guy said, gunning his best smile in her direction, 'look immensely doable.'

'Thanks, Lonnie.'

'Nah, I mean it. Immensely doable.'

Lonnie Berger was her teaching assistant, though he was her age. He was permanently caught in that education trap, getting a new degree, hanging out on campus, the telltale sign of age round the eyes.

'Seriously, chief, when was the last time you got some?'

'It's been eight months, six days and about'—Lucy checked her watch— 'four hours.'

He laughed. 'I printed out the journals,' he said.

The anonymous journals.

She was teaching a class that the university had dubbed Creative Reasoning, a combination of cutting-edge psychological trauma with creative writing and philosophy. Truth be told, Lucy loved it. Current assignment: each student was supposed to write on a traumatic event in their lives—something that they would not normally share with anyone. No names were to be used. No grades given.

'Did you start reading them?' she asked.

Lonnie nodded and sat in the seat that Sylvia had occupied a few minutes ago. He threw his feet up on the desk. 'The usual,' he said.

'Bad erotica?'

'I'd say more like soft porn.'

He handed her a few of the journals. They both started digging in. Five minutes later, Lonnie shook his head.

Lucy said, 'What?'

'How old are most of these kids?' Lonnie asked. 'Maybe twenty, right?'

'Right.'

'And their sexual escapades always last, like, two hours?'

Lucy smiled. 'Active imagination.'

They went back to reading. Half an hour later, Lonnie sat forward and said. 'Read this one.'

She put down the journal she'd been reading—yet another story of a girl who'd got drunk with her new boyfriend and ended up in a threesome. Lucy had read lots of stories of threesomes.

But a minute later she forgot all about that. She forgot that she lived alone or that she was a college professor or that Lonnie was still sitting in front of her. Lucy Gold was gone. And in her place was a girl with a different name, a girl on the verge of adulthood but still so very much a girl.

This happened when I was seventeen. I was at summer camp, working as a counsellor. My dad owned the place . . .

Lucy stopped. She looked at the front sheet. There was no name, of course. The students emailed the papers in, and there was supposed to be no way to know who sent what paper. It was part of the comfort. You just hit the anonymous Send button.

It was the best summer of my life. At least it was until that final night. Weird, right? But I know. I know that I will never, ever, be that happy again.

I loved a boy that summer. I will call him P for this story. He was a year older than me and a junior counsellor. His whole family was at the camp. His sister worked there and his father was the camp doctor. But I barely noticed them because the moment I met P, I felt my stomach clench.

I know what you're thinking. It was just a dumb summer romance. But it wasn't. And now I'm scared that I will never love someone like I loved him, that I had one chance at happiness and I blew it.

A hole in Lucy's heart started opening, expanding.

One night, we went into the woods. We weren't supposed to. There were strict rules about it. P was on 'night' duty and he didn't want to go into the woods because he thought he should keep watch, but hey, I knew how to entice him. I regret that now, of course. But I did it. So we headed into the woods, just the two of us. I knew the way. P was holding my hand. It was so dark. You can't see more than ten feet in front of you. We heard a rustling noise and realised that someone was in the woods. I froze, but I remember

P smiling in the dark and shaking his head in a funny way. You see, the only reason campers met up in the woods was, well, it was a co-ed camp. You figure it out.

P sighed. 'We better check it out,' he said. Or something like that.

But I didn't want to. I wanted to be alone with him.

My flashlight was out of batteries. I can still remember how fast my heart was beating as we stepped into the trees. There I was, in the dark, holding hands with the guy I loved. He would touch me and I would just melt. You know that feeling? When you can't stand to be away from a guy for even five minutes? It is a crazy feeling. It is wonderful but it also hurts.

'Shh,' he whispers. 'Just stop.'

We do. We stop.

P pulls me behind a tree. He cups my face in both of his hands. He has big hands and I love the way that feels. He tilts my face up and then he kisses me. I feel it everywhere, a fluttering that begins in the centre of my heart and then spreads. He takes his hand away from my face. He puts it on my rib cage, right next to my breast. I start to anticipate. I groan out loud.

We kept kissing. It was so passionate. Every part of me felt on fire. I forgot about the rustling in the woods. We made love.

I was so lost in us, in what we were doing, that at first I didn't even hear the screams. I don't think P did either.

But the screams kept coming and you know how people describe near-death experiences? That was what it was like, but in reverse. It was like we were both headed for some wonderful light and the screams were like a rope trying to pull us back, though we didn't want to go back.

He stopped kissing me. And here is the terrible thing.

He never kissed me again.

Lucy turned the page, but there were no more. She snapped her head up. 'Where's the rest?'

'That's it. You said to send it in parts, remember. You OK, Luce?'

'You're good with computers, aren't you, Lonnie?'

'Yeah, I'm good with computers. Why?'

'I need to find out who wrote this.'

'But—' He met her eye. He studied her face for a second. She knew what he wanted to say. It betrayed everything that they were about. They had read horrible stories in here, one this year about father-daughter incest even, and they had never tried to track the person down.

Lonnie said, 'Do you want to tell me what this is about?'

'No.'

'That bad?'

She just looked at him.

'Ah, what the hell,' Lonnie said. 'I'll see what I can do.'

'I'M TELLING YOU,' I said yet again. 'It's Gil Perez.'

'The guy who died with your sister twenty years ago.'

'Obviously,' I said, 'he didn't die.'

I don't think they believed me.

'Maybe it's his brother,' York tried.

'With my sister's ring?'

Dillon added, 'That ring isn't unusual. Twenty years ago they were all the rage. We don't know for sure.'

They would be in touch, they said. They'd find Gil Perez's family, see if they could make a positive ID. I felt numb and confused.

My BlackBerry and cellphone were going nuts. I was late now for an appointment with the defence team in the biggest case of my career. Two wealthy collegiate tennis players from the ritzy suburb of Short Hills stood accused of raping a sixteen-year-old African-American girl from Irvington, Chamique Johnson. The trial had already started, had hit a delay, and now I hoped to cut a jail-time deal before we had to start up again.

The cops gave me a lift to my office in Newark. I knew that opposing counsel would think my tardiness was a ploy, but there wasn't much to be done about that. When I entered my office, the two lead defence lawyers were already there.

One, Mort Pubin, stood and started bellowing. 'You son of a bitch! We've been sitting here for an hour!'

The other lawyer, Flair Hickory, just sat there, legs crossed, not a care in the world. He let Mort rant for another minute or two, then he raised his hand and silenced him with a fluttery wave.

'Enough,' Flair said.

He wore a purple suit. The shirt was the same colour. So was the solid tie. So were—good Lord—the shoes. Flair noticed me noticing the clothes.

'You like it?' Flair asked me.

'Barney joins the Village People,' I said.

Flair frowned at me. 'Could you possibly come up with two more dated, overused pop references?' He crossed his arms and sighed. 'So now that we are all here, can we just let our clients walk and be done with this?'

I met his eye. 'They did it, Flair.'

He wouldn't deny it. 'Are you really going to put that deranged stripper-cum-prostitute on the stand?'

'I am.'

Flair tried not to smile. 'I will,' he said, 'destroy her.'

He would. I knew that. Flair was the defence attorney I feared like no other. He was not what anyone expected. In the first place, he was gay. OK, that wasn't a big deal. Plenty of attorneys are gay, but Flair was *gay* gay, like the love child of Liberace and Liza Minnelli. You'd think at least some of the jury would consist of homophobes and that they'd hate or fear him. But that wasn't how it worked with Flair. The female jurors wanted to go shopping with him and tell him about their husbands' inadequacies. The men found him so nonthreatening that they thought there was no way he could pull anything over on them. It made for a lethal defence.

'What are you looking for?' I asked.

Flair grinned. 'You're nervous, aren't you?'

At that moment the door opened and Loren Muse, my chief investigator, walked in. Muse was my age, mid-thirties, and had been a homicide investigator under my predecessor, Ed Steinberg.

Muse sat down without a word or even a wave.

I turned back to Flair. 'What do you want?' I asked again.

'For starters,' Flair said, 'I want Ms Chamique Johnson to apologise for destroying the reputation of two fine, upstanding boys.'

I just looked at him.

'But we'll settle for an immediate dropping of all charges.'

'Dream on.'

'Cope, Cope, Cope.' Flair shook his head and tsk-tsked.

'I said no.'

'You're adorable when you're macho, but you know that already, don't you?' Flair looked over at Loren Muse. A stricken expression crossed his face. 'Dear God, what are you wearing?'

Muse sat up. 'What?'

'Your wardrobe. It's like a frightening new Fox reality show: *When Policewomen Dress Themselves*. Dear God. And those shoes . . .'

'They're practical,' Muse said.

'Sweetheart, fashion rule one: The words *shoes* and *practical* should never be in the same sentence.' Without blinking an eye, Flair turned back to me: 'Our clients cop to a misdemeanour and you give them probation.'

'No.'

'Can I just say two words to you? Cal and Jim.'

He paused. I glanced at Muse. She shifted in her seat.

'Those two little names,' Flair went on. 'Cal and Jim. Music to my ears. Do you know what I'm saying, Cope?'

I didn't take the bait.

'In your alleged victim's statement she says that her rapists were named Cal and Jim. Our clients are named Barry Marantz and Edward Jenrette.'

'It means nothing,' I said. 'Barry Marantz's semen was found in her.'

'Ah, yes, but young Barry—a handsome boy, by the way, and we both know that matters—admits to a consensual sex act with your eager, young Ms Johnson earlier in the evening. We all know that Chamique was at their fraternity house—that's not in dispute, is it?'

I didn't like it, but I said, 'No, that's not in dispute.'

'Chamique Johnson had worked there the week before as a stripper.'

'Exotic dancer,' I corrected.

He just looked at me. 'And so she returned. Without the benefit of money being exchanged. We can agree on that too, can't we?' He didn't bother waiting for me. 'And I can get five, six boys to say she was acting very friendly with Barry. Come on, Cope. You've been round this block before. She's a stripper. She's underage. She got nailed by the handsome rich kid. He, what, blew her off or didn't call or whatever. She got upset.'

'And plenty of bruises,' I said.

Mort pounded the table with a fist that looked like roadkill. 'She's just looking for a big payday,' he said. 'She's already got a lawyer. Going to shake our boys down. The only reason you're prosecuting them is because they're wealthy. Don't pretend you aren't. You know what sucks about that? It is now an encouraged prejudice in our society—to hate rich people. If I ever said, "Hey, I hate poor people," I'd be strung up. But call the rich names? Well, you have a free pass. Everyone is allowed to hate the rich.'

I looked at him. 'Maybe they should form a support group.'

'Up yours, Cope.'

'No, I mean it. The world hasn't been fair to them. Maybe they should hold a telethon or something.'

Flair Hickory rose theatrically. 'I think we're done here. See you tomorrow, handsome. And you'—he looked at Loren Muse, shuddered.

'Flair?'

He looked at me.

'That Cal and Jim thing,' I said. 'It just proves she's telling the truth.'

Flair smiled. 'How's that, exactly?'

'Your boys were smart. They called themselves Cal and Jim, so she'd say that. I mean, if Chamique wanted to set your clients up, why wouldn't she use their correct names? Why would she make up all that dialogue with Cal and Jim? Why would she make that all up?'

Mort took that one. 'Because she's a dumb money-hungry whore?'

But I could see that I'd scored a point with Flair.

Flair leaned towards me. 'Perhaps you're right, Cope. Perhaps it doesn't make sense. But see, that leads to confusion. And confusion has the major hots for my favourite hunk, Mr Reasonable Doubt.' He smiled. 'You might have some physical evidence. But, well, you put that girl on the stand, I will not hold back. It will be game, set, match. We both know that.'

They headed to the door.

'Toodles, my friend. See you in court.'

MUSE AND I said nothing for a few moments.

Cal and Jim. The names deflated us.

The position of chief investigator was almost always held by a male. It would be that man's job to manoeuvre the guileless county prosecutor, a political appointee like me, through the rings of the Essex County legal system. Loren Muse was maybe five feet tall and weighed about as much as your average fourth grader. My choosing Muse had caused some ripples among the veterans, but I prefer hiring single women of a certain age. They work harder and are more loyal. Muse was also an incredibly gifted investigator. I liked talking things out with her. I would say 'muse'-ing them over, but then you'd understandably groan. Right now she was staring at the floor.

'What's on your mind?' I asked her.

'Put simply,' she said, 'if we don't find a way to explain Cal and Jim, we're screwed.'

'You questioned Chamique again?'

'I did. Her story is frighteningly consistent. I think you're right. They simply did that as a cover—so her story would sound idiotic.'

'But why those two names?' I asked for the umpteenth time. 'We're missing something, Muse.'

She nodded. 'I know.'

I have always been pretty good about partitioning my life. We all are, but I am especially good at it. I can deal with one aspect of my life and not have it interfere with another in any way. Some people watch a gangster movie and wonder how the mobster can be so violent on the streets and so loving at home. I get that. I have that ability. It is not necessarily a great attribute. It protects, yes, but I have seen what actions it can justify.

So for the past half-hour I had been pushing away the obvious questions. If Gil Perez had been alive this whole time, where had he been? And if Gil Perez had survived that awful night . . .

Had my sister survived too?

'Cope?'

It was Muse.

'What's going on?'

I wanted to tell her. But now was not the time. I needed to sort it through.

'Cal and Jim,' I said. 'We have to figure out what the hell that's all about—and fast.'

CHAPTER 2

My wife's sister, Greta, and her husband, Bob, lived in a McMansion in a new cul-de-sac that looks almost precisely the same as every other new cul-de-sac in North America. The lots are too small for the ginormous brick edifices that stretch across them. The houses have a variety of shapes and shades but somehow still look exactly the same.

I had met Greta first, before my wife. I don't want to sound unkind but Greta was the ugly sister. They looked alike, she and my lovely dead bride. But everything that worked physically with my Jane just doesn't quite make it on Greta. My mother ran away before I turned twenty, but I remember something she told me. We were the poorest citizens in our rather mixed town. We were immigrants who had come over from the old Soviet Union when I was four. We had started out OK but things turned very bad very quickly. My father, Vladimir Copinsky (he anglicised it to Copeland), who had once been a doctor in Leningrad, couldn't get a licence to practise in this country. He ended up working as a house painter. My mother, a frail beauty named Natasha, the well-educated daughter of aristocratic college professors, took on a variety of cleaning jobs for the wealthier families in Short Hills and Livingston but could never hold on to one for very long.

'There is an old Russian expression,' my mother said. 'A rich girl is beautiful when she stands on her money.' That was the first thought that came through my mind when I met Greta. Her parents—my former in-laws, still the grandparents of my Cara—are loaded. My wife came from money. It's all in trust for Cara. I'm the executor.

Cara and Madison, my niece, were playing in the driveway. The days were starting to get longer now. Madison sat on the asphalt and drew with pieces of chalk. My own daughter rode one of those motorised, slow-moving minicars that are all the rage with today's under-six crowd. The kids who own them never play on them. Only their visitors do.

I stepped out of the car and shouted, 'Hey, kiddos.'

I waited for the two six-year-old girls to stop what they were doing and sprint over to me and wrap me in big hugs. Yeah, right. Madison glanced my way, but she couldn't have looked less interested without some sort of surgical cerebral disconnect. My own daughter pretended not to hear.

Greta pushed open the screen door. 'Hey.'

'Hey,' I said. 'So how was the rest of the gymnastics show?'

'Don't worry,' Greta said. 'I have the whole thing on video. So what was up with those two cops?'

I shrugged. 'Just work.'

She didn't buy it but she didn't press. 'I have Cara's backpack inside.'

She let the door close behind her. There were workers walking round from the back. Bob and Greta were putting in a swimming pool with matching landscaping. They'd been thinking about it for several years but wanted to wait until Madison was old enough to be safe.

'Come on,' I said to my daughter, 'we need to go.'

Cara ignored me again, pretending that the whirr of the pink Barbie Jeep, was overwhelming her aural faculties. The battery was fading fast. I frowned and started towards her. Cara was ridiculously stubborn. I would like to say, 'like her mother', but my Jane was the most patient and under-standing woman you ever met. It was amazing. All the negative qualities in Cara seemed to emanate from her father.

Greta came out with the backpack. 'We already did the homework.'

'Thank you.'

She waved it off. 'Cara, sweetheart? Your father is here.'

Cara ignored her too. I knew that a tantrum was coming. I braced for the confrontation but fortunately the gods interceded. The Barbie battery went totally dead. The pink Jeep stopped. Cara tried to move the vehicle another foot or two, but Barbie wouldn't budge. Cara sighed, stepped out of the Jeep, and started for the car.

'Say goodbye to Aunt Greta and your cousin.'

She did so in a voice sullen enough to make a teenager envious.

When we got home, Cara snapped on the TV without asking permission and settled in for an episode of *SpongeBob*. I was going to say something, but I let it go. Right now I just wanted her distracted. I was still trying to put together what was going on with both the rape case and now the murder of Gil Perez. I confess that my big case was getting the short end of the stick.

I started preparing dinner. I do have a nanny-housekeeper, but today was her day off.

The phone rang. I picked it up.

'Mr Copeland? This is Detective Tucker York.'

'Yes, Detective, what can I do for you?'

'We located Gil Perez's parents, and we're bringing them in tomorrow morning to see if we can get an ID. Maybe you should be here, you know, in case any weird questions come up.'

'I'll be there.'

A FEW HOURS LATER I tucked my daughter into bed.

Cara never gives me trouble at bedtime. We have a wonderful routine. I read to her. She adores it. I am reading Roald Dahl to her right now. Last year, when I took her to see the stage production of *The Lion King*, I bought her a terribly overpriced Timon doll. She has it gripped in her right arm. Timon is a pretty avid listener too.

I finished reading and gave Cara a kiss on the cheek. She smelt like baby shampoo. 'Good night, Daddy,' she said.

'Good night, Pumpkin.'

Kids. One moment they're like Medea having a bad mood swing, the next they are God-kissed angels.

I snapped off her light and headed to my home office. I have a hookup to my work computer files. I opened up the rape case of Chamique Johnson and started poring over it. Cal and Jim.

My victim wasn't what we call jury-pool sympathetic. Chamique was sixteen and had a child out of wedlock. She had been arrested twice for solicitation, once for possession of marijuana. She worked parties as an exotic dancer, and yes, that is a euphemism for stripper. But that did not discourage me. It makes me fight harder. Not because I care about political correctness, but because I am into—very into—justice.

Chamique was a person, a human being. She did not deserve what Barry Marantz and Edward Jenrette did to her.

I thought about my victim's statement—I didn't have to read it again. It was disgusting and rather specific. The two boys had made Chamique do things, had put her in different positions, had talked the whole time. Something about it all, the way they moved her around . . .

What was I missing? You know that feeling, when something you know is just out of reach, like the name of the boxer Mr T played in *Rocky III*? The answer was there somewhere, just hiding, just round that mental corner.

EARLY THE NEXT MORNING Detective York led Mr and Mrs Perez down the corridor at the morgue.

I followed at a discreet distance. Dillon stayed with me. Mrs Perez held her head high. She was gripping her handbag tight against her. She stayed a step ahead of her husband, who seemed to shrink with every step.

I'd seen Mrs Perez only once since the tragedy. There had been a meeting of the victims' families—the wealthy Greens, the wealthier Billinghams, the poor Copelands, the poorer Perezes—in a big fancy law office. The case had gone class action with the four families against the camp owner. The Perezes had barely spoken that day. They'd sat and listened and let the others rant and take the lead.

With its linoleum floor and walls of scrape-the-skin concrete, the corridor couldn't have looked more institutional. I could hear the echo of the footsteps. Mrs Perez wore heavy gold bracelets. I could hear them clank in rhythm with the walking.

When they turned right at the same window I had stood in front of yesterday, Dillon stuck out his hand in front of me, almost in a protective way. We stayed a good ten yards back, out of their line of vision.

It was hard to see their faces. Mr and Mrs Perez stood next to each other. They did not touch. I could see Mr Perez lower his head. He was wearing a blue blazer. Mrs Perez had on a dark blouse almost the colour of dried blood. A man wheeled the gurney towards the window.

When it was in place, the man carefully lifted the sheet, as if there were something fragile underneath. I was afraid to make a sound, but I still tilted my body a little to the left. I wanted to see some of Mrs Perez's face.

She took the blow with a small shudder, nothing more. Mr Perez's eyes were on the floor. They were wet. I could see the quake cross his lips.

Without looking away, Mrs Perez said, 'That's not our son.'

Silence. I had not expected that.

York said, 'Are you sure, Mrs Perez? He was a teenager when you last saw him. It's been a lot of years. Please take your time.'

Mrs Perez finally wrested her eyes from the body.

'That's not Gil,' she said again.

York swallowed, looked towards the father. 'Mr Perez?'

He managed a nod, cleared his throat. 'There's not even a resemblance.' His eyes closed and another quake ran across his face. 'It's just . . .'

'It's the right age,' Mrs Perez finished for him.

York said, 'I'm not sure I follow.'

'When you lose a son like that, you always wonder. For us, he'll be forever a teenager. But if he had lived, he would be, yes, the same age as this husky man. So you wonder what he'd be like. What he would look like.'

'And you're certain this man isn't your son?'

She smiled the saddest smile I had ever seen. 'I am certain.'

York nodded. 'I'm sorry to bring you out here.'

They began to turn away when I said, 'Show them the arm.'

Everyone turned in my direction. Mrs Perez's laser gaze zeroed in on me. There was something there, a challenge maybe. Mr Perez spoke first.

'Who are you?' he asked.

I had my eyes on Mrs Perez. Her sad smile returned. 'You're the Copeland boy, aren't you?'

'Yes, ma'am. Camille Copeland's brother.'

'Are you the one who made the identification?'

I wanted to explain about the clippings and the ring, but I felt I was running out of time. 'The arm,' I said. 'Gil had that awful scar on his arm.'

Mrs Perez nodded. 'One of our neighbours kept llamas. He had a barbed-wire fence. Gil was always a good climber. He tried to get into the pen when he was eight years old. He slipped and the wire dug deep into his shoulder.'

'I remembered it from camp,' I said. I gestured with my chin back towards the glass. 'Look at his arm.'

Mr Perez shook his head. 'But we already said—'

His wife put a hand up, quieting him.

'Show me,' she said, turning back to the glass.

Her husband looked confused, but he joined her at the window. This time she took his hand and held it.

York hit the intercom button. 'Please show them his arms.'

The man pulled back the sheet again. The scar was there, an angry slash. A smile returned to Mrs Perez's face, but what type—sad, happy, confused, fake, practised, spontaneous?—I couldn't say.

She turned to me. 'This scar is on the left arm,' she said. 'Gil's was on the right. And Gil's wasn't that long or deep.' Mrs Perez put a hand on my arm. 'It's not him, Mr Copeland. I understand why you'd so much want it to be Gil. But it's not. He isn't coming back to us. And neither is your sister.'

WHEN I GOT BACK to my house, Loren Muse was pacing like a lion near a wounded gazelle. Cara was at a dance class. Our nanny, Estelle, had taken her.

I pulled into my driveway. The house was a three-bedroom split-level that had all the personality of that morgue corridor. It was our 'starter' house. Jane had wanted to upgrade to a McMansion. I didn't care where we lived. I would pretty much let Jane have her way on that kind of stuff.

I missed my wife.

Loren Muse had a something-eating grin locked onto her face. No poker player was Muse. 'I got all the bills. Computer records too. The works.'

Muse and I spread everything out on the den floor—witness statements, police reports, phone records, all the fraternity house bills. We started with the frat bills, and man, there were a ton. Every cellphone. Every beer order. Every online purchase.

'So,' Muse said, 'what are we looking for?'

'Damned if I know. It's just a feeling.'

'Please don't tell me you're playing a hunch.'

'I would never,' I said. 'But the answer is here. I can almost see it.'

'Oookay,' she said, managing with great effort not to roll her eyes.

We kept looking. They ordered pizza pretty much every night, eight pies, from Pizza-To-Go. They had Netflix so that they could rent regular DVD movies, and something called HotFlixxx, so they could do the same with dirty ones. They ordered fraternity frat-logo golf shirts and golf balls, tons of them. We tried to put them in some kind of order. I don't have a clue why.

I lifted the HotFlixxx bill and showed it to Muse. 'Cheap,' I said.

'The Internet makes porn affordable to the masses.'

'Good to know,' I said.

'But this might be an opening,' Muse said. 'Young boys, hot women. Or in this case, wom*a*n.'

'Explain,' I said.

'I want to hire someone outside the office. A private eye named Cingle Shaker. She has a body that not only stops traffic, it pulls up the road and bulldozes highway dividers. And she's very good. If anyone can get lawyered-up frat boys to spill, it's Cingle.'

'OK,' I said.

Hours later—I can't even tell you how many—Muse started to rise. 'There's nothing here, Cope.'

'Seems that way, doesn't it?'

'You have Chamique's direct first thing in the morning?'

'Yes.'

She stood over me. 'Your time would be better spent working on that.'

I did a mock 'yes, sir' salute in her direction.

'I'll get you what I can,' Muse said.

She stomped out of the door in her best lick-da-world mode.

Estelle made dinner—spaghetti and meatballs. Estelle is not a great cook, but it went down. Afterwards, I took Cara out for Van Dyke's ice cream, a special treat. In the rearview mirror, I could see her strapped into the car seat. When I was a kid, we were allowed to sit in the front seat. Now you had to be of drinking age before that was permissible.

I tried to listen to what she was saying but Cara was just yakking nonsense the way kids do. Brittany had been mean to Morgan so Kyle threw an eraser and how come Kylie—Kylie N, not Kylie G—didn't want to go on the swings at recess unless Kiera was on one too? I kept glancing at her face, scrunched up as though imitating an adult. I got hit with that overwhelming feeling. Parents get it from time to time. You are looking at your child and it is an ordinary moment, not like they are onstage or hitting a winning shot, just sitting there, and you know that they are your whole life, and that moves you and scares you and makes you want to stop time.

I had lost a sister. I had lost a wife. And most recently, I had lost my father. In all three cases I had got back up off the canvas. But as I looked at Cara, I knew that there was one blow from which I could never rise.

I thought about my father. In the woods. With that shovel. His heart broken. Searching for his little girl. I thought about my mother. She had run away. I didn't know where she was. Sometimes I still think about searching her out. But not that often any more. For years I had hated her. Maybe I still do. Or maybe now that I have a child I understand a little better about the pain she must have been going though.

When we walked back into the house, the phone rang. Estelle took Cara from me. I picked it up and said hello.

'We got a problem, Cope.'

It was my brother-in-law, Bob, Greta's husband. He was chairman of the charitable fund JaneCare. Greta, Bob and I had founded it after my wife's death. My living memorial to my lovely, beautiful, gentle wife.

'What's the matter?' I asked.

'Your rape case is costing us big-time. Edward Jenrette's father has got several of his friends to back out of their commitments.'

I closed my eyes. 'Classy.'

'Worse, he's making noises that we've embezzled funds. EJ Jenrette is a well-connected son of a bitch. I'm already getting calls.'

'So we open our books,' I said. 'They won't find anything.'

'Don't be naive. If there is even a whiff of a scandal, we're finished.'

'Not much we can do about it, Bob.'

'I know. It's just that . . . we're doing a lot of good here, Cope.'

'What are you suggesting?'

'Nothing.' Bob hesitated and I could tell he had more to say. So I waited. 'But come on, Cope, you guys plea-bargain all the time, right?'

'When we have to.'

'Look, I'm not saying that these kids don't deserve to be punished, but sometimes you have to trade. The greater good. JaneCare is making big strides. It might be the greater good. That's all I'm saying.'

'Good night, Bob.'

'No offence, Cope. I'm just trying to help.'

'I know. Good night, Bob.'

I hung up. My hands were shaking. Jenrette, that son of a bitch, hadn't gone after me. He had gone after my wife's memory. I started upstairs. Rage consumed me. I would channel it. I sat at my desk.

There were only two pictures on it. One was the current school photo of Cara. It had a prized spot, dead centre. The second was a grainy photograph of my Noni and Popi from the old country, Russia. They died in a gulag when I was very young, when we still lived in Leningrad.

Why, I often wondered, do I keep this picture out? Their daughter, my mother, had abandoned me, right? Somehow, despite the obvious pain intertwined, I find the picture oddly relevant. I would look at it and wonder about ripples and family curses and where it all might have started.

Finally I allowed my mind to go where it wanted to—my sister, Camille, Gil Perez, that awful, magical summer. I flashed back to camp. I thought about Camille. I thought about that night. And for the first time in several years, I let myself think about Lucy.

A sad smile crossed my face. Lucy Silverstein had been my first real girl-friend. We'd had it so good, a fairy-tale summer romance, until that night. We never had the chance to break up—we were, instead, ripped apart by bloody murders. We were torn away while still enmeshed in each other at a point where our love—as silly and immature as it was supposed to have been—was still rising and growing.

Lucy was the past. I had shut her out. She was probably married now—like I had been. She was probably happy. I hoped so.

I pushed that all away. Right now I needed to think about Gil Perez. I closed my eyes and went back. I thought about him at camp, how we horsed around, how I used to fun-punch him in the arm and he'd say, 'Wimp! I didn't even feel that . . .' I could see him now, with the skinny torso, his shorts too baggy before that was a fashionable look, the smile that needed major orthodontia, the . . . My eyes opened. Something felt wrong.

I headed into the basement. I found the cardboard box right away, the photographs from that long-ago summer.

There were none of Lucy. I had wisely thrown them all away years ago. I sifted through the stack of pictures until I found one of my sister taken three days before she died. Doug was in the picture—her boyfriend. A rich kid. The camp was an odd social mix of privileged and poor. That was how the guy who ran the camp, Lucy's fun-loving hippie dad, Ira, wanted it.

Margot Green, another rich kid, was smack in the middle. She had been the camp hottie and knew it. She was blonde and busty and worked it constantly. She always dated older guys, until Gil anyway.

Gil was in the photograph too. And that was why I was here.

I pointed my desk light and took a closer look.

Upstairs, I'd remembered something. I am right-handed, but when I fun-punched Gil on the arm, I used my left hand. I did this to avoid touching that awful scar. Like I was afraid it might tear open anew. I squinted and moved closer. I could see the bottom of the scar peaking out beneath the T-shirt. Gil Perez's scar was on his left arm. Mrs Perez had lied.

I ARRIVED IN MY OFFICE early the next morning. In half an hour, I would have Chamique Johnson on the stand. I called Detective York.

'Mrs Perez lied,' I said.

He listened to my explanation.

'Lied,' York repeated when I finished. 'Isn't that a little strong? Maybe she just made a mistake?'

I wasn't buying it. 'Have you got anything new on the case?'

'We think Santiago was living in New Jersey.'

'You have an address?'

'Nope. But we have a girlfriend. Or at least we think she's a girlfriend.'

'How did you find her?'

'That empty cellphone. She called it looking for him. She only knew him as Santiago. Oh, and something else important.'

'What?'

'His body was moved. The medical examiner says Santiago was probably dead an hour before he got dumped. There are some carpet fibres, stuff like that. Preliminary shows that they're from a car.'

'Do you have a make on the car?'

'Not yet. They're working on it. But our guy says it's something old.'

'This girlfriend,' I said. 'Do you have a name?'

'Raya Singh.'

'How about an address?'

'You going to talk to her?'

'You mind?'

'As long as you don't screw up my case, you can do whatever you want. But can I give you a piece of friendly advice?'

'Sure.'

'That lunatic, the Summer Slasher. Wayne Steubens. He's still looking to overturn his conviction.'

'He was never tried for those first four murders,' I said.

'I know. But if it really is Gil Perez and Steubens was to hear, well, it would help him. You know what I'm saying?'

He was saying to keep it quiet until I knew something for sure. I got that. The last thing I wanted to do was help Wayne Steubens.

We hung up. Loren Muse stuck her head in my office. 'You ready?'

'I am.'

'Then come on. It's show time.'

CHAPTER 3

'The People call Chamique Johnson.'

Chamique was dressed on the conservative side but not ridiculously so. You could still see the street. You could still see the curves. I even had her wear high heels. There are times when you know that your only chance is for the jury to see the entire picture, warts and all. If you are going to go down, go down with the truth.

Chamique stated her name and swore on the Bible and sat down. I smiled at her and she offered me a little nod, giving me the OK to go ahead.

'You work as a stripper, isn't that right?'

Opening up with a question like that—without any preliminaries—surprised the gallery. There were a few gasps. Chamique blinked.

'Part time,' she said.

I didn't like that answer. It seemed too wary.

'But you do take off your clothes for money, right?'

'Yeah.'

That was more like it. No hesitation.

'Do you strip in clubs or at private parties?'

'Both.'

'How old are you?' I asked.

'Sixteen.'

'Don't you have to be eighteen to strip?'

'Yeah.'

'So how do you get round that?'

Chamique shrugged. 'I got a fake ID, says I'm twenty-one.'

'So you break the law?'

'Yeah. Guess so.'

I looked over at the defence table. Mort Pubin stared at me as if I were out of my mind. Flair Hickory had his palms pressed together, his index fingers resting on his lips. Their two clients, Barry Marantz and Edward Jenrette, wore blue blazers and pale faces. They looked contrite and scared. The cynic would say that this was intentional—that their lawyers had told them what expressions to wear. But I knew better.

I smiled at my witness. 'You're not the only one, Chamique. We found a bunch of fake IDs at your rapists' frat house—so that they could all do a little underage partying. At least you broke the law to make a living.'

Mort was on his feet. 'Objection!'

'Sustained.'

But it was in. As the old saw goes, 'You can't unring a bell.'

'Miss Johnson,' I continued, 'you're not a virgin, are you?'

'No.'

'In fact, you have a fifteen-month-old son out of wedlock.'

'I do.'

'Tell me, Miss Johnson. Does the fact that you're not a virgin and have a son out of marriage make you less of a human being?'

'Objection!'

'Sustained.' The judge, a man named Arnold Pierce, frowned at me.

'I'm just pointing out the obvious, Your Honour. If Miss Johnson were an upper-class blonde from Short Hills or Livingston—'

'Save it for the summation, Mr Copeland.'

I would. And I had used it in the opening.

I turned back to my victim. 'You weren't stripping the night you were raped, were you?'

'Objection!'

'Alleged rape,' I corrected.

'No,' Chamique said. 'I was invited.'

'You were invited to a party at the frat house where Mr Marantz and Mr Jenrette live?'

'That's right.'

'Who invited you?'

'Another boy who lived there. Jerry Flynn.'

'I see. How did you meet Mr Flynn?'

'I worked the frat the week before.'

'When you say you worked the frat—'

'I stripped for them,' Chamique finished for me. I liked that. We were getting a rhythm.

'And Mr Flynn was there?'

'They all were.'

'When you say "they all"—'

She pointed at the two defendants. 'They were there too. A bunch of twenty, twenty-five other guys.'

'OK, but it was Mr Flynn who invited you to the party a week later?'

'Yes.'

'Why did you choose to go?'

'It would be like a billionaire inviting you on his yacht.'

'You were impressed with them?'

'Yeah. 'Course.'

'And their money?'

'That too,' she said.

I loved her for that answer.

'And,' she went on, 'Jerry was sweet to me when I was stripping.'

'Mr Flynn treated you nicely?'

'Yeah.'

I nodded. I was entering trickier territory now but I went for it. 'Going back to the night you were hired to strip, did you perform other services on any of the men in attendance?

She swallowed but she held it together. Her voice was soft. 'Yeah.'

'Were these favours of a sexual nature?'

'Yeah.' She lowered her head.

'Don't be ashamed,' I said. 'You needed the money. What's their excuse?'

Mort Rubin turned red. 'Objection.'

'Sustained,' the judge said.

I held up my hand to the judge, signalling that I would cease. I am a firm believer in getting all the bad news out of the way.

'Were you interested in Mr Flynn as a potential boyfriend?'

Mort Pubin again: 'Objection! Relevance?'

'Mr Copeland?'

'Of course it's relevant. They are going to say that Miss Johnson is making up these charges to shake down their clients financially. I'm trying to establish her frame of mind on that night.'

'I'll allow it,' Judge Pierce said.

I repeated the question.

Chamique squirmed a little and it made her look her age. 'Jerry was out of my league. But I had never met anyone like him. He held a door for me. He was so nice. I'm not used to that.'

'And he's rich. Did that mean something to you?'

'Sure.' Chamique's eyes darted towards the jury box. The defiant expression was back. 'I got dreams too.'

I let that echo a few moments before following up. 'And what was your dream that night, Chamique?'

Mort was about to object again but Flair Hickory put his hand on Mort's forearm. By and large, juries don't like objections. They think you're hiding something from them. Flair wanted to stay liked.

Chamique shrugged. 'It's stupid.'

'Tell me anyway.'

'I thought maybe . . . I thought maybe he'd like me, you know?'

'I do,' I said. 'And when you arrived at the party was Mr Flynn still sweet?'

'At first, yeah.' A tear escaped. 'He was real sweet. It was—' She stopped.

'It was what, Chamique?'

'In the beginning'—another tear ran down her cheek—'it was the best night of my life.'

I let the words hang and echo. A third tear escaped.

'Are you OK?' I asked.

Chamique wiped the tear. 'I'm fine.' Her voice was hard again. 'Ask your question, Mr Copeland.'

She was wonderful. The jury had their heads up, listening to every word.

'When did Mr Flynn's behaviour towards you change?'

'I saw him whispering with that one over there.' She pointed towards Edward Jenrette.

'Mr Jenrette?'

'Yeah. Him.'

Jenrette tried not to shrink from her gaze. He was half successful.

'Then what happened?'

'Jerry asked me if I wanted to take a walk outside. They had a keg. He asked me if I wanted a beer. I said no. He was acting all jumpy and stuff. Something was different. He wouldn't look at me no more. I asked him if he was OK. He said, sure, everything was great. And then'—her voice didn't catch, but it came awfully close—'he said I had a hot bod and that he liked watching me take off my clothes.'

'Did that surprise you?'

'Yeah. I mean, he never talked like that before. His voice was all rough now.' She swallowed. 'Like the others.'

'Go on.'

'He said, "You wanna go upstairs and see my room?"'

'What did you say?'

'I said OK.'

'Did you want to go to his room?'

Chamique closed her eyes. Another tear leaked out. 'No.'

'Why did you go?'

'I wanted him to like me.'

'And you thought he would like you if you went upstairs with him?'

Chamique's voice was soft. 'I knew he wouldn't if I said no.'

I moved back to my table. I wanted to give the jury time to digest. Chamique kept her chin high, but you could feel the hurt emanating from her.

'What happened when you got upstairs?'

'I walked past a door.' She turned her eyes back to Jenrette. 'And then he grabbed me.'

Again I made her point out Edward Jenrette and identify him by name.

'Was anyone else in the room?'

'Yeah. Him.'

She pointed to Barry Marantz. I noticed the two families behind the defendants. The parents had those death-mask faces, where the cheekbones appear too prominent, the eyes sunken and shattered. They were devastated. I felt bad for them. But too bad. Edward Jenrette and Barry Marantz had people to protect them. Chamique Johnson had no one.

'OK,' I said, 'what happened next?'

'He closed the door.' She pointed to Marantz.

'Chamique, to make this easier, could you call him Mr Marantz and the other one Mr Jenrette?'

She nodded.

'So Mr Marantz closed the door. And where was Mr Flynn at this point?'

'I don't know. He didn't come in the room.'

I asked Chamique what happened next. I walked her through the assault, what they had said, how they had laughed, what they had done to her. I needed her to try to be as specific as possible. It was numbing.

When we finished the testimony on the assault, I gave it a few seconds and then approached our trickiest problem. 'In your testimony, you claimed your attackers used the names Cal and Jim.'

'Objection, Your Honour.'

It was Flair Hickory, speaking up for the first time.

'She did not claim they *used* the names Cal and Jim,' Flair said. 'She claimed, in both her testimony and statements, that they *were* Cal and Jim.'

'I'll rephrase,' I said with a tone of exasperation. 'Which one *was* Cal and which one *was* Jim?'

Chamique identified Barry Marantz as Cal and Edward Jenrette as Jim.

'How did you know their names? Did they introduce themselves to you?'

'They used them with each other.'

'You are aware,' I said, 'that neither defendant is named Cal or Jim.'

'I know,' she said. 'I'm just telling you what they said.'

No hesitation, no excuses—it was a good answer. I left it alone.

'What happened after they raped you?'

'They stuck me in a shower. Made me clean up. Then they took my clothes—they said they were going to burn them. Then they gave me a T-shirt and shorts.'

'What happened next?'

'Jerry walked me to the bus-stop.'

'Did you say anything to Mr Flynn during the walk?'

'No.'

I looked surprised. 'You didn't tell him you were raped?'

She smiled for the first time. 'You don't think he knew that?'

I let that go too. I wanted to shift gears again.

'Have you hired a lawyer, Chamique?'

'Yeah. Horace Foley. I want to make them pay,' she said.

'Isn't that what we're doing here? Finding a way to punish them?'

'Yeah. But the lawsuit is about money.'

I made a face as though I didn't understand. 'But the defence is going to claim that you made up these charges to extort money. They're going to say that your lawsuit proves that you're interested in money.'

'Can't do nothing about that,' she said. 'See, if I say I don't care about money, that would be a lie.' She looked at the jury. 'If I sat here and told you, money means nothing to me, would you believe me? 'Course not. They raped me. I want them to go to jail for that. And if I can get some money from them too, why not? I could use it.'

I stepped back. Candour—real candour—smells like nothing else.

'Nothing further,' I said.

CHAPTER 4

The trial broke for lunch.

Lunch is usually a time to discuss strategy with my subordinates. But I didn't want that right now. I wanted to be alone. I wanted to rework the direct in my head, see what I missed, figure out what Flair was going to do.

I ordered a cheeseburger and a beer.

The waitress dropped the burger in front of me. I eyed it. It looked so greasy I almost ordered a side of angiogram. But in truth, it was just what I'd wanted. I put both hands on it and felt my fingers sink into the bun.

'Mr Copeland?'

I didn't recognise the young man standing over me.

'This is for you.'

He dropped a note on the table and left. I opened it. It said: *Please meet me in the back booth on your right. EJ Jenrette.*

It was Edward's father. I looked down at my beloved burger. I hate eating cold food. So I ate it. I was starving. The beer tasted damn good.

When I was done I rose and headed towards the back booth on my right. EJ Jenrette was there, a glass of what looked like Scotch on the table in front of him. If he was upset by my tardiness he was hiding it well.

'You wanted to see me?' I said, sliding into the booth.

EJ nodded. He was a big man, ex-athlete type. I waited.

'You have a child,' he said. 'What would you do to protect her?'

'For one,' I said, 'I'd never let her go to a party at your son's frat house.'

'That's not funny. Do you really want my son to spend the next ten years in prison?'

'Yes. But the judge will decide the sentence.'

'He's just a kid. At worst, he got carried away.'

'You have a daughter, don't you, Mr Jenrette? If a couple of black kids from Irvington did those things to her, would you want it swept under the rug?'

'My daughter isn't a stripper.'

I raised my eyebrows. 'What Chamique Johnson does or doesn't do for a living is totally irrelevant to her being raped. The fact that she's forced to strip and sell herself doesn't make Edward less culpable.'

'I can make it hard on you.'

'Seems like you're already trying that.'

'The fund stoppage?' He shrugged. 'That was nothing. A muscle flex.'

He met my eye and held it. This had gone far enough.

'Goodbye, Mr Jenrette.'

He reached out and grabbed my forearm. 'My son and the Marantz boy will plead to whatever charge you come up with so long as there is no jail time. They can be on strict probation for as long as you want. In addition, I will help support this troubled woman. It's a win-win.'

'No,' I said.

'Do you really think these boys will do something like this again?'

'Truth?' I said. 'Probably not. But I'm big on justice.'

'Have you ever made a mistake, Mr Copeland? Because I'm going to dig. I'm going to dig until I find every mistake you ever made. And I'll use them. You got skeletons, Mr Copeland. I'm going to drag them out for all the world to see.' He seemed to be gaining confidence now. I didn't like that. 'At worst, my son made a big mistake. We're trying to find a way to make amends for what he did without destroying his life. Can you understand that?'

'I have nothing more to say to you,' I said.

He kept hold of my arm. 'Last warning, Mr Copeland. I will do whatever I can to protect my child.'

THE TRIAL WAS POSTPONED for the afternoon.

There were those who would argue that this made a difference in the case—that the jury would be left overnight with my direct and that it would settle in, blah, blah, blah. That sort of strategising was nonsense. If there was a positive in this development, it would be offset by the fact that Flair Hickory would now have more time to prepare his cross-examination. Trials work like that—stuff like this tends to even out.

I called Loren Muse on my cell. 'You have anything yet?'

'Still working on it.'

I hung up and saw there was a message from Detective York.

'You asked about Raya Singh, the victim's girlfriend. She works at an Indian restaurant.' He gave me the address. 'She's there all day. If you learn anything about Santiago's real name, let me know.'

I headed to my car, and as soon as I started to slide in, I realised something was very wrong. There was a manila envelope sitting on the driver's seat. I knew I hadn't left it there. I was sure that I had locked my car doors.

Someone had broken into my car.

I picked up the envelope. No address, no postage. The front was blank. I sat down in the front seat and closed the door behind me, then I slit the envelope open with my index finger, reached in and plucked out the contents.

Ice poured in my veins when I saw what it was: a photograph of my father. On the bottom, neatly typed on the white border, was my father's name and the year. That was all.

I just sat there for a moment. I stared at the photograph of my beloved father. I thought about how he had been a young doctor in Leningrad, how so much had been taken away from him, how his life ended up being an endless series of disappointments. I remembered him arguing with my mother, both of them wounded with no one to strike at but each other.

I didn't get it. Why was this photograph . . . ?

There was something else in the envelope. I dug with my hand to the bottom. It felt like an index card. I pulled it into view. On one side someone had typed three words: THE FIRST SKELETON.

'YOU FOUND OUT who sent the journal?' Lucy asked.

'Not yet,' Lonnie said. 'But I will.'

Lonnie kept his head down. Gone was the confident swagger. Lucy felt bad about that. He didn't like what she was making him do. She didn't like it either. But there was no choice here. She had worked hard to conceal her past. She had changed her name. She had got rid of her naturally blonde hair—man, how many women her age had naturally blonde hair?—and replaced it with this brown mess.

'OK,' she said. 'You'll be here when I get back?'

He nodded. Lucy headed down the stairs to her car.

Ira Silverstein, her father, lived in a halfway house ten miles from Reston University. The house, a converted mansion on a large tract of land, was nicer than most. Lucy's entire salary pretty much went here.

She parked near her father's old car, a rusted-out yellow VW Beetle. She doubted that it had moved from there in the past year. Her father had freedom here. He could check himself in and out. But the sad fact was, he almost never left his room. Lucy had a copy of the VW key and every once in a while she started it up, just to keep the battery in operating order.

She signed in at the front desk. This house catered for older residents with lifelong drug and mental issues. There seemed to be a tremendous range in here, everything from those who appeared totally 'normal' to people who could double as extras in *One Flew Over the Cuckoo's Nest*.

Ira was a little of both.

The slide into early dementia had been gradual. That was what the doctors said. But Lucy knew that the initial push down the slide had occurred that summer. Ira took a lot of the blame for what happened in those woods. It was his camp. He should have done more to protect his campers. The media went after him but not as hard as the families. Ira was too sweet a man to handle it. It broke him.

The doctor had explained that this sort of dementia—from age or drug use, no one could say—did not improve with time, so you want the patient to be as happy and stress free as possible, even if that means living something of a lie. Long after everyone else had turned in their hippie tie-dyes and peace beads, after the others had got haircuts and shaved off their beards, Ira stayed true to the cause. Half the time he actually thought it was still 1968. That was where he was happiest. So why fight it?

She stopped in his doorway. Ira's back was to her. He wore the familiar hemp poncho. His hair was in every-direction shock. 'Let's Live for Today', a classic from 1967, boomed from what her father still called a 'hi-fi'.

'Hey, Ira.' He had never wanted her to call him 'Dad'. He turned towards her voice and waved. 'Hey, Luce.'

She blinked away the tears. He always knew who she was.

'I'm so happy you're here . . .' Ira said, half stumbling towards her.

She took a step in and embraced him.

'How are you feeling, Ira?'

'Great. Never better.'

He opened a bottle and took a vitamin. Ira did that a lot. Despite his non-capitalist ways, her father had made a small fortune in vitamins during the early seventies. He cashed out and bought that property on the Pennsylvania–New Jersey border. For a while he ran it as a commune. But that didn't last. So he turned it into a summer camp.

'How are you?' she asked.

'Never better, Luce.'

And then he started crying. Lucy sat with him and held his hand. He cried, then he laughed, then he cried again. He kept telling her over and over how much he loved her.

'You're the world, Luce,' he said.

'I love you too, Ira.'

She couldn't stay long. She needed to get back to her office and see what Lonnie had learned. Ira's head was on her shoulder. When a nurse came in, Lucy used the interruption to extricate herself from him.

'I'll be back next week, OK?'

Ira nodded. He was smiling when she left.

In the corridor the nurse was waiting.

'How has he been?' Lucy asked.

Normally the nurse would say, 'Oh, he's doing just fine,' but this time, she said, 'Your father has been more agitated lately.'

'How so?'

'Ira is normally the sweetest, most gentle man in the universe. But his mood swings—'

'He's always had mood swings.'

'Not like these . . . He talks a lot about a summer camp. And then he loses it. He starts ranting about blood and the woods and the dark, stuff like that. Then he clams up. It's creepy.'

From down the hall another nurse called, 'Rebecca?'

The nurse said, 'I have to run.'

Lucy looked into the room. Her father's back was to her. He was staring at the wall. She wondered what was going on in his head. What he really knew about that night.

She tore herself away and headed towards the exit. The receptionist asked her to sign out. Each patient had his own page, and Lucy was about to do the same absent-minded scribble she had done on the way in when she stopped. There was another name there. Last week, Ira had another visitor. His first and only visitor besides her. Ever. She frowned. The name was wholly unfamiliar.

Who the hell was Manolo Santiago?

I NEEDED NOW to make a detour on the way to my visit with Raya Singh. There was only one person who could help me when it came to my dad and his potential skeletons. I took out my cellphone and dialled.

He answered on the first ring in his low rumble of a voice. 'Paul.'

'Hi, Uncle Sosh.'

Sosh wasn't really my uncle. He was a close family friend from the old country. I hadn't seen him in three months, not since my father's funeral, but as soon as I heard his voice, I instantly saw the big bear of a man. My father said that Uncle Sosh had been the most powerful and feared man in Pulkovo, the town on the outskirts of Leningrad where he and my father had been raised.

'I hoped you would call today.'

That surprised me. 'Why?'

'Because, my young nephew, we need to talk.'

'About what?'

'I never talk about anything on the phone. When can you be here?'

Sosh had an expansive penthouse on 36th Street in Manhattan. 'Half an hour if there's no traffic,' I said.

THERE WAS NO TRAFFIC, so the ride to Uncle Sosh's was closer to twenty-five minutes. The doorman wore one of those ridiculous uniforms with rope tassels. He had been told that I was arriving. If the doorman isn't told in advance, he doesn't ring up. You just don't get in. He held the elevator door open.

I stepped out into the huge penthouse. Uncle Sosh's face lit up when he saw me. He spread his hands wide. One of my most vivid childhood memories was the size of those hands. They were still huge. He had greyed over the years, but even now in his early seventies strength emanated from him. He pulled me close in a bear hug and I felt as though he could simply tighten his grip and snap my spine.

After a few seconds, Sosh held me at arm's length so he could take a good look. 'Your father,' he said, his voice thick with more than accent. 'You look just like your father.'

Sosh had arrived from the Soviet Union not long after we did. He worked for InTourist, the Soviet tour company, in their Manhattan office. His job was to help facilitate American tourists who wished to visit Leningrad. Since the fall of the Soviet government, he dabbled in 'import-export'. I never knew what that meant exactly, but it had paid for this penthouse.

Uncle Sosh was not one for casual talk. He looked me hard in the eye and said, 'I have been getting calls from friends in the old country.'

'I'm not sure I follow.'

'People have been asking questions. Americans. They are in Moscow and throwing money around and asking questions about your father.'

'What kind of questions?'

'You remember the old rumours?'

'You're kidding me.'

But he wasn't. It made sense. The First Skeleton. I should have guessed. I remembered the rumours, of course. They nearly destroyed my family.

My sister and I were born during the Cold War. My father was a doctor but lost his licence on charges of incompetence trumped up because he was Jewish. That was how it was in those days. At the same time, a reform synagogue here in the United States—Skokie, Illinois, to be more specific—was working hard on behalf of Soviet Jewry. We got lucky. They got us out.

For a long time we were heralded in our new land as heroes. My father spoke passionately at Friday-night services about the plight of the Soviet Jew. Money was donated. But about a year into our stay, my father and the head rabbi had a falling-out, and suddenly there were whispers that my father had got out of the Soviet Union because he was KGB, that it was all a ruse. The charges were pathetic and false.

I shook my head. 'They're trying to prove that my father was KGB?'

'Yes.'

I got it. Friggin' Jenrette. I was something of a public figure now. The charges, even if ultimately proven false, would be damaging. I should know. Twenty-five years ago my family lost pretty much everything because of those accusations. We left Skokie, moved east to Newark. Our family was never the same.

'So,' I said, 'they must have something.'

The big man did not reply. I watched his face. And it was as if my entire world, everything I grew up believing, slowly shifted.

'Was he KGB, Sosh?' I asked.

'It was a long time ago,' Sosh said.

'Does that mean yes?'

Sosh smiled slowly. 'Do you know how I came to this country?'

'You worked for a travel company.'

'It was the Soviet Union, Pavel,' he said, using my Russian name. 'There were no companies. InTourist was run by the government. So when the government had a chance to send someone to live in New York, do you think they sent the man who was most competent in booking vacations? Or do you think they sent someone who might help them in other ways?'

I thought about the size of his hands, his strength. 'So you were KGB?'

'I was a colonel in the military. We didn't call it KGB. But yes, I guess you would call me a spy. I would meet with American officials. I would try to bribe them. We learned nothing relevant. Not ever. The American spies never learned anything about us either. We passed nonsense from side to side. It was a silly game.'

'And my father?'

'The Soviet government let him out. Your Jewish friends think that they applied enough pressure. But please. Did a bunch of Jews really think they could pressure a government that answered to no one? It's almost funny.'

'So you're saying . . .?'

'I'm just telling you how it was. Did your father promise he would help the regime? Of course. But it was just to get out. You can't imagine what it was like for him. Your father was a good doctor and a better man. The government took away his licence. Then your grandmother and grandfather . . . you're too young to remember—'

'I remember,' I said.

But did I? I was three when they were taken away. Did I really remember them, or has that old photo I still keep out come to life?

'Your grandparents were intellectuals—university professors. Your grandfather headed the history department. Your grandmother was a mathematician. The most brilliant academics sought them out. But, of course, that drew the attention of the government. They were labelled radicals. They were considered dangerous. Do you remember when they were arrested? A traitor had turned them in.'

'I remember,' I said, 'the aftermath.'

He closed his eyes for a long second. 'So here he was, your father. He had lost so much—his career, his reputation, his licence and now your mother's parents. And suddenly the government gave your father a way out. A chance for a fresh start in the USA.'

'And all he had to do was spy?'

Sosh waved a dismissive hand in my direction. 'What could a man like your father learn? Even if he tried—which he didn't.'

'And my mother?'

'Natasha was just a woman to them. The government cared nothing for the woman. But when her parents were taken and, well, put to death, really, she was never the same.'

'What happened, Sosh?'

'They were sent to a gulag—a work camp. The conditions were terrible. Your grandfather had a heart condition. They wouldn't treat him. Wouldn't even give him his medicine. He was dead within three months.'

I waited.

'So what aren't you telling me, Sosh?'

'Do you know what happened to your grandmother?'

'I know what my mother told me. With her husband gone, her heart sorta gave out.'

'Your grandmother committed suicide. She hanged herself with a sheet.'

My body stiffened. I started shaking my head. I thought of that picture of my Noni. I thought of the stories my mother told me about her, about her sharp mind and sharper tongue. Suicide.

'Did my mother know?' I asked.

'Yes.'

'She never told me.'

'Maybe I shouldn't have either. I guess I wanted you to know how it was,' he said. 'For your mother. So maybe you'd understand more.'

Sosh turned away from me then. He moved over to the window. He had a great view of the Hudson. There were two mega-cruise ships in port.

'Do you know where my mother is?'

The big man didn't answer for a long time.

'Sosh?'

'She ran back to Russia.'

'Why?'

'You can't blame her, Pavel. You hate your government but never your people. Your homeland is your homeland. Always.'

He turned to me. Our eyes locked.

'That was her reasoning? Because her homeland was always her homeland?' I said, almost shouting. I felt something in my blood tick. 'How about your family is your family? Or more to the point, how about your son is your son? What about me and Dad?'

'I don't have an answer for you, Pavel.'

'Do you know where she is now?'

'No.'

'But you could find her, couldn't you? Would you find her for me?'

He didn't nod but he didn't shake his head either.

'The past is for the dead, Pavel. You don't want to bring the dead back. You want to bury them and move on.'

'My mother isn't dead,' I said. 'Is she?'

'I don't know.'

'So why are you talking about the dead? And while we're talking about the dead, here's one more thing to chew over'—I couldn't stop myself, so I just said it—'I'm not even sure my sister is dead any more.'

I expected to see shock on his face. I didn't. He barely seemed surprised.

'To you,' he said, 'they should both be dead.'

CHAPTER 5

I shook off Uncle Sosh's words and headed back. I needed to focus on two things and two things only: Focus One, convict those two damned sons of bitches who had raped Chamique Johnson. And Focus Two, find out where Gil Perez had been for the past twenty years.

I checked the address Detective York had given me for the witness/girlfriend. Raya Singh worked at an Indian restaurant called Curry Up and Wait. I hate pun titles. Or do I love them? Let's go with love.

When I arrived at the restaurant, I parked the car and called Loren Muse. She answered and I said, 'I may have a small problem.'

'What's that?' Muse asked.

'Jenrette's father is coming after me. He's digging into my past.'

'Will he find anything?'

'You dig into anybody's past,' I said, 'you find something.'

'OK, cut to the chase then. What do you need from me?'

'You're friends with some of the local private eyes, right? Can you call around, see if you can find out who's on me?'

'OK, I'm on it.'

'Muse, how do you think we did today?'

'It was a good day for the good guys,' she said. 'But probably not good enough.'

'Cal and Jim?'

'I'm in the mood to gun down every man with those names.'

'Get on it,' I said and hung up.

The interior of the restaurant was very bright and colourful in the pseudo-style of a Hindu temple, with faux-mosaic statues of Ganesh and other deities, and waitresses costumed in belly-revealing aqua outfits.

The hostess frowned when I entered. 'How many?' she asked.

'I'm not here to eat,' I said. 'Is Raya Singh here?'

'Who?'

I repeated the name.

'I don't . . . oh, wait, she's the new girl. Who wants to know?'

I handed her a business card. She read it and then shouted out, 'Raya!'

Raya Singh stepped forward and I stepped back. She was younger than I'd expected, early twenties, and absolutely stunning. The first thing you noticed was that Raya Singh had more curves than seemed anatomically possible. Her skin was more gold than brown and she had almond eyes that a man could slip into and never find his way back out.

'Raya Singh?' I said.

'Yes.'

'My name is Paul Copeland. I'm the prosecutor for Essex County in New Jersey. Could we talk a moment?'

'Is this about the murder?'

'Yes.'

'Then of course.'

Her voice was polished with a hint of a New England–boarding-school accent that shouted refinement over geographical locale. I was trying not to stare. She saw that and smiled a little.

She led me outside onto the street, where it was quieter. She wrapped her arms around herself as though she were cold. I was tempted to offer her my coat or something, but it wasn't cold at all. Oh, and I wasn't wearing a coat.

'Do you know a man named Manolo Santiago?' I asked.

'He was murdered,' she said.

Her voice had a strange lilt to it, as if she were reading for a part.

'Were you lovers?'

'Not yet. Our relationship,' she said, 'was platonic.'

'Do you know where Mr Santiago lived?'

'No, I'm sorry, I don't.'

'How did you two meet?'

'He approached me on the street and asked me if I would like to grab a cup of coffee.'

'And you did?'

'Yes.'

'Do you always do that?' I asked. 'Meet a stranger and accept his invitation to grab coffee with him?'

That seemed to amuse her. 'Do I need to justify my behaviour to you, Mr Copeland?'

'No. Manolo Santiago was an alias. I'm trying to find out his real name.'

'I wouldn't know it.'

'At the risk of overstepping my bounds,' I said, 'I'm having trouble here. Men must hit on you all the time, so why did you go with him?'

'Does it matter?'

'It might tell me something about him.'

'Suppose I told you that I found him handsome. Would that help?'

'Did you?'

The smile was knowing. 'You almost sound jealous.'

'Ms Singh, I'm investigating a murder. Can we stop the head games?'

'Well, OK then,' she said. 'Fair enough.'

'Can you help me figure out who he really was?'

She thought about it. 'Maybe through his cellphone records?'

'We checked the one he had on him. Your call was the only one on it. Can you think of anything else?'

'Not really.'

I took out a card and wrote down my mobile phone number. 'If you do remember something, will you call me?'

'Of course.'

I handed it to her. She looked at me with those eyes and smiled. 'Why don't you ask me out?' she asked.

'Excuse me?'

'I know you think I'm pretty. Why don't you ask me out?'

'I don't mix my work life with my personal,' I said.

'I came here from Calcutta. Have you been?'

The change in subjects threw me for a second. I told her I had never been, but I obviously knew of it.

'What you've heard,' she said. 'It's even worse.'

I said nothing, wondering where she was going with this.

'I have a life plan,' she said. 'The first part was getting here, to the US.'

'And the second part?'

'I know my assets. I am beautiful. I am also a nice person and I have learned how to be'—she considered her words—'good for a man. I will make a man incredibly happy. I will give myself to him whenever he wants and in whatever way he wants. And I will do it gladly.'

Oookay, I thought. My mouth felt very dry.

'Manolo Santiago,' I said in a voice that sounded far away. 'Did you think he might be that man?'

'I thought he might be,' she said. 'But he wasn't. You seem nice. Like you would treat a woman well.' Raya Singh might have moved towards me, I can't be sure. But she suddenly seemed closer. 'So how do you know that I'm not the one? The one who will make you deliriously happy.'

Whoa. 'I don't,' I said.

She just looked at me. Oh, I was being played. I knew that, yet I found it oddly endearing. Or maybe it was the blinded-by-beauty thing again.

'I have to go,' I said. 'You have my number.'

'Goodbye, Mr Copeland.' She gave me one more smile that made me feel like a fish dropped on a dock. 'I hope you find what you're looking for.'

LUCY WANTED TO Google the name 'Manolo Santiago'—he was probably a reporter doing a story on Wayne Steubens—but Lonnie was waiting for her in the office. He didn't look up.

'You know who sent the journals,' she said as she entered.

'I can't be sure.'

'But?'

Lonnie took a deep breath, readying himself, she hoped, to take the plunge. 'There are ways of sending email anonymously. But usually, even if you do that, there are some footprints.'

'Great, Lonnie, super.' He was stalling. 'So can I assume you found some of these footprints in the email with that journal attached?'

'Yes,' Lonnie said. He looked up now and managed a smile. 'I'm not going to ask you why you want the name any more. Because I know you, Lucy. Like most hot chicks, you're a major pain in the ass. But you're also frighteningly ethical. If you need to betray the trust of your students there must be a good reason.'

'Just tell me, Lonnie.'

'The email came from a bank of computers at the Frost Library.'

'There must be, what, fifty computers in there? We'll never figure out who sent it.'

Lonnie made a yes-and-no gesture with a head tilt. 'We know what time it was sent. Six forty-two p.m. the day before yesterday. The students who use the computer need to sign in. So I went to the library and got the time sheets. There was only one student in this class who had signed up for a computer during the hour between six and seven p.m.'

'Who?'

Lonnie walked over to the window. He looked down at the quad. 'I'll give you a hint,' he said.

'Lonnie, I'm not in the mood—'

'Her nose,' he said, 'is brown.'

Lucy froze. 'Sylvia Potter?'

His back was still to her. 'Yes,' he said.

'HEY.'

It was Loren Muse. I was back in the courthouse the next morning. Flair Hickory's cross-examination would start in a few minutes.

'Hey,' I said.

'You look like hell. You worried about this cross?'

'Of course.'

'Chamique will be fine. You did a helluva job.'

I nodded, tried to get my head back into the game.

'Oh,' she said, walking next to me. 'You heard of MVD?'

'Most Valuable Detection,' I said.

'Right, biggest private-eye firm in the state. Cingle Shaker, the woman I have on the frat boys, used to work there. Rumour has it they got a no-expense-spared, seek-'n'-destroy investigation going on with you.'

We entered the courtroom. 'Super.' I handed her an old picture of Gil Perez. She looked at it. 'What?'

'Do we still have Farrell Lynch doing the computer work?'

'We do.'

'Ask him to do an age progression on this. Age him twenty years. Tell Farrell to give him a shaved head too.'

Loren Muse was about to follow up, but something in my face stopped her. She shrugged and peeled off. I sat down. Judge Pierce came in. We all rose. And then Chamique Johnson took the stand.

Flair Hickory stood and carefully buttoned his jacket. I frowned. The last time I'd seen a powder-blue suit in that shade was in 1978.

He smiled at Chamique. 'Good morning, Miss Johnson.'

Chamique looked terrified. 'Morning,' she managed.

Flair introduced himself as if they'd just stumbled across each other at a cocktail party. He segued into Chamique's criminal record. She had been arrested for prostitution, correct? She had been arrested for drugs, correct?

I didn't object. I had raised much of this during my own examination.

After twenty minutes, Flair began his cross in earnest. 'You have smoked marijuana, have you not?'

Chamique said, 'Yeah.'

'Did you smoke any the night of your alleged attack?'

'No.'

'No?' Flair put his hand on his chest as though this answer shocked him to the core. 'Hmm. Did you drink any alcohol? A beer or wine maybe?'

'No.'

'Nothing. How about a regular drink? Maybe a soda?'

I was going to object, but again my strategy was to let her handle this as much as she could.

'I had some punch,' Chamique said.

'Punch, I see. And it was non-alcoholic?'

'That's what the guys said.'

'Which guys?'

She hesitated. 'Jerry.'

'Jerry Flynn?'

'Yeah.'

'How many glasses did you have?'

'I don't know.'

'More than one?'

'I guess.'

'Please don't guess, Miss Johnson. Would you say more than one?'

'Probably, yeah.'

'More than two?'

'I don't think so. Probably two. Maybe not even that much.'

'And the only person who told you that the punch was non-alcoholic was Jerry Flynn. Is that correct?'

'I think.'

'Before you said "guys" as in more than one. But now you're saying just one person. Are you changing your testimony?'

I stood. 'Objection.'

Flair waved me off. 'He's right, small matter, let's move on.' He cleared his throat. 'Did you take any drugs that night?'

'No.'

'So when did you last do any sort of drugs?'

'I don't remember.'

'Let me see if I can help nail down the timetable. Have you done any illegal drugs since your son's been born?'

Her voice was very quiet. 'Yeah.'

'Can you tell us what kind?'

I stood yet again. 'I object. We get the point. Ms Johnson has done drugs in the past. No one denies that. What's the difference when?'

The judge looked at Flair. 'Mr Hickory?'

'We believe that Ms Johnson is a habitual drug user. We believe that she was high that night and the jury should understand that when assessing the integrity of her testimony.'

'Ms Johnson has already stated that she had not taken any drugs that night or drunk any alcohol.'

'And I,' Flair said, 'have the right to cast doubt on her recollections. The punch was indeed spiked. I will produce Mr Flynn, who will testify that the defendant knew that. I also want to establish that this is a woman who did not hesitate to do drugs, even when she was mothering a child—'

'Your Honour!' I shouted.

'OK, that'enough.' The judge cracked the gavel. 'Can we move along, Mr Hickory?'

I sat down. My objection had been stupid. It looked as if I was trying to get in the way and worse, I had given Flair the chance to offer more narrative. My strategy had been to stay silent. Losing my discipline had cost us.

'Ms Johnson, you are accusing these boys of raping you, is that correct?'

'Yeah.'

'Uh-huh. And tell me, Ms Johnson, do you know any rapists?'

I was up again. 'You mean, besides your clients?'

Flair just gave me a look and then turned to the jury as if to say, *My, wasn't that the lowest cheap shot ever?* And truth: it was.

For her part, Chamique said, 'I don't understand what you mean.'

'No matter, my dear,' Flair said, as if her answer would bore him. 'I'll get back to that later.'

I hate when Flair says that.

'During this purported attack, did my clients, Mr Jenrette and Mr Marantz, did they wear masks or try to hide their faces?'

'No.'

Flair Hickory shook his head as if this was the most puzzling thing he had ever heard.

'So it is your testimony that two men raped you, that they didn't wear masks or disguise themselves, that they did this in their room with at least one witness watching you being forced to enter that room. Correct?'

'That sounds right, yeah.'

'And yet, for some reason'—again Flair looked like the most perplexed man imaginable—'they used aliases? Your attackers used the names Cal and Jim instead of their own. That's your testimony, is it not?'

'It is.'

'Does that make any sense to you?'

'Objection,' I said. 'Nothing about this brutal crime makes sense to her.'

'Oh, I understand that,' Flair said. 'I was just hoping that Ms Johnson might have a theory on why they would let their faces be seen and yet use aliases.' He smiled sweetly. 'Do you have one, Miss Johnson?'

'No.'

Flair Hickory walked back to his desk. 'Before I asked you if you knew any rapists. Do you remember that?'

'Yeah.'

'Good. Do you?'

'I don't think so.'

Flair nodded and picked up a sheet of paper. 'How about a man currently being incarcerated in Rahway on charges of sexual battery named—and please pay attention, Ms Johnson—*Jim* Broodway?'

Chamique's eyes grew wide. 'You mean James?'

'I mean, Jim—or James, if you want the formal name—Broodway of Newark, New Jersey. Do you know him?'

'Yeah.' Her voice was soft. 'I used to know him.'

'Have you ever had sex with Jim Broodway?'

'His name is James!' Chamique said again.

'Let's call him "Mr Broodway" for the sake of this discussion, shall we? Have you ever had sex with Mr Broodway?'

I couldn't just let this go. 'Objection. Her sex life is irrelevant to this case. The law is clear here.'

Judge Pierce looked at Flair. 'Mr Hickory?'

'I am not trying to imply that Miss Johnson is a woman of loose morals,' Flair said. 'Opposing counsel already explained that she has worked as a prostitute and has engaged in a variety of sexual activities.'

When will I learn to keep my mouth shut?

'The point I am trying to raise is a different one. Chamique Johnson has testified that a man named Jim raped her. What I am asking is this: did she ever have sex with Mr Jim Broodway—or James, if she prefers—who is currently serving time in a state penitentiary for sexual battery?'

I saw now where this was going. And it wasn't good.

'I'll allow it,' the judge said.

'Miss Johnson, have you ever had sexual relations with Mr Broodway?'

A tear rolled down her cheek. 'Yeah.'

'More than once?'

'Yeah.' She was crying harder now.

'Was there ever another man involved in those sexual encounters?'

The courtroom exploded.

'Your Honour!' I shouted.

'Order!' The judge used the gavel. 'Order!'

The room quieted quickly. Judge Pierce looked down at me. 'I know how hard this is to listen to, but I'm going to allow this question.' He turned to Chamique. 'Please answer.'

The court stenographer read the question again. Tears spilled down Chamique's face. When the stenographer finished, she said, 'No.'

'Mr Broodway will testify that—'

'He let some friend of his watch!' Chamique cried out. 'That's all. I never let him touch me! You hear me? Not ever!'

I tried to keep my head up, tried not to close my eyes.

'So,' Flair Hickory said, 'you had sex with a man named Jim—'

'James! His name is James!'

'—and another man was in the room and yet you don't know how you came up with the names Jim and Cal?'

'I don't know no Cal. And his name is James.'

Flair Hickory moved closer to her, his face showing concern.

'I don't necessarily say you're lying,' he went on, 'but isn't there a chance that maybe you had too much punch—not your fault, you thought it was non-alcoholic—and then you engaged in a consensual act and just flashed back to some other time period? Wouldn't that explain your insisting that the two men who raped you were named Jim and Cal?'

I was up on my feet to say that was two questions, but Flair again knew what he was doing.

'Withdrawn,' Flair Hickory said, as if this whole thing was just the saddest thing for all parties involved. 'I have no further questions.'

CHAPTER 6

Lucy Gold called Sylvia Potter's room. There was no answer. She checked the school phone directory, but they didn't list mobile numbers. Lucy remembered seeing Sylvia using a BlackBerry, so she emailed a brief message asking her to call as soon as possible.

While she waited for Sylvia to call, she tried to Google the name 'Manolo Santiago'. There were lots of hits, but nothing that helped. So who was he? She could ask Ira, of course. If he remembered.

Two hours passed. She called Sylvia's room. She tried emailing again. No answer.

Lucy checked the student directory. Sylvia lived in Stone House down in the social quad. She decided to walk over and see what she could find.

Her entrance drew a few stares but not too many. She took the centre stairwell. Sylvia Potter lived in a single on the first floor. Lucy found her door and knocked. There was no reply. She tried the knob. It was locked. She thought about leaving a note on the door—there was an erasable board—but it seemed a little desperate. She had started back down the stairs when the front door of Stone House opened and Sylvia Potter entered.

'Oh, hi, Professor Gold. Class ran late, I'm so sorry. I figured you'd be gone. Shall I stop by tomorrow?' Sylvia asked.

'Do you have time now?'

Sylvia looked at her watch without really looking at it. 'I'm really so crazy with this project. Can it wait until tomorrow?'

'It's about your journal.'

'My . . ?' She shook her head. 'But I sent it in anonymously. How would you know which is mine?'

'Please, Sylvia—'

'You said! You promised! They were anonymous. You said that.'

'I know what I said. But this is really important.'

'No, it's not. I don't want to talk to you. You can't make me. And if you say anything about it, I will tell the dean what you did. Leave me alone!'

Sylvia Potter turned, opened the door and ran away.

AFTER FLAIR HICKORY finished with Chamique, the Judge called the court day over. I met Loren Muse in my office.

'Wow,' Loren said. 'That sucked.'

'Get on that name thing,' I said. 'Find out if Broodway is known as "Jim".'

Muse frowned. 'You think that's going to help?'

'It can't hurt,' I said. 'Has your friend Cingle learned anything?'

'Not yet.'

My cellphone rang. I looked at the caller ID. I didn't recognise the number. I put the phone to my ear and said, 'Hello?'

'It is Raya.'

Raya Singh. The comely Indian waitress. I felt my throat go dry.

'How are you?'

'Fine.'

'Did you think of something?'

Muse looked at me. I tried to look at her as if to say, this is private. For an investigator, she could be slow on the pick-up. Or maybe that was intentional.

'I probably should have said something earlier,' Raya Singh said. 'But you showing up like that surprised me.'

'Raya,' I said, 'I have no idea what you're talking about.'

'He mentioned your name.'

'Manolo Santiago mentioned my name? And you didn't think you should tell me this before?'

'I didn't know if I could trust you.'

'And what changed your mind?'

'I looked you up on the Internet. You really are the county prosecutor.'

'What did Santiago say about me?'

'He said you lied about something.'

'About what?'

'I don't know.'

I pushed ahead. 'Who did he say it to?'

'A man. I don't know his name. He also had clippings about you in his apartment.'

'His apartment? I thought you said you didn't know where he lived.'

'That's when I didn't trust you.'

'And you do now?'

She did not reply to that one directly. 'Pick me up at the restaurant in one hour,' Raya Singh said, 'and I'll show you where Manolo lived.'

WHEN LUCY CAME back to her office, Lonnie was there, holding up sheets of paper. 'What's that?' she asked.

'More of that journal.'

She tried hard not to snap the pages from his hand.

'Did you find Sylvia?' he asked.

'Yes. She went crazy on me and won't talk. Did you read it already?'

'Yep,' he said, and passed the sheets to her.

She just nodded and started in for herself.

P broke our embrace and darted towards the scream.

I called after him, but he didn't stop. Two seconds later, it was like the night had swallowed him whole. I tried to follow. But it was dark. The screaming voice had been a girl's. That much I could tell. I was scared.

I trekked through the woods in the moonlight. Moonlight in the woods changes the colour of everything. So when I finally found P and I saw the strange colour on his shirt, I didn't recognise what it was at first. I couldn't tell the shade of crimson. It looked more like liquid blue. He looked at me. His eyes were wide.

'We have to go,' he said. 'And we can't tell anyone we were out here . . .'

That was it. Lucy put the story down. Lonnie was watching her.

'So,' he said, 'I assume that you are the narrator of this little tale?'

'What?'

'I've been trying to figure this out, and I've only come up with one possible explanation. You're the girl in the story. Someone is writing about you.'

'That's ridiculous,' she said.

'Come on, Luce. We have tales of incest in that pile and we aren't searching those kids out. Yet you're all uptight about this scream-in-the-woods story?'

'Let it go, Lonnie.'

He shook his head. 'Sorry, not my nature. I'd like to help if I can.'

'You can't.'

'I know more than you think.'

Lucy looked up at him and waited.

'Something about this journal kept bugging me,' he went on. 'This stuff about a camp. I was young, but I remember hearing about the Summer Slasher. So I did a little research.' He tried to give her the cocky smile. 'Lucy Gold isn't your real name. You changed it.'

'It was a tough time in my life. That's why I changed my name.'

'I can imagine. Your family took a big hit. You wanted to get out from under that.'

'Yes.'

'And now, for some weird reason, it's coming back.'

She nodded.

'Who is P? It's Paul Copeland, right? He's a DA or something now.'

She shook her head.

'You're not making this easy,' he said.

She kept her mouth closed.

'OK,' he said, standing. 'I'll help anyway. I'll get Sylvia Potter to talk.'

'How?'

Lonnie headed for the door. 'I got my ways.'

On the way back to the Indian restaurant, I took a detour and visited Jane's grave. I was not sure why. I did not do it that often.

I sat on a concrete bench. I didn't talk to her. I don't really feel my wife's presence here. It was so bad in the end. Jane suffered. I watched. For a while anyway. We got hospice care—Jane wanted to die at home—but then there was her weight loss and the smell and the groans. The sound that I remembered most was the awful coughing noise, more a choke really, when Jane couldn't get the phlegm up and it would hurt so much. It went on for months and months and I tried to be strong but I wasn't as strong as Jane and she knew that.

There was a time early in our relationship when she knew that I was having doubts. I had lost a sister. My mother had run off on me. And now, for the first time in a long time, I was letting a woman into my life.

'I'm not her,' Jane said one night, as if she could read my thoughts. 'I will never abandon you.' But in the end, she did.

I had dated since her death. I have even had some fairly intense emotional commitments. One day I hope to remarry. But right now, as I thought about that night, I realised that it would probably not happen.

I'm not her, my wife had said. And, of course, she meant my mother.

RAYA SINGH WAS WAITING for me in the restaurant parking lot. She had turned in the aqua waitress uniform for jeans and a dark blue blouse. Her hair was pulled back in a ponytail. The effect was no less dazzling.

She slipped into the passenger seat. She smelt great.

'Where to?' I asked.

'Do you know where Route 17 is?'

'Yes.'

'Take it north.'

I pulled out of the lot. 'Do you want to start telling me the truth?' I asked.

'I never lied to you,' she said. 'I decided not to tell you certain things.'

'Tell me about hearing Santiago say my name,' I said.

She took a deep breath. 'Manolo said you lied about something involving'—she hesitated—'involving woods or a forest or something like that.'

I felt my heart lurch across my chest. 'What were his exact words?'

'I don't remember.'

'Try.'

'"Paul Copeland lied about what happened in those woods."' Then she tilted her head. 'Oh, wait.'

I did.

'That was the other name. He said, "So did Lucy."'

Now it was my turn to be struck silent.

'Paul,' Raya said, 'who is this Lucy?'

WE TOOK THE REST of the ride in silence.

I was lost in thoughts of Lucy. I tried to remember the feel of her flaxen hair, the wondrous smell of it. But I couldn't. I just remembered the wonder. I remembered the lust. We were both clumsy, both inexperienced, but God, that lust. And when did that lust segue into love?

Summer romances come to an end. That was part of the deal. I thought Luce and I would be different. We were, I guess, but not in the way that I thought. I truly believed that we would never let each other go.

The apartment was in Ramsey, New Jersey. Raya had a key. She opened the door to a room on the second floor. I would describe the decor to you except that the only word to describe it would be *nondescript*.

When we stepped into the room, Raya let out a little gasp.

'What?' I said.

Her eyes took in the whole room. 'There were tons of papers on that table,' she said.

We did a pretty thorough search. Everything was gone—there were no clothes, no personal items.

'Someone cleared this place out.'

'When were you here last?'

'Three days ago.'

I started for the door. 'Come on. I'm going to talk to someone at the front desk.'

But there was a kid working there. He gave us pretty much nothing. The occupant had signed in as Manolo Santiago. The room had been paid for in cash, until the end of the month. And no, the kid didn't remember what Mr Santiago looked like or anything about him.

Raya and I headed back to Santiago's room.

'You said there were papers? What did they say?'

'I didn't pry.'

'Raya,' I said. 'I have to be honest here. I'm not buying the ignorant act.'

She just looked at me with those damn eyes. 'Why should I trust you? When we met you said you were just investigating his murder, like a regular detective. But that wasn't true, was it?'

I said nothing.

'Manolo didn't trust you. I read those articles. I know something happened to all of you in those woods twenty years ago. He thought you lied about it. If you were in my position, would you tell everything you knew?'

I took a second. She had a point. 'If you saw those articles, then you know that my sister disappeared that night. That's why I'm here.'

'You're here to avenge your sister?'

'No,' I said. 'I'm here to find her.'

'But I thought she was dead. Wayne Steubens murdered her.'

'That was what I used to think.'

Raya turned away for a moment. Then she looked right through me. 'Who is Lucy? What's her connection to this?'

'Her father owned the camp,' I said. Then I added, 'She was also my girlfriend at the time.'

'And how did you both lie?'

'We didn't lie.'

'So what was Manolo talking about?'

'Damned if I know. That's what I'm trying to find out.'

'I don't understand. What makes you so sure your sister is alive?'

'I'm not sure,' I said. 'But I think there's a decent enough chance.'

'Why?'

'Because of Manolo.'

'What about him?

I studied her face and wondered if I was being played here. 'Do you know why he was looking into what happened that night? Weren't you curious?'

She shrugged. 'He said it was business.'

'Raya,' I said. 'Manolo Santiago wasn't his real name. His real name was Gil Perez.'

She took a second to process this. 'The boy from the woods? You're telling me he was alive this whole time?'

I nodded.

'And if he was alive . . .' Raya Singh stopped. So I finished it for her.

'Maybe my sister is too.'

'Or maybe,' she said, 'Manolo—Gil, whatever—killed them all.'

I hadn't thought of that. It made some sense. Gil kills them all, leaves evidence he was a victim too. But how do you explain Wayne Steubens?

'If that's the case,' I said, 'then I'll find that out.'

Raya frowned. 'Manolo said you and Lucy were lying. If he killed them, why would he be looking into what happened?'

She crossed the room and stood directly in front of me. So beautiful. I actually wanted to kiss her.

'What aren't you telling me?' she asked.

My cellphone rang. I glanced at the caller ID. It was Loren Muse. I hit the On button and said, 'What's up?'

'We got a problem,' Muse said. 'Chamique wants to recant.'

CHAMIQUE SAT in my office. She was so damned young, but you could see the hard written on her face. Life had not been easy for this girl. Her attorney, Horace Foley, wore too much cologne and had eyes spaced too widely apart. I was fairly confident that if an ambulance drove by, this guy would jump through my second-floor window to slow it down.

'We would like to see you drop the charges on Mr Jenrette and Mr Marantz,' Foley said.

'Can't do that,' I said. I looked at Chamique. She wasn't exactly clamouring for eye contact. 'Did you lie on the stand yesterday?' I asked her.

'My client would never lie,' Foley said.

I ignored him, met Chamique's eyes. She said, 'You're never going to convict them anyway.'

'You don't know that.'

Chamique smiled at me, as if I were the most naive creature that God had ever created. 'You don't understand, do you?'

'Oh, I understand. They're offering money if you recant. The sum has now reached a level where your attorney here, Mr Who-Needs-A-Shower-When-There's-Cologne, thinks it makes sense to do it.'

'What did you call me?'

I looked at Muse. 'Open a window, will you?'

'Got it, Cope.'

'Hey, what did you call me?

'The window is open. Feel free to jump out.' I looked back at Chamique. 'If you recant now, that means your testimony today and yesterday was a lie. It means you committed perjury. That's a crime. You'll go to jail.'

Foley said, 'Talk to me, Mr Copeland, not my client.'

'Don't do this,' I said to Chamique.

'I have to.'

'Then I'll charge you.'

Her attorney was ready to do battle again, but Chamique put her hand on his arm. 'You won't do that, Mr Copeland.'

'I will.'

But she knew I was bluffing. She was a poor, scared rape victim who had a chance of cashing in—making more money than she would probably see again in her lifetime. Who was I to lecture her on values and justice?

She and her attorney stood. Horace Foley said, 'We sign the agreement in the morning.'

I didn't say anything. Part of me felt relief, and that shamed me. JaneCare would survive now. My father's memory—OK, my political career—wouldn't take a hit. Best off, it wasn't my doing.

Chamique offered me her hand. I took it. 'Thank you,' she said.

I GOT HOME and had dinner with Cara. She had a 'homework' assignment that consisted of finding things that were red in magazines and cutting them out. As she went to work with the scissors she started singing a song. The song was from a cartoon TV show called *Dora the Explorer* and basically consisted of singing the word *backpack* over and over again until the head of a nearby parent exploded into a million pieces.

I had made the mistake about two months ago of buying her a Dora the Explorer Talking Backpack with matching talking Map (song: 'I'm the map, I'm the map, I'm the map,' repeat). When Madison came over, they would often play Dora the Explorer. One of them would play the role of Dora. The other would be a monkey with the rather interesting moniker 'Boots'.

I was thinking about that, about Boots, about the way Cara and her cousin would argue over who would be Dora and who would be Boots, when it struck me like the proverbial thunderbolt.

I froze. I actually stopped and just sat there. Even Cara saw it.

'Daddy?'

'One second, kitten.'

I ran to the den. Where the hell were those bills from the frat house? I started tearing apart the room. It took me a few minutes to find them—I had been ready to throw them all away. Bang, there they were. I rifled through them. I found the online charges, the monthly ones, and called Muse. She answered on the first ring.

'What's up?'

'I have an idea, but I don't know if we have the time.'

'Don't worry about the time. What's the idea concerning?'

'It concerns,' I said, 'our old buddies Cal and Jim.'

I GOT COLOGNE Lawyer Foley's home number and woke him up.

'Don't sign those papers until the afternoon,' I said.

'Why?'

'Because if you do, I will make sure my office comes down on you as hard as they can. I will let it be known that we don't cut deals with Horace Foley, that we always make sure your clients serve the maximum time.'

'You can't do that, and anyway I have an obligation to my client.'

'Tell her I asked for the extra time. Tell her it's in her best interest.'

'And what do I say to the other side?'

'I don't know. Find something wrong with the paperwork, whatever.'

'And how is that in my client's best interest?'

'If I get lucky, you can renegotiate. More moolah in your pockets.'

He paused. Then: 'She's a strange kid. Chamique. I mean, until they sandbagged her with that Jim/James thing yesterday, she was more interested in them going to jail than the financial payoff. She really wanted justice.'

'And that surprises you?'

'Yeah, it surprised the hell out of me. Most of them would have taken the money right away. But Chamique is different. This is life-changing money for her. So whatever you're up to, Mr Prosecutor, don't screw it up for her.'

LUCY DRANK ALONE. It was night. Lucy lived on campus in faculty housing. The place was beyond depressing. Before her, an English-lit professor had spent three decades of spinsterhood in this very unit. Lung cancer cut her down at the age of fifty-eight. Despite recarpeting and repainting, the cigarette stench remained. It was a little like living in an ashtray.

Lucy was a vodka girl. She looked out of the window. Rain fell outside. In the distance, she heard music. She checked her watch. Midnight.

She flipped on her iPod stereo and set it on a playlist she called 'Mellow'. Each song was a total heart ripper. She closed her eyes.

The past was rising up again. Lucy had spent her entire adult life running away from those damn woods at her father's camp. She had fled across the country, all the way to California, and she had fled all the way back again. But in the end that awful night always found her.

But this time . . . how? How could those journal entries exist? Sylvia had barely been born when the Summer Slasher struck. What could she know about it? Of course, like Lonnie, she might have gone online, done some research. Or maybe someone had told her something. But still. Only one person knew that Lucy had lied about what happened that night.

And, of course, Paul wouldn't say anything.

She stared through the clear liquid in her glass. Paul. Paul Copeland. She could still see him with those gangly legs, that long hair, that knock-a-girl-back smile. They had met through their fathers. Paul's old man, an ob-gyn, had escaped repression in the Soviet Union only to find plenty of it here in the good ol' USA. Ira, Lucy's bleeding-heart father, could never resist a tale of woe like that. So he hired Vladimir Copeland to be camp doctor.

Lucy could still see it—their car, a broken-down Oldsmobile, kicking up the dirt road, coming to a stop, the four doors opening and the family of four stepping out as one. At that moment, when Lucy first saw Paul and their eyes met, it was boom, crack, thunderbolt. And she could see that he felt the same. There are those rare moments in life—when you feel that jolt and suddenly colours seem brighter and sounds have more clarity and you never, not even for a minute, stop thinking about him and you know that he is feeling exactly the same way about you.

Six years ago, Lucy had looked him up on the Internet. What she'd found was both sobering and unsurprising. Paul was married. He worked as an attorney. He had a daughter. Lucy had even managed to find a picture of his wife at some charity function. Another swig of her vodka and tonic.

Things might have changed in six years, but back then Paul was living in Ridgewood, New Jersey, a scant twenty miles from where Lucy now was.

Paul should be told about the journal entries, shouldn't he?

And it would be no problem to do another quick Google search. Get a phone number for him.

She put down her drink. Her computer was already on. She was about to type when she heard the knock on the door. Lucy checked her watch: 12.17 a.m. Awfully late for a visitor.

'Who is it?'

'It's Sylvia Potter.'

There were tears in that voice. Lucy stood and stumbled to the kitchen. She dumped the rest of her drink into the sink. Vodka didn't smell, at least not that much, so she was OK on that score.

'Coming.'

She opened the door and Sylvia tumbled in as if she'd been leaning against it. The girl was soaked.

Sylvia said, 'I'm sorry it's so late.'

'Don't worry about it. I was up.'

She stopped in the centre of the room. 'I'm sorry about before.'

'That's OK.' Lucy gestured for Sylvia to have a seat on the couch.

'How did you find out I wrote that journal?' the girl asked.

'It's not important.'

'You said they would be confidential.'

'I know. I'm sorry about that.'

Sylvia wiped her nose. Her hair was still dripping. She did not say anything. Lucy remembered that Lonnie said he would help get her to talk.

'Did Lonnie visit you tonight?'

'Lonnie Berger? Why would Lonnie visit me?'

'It doesn't matter. So you just came here on your own?'

Sylvia swallowed and looked unsure of herself. 'Was I wrong to?'

'No, not at all. I'm glad you're here.'

'What do you think I should do?'

'Tell me everything, OK?'

'I have. I mean, the majority of it.'

Lucy wondered how to play this. 'Who is P?'

Sylvia frowned. 'What?'

'In your journal. You talk about a boy named P. Who is P?'

Sylvia was being cagey. 'I didn't call anyone P. I said straight out that it was . . .' The words stuck in her throat. She closed her eyes and whispered, 'my father.' The dam broke. The tears came down like the rain, in sheets.

Lucy closed her eyes. The incest story. The one that had struck her and Lonnie with such horror. Damn. Lonnie had got it wrong.

Lucy reached out to this poor girl and held her.

CHAPTER 7

When the judge called us to order the next morning, I called a—gasp—surprise witness.

'The People call Gerald Flynn.'

Flynn had been the 'nice' boy who'd invited Chamique Johnson to the party. He looked the part, too, what with his too-smooth skin, nicely parted blond locks, wide blue eyes that seemed to gaze at everything with naiveté. Because he was the defence's key witness—Flynn had steadfastly backed his fraternity brothers—they had made sure he was waiting.

I asked him to say his name for the record.

'Gerald Flynn.'

'But you go by Jerry, isn't that correct?'

'Yes.'

'Fine, let's start from the beginning, shall we? When did you first meet the defendant, Ms Chamique Johnson?'

Chamique was sitting in the second-to-last row near Horace Foley. The Jenrette and Marantz families were not pleased with the last-minute snafu in their Chamique retraction, but their court faces, concerned, serious, engaged, were back in place. It was a temporary delay, they figured.

'When she came to the fraternity house on October 12th,' he replied.

'Why was Ms Johnson at your fraternity house?'

'She was hired as an exotic dancer.'

'And you watched this dance?'

'I did.'

'What did you think of it?'

Mort Pubin was up. 'Objection!'

The judge was already scowling in my direction. 'Mr Copeland?'

'According to Ms Johnson, Mr Flynn here invited her to the party where the rape took place. I am trying to understand why he would do that.'

Judge Pierce said, 'So ask him that.'

I turned back to Flynn. 'Did you think Ms Johnson was attractive?'

'Yeah, I mean, I guess so.'

'Yes or no?'

'Objection!' Pubin again. 'Maybe he thought she was mildly attractive. It isn't always yes or no.'

'I agree, Mort,' I said, surprising him. 'Let me rephrase, Mr Flynn—how would you describe her attractiveness?'

'Like on a one-to-ten scale?'

'That would be splendid, Mr Flynn. On a one-to-ten scale.'

He thought about it. 'Seven, maybe an eight.'

'Fine, thank you. Did you talk to Ms Johnson during the evening?'

'Yes.'

'What did you talk about?'

'I asked her where she lived. I asked her if she went to school or if she had a boyfriend. That kinda thing. She told me about having a kid. She asked me what I was studying. I said I wanted to go to medical school.'

'Did you ask Ms Johnson for her phone number?'

'Yes.'

'Why?'

'I thought I might call her.'

'Did there come a time when you called Ms Johnson?'

'Yes. Ten days later I called and asked her if she wanted to come to a party at the fraternity.'

'Did you want her to dance exotically again?'

'No,' Flynn said. I saw him swallow. 'I asked her as a guest.'

I looked at Jerry Flynn. I let the jury look at him. There was something in his face. Had he liked Chamique Johnson? I let the moment linger, because I was confused. I had thought that Jerry Flynn was part of it—that he had called Chamique and set her up. I tried to work it through in my head.

'Did Ms Johnson accept your invitation?'

'Yes.'

I followed him through meeting her and getting her punch.

'Did you tell her it was spiked with alcohol?' I asked.

'Yes.'

It was a lie. And it looked like a lie, but I wanted to emphasise the ridiculousness of that claim.

'Tell me how that conversation went,' I said.

'I don't understand the question.'

'Did you ask Ms Johnson if she wanted something to drink?'

'Yes. I asked her if she wanted some punch.'

'And what did she say?'

'She said yes.'

'And then what?'

He shifted in his chair. 'I said it was spiked.'

I arched an eyebrow. 'Just like that?'

'Objection!' Pubin rose. 'He said it was spiked. Asked and answered.'

He was right. Leave them with the obvious lie. I waved to the judge that I would let it go. I started walking him through the night. Flynn stuck to the story he'd already told, about how Chamique got drunk, how she started flirting with Edward Jenrette.

'How did you react when that happened?'

He shrugged. 'Edward is a senior, I'm a freshman. It happens.'

'So you think Chamique was impressed because Mr Jenrette was older?'

'I don't know,' Flynn said. 'Maybe.'

Flynn continued to weave his tale. He started partying with his friends. He saw Chamique start up the stairs holding hands with Jenrette. He didn't know what happened after that. Then later that night, he met up with Chamique again and walked her to the bus-stop.

'Did she seem upset?' I asked.

Flynn said no, just the opposite. Chamique was 'smiling' and 'happy' and light as air. His Pollyanna description was overkill.

'So when Ms Johnson talked about going out to the keg with you and then walking upstairs and being grabbed,' I said, 'that was all a lie?'

Flynn was smart enough not to bite. 'I'm telling you what I saw.'

'Are you aware that Ms Johnson claimed the men who raped her were named Cal and Jim?'

He was wondering how to handle that one. He went with the truth. 'I heard that.'

'Was there anyone named Cal or Jim at the party?'

'Not that I'm aware of.'

'I see. And would you know any reason why Mr Jenrette and Mr Marantz would call themselves that?'

'No.'

'Ever heard those two names together? I mean, before the alleged rape?'

'Not that I can recall.'

I looked back at Loren Muse. Her head was down, fiddling with her BlackBerry. She glanced up, met my eye, nodded once.

'Your Honour,' I said, 'I have more questions for this witness but this might make a good place to break for lunch.'

Judge Pierce agreed.

I tried not to sprint over to Loren Muse.

'We got it,' she said with a grin. 'The fax is in your office.'

LUCY HAD NO morning class. She had stayed in bed until noon. When she rose, she placed a call to one of the school counsellors, Katherine Lucas, a therapist Lucy had always thought was really good. She explained the situation with Sylvia. Lucas would have a better idea what to do.

She thought about the journal entry that had started all this. The woods. The screams. The blood. Sylvia Potter hadn't sent it. So who had?

No clue.

Last night, she had decided Paul needed to know about this. She found his work number on the computer. He was the Essex County prosecutor and a widower. Lucy wondered how she felt about that, but there was no way she could sort through it now. With a shaking hand she dialled the number. When she reached the switchboard operator, she asked to speak to Paul Copeland.

'May I ask who's calling?'

'My name is Lucy. Just tell him that. A friend from twenty years ago.'

'Prosecutor Copeland isn't in the office at the moment. Would you like to leave a number so he can return your call?'

Lucy gave her the numbers for her home, her office, her mobile.

'May I tell him what this is in reference to?'

'Just tell him that it's Lucy. And that it's important.'

MUSE AND I were in my office. We had ordered in deli sandwiches for lunch. I was having chicken salad on wholewheat. Muse was downing a meatball sub that was the approximate size of a surfboard.

I had the fax in my hands. 'Where is your private eye? Cingle whatever?'

'Shaker. Cingle Shaker. She'll be here.'

Muse lifted the sandwich. I was surprised that she could do it without the use of an industrial crane.

'I hate to say this, Cope, you being my boss and all, but you're a doggone genius,' she said, teeth-diving into the sandwich.

'Yeah,' I said. 'I guess I am.' I looked at my notes.

'So'—more chewing, some swallowing—'would it distract you if I raised another issue, one that doesn't involve this case?'

I looked up. 'Actually, I could use the distraction. What's on your mind?'

'I have some friends in Manhattan homicide.'

I had an idea where this was going. 'Let me guess. One of your homicide friends told you about the murder of Manolo Santiago?'

'Yeah.'

'Did they tell you my theory about him being one of the boys murdered at that camp, even though his parents say it's not him?'

'Yeah, they told me,' Muse said. 'So I want in.'

I took a delicate bite of my sandwich. 'In on what?'

'You know what. You're going to investigate, right? You're going to see if you can figure out what really happened in those woods?'

'I can't have you taking up county time with my personal affairs.'

'I am hired to work forty hours a week. I do closer to eighty. You know that. So what I do outside of those forty hours is up to me. And before you ask, no, this isn't just a favour for my boss. Let's face it, I'm an investigator. Solving the case would be a heck of a feather in my cap. What do you say?'

I shrugged. 'What the hell.'

'I'm in?'

'You're in.'

She looked very pleased. 'So what's step one?'

I thought about it. There was something I had to do. I had avoided it. I couldn't avoid it any longer.

'Wayne Steubens,' I said. 'I need to see him.'

'I think I read that he doesn't allow visitors.'

'We need to change his mind,' I said.

'He's in a maximum security facility in Virginia,' Muse said. 'I can make some calls.'

Muse already knew where Steubens was being held. Incredible.

'Do that,' I said.

There was a knock on my door and Jocelyn Durels, my secretary, stuck her head in the door. 'Messages,' she said.

I waved my fingers for her to hand them to me. 'Anything important?'

'Not really. A fair amount from media.'

I took the messages and started sorting through them. One caught my eye: *Lucy??*

I stared at the name for a moment. Lucy. It couldn't be.

There was a work number, a home number and a mobile. All had New Jersey area codes. I grabbed the phone and hit the intercom.

'Jocelyn? I'm seeing a message here from someone named Lucy,' I said. 'You didn't write a last name.'

'She wouldn't give one. That's why I put the question marks. Did you read my notes at the bottom of the page?'

'No.' I scanned down the sheet and read: *Says she's an old friend from twenty years ago.* I read the note again. And again.

'Ground control to Major Cope.'

It was Muse. She hadn't said the words—she sang them, using the old David Bowie tune. I startled up. 'You sing,' I said, 'like you pick out shoes.'

'Very funny.' She gestured at the message and arched one eyebrow. 'So who is this Lucy? An old lover?'

I said nothing. Muse saw me looking down at the note.

'A friend from twenty years ago,' Muse said. 'That's when the camp murders occurred.'

I looked at her.

'It's connected, isn't it?'

'I don't know,' I said. 'But probably.'

'What's her last name?'

'Silverstein. Lucy Silverstein.'

'She was your girlfriend,' Muse said.

'How did you figure that?'

'I brushed up on the case before I told you I wanted in.'

I wasn't surprised. 'Summer romance,' I said. 'We were kids.'

'When was the last time you heard from her?'

'It's been a long time.'

We just sat there for a moment. Muse's gaze turned to the clock behind me. I looked too. Lunch was over. This would have to wait.

'Showtime,' Muse said.

I nodded. More than showtime. I was going to destroy those sons of bitches. And I was going to try like hell not to enjoy it too much.

JERRY FLYNN looked fairly composed. I had done little damage in the morning. There was no reason to think the afternoon would be any different.

'Mr Flynn,' I began, 'do you like pornography?'

I didn't even wait for the obvious. I turned to Mort Pubin and made a sarcastic hand gesture, as though I was ushering him onstage.

'Objection!'

Pubin didn't need to elaborate. The judge gave me a disapproving look. I shrugged and said, 'Exhibit eighteen.' I picked up the fax. 'This is a bill sent to the fraternity house for online expenses. Do you recognise it?'

He looked at it. 'I don't pay the bills. The treasurer does.'

'Yes, Mr Rich Devin, who testified that this is indeed the fraternity bill.' I pointed to a line near the top. 'Do you see this entry here? Can you read what it says?'

Flynn cleared his throat. 'HotFlixxx,' he said.

He looked as though he was about to be sick.

'Can you tell me what HotFlixxx is?'

'It's a DVD movie rental service.'

'What kind of movies?'

'Um, well, adult movies.'

'I see. So before I asked if you liked pornography—perhaps a better question would have been, do you ever watch pornographic movies?'

He squirmed. 'Sometimes,' he said.

'Nothing wrong with that, son. Is there any pornographic movie in particular that you like?'

The colour drained from his face. His head swivelled towards the defence table. 'Can I plead the Fifth?' he said.

'For what?' I asked.

Flair Hickory stood. 'The witness has asked for counsel. Can we have a ten-minute recess?'

'Your Honour,' I said, 'when I went to law school, we learned that the Fifth Amendment was to be used to prevent self-incrimination and—correct me if I'm wrong here—but, well, is there a law on the books against having a favourite pornographic movie?'

Judge Pierce took his time. If Flair got him off the stand, I would be in trouble. They would come up with something.

'No recess,' the judge said.

Flair Hickory wilted back into his seat.

I went back to Flynn. 'Do you have a favourite pornographic movie?'

'No,' he said.

'Have you ever heard of a pornographic movie called'—I pretended now to be checking a piece of paper but I knew the name by heart—'a movie called *Romancing His Bone*?'

He must have seen it coming, but the question still zapped him like a cattle prod. 'Uh, I'm not sure. I'm not good with movie titles.'

'Well, let's see if I can refresh your recollection.'

I passed a copy of the fax Muse had given me to opposing counsel and made it an exhibit. Then I started back in: 'According to HotFlixxx, a copy of that DVD had been in the possession of the fraternity house for the past six months. It was mailed back to them the day *after* Ms Johnson reported the assault to the police. Does that refresh your memory?'

'I don't know.'

'You don't know? Then let's try something else.'

I looked towards the back of the room. Loren Muse was standing by the door. She was grinning. I nodded. She opened the door and Muse's private eye, Cingle Shaker, strutted into the room like a gorgeous Amazon in a B movie. The room itself seemed to gasp at the sight.

I said, 'Do you recognise the woman who just walked into the room?'

He did not reply. The judge said, 'Mr Flynn?'

'Yes.' Flynn cleared his throat to gain time. 'I met her at a bar last night.'

'I see. And did you two talk about the movie *Romancing His Bone*?'

Cingle had pretended to be an ex-porno actress. She had got several frat boys to open up.

Flynn said, 'We might have said something about it.'

'Hmm,' I said, as if this were a curious development. 'So now, with Ms Shaker out there as a catalyst, do you remember telling her that it was the entire fraternity's favourite porno flick?'

He hesitated.

'It's OK, Jerry. Three of your brothers told Ms Shaker the same thing.'

I looked back at Cingle Shaker, who smiled and waved as though she were a celebrity and had just been introduced to an audience. I wheeled out the TV with a DVD player. The offending DVD was already in it.

'Your Honour, last night one of my investigators visited King David's Smut Palace in New York City.' I looked at the jury and said, 'See, it's open twenty-four hours, though why someone might need to go there at, say, three in the morning is beyond me—'

'Mr Copeland.'

The judge correctly stopped me with a disapproving gaze, but the jury had smiled. That was good. I wanted the mood loose. And then, when the contrast came, when they saw what was on that DVD, I wanted to wallop them.

'Anyway, my investigator purchased all of the X-rated movies ordered on HotFlixxx by the frat house in the past six months, including *Romancing His Bone*. I would now like to show a scene I believe is relevant.'

Everything stopped. All eyes turned towards the judge's bench. Arnold Pierce took his time. He stroked his chin.

Then he simply nodded and said, 'Go ahead. I'll allow it.'

'Wait!' Mort Pubin objected, did everything he could, wanted *voir dire* and all that. But it was a waste of energy. Eventually the courtroom curtains were closed to shut out the glare and I hit the Play button.

The setting was a run-of-the-mill bedroom. Looked like a king-size bed. Three participants. A rough ménage à trois started up. There were two men. There was one girl.

The two men were white. The girl was black.

The white men tossed her about like a plaything. They sneered and laughed and talked to each other throughout: '*Turn her over, Cal* . . . *Yeah, Jim, like that* . . .'

Children play-act. My daughter and niece acted out *Dora the Explorer*. Jenrette and Marantz, as sick as it was, had acted out a scene from a pornographic movie. The courtroom was tomb still. I watched the faces in the gallery collapse, even those behind Jenrette and Marantz, as the black girl in the movie screamed, as the two white men used their names and laughed cruelly. On and on. Cal and Jim. Their voices were cruel, awful, hell-spawned. I looked towards the back of the room and found Chamique Johnson.

Chamique met my eye and nodded. I nodded back. There were tears on her cheeks. I couldn't be sure, but I think there were tears on mine too.

FLAIR HICKORY did everything in his considerable power to prevent me from finishing the job. He called for a recess, claiming that the film should have been given to them during discovery, it was unfair, blah, blah, blah.

But it didn't work.

I could tell you that Flynn probably wasn't a bad kid. The truth was he had liked Chamique. He had asked her out legitimately on a date. But when the upperclassmen got wind of it, they bullied him into going along with their sick 'movie re-enactment' plan. And Flynn the Freshman folded.

'I hated myself for doing it,' he said. 'But you have to understand.'

No, I don't, I wanted to say. But I didn't. I just looked at him until he lowered his eyes. Then I looked at the jury with a slight challenge in my eyes.

Finally I turned to Flair Hickory and said, 'Your witness.'

IT TOOK ME A WHILE before I was alone in my office. I had managed to do my brain-partition thing during my Flynn questioning. I had kept Lucy out. But now, as much as I wanted to spend a few minutes basking in the glory of the moment, the message from Lucy was calling out to me again.

I decided to do some amateur sleuthing. I Googled Lucy's phone numbers. Two gave me nothing, but the third, her work number, showed me that it was the direct line to a professor at Reston University named Lucy Gold.

Gold. *Silver*-stein. Cute.

I had already known it was 'my' Lucy, but this confirmed it.

I was not big on coincidence. I hadn't heard a word from this woman in twenty years. Now suddenly she calls. It had to be connected to Gil Perez's death. It had to be connected to the camp incident.

I had closed that door. Lucy was gone. It took me a long time to accept that. But I did and I kept that damn door shut.

Now I would have to open it.

I picked up the phone and dialled her home. A woman's voice said, 'I'm not home, but at the beep please leave a message.'

The beep came too fast. I wasn't ready for it. So I hung up.

My head swam. It had been twenty years. Lucy would be thirty-seven now. I wondered if she was still as beautiful. Her voice sounded exactly the same . . . it was like nothing had changed. I was eighteen again.

I took a few deep breaths. There was a knock on the door.

'Come in.'

Muse stuck her head in the room. 'Did you call her yet?'

'I tried her home number. No answer.'

'You probably won't get her now,' Muse said. 'She's in class.'

'And you know this because?'

'Because you said I was in on this, remember?'

She sat down at the table. She studied my face and didn't speak. I kept quiet too. Finally she said, 'You want me to leave?'

'Tell me what you got first.'

'She changed her name seventeen years ago. It's Lucy Gold now.'

I nodded. 'That would have been right after the settlement.'

'What settlement? Oh, wait, you guys sued the camp, right? And Lucy's father owned the camp.'

'Right. It was a summer camp with practically no security.' I squirmed when I said that. 'The victims' families got Silverstein's biggest asset, the camp. We sold the land to a developer.'

'How much did you guys get?'

'After fees, each family ended up with more than eight hundred grand.'

Her eyes widened. 'Wow.'

'Yeah. Losing a child is a great moneymaker.'

'I didn't mean—'

I waved her off. 'I know. I'm just being an ass.'

She didn't argue. 'It must have changed things,' Muse said.

I didn't answer right away. The money had been held in a joint account. My mother took off with a hundred grand. She left the rest for us. Dad and I moved to a decent place in Montclair. I had already got a scholarship to Rutgers, but now I set my sights on Columbia Law School.

'Yeah,' I said. 'It changed things.'

'Do you want to know more about your old flame?'

I nodded.

'She went to UCLA. Majored in psychology. She got another degree in English from Stanford. She's currently down the road at Reston U. She, uh, she got two DUIs when she lived in California.'

I sat there. DUI. That didn't sound like Lucy. Her father, Ira, had been a major stoner—so much so that she'd had no interest in anything that would provide a high. Now she had two convictions for drinking and driving.

'Another thing,' Muse said. She shifted in the seat, aiming for nonchalance. 'Lucy Silverstein, a.k.a Gold, isn't married. Never has been.'

That pierced me. She was such a lively thing, so bright and energetic and so damn easy to love. How could she have remained single all these years?

'What time does her class end?' I asked.

'Twenty minutes.'

'OK. I'll call her then. Anything else?'

'I'm working on your prison visit to Wayne Steubens.'

'Thank you.'

She stood. 'Oh, one more thing,' she said. 'There are pictures of all the professors on the university's website.' She held up a small piece of paper. 'I got the URL right here.' She dropped the address on the table and left.

I HAD TWENTY MINUTES. Why not? I typed in the Reston University website page Muse had given me. And there she was.

It wasn't Lucy's most flattering photograph. Her smile was tight, her expression grim. The blonde hair was gone. That happens with age, I know, but I had a feeling it was intentional. The colour didn't look right on her. She was older—duh—but it worked on her. Her face was thinner. The high cheekbones were more pronounced.

And damn if she didn't still look beautiful.

Looking at her face, something long dormant came alive and started twisting in my gut. I didn't need that now. There were enough complications in my life. I read her short bio, learned nothing. Nowadays students rank classes and professors. You could often find that information online. I did. Lucy was clearly beloved by her students. Her rankings were incredible. I smiled and felt a strange sense of pride.

Twenty minutes passed.

I gave it another five, then dialled Lucy's cellphone. On the third ring I heard her voice say, 'Hello?'

My heart leapt into my throat but I managed to say, 'It's me, Luce.'

And then, a few seconds later, I heard her start to cry.

'LUCE?' I SAID into the phone. 'You OK?'

'I'm fine. I can't believe I did that.'

'You always were an easy cry,' I said.

She snorted a laugh. 'Not any more,' she said.

Silence.

'I'm sorry about leaving such a cryptic message. I don't go by Silverstein any more.'

I didn't want her to know I already knew this. But I didn't want to lie either. So I gave a noncommittal 'Oh.'

More silence.

She broke it this time. 'Man, this is awkward. I feel like a big dope. Like I'm sixteen again and worried about a new zit.'

I smiled. 'Same here,' I said. 'It's good to hear your voice, Luce.'

'Yours too.'

'I was calling because . . .' Lucy stopped. Then: 'I don't know how to say this, so let me ask a question. Has anything strange happened to you lately?'

'Strange how?'

'Strange as in about-that-night strange.'

I should have expected her to say something like that—knew it was coming—but the smile still fled as if I'd been punched. 'Yes.'

'What the hell is going on, Paul?'

'I don't know.'

'Do you want to meet? I mean, I think we should discuss this, don't you?'

'I do,' I said. 'Where should we meet?'

'Do you know where Reston University is?'

'Yes.'

'I have student appointments until seven thirty. Do you want to meet me at my office? It's in the Armstrong Building. Say, eight o'clock?'

'I'll be there.'

WHEN I ARRIVED HOME I was surprised to find the press camped out in front of my house. You often hear about that—about the press doing stuff like that—but this was my first experience with it.

Greta gave me the conquering-hero welcome. She was full of hugs and congratulations. I love Greta. There are some people you know are pure good, who are always on your side. There aren't many of them.

'Where's Cara?' I asked.

'Bob took Cara and Madison to Baumgart's for dinner.'

Estelle was in the kitchen. 'I need to go out tonight,' I said to her.

'No problem.'

Greta followed me into the den. The front door opened and Bob came in with the two girls. I swept my daughter up in my arms and kissed her hard.

Bob slapped my back. 'Congrats on the trial,' he said. 'It should get that Jenrette off our back.'

'Or more desperate.'

His face paled a little. If you were to cast Bob in a movie, he'd be the bad-guy rich Republican. His complexion was ruddy, his jowls thick, his fingers short and stubby. But appearances could be deceiving. Bob's background was totally blue collar. He studied and worked hard. Nothing had ever been given to him or made easy.

Cara came back into the room carrying a DVD. Remembering what day of the week it was, I cursed to myself. Then I said to her, 'It's movie night.'

She held up the DVD. Her eyes were wide. She was smiling. On the cover was something computer-generated with talking cars or maybe farm animals, something I had seen a hundred times already.

I knelt down so I was at her eye level. 'Honey, Daddy has to go out tonight. I'm sorry, sweetie.' I waited for the tears.

'Can Estelle watch it with me?'

'Sure, honey.'

'Cool.'

I'd been hoping for a little crestfallen. No go.

Cara skipped away. I looked at Bob.

'On the inside,' I said, gesturing towards my daughter, 'she's crushed.'

Bob laughed as my cellphone buzzed. I recognised the number and felt a little jolt. I picked it up and said, 'Hello?'

'Nice job today, All-Star.'

I smiled. I first met Dave (now Governor) Markie at a party during my freshman year at Rutgers. I was the immigrant's son. His father was a United States senator. But that was the beauty of college. It is made for strange bedfellows. We ended up becoming close friends.

Dave's critics could not help but notice this friendship when he appointed me to my current post as Essex County prosecutor. I had got very good press already, and today should have helped my possible bid for a congressional seat.

'So, big day, no? You da man. Go, Cope, go, Cope, it's your birthday.'

'Trying to appeal to your hip-hop constituency?'

'Trying to understand my teenage daughter. Anyway, congrats.'

'Thanks.'

'So how is everything, Cope? You dating?'

'Some.'

'Dude, you're single. You're good-looking. You got some money in the bank. Do you see where I'm going with this?'

'You're subtle, Dave, but I think I can follow.'

Dave Markie had always been a lady slayer. He was OK-looking, but the man had a gift for pick-up that could be conservatively called dazzling. Dave was married now, of course, had two polished children, but I had little doubt that there was some side action.

'I'm coming up to Newark to see you. It's been too long,' he said.

'What's up, Dave? I'm kinda busy with this case.'

'It involves what we talked about before.'

My possible congressional run. 'Good news?' I said.

'No.'

Silence.

'I think there's a problem,' he said. Then his voice switched back to jovial. 'Could be nothing, Cope. We'll talk. Let's make it your office. Say, tomorrow lunchtime?'

'OK.'

'See you then.'

LUCY GOLD'S OFFICE BUILDING was the otherwise-lovely quad's resident eyesore, a seventies structure that was supposed to look futuristic but somehow looked dated three years after completion. The rest of the quad edifices were handsome brick that begged for more ivy. I parked in the lot in the southwest corner. I tilted the rearview mirror and then, to paraphrase Bruce Springsteen, I checked my look in that mirror and wanted to change my clothes, my hair, my face. I wore an untucked white shirt, blue jeans, blue blazer, Ferragamo loafers. Mr Casual Chic.

I got out of the car and walked across the grounds. As I approached the building, I could actually feel my body shaking. I scolded myself. I was a grown man. I had been married. I was a father and a widower. I had last seen this woman more than half my life ago. When do we grow out of this?

I found her office. I knocked, two sharp raps. Confident, I thought. Manly. God, I'm pathetic.

'Come in.'

Her voice made my stomach drop. I opened the door and stepped into the room. She stood near the window. The sun was still out, and a shadow cut across her. She was still damn beautiful. For a moment we just stood there.

'How's the lighting?' she said.

'Excuse me?'

'I was trying to figure out where to be. You know, when you knocked. I had a friend of mine help me test out all the angles. He thought I looked best with this one—across the room, the shade half drawn.'

I smiled. 'You look terrific.'

'So do you. Come in.'

'Should we, I don't know, hug or something?'

'Not yet.'

Lucy sat at her desk chair. I sat in the chair in front of the desk.

'I saw online about your wife,' she said. 'I'm sorry.'

I nodded. 'How's your father?'

'Not well. All that free love and drugs—eventually they take a toll. Ira also . . . he never got over what happened, you know?'

I guessed that I did. 'I'm sorry to hear that.'

'How about your parents?' Lucy asked.

'My father died a few months ago.'

'I'm sorry. I remember him so well from that summer.'

'It was the last time he was happy,' I said.

'Because of your sister?'

'Because of a lot of things. Ira gave him the chance to be a doctor again. He loved that—practising medicine. He never got to do it again.'

'I'm sorry.'

'My father really didn't want to be part of the lawsuit—he adored Ira—but my mom pushed him. All the other families were on board.'

'You don't need to explain.'

I stopped. She was right.

'And your mother?' she asked.

'Their marriage didn't survive.'

The answer did not seem to surprise her. 'Losing a child is a ridiculous strain on a marriage,' Lucy said. 'Do you still have a good relationship with her?'

'I haven't seen her in eighteen years.'

'You've lost a lot of people, Paul.'

'You're not going to psychoanalyse me, are you?'

'No, nothing like that.' She sat back and looked up and away. It was a look that sent me right back. We would sit out in the camp's old baseball field, where the grass was overgrown, and I would hold her and she would look up and away like that.

Then she turned and smiled at me. 'This is so weird, isn't it? I mean, we were together for, what, six weeks, and it was just a summer fling. You've probably had dozens of girls since then.'

'Dozens?' I repeated.

'What, more like hundreds?'

'At the very least,' I said.

Silence. I felt something well up in my chest.

'But you were special, Lucy. You were . . .' I stopped.

'Yeah, I know,' she said. 'So were you. That's why this is awkward. I want to know everything about you. But I'm not sure now is the time.'

It was as if a surgeon was at work, a time-warping plastic surgeon maybe, and he had snipped off the last twenty years, almost seamlessly.

'You haven't changed, Luce.'

'Yeah, Cope. I've changed. You wouldn't believe how much.'

Our eyes met, really met, for the first time since I entered the room. She was telling me something there, a tale, and the tale had a lot of pain in it.

I didn't want any lies between the two of us.

'Do you know what I do now?' I asked.

'You're the county prosecutor. I saw that online.'

'Right. That gives me access to information. One of my investigators did a quick background check on you.'

'I see. So you know about my drinking and driving?'

'Not my business.'

'No, it's not. But I'm glad you told me. So what's the strange thing that's happened to you, Cope?'

'A few days ago, a couple of Manhattan homicide detectives showed me an unidentified male victim,' I said. 'I think the man was Gil Perez.'

Her jaw dropped. 'How the hell is that possible?'

'I don't know.'

'He's been alive all this time?'

'Apparently.'

She stopped and shook her head. 'Wait, did you tell his parents?'

'The police brought them in to ID him. They said it wasn't Gil. That Gil died twenty years ago.'

'Wow.' She collapsed back in the chair, mulling it over. So his parents are either lying or in denial. Which one?'

'I'm not sure. But I'm leaning towards lying.'

'What has Gil been doing all this time? What else have you learned?'

'Not much.' I shifted in my seat. 'How about you? What happened?'

'My students write anonymous journals. I got one that pretty much described what happened to us that night. How we went into the woods. How we were messing around. How we heard the scream.'

I thought I was hearing wrong. 'Written by one of your students?'

'Yeah.'

'And you have no idea who wrote it?'

'Nope.'

I asked, 'Do you have the journal here?'

'I made you a copy.'

She handed the pages across the desk. I read them. It brought it back. It hurt, reading it. I wondered about the heart stuff, about never getting over the mysterious 'P'. But when I put it down, the first thing I said to her was, 'This isn't what happened.'

'I know. But it's close.'

'I met this young woman who knew Gil,' I told her. 'She said she overheard him talking about us. He said that we lied.'

Lucy kept still for a moment. 'We did.'

'Not about anything that mattered,' I said.

'We were making love,' she said, 'while they were being murdered.'

I said nothing. I partitioned again. That was how I got through my day. Because if I didn't, I would remember that I was the counsellor on guard duty that night. That I shouldn't have sneaked off with my girlfriend. That if I had been a responsible kid, I wouldn't have lied about it the next morning.

Lucy said, 'We were just kids, Cope.'

Still nothing.

'They would have sneaked out if we were there or not.'

I would have spotted them, I thought. Or I would have noticed empty beds when I did my rounds. I did none of that. I went off and had a good time with my girlfriend. And the next morning, I lied. I said I'd checked the cabins and that they'd been safely tucked away. I said I was alone that night because I wanted to protect Lucy. Once Margot Green was found, I admitted most of the truth—that I'd been negligent on guard duty. But I left off Lucy's role. And once I stuck with that lie, I was afraid to go back and tell the whole truth. They were suspicious of me already—I still remember Sheriff Lowell's sceptical face—and if I admitted it later, the police would wonder why I lied in the first place.

Anyway, what difference did it make if I was alone or with somebody? Either way, I didn't watch out for them.

During the lawsuit, Ira Silverstein's lawyer tried to lay some of the blame on me. But I was only a kid. And even if I had been in position, it would have been easy enough to sneak out. The security was inadequate. That was true. Legally, it wasn't my fault.

'My father used to go back to those woods,' I said. 'For two years he would go digging. For my sister. He told us he was going fishing. But I knew.'

'What made him stop?'

'My mother left us. I think he figured that his obsession had cost him too much already.'

'And what about your mother?'

'She grew more and more distant. My parents never had the greatest marriage. There were cracks already. When my sister died—or whatever the hell happened—she totally withdrew from him.'

We both went quiet. The last remnants of sunlight were fading away. The sky was turning into a purple swirl. I looked out of the window. She looked out too. We sat there, the closest we had been in twenty years.

The sadness was back. I could see it on her. The long-lasting destruction to my family from that night was obvious. I had hoped that Lucy had been able to get past it. But she hadn't. There hadn't been closure for her either.

'What do we do now?' She was still looking out of the window.

'We find out what really happened in those woods.'

CHAPTER 8

I remember on a trip to Italy seeing tapestries that seem to change perspective depending on where you stand. If you move to the right, the table appears to be facing the right. If you move to the left, the table follows you. Governor Dave Markie was the human embodiment of that. When he walked into a room he had the ability to make every person feel as though he were looking at them. I had seen him score with many women, because he seemed so interested in them.

He brought that into my office. Jocelyn Durels, my secretary, tittered. Loren Muse's face flushed. Even the US Attorney, Joan Thurston, had a smile on her face that showed me what she must have looked like when she had her first kiss in the seventh grade.

We greeted each other with a hug. I noticed that guys did that now— hugged as a greeting. I liked it, the true human contact.

'You don't want all these people here,' Dave whispered to me.

We pulled back from the embrace. He had a smile on his face, but I got the message. I cleared everyone out of my office. Joan Thurston stayed behind. I knew her pretty well. The US Attorney's office was right down the street. We tried to cooperate, though she was only interested in the big stuff. Right now that mostly meant terrorism and political corruption.

As soon as the door closed, leaving the three of us alone, the smile slipped off Dave's face. We sat at my conference table.

'Bad?' I said.

'Very.'

Dave looked at Joan Thurston. She cleared her throat.

'As we speak, my detectives are entering the offices of the charitable institution known as JaneCare. They have a warrant. I had hoped to keep it quiet, but the media already has a hold of it.'

I felt my pulse do a two-step. 'This is crap. It's Jenrette. He's pressuring me to go easy on his son.'

'We know,' Dave said. He looked over at Thurston again.

'That doesn't make the charges untrue.'

'What the hell are you talking about?'

'Jenrette's investigators found improprieties. They brought them to the attention of one of my best people. My guy did more digging. Your brother-in-law has been skimming.'

'Bob? No way.'

'He's diverted at least a hundred grand.'

She handed me two sheets of paper. I scanned down them.

'Your brother-in-law is putting in a pool, right? Fifty grand was given to Marston Pools in various payments and listed here as a building expansion. Another thirty grand was given to Barry's Landscaping. Did JaneCare have a building expansion?'

Our office was half a converted two-house dwelling in downtown Newark. There were no plans to expand. We were concentrating on raising money for treatments and cures. I felt sick.

Dave said, 'We can't play favourites. You know that.'

'I do,' I said.

'And even if we wanted to keep it quiet for friendship's sake, we couldn't. The media has been tipped off. Joan is about to hold a press conference.'

'Are you going to arrest him?'

'He's in custody now,' Joan said. 'We picked him up an hour ago.'

I thought about Greta. I thought about Madison. A pool. Bob had stolen from my wife's charity to build a goddamn pool.

Dave rose. Joan Thurston followed. 'Get him somebody good, Cope. It's going to be ugly, I think.'

I FLICKED ON THE TV and watched Bob's perp walk. No, it wasn't carried live on CNN or Fox, but News 12 New Jersey, our local news station, carried it.

Bob looked, as so many do, dazed and childlike. I felt nauseous. I called Greta at home and on her cell. No answer. I left messages on both.

Muse sat with me throughout. When they moved on to another story, she said, 'That sucked.'

'It did.'

I kept thinking about Greta, sweet, kind Greta, and how this was going to destroy her. I thought about my wife, my Jane, how this charity I had set up as a memorial to her was about to be levelled.

'You in the mood to talk about Gil Perez and your sister?'

I nodded.

'Farrell Lynch finished the age progression.'

She handed me two photographs. The first was a morgue shot of Manolo Santiago. The second was the age-progression shot derived from the photograph I'd given her of Gil Perez. A total match.

'Wow,' I said.

'I got the address for Perez's parents.' She handed me a slip of paper. 'You want me to go?'

I shook my head. Lucy had already insisted on joining me.

'I also have a thought,' she said.

'What's that?'

'The technology in finding buried bodies is much better now than it was twenty years ago. Do you remember Andrew Barrett?'

'Lab guy at John Jay? Talkative and strange.'

'And a genius. Right, that's him. He's probably the country's top expert in this new ground-penetrating radar machine. He pretty much invented it and he's dying to try this new baby out. He says he needs the fieldwork.'

'Sure, why not?' I glanced at the TV. They were replaying Bob's perp walk.

'Cope?'

I looked at her.

'We gotta go to court,' Muse said.

I nodded, rose without speaking. She opened the door.

SOME DAYS, court is about sound and fury signifying nothing. This was one of them. Flair and Mort knew that they were in deep trouble. They wanted to exclude the pornographic DVD because we hadn't produced it earlier. They tried for a mistrial. They made motions and handed in findings and research. Their paralegals must have been up all night.

Judge Pierce listened, his bushy eyebrows low. He had his hand on his chin and looked very, well, judicial. I wasn't worried. They had nothing. But a thought began to worm its way in and gnaw. They had gone after me. Might they not do the same with the judge? I looked at his eyes, looked for some sort of telltale sign that he wasn't sleeping. There was nothing there, but that didn't mean anything.

We finished up by 3 p.m. I went back to my office and checked my messages. Nothing from Greta. I called her again. Still no answer.

Then I called Lucy. She picked up on the first ring.

'Hey,' Lucy answered. Today there was a lilt in her voice.

'Hey.'

There was a weird, almost happy pause.

'I got the address for the Perezes,' I said. 'I can pick you up on the way.'

'I'll be ready.'

LUCY LOOKED FABULOUS. She wore a green snug pullover that clung exactly as it should. Her hair was tied back in a ponytail. She tucked a strand behind her ear as she got into the car.

The Perezes lived in a condo development in Park Ridge.

'Are they expecting us?' Lucy asked.

'No.'

'How do you know they're home?' she asked.

'I called right before I picked you up. When I heard Mrs Perez answer, I said I had the wrong number.'

'Wow, you're good at this.'

'I try to remain humble.'

We headed out of the car. The door opened before I could knock. It was Mrs Perez. She did not say hi or offer up a greeting. She looked at me with hooded eyes and waited.

'We need to talk,' I said. 'May we come in?'

Her eyes moved towards Lucy. 'Who are you?'

'Lucy Silverstein,' she said.

Mrs Perez closed her eyes. 'Ira's daughter.'

'Yes.'

Her shoulders seemed to sag. She stepped back and we entered. The air was syrupy with some kind of strong, cloying smell, like someone had spilled cheap shampoo. She closed the door and led us to a couch.

'Is Mr Perez home?'

'No.'

I looked around the room. Everything was so in place, so coordinated, you would swear they bought the model unit.

The unit had a fireplace. I stood and walked over to the mantel. There were family photographs. There were no pictures of Gil. The mantel was full of images of people I assumed to be Gil's two brothers and one sister. One brother was in a wheelchair.

'That's Tomás,' she said, pointing to a picture of the smiling boy in the wheelchair graduating from Kean University. 'He has cerebral palsy.'

'How old is he?'

'Tomás is thirty-three now.'

'And who's that?'

'Eduardo,' she said. Her expression said not to press it. I remembered Gil telling me that his brother was a gang member or something. Eduardo looked like a hard case.

I pointed to the girl. 'I remember Gil talking about her,' I said. 'She was trying to get into college or something.'

'Glenda is a lawyer,' Mrs Perez said, and her chest puffed out. 'She went to Columbia Law School.'

'Really? So did I,' I said.

Mrs Perez smiled. She moved back to the couch. 'Tomás lives in the unit next door. We knocked down a common wall.'

'He can live on his own?'

'I take care of him. We also have nursing.'

I nodded, sat back down.

Lucy had not left her seat. She remained quiet, letting me take the lead. She was soaking in everything, probably putting on her psychology suit.

Mrs Perez looked at me. 'Why are you here?'

'The body we found belonged to Gil.'

'I already explained to you—'

I reached into a manila envelope and slipped out the old photograph from camp. I put it on the coffee table. She stared down at the image of her son. I watched her face to see the reaction. One moment she looked OK. Then the mask cracked, laying the devastation bare.

She closed her eyes. 'Why are you showing me this?'

'You said Gil's scar was on the right arm. But look, it was on the left.'

'My son was murdered by Wayne Steubens twenty years ago.'

'No.' I reached into the envelope again. 'This is Manolo Santiago, the man in the morgue.'

Lucy startled up. 'What was his name?'

'Manolo Santiago.'

Lucy looked stunned.

'What?' I said.

She shook me off. I continued.

'And this'—I plucked out the final photograph—'is a computer render-ing using age-progression software. In other words, my lab guy took the old photograph of Gil and aged him twenty years. Then he matched the shaved head and facial hair of Manolo Santiago.' I put the pictures next to one another. 'Take a look, Mrs Perez.'

She did. She looked for a long time. 'He looks like him maybe. That's all.'

'Mrs Perez?'

It was Lucy, speaking directly to Gil's mother for the first time. 'We got the results on the DNA test on the way over here. It's your son.'

Man, I thought, she's good.

'DNA?' Mrs Perez shouted. 'I didn't give permission to run a DNA test.'

'The police don't need your permission,' Lucy said. 'After all, according to you, Manolo Santiago is not your son.'

'But . . . but how did they get my DNA?'

I took that one. 'We're not at liberty to say.'

Mrs Perez sat back. For a long time she didn't speak. We waited her out.

'You're lying,' she said, 'or the DNA test is wrong. That man is not my son. My son was murdered twenty years ago. So was your sister. They died at your father's summer camp. You are both chasing ghosts, that's all.'

I looked over at Lucy, hoping she would have a clue here, but she shook me off.

Mrs Perez rose. 'I want you to leave now. Let me grieve in peace.'

'I thought your son died twenty years ago.'

'You never get over it,' Mrs Perez said, walking us to the door.

We headed back to my car. After we slipped into it, I said, 'Well?'

'Mrs Perez is definitely lying.'

'NICE BLUFF,' I SAID.

'The DNA test?'

'Yeah.'

Lucy let that go. 'In there. You mentioned the name Manolo Santiago.'

'That was Gil's alias.'

'I visited my father yesterday at his home. I checked the logbook. He's had only one visitor other than me in the past month. Manolo Santiago.'

'Whoa,' I said. 'Why would Gil visit your father?'

'Good question.'

'Can you ask Ira?'

'I'll try. He's not well. His mind has a habit of wandering.'

'Worth a try.'

She nodded. I made a right turn, decided to change subjects.

'What makes you so sure Mrs Perez is lying?' I asked.

'She's grieving, for one thing. That smell? It's candles. She was wearing black. You could see the red in the eyes. All that. Second, the pictures.'

'What about them?'

'I've counselled parents who are grieving. It is very unusual to have pictures on display dating back to childhood and leaving out a dead child. And did you notice the funny spacing? There weren't enough pictures for that mantel. My guess is, she took away the pictures with Gil in them. I think she was getting rid of evidence.'

I thought about it.

'Her reactions were all wrong, Cope. She's lying.'

'So the question is, what was she lying about?'

Lucy shrugged. 'Gil helped Wayne kill them. That would explain everything. People always assumed that Steubens had an accomplice. Maybe Wayne and Gil staged it to look like Gil died too. Who knows?'

'If that's the case,' I said, 'then my sister is dead.'

'I know.'

I said nothing.

'Cope?'

'What?'

'It's not your fault.'

I said nothing.

'If anything,' she said, 'it's mine. I'm the one who lured you into the woods. You wanted to stay and work guard duty.'

'I had a mind of my own, Lucy. You didn't make me do anything.'

She stayed quiet. Then she said, 'You still blame yourself.'

I felt my grip tighten on the wheel. 'No, I don't.'

'Yeah, Cope, you do. You knew that your sister had to be dead. You were hoping for a second chance. You were hoping to still find redemption.'

'That psychology degree of yours,' I said. 'It's really paying off, huh?'

'I don't mean to—'

'How about you, Luce?' My voice had more bite than I intended. 'Do you blame yourself? Is that why you drink so damn much?'

Silence.

'I shouldn't have said that,' I said.

Her voice was soft. 'You don't know anything about my life.'

'I know. I'm sorry.'

She turned away and looked out of the window. We drove in silence.

'You may be right,' I said.

Her eyes stayed on the window.

'Here is something I've never told anyone,' I said. I felt my face flush and the tears push against my eyes. 'After the night in the woods, my father never looked at me the same.'

She turned towards me.

'I could have been projecting. I mean, you're right. I did blame myself to some degree. What if we hadn't gone off? What if I had just stayed where I was supposed to? And maybe the look on his face was just the pure devastation of a parent losing a child. But I always thought there was something more in it. Something almost accusatory.'

She put a hand on my arm. 'Oh, Cope.'

I kept driving. 'So maybe I do need to make amends for the past. But what about you? Why are you delving into this? What do you hope to gain?'

'Are you kidding? The life I knew ended that night. Don't you get that? The families—including yours—dragged my father into court. You took away everything we had. Ira couldn't take the stress.'

'I understand that,' I said. 'But what are you after now?'

She didn't reply. I drove some more. The skies were starting to darken.

Finally she said, 'Sometimes it feels like I was pushed down a hill that night and I've been stumbling down it ever since. That sometimes I sort of get my bearings but the hill is so steep that I can never really get balanced and I start tumbling again. So perhaps—I don't know—perhaps if I figure out what really happened that night, I'll stop tumbling.'

She had been so magnificent when I knew her. I wanted to remind her of that. I wanted to tell her that she was being melodramatic, that she was still beautiful and that she still had so much going for her. I wanted to reach out and take her hand, but I knew for both of us right now, it was too raw, that even a move like that would be too much and not enough.

I DROPPED LUCY back at her office. She had a bunch of papers to correct.

'In the morning,' she said, 'I'll visit Ira and see what he can tell me about Manolo Santiago.'

'OK.'

Lucy slipped out of the car. As I watched her walk towards the door my cellphone rang. I looked at the caller ID and saw it was Muse.

'How did it go with Perez's mother?' Muse asked.

'I think she's lying.'

'I got something you might find interesting. Mr Perez hangs out at a local bar called Smith Brothers. Plays some darts, that kind of thing. Moderate drinker from what I hear. But the last two nights, he got really lit up. Started crying and picking fights.'

'Grieving,' I said.

At the morgue, Mrs Perez had been the strong one. He had leaned on her. I remembered that I could see the cracks there.

'He's there now, by the way. Might be a good place to take a run at him.'

'On my way.'

'There is one more thing. Wayne Steubens will see you.'

I think I stopped breathing. 'When?'

'Tomorrow. He's serving his time at Red Onion State Prison in Virginia.'

'Can't. We have court.'

'Can. One of your associates can handle it. I have you booked on the morning flight.'

IN MY DAY, they would have called the bar a yuppie bar. There were young men in loosened ties and women trying hard to look business-y. The men drank beer out of bottles, trying hard to look like they were having a good time with their buddies while checking out the ladies. The ladies drank wine or faux martinis and eyed the guys more surreptitiously.

This didn't look like a hangout for a guy like Jorge Perez, but I found him towards the back. He sat at the bar with four or five comrades-in-arms, all men who knew how to drink. They watched the twenty-first-century yuppies milling about them with hooded eyes.

I came up behind Mr Perez and put a hand on his shoulder. He turned towards me slowly. So did his comrades. His eyes were red and runny.

'My condolences,' I said.

He seemed puzzled. The other guys with him, all tough Latino men in their late fifties, looked at me as though I'd been ogling their daughters.

'What do you want?' he asked me.

'Why are you lying about Gil? That was your son in the morgue.'

He turned away from me and grabbed his beer. 'Get out of here.'

'I'm not going anywhere.'

The other men glared at me. One slid off his bar stool.

'Sit down,' I said to him.

He didn't move. I met his eyes and held it. Another man stood up.

'Do you know who I am?' I said. I reached into my pocket and pulled out my prosecutor badge. 'You all better be legal,' I said. 'Your family better be legal, your friends better be legal. Let me see some ID,' I said. 'All of you.'

The one who had stood first said, 'Hey, we don't want no trouble.'

'Then get lost.'

They threw down some bills and left. Normally I would feel bad about abusing my power like that, but they had asked for it.

Perez turned to me, clearly unhappy. 'Haven't you done enough?'

The bar stool next to him was free. I took it. I signalled for the bartender and ordered a draught of 'whatever he's having', pointing to Jorge Perez's mug.

'What do you want?' Perez asked me.

'I saw your face at the morgue. Why are you lying about Gil?'

His eyes narrowed. 'Who are you calling a liar?'

'That was your son in the morgue,' I said. 'I could show you the proof, but we both know it.'

My beer arrived and I took a deep sip of what on a hot day could only be called God's nectar.

'There are two ways to play it,' I went on. 'You keep pretending it's not him. I've already ordered a DNA test. So you know it won't be a problem for us to prove that Manolo Santiago was Gil.'

Perez took a sip of his beer. His hand shook.

'So the question is, once we prove it's your son, what happens? My guess is, you and your wife will try to peddle some "gasp!—we had no idea" crap. But that won't hold. You start off looking like liars. Then my people start investigating for real. We check all the phone records, all the bank records, we ask your friends about you, we ask about your children—'

'Leave my children out of it. That's not right.'

'What's not right is you lying about your son.'

He shook his head. 'You don't understand.'

'Like hell I don't. My sister was in those woods that night too.'

Tears filled his eyes.

'What happened, Mr Perez? Did your son kill my sister? Is that what you're trying to cover up?'

'We're not covering up anything.'

He stared at his beer. The tears escaped and trickled down his face. He didn't wipe them away.

'I'm not making idle threats here, Mr Perez. I'll go after you. I'll go after your children.'

His hands moved so fast I didn't have time to react. He grabbed my lapels and pulled me close. He had a good twenty years on me, but I could feel his strength. I got my bearings quickly enough and, remembering one of the martial arts moves I learned when I was a kid, slashed down on his forearms.

He released me, then he stood. I stood too. The bartender was watching us now.

'You need help, Mr Perez?' he asked.

I had the badge out again. 'You reporting all your tips to the IRS?'

He backed off. Everyone has stuff they keep buried.

Perez and I stared at each other. Then Perez said, 'I'm going to make this simple for you. If you go after my children, I'll go after yours.'

I felt my blood tick. 'What the hell does that mean?'

'It means,' he said, 'I don't care what sort of badge you carry. You don't threaten to go after a man's children.' He walked out of the door.

I picked up my cellphone and called Muse.

'Dig up everything you can on the Perezes,' I said.

CHAPTER 9

Greta finally returned my call. I was on my way home, still in the car. I struggled to find that damn 'hands-free' so that the Essex County prosecutor would not be caught breaking the law.

'Where are you?' Greta asked. I could hear the tears in her voice.

'I'm on my way home.'

'Do you mind if I meet you there?'

'Of course not. Did Bob make bail?'

'Yes. He's upstairs getting Madison to bed. I'll see you in an hour, OK?' Greta hung up before I could answer.

Cara was still awake when I got home. I was glad for that. I put her to bed and we played her new favourite game, called 'Ghost'. Ghost is basically hide-and-seek and tag combined. One person hides. When that person is found, he tries to tag the finder before the finder gets back to home base. What made our version of the game extra-silly was that we played it in her bed. This severely limited your hiding spots and chances to reach home base. It was dumb and silly and we both laughed, well, like children.

By the time Greta arrived, using the key I had given her years ago, I was so lost in the bliss of my daughter that I'd almost forgotten everything— young men who rape, young girls who vanish in the woods, serial killers who slit throats. But the jangle in the door brought it all back to me.

'I have to go,' I told Cara. 'Aunt Greta is here. I need to talk to her, OK?' I kissed her cheek and left her.

Greta wasn't pale. Her eyes were dry. Her mouth was a straight line.

'Isn't Bob coming?' I asked.

'He's watching Madison. And his lawyer is coming over.'

'Who does he have?'

'Hester Crimstein.'

I knew her. She was very good.

Greta moved towards the den. I followed. We sat on the couch. I took her hands in mine. My heart broke for her.

'You need to help Bob,' she said. Then: 'Help us.'

'I will do whatever I can. You know that.'

Her hands felt ice cold. She looked straight at me.

'You have to say you loaned us the money,' Greta said in pure monotone. 'That you knew about it. That we agreed to pay you back with interest.'

I just sat there.

'Paul?'

'You want me to lie?'

'You just said you would do whatever you could.'

'Are you saying'—I had to stop—'Are you saying Bob took the money? That he stole from the charity?'

Her voice was firm. 'He borrowed the money, Paul.'

'You're kidding, right?'

Greta took her hands away. 'He'll go to jail,' she said. 'My husband. Madison's father. It will ruin all our lives.'

'Bob should have thought of that before he stole from a charity.'

'He didn't steal. He borrowed. It's been tough for him at work. Did you know he lost his two biggest accounts?'

'So he thought the answer was to steal?'

'It's not that simple. We had signed the papers and committed to the pool. We made a mistake. We overextended.'

'What about your family money?'

'After Jane died, my parents thought it best to keep everything in trust. I can't touch it.'

I shook my head. 'So he stole?'

'Will you stop saying that? Look.' She handed me photocopied sheets. 'Bob was keeping tabs on every cent he took. He would pay it all back once he got on his feet. It was just a way of tiding us over.'

I scanned through the papers. They were just handwritten notes that could have been put there at any time. My heart sank.

'Did you know about this?' I asked her.

'No,' she said. 'He didn't tell me where the money came from. But listen, Bob's a good man. He would have returned the money. This type of thing is done all the time. But because of who you are and this damn rape case, they will make an example of him. They'll destroy the man I love. And if they destroy him, they destroy me and my family. Do you get that, Paul?'

I did get it. I had seen it done before. She was right. They would put the entire family through the wringer.

'I wish I could help, Greta.'

'You're turning your back on us?'

'I'm not turning my back. But I can't lie for you.'

She just stared at me. 'I would do it for you. You know that.'

I said nothing.

'You've failed everyone in your life,' Greta said. 'You didn't look out for your sister at that camp. And in the end, when my sister was suffering the most . . .' She stopped.

The room temperature dialled down ten degrees. That sleeping snake in my belly woke up and started to slither.

I met her eyes. 'Say it. Go ahead, say it.'

'JaneCare wasn't about Jane. It was about you and your guilt. My sister was dying. She was in pain. I was there, at her deathbed. You weren't.'

The unending suffering. Days turned to weeks, weeks to months. I watched the woman I adored, my tower of strength, wither away. I watched the light dim from her eyes. And towards the end, I couldn't take it. I couldn't watch the final light go out. My Jane died without me. Greta was right. I had failed to stay on watch. Again. And the guilt did indeed drive me to start up JaneCare.

Greta stood. 'You won't help us?'

'I'll help. I won't lie.'

'That's pretty typical of you, Cope. You're willing to do anything for the dead. It's the living you're not so good with.'

MUSE HAD FAXED me a three-page summary on Wayne Steubens.

Count on Muse She had read the file herself and given me the main points. Most of it I knew. I remember that when Wayne was arrested, many wondered why he decided to kill campers. Did he have a bad experience at a summer camp? One psychiatrist surmised that it was just the ease of the kill: Steubens had slaughtered his first four victims and got away with it. He associated that rush with summer camps and thus continued the pattern.

Wayne hadn't worked at the other camps. That would have been too obvious, of course. But circumstances had been his undoing. He had been under moderate suspicion for those first four murders. By the time the boy was slaughtered in Indiana, the FBI was looking at anyone who could have been in all those spots at the same time, starting with the camp counsellors.

Originally they found nothing in Indiana, the site of the second murder, but there had been an ATM withdrawal in Wayne Steubens's name two towns away from the murder of the boy in Virginia. That was the big break. They did more digging. Wayne Steubens hadn't made any ATM withdrawals in Indiana, but there was one in Everett, Pennsylvania, and another in Columbus, Ohio, in a pattern that suggested that he had driven from his home in New York out that way. He had no alibi and eventually they found a small motel owner near Muncie who positively identified him. The FBI got a warrant and found souvenirs buried in Steubens's yard.

Wayne claimed innocence. He said that he'd been set up.

They convicted him of the Virginia and Indiana murders. That was where the most evidence was. They didn't have enough for the camp. And there were problems with that case. He had only used a knife. How had he managed to kill four of them? How had he disposed of the other two bodies? The case wasn't neat. With the other murders, it was open and shut.

Lucy called at near midnight.

'How did it go with Jorge Perez?' she asked.

'You're right. They're lying. But he wouldn't talk either.'

'So what's the next step?'

'I meet with Wayne Steubens.'

'When?'

'Tomorrow morning.'

'One thing I remember about him,' she said.

'What?'

'Wayne was a pathological liar. I mean, now that I have that big-time psychology degree I know the technical term for it. But even then. Do you remember? He would lie about anything. It was his natural reaction. He would lie about what he had for breakfast.'

I thought about it. 'Yeah, I do remember. Part of it was normal camp boasting. He was this rich kid and he'd try to fit in with us wrong-siders. He was a drug dealer, he said. He was in a gang. He had this girlfriend who posed in *Playboy*. Everything he said was crap.'

'Remember that,' she said, 'when you talk to him.'

SERIAL KILLING must be pretty stress free, because Wayne Steubens had barely aged in twenty years. He had been a good-looking guy back when I knew him. He still was. He had a buzz cut now as opposed to those wavy, out-sailing-with-Mummy locks, but it looked good on him.

He gave me a winning, near-perfect smile. 'Are you here to invite me to a camp reunion?'

'We're having it in the Rainbow Room in Manhattan. Gosh, I hope you can attend.'

He howled with laughter as if I had just cracked the gem of gems. It wasn't, of course, but this interrogation was going to be a dance. He knew every trick in The Psychopath's Handbook. Normal approaches wouldn't work here. We had a past. We had even been somewhat friendly. I needed to use that.

Then his laughter slipped away. 'So how are you, Cope?'

'Groovy,' I said.

'Groovy,' Wayne repeated. 'You sound like Uncle Ira.'

At camp we used to call the elders Uncle and Aunt.

'Ira was one crazy dude, wasn't he, Cope?'

'He was out there.'

'That he was.' Wayne looked off.

I tried to focus in on his powder-blue eyes, but they kept darting around. He seemed a bit manic, but I had expected him to be more outwardly crazy or obvious. I mean the piercing gaze, the intensity, the hands clenching and unclenching, the rage right under the surface. But I didn't feel any of that with Wayne.

What I got from him was something far more frightening. Sitting here and talking to him—the man who in all likelihood had murdered my sister and at least seven others—felt normal. OK, even.

'I need to know what happened in those woods, Wayne.'

'Why now?'

'I'm not sure,' I said.

His eyes met mine: the psychotic was trying to read me for a lie.

'The timing is very interesting. Because you're not my only recent surprise visitor.'

I nodded slowly, trying not to seem too anxious. 'Who else came?'

'Why should I tell you?'

'Why not?'

Wayne Steubens sat back. 'You're still a good-looking guy, Cope.'

'So are you,' I said. 'But I think us dating is out of the question.'

'I should be angry with you, really.'

'Oh?'

'You spoilt that summer for me.'

Partitioning. I talked about that before. I know that my face showed nothing, but it was like razors were slicing through my gut.

I kept my breath steady. 'How did I do that?' I asked.

'Lucy would have been mine, if you weren't there. I had more than an inside track, if you know what I mean.'

I wasn't sure what to say to that, but I waded in. 'I thought you were interested in Margot Green.'

He smiled. 'She had some bod, huh?'

'Indeed.' Margot was the camp va-va-voom, and man, did she know it.

'Such a major tease. You do know that she dumped Gil?'

'Margot?'

'Yep. Right before the murder.' He arched an eyebrow. 'Makes you wonder, doesn't it?'

I didn't move, let him talk, hoped he'd say more. He did.

'I had her, you know. Margot. But she wasn't as good as Lucy.' He put his hand to his mouth as though he had said too much. 'You do know that we had a fling before you arrived that summer, right? Lucy and me.'

'Uh-huh.'

'You look a little green, Cope. You aren't jealous, are you?'

'It was twenty years ago.'

'It was, yes. And to be honest, I only got to second base. Bet you got further, Cope. Bet you popped that cherry, didn't you?'

He was trying to get a rise out of me. I wouldn't play that game.

'What happened in those woods, Wayne?'

'People died.'

'Don't play games with me.'

'Only one of us is playing games, Cope. If you want the truth, let's start with you. Why are you here today? The timing isn't coincidental.'

I looked behind me. I knew that we were being watched. I had requested no eavesdropping. I signalled for a guard to come in.

'Sir?' the guard said to me.

'Can you get me the names of any visitors Mr Steubens has had over the past, say, two weeks?'

'Yes, sir.'

The guard left. I looked back at Wayne. 'There's no need,' he said. 'I will tell you. A man named Curt Smith. He works for a company called MVD.'

'A private detective?'

'Yes.'

'And he came because he wanted'—I saw it now, those damn sons of bitches—'he wanted dirt on me.'

Wayne Steubens touched his nose and then pointed at me.

'What did he offer you?' I asked.

'His boss used to be a big fed. He said he could get me better treatment.'

'Did you tell him anything?'

'No. For two reasons. One, an ex-fed can't do anything for me.'

'And two?'

Wayne Steubens leaned forward. He made sure I was looking him square in the eye. 'I have done a lot of bad things in my life. I won't go into details.

I have spent the past eighteen years in this hellhole paying for them. I won't talk about Indiana or Virginia or any of that. The people who died there—I didn't know them. They were strangers. But I have no idea what happened in those woods twenty years ago. Because I wasn't there. I don't know what happened to my friends—not *strangers*, Cope, friends.'

I said nothing.

'You are a prosecutor now, right?'

I nodded.

'People are digging into your past. I understand that. I wouldn't really pay too much attention. Except now you're here too. Which means something happened. Something new. Something involving that night.'

'What's your point, Wayne?'

'Something has changed. I can see it in your face. For the first time you seriously wonder if I had something to do with that night. And if you have learned something new, you have an obligation to tell me about it.'

'I have no obligations, Wayne. You weren't tried for those murders. You were tried and convicted for murders in Indiana and Virginia.'

He spread his arms. 'Then where's the harm in telling me?'

I thought about that. He had a point. I chose discretion for now. Until we had a positive ID on Gil Perez, there was no reason to say anything anyway. I looked at him. Was he a lunatic? I thought so. But how the hell could I be sure? Either way, I had learned all I could today. So I stood.

'Goodbye, Wayne.'

'You know I didn't kill them, don't you?'

I did not reply. I started for the door.

'And if I didn't kill them,' he went on, 'you have to wonder about everything that happened that night—not only to Margot, Doug, Gil and Camille. But what happened to me. And to you.'

'IRA, LOOK AT ME a second.'

Lucy had waited until her father seemed his most lucid. She sat across from him in his room. He was smiling at an old picture from their camp days. The yellow VW Beetle had been decorated by some of the older girls. They put flowers and peace signs all over it. Ira was standing in the middle. The girls surrounded the car. Lucy remembered that day. It had been a good one, one of those you stick in a box and put in a bottom drawer and take out and look at when you're feeling blue.

'Ira?'

He turned towards her. 'I'm listening.'

Ira's beard was trimmed today. His hair was still unruly. His hands shook and Lucy wondered if maybe Parkinson's was on the horizon. His last years, she knew, would not be good. But then again, there really hadn't been many good ones in the past twenty.

'What is it, honey?'

His concern was so apparent. It had been one of Ira's great and honest charms—he so genuinely cared about people. Everyone felt that empathy with Ira. But when you were his only child, it was like the warmest blanket on the coldest day. He'd been such a magnificent father. She missed that man so much.

'In the logbook, it says that a man named Manolo Santiago visited you.' She tilted her head. 'Do you remember that, Ira?'

His smile slid away. 'Yeah,' he said. 'I remember.'

'What did he want?'

'To talk.'

'To talk about what?'

He shook his head.

'Please tell me,' she said.

Ira's mouth opened but nothing came out. When he finally spoke his voice was a hush. 'You know what he wanted to talk about.'

'The camp?' Lucy said.

He nodded.

'What did he want to know?'

He started to cry.

'Ira?'

'I didn't want to go back there,' he said. 'I let everyone down.'

'No, you didn't.'

He had his face in his hands and his sobs were uncontrollable now. Lucy got on her knees in front of him. She felt the tears push against her eyes too.

'Please, Dad, look at me.'

He wouldn't. The nurse, Rebecca, stuck her head in the doorway.

'I'll go get something to calm him down,' the nurse said.

Lucy held a hand up. 'No. He's getting emotional, that's all.'

'I'll get the doctor.'

Lucy was about to tell her not to, but she was gone.

'Ira, please listen to me. What did you say to him?'

Ira let out cry. 'I could only protect so many. Do you understand?'

She didn't. She put her hands on his cheeks and tried to lift his head. His scream almost knocked her backward. She let go. He stood, knocking the chair to the ground, then huddled in the corner. 'No . . . !'

'It's OK, Dad. It's—'

Nurse Rebecca came back with two other women. One Lucy recognised as Dr Julie Contrucci. The other, another nurse, had a hypodermic needle.

Rebecca said, 'It's OK, Ira.'

They started to approach him. Lucy stepped in the way. 'Get out,' she said. 'He's fine. I need him lucid for a few more minutes.'

'You call this lucid?' Dr Contrucci asked.

'I need time with him.'

Ira let out another sob.

Contrucci looked at Ira. 'Do you want a sedative, Mr Silverstein?'

Ira's eyes darted back and forth like the cornered animal he suddenly was. 'Mr Silverstein?'

He stared at his daughter. 'I didn't say anything, Lucy. What could I tell him?' He started sobbing again. 'I love you, Luce.'

'I love you too.'

The nurses went over. Ira stuck out his arm. The needle went in.

A LITTLE OVER AN HOUR after I left Wayne Steubens, I was sitting on a plane. The door had not yet closed when Muse called me.

'How did it go with Steubens?' she asked.

'I'll tell you about it later. How was court?'

'Motions and nothingness from what I hear. They used the phrase "under advisement" a lot. Being a lawyer must be so friggin' boring. The judge wants to see all counsel in chambers first thing Thursday morning. Listen, I have something else for you.'

'What?'

'I had our best computer weenie comb through those journals sent to your friend Lucy. I took the information he gleaned and then I did some digging. I think I know who sent them.'

'Who?'

'Do you have your BlackBerry with you? Might be easier if I email you all the details. I'd rather see if you come up with the same answer I do.'

FOUR HOURS AFTER I left Virginia, I sat in the office adjacent to Lucy's, one normally used by an English professor, who was on sabbatical. Lucy had the key. She was looking out of the window when her teaching assistant, a guy named Lonnie Berger, came in without knocking.

'What's up, Luce? And why are we in Professor Mitnick's office? . . .' Lonnie spotted me and his voice sort of faded away. 'Who's this?'

Lucy was still looking out of the window.

'I'm Paul Copeland,' I said.

I stuck out my hand. He shook it.

'Whoa,' Lonnie said. 'You're the guy in the story, right? Mr P or whatever. I mean, I read about the case online and—'

'Yes, Lucy filled me in on your amateur sleuthing. As you probably know, I have some pretty good investigators working for me.'

He let go of my hand.

'Anything you want to share with us?' I said.

'What are you talking about?'

'You were right, by the way. The email did come from the Frost Library computers at six forty-two p.m. But Sylvia Potter wasn't there then.'

He started backing away.

'You were, Lonnie.'

He put on a crooked smile and shook his head. Buying time. 'That's a bunch of crap. Hey, wait a second here. . . .' The smile fled as he faked shock and offence. 'C'mon, Luce, you can't believe that I . . .'

Lucy finally turned towards him. She didn't say anything.

Lonnie pointed at me. 'You don't believe this guy, do you? He's—'

'I'm what?'

No reply. Lucy just stared at him. He eventually collapsed into a chair. 'Damn,' he said.

'Why did you send Lucy the journal?' I said.

He started fiddling with an earring. 'I don't have to tell you a thing.'

'Sure you do,' I said. 'I can have you arrested for harassment.'

'No, you can't. First off, you can't prove I sent anything.'

'Sure I can. You may think you're knowledgeable about computers, but the experts in my office—they're trained professionals. We already know you sent it. We already have the proof.'

He considered that. 'So what? Even if I did send it, how can it be harassment to send a fictional story to a college professor?'

He had a point.

Lucy said, 'I can have you fired.'

'Maybe, maybe not. But you're the one who lied about your background. You'd have a lot more to explain than I do, Luce.'

Lonnie liked that argument. He sat up now and crossed his arms and looked very smug. I wanted very badly to punch him in the face.

'Is that so?' I held up my BlackBerry. 'I have your arrest records here. You want me to start listing them for you?'

That made the smug go bye-bye.

'I'm a powerful and angry cop, Lonnie. I can screw with you five ways to Sunday. So cut the crap and tell me why you sent the journal.'

He looked at Lucy. 'Truth is, I did it for you, Luce. To protect you. And, OK, myself. See, I didn't list those arrests on my Reston application. If the school found out, I'd be out. Just like that. That's what he told me.'

'Who told you?' I said.

'I don't know the names. They didn't say.'

'So what did they say?'

'They promised me that this wouldn't hurt Lucy. They said what I was doing would be for her good, too, that they were trying to catch a killer. They were private eyes. They'd been hired by one of the victims' families.'

One of the victims' families. A lie. A bald-faced lie. It was MVD, the private investigation firm. Suddenly it was all starting to make a lot of sense.

'Wonderful, thank you. What else did they say?'

'They told me that their firm was looking into the murders. That they didn't believe the official version, blaming them on the Summer Slasher.'

I looked at Lucy. I had filled her in on my visit with Wayne Steubens. We had talked about that night, the mistakes we made, the past certainty that all four were dead and that Wayne Steubens had killed them.

We had no idea what to think any more.

'Anything else?'

'That's it.'

'Oh, come on now, Lonnie. These guys sent Lucy the journal to get her to react, right? You were supposed to watch her. You were supposed to worm your way into her good graces and tell them what she said and did. Did they offer you a bonus if you got some dirt?'

'A bonus? I didn't do this for money.'

I shook my head. 'Let's not pretend it was all about fear of being exposed. The same investigators who dig up old arrests have access to bank accounts. They can find, for example, five-thousand-dollar cash deposits. Like the one you made five days ago at the Chase in West Orange.'

I had to hand it to Muse. Her investigating skills are incredible.

'I didn't do anything illegal,' he said.

'That's debatable, but I'm not in the mood right now. Who wrote the journal? Did they tell you how they got that information?'

'They said they had sources. They knew everything about Lucy. But they wanted *you*, pal. Anything I could get her to say about Paul Copeland—that was their main concern. They think maybe you're a killer.'

'No, they don't, Lonnie. They think maybe you're an idiot who can muddy up my name.'

Lonnie worked very hard at looking perplexed. He looked at Lucy. 'I'm really sorry. I would never do anything to hurt you. You know that.'

'Do me a favour, Lonnie,' she said. 'Just get the hell out of my face.'

ALEXANDER 'SOSH' SIEKIERKY stood alone in his penthouse.

Man gets used to his environment. That was how it was. He was getting comfortable. Too comfortable for a man with his beginnings. He wondered if he was still as tough as he once was, if he could still walk into those dens, those lairs, and lay waste without fear. The answer, he was certain, was no. It wasn't age that had weakened him. It was comfort.

As a young child, Sosh's family had got ensnared in the horrible siege of Leningrad. The Nazis surrounded the city and caused unspeakable suffering. Sosh had turned five on October 21, 1941, a month after the blockade began. He would turn six and seven with the siege still on. In January 1942, Sosh's brother, Gavrel, aged twelve, and his sister, Aline, aged eight, died of starvation. Sosh survived by eating stray animals. Cats mostly. People hear the stories but they can't fathom the terror, the agony. But even that, even the horror—you get used to it. Like comfort, suffering can become the norm.

Sosh remembered when he first came to the USA. You could buy food anywhere. There were no shortages. He remembered buying a chicken. He kept it in his freezer. He couldn't believe it. He would wake up at night and run to the freezer and open it up and just stare at the chicken.

He still did that. You don't worry about happiness and fulfilment when you're starving. It is good to remember that.

Most of his Soviet colleagues missed the old days. They missed the power. A few had returned to the old country, but most had stayed. They were bitter men. Sosh hired some of his former colleagues because he trusted them and wanted to help.

The message had come in on his computer.

That was how it worked nowadays. Computers, emails. He wondered how the old Soviet regime would have handled the Internet. Controlling information had been such a large part of what they did. But how do you control it with something like the Internet? Or maybe it wasn't that big a difference. In the end, the way you rounded up your enemies was through leaks. People talked, sold one another out. Sometimes for a hunk of bread. Sometimes for a ticket to freedom. It all depended on how hungry you were.

Sosh read the message again: *We found her.*

And now he wondered what he should do about it.

I PUT A CALL in to Muse. 'Can you find Cingle Shaker for me? I want to ask her some questions about how MVD works.'

'I'm on it.'

I hung up and turned back to Lucy. She was still looking out of the window. 'You OK?'

'Lonnie Berger was probably my closest friend. I trusted him.'

I was going to say I'm sorry or something equally hackneyed, but I decided to keep it to myself.

'By the way, how's my self-pity act? Pretty attractive, right?'

'Actually,' I said, 'it is.'

She turned away from the window and looked at me.

'Are we going to try again, Cope? I mean, after this is all done and we figure out what happened to your sister. Are we going back to our lives—or are we going to try to see what could happen here?'

'I love when you beat around the bush.'

Lucy wasn't smiling.

'Yeah,' I said. 'I want to try.'

'Good answer. Very good. So who killed Margot and Doug?' she asked.

'Wow, that was a quick segue.'

'Yeah, well, the faster we figure out what happened . . .' She shrugged.

'You know, it's just so damn easy to remember why I fell for you.'

Lucy turned away. 'I am not going to cry, I am not going to cry . . .'

'I don't know who killed them any more,' I said.

'OK. How about Wayne Steubens? We know that he didn't kill Gil Perez. Do you think he told you the truth?'

'He said he hooked up with you. But that he only got to second base.'

'If he counts the time he intentionally bumped into me during a softball game and copped a feel, well, then technically he's telling the truth.'

'He also said he slept with Margot.'

'That's probably true. Lots of guys had Margot.'

'Not me.'

'That's because I snagged you as soon as you arrived.'

'That you did. He also said that Gil and Margot had broken up. Do you think that's true?'

'You know how camp was. People were always going out and then breaking up and then finding someone new.'

'True. But the common theory was that both couples went into the woods to, uh, mess around. If Gil and Margot were no longer together, why would they have been sneaking into the woods?' I thought about what Raya Singh had suggested. 'Maybe Gil killed Margot. Maybe Camille and Doug just stumbled across that.'

'So Gil silenced them.'

'Right. Now he's in trouble. So he faked like he died too.'

We both sat there.

'We're missing something,' she said.

'I know.'

'We might be getting close.'

'Or we might be way off.'

'One of the two,' Lucy agreed.

Man, it felt good to be with her.

'Something else,' I said. 'That journal. What were they talking about— you finding me covered with blood and me saying we can't tell anyone?'

'I don't know.'

'Let's start with the first part—the part they got right. About how we sneaked away. How would they know that?'

'I don't know,' she said.

'How would they know you led me away?'

'Or'—she stopped, swallowed—'how I felt about you?'

'I'm trying hard to focus here and not smile.'

'Don't try too hard,' she said. 'Anyway, let's move on to part two.'

'The stuff about me covered in blood. Where did that come from?'

'No idea. But you know what really creeps me out? That they knew we got separated. That we did lose sight of each other.'

I had wondered about that too.

'Who would know about that?' I asked. 'I never told a soul.'

'Neither did I.'

'Someone could have guessed,' Lucy said. She stopped. 'Or . . .' She looked straight at me. 'Someone saw us that night.'

Silence.

'Gil maybe,' I said. 'Or Wayne. They're our two murder suspects, right?'

'Right. Then who murdered Gil?'

'FOUND HER,' Muse said, as she walked into my office.

Cingle Shaker followed. Cingle knew how to make an entrance, but I wasn't sure that was a conscious effort on her part. There was something fierce in her movements, as if the air itself better make way. Muse was no potted plant, but she looked like one next to Cingle Shaker.

They both sat. Cingle crossed her long legs.

'So,' Cingle said. 'MVD is after you big-time.'

'Looks that way.'

'It is that way. I've checked. It's a scorched-earth operation. No expense spared. They destroyed your brother-in-law already. They sent a guy to Russia. They had someone try to bribe Wayne Steubens. In short, they're going to carve out any piece of your ass they can get their blade into.'

'Any word on what they got?'

'Not yet, no. Just what you already know.'

I told her about the journal. 'A lot is wrong. I never stumbled across blood or said we have to keep this secret or anything like that. But they know how we felt about each other. They know we sneaked away and how and all that.'

'Interesting.'

'How would they have got their information?'

'Hard to say.'

'Any thoughts?'

She mulled it over for a few moments. 'This is how they operate. They want to stir something up. It doesn't matter if it's the truth or not. Sometimes you need to shift reality. For example, when I first got to MVD,

I was hired to catch cheating spouses. Some wives don't want the truth. They want their husbands to be cheating.'

I looked at Muse. 'I'm lost.'

'No, you're not. If a wife wanted to nail her husband for cheating, my job would be to seduce him. That's how MVD worked. The husband would be at a bar or something. They would send me out as a'—she made quote marks with her fingers—'fidelity test.'

'So?'

'So I hate to sound immodest, but take a look.' Cingle spread her arms. Even dressed down in a loose sweater, the sight was indeed impressive. 'If that's not unfair entrapment, I don't know what is.'

'If the guy's committed, it shouldn't make a difference how attractive the woman is.'

Cingle Shaker looked at Muse. 'Is he for real?'

Muse shrugged.

'Let me put it this way,' Cingle said. 'I probably ran, oh, thirty or forty of these so-called fidelity tests. Guess how many guys turned me down?'

'I have no idea.'

'Two. Do you know why? They realised something had to be up. They saw the trap. The point is this: MVD wants dirt, any way they can get it. If the current reality isn't providing any they'll shift the reality. Do you get it now?'

'I think so. I have to be careful not only about what I might have done, but what I appear to be doing or might get entrapped into doing.'

'Bingo.' She stood. 'Anything else I can help you with?'

'No, Cingle, I think that covers it.'

'Cool. By the way, I have my bill here for the Jenrette-Marantz case.' Cingle handed it to me and smiled. 'I liked watching you in court, Cope. You nailed those sons of bitches but good.'

'Couldn't have done it without you,' I said. 'MVD must miss you.'

'I hear they got a new hottie. I might try to steal her from them. I could use a second hottie, and she appeals to a slightly different demographic.'

'How's that?'

'I'm a blonde. MVD's new girl is dark-skinned.'

'African-American?'

'No.'

And then I felt the floor underneath me give way as Cingle Shaker added, 'I think she's from India.'

THE NEXT MORNING Raya was waiting for me in front of Bistro Janice in Hohokus, a small town in northeast New Jersey.

She wore dark jeans and a white blouse open at the throat. A killer. Even though I now knew what she was about, I couldn't help feeling an attraction and hating myself for it. On the other hand, as beautiful as she was, I couldn't help thinking that she wasn't in Lucy's league. I liked feeling that. I held on to it. I thought about Lucy and a funny smile crept onto my face.

'I'm so glad you called,' Raya said.

She bussed my cheek. A subtle whiff of lavender came off her. We moved towards a booth in the back of the bistro and sat down. Raya gave me her best melt-'em smile. I thought about Lucy. It knocked away the effect.

'So,' I said, 'you're a private eye.'

Subtlety wasn't going to work here. I didn't have the time or the patience for it. I kept going before she could start with the denials.

'You work for Most Valuable Detection of Newark, New Jersey. You don't really work for that Indian restaurant. I should have picked up on that when the woman at the desk didn't know who you were.'

She shrugged. 'How did you figure me out?'

'I'll tell you later. How much of what you said to me was a lie?'

'Not much, actually.'

'Are you still going to stick with that story about not knowing who Manolo Santiago really was?'

'That part was true. I didn't know he was Gil Perez until you told me.'

That confused me.

'How did you two really meet?' I asked.

'I met him on the street,' she said. 'Just like I told you.'

'But not by accident.'

'No, not by accident. My job was to get closer to him.'

'Why him?'

'He claimed to have information on you.'

'I don't understand. Gil Perez comes to MVD—'

'He was Manolo Santiago to us.'

'Right, OK, he comes to you and says he can help you find dirt on me.'

'Dirt is a bit strong, Paul.'

'Call me Prosecutor Copeland,' I said. 'That was your task, right? Find something incriminating on me? Try to get me to back off?'

She did not reply. She didn't have to.

'So he says he has information on me. Then what?'

'He won't say exactly what it is. He gets coy. He wants money, lots of it.'

'And Jenrette is willing to pay it. So go on from there.'

'We insist on proof. Manolo starts talking about how he still needs to nail down details. But we've checked up on him now. We know his name isn't really Manolo Santiago. But we also know that he's onto something big.'

'Like what?'

'He told us that he knew what really happened the night those four kids died in the woods. He told us that he could prove you lied about it.'

'How did he find you?' I asked.

'What do you mean?'

But I thought about it. 'MVD knew about those old murders . . . that the sheriff even questioned me.' I saw it now. 'So you questioned everyone involved in that case. I know you guys sent someone down to visit Wayne Steubens. And that means you went to the Perez family too, right?'

'I don't know, but that makes sense.'

'And that's how Gil heard about it. He sees a way to score some money. He goes to you. He doesn't tell you who he really is. But he has enough information that you're curious. So they send you to, what, seduce him?'

'Get close to him. Not seduce.'

'You say "tomato," I say "tomahto". Did he take the bait?'

'Men usually do.'

'And what did he tell you?'

'Almost nothing. He told us you were with a girl that night. Someone named Lucy. That's all I knew—what I told you. The day after we met, I called him on his cell. Detective York answered. You know the rest.'

'So Gil was trying to get you proof? In order to score this big payday?'

'Yes.'

I thought about that. He had visited Ira. What could Ira have told him?

'Did Gil say anything about my sister?'

'No.'

'Did he say anything about, well, any of the victims?'

'Nothing. He was coy, like I said. But it was clear he had something big.'

'And then he ends up dead.'

She smiled. 'You can imagine what we thought.'

The waiter came over. He took our order. I got the salad special. Raya ordered a cheeseburger, rare.

I skipped the obvious answer. 'So when Gil was found dead, your assignment changed. You were supposed to get close to me.'

'Yes. I thought my helpless Calcutta story would get to you. But then you didn't call, so I called you.'

'That apartment in Ramsey. The one you said Gil lived in—'

'We rented that room. I was trying to get you to admit to something.'

'And I did tell you some stuff.'

'Yes. But we weren't sure you were being accurate or truthful. Nobody really believed that Manolo Santiago was Gil Perez.'

'I told you about Lucy being my girlfriend.'

'We already knew about that. In fact, we'd already found her.'

'How?'

'We're a detective agency, that's how. But according to Santiago, she was lying about something that happened back then too. So we figured a direct interrogation wouldn't work.'

'You sent her a journal instead, through Lonnie Berger.'

'Yes.'

'How did you get that information?'

'That I don't know,' she said. 'Actually, this is kind of a relief, you finding out. It felt OK when I thought you might be a killer. Now it just feels sleazy.'

I rose. 'I might want you to testify.'

'I won't.'

'Yeah,' I said. 'I hear that all the time.'

CHAPTER 10

Loren Muse was doing research on the Perez family.

Funny thing she noticed right away. The Perezes owned that bar, the one where Cope had met up with Mr Perez. Muse found that interesting. They'd been a family of poor immigrants, and now they had a net worth in excess of more than $4 million.

She was wondering what that meant, if anything, when the phone call came in. 'Muse here.'

'Yo, sweetums, it's Andrew.'

Andrew Barrett was the guy with the new radar machine. He was supposed to go out this morning to the old campsite and start searching.

'Sweetums?'

'I only work with machines,' he said. 'I'm not good with people.'

'I see. So is there a problem?'

'Uh, not really.' There was a funny hum in his voice.

'Have you got out to the site yet?' she asked.

'You kidding? Of course we did. Soon as you gave me the OK, I was, like, so there. Started working at first light.'

'So?'

'So you know how I said this new radar machine is a miracle worker?'

'Yes.'

'Well, I was right. You should get out here pronto. The ME is on her way.'

DETECTIVE YORK'S phone rang. He picked it up. 'York.'

'Hey, it's Max down at the lab.'

Max Reynolds was their lab liaison on this case. York liked this kid. He was smart.

'What's up, Max?'

'I got the results back on the carpet-fibre test. You know, the one on your Manolo Santiago corpse.'

Usually the liaison just sent a report.

'Something unusual?'

'Yes. The fibres are old. The car they're from has to be more than thirty years old. This particular carpeting was used between 1968 and 1974.'

'Wow. Anything else?'

'The manufacturer,' Reynolds said, 'was German.'

'Mercedes-Benz?'

'Not that upscale,' he said. 'My guess? Probably Volkswagen.'

LUCY DECIDED to give it one more try with her father.

Ira was painting when she arrived. Nurse Rebecca was with him. The nurse gave Lucy a look when she entered the room. Ira had his back to her.

'Ira?'

When he turned, she almost took a step back. He looked horrible. The colour was gone from his face. His hair, always unruly, now looked like the result of too many years of living among the homeless.

'How are you feeling?' Lucy asked.

Nurse Rebecca gave her an I-warned-you glare.

'Not so good,' he said.

'What are you working on?'

Lucy walked over to the canvas. She pulled up when she saw what it was. Woods.

Their woods, of course. The old campsite. He had got every detail right. Amazing. The painting was a night view. The moon lit up the treetops.

Lucy looked at her father. Her father looked at her.

'We'd like to be alone,' Lucy said to the nurse.

'I don't think that's a good idea.'

Nurse Rebecca thought that talking would make him worse. The truth was just the opposite. Something was locked up there, in Ira's head. They had to confront it now, finally, after all these years.

Ira said, 'Rebecca, get out.'

Just like that. The voice wasn't cold, but it hadn't been inviting either. Rebecca took her time. 'If you need me,' she said, 'just call. OK, Ira?'

Ira said nothing. Rebecca left. She did not close the door.

Ira closed his eyes. Lucy sat next to him and took his hands in hers.

'I love you,' she said.

'I love you too. More than anything. Always. For ever.'

Lucy waited. He just kept his eyes closed.

'You're thinking back to that summer,' she said.

His eyes stayed closed.

'When Manolo Santiago came to see you—'

'How did you know that he visited me?'

'It was in the logbook.'

He finally opened his eyes. 'Did he visit you too?'

'No.'

He seemed puzzled by this. Lucy decided to try another avenue.

'Do you remember Paul Copeland?' she asked.

He closed his eyes again, as though that hurt. 'Of course.'

'He visited me.'

The eyes popped open. 'What?'

'Something is happening, Ira. Something is bringing this all back after all these years. I need to find out what. Help me, OK?'

'Why . . .?' His voice faltered. 'Why did Paul Copeland visit you?'

'Because he wants to know what really happened that night.' She tilted her head. 'What did you tell Manolo Santiago?'

'Nothing!' he shouted. 'Absolutely nothing!'

He was growing agitated. She made her voice soft.

'Ira, what's wrong?'

He turned and stared at his painting. Tears came to his eyes. He reached his hand towards the woods, as if he could disappear into them.

'I want to see Paul Copeland,' he said.

'You want me to come too?'

He shook his head. 'Tell him to come here. Alone. I'll tell him what he needs to hear. And then, maybe, the ghosts will go back to sleep.'

WHEN I GOT BACK to my office, I got yet another shock.

'Glenda Perez is here,' Jocelyn Durels said.

'Who?'

'She's an attorney. Says you'll know her better as Gil Perez's sister.'

I beelined into my waiting area and spotted her right away. Glenda Perez looked the same as she had in those pictures on the mantelpiece.

'Ms Perez?'

She rose and gave me a perfunctory handshake. 'I assume you have time to see me.'

She did not wait for me to lead the way. She walked head high into my office. I followed her and closed the door.

I waved for her to take a seat. She didn't. I moved round my desk and sat down. She put her hands on her hips and glared down at me.

'Tell me, Mr Copeland, do you enjoy threatening old people?'

'Not at first, no. But once you get the hang of it, yeah, it's kinda fun.'

The hands dropped from her hips. 'You think this is funny?'

'Why don't you sit down, Ms Perez?'

'Did you threaten my parents?'

'No. Wait, yes. Your father. I did say that if he didn't tell me the truth I would rip his world apart and go after him and his children. If you call that a threat, then yes, I made it.'

I smiled at her. She had expected denials and apologies. I hadn't given her any, hadn't fuelled her fire. She opened her mouth, closed it, sat.

'So,' I said, 'let's skip the posturing. Your brother walked out of those woods twenty years ago. I need to know what happened.'

Glenda Perez wore a grey business suit. She crossed her legs and tried to look relaxed. She wasn't pulling it off. I waited.

'That's not true. My brother was murdered with your sister.'

'I thought we were going to skip the posturing.'

She sat and tapped her lip.

'Are you really going to go after my family?'

'This is my sister's murder we're talking about. You, Ms Perez, should understand that.'

She tapped her lip some more. I waited some more.

'How about if I lay a hypothetical on you?'

I spread my hands. 'I'm all for hypotheticals.'

'Suppose,' Glenda Perez began, 'this dead man, this Manolo Santiago, was indeed my brother. What do you think it would mean to my family?'

'That you lied to me.'

'Not just to you, though.'

I sat back. 'Who else?'

'As you know, all of our families engaged in a lawsuit. We won millions. That would now be a case of fraud, wouldn't it? Hypothetically speaking.'

I said nothing.

'We used that money to invest, for my education, for my brother. Tomás would be in a home if we hadn't won that money. Do you understand?'

'I do.'

'And, hypothetically speaking, if Gil was alive and we knew it, then the entire case was based on a lie. We would be open to prosecution. Do you see?'

We looked at each other. Now she was doing the waiting.

'There is another problem with your hypothetical,' I said.

'What's that?'

'Four people go into the woods. One comes out alive. He keeps the fact that he's alive a secret. One would have to conclude, based on your hypothetical, that he killed the other three.'

Tapping the lip. 'I can see how your mind might go in that direction. But he didn't.'

'I just take your word for that?'

'If my brother killed them, then this is over, isn't it? He's dead. You can't bring him back and try him.'

'You have a point.'

'Thank you.'

'Who did kill my sister?'

Glenda Perez stood. 'For a long time, I didn't know. In our hypothetical, I didn't know that my brother was alive.'

'Did your parents?'

'I'm not here to talk about them.'

'I need to know—'

'Who killed your sister. I get that. So I'm going to tell you one more thing. And that's it. I will tell you this under one condition.'

'What?'

'That this always stays hypothetical. That you stop telling the authorities that Santiago is my brother. That you leave my parents alone.'

'I can't promise that.'

'Then I can't tell you what I know about your sister.'

Silence. There it was. The impasse. Glenda Perez rose to leave.

'I know something about what happened to your sister that night. If you want to know what it is, you'll make the deal.'

'I won't tell,' I said, 'unless I absolutely have to. I have no interest in harming you or your family. I promise to do my best. But we both know that's all I can do.'

Glenda Perez hesitated. Then she headed to my door. She put her hand on the knob and turned towards me.

'Still hypothetically speaking?' she said.

'Yes.'

'If my brother walked out of those woods, he didn't walk out alone.'

My whole body went cold. I couldn't move. I tried to say something but nothing came out. I met Glenda Perez's eye. She nodded and I could see her eyes were wet. She turned away.

'Don't play games with me, Glenda.'

'I'm not, Paul. That's all I know. My brother survived that night. And so did your sister.'

DAY WAS SURRENDERING to the shadows when Loren Muse reached the old campsite.

Muse hated the woods. She loved sports but hated the supposedly grey outdoors. She hated bugs and fishing and wading and taking hikes and dirt and everything else she considered 'rural'.

She stopped at the sign that said Lake Charmaine Condominium Centre.

There were flashing lights up ahead. A bunch of parked police cars, she figured. Probably every cop within a fifty-mile radius wanted in on this one.

The adrenaline was kicking in now. She was anxious to know what Andrew Barrett had found. Judging by the amount of flashing lights, it had to be something big.

Like a body.

A man in uniform sauntered towards her vehicle. He wore a big-brimmed hat and had a sheriff's badge. His name tag read Lowell.

'Can I help you, miss?'

She flashed her ID. 'Loren Muse, chief investigator for Essex County.'

Sheriff Lowell sighed and wiped his nose with a handkerchief. His nose was bulbous and rather huge. So were all his features—long and droopy, as if someone had drawn a caricature of him and then let it melt in the sun.

He examined the ID, then said, 'Park to the right. We have to hike up to the site. I'll take you.'

She parked and Lowell handed her a flashlight.

'To the right. Come on.'

Muse counted seven cop cars and three other emergency vehicles of one kind or another. All had lights flashing. Why they needed their lights on she had no idea. The residents, a mix of old folks and young families, gathered, drawn by the unnecessary flashing lights, and watched nothing.

'How far is the walk?' Muse asked.

'Mile and a half maybe. You want a tour as we go along? We'll be passing where they found one of the bodies twenty years ago.'

'Were you on that case?'

'Peripherally,' he said.

The path grew thinner until it practically disappeared. They were climbing on rocks and round trees. Muse had always been something of a tomboy. She enjoyed the activity. And—Flair Hickory be damned—her shoes could handle it.

'Hold up,' Lowell said.

The sun continued to dip. Lowell's profile was in silhouette. He took off his hat. 'This is where the Billingham kid was found.'

The woods seemed to settle at the words, and then the wind whispered an old song. Muse looked down. A kid. Doug Billingham had been seventeen. He had been found with eight stab wounds, mostly defensive. He had fought his assailant. She looked at Lowell. His head was lowered, his eyes closed.

Muse remembered something else—something from the file. Lowell. That name. 'Peripherally, my ass,' she said. 'You were the lead.'

Lowell did not reply.

'I don't get it. Why didn't you tell me?'

He shrugged. 'Why didn't you tell me you were reopening my case?'

'We weren't really. I mean, I didn't think we had anything yet.'

'So your guys hitting pay dirt,' he said. 'That was just dumb luck? You sent men in to my county without informing me?'

Muse didn't like where this was going.

'How far are we from where Margot Green was found?' she asked.

'A half-mile due south.'

'Margot Green was found first, right?'

'Yep. See, where you came in? The condos? That used to be where the girls' side of the camp was. You know. Their cabins. The boys were to the south. The Green girl was found near there.'

'How long after you found Green did you locate the Billingham boy?'

'Thirty-six hours. He was buried in a shallow grave. That's probably why it was missed the first time. You know how it is. Everybody hears about missing kids and they come out and help us cover ground. They walked right over him.'

There was a beat-up cross like those makeshift memorials for car-accident deaths. There was no picture of Billingham. No keepsakes or flowers. Just the cross. Alone out here in the woods. Muse almost shivered.

'The killer—you probably know this—his name was Wayne Steubens. There are a lot of theories on what happened that night, but the consensus seems to be that Steubens worked on the vanished kids—Perez and Copeland—first. He buried them. He started to dig a grave for Douglas Billingham when Margot Green was found. So he took off.'

She knew that too. 'Did you ever question Wayne Steubens?'

'We talked to everyone at that camp.'

He said that slowly, carefully. A bell rang in Muse's head.

'And yes,' he continued, 'the Steubens kid gave me the creeps. But maybe that's hindsight, I don't know any more. There was no evidence linking Steubens to the murders. There was nothing linking anybody, really. Plus Steubens was rich. His family hired a lawyer. As you can imagine the camp broke up right away. All the kids went home.'

Muse still had her eyes on the cross.

'You ready to keep moving?'

She nodded. They started hiking again.

'Have you met any of the victims' families?' he asked after a while.

She thought about that. 'One is my boss, actually. Paul Copeland. You remember him?'

'Like I said, I questioned everybody at that camp.'

The bell in Muse's head sounded again.

'Is he the one who got you to look into the case?' Lowell asked.

She didn't reply.

'Murder is unjust,' he went on. 'It's like God had this plan and there is this natural order. Then someone took it upon themselves to mess with that. If you solve the case, sure, it helps. But it's like you crumpled up a piece of aluminium foil. Finding the killer helps you spread it out again, but for the family, it never really regains its form.'

'You're quite the philosopher, Sheriff.'

'Look into your boss's eyes. Whatever happened in these woods that night? It's still there. There are some old-timers who think a sound echoes for ever in here. Makes sense when you think about it. This Billingham kid. I'm sure he screamed. It echoes, just bounces back and forth, the sound getting smaller and smaller, never entirely disappearing. Like a part of him is still calling out, even now. Murder echoes like that, doesn't it?'

'I don't know,' Muse said.

'And I don't know if you should be here.'

'Why's that?'

'Because I did question your boss that night.'

Muse stopped walking. 'Are you saying there's a conflict of interest?'

'I think that might be exactly what I'm saying.'

'Paul Copeland was a suspect?'

'It is still an open case. It is still, despite your interference, my case. So I won't answer that. But I will tell you this. He lied about what happened.'

'He was a kid on guard duty. He didn't know how serious it was.'

'That's no excuse.'

'He came clean later, right?'

Lowell did not respond.

'I read the file,' Muse said. 'He goofed off and didn't do what he was supposed to do on guard duty. How about the guilt he must feel over that? He misses his sister, sure. But I think the guilt eats at him more.'

'Interesting.'

'What?'

'You said the guilt eats at him. What kind of guilt?'

Muse kept walking.

'And it's curious, don't you think?' Lowell said. 'That he left his post that night. I mean, think about it. Here he is, a responsible kid. Everyone said so. And suddenly, on the night that these campers sneak out, on the night that Wayne Steubens plans on committing murder, Paul Copeland chooses to slack off. That's always struck me as a hell of a coincidence.'

Muse said nothing.

Lowell smiled and turned away.

'Come on,' he said. 'It's getting dark and you're going to want to see what your friend Barrett found.'

AFTER GLENDA PEREZ LEFT, I sat in my office, alone, stunned, not sure what to do or think or feel. My body was shuddering. I actually did that thing when you wonder if you're dreaming. I did all the checks. I wasn't. This was real. Camille was alive.

I called Lucy on her cellphone.

'Hey,' she said.

'You're not going to believe what Gil Perez's sister just told me.'

'What?'

I filled her in. When I got to the part about Camille walking out of those woods, Lucy gasped out loud.

'Do you believe her?' Lucy asked.

'Why would she say that if it wasn't true?'

Silence.

'What is it, Lucy?'

'It's just odd. If your sister is alive, where the hell has she been?'

'I don't know.'

'So what are you going to do now?'

It was a good question. What next? Where do I go from here?

Lucy said, 'I talked to my father again. And he remembers something about that night. He won't tell me what it is. He said he'd only tell you.'

'Me?'

'Yep. Ira said he wanted to see you.'

'Now?'

'If you want.'

'I want. Should I pick you up?'

She hesitated. 'Ira said he wanted to see you alone.'

'OK.'

'Pick me up anyway. I'll wait in the car while you go in.'

HOMICIDE DETECTIVES York and Dillon sat in the 'tech room', eating pizza. The tech room was actually a meeting space where they wheeled in televisions and VCRs and the like.

Max Reynolds entered. 'How are you guys?'

Dillon said, 'This pizza is awful. We're in New York, for crying out loud. The home of pizza. And this tastes like something that disobeyed a pooper-scooper law.'

Reynolds turned on the television. 'I'm sorry the cuisine does not measure up to your standards.'

'Am I exaggerating?' Dillon asked York.

York said, 'That's your third slice.' He turned to Max Reynolds. 'What have you got for us?'

'I think I found our guy. Or at least, his car,' he began. 'Two blocks from where you found the body there is a convenience store. The owner has been having problems with shoplifters grabbing items he keeps outside, so he aims his camera out that way. It gives us a partial of the street, as well. So we started checking for cars around that age—more than thirty years old—and look what we found.'

Reynolds already had the tape keyed up. An old Volkswagen Beetle drove by. He hit the freeze button.

'That's our car?' York asked.

'A 1971 Volkswagen Beetle. More important, this type of car matches the carpet fibres we found on Mr Santiago's clothing.'

'Hot damn,' Dillon said.

'Can you make out the licence plate?' York asked.

'No. We only get a side view. Not a partial, not even the state.'

'But how many original Volkswagen bugs in yellow can there be on the road?' York said. He turned back to Reynolds. 'Anything else?'

Reynolds hit a button and the picture zoomed. 'Here's the guy.'

Dillon squinted. 'He looks like Jerry Garcia or something.'

'Long grey hair, long grey beard,' Reynolds agreed.

'That it?'

'That's it.'

York said to Dillon, 'Let's start checking the motor vehicles record. This car can't be that hard to find.'

SHERIFF LOWELL'S ACCUSATIONS echoed in the still of the woods. Lowell thought Paul Copeland had lied about the murders. Had he? Did it matter?

Muse thought about that. She liked Cope, no question. But this was a homicide case. Like any other. It leads where it leads, even if that means back to her boss. No favourites.

A few minutes later Muse spotted Andrew Barrett dragging what looked like a baby carriage behind him. Muse called out to him. He looked up, clearly displeased with the interruption. When he saw who it was, his face lit up.

'Hey, Muse!'

'Andrew.'

'Wow, great to see you.'

'Uh-huh,' she said. 'What are you doing?'

'What do you mean, what am I doing? I'm looking for graves.'

'I thought you found something.'

'I did. It's up ahead another hundred yards. But I thought there were two bodies missing, so I figured, hey, why rest on my laurels.'

Muse swallowed. 'You found a body?'

'Muse, this machine. Oh my, it's just amazing. We got lucky, of course. There hasn't been any rain in this area in, I don't know, how long, Sheriff?'

'Two, three weeks,' Lowell said.

'See, that helps. Dry ground. You know anything about how ground-penetrating radar works? I stuck an 800 MHz on this baby. That lets me—'

'Barrett?' Muse said. 'Do I look like I give the smallest rat's buttock *how* your toy works? Please just tell me what you found before I shoot someone?'

'Bones, Muse,' he said with a smile. 'We found bones.'

'Human, right?'

'Definitely. In fact, the first thing we found was a skull. That's when we stopped digging. The pros are excavating now.'

Muse hurried past him. Lowell followed. Up ahead she could make out big spotlights, almost like a movie set. Lowell pointed towards an attractive woman wearing rubber gloves.

'That's Doc O'Neill,' Lowell said.

'She's your coroner?'

'Yep.'

As Muse got closer, she could see that 'attractive' may have been under-stating it. Tara O'Neill was a knockout. Muse stepped quickly towards her.

'I'm Loren Muse, chief investigator for Essex County.'

The woman offered the glove hand. 'Tara O'Neill, coroner.'

'What can you tell me about the body?'

O'Neill looked wary for a second, but Lowell nodded that it was OK. 'Are you the one who sent Mr Barrett out here?' she asked.

'I am.'

'We're still working on it, but from what I can see we have a fairly complete skeleton. It was found three feet down. I'll need to get the bones to the lab to make a positive ID.'

'What can you tell me now?'

'Come this way.'

She walked Muse over to the other side of the dig. The bones were tagged and laid out on a blue tarmac.

'No clothing?' Muse said.

'None.'

'Did they disintegrate or was the body buried naked?'

'I can't say for sure. But since there are no coins or jewellery or buttons or zippers or even footwear, my guess would be naked.'

Muse just stared at the brown skull. 'Cause of death?'

'Too early to tell. But there are some things we know. The bones are in pretty bad shape, and they've been here a while.'

'How long?'

'It's hard to say. My best estimate would be at least fifteen years. In short, it is consistent with the time frame of the murders that took place in these woods twenty years ago.'

Muse swallowed. 'Can you tell gender? Do the bones belong to someone male or female?'

'Let me show you.'

Tara O'Neill got down on her haunches. So did Muse. O'Neill pointed her flashlight towards the skull.

'To tell the difference between the male and female skeleton, one of the things we go by is the size and density of the bones. First off, the bones appear to be on the lighter side. Second, check out the spot below where the eyebrows would have been.'

'OK.'

'That's the supraorbital ridge. It's more pronounced in males. Now, this skull has been worn down, but you can see the ridge is not pronounced. But the real key is in the pelvic cavity.' She shifted the flashlight. 'Do you see it?'

'Yeah, I see it, I guess. So?'

'It's pretty wide.' Tara O'Neill snapped off the flashlight. 'Which means,' she said, getting back to her feet, 'that your victim is Caucasian, about five foot seven—the same height as Camille Copeland, by the way—and female.'

DILLON SAID, 'You're not going to believe this.'

York looked up. 'What?'

'I got a computer hit on that Volkswagen. There are only fourteen in the tristate area that fit the bill. But here's the kicker. One is registered to a guy named Ira Silverstein. That name ring a bell?'

'Isn't he the guy who owned that camp?'

'That's it.'

'Are you telling me that Copeland might have been right all along?'

'I got Silverstein's address,' Dillon said. 'Some rehab place.'

'So what are we waiting for?' York said. 'Let's haul ass.'

CHAPTER 11

When Lucy got into the car, I pressed the button for the CD player. Bruce Springsteen's 'Back In Your Arms' came on. She smiled. 'That song always makes me cry.'

'All songs make you cry,' I said.

'God, you know me so well.'

I smiled.

'You seem calm for a man who just learned that his dead sister might be alive.'

'I put things in different boxes. It's how I get through the craziness. I just put it somewhere else for a while. Partitioning.'

'We psychological types have another term for it,' Lucy said. 'We call it "Big-Time Denial".'

'Call it what you will. There's a flow here now, Luce. We're going to find Camille. She's going to be OK.'

We drove some more.

'What could your father possibly remember now?' I asked.

'I don't know. But we know that Gil Perez visited him. My guess is, that visit stirred something in Ira's head. I don't know what. It might be nothing. He's not well. It might be something he imagined or even made up.'

We parked in a spot near Ira's Volkswagen Beetle. Funny seeing that old car. It should have brought me back. He used to drive it around the camp all the time. But right now the old Volkswagen did nothing for me.

My partitioning was breaking down.

Because I had hope.

I had hope that I would find my sister. I had hope that I was truly connecting with a woman for the first time since Jane died.

I tried to warn myself. I tried to remember that hope was the cruellest of all mistresses, that it could crush your soul as if it were a Styrofoam cup. But right now I didn't want to go there. I wanted the hope. I wanted to hold on to it and just let it make me feel light for a little while.

I looked at Lucy. She smiled and I felt it rip open my chest. It had been so long since I felt like this, felt that heady rush.

'You better go in,' she said.

'You're going to stay here?'

'Ira made it clear. You, alone. I'll probably start up his car, make sure the battery is still charged.'

I got out and floated up the path. The setting for the house was peaceful and green. The mansion was Georgian brick, I guessed, almost perfectly rectangular with white columns in the front.

There was a woman at the desk. I gave her my name. She asked me to sign in. I did. She placed a call and I waited.

A redheaded woman dressed in civilian clothes came down to see me.

'I'm Rebecca,' she said. 'I'll bring you to Mr Silverstein.'

'Thank you.'

I expected her to lead me down the corridor, but we walked through the back and straight outside. The gardens were well tended. A thick row of hedges surrounded the premises like guard dogs.

I spotted Ira right away. He had changed and yet he hadn't changed at all. You know people like that. They get older, they grey, they widen, they slump, and yet they are exactly the same. That was how it was with Ira.

'Ira?'

He wore a poncho I'd last seen in a Woodstock documentary. He had sandals on his feet. Ira stood slowly and put his arms out towards me. I stepped into his embrace. He held me tight, with all his strength.

He let go of me and said to Rebecca, 'Leave us alone.'

Rebecca turned away and he led me to a bench. We sat.

'You look the same, Cope,' he said.

He'd remembered my nickname. 'So do you.'

'So what do you do now?'

'I'm the county prosecutor.'

He frowned. 'Really? That's kind of establishment.'

Still Ira.

'I'm not prosecuting antiwar protestors,' I assured him. 'I go after murderers and rapists. People like that.'

He squinted. 'Is that why you're here?'

I didn't know what to make of that so I went with the flow. 'In a way, I guess. I'm trying to learn what happened that night in the woods.'

Ira's eyes closed. 'You broke Lucy's heart, you know.'

'I wrote her. I tried to call. She wouldn't call me back.'

'Still. She was in pain.'

'I never meant for that to happen.'

'So why are you here now?'

'I'm here,' I said slowly, 'because you asked to see me.'

'Not *here* here. Here, as in back in our lives. Why now?'

'I want to find out what happened to my sister.'

'She was murdered. Like the others.'

'No, she wasn't. Gil Perez didn't die that night either. He came back. He visited you, didn't he?'

Ira's eyes took on that thousand-yard stare. He stood up and started to walk. I caught up with him.

'Was he here, Ira?'

'He didn't tell me who he was. Not at first. He said his name was Manolo something. But I knew who he was. He didn't really look the same but there was something in his mannerisms, you know?'

He kept walking. I noticed that he limped. His face pinched up in pain.

'Are you OK?' I asked him.

'I need to walk. In the woods. Come.'

The garden wasn't fenced in. Ira slipped past a break in the hedges. I followed. There was a wooded hill in front of us. Ira started up the path.

'Are you allowed to leave?'

'Of course. I'm here on a voluntary basis. I can come and go as I please.'

'So what did Gil say to you?' I asked.

'He wanted to know what happened that night.'

'He didn't know?'

'He knew some. He wanted to know more.'

'I don't understand.'

'You don't have to.'

'Yes, Ira, I do. Did he mention my sister?'

He stopped for a second. His smile was sad. 'Camille. Poor Camille.'

'Yes. Camille. Did he say anything about her?'

Ira started to climb again. 'So much blood that night.'

'Please, Ira, I need you to focus. Did Gil say anything about Camille?'

'No. They're dead, Cope. The killer is in jail. You should let the dead rest.'

'Gil wasn't dead.'

'Until that day, the day he visited me, he was. Do you understand?'

'No.'

'It's over. The dead are gone. The living are safe.'

I reached out and grabbed his arm. 'Ira, what did Gil Perez say to you?'

We stopped. Ira looked down the hill. I followed his gaze. I could only make out the roof of the house now. We were in the thick of the woods.

'You won't leave it alone, will you?' Ira said.

'No. I won't leave it alone.'

Ira nodded. He looked very sad. Then he reached underneath his poncho, pulled out a gun, and without saying another word, fired at me.

'WHAT WE HAVE HERE is a problem.' Sheriff Lowell wiped his nose with a handkerchief that looked large enough to be a clown's prop. His station building was new, more modern than Muse had expected, the design sleek and clean with computer monitors and cubicles. Lots of whites and greys.

'What's our problem?' Muse asked.

'We just found a body that's been in the woods, by early estimates, a pretty long time. We know three things: Caucasian, female, height of five-seven. That's all we know for now. I have already combed through the records. There were no missing or unaccounted girls within a fifty-mile radius who match that description.'

'We both know who it is,' Muse said.

'Not yet we don't. We don't have a definite ID. Doc O'Neill is working on it. We've ordered Camille Copeland's dental records. We should know for sure in a day or two. No rush. We have other cases.'

'No rush?'

'That's what I said.'

'Then I'm not following.'

'See, this is where I have to wonder, Investigator Muse—what are you first and foremost? Are you a law enforcement officer or a political crony?'

'What the hell does that mean?'

'If this was your case and I came waltzing in and you knew that I was going to run right home and tell my boss—someone who was, at the very least, involved—what would you do?'

Muse sat back. 'Fair enough,' she said. 'So how can I comfort you?'

'You can let me take my time identifying the body. Copeland's waited twenty years. What's another day or two? Something else I want too,' Lowell went on. 'I need you to tell me why that Barrett guy was out there with his little toy looking for long-dead bodies.'

'I told you. They wanted to test this machine in the field.'

'You work in Newark, New Jersey. Are you telling me there are no possible burial sites in that area you could have sent them to?'

He was right, of course. Time to come clean.

'A man was found murdered in New York City,' Muse said. 'My boss thinks it was Gil Perez.'

Lowell dropped the poker face. 'Come again?'

She was about to explain when Tara O'Neill rushed in. Lowell looked annoyed by the interruption but kept his voice neutral. 'What's up, Tara?'

'I found something on the body,' she said. 'Something important, I think.'

AFTER COPE LEFT the car, Lucy sat alone for a good five minutes with the trace of a smile on her lips. The way he looked at her . . . it was as though her heart had not only started beating again but had taken flight.

It was wonderful. It was scary.

She checked through his CD collection, found one by Ben Folds, put on the song 'Brick'. She had never been sure what the song was about—a drug overdose, an abortion, a mental collapse—but in the end, the woman is a brick and she's drowning him.

Sad music was better than drinking, she guessed. But not much.

She thought about her life, about the mistakes she'd made. Maybe she should have tried to work through what happened that night right away. Instead you bury it. You're scared of confrontation so you find other ways to hide.

As she turned off the engine, she saw a green car, a Ford with New York licence plates, pull up right to the front of the building. Two men got out—one tall, one built like a square—and strolled inside. Lucy didn't know what to make of it. It was probably nothing.

The keys to Ira's Beetle were in her bag. She rummaged through the bag and found them. Then she got out of the car and started towards the old Volkswagen. The lock was rusted and she had to twist hard but it popped up.

She slid into the driver's seat and immediately the smell hit her.

Lucy turned and looked in the back seat.

There was blood on the floor.

And then, in the distance, she heard a crack of gunfire.

THE SKELETAL REMAINS were laid out on a silver table with tiny holes in it. The holes made it easier to clean by simply spraying it with a hose. Lowell stood on one side of the table, Muse on the other with Tara O'Neill.

'So what's up?' Lowell asked.

'First off, we're missing some small bones. I'll go out later and take another look. That's normal in a case like this. I was about to run some X-rays, check the ossification centres, especially up at the clavicle.'

'What will that tell us?'

'It gives us an idea of age. The last place of ossification is up there, pretty much where the clavicle meets the sternum. The process stops around the age of twenty-one. But that's not important right now.'

'So what's the big thing you found?'

'This.' O'Neill pointed to the pelvis.

Muse said, 'You showed me that before. That's the proof that the skeleton belonged to a female.'

'Well, yes. There is no doubt in my mind that the remains are female.'

'So what are you showing us?'

'The pubic bone. You see here? This notching? That's formed on the cartilaginous surface where the bones once met and then separated.'

O'Neill looked up at them. Her face was glowing.

'The notches are formed when the cartilage is strained. When the pubic bones separate.'

Muse looked at Lowell. Lowell shrugged.

'And that means?' Muse tried.

'That means that at some point in her life your victim gave birth.'

THINGS DO NOT slow down when you have a gun pointed at you.

To the contrary, they speed up. When Ira pointed the gun at me, I expected to have time to react. I started to raise my hands. My mouth began to open to try to talk my way through this, to tell him I would do what he wanted. But I didn't have time for any of that. I didn't have time to ask him why.

Because Ira was already pulling the trigger.

Maybe it was something in his stance or the way he pulled out the gun or whatever made me realise instinctively that there would indeed be no talking to him, that he was going to fire and that I was going to die. Something made me jump right away.

But the bullet still hit me.

He had aimed for the centre of my chest. The bullet hit my side, ripping across my waist like a hot lance. I fell hard on my side and tried to roll behind a tree. Ira fired again. He missed this time. I kept rolling.

I realised now that this had been Ira's plan all along. This was why he wanted to see me alone. This was why he had taken me into the woods. He wanted to shoot me.

I looked behind me. He was only six, eight feet away. He had a gun. I was already hit, could feel the blood leaking out of me. I was going to die.

We were stumbling down the hill, me still rolling, Ira trying to gain enough balance to take another shot. I knew I had only a few seconds.

My only chance was to reverse direction. I grabbed the ground and made myself break. Ira tried to slow. I grabbed a tree with both hands and whipped my legs towards him. It was a pathetic move, I thought, a bad gymnast on a pommel horse. But my feet hit against the side of Ira's right ankle. Not all that hard. But hard enough to knock him off balance.

Ira let out a shout and tumbled to the ground.

The gun, I thought. Get the gun.

I scrambled towards him. I was younger. I was in much better condition. There was still power in his arms and his legs. But the years and the drug abuse had slowed the reflexes down. I grabbed his right arm with both my hands, rolled my body on it then bent it back.

The hand was empty.

I had been so preoccupied with the right hand that I never saw the left coming. He swung in a long arc. The gun must have dropped when he fell. He had it now in his left hand, gripping it like a rock. He crashed the butt against my forehead.

It was like a lightning bolt had seared through my skull. My body convulsed. I let go of him and looked up. He had the gun pointed at me.

'Freeze. Police!'

I recognised the voice. It was York.

The air stopped, crackled. I moved my gaze from the gun to Ira's eyes. And I saw it. He was going to shoot and kill me. The police were here. It was over for him. He had to know that. But he was going to kill me anyway.

'Dad! No!'

It was Lucy. He heard her voice and something in those eyes changed.

'Drop the gun now! Do it! Now!' shouted York.

Ira kept his eyes on me. 'Your sister is dead,' he said.

Then he turned the gun away from me, put it in his own mouth and pulled the trigger.

CHAPTER 12

'Mr Copeland?'

I blinked my eyes open. I was in a bed. A hospital room.

'My name is Dr McFadden.'

I let my gaze travel the room. I saw York behind him.

'You were shot in the side. We stitched you up. You're going to be fine, but there will be soreness—'

'Doc?'

McFadden hadn't been expecting an interruption. He frowned. 'Yes?'

'Can we talk about this later? I really need to speak to that officer.'

York hid a smile. I expected an argument. Doctors are even more arrogant than attorneys. But he didn't give me one. He shrugged and said, 'Sure. Have the nurse page me when you're done.'

He left without another word. York moved closer to the bed.

'How did you know about Ira?' I asked.

'The lab guys matched carpet fibres found on the body of, uh . . .' York's voice drifted off. 'We can call him Gil Perez, if you want.'

'That would be good.'

'Right, anyway, we knew that these carpet fibres came from an old car. We saw a yellow Volkswagen on a security camera near where the body was dumped, we matched it to Silverstein. So we hurried over.'

'Where's Lucy?'

'Dillon's asking her some questions.'

'I don't get it. Ira killed Gil Perez?'

'Yep. First off, we found blood in the back seat of the Volkswagen. My guess is, it'll match Perez. Two, the staff at that halfway house confirmed that Perez—signing in as Manolo Santiago—visited Silverstein the day before the murder. The staff also confirmed that they saw Silverstein leave in the Volkswagen the next morning. First time he'd been out in six months.'

'I don't get it. Why would Ira kill him?'

'The same reason he wanted to kill you, I guess. You were both looking into what happened at that camp twenty years ago. He didn't want that.'

'So he killed Margot Green and Doug Billingham?'

York waited a second, expecting me to add my sister to the list. I didn't.

'Could be.'

'And what about Wayne Steubens?'

'They probably worked together somehow, I don't know. What I do know is, Ira Silverstein killed *my* guy. Oh, another thing: the gun Ira shot you with? It's the same calibre as the one used to shoot Gil Perez. We're running a ballistic test now, but you know it'll be a match. Ira Silverstein is dead, though, and it is very difficult to try a dead man. As for what he did or didn't do twenty years ago'—York shrugged—'hey, I'm curious too. But that's someone else's mystery to solve.'

'You'll help, if we need it?'

'Sure. Love to. And when you do figure it all out, why don't you come into the city and I'll take you for a steak dinner?'

'Deal.'

We shook hands.

'I should thank you for saving my life,' I said.

'Yeah, you should. Except I don't think I did.'

I remembered the look on Ira's face, his determination to kill me. Lucy's voice had been what saved me more than York's gun.

York left then. My thoughts turned to Lucy. I thought about what she must be going through, watching her beloved father blow his head off, wondering about the whys and hows of it all. I wanted to comfort her.

There was a knock on my door. 'Come in.'

It was Muse. I smiled at her. I expected her to smile back. She didn't.

'Don't look so glum,' I said. 'I'm fine.'

Muse moved closer to the bed. She grabbed a chair, pulled it next to the bed. 'We need to talk.'

I HAD SEEN LOREN MUSE make this face before.

It was her I'm-gonna-nail-da-bastard face. It was her try-to-lie-and-I'll-spot-it face. I had seen her direct this look at murderers and rapists and carjackers. Now she was aiming it at me.

'What's the matter, Muse?'

'I talked to Sheriff Lowell today.'

I knew Muse was thorough. It would be natural for her to have contacted the lead from those murders.

'Let me guess,' I said. 'He thinks I lied about that night.'

Muse did not say yes or no. 'It is odd, don't you think? You not staying on guard duty the night of the murder.'

'You know why. You read the journal.'

'Yes, I did. You sneaked off with your girlfriend. And then you didn't want to get her in trouble.'

'Right.'

'But the journal also said that you were covered with blood. Is that true too?'

I looked at her. 'What the hell is going on?'

'I'm pretending that you aren't my boss.'

I tried to sit up. The stitches in my side hurt like hell.

'Did Lowell say I was a suspect?'

'He doesn't have to. And you don't have to be a suspect for me to ask these questions. Put yourself in my position. I need to handle this case with no agenda or bias, Cope. If you were me, wouldn't you ask these questions?'

I thought about it. 'I get it, OK, fine. Ask me whatever you want.'

'Was your sister ever pregnant?'

The question hit me like a surprise left hook. Probably her intent.

'Are you serious?'

'Just answer the question.'

'No, my sister was never pregnant.'

'Are you sure?'

'I think I'd know. Why are you asking?'

She searched my face, her eyes crawling on me like slimy worms.

'Cut that out,' I said.

'You have to recuse yourself, Cope. You know that.'

'I don't have to do anything.'

'Yeah, you do. Lowell is still running the show. But I've got his OK to talk to you.'

'Fine, play it that way. Look, I promised Glenda Perez that I would try to keep her family out of it. But tell Lowell about it. The key thing is, Glenda Perez said my sister walked out of those woods alive.'

'And,' Muse said, 'Ira Silverstein said she was dead.'

I looked at her hard. 'What the hell is going on, Muse?'

She held my gaze. I didn't like what I saw.

'Do you remember my sending Andrew Barrett up to the campsite?'

'Of course,' I said.

Muse looked at me. That was all she did. I saw her eyes go wet. Then she nodded at me. It was the saddest nod I have ever seen.

I felt my world drop with a splat.

The hope I had been gently cradling in my heart was crushed.

'They discovered old remains not far from where the other two bodies were found,' Muse said.

I shook my head. Not now. Not after all this.

'Female, five foot seven, probably been in the ground between fifteen and thirty years.'

I shook my head some more, trying to clear my thoughts. Muse stopped, waiting for me to get my bearings. Then I remembered something.

'Wait, you asked me if Camille was pregnant. Are you saying this body. . . that they can tell that she was pregnant?'

'Not just pregnant,' Muse said. 'She gave birth.'

I tried to take it in. I couldn't. It was one thing to hear that she'd been pregnant. That could have happened. She could have had an abortion or something, I don't know. But that she delivered a baby, and that now she was dead . . .

'Find out what happened, Muse.'

'I will.'

'And if there is a baby out there . . .'

'We'll find that too.'

DR McFADDEN RETURNED and told me that I was lucky, that the bullet went through my side without hitting any internal organs.

'I'm more worried about the blow to your head,' he said.

'But I can go home?'

'Let's let you sleep a while, OK? See how you feel when you wake up. I think you should stay overnight.'

I was going to argue but there was nothing to be gained by going home. I felt sore and sick and achy. I probably looked like hell and would scare Cara with my appearance.

I reached for the phone and dialled home to check up on my daughter. I was surprised when Greta answered with a friendly 'Hello'.

'Hi,' I said.

The friendly fled. 'I hear you're going to be fine.'

'That's what they tell me.'

'I'm here with Cara now,' Greta said, all business. 'I can have her stay at my place tonight, if you'd like.'

'That would be great, thanks.'

There was a brief lull.

'Paul?'

She usually called me Cope. I didn't like that. 'Yes?'

'Cara's welfare is very important to me. She is still my niece. She is still the daughter of my sister.'

'I understand that.'

'You, on the other hand, mean nothing to me.'

She hung up the phone.

I sat back and tried to wrap my brain around the fact that they had found a body in the woods.

Muse had faxed the preliminary autopsy to the hospital. It was hard to believe that it wasn't my sister. Muse had done a more thorough examination of missing women from the area. The search had been fruitless—the only preliminary match for the computer records was my sister.

So far the coroner had come up with no cause of death. That wasn't unusual in a skeleton in this shape. If he had sliced her throat or buried her alive, they probably would never know.

I skipped down to the key item. The pitting of the pubic bone. The victim had given birth. I again wondered about that. But if it wasn't my sister they'd dug up, what could I conclude exactly?

I was missing something. I was missing a lot.

I took out my cellphone. There was no service in the hospital but I looked up York's number on it. I used my room phone to make the call.

'Anything new?' I asked him.

'Do you know what time it is?'

I checked the clock. 'It's a few minutes after ten. Anything new?'

He sighed. 'Ballistics confirmed that the gun Silverstein shot you with is the same one he used to kill Gil Perez. And the blood type in the back of the Volkswagen matches Perez's. In sports terms, I'd call that game, set, match.'

'What did Lucy say?'

'Dillon said she wasn't much of a help. She was in shock. Said her father was not well, that he probably imagined some kind of threat.'

'Dillon buy that?'

'Sure, why not? Either way our case is closed.'

'OK, thanks.'

I hung up and dialled Lucy's number. It went into her voicemail. I left a message. Then I called Muse's mobile.

'Where are you?' I asked.

'Heading home, why?'

'I thought maybe you'd be going to Reston U to question Lucy.'

'I already went.'

'And?'

'She didn't open the door. But I could see lights on. She's in there.'

I didn't like it. Her father died and she was alone in her apartment. 'How far are you from the hospital?'

'Fifteen minutes.'

'How about picking me up?'

'Are you, my boss, asking me to drive you to your girlfriend's house?'

'No. I, the county prosecutor, am asking you to drive me to the home of a major person of interest in a recent homicide.'

'Either way,' Muse said, 'I'm so very there.'

No ONE STOPPED ME from leaving the hospital.

I didn't feel well, but I had felt worse. I was worried about Lucy and I realised with growing certainty that it was more than normal worry.

I missed her. I liked being with her. I liked the way it felt. I liked being with her the way you like being with someone you're falling in love with. There was no need to explain further.

Muse drove. Her car was small and cramped. I was not much of a car guy and I had no idea what kind of car it was, but I wished she'd drive faster.

'Will you be OK for court tomorrow?' she asked.

'I think so, yeah.'

'Judge Pierce wanted to meet with counsel in his chambers at nine a.m. sharp. You want me to pick you up?'

'I do.'

'Cool.' She drove some more. 'I'm sorry about your sister.'

I said nothing. I was still having a hard time reacting to that. Maybe I needed to hear that the ID was confirmed. Or maybe I had already done twenty years of mourning and didn't have that much left. Or maybe, most likely, I was putting my emotions on the back burner.

The faculty housing at Reston University was depressing. The buildings were dated brick and shoved together. The lighting was bad, but I think that might have been a good thing.

'You mind staying in the car?' I said.

'I have to run a quick errand,' Muse said. 'I'll be right back.'

I headed up the walk. The lights were out, but I could hear music. I recognised the song. 'Somebody' by Bonnie McKee. Depressing as hell— the 'somebody' being this perfect love she knows is out there but will never find—but that was Lucy. She adored the heartbreakers.

I knocked on the door. There was no answer.

'Luce!'

I knocked some more. Whatever the doctor had given me was wearing off. I could feel the stitches in my side.

'Luce! Come on, I know you're in there.'

I heard a car behind me. It was Muse. She pulled to a stop and got out.

'Here,' she said. 'Master key. I got it from campus security.' She tossed it to me and headed back to the car.

I put the key in the lock, knocked again, turned it and stepped inside.

'Don't turn on the light.' It was Lucy. 'Leave me alone, Cope, OK?'

'You should do one of those K-tel collections,' I said. 'You know, like *Time Life* presents *The Most Depressing Songs of All Time*.'

I heard her snort a laugh. My eyes were adjusting. I could see her sitting on the couch now. I moved closer.

'Don't,' she said.

But I kept walking. I sat next to her. There was a bottle of vodka in her hand. It was half empty. I looked around her apartment. There was nothing personal, nothing new, nothing bright or happy.

'Ira,' she said.

'I'm so sorry.'

'The cops said he killed Gil.'

'What do you think?'

'I saw blood in his car. He shot you. So yeah, I think he killed Gil.' She took another long swig.

'Why don't you give me that?' I said.

'This is what I am, Cope. You can't rescue me.'

I had a few replies to that but every one reeked of cliché. I let it go.

'I love you,' she said. 'I mean, I never stopped. I've been with other men. I've had relationships. But you've always been there. It's stupid and dumb and we were just kids, but that's the way it is.'

'I get it,' I said.

'They think maybe Ira was the one who killed Margot and Doug.'

'You don't?'

'He just wanted it to go away. You know? It hurt so much, caused so much destruction. And then, when he saw Gil, it must have been like a ghost was coming back to haunt him.'

'I'm sorry,' I said again.

'Go home, Cope.'

'I'd rather stay. I don't like leaving you like this.'

'This is what I do. I drink in the dark and play these damn songs. I don't want you here. It will just make it worse.'

'But—'

'Please,' she said, and her voice was a plea. 'We can start again tomorrow.'

DR TARA O'NEILL was back in the woods by 6 a.m., at first daylight. She loved these woods—any woods, really. This—out in the woods like this—was where she was happiest.

She carried her tool case, but of all the fancy new gismos that the public had helped pay for, the one she found most useful was the simplest: a strainer. She took it out and started in the dirt.

The strainer's job was to find teeth and small bones.

It was painstaking work, not unlike an archaeological dig she had done after high school. She worked through this burial site with the same patience—work most people would find mind-deadeningly tedious.

An hour later, she found the small piece of bone.

She felt her pulse quicken. She had realised that it was a possibility after the ossification X-rays. But still. To find the missing piece . . . Tara O'Neill's face broke into a beatific smile and she shook her head in awe.

It was the hyoid bone.

Half of it anyway. O'Neill went back to her search. Five minutes later, she found the other half. She held up both pieces. Even after all those years, the bone fragments fitted together like a jigsaw. For a moment she stared at her own handiwork, then she took out her cellphone and pressed Sheriff Lowell's number. He picked up on the second ring.

'I found something at the burial site,' Tara O'Neill said.

'And?'

'And it changes everything we thought about this case.'

ONE OF THOSE RANDOM hospital beeping noises woke me. I stirred slowly, blinked open my eyes and saw Mrs Perez sitting with me.

She had pulled the chair right next to my bed. The handbag was in her lap. Her back was straight. I looked into her eyes. She'd been crying.

'I heard about Mr Silverstein,' she said.

I waited.

'They say that he murdered my Gil. Do you think that's true?'

My Gil. So the pretence was down. No more hiding behind a lie or a daughter. No more hypothetical.

'Yes.'

She nodded. 'Sometimes I think Gil really did die in those woods. That was how it was supposed to be. Part of him never escaped.'

'Tell me what happened,' I said.

'You were at the camp that summer. You knew my Gil.'

'Yes.'

'And you knew this girl. This Margot Green.'

I said that I did.

'Gil fell for her hard. He was this poor boy. We lived in a burnt-out section of Irvington. Mr Silverstein had a programme where children of workers got to attend. I worked in the laundry room. You know this.'

I did.

'I liked your mother. She was so smart. We talked a lot. About books, about life, about our disappointments. Natasha was what we call an old soul. She was so beautiful but it was fragile. Do you understand?'

'I think so, yes.'

'Anyway, Gil fell very hard for Margot Green. She was practically a magazine model in his eyes. That's how it is with men. They are so driven by lust. But she broke his heart. That too is common. He should have just suffered for a few weeks and then moved on. He probably would have.'

She stopped.

'So what happened?' I asked.

'Wayne Steubens. He whispered in Gil's ear. He told him that he shouldn't let Margot get away with it. Margot had been strutting all over camp. He appealed to Gil's machismo. Margot, he said, was laughing at Gil. You need to pay that tease back, he whispered. And after a while—I don't know how long—Gil agreed.

'Wayne planned it all very carefully, Gil said. They were going to draw Margot out to the woods. It was going to be a prank. There were many kids who wanted to knock her down a peg. My son, of course. Doug Billingham too. Maybe your sister. She was there, but that might have been because Doug talked her into it. Your sister helped with the lure. She said that they were going to meet some cute boys. Gil put a mask on his head. He grabbed Margot. He tied her up. That was supposed to be the end of it. They'd leave her there for a few minutes. She'd either escape from the rope or they'd untie her. It was dumb, very immature, but these things happen.'

I knew that they did. Camp was full of 'pranks' back then. Tying up a total tease and leaving her in the woods for a little while . . . that wouldn't have surprised me at all.

'Margot played along. She let Gil tie her up. Then she started mocking my son. Made fun of him, said he didn't know how to handle a real woman.

Gil didn't do anything. What could he do? Then something went very wrong,' Mrs Perez said.

I waited. A tear escaped Mrs Perez's eye. She reached into her bag and pulled out a wad of tissues. She dabbed her eyes, fought them back.

'Wayne Steubens took out a razor blade.'

I think my eyes widened a little when she said that. I could almost see the scene. I could see the five of them out in the woods, picture their surprise.

'At first, Gil thought it was part of the act. To scare Margot. But then Wayne walked over to her and slashed her neck from ear to ear.'

I closed my eyes. I saw it again. I saw the blade going across that young skin, the blood spurting, the life force leaving her. I thought about it. While Margot Green was being slaughtered, I was only a few hundred yards away making love to my girlfriend.

'For a moment no one moved. They all just stood there. Wayne smiled at them and said, "Thanks for the help." Then he lifted the blade. Gil said they could see how much Wayne liked what he had done. He had a thirst now. He started towards them. And they ran. They ran in different directions. Wayne chased them. Gil ran for miles and miles. I don't know what happened exactly. But we can guess. Wayne caught up to Doug. He killed him. But Gil and your sister got away.'

Mrs Perez looked around the room as if she'd just noticed where she was. I was afraid I was going to lose her.

'It's OK,' I said.

She nodded. 'Gil was terrified, of course. So was your sister. You have to see it from their viewpoint. They were young. They had watched Margot Green get slaughtered. They were nearly killed. But maybe most of all, Wayne's words haunted them. "Thanks for the help." You understand?'

'He had made them a part of it.'

'Yes.'

'So what did they do?'

'They hid. Your mother and I were worried sick. My husband was home in Irvington. Your father was out with the search parties. Gil knew the number of the payphone in the back of the camp kitchen. He dialled it three different times but he hung up when someone else answered. Then, more than a day after they went missing, I picked it up.'

'Gil told you what happened?'

'Yes.'

'You told my mother?'

She nodded. I was starting to see it.

'Did you approach Wayne Steubens?' I asked.

'We didn't have to. He'd already approached your mother. Made it clear. He had set up an alibi for that night. And you see, we knew already. Mothers are like that.'

'You knew what?'

'Gil's brother, my Eduardo, was serving time. Your family was poor, my family was poor. There would be fingerprints on the rope. The police would wonder why your sister had led Margot Green into the woods. Wayne had got rid of the evidence against him. He was rich and could hire the best attorneys. You're a prosecutor, Mr Copeland. You tell me. If Gil and Camille came forward, who would have believed them?'

I closed my eyes. 'So you told them to stay hidden.'

'Yes.'

'Who planted their clothes with the blood?'

'I did that. I met Gil. He was still in the woods.'

'Did you see my sister?'

'No. He gave me the clothes. He cut himself, pressed his shirt against the wound. I told him to stay hidden until we came up with a plan. Your mother and I tried to figure a way to turn it around, to get the police to learn the truth. But nothing came to us. Days passed.'

I saw something else. 'You had a handicapped son. And you needed money. To take care of him. And maybe to pay for Glenda to go to a decent school.' My eyes found hers. 'When did you realise that you could cash in with that lawsuit?'

'That came later—when Billingham's father started screaming about how Mr Silverstein didn't protect his son. So yes, I saw an opportunity. So did your mother.'

My head was spinning. 'Are you telling me . . .' I stopped. 'Are you telling me that my parents knew that my sister was alive?'

'Not your parents,' she said.

And I felt the cold gust hit my heart.

'She didn't tell my father, did she?'

'No.'

'Why not?'

'Because she hated him.'

I just sat there. I thought about the fights, the bitterness, the unhappiness. Did she hate my father so much that she'd let him think his own daughter was dead?

It started to hit me, like heavy raindrops. Big thuds. 'She bided her time, didn't she? She hid my sister until the settlement money came through. And as soon as it did . . . she ran. She took enough money and ran and met up with my sister.'

'That was . . . that was her plan, yes.'

I blurted out the next question. 'Why didn't she take me?'

Mrs Perez just looked at me. I thought about it. Why? And then I realised something. 'If she took me, my father would never stop looking. He'd get Uncle Sosh and all his old KGB cronies on it. He might let my mother go— he had probably fallen out of love with her too. But not me . . .'

I remembered what Uncle Sosh said, about her returning to Russia. Were they both there? Did that make sense? I didn't know what to think.

'Gil changed his name,' she went on. 'He travelled around. His life was less than spectacular. And when those private detectives came round to our house and asked questions, he got wind of it. He saw it as a way of cashing in again. You see, it was odd. He blamed you too. Because you didn't stay on guard duty that night.'

I said nothing.

'He thought that maybe this was a good time for payback.'

It added up. It fitted in perfectly with what Raya Singh had told me.

She stood. 'That's all I know.'

'Mrs Perez? Did you ever see Camille yourself?'

'No,' she said. 'I never saw your sister.'

FIVE MINUTES AFTER Mrs Perez left my room, Muse entered. I was being released that morning.

We checked out of the hospital without fuss. I had an extra suit in my office. I changed into it. And then I headed to Judge Pierce's chamber. Flair Hickory and Mort Pubin were already there.

'Gentlemen,' the judge said. 'I'm hoping we can find a way of settling this case.'

I was in no mood. 'That's what this is about?'

'It is.'

I looked at the judge. He looked at me. I shook my head. It made sense.

If they had tried to pressure me by digging up dirt, what would have stopped them from doing the same with the judge?

'The People aren't interested in a deal,' I said.

I stood.

'Sit down, Mr Copeland,' Judge Pierce said. 'There may be problems with your DVD evidence. I may have to exclude it.'

I started for the door.

'Mr Copeland!'

'I'm not staying,' I said. 'It's on me, Judge. You did your part. Blame me.'

I reached for the doorknob.

Flair Hickory frowned. 'What are you talking about?'

'Sit down, Mr Copeland, or be in contempt.'

'Because I don't want to settle?'

I turned and looked at Arnold Pierce. There was a quiver in his lower lip.

I nodded to Pierce that I understood. But I wasn't about to give in. I turned the knob and left. I started down the hallway. My wounded side ached. My head throbbed. I wanted to sit down and cry. I wanted to sit down and ponder what I had just learned about my mother and my sister.

'I didn't think it would work.'

I turned. It was EJ Jenrette. He had a manila folder in his hand.

'I'm just trying to save my son,' he said.

'Your son raped a girl.'

'Everyone makes mistakes. You know he'd never do it again. He screwed up. He thought he was invincible. He knows better now.'

'We're not getting into this again,' I said.

'I never went after your child,' Jenrette said. 'I went after you. I went after your past. I even went after your brother-in-law. But I never went near your child. That was my own personal line.'

'You're a prince,' I said. 'So what do you have on Judge Pierce?'

'It's not important.'

He was right. I didn't need to know.

EJ Jenrette held up the envelope. 'A man does what he can to protect his children. Maybe that was your father's excuse.'

'My father's?'

'This is a summary of his KGB file, translated into English. If you want to see how far a father might go to make a better life for his children, you should read this. Maybe you'll understand me a little better.'

'I don't want to understand you.'

EJ Jenrette just held the file out. Eventually I took it. He walked away without another word.

I headed back to my office, sat at my desk and started reading. And yet again, just when I thought I couldn't hurt any more, the words tore open my chest and shredded me apart.

Muse came in without knocking.

'The skeleton they found at that camp,' she said. 'It's not your sister.'

I couldn't speak.

'See, this Dr O'Neill found something called a hyoid bone. That's in the throat. It was snapped in half. That means the victim was probably manually strangled. But see, the hyoid bone isn't this brittle in young people— it's more like a cartilage, I guess. In short, it is much more likely that the skeleton belonged to a woman in her forties, maybe even her fifties, than someone Camille's age.'

I said nothing. I just stared at the page in front of me.

'Cope? Don't you get it? It's not your sister.'

I closed my eyes. My heart felt so damn heavy.

'I know,' I said. 'It's not my sister in the woods,' I said. 'It's my mother.'

SOSH WASN'T SURPRISED to see me.

'You knew, didn't you?'

He was on the phone. He put his hand over the mouthpiece.

'Sit down, Pavel.'

He finished his call and put the phone back in the cradle. Then he saw the manila envelope in my hand. 'What's that?'

'It's a summary of my father's KGB file.'

His shoulders slumped. 'You can't believe everything in those.'

'He turned in my Noni and Popi, didn't he? He was the source that betrayed them. My own father.'

Sosh just looked at me.

'Answer me, dammit. Yes or no?'

'Your father had been accused of botching a delivery. I don't know if he did or not. It makes no difference. The government wanted him. They would have destroyed your entire family.'

'So he sold out my grandparents to save his own skin?'

'The government would have got them anyway. But yes, OK, Vladimir chose to save his own children over his elderly in-laws. He figured they'd hold them for a few weeks at the most. And in exchange, your family would get a second chance. Don't you see?'

'No, I don't. People don't sell out their own family members. You should know. You survived that blockade. The people of Leningrad wouldn't surrender. No matter what the Nazis did, you took it and held your head high.'

'And you think that was smart?' he snapped. His hands formed two fists. 'My God, you are so naive. My brother and sister starved to death. Do you understand that? If we had surrendered, Gavrel and Aline would still be alive. They would have had lives—children, grandchildren. Instead . . .' He turned away.

'When did my mother find out about what he'd done?' I asked.

'I think part of your mother had always wondered. I think that was why she had such contempt for him. But the night your sister vanished, he crumbled. He confessed the truth.'

It made sense. Horrible sense. Once my mother had learned what my father had done, she could never forgive him for betraying her beloved parents. She would think nothing of making him suffer, of letting him think that his own daughter was dead.

'So,' I said, 'my mother hid my sister. She waited until she had enough money from the settlement. Then she planned on disappearing with her.'

'Yes.'

'I spent my whole life thinking my mother didn't care enough about me. That she just ran off and never looked back. How could you let me believe that, Sosh?'

'You think the truth is better?'

I thought of how I spied on my father in those woods. He dug and dug for his daughter. And then one day he stopped. I thought that he stopped because my mother ran off. I remembered how he told me not to follow him: *Not today, Paul. Today I go alone* . . .

He dug his last hole that day. Not to find my sister. But to bury my mother.

'Dad found out she planned to run.'

'Yes.'

'How?'

'I told him.'

Sosh met my eye. I said nothing.

'I learned that your mother had transferred a hundred thousand dollars out of their joint account. It was common KGB protocol to keep an eye on one another. I asked your father about it.'

'And he confronted her.'

'Yes.'

'And my mother . . .' There was a choke in my voice. I blinked, tried again. 'My mother never planned on abandoning me,' I said. 'She was going to take me too.'

Sosh held my gaze and nodded.

'Did you know he killed her, Sosh?'

'Yes.'

'And you didn't do anything about it?'

'We were still working for the government,' Sosh said. 'If it came out that he was a murderer, our cover would have been blown and we could all be in danger.'

'So you let him get away with it.'

'Your father never meant to kill her. He snapped. Natasha was going to run away. She was going to take his children and disappear for ever.'

I remembered now my father's last words, on that deathbed: '*Paul, we still need to find her* . . .' Did he mean Camille's body? Or Camille herself?

'My father found out my sister was alive.'

'It's not that simple. You talk about brave, about being able to withstand hardships. Your mother wouldn't speak, no matter what your father did to her.

'Then how did he find out?'

'After he killed her, he searched through her papers, through phone records. He put it together—or at least he had his suspicions.'

'Did he search for Camille?' I asked.

'You spoke before about the siege of Leningrad,' he said. 'Do you know what it taught me? The dead are nothing. They are gone. You bury them and you move on. You went on this quest. You wouldn't leave the dead alone. And now where are you? Two more have been killed. You learned that your beloved father murdered your mother. Was it worth it, Pavel?'

'It depends,' I said, 'on what happened to my sister.'

My father's last words came to me: '*Did you know?*'

I'd thought he was accusing me, that he saw guilt on my face. But that wasn't it. Did I know about the real fate of my sister? Did I know what he'd done? Did I know that he murdered my mother and buried her in the woods?

'What happened to my sister, Sosh?'

'You have to understand. Your father was never sure. All he knew for certain was that she was going to run with the money and take you with her. So he asked me for help. He asked me to find Camille.'

I looked at him. 'Did you?'

'I looked into it, yes.' He took a step towards me. 'And when I was finished, I told your father that he got it wrong. That she had died that night in the woods.'

'What?' I was confused. 'Did she?'

'No, Pavel. She didn't die that night.'

I felt my heart start to expand in my chest.

'Your sister knew what your father had done. She couldn't come forward as there was still the matter of why she had disappeared in the first place. And of course, she feared your father. How could she return to the man who murdered her mother?'

'Where is she now?' I asked.

'We lost touch years ago. You know, Camille didn't want to hurt you. She thought about taking you away. But that was impractical. She knew how much you loved your father. And then later, when you became a public figure, she knew what her return, what this scandal, would do to you. Your career would be over.'

'It already is.'

'Yes. We know that now.'

We, he said. We. Hope again filled my chest.

'Where is Camille?' I asked.

'It took a while to find her after all these years,' he said. 'But I did. We talked. Once she knew your father had died, it changed everything.'

'Wait a second. You . . .' I stopped. 'You and Camille talked?'

It was my voice, I think.

'Yes, Pavel. When you came in, that was her on the phone.'

My body went cold.

'She's staying at a hotel two blocks away. I told her to come over.' He looked at the elevator. 'That's her now. On her way up.'

I slowly turned and watched the numbers climb above the elevator. I didn't believe it.

The elevator stopped.

And then, twenty years after vanishing into those woods, my sister, Camille, stepped back into my life.

EPILOGUE
One Month Later

L ucy does not want me to take this trip.

'You don't need to face him again, Cope. It's over.'

'I do. I need some final answers.'

Lucy closes her eyes. 'It's all so fragile, you know? I'm afraid you'll shift the ground again.'

I understand. But this needs to be done.

An hour later, I am looking out of the window of a plane. Over the past month, life has returned to quasi-normal. The Jenrette and Marantz case took some wild and weird twists towards its rather glorious ending. The families applied pressure on Judge Arnold Pierce and he broke. He threw out the porno DVD, claiming we didn't produce it in a timely enough fashion. But the jury saw through it—they often do—and came back with guilty verdicts. Flair and Mort are appealing, of course.

I want to prosecute Judge Pierce, but I'll never get him. I want to prosecute EJ Jenrette and MVD for blackmail. I doubt I'll get that either. But Chamique's lawsuit is going well. Rumour has it that they want her out of the way quickly. A seven-figure settlement is being bandied about.

My brother-in-law, Bob, is out on bail. I caved in on that one. I told the federal authorities that while my recollections were 'fuzzy', I do believe Bob told me that he needed a loan and that I approved it. I don't know if I'm doing the right thing (probably not) but I don't want Greta and her family destroyed. Feel free to call me a hypocrite—I am—but that line between right and wrong grows so blurry sometimes in the bright sunshine of the real world. And, of course, it grows blurry in the dark of those woods.

Here is the quick yet thorough update on Loren Muse: Muse remains Muse. And I'm thankful for that. Governor Dave Markie hasn't called for my resignation yet and, right now, I'm hanging in.

The plane lands. I get off. I check my BlackBerry. There is a short message from my sister, Camille: *Hey, bro—Cara and I are going to have lunch in the city and shop. Miss and love you, Camille.*

My sister, Camille. It is fantastic to have her back. I can't believe how quickly she had become a fully fledged and integral part of our lives. I still don't have her entire backstory. I know that she started with a new identity in Moscow, but didn't stay long. There were two years in Prague and another on the Costa Brava in Spain. She came back to the United States, moved around some more, got married and settled outside Atlanta, ended up divorced three years later.

She never had kids, but she is already the world's greatest aunt. She loves Cara, and the feeling is more than reciprocated. Camille is living with us. It is wonderful—better than I could have hoped.

Part of me, of course, wonders why it took so long for my sister to come home. She chose to keep silent about what happened in those woods. Her choice, right or wrong, left Wayne free to murder more people. You could argue that Wayne might still have got away with it, that he might have run off. Who knows? But Camille thought that she could bury those lies. Maybe we all did.

But none of us got out of those woods unscathed.

As for my romantic life, well, I am in love. Simple as that. I love Lucy with all my heart. We are not taking it slow—we plunged right in, as if trying to make up for lost time. We see a lot of each other, and when we're not together I feel lost and want to be with her again. But that's love, right?

Lucy is funny and goofy and warm and smart and beautiful and she overwhelms me in the best way. We seem to agree on everything.

Except, of course, my taking this trip.

I understand her fear. I know all too well how fragile this all is. But you can't live on thin ice either. So here I am again, in Red Onion State Prison, Virginia, waiting to learn a few last truths.

Wayne Steubens enters. We are in the same room as our last meeting.

'My, my,' he says to me. 'You've been a busy boy, Cope.'

'You killed them,' I say. 'After all is said and done, you did it.'

Wayne smiles.

'You planned it all along, didn't you?'

'Is anyone listening in to this?'

'No.'

'Then, sure, why not. I did, yes. I planned the killings.'

So there it is. He too has decided that the past needs to be faced.

'And you carried it out, just like Mrs Perez said. You slaughtered Margot. Gil, Camille and Doug ran. You caught up to Doug. Murdered him too.'

He raises his index finger. 'I made a miscalculation there. See, I jumped the gun with Margot. I meant her to be last because she was already tied up. But her neck was so open, so vulnerable . . . I couldn't resist.'

'There are a few things I couldn't figure out at first,' I say. 'The journal the private detectives sent to Lucy. I wondered who saw us in the woods, but Lucy got that one right. Only one person could have known: the killer. You, Wayne. And you were the one who gave MVD the information they used in the journal.'

He spreads his hands. 'Modesty prevents me from saying more.'

He is enjoying this.

'How did you get Ira to help?' I ask.

'Dear Uncle Ira. That addle-brained hippie. He didn't help much. I just needed him out of the way. You see, Ira did drugs and I had proof. If it came out, his camp would have been ruined.'

He smiles some more.

'So when Gil and I threatened to bring it all back,' I say, 'Ira got scared. You said he was addle-brained then—he was a lot worse now. Paranoia clouded his thinking. He panicked. He silenced Gil and tried to silence me.'

Another smile from Wayne.

But there is something different in the smile now.

'You're still missing something, Cope,' he says. 'One teensy-weensy thing.'

I am holding my breath. He just smiles.

'What?' I ask.

He leans forward. 'You're forgetting your part in this, Cope.'

'I know my part,' I say. 'I left my post. Is that what you wanted to hear, Wayne? That I feel partially responsible?'

'No.' He shakes his head. 'You're missing the point.'

'What point?'

He cups his hands around his mouth and his voice drops to a whisper.

'How did I *know* you wouldn't be at your post that night?'

LUCY AND I DRIVE OUT to the woods.

Lucy's father, her dear Ira, had owned all this land. He had come up here all those years ago and realised his lifelong dream: a camp, a commune, a natural habitat free from the sins of man, a place of peace and harmony.

Poor Ira.

Lucy carries flowers, but she should know better. We don't place flowers on tombstones in our tradition. We place stones. I also don't know who the flowers are for—my mother or her father. Probably both.

We take the old trail—yes, it is still there, though it's pretty overgrown—to where Barrett found my mother's bones. The remnants of yellow crime-scene tape blow in the breeze.

Lucy kneels down. I listen to the wind, wonder if I hear the cries. I don't. I don't hear anything but the hollow of my heart.

'Why did we go into the woods that night, Lucy?'

She doesn't look up at me.

'I never really thought about that. Everyone else wondered how I could have been so irresponsible. But to me, it was obvious. I was in love. I was sneaking away with my girlfriend. What could be more natural?'

She puts the flowers down carefully. She still won't look at me.

'Ira didn't help Wayne that night,' I say to the woman I love. 'You did.'

I hear the prosecutor in my voice. I want him to shut up. But he won't.

'How did Wayne know I wouldn't be at my post? Because it was your job to make sure that I wasn't.'

I can see her start to grow smaller, wither.

'That's why you could never face me,' I say. 'That's why you feel like you're still tumbling down a hill and can't stop. It's not that your family lost the camp or their money. It's that you helped Wayne Steubens.'

I wait. Lucy lowers her head into her hands. She sobs. I hear her cries, and my heart breaks in two. I take a step towards her. The hell with this, I think. Uncle Sosh is right. I don't need to bring it all back.

I just need her. So I take that step.

Lucy holds up a hand to stop me. She gathers herself a piece at a time.

'He said he'd have Ira arrested if I didn't help. I thought . . . I thought he was just going to scare Margot. You know. A stupid prank.'

Something catches in my throat. 'Wayne knew we got separated.'

She nods. 'He saw me.'

'You,' I say. 'Not us.'

She nods again.

'You found the body, didn't you? Margot's, I mean. That was the blood in the journal. Wayne wasn't talking about me. He was talking about you.'

'Yes.'

I think about it, about how scared she must have been, how she probably ran to her father, covered in blood. How Ira would have panicked too.

'Ira wouldn't kill Gil and me to protect himself,' I say. 'But he was a father. In the end, with all his peace, love and understanding, Ira was first and foremost a father. And so he'd kill to protect his little girl.'

She sobs again.

Everyone had kept quiet. Everyone had been afraid—my sister, my mother, Gil, his family, Lucy. They all bear some of the blame, and they all paid a stiff price. And what about me? I excuse myself by claiming youth. But I had a responsibility to watch the campers that night. I shirked it.

The trees seem to close in on us. I look up at them and then I look at Lucy's face. I see the beauty. I see the damage. I want to go to her. I know it is the right thing to do. But I can't.

I turn instead and walk away from the woman I love. I expect her to call out for me to stop. But she doesn't. She lets me go. I hear her sobs. I walk some more. I walk until I am out of the woods and back by the car. I sit on the kerb and close my eyes. Eventually she will have to come back here. So I sit and wait for her. I wonder where we will go after she comes out. I wonder if we will drive off together or if these woods, after all these years, will have claimed one last victim.

HARLAN COBEN

Born: New Jersey, January 7, 1962
Favourite author: Philip Roth
Series detective: Myron Bolitar

RD: Fourteen novels down the line, what would you say is the best thing about being an author?

HC: Pretty much everything. I am very lucky that I get to tell stories for a living. I love being able to grab people's attention, to keep them turning the pages, to make them stay awake all night. I want to stir the pulse, yes, but also to stir the heart. I hope *The Woods* does that.

RD: What was the inspiration for this new book?

HC: When I was seventeen, I worked as a counsellor at a co-ed sleep-away camp for eight weeks. I loved it but it could be harrowing—it was far too much responsibility for someone my age. I started thinking about that. Then an image came to my mind, which ended up being the first sentence of the book: 'I see my father with that shovel.' And I was off and writing.

RD: What keeps you motivated from one novel to the next?

HC: When you like something and you're pretty good at it and you can make a living doing it, you don't ask why. You just count your blessings and go with it.

RD: How do you come up with such fantastic plot twists?

HC: You got me. I work hard on them and think about them constantly. The book is never far from my mind.

RD: Is your writing usually done at home?

HC: I can write pretty much anywhere if you give me time and some quiet. The home is not usually the best place because I have four children. It's usually pandemonium around here!

RD: You live with your family in Newark, New Jersey where you were born. Could you imagine moving anywhere else?

HC: Sure, but my guess is, we'll stay here in New Jersey, right outside New York City. The state of New Jersey is really two places—terrible cities and wonderful suburbs. I live in the suburbs, the final battleground of the American dream, where people get married and have kids and try to scratch out a happy life for themselves. It's very romantic in that way, but a bit naive. I like to play with that in my work.

RD: What was your own New Jersey childhood like?

HC: Normal, I guess. Two brothers, good parents, a house in Livingston—actually the same house in which several of my characters, including Myron Bolitar, grew up.

RD: Your novel *Tell No One* has just been made into a French language film, *Ne Le Dis à Personne*. What do you think of it?

HC: It is an excellent film. The French cast is wonderful and readers will get a kick out of Kristin Scott Thomas appearing in what is a very different role for her.

RD: Did you get involved in the production at all?

HC: A little. I mostly gave director Guillaume Canet a free rein—it is his movie—but he kept me involved in the process. I appreciated that. I even have a cameo role. You can see me following the actor François Cluzet in the trailer, if you don't blink. We had a great deal of fun making it.

RD: Did you feel very protective of your words and characters?

HC: To some degree. But a movie is not a book, and shouldn't be. The best movie adaptations keep to the spirit of the original but aren't totally faithful re-creations. *Tell No One* is very close to the novel that inspired it, but Guillaume altered the ending in a way I agreed with. It wouldn't have worked as I'd written it.

RD: Hasn't the film recently won the French equivalent of the Oscar?

HC: Yes. Guillaume and I joked when we first started work that if the movie was nominated for even one César, I would fly over for the ceremony. Well, it ended up being nominated for nine and winning four, including Best Actor, Best Director and Best Soundtrack!

RD: Are there any more adaptations of your books in the pipeline?

HC: Most of the books have been optioned, but you never know with Hollywood.

RD: Do you still enjoy writing as much you did when you started?

HC: Some days I enjoy it more, some days I enjoy it less. Most days I remember the old adage: 'I don't like writing. I like having written.'

'Part pathology, part archaeology, what I do goes beyond either. Because even after a human life is reduced to decay and old, dry bones, the dead can still bear witness. They can still tell a story, if only you know how to interpret it.

That's what I do.

Coax the dead to tell their story.'

Dr David Hunter, forensic anthropologist

CHAPTER 1

Given the right temperature, everything burns. Wood. Clothing. People.

At 250° Celsius, flesh will ignite. Skin blackens and splits. The subcutaneous fat below it starts to liquefy, like grease in a hot pan. Fuelled by it, the body starts to burn. Arms and legs catch first, acting as kindling to the greater mass of the torso. Tendons and muscle fibres contract, causing the burning limbs to move in an obscene parody of life. Last to go are the organs. Cocooned in moisture, they often remain even after the rest of the soft tissue has been consumed.

But bone is, quite literally, a different matter. Bone stubbornly resists all but the hottest fires. And even when the carbon has burned from it, leaving it as lifeless as pumice, bone will still retain its shape. Now, though, it is a ghost of its former self, and will easily crumble. It's a process that, with few variations, inevitably follows the same pattern.

But not always.

The peace of the old cottage is broken by a footfall. The rotting door is pushed open, its rusted hinges protesting the disturbance. Daylight falls into the room, then is blocked out as a shadow fills the doorway. The man ducks to see into the darkened interior. The old dog with him hesitates, its senses alert. Now the man, too, pauses, as though reluctant to cross the threshold. When the dog begins to venture inside he recalls it with a word.

'Here.'

Obediently, the dog returns, glancing nervously, with eyes grown opaque with cataracts, at the man.

'Stay.'

The dog watches, anxiously, as the man advances further into the derelict cottage. The odour of damp envelops him. And now another smell is making itself known. Slowly, almost reluctantly, the man crosses to a low door set in the back wall. He puts out his hand to push it open, then pauses again. Behind him, the dog gives a low whine. Gently, he eases open the door.

At first he sees nothing. The room is dim, the only light coming from a small window, through glass cobwebbed with decades of dirt. But the man's eyes adjust, and details begin to emerge from the gloom.

And he sees what's lying in the room.

He sucks in a breath as though punched, taking an involuntary step backwards. His face pales, and he backs out of the doorway as if reluctant to turn away from the object on the floor. Only when the warped door has creaked shut again, cutting off his view of the other room, does he turn his back.

His gait is unsteady as he goes outside the cottage. The old dog greets him, but is ignored as the man reaches inside his coat and fumbles out a pack of cigarettes. His hands are trembling, and it takes three attempts for him to ignite the lighter. But he draws the smoke deep into his lungs, and by the time the cigarette is finished his trembling has steadied.

He drops the cigarette stub onto the grass and treads it out before bending down to retrieve it. Then, slipping it into his coat pocket, he takes a deep breath and goes to make the phone call.

I WAS ON MY WAY to Glasgow airport in a taxi when the call came. It was a foul February morning: brooding grey skies and a depressing mizzle driven by cold winds. The east coast was being lashed by storms, and I only hoped the worst would hold off long enough for me to catch my flight.

I was returning to London, having spent the previous week first recovering, then examining, a body from a moorland grave out on the Grampian Highlands. It had been a thankless task. The mutilated victim had been a young woman, who still hadn't been identified. It was the second such body I'd been asked to recover from the Grampians in recent months. No one on the investigating team was in any doubt that the same killer was responsible for both. One who would kill again if he wasn't caught.

It had been a gruelling trip, and I was looking forward to going home. For the past eighteen months I'd been living in London, based at the Forensic Science department of the university, but in recent weeks I'd spent far more time working out in the field than I had in my office. I'd promised Jenny, my girlfriend, that we'd be able to spend some time together after this. It wasn't the first time I'd made that promise, but this time I was determined to keep it.

When my phone rang I thought it would be her, calling to make sure I was on my way home. But the number on the caller display wasn't one I recognised. When I answered, the voice at the other end was gruff.

'Sorry to disturb you, Dr Hunter. I'm Detective Superintendent Graham Wallace, at Northern Force Headquarters in Inverness. Can you spare me a few minutes?' He had the tone of someone used to getting his own way.

'Just a few. I'm on my way to catch a flight.'

'I know. I've just spoken to DCI Allan Campbell at Grampian Police, and he told me you'd finished up here. I'm glad I've caught you.'

Campbell was the Senior Investigating Officer I'd been working with on the body recovery. I glanced at the taxi driver, conscious of being overheard. 'What can I do for you?' I asked.

'I'm looking for a favour.' Wallace clipped the words out. 'You'll have seen about the train crash this morning?'

I had. At my hotel before I'd left I'd watched the news reports of a West Coast commuter express that had derailed after hitting a van left on the line. From the TV footage it looked bad, the train carriages lying mangled and twisted by the track. No one knew yet how many people had been killed.

'There's a chance the derailment was deliberate, so we're having to treat the whole area as a crime scene,' Wallace continued. 'We're calling in help from other forces, but right now we're running at full stretch.'

I could guess what was coming. According to the news reports, some of the carriages had caught fire, which would make victim identification a forensic nightmare. But before that could begin, the bodies would have to be recovered, and from what I'd seen that was still some way off.

'I'm not sure how much help I'd be at the moment,' I told him.

'It isn't the crash I'm calling about,' he said impatiently. 'We've got a report of a fire death on Runa, a small island in the Outer Hebrides.'

'Suspicious?' I asked.

'Doesn't sound like it. Might be suicide, but more likely to be a drunk or vagrant who fell asleep too close to a campfire. Dog walker found it at an abandoned croft and called it in. He's a retired DI, lives out there now. I've worked with him. Used to be a good man.'

I wondered if the *used to be* was significant. 'So what else did he say about it?'

There was a beat before he replied. 'Just that it's badly burnt. But I don't want to pull resources away from a major incident unless I have to. A couple of the local boys from Stornoway are going out by ferry later today, and I'd like you to go with them and take a look. See if you think I need to send a SOC team. I'd like an expert assessment before I press the panic button, and Allan Campbell says you're bloody good.'

The flattery sat awkwardly with his bluff manner. I'd also noted his hesitation when I asked about the body, and wondered if there was something he wasn't telling me. But if Wallace thought there was anything suspicious about the death, he'd be sending a scene-of-crime team, train crash or not.

The taxi was almost at the airport. I had every reason to say no. This sounded fairly mundane: the sort of everyday tragedy that never makes it into the newspapers. I thought about having to tell Jenny that I wouldn't be back today after all. I knew that wouldn't go down well.

Wallace sensed my reluctance. 'Should only take a couple of days. The thing is, it sounds as if there might be something . . . odd about it.'

'I thought you said it wasn't suspicious,' I said, frowning.

'It isn't. At least, nothing I've heard makes me think it is. Look, I don't want to say too much, but I'd like an expert to take a look.'

I hate being manipulated. But I couldn't deny that my curiosity had been aroused. 'I'll have to get back to you,' I said. 'Give me five minutes.'

He didn't like that, but he could hardly object. I rang off and dialled Jenny's number. I smiled at the sound of her voice, even though I wasn't looking forward to the conversation we were about to have.

'David! I was just on my way to work. Where are you?'

'On my way to the airport.'

I heard her laugh. 'Thank God for that. I thought you were phoning to say you were weren't coming back today after all.'

I felt my stomach sink. 'That's what I was calling about,' I said. 'The thing is, I've just been asked to go on another job. It's only for a day or two. In the Outer Hebrides. But there's no one else to do it right now.'

There was a pause. 'So what did you say?' I hated the way the laughter had gone from Jenny's voice.

'That I'd let them know. I wanted to talk to you first.'

'Why? We both know you've already made up your mind.'

I'd not wanted this to develop into an argument. 'Look, Jenny—'

'I've got to go. I'll be late for work.' There was a click as she hung up.

I sighed. This wasn't how I'd expected the morning to go. *So call her back and say you'll turn it down.* My finger poised over the phone.

'Don't worry, pal. My wife's always giving me a hard time, too,' the taxi driver said over his shoulder. 'She'll get over it, eh?'

I made a noncommittal comment. In the distance I could see a plane taking off from the airport. The driver indicated to turn off as I keyed in the number. It was answered on the first ring.

'How do I get there?' I asked Wallace.

I SPEND MOST of my working day with the dead. The long dead, sometimes. I'm a forensic anthropologist. It's a field of expertise, and a fact of life, that most people prefer not to confront. Not until they have to. For a while I was one of them. When my wife and daughter were killed in a car crash, working in a field that reminded me, every day, of what I'd lost was too painful. So I became a GP, tending to the living rather than the dead.

But then events forced me to return to my original vocation. My calling, you might say. Part pathology, part archaeology, what I do goes beyond either. Because even after a human life is reduced to decay and old, dry bones, the dead can still bear witness. They can still tell a story, if only you know how to interpret it. That's what I do.

Coax the dead to tell their story.

Wallace had booked a seat for me on a flight to Lewis, the main island in the Outer Hebrides. It was a bumpy ride, whose only redeeming feature was that it was short. The day was half gone by the time I caught a taxi from the airport to the ferry terminal at Stornoway. The dock where I was dropped off was misty and cold, pungent with the usual harbour fug of diesel and fish. I'd been expecting to board one of the big car ferries that belched smoke into the rainy sky, but the boat I found myself standing before looked more like a small fishing vessel. Only the presence of a police Range Rover taking up most of the deck told me I was at the right place.

The boarding ramp rocked queasily in the heavy swell. A uniformed police sergeant was standing at the bottom, hands stuffed into the pockets of his coat. His cheeks and nose had the permanent flush of broken capillaries. Pouchy eyes regarded me balefully over a pepper-and-salt moustache.

'You Dr Hunter? I'm Sergeant Fraser,' he informed me gruffly. There was no first name, and his hands remained in his pockets. 'We've been waiting for you to turn up.'

With that, he went back up the ramp, making no offer to help with my heavy luggage. I hefted my shoulder bag and aluminium flight case and started up after him. The ramp was wet and slippery, and I struggled to keep my footing. Then someone was trotting down the ramp to help. A young uniformed constable took the flight case from my hand.

'Here, I'll take that.' He loaded my aluminium case into the back of the Range Rover. 'What have you got in here, a body?' he asked cheerfully.

I put my bag in with the case. 'No, it just feels like it. Thanks.'

'No problem.' He couldn't have been much older than twenty. He had a friendly, open face and his handshake was enthusiastic. 'I'm PC McKinney, but just call me Duncan. So you're the forensic man?'

'Afraid so.'

'Great! I mean, not great, but . . . well, you know. Let's get out of the rain.'

The passenger cabin was a glassed-in section below the wheelhouse. Outside it, Fraser was talking heatedly to a bearded man in oilskins. Behind him a tall teenage boy, face rippled with acne, looked on sullenly as Fraser jabbed the air with a finger.

'. . . waited long enough as it is, and now you're saying you're not ready to go?'

The bearded man stared back impassively. 'There's another passenger. We're not leaving till she's arrived.'

Fraser's red face darkened further. 'This isn't a bloody pleasure cruise. We're already behind schedule, so get that ramp pulled up, OK?'

The other man's eyes stared out above the dark beard, giving him the feral look of a wild animal. 'This is my boat, and I set the schedules.'

As Fraser prepared to assert himself, there was a clattering from the ramp. A diminutive young woman was hurrying up, struggling under the weight of a heavy-looking bag. She wore a bright red, down-filled coat that looked at least two sizes too big for her. A woollen hat was pulled over her ears. With her sandy hair and pointed chin, it gave her an appealing, elfin appearance.

'Hi, gents. Anyone care to give me a hand here?' she panted.

Duncan had started forward but the bearded man beat him to it. He grinned at the new arrival, white teeth gleaming as he took the bag from her.

'About time you showed up, Maggie. We were about to go without you.'

'Good job you didn't, or my gran would have killed you.' She stood with her hands on her hips, regarding them as she caught her breath. 'Hi, Kevin, how's it going? Your dad here still working you too hard?'

The teenager blushed and looked down. 'Aye.'

'Now you're eighteen, you'll have to put in for a pay rise.' She eyed the police Range Rover. 'So what's going on? Something happened I should know about?'

The bearded man jerked his head dismissively towards us. 'Try asking them. They won't tell us anything about it.'

The woman's grin faltered when she saw Fraser. Then she recovered herself. 'Hello, Sergeant Fraser. What takes you out to Runa?'

'Police business,' Fraser said flatly, and turned away. Whoever the young woman was, he wasn't pleased to see her.

As the ferry captain and his son busied themselves on deck, the woman went into the wheelhouse. There was a motorised whine as the ramp was winched up. Then, with a belch of diesel, the ferry chugged out of the harbour.

WHAT SHOULD HAVE BEEN a two-hour crossing took almost three. Once we'd left the protection of Stornoway harbour, the Atlantic became a turbulent grey plain of angry waves, into which the ferry smacked head on. The only shelter was in the cramped passenger cabin, where diesel fumes and burning-hot radiators made for an uncomfortable combination. Fraser and Duncan sat for the most part in miserable silence. I'd tried to draw out Fraser about the body, but he obviously knew little more than I did.

'Some drunk fell asleep too close to his campfire, most likely,' he grunted.

'Wallace told me a retired DI had found it. Who is he?'

'That's Andrew Brody,' Duncan piped up. 'My dad used to work with him on the mainland. Said he was a damn good police officer.'

'Aye, "was",' Fraser said. 'Didn't like being a team player. I heard he lost it completely after his wife and daughter ran off; that's why he retired.'

Duncan looked embarrassed. 'It was stress, my dad said.'

Fraser waved away the distinction. 'Same thing. Just so long as he remembers he's not a DI any more.' He stiffened as the boat suddenly shuddered and yawed over another mountainous swell.

I stayed in the cabin for an hour or so more, then went on deck. The wind blustered against me, peppering my face with rain, but it was a relief after the sour, overheated cabin. The island was visible now, a dark mass rising from the sea as the ferry chugged towards it.

A flash of red caught the corner of my eye, and I turned to see the young woman unsteadily making her way across the deck towards me. A sudden dip sent her running the last few steps, and I put out my arm to steady her.

'Thanks.'

She gave me a gamine smile as she joined me at the railing. 'It's a rough one. Iain says it's going to be fun trying to dock in this.'

Her accent was a softer, more lilting version of Fraser's. 'Iain?'

'Iain Kinross, the skipper. He's an old neighbour, from Runa.'

'Is that where you live?'

'Not any more. My family moved to Stornoway, except for my gran. We take it in turns to visit her. So you're here with the police, then?'

She asked the question with an innocence I didn't entirely trust.

'More or less.'

'Iain said they called you "Dr". Is there someone injured out here?'

'Not as far as I know.'

'What's a doctor doing coming out to Runa with the police?'

'You'd better ask Sergeant Fraser.'

She grimaced. 'Aye, that'll happen.'

'So what do you do on Stornoway?' I asked.

'Oh . . . I'm a writer, working on a novel. I'm Maggie Cassidy, by the way.'

'David. David Hunter.'

She seemed to file the information away. We were silent for a while, watching the island gradually take form in the fading light: grey cliffs rising from the sea, topped with featureless green. A tall sea stack, a natural tower of black rock, thrust up from the waves in front of the cliffs.

'Nearly there,' Maggie said. 'The harbour's just behind Stac Ross, that big rock thingy.' She stood up from the railing. 'Well, nice meeting you, David. Perhaps see you again before you go.'

She made her way back across the deck to rejoin Kinross and his son in the wheelhouse. I noticed that she seemed much steadier on her feet than she had when she'd come out.

As I turned my attention back to the island, a sharp whistle came from behind me, carrying even above the wind and the sound of the engine. I turned to see Kinross gesturing angrily.

'Get inside!'

I didn't need to be told twice. The sea was becoming more violent as the waves were funnelled in between the tall cliffs that bracketed the harbour. Grabbing at handholds to steady myself, I made my way back to the over-heated cabin and waited with Duncan and a pale-faced Fraser as the ferry manoeuvred into the harbour. It took three attempts to dock, the entire boat vibrating as the engine revved to hold us in place.

We left the cabin, walking with difficulty on the still-swaying deck. Gulls wheeled and cried overhead, while on the jetty men were scurrying about, securing ropes and rubber fenders.

Despite the cliffs, the harbour was fully open to the sea, with only a single breakwater jutting out to blunt the force of the waves. A scattering of low houses and cottages clung barnacle-like to the steep hillside that dropped down to the harbour. In the distance, the skyline was dominated by a brooding peak, its tip lost in the mist of low clouds.

Maggie Cassidy hurried off the ferry as soon as the ramp was lowered. Behind me, the police Range Rover's engine started up. Aware of the stares of the men who had helped fasten the moorings, I climbed into the back. Fraser let the young PC drive, and he eased the vehicle carefully down the undulating ramp.

A craggy-faced man was waiting for us on the jetty. He was mid-fifties, tall and powerfully built, and I didn't need to be told that this was the retired detective inspector who had found the body.

Fraser wound down the window. 'Andrew Brody?'

The man nodded. The wind ruffled his grey hair as he looked at the three of us inside the car. 'This all of you?' he asked, his disapproval obvious.

Fraser gave a stiff nod. 'Aye, for now.'

'What about SOC? When are they coming out?'

'We don't know they are, yet,' Fraser retorted. 'A DC's going to follow on from Stornoway after Dr Hunter here has taken a look at the body. He's a forensic . . . a forensic expert.'

Until now Brody hadn't paid me any attention. Now he looked at me with more interest. His eyes were sharp and intelligent.

'There's not much light left,' he said, glancing at the darkening sky. 'It's only fifteen minutes drive, but it'll be dark by the time we get out there. Perhaps you'd like to ride with me, Dr Hunter. I can brief you on the way.'

His car was parked on the quayside, a newish-looking Volvo saloon. The inside was spotless. It smelt of air freshener and, more faintly, of cigarettes. An old border collie was on a blanket in the back, black muzzle greyed with age. It stood up excitedly when Brody got into the car.

'Down, Bess,' he said mildly, and the dog immediately settled.

The headlights of the police Range Rover told us that Fraser and Duncan were following as we drove along a narrow road from the seafront to the village. Even from the little I could see of it, it was apparent that Runa wasn't the backwater I'd expected. Most of the doors and windows in the old stone cottages we passed looked new, as though they'd recently been replaced. There was a handful of shops, a small but modern school, and a little further out the timber structure of the community hall boasted a new extension that bore a sign saying RUNA MEDICAL CLINIC.

The road climbed steeply through the village, then levelled out as we passed the last few houses. On a hilltop overlooking them, silhouetted against the darkening sky, was a tall and crooked standing stone, rising from the grass like an accusing finger.

'That's Bodach Runa,' said Brody. 'The Old Man of Runa. Legend is he went out there to watch for the return of his son, who'd gone to sea. But the son never came back, and the old man stood there so long he turned to stone.'

'In this weather I can believe it.'

He smiled, but it quickly died. After wanting me to ride with him, he now seemed uncomfortable. I took out my mobile to check for messages.

'You'll not get a signal out here,' Brody warned. 'If you want to call out you'll have to use either a land line or a police radio.'

I put my phone away. I'd half hoped Jenny might have left a message, though I didn't really expect it.

'So what sort of "forensic expert" are you?' Brody asked.

'I'm a forensic anthropologist.'

Brody seemed satisfied. 'Good. At least we'll have one person out here who knows what he's doing. How much did Wallace tell you?'

'Just that it was a fire death, and that there was something odd about it. He wouldn't say what, except that it wasn't suspicious.'

His jaw set in disapproval. 'Did he, now?'

I was starting to have a bad feeling about this. Normally I wouldn't get involved before a scene-of-crime team had processed the site. I hoped Wallace hadn't let his preoccupation with the train crash cloud his judgment.

I remembered what he'd said about Brody. *Used to be a good man.* Retired police officers often found it hard being out of the loop. Brody wouldn't be the first to exaggerate in order to feel in the thick of things again.

'All he wants me to do is take a look,' I said. 'If I see anything that suggests it might not be accidental, then I'll back off until SOC gets out here.'

'That'll have to do, I suppose,' Brody said grudgingly.

'How did you find the body?' I asked.

'The dog caught the scent when I was taking her out for a walk this morning. It's in an abandoned crofter's cottage,' he said. 'And before you ask, no, I didn't touch anything. I might be retired, but I know better than that.'

I didn't doubt it. 'Any idea who it might be?'

'Not a clue. Far as I know, no one from the island's been reported missing. And there's less than two hundred people live out here, so it'd be hard for anyone to disappear without it being noticed.'

'Do you get many people from the mainland coming here?'

'Not many, but some. The odd naturalist or archaeologist. All the islands are peppered with ruins—Stone Age, Bronze Age and God knows what. And there's been quite a lot of renovation work going on, so we've had builders and contractors coming out. But not since the weather turned.'

'Who else knows about the body?'

'No one, as far as I'm aware. The only person I told was Wallace.'

'Wallace told me you used to work with him.'

'I did a stint at HQ in Inverness.'

'Runa must have been quite a change after that.'

'Aye, but for the better. It's a good place to live. Quiet. There's time and space to think.'

'Are you from here originally?'

'God, no. No, I'm an "incomer",' he said with a smile. 'Wanted to get away from it all when I took early retirement. And it doesn't get much further away than this.'

There was no disputing that. Once we had left the village, the only sign of habitation we'd passed was an imposing old house, set well back from the road. Other than that there had been only the occasional ruined cottage and sheep. In the gathering twilight, Runa looked beautiful, but desolate.

It would be a lonely place to die.

There was a jolt as Brody turned off the road and bumped down an overgrown track. Ahead of us, the car's headlights picked out a crumbling old cottage. He pulled up outside and turned off the engine.

'Stay, Bess,' he ordered the border collie.

We climbed out of the car as the Range Rover drew up behind us. The croft cottage was a squat, single-storey building. Looming up behind it in the encroaching darkness was the peak I'd seen earlier.

'That's Beinn Tuiridh,' Brody told me. 'It's what passes for a mountain out here. They say there's an old watchtower and burial cairns up there.'

He took a Maglite from his glove compartment, and we waited beside the car for Fraser and Duncan. Then we made our way towards the cottage, torch beams bouncing and crisscrossing in the darkness. It was little more than a stone shack, and the doorway was so low I had to stoop to go inside.

I paused and shone my torch around. The place was obviously long abandoned. Water dripped from a hole in the roof, and a low ceiling added to the claustrophobic feel. We were in what had once been a kitchen. There was an old range, a dusty cast-iron pan still standing on one of its cold plates. A rickety wooden table stood in the middle of the flagstone floor. A few cans and bottles were scattered around, evidence that the place hadn't been entirely untenanted. It had the musty smell of age and damp, but nothing else. For a fire death there seemed remarkably little sign of any fire.

'Through there,' Brody said, shining his torch on another doorway.

As I approached it I caught the first faint, sooty whiff of combustion. The door was broken, its rusted hinges protesting as it was pushed open. The stink of fire was unmistakable now. The torchlight showed ancient, crumbling plaster on the bare walls, in one of which was the gaping mouth of a fireplace. But the smell didn't come from that. Its source was in the centre of the room, and as I shone my torch on it my breath caught in my throat.

There was precious little left of what had once been a living person. Even the white heat of a crematorium isn't enough to reduce a human body to ash, yet this fire had somehow done just that.

A pile of greasy ash and cinders lay on the floor. Only the larger bones remained, emerging like dead branches from a snowdrift. The carbon had burned from them until they were grey and brittle. Presiding over all like a broken eggshell was a skull, its jawbone canted off to one side.

And yet, apart from the body, nothing else in the room had been damaged. The fire that had all but incinerated a human being had somehow done so without burning anything else. The stone flags below the remains were blackened, but a few feet away a tattered mattress lay untouched.

But that wasn't the worst of it. What had shocked me to silence was the sight of two unburnt feet and a single hand protruding from the ashes. The bones jutting from them were scorched to black sticks, yet they were completely unmarked.

Brody came and stood beside me.

'Well, Dr Hunter? Still think there's nothing suspicious about it?'

CHAPTER 2

The wind moaned fitfully outside the old cottage, an eerie background music to the macabre scene. I was aware of Duncan's indrawn breath from the doorway as he and Fraser saw what was lying on the floor.

'Is there any chance of getting some more light in here?' I asked.

'We've got a portable floodlight in the car,' Fraser said, tearing his eyes from the pile of bone and ashes. 'Go and get it, Duncan. *Duncan.*'

The PC was still staring at the remains. The colour had left his face.

'Aye. Sorry.' He hurried out.

'I told Wallace it was a strange one,' Brody said, 'but I don't think he believed me. Dare say he thought I'd gone a bit soft.'

He was probably right, I thought, remembering the doubts I'd harboured myself only a few minutes before. But I couldn't blame Wallace for being sceptical. What I was looking at was freakish enough to flout all logic.

The body—what was left of it—was lying face down. I played my torch on the feet. They were intact from just above the ankle, and both were still wearing trainers. The charred shafts of the tibia and fibula came to an abrupt halt halfway up the shin.

I moved the torch beam until it shone on the hand. It was the right one, and could have belonged to either a small man or a large woman. There were no rings, and the fingernails were unvarnished. The radius and ulna protruded from the exposed tissue of the wrist, burned a dark amber close to the flesh, and blackened after that. The bones had burned right through just before where they should have joined the elbow.

Other than that, the surviving limbs showed little evidence of the fire that had destroyed the rest of the body. The main damage was from where rodents or other small animals had gnawed at the flesh and unburnt bone. The soft tissue was starting to decompose normally, a marbling effect evident beneath the darkened skin.

I shone the torch at the ceiling above the body. The cracked plaster was smoke-blackened, but not burned. It was coated with an oily brownish deposit. The same fatty residue was also on the floor around the remains.

'What's all that brown stuff?' Fraser asked.

'It's fat. From the body, as it burned.'

He grimaced. 'Bit like you get with a chip-pan fire, eh?'

'Something like that.'

Duncan had returned with the floodlight. He stared wide-eyed at the remains as he set it on the floor. 'I've read about this sort of thing,' he blurted. 'Where people burst into flames for no reason. Without burning anything else around them.'

'Stop talking rubbish,' Fraser snapped.

But I'd been expecting this ever since I'd seen the remains. 'It's all right,' I told Duncan. 'You're talking about spontaneous combustion.'

He nodded eagerly. 'Aye, that's it!'

Spontaneous human combustion was generally thought of as a paranormal phenomenon for which there was no real explanation. Yet there were well-documented cases of individuals found incinerated in a room otherwise untouched by fire, often with hands or lower legs partially intact among the ashes. A range of theories had been put forward to explain it, from demonic possession to microwaves. But the popular consensus was that its cause had to be something inexplicable to known science.

I didn't believe in it for a moment.

Fraser was scowling at Duncan 'What the hell do you know about it?'

Duncan gave me a sheepish glance. 'I've seen photographs. There was one woman who was burned up, just like this. All that was left was one of her legs, with the shoe still on. They call her "the cinder woman".'

'Her real name was Mary Reeser,' I told him. 'She was an elderly widow in Florida back in the 1950s. There was almost nothing left of her except for one leg from the shin down, and the foot still had a slipper on it. The armchair she was sitting on was destroyed, and a nearby table and lamp, but nothing else in the room was damaged. Is that the one?'

Duncan looked taken aback. 'Aye. And I've read about others.'

'They crop up now and again,' I agreed. 'But people don't just burst into flames for no reason. And whatever happened to this woman, there was nothing supernatural or paranormal about it.'

Brody had been watching us during the exchange. Now he spoke up.

'How do you know it's a woman?'

'Because of the skeleton.' I shone the torch onto what was left of the pelvis, obscured by ash but still visible. 'The hipbone's obviously too wide for a man's. And the head of the humerus—that's the ball where the upper arm bone fits into the shoulder—is too small. Whoever this was, she was big-boned but definitely female.'

'Any idea how long the body might have been here?' he asked.

For an accurate time since death you need to trace the extent of decomposition in muscle proteins, amino and volatile fatty acids, all of which are normally destroyed by fire. This body had enough soft tissue to run tests that weren't possible for most fire deaths, but that would have to wait till I was back in a lab. Still, I could make an educated guess.

'The cold weather will have slowed the rate of decay,' I told him. 'But I'd say we're looking at around four or five weeks.'

'The contractors had all finished work long before then,' Brody mused. 'Can't be anyone who came out with them.'

Fraser had been listening with mounting irritation, not liking the way the former DI was taking over. 'Aye, well, if it's nobody local I dare say we'll be able to find out who it is from the ferry's passenger list.'

Brody smiled. 'Did it strike you as the sort of service that keeps records? Besides, a dozen or so other boats shuttle between Runa and Stornoway. No one keeps track of who comes and goes.' He turned to me, dismissing the police sergeant. 'So will you tell Wallace to send out a SOC team now?'

Fraser butted in angrily before I could answer. 'We're not doing anything until Dr Hunter's finished what he came to do. For all we know this was probably just some wino who fell asleep too close to the campfire.'

Brody's expression was unreadable. He shone his torch onto the skull. It lay face down, tilted slightly to one side among the ashes, the back of its once-smooth crown marred by a gaping hole.

'You think she might have smashed in her own head as well?'

I intervened before tempers frayed still more. 'Actually, the skull often shatters in a hot fire like this. It's basically a sealed container of fluid and jelly, so when it's heated it acts like a pressure cooker. You get a build-up of gas that eventually makes it explode.'

Fraser blanched. 'Christ.'

'So you still think it could be accidental?' Brody asked dubiously.

'It's possible,' I hedged. 'I know this looks bizarre, but nothing here immediately screams "murder". Other than the skull, there's no obvious trauma.'

Brody frowned. 'Fair enough. But I was a police officer for thirty years. I saw my share of fire deaths, accidental and otherwise, but it's hard to see how this could happen without an accelerant being used.'

Under normal circumstances he would be right. But the circumstances here were far from normal.

'An accelerant like petrol couldn't have done this,' I told him. 'It doesn't burn hotly enough. And to incinerate a body to anything like this extent would have taken so much that the whole cottage would have gone up.'

'So what could have caused it?'

I had an idea, but I didn't want to speculate just yet. 'That's what I'm here to find out. In the meantime, let's play safe anyway.' I turned to Fraser. 'Can you tape off a walkway from the doorway, and cordon off the body?'

The sergeant jerked his head at Duncan. 'Go on, go and get the incident tape. We don't have all night.'

He made a point of saying 'incident' rather than 'crime scene', I noticed. Brody hadn't missed it, either. His jaw muscles bunched.

As Duncan headed towards the door, the room was suddenly lit up as headlights spilled through the small window. The sound of a car engine being switched off came from outside the cottage.

'Looks like we've got visitors,' Brody commented.

Fraser motioned angrily to Duncan. 'Get out there. Don't let anyone in.'

But it was too late. As we hurried from the room a figure was already in the front doorway. It was the young woman I'd spoken to on the ferry, her red coat a vivid shout of colour in the depressing sepia of the cottage.

'Get her out,' Fraser snarled to Duncan.

She lowered her torch, shielding her eyes as Fraser shone his in her face. 'Now that's no way to treat a member of the press, is it?'

Press? I thought, dismayed. She'd told me she was a novelist. The woman was already looking behind us, trying to see into the other room. Brody tried to close the door, but its rusted hinges seemed to have frozen. They gave an explosive creak, but refused to shut.

She smiled at him. 'You must be Andrew Brody. Heard about you from my gran. I'm Maggie Cassidy, *Lewis Gazette*.'

Brody appeared unruffled. 'What do you want, Maggie?'

'To find out what's going on, obviously.' She grinned. 'You don't get police coming out to Runa every day.'

Now I knew why she'd rushed off the ferry so quickly; she'd gone to get a car. With only one road and the police Range Rover parked outside the cottage, she wouldn't have had much difficulty finding us.

She turned to me. 'Hello again, Dr Hunter. Not got a patient here, surely?'

'Never mind that,' Fraser said, his face livid. 'I want you out! Now! Before I throw you out on your arse.'

'That'd be assault, Sergeant Fraser.' She rummaged in her bag, emerging with a voice recorder. 'Just a few comments, that's all I'm asking. It's not every day a body's found on Runa. That *is* what's in there, isn't it? A body?'

Fraser had balled his fists. 'Duncan, get her out.'

She brandished the recorder towards us. 'Any idea who it is?'

Duncan reached out to take hold of her arm. 'Come on, miss . . .' he said.

Maggie gave a resigned shrug. 'Ah, well. Can't blame a girl for trying.'

She made as if to go, but as she did so her bag slipped from her shoulder. Duncan automatically bent to pick it up, and she suddenly ducked to one side, peering round him into the other room.

Her eyes widened with shock. 'Oh my God!'

'Right. Out!' Fraser pushed past Duncan and grabbed her by the arm.

'Ow! You're hurting!' She raised the voice recorder. 'I'm being physically thrown out by Sergeant Neil Fraser . . .'.

Fraser took no notice. He steered her firmly towards the door. 'I see you hanging round here again, you'll be under arrest. Clear?'

'This is assault . . .!'

But Fraser had already thrust her out of the cottage. He turned on Duncan. 'Get her in her car and see she leaves.'

Duncan hurried out.

'Great!' Fraser fumed. 'Just what we need, a bloody hack!'

'She seemed to know you,' Brody said.

Fraser glared at him. 'I'll take your statement now, *Mr* Brody.' The emphasis was deliberately insulting. 'We'll not be needing you after that.'

Brody's jaw set, but that was the only sign of annoyance. 'What are you planning on using for a command post while you're here?'

Fraser blinked, suspiciously. 'What?'

'You can't leave this place unattended. If one of you wants to come back to town with me, I've got a camper van you can use.' His eyebrows went up. 'Unless you were planning on staying out here all night in the car?'

The sergeant's expression made it plain he hadn't thought that far ahead. 'I'll send Duncan with you to get it,' he said gruffly.

There was humour in Brody's eyes as he gave me a nod. 'Pleasure meeting you, Dr Hunter. Good luck.'

He and Fraser went out. When they'd gone, I went back into the room where the remains of the dead woman lay. As I started to plan what I had to do, I felt the hairs on the back of my neck begin to prickle. I quickly turned round, expecting to find that Duncan or Fraser had returned.

But, except for the shadows, the room was empty.

WHILE FRASER taped off the cottage, I used his radio to brief Wallace. The superintendent sounded even more harried than he had that morning as I outlined what I knew so far.

'So Brody wasn't exaggerating,' Wallace said, sounding surprised.

'No.' I took a deep breath. 'Look, you're not going to like this, but you might want to think about getting SOC out here.'

'You're saying you think it's murder?' he asked sharply.

'No, just that I can't say for certain it isn't.'

Wallace sighed. 'Under normal circumstances I'd have a team out there with you first thing tomorrow. But right now this train crash takes priority. There are still people trapped. I can't take SOCOs off that for something that in all likelihood's going to be an accidental death.'

'All right. But if I find anything I don't like then I'm backing off until SOC arrive,' I said. 'And one more thing. It might help if you can send me details from the Missing Persons data base of any young women who fit the dead woman's basic profile. Race, size, age, that sort of thing.'

Wallace said he'd have the Missing Persons files emailed to me, then ended the call without ceremony.

There wasn't much more I could do without the generator-fed lamps that would normally illuminate this sort of scene, so I decided to wait for daylight to carry out any sort of real assessment. I took my digital camera from the flight case and began photographing the remains.

As I worked I tried to ignore the irrational unease I felt. It had nothing to do with the pitiful mound of bones and ash in the centre of the room. I don't believe in ghosts. But there was something unnerving about being out there. I put it down to tiredness and the mournful circling of the wind. I told myself that the biggest danger was that the remains would be compromised by the cottage's ancient roof. The whole thing looked unsafe, and with the weather getting worse I didn't want a sudden collapse to damage the fragile bones before I'd examined them.

I'd just finished taking photographs when Duncan returned with Brody's camper van, with its scrupulously clean, self-contained living quarters.

'You'll be fine. Nice and cosy in here,' Fraser told Duncan, patting the side of the van. He jerked his head towards the cottage. 'If she comes out to bother you, you've my permission to arrest her.'

'Aye, thanks a bunch,' the young PC said unhappily.

Fraser gave a wheezing chuckle. Promising to bring Duncan out some supper, we started back to the village.

We'd been driving for about ten minutes when I saw something standing out like a lighthouse in the darkness. It was the imposing house I'd noticed on the way to the cottage, now lit up by spotlights.

'Must be nice to have money to burn,' Fraser commented sourly.

'Who lives there?'

'Guy called Strachan. Locals think the sun shines out of his arse, by all accounts. Came here a few years ago and started chucking money around. Fixed up the roads and houses, paid for a new school and medical clinic. Absolutely loaded. Got his own yacht, and his wife's supposed to be a stunner.' He gave a derisive snort. 'Some people have all the luck.'

I looked at the gaily lit windows, suspended in the darkness, and wondered briefly why life and luck should favour some and victimise others. Then we rounded a bend, and the house was lost from view.

We reached the village not long afterwards. Fraser followed the main road down to the harbour, then turned off back up a narrow side street. Standing by itself at the top was a tall, old building on which was hung a neat sign that said RUNA HOTEL. As we pulled up outside I thought it looked snug and welcoming. I climbed out of the car. The rain had eased and shredded clouds streamed across an ink-black sky, giving glimpses of bright stars and a sickle moon. The night was cold and quiet.

I followed Fraser up the steps and through the double doors. An appealing scent of beeswax and freshly baked bread engulfed me as I found myself in a long, warmly lit hallway. The bare floorboards had been polished to the colour of cinnamon by generations of feet, and the walls and ceiling were clad in old pine panels, so that it was like walking into an old ship. An ancient grandfather clock ticktocked away against one wall.

A young woman emerged through a swing door at the far end. She looked in her late twenties, tall and slim in jeans and a blue sweater that complemented her dark red hair. A constellation of freckles dappled her nose and cheekbones, above which were striking sea-green eyes.

'Good evening,' she said. 'You must be Sergeant Fraser and Dr Hunter.'

'Aye,' Fraser answered, but his attention was on the bar visible through an open doorway. An inviting murmur of voices filtered from inside.

'I'm Ellen McLeod. I wasn't sure what time you'd be here, but your rooms are ready. Have you eaten?'

Fraser reluctantly tore his eyes away from the bar. 'Not yet. Something hot would be welcome when we've dumped our bags.'

'What about Duncan?' I reminded him.

'Oh. Right,' Fraser said, with little enthusiasm. 'I've got a PC outside on duty. Could you organise a plate of something I can take out to him?'

'Of course.'

Fraser was heading for the bar. 'Look, you might as well see to Dr Hunter. I'll, er . . . I'll be waiting in here.'

The broken capillaries in his cheeks and nose hadn't lied, I thought.

'He'll be disappointed if he's wanting a drink. There's only me here.' Ellen gave me a conspiratorial smile. 'I'll show you to your room.'

The stairs creaked as they took our weight, but there was a reassuring solidity to them. The dark red carpet was worn, but clean.

A flash of something white caught my eye as I followed Ellen along the first-floor landing. It came from the landing on the unlit floor above. I looked up and saw a little girl watching me through the banister spindles.

I felt my heart stutter.

'Anna, it's past your bedtime,' Ellen said sternly. 'Go back to bed.'

The little girl took this as an invitation to come down the stairs. As she emerged from the shadows in her nightgown the shock I'd felt at seeing her was already fading. I could see now that the resemblance to my own daughter was only superficial. Alice had been older, and her hair had been blonde. *Like her mother's.* This little girl was only four or five, her hair the same dark red as the young woman's.

'I can't sleep,' the little girl said, staring at me with open curiosity. 'I'm scared of the wind.'

'Funny, you've never been bothered by it before,' Ellen said drily. 'Go on, off to bed. I'll call in to see you after I've shown Dr Hunter his room.'

With a final look at me, the little girl did as she was told.

'Sorry about that,' Ellen said, continuing down the hallway. 'My daughter's got what I think's called a "healthy curiosity".'

I managed a smile. 'Glad to hear it. And the name's David. How old is she? Five?'

'Four. She's big for her age.' There was a quiet note of pride in her voice. 'Do you have children?'

I felt my face stiffen. 'No.'

'Are you married?'

'I used to be. My wife died.'

Ellen's hand went to her mouth. 'Oh, I'm sorry . . .'

'It's all right.'

But she was looking at me now with realisation. 'It wasn't just your wife, was it? That's why you looked so shocked when you saw Anna.'

'They were about the same age, that's all,' I said, as neutrally as I could. I smiled. 'Anna looks a lovely little girl.'

Ellen took the hint. 'You wouldn't say that if you saw her when she can't get her own way. She can be a madam when the mood takes her.'

I wondered where the little girl's father was. Ellen didn't wear a wedding ring, and from the way she'd spoken earlier it sounded as if she was alone here with her daughter. Not that it was any of my business, I told myself.

She opened a door at the far end of the hall. 'Here we are. Not very grand, I'm afraid.'

'It's fine,' I told her. And it was. The room was spartan, but clean and comfortable. A single brass bedstead was flanked by an old pine dresser on one side and a wardrobe on the other, and its tartan counterpane was neatly turned down to reveal crisp white sheets.

'The bathroom is at the end of the hall. Shared, but only between you and Sergeant Fraser. I'll leave you to sort yourself out. Just come down to the bar when you're ready for supper.'

There was a telephone on the dresser, so at least I'd be able to call Jenny. 'Is there anywhere I can log on to the Internet? I'd like to check my emails.'

'If you've got a laptop you can use the phone line in here. We're not wireless yet, but there's a broadband connection.'

'You've got broadband?' I asked, surprised.

'We can still lose power and phones if the weather's bad, so we're not that sophisticated yet, but it works fine most of the time.'

When she'd gone I sat down heavily on the bed. Its springs made a metallic rustling as they took my weight. *God.* I was more tired than I'd thought. The incident on the stairs had struck through the defences I'd painstakingly built up after Kara and Alice had died. It had taken a long time to reach a state of truce with the cold fact that I was still alive, while my wife and daughter weren't. Jenny had played a large part in that, and I was deeply thankful to have been given a second chance. But every now and then the loss would still hit home with a force that took my breath away.

I took my laptop from my bag and put it on the dresser. I picked up the phone to call Jenny as I waited for it to boot up. She should be back from work by now. We were unofficially living together at her flat in Clapham. Unofficially, because I still had my own flat in east London, although I hardly ever stayed there. We both felt it would be good for us to keep some degree of independence. For the most part it had worked out.

It was only recently that the first fault lines had begun to appear in our relationship.

I knew I was largely to blame. When Jenny and I had met I'd been a GP. The work I did now was very different. It increasingly took me away from home, creating a conflict I had no idea how to resolve. My work was as much a part of me as breathing, but I couldn't imagine losing Jenny. I was beginning to think that soon I'd have to choose between them.

The phone rang for a while before she answered.

'Hi, it's me,' I said.

'Hi.' There was a strained pause. 'So. How are the Outer Hebrides?'

'Cold and wet. How was your day?'

'Fine.'

Jenny worked part-time as a teacher in a nursery school. She was good at her job, and good with children. I knew she wanted some of her own one day. That was something else I wasn't sure about.

'Listen, I'm sorry about earlier,' I said.

'It doesn't matter.'

'No, it does. I just wanted to explain—'

'Don't. Please,' she added, less forcefully. 'There's no point. You're there now. I was just disappointed you wouldn't be coming back today.'

'It'll only be another day or two,' I said.

There was a pause. 'OK.'

'I'd better go,' I said. 'I'll call you tomorrow.'

I heard her sigh. 'David . . .'

My stomach knotted. 'What?'

Another pause. 'Nothing. I'm looking forward to seeing you, that's all.'

I told her the same and reluctantly broke the connection. After I'd hung up I stayed on the bed, wondering what it was she'd been about to say.

Sighing, I connected my camera to the laptop and downloaded the photographs from the cottage. There were over a hundred shots of the remains, capturing them from every angle.

I backed up the files onto a USB memory stick, then lay on the bed and closed my eyes. I could easily have fallen asleep if my stomach hadn't rumbled noisily to remind me that, tired or not, I needed to eat.

I pushed myself off the bed, switched off the light and headed downstairs.

THE BAR WAS little more than a snug into which a few tables had been squeezed. Like the hallway, it was clad in pine panels. Set against one wall was a fireplace covered completely in seashells. A peat block burned in its hearth, filling the air with a rich, spicy scent.

There were fewer than a dozen customers, but it was enough to make the place feel busy. The voices were a curious blend of lilting Scots and the harsher consonants of Gaelic. I received a few curious looks as I went in, then everyone went back to what they were doing. Two old men were playing dominoes by the window. Kinross, the bearded ferry captain, was talking at the bar to a huge man with a ponderous gut. A blowzy woman in her forties was with them, her raucous laugh carrying above the hubbub.

There was no sign of Fraser, so I guessed he had gone to take Duncan's supper out to the camper van.

'Dr Hunter.' Brody was sitting at a table by the fire, hand raised to attract my attention. The old border collie was curled asleep on the floor at his feet. 'Won't you join me?'

'Thanks.' Glad to see a familiar face, I went over, easing my way past the domino players.

'Can I get you a drink?' Brody asked.

'A whisky, please.'

He went to the bar. As there was no one serving, he poured a measure of whisky into a glass, then chalked it up on a slate hanging by the bar.

'Here you go. Fifteen-year-old Islay malt,' he said, setting the glass in front of me with a small jug of water.

I looked at the mug of tea in front of him. 'You don't drink yourself?'

'Not any more.' He raised his mug. '*Slàinte*.'

I added a little water to the malt. 'Cheers.'

'So how are they settling into the camper?'

'All right, I think. At least, Duncan is.'

Brody smiled. 'Drew the short straw, did he? Ah, well, he'll stay in worse places before he's finished.'

'Duncan was saying you used to work with his father.'

His smile grew reflective. 'Aye. We served in the Territorial Army together when we were both green. Last time I saw Sandy his lad was still at school.' Brody shook his head. 'Where's the time go, eh? One minute you're chasing crooks, the next—' He broke off, brightening as Ellen came over.

'Can I get you something to eat, Dr Hunter?' she asked.

'That sounds good. And, please, it's David.'

'David,' she corrected herself, smiling. 'I hope Andrew here's not bothering you. You know what these ex-policemen are like.'

Brody wagged a finger, mock-stern. 'Careful, that's slander.'

The big man who was with Kinross suddenly raised his voice. 'Another couple of drams here, Ellen.'

'In a minute, Sean.'

'Shall we help ourselves, then? We're dying of thirst.'

It was the woman at the bar who'd spoken. She was drunk, a condition I guessed from the look of her wasn't unusual. Years ago she might have been attractive, but now her features were puffy and etched with bitterness.

'The last time you helped yourself, Karen, you forgot to chalk it up,' Ellen retorted. 'I'm sure you can survive for a few more minutes.' She turned back to us, and missed the anger that clouded the woman's face. 'Sorry about that. A few drinks and some people forget their manners. Now, what do you want to eat? There's mutton stew, or I can make you a sandwich if you'd rather.'

'Mutton stew sounds good. But I don't mind if you serve them first.'

'They can wait. It'll do them good.'

'Ellen . . .' Brody said quietly.

She sighed, then gave him a tired smile. 'Aye, all right. I know.'

He watched her go to the bar to serve them. 'Ellen can be a little . . . fiery,' he said with affection. 'But the hotel's the only watering hole on Runa, so everyone either abides by her rules or stays home. She's a good cook, too. I eat here most nights.'

'Does she run this place by herself?'

'Aye. Not easy, but she manages.'

'What happened to her husband?'

His face closed down. 'There wasn't one. Anna's father was someone Ellen met on the mainland. She doesn't talk about it.' He cleared his throat and nodded towards the group at the bar. 'Anyway, let me tell you about some of Runa's local colour. Kinross you'll have met on the boat. Surly bugger, but he's had it rough. Wife died a couple of years ago, so now there's just him and his lad. The loudmouth with the beer belly is Sean Guthrie. Used to be a fisherman but lost his boat to the bank. He's got an old one he's trying to patch up, but he scrapes a living doing odd jobs and helping Kinross run the ferry. Keep clear of him when he's had too many.'

He was interrupted by a raucous laugh from the woman.

'That's Karen Tait. Runs the general store, when she's sober and can be bothered. Got a sixteen-year-old daughter, Mary, who . . . well, she isn't what she should be. You'd think Karen would be at home with her, but she'd rather prop up the bar in here every night.'

A blast of cold air swept into the bar as the outside door was opened. A moment later a golden retriever burst inside in a scrabble of claws.

'Oscar! *Oscar!*'

A man came in after it. He looked about forty, with chiselled good looks and dark hair winged with premature grey above the ears. His weatherproof coat was black and obviously expensive.

His entrance had silenced everyone in the room. The man casually snapped his fingers at the dog. It trotted back to him, wagging its tail.

'Sorry about that, Ellen,' he said with an easy confidence, the clipped vowels of a South African evident in his voice. 'He shot straight in as soon as I opened the door.'

Ellen looked unimpressed with both the newcomer and his apology. 'You should keep hold of him, then. This is a hotel, not a kennel.'

'I know. It won't happen again.'

He looked contrite, but as she turned away I saw him flash a quick smile and wink at the drinkers at the bar. There were grins in reply.

'Evening, everyone. It's a raw one out there tonight,' he said, shrugging out of his coat.

There was a chorus of '*Oidhche mhath*' and 'aye's'. I had the impression he could have said it was a beautiful evening and they would have just as readily agreed with him.

'Will you take a drink, Mr Strachan?' Kinross asked, awkwardly formal.

'No, thank you, Iain. But I'll gladly buy a round myself. Help yourselves, and mark it up on my tab.' He gave the woman at the bar a smile. 'Hello, Karen. I've not seen you for a while. Are you and Mary keeping well?'

She was more susceptible to his charm than Ellen had been. 'Yes, thank you,' she said, her blush visible even from where I sat.

Only now did the man turn towards Brody and me. 'Evening, Andrew.'

Brody gave a stiff nod in return, his expression hard as granite. He shifted his legs to put them between his border collie bitch and the golden retriever, which was sniffing around her.

The newcomer swatted the retriever with his gloves. 'Leave her alone Oscar, you hound.' As the dog came away, tail wagging, his owner gave me an engaging grin. 'And you must be one of the visitors I've been hearing about. I'm Michael Strachan.'

I'd already guessed this must be Runa's unofficial laird, and the owner of the big house we'd passed on the way back from the cottage.

'David Hunter,' I said, shaking the offered hand. He had a strong grip.

'Can I buy you both a drink as well?' he asked.

'Not for me, thanks,' I said.

Brody rose to his feet, his expression stony. 'I was just leaving. Nice seeing you again, Dr Hunter. Come on, Bess.'

The dog obediently trotted out after him. Strachan watched him go, his mouth curved in a faint smile, before turning back to me.

'Mind if I join you?'

He was already sliding into Brody's seat, casually tossing his gloves onto the table. The golden retriever flopped down beside him, as close to the crackling fire as he could get. Strachan reached down and scratched his ears.

'Are you a friend of Andrew Brody's?' he asked.

'We only met today.'

He grinned. 'I'm afraid he doesn't approve of me, as you've probably noticed. I'm sure he was a good policeman, but God, the man's dour!'

I didn't say anything. I'd been quite impressed by Brody so far. Strachan slouched easily in his chair, casually resting one foot on his knee.

'I gather you're a . . . what is it? A forensic anthropologist?' He smiled at my surprise. 'It's hard to keep anything a secret on Runa. Especially when we've got a reporter whose grandmother lives on the island.'

I thought back to how Maggie Cassidy had stumbled against me on the ferry, pretending to be a novelist as she'd pumped me for information.

And I'd fallen for it.

'Don't feel bad,' Strachan said, interpreting my expression. 'It isn't often there's a body found out here. What was it, some kind of accident?'

'Sorry, I can't really say.'

Strachan gave an apologetic smile. 'No, of course. You'll have to excuse my curiosity. It's just that I'm responsible for a lot of redevelopment here. It's brought a lot more people to the island than we're used to—contractors and so on. I'd hate to think I'd imported big-town troubles as well.'

He seemed genuinely concerned, but I wasn't going to let myself be drawn. 'You don't sound like a local,' I said.

'The accent's a bit of a giveaway, eh? My family's Scottish originally, but I grew up near Johannesburg. My wife and I moved to Runa five years ago.'

'It's a long way from South Africa.'

Strachan tousled his dog's ears. 'I suppose it is. But we'd been travelling round a lot, so it was time to put down roots. I liked the remoteness of this place. Reminded me in some ways of where I grew up. Place was pretty depressed back then, of course. No local economy to speak of.'

'You seem to have helped turn it round,' I said.

He looked embarrassed. 'I don't want to make out it's all down to me. But Runa's our home now. Grace, my wife, helps out at the school, and we do what we can in other ways as well. Hello, what's up, Oscar?'

The golden retriever was looking expectantly at the doorway, his tail thumping against the floor.

'I don't know how he does that, but he always knows,' Strachan said, shaking his head.

Knows what? I wondered, and then a woman came into the bar. I didn't need to be told she was Strachan's wife. It wasn't just that she was beautiful, although she was certainly that. Her white Prada parka was flecked with rain, setting off thick, shoulder-length hair that was raven-black. Her skin was white and flawless, with a full mouth it was hard to take your eyes from.

But there was also an energy to her, a sheer physical presence that seemed to draw all the light in the room. She'd had a tentative smile as she came into the bar, but when she saw Strachan it bloomed into something dazzling.

'Caught you! So this is where you end up when you go out on "business".' She had the same faint South African accent as her husband.

Strachan rose to give her a kiss. 'Guilty. How did you know I was here?'

'I came to get some things from the store, but it was shut,' she said, taking off her gloves. On her left hand she wore a plain gold wedding band, and a diamond ring whose single stone danced with blue light. 'Next time you want to sneak a drink, don't leave your car outside.'

'Blame Oscar. He dragged me here.'

She looked across at me, waiting for an introduction. Her brown eyes were so dark they were almost black.

'This is David Hunter,' Strachan said. 'David, this is my wife, Grace.'

She smiled and held out her hand. 'Pleased to meet you, David.'

As I took it I could smell her perfume: a subtle, delicately spiced musk.

'David's a forensic expert. He's with the police,' Strachan explained.

'God, what an awful business,' she said. 'I just hope it's no one from here. I know that sounds selfish, but . . . well, you know what I mean.'

I did. When it comes to ill fortune we're all selfish at heart.

Strachan had got to his feet. 'Well, nice meeting you, Dr Hunter.'

Grace arched an eyebrow. 'Don't I even get a drink now I'm here?'

'I'll buy you a drink, Mrs Strachan.'

The offer came from Guthrie, the man with the ponderous gut. I had the impression that he'd beaten Kinross and several others to the punch.

Grace Strachan gave the big man a warm smile. 'Thank you, Sean, but I can see Michael's raring to go.'

'Sorry, darling, I thought you wanted to get back,' Strachan apologised. 'I was planning to cook mussels for dinner. But if you're not hungry . . .'

'Sounds like blackmail to me.' The smile she gave him was intimate.

He turned to me. 'If you get a chance, you should take a look at the burial cairns on the mountain. Neolithic. They're quite something.'

Grace shook her head in mock exasperation. 'I think Michael would rather have those old ruins than me, sometimes.'

'It's just an interest,' Strachan said, growing self-conscious. 'Come on, Oscar, you lazy brute. Time to go.'

He raised his hand in response to the respectful 'good night's' that accompanied them to the door. As they went out they almost bumped into Ellen coming the other way carrying a steaming dish of stew.

'Sorry, our fault,' Strachan said, putting his arm round Grace's waist.

'Not at all.' Ellen gave them both a polite smile. I thought I saw a flicker of something else on her face as she looked at the other woman, but it was gone before I could be sure. 'Evening, Mrs Strachan.'

There was a reserve there, but Grace didn't appear to notice. 'Hello, Ellen. Did you like the painting Anna did at school the other day?'

'It's on the fridge door, with the rest of the gallery.'

'She's got real promise. You should be proud of her.'

'I am.'

Strachan moved towards the door. He seemed impatient to leave.

'Well, we'll let you get on. Night.'

Ellen's face was so devoid of emotion it might have been a mask as she set the plate in front of me. She acknowledged my thanks with a perfunctory smile, and as she turned away I reflected that Brody was not the only person on Runa who wasn't overly impressed by the island's golden couple.

CHAPTER 3

A grudging daylight was only just seeping into the sky as I showered and shaved the next morning. There had been no letup in the rain overnight, and I hoped the remains were still all right beneath the cottage's crumbling roof.

I hadn't slept well, and I felt grainy and tired as I went down for breakfast. The bar doubled as the dining room, and I'd nearly finished eating by the time Fraser trudged in, looking red-eyed and hung over. After he'd returned from the cottage the evening before, he'd settled himself in the bar with the air of a man getting down to business. I'd left him there when I went to bed and he'd obviously made a night of it.

I tried not to smile as he queasily regarded the plate of fried eggs, bacon and sausage that Ellen set down in front of him.

'How long will you be?' I asked. I was keen to make a start, conscious of how short the days were up here at this time of year.

'Not long,' he muttered, hand shaking as he lifted a forkful of dripping egg.

Ellen was clearing my breakfast plate from the table. 'If you want, you can take my car. I won't be using it today.'

'Good idea,' Fraser agreed quickly, through a full mouth. 'There's things I need to do in the village anyway. Start asking round, see if anyone knows who the dead woman is.'

It hadn't been made public yet that the body was a woman's. I glanced at Ellen, and saw that the slip hadn't gone unnoticed.

She gave me a knowing look. 'If you're ready I'll get you the car keys.'

I followed her from the bar. 'Look, about what Sergeant Fraser said . . .'

'Don't worry, I won't say anything,' she said, smiling as she went into the kitchen. 'You run a hotel, you learn to keep secrets.'

The kitchen was a single-storey extension, much newer than the rest of the hotel. Heavy saucepans stood on an old gas cooker, blackened with use, while a tall pine dresser was laden with mismatched crockery. Ellen rooted in a drawer for the car keys, then led me out through a door into a small yard. Parked in the lane just beyond the wall was an old VW Beetle.

'It's not much to look at, but it's reliable enough,' she said, giving me the keys. 'And I've made a flask of tea and sandwiches for you all.'

I thanked her as I took them. The VW grated and whined when I started it, but rattled along happily enough. The weather hadn't improved since the day before, but at least the village was more alive now. There were people in the street, and children were filing through the school gate.

After leaving the village, I passed the hill where Bodach Runa, the ancient standing stone Brody had pointed out, stood watch. The island could never be described as picturesque, but it was starkly impressive: a landscape of hills and dark peat moors, dotted with sheep.

Brody's Volvo was already parked outside the cottage when I arrived. The ex-inspector and Duncan were in the camper van. A kettle was hissing away on the small cooking ring. Wedged in one corner was a paraffin heater, and the cramped cabin smelt of its fumes.

'Morning,' Brody greeted me. He was sitting on a padded bench that butted up to a fold-down table, his old dog asleep at his feet. Somehow, I wasn't surprised to find him here. 'Sergeant Fraser not with you?'

'He had things to do in the village.'

I saw disapproval register on his face, but he made no comment. 'Don't mind my coming out again, do you?' he asked, as though reading my mind. 'I spoke to Wallace this morning. He said it was your call.'

'In that case it's fine by me.'

I guessed Wallace was probably glad the former DI was prepared to stick around. If it came to that, so was I. It might have ruffled Fraser's feathers, but it didn't hurt to have someone with Brody's experience on hand.

Duncan yawned. He looked as though he hadn't slept well. But when I gave him the bacon and egg sandwich that Ellen had sent, he began unwrapping it with the enthusiasm of a child at Christmas.

'Apparently we had a visitor last night,' Brody told me. 'Maggie Cassidy was out here again, trying to get photographs through the cottage window.'

'She didn't get any,' Duncan insisted. 'Well, just a few blurred images on her mobile phone, but I made her delete them. And I made her promise she wouldn't try again.'

Brody raised an eyebrow sceptically, but said nothing.

A thick criminology textbook sat on the table in front of Duncan, a bookmark tucked into the first few pages.

'Been studying?' I asked.

He blushed. 'Not really. Just something to read, you know.'

'Duncan was just saying he wants to apply for CID,' Brody added.

'Eventually,' Duncan said quickly, still looking embarrassed. 'I've not put enough time in yet.'

I opened the flight case I'd brought with me. Inside was the basic field kit I always took with me on a job. Disposable overalls, shoes and masks, latex gloves, trowels, brushes and sieves. And lots of plastic evidence bags.

I was down to my last few pairs of disposable gloves and overalls, having used most of them on the Grampian job. I struggled into the overalls and snapped protective shoes over my boots, then pulled the latex gloves on top of a pair of silk liners.

Duncan had been watching me get ready. Now he put down his sandwich. 'Doesn't it bother you? Working with dead bodies, I mean?'

'Don't be impertinent, lad,' Brody said reprovingly.

'That's all right,' I reassured him. 'Someone needs to do it. As for the rest . . . You get used to it.'

But his words stayed with me. *Doesn't it bother you?* There was no easy answer. I was well aware of what many people would regard as the gruesome nature of my work, but it was what I did. What I was.

So what did that make me?

The question was still troubling me as I stepped out of the camper van and saw a sleek silver-grey Saab coming along the track towards the cottage. Brody and Duncan came out as it pulled up next to Ellen's VW.

'What the hell is he doing here?' Brody asked irritably, as Strachan climbed out.

'Morning,' he greeted us, as his golden retriever jumped out of the Saab.

'Get that dog back in the car!' Brody snapped.

The retriever was sniffing the air intently. He suddenly caught a scent and bounded straight for the cottage.

'Bloody hell!' Brody swore, and raced to cut it off.

He was surprisingly fast for a man his size and age. He grabbed hold of the dog's collar, almost yanking him off his feet as he pulled him back.

Strachan ran up, his face shocked. 'God, I'm sorry!'

Brody kept hold of the retriever's collar, suspending his front paws off the ground as he yelped and struggled.

'I'll take him now,' Strachan said, holding out his hand.

For a moment I thought Brody wasn't going to pass the dog over. Then he thrust the animal at Strachan. 'You shouldn't be out here.'

Strachan soothed his pet, keeping hold of his collar. 'I apologise. I didn't mean to let him out. I just wanted to see if I could do anything.'

'You can get back in your car and leave. This is police business.'

Now Strachan was growing angry. 'Funny, I thought you'd retired.'

Brody's jaw muscles bunched with the effort of restraint. 'Constable McKinney, why don't you escort this gentleman back to his car?'

Duncan was looking worried, out of his depth.

'No need. I'm going,' Strachan said. There were twin patches of colour on his cheeks. 'Morning, Dr Hunter. Sorry about this.'

'That's OK. It's just better not to have many people around,' I said.

'No, I appreciate that. But if there *is* anything I can do to help, then please let me know. Anything at all.'

Brody watched him lead the dog back to the car, his expression stern.

Duncan began to stammer an apology. 'Sorry, I wasn't sure what—'

'No need to apologise. Shouldn't have lost my temper like that.' Brody took a packet of cigarettes and a lighter from his pocket, clearly still rattled.

In the camper van, the kettle had boiled. I waited till Duncan had gone back inside to make the tea, then turned to Brody.

'You don't like Strachan much, do you?'

Brody smiled. 'That obvious, is it?'

'What have you got against him?'

He lit a cigarette and took a long drag. 'I don't approve of his sort. Privileged types who think because they've got money they can do as they like. He didn't even earn it himself; he inherited it. His family made their fortune in gold mining out in South Africa during apartheid. You think they were so keen to share it with their workers over there?'

'You can't blame him for what his family did.'

'Perhaps not. But he's too cocksure. You saw him last night turning his charm on for Karen Tait. A wife like that, and he's still got a roving eye.'

I remembered what Fraser had told me about Brody's own wife leaving him, and wondered if his dislike of Strachan was coloured with envy. 'What about what he's done for the island?'

'I was a policeman long enough to know that, whatever people do, there's always a reason. And one way or another it's usually self-interest. Strachan's made people here more comfortable, I'll grant him that. Better houses, better roads. You won't find anyone has a bad word to say about him.' He shrugged. 'I just don't believe in something for nothing. There's always a price to pay.'

THE COTTAGE DIDN'T LOOK any more prepossessing by daylight. Its roof was swaybacked and gaping in places, its windows cracked and thick with decades of grime. Behind it rose the imposing bulk of Beinn Tuiridh, now visible as a misshapen tumble of rocks smeared with dirty traces of snow.

A corridor of incident tape had been run from the front door into the room where the burnt remains lay. The ceiling looked on the verge of collapse, although as yet no rain had leaked onto the ash and bones. In the murky light they looked even more pathetic than I remembered.

Since this wasn't as yet a crime scene, there was no real reason for me to grid out the remains. That was usually done to record the position of any evidence found. But I did it anyway. The stone floor prevented me from hammering pegs into the ground, but I carried drilled wooden blocks for that purpose. I arranged them in a square round the body, placing a peg in each one, then strung a grid of nylon cord between the pegs. Using a trowel and fine brush, I began clearing away the covering layer of talc-like ash.

Gradually, what was left of the skeleton was laid bare.

Our lives, and sometimes deaths, are stories written in bone. It provides a telltale record of injuries, neglect or abuse. But in order to find what was written here, first I had to be able to see it. It was a slow, painstaking business. Working on one square of the grid at a time, I carefully removed and sifted the ash, plotting the location of bone fragments onto graph paper before sealing everything in evidence bags. Time passed without my noticing. The world narrowed down to a pile of ash and desiccated bones, so that I was startled when I heard someone clearing his throat behind me.

I looked up to see Duncan standing in the doorway. He held up a mug of steaming tea. 'Thought you could use this.'

I checked my watch and saw it was nearly three o'clock. I'd worked right through lunchtime without realising.

I stood up. 'Thanks,' I said, stripping off my gloves as I went over.

'Sergeant Fraser's called in, wanting to know how you were getting on.'

Fraser had put in a brief appearance earlier, but hadn't stayed long, claiming he needed to carry on interviewing the locals.

'Slowly,' I told Duncan, letting the hot mug warm my frozen hands.

He lingered in the doorway. 'So have you . . . found anything so far?'

'Well, it's definitely a woman, under thirty, and about five feet seven.'

He stared at the remains. 'Seriously?'

I indicated the hips, now cleaned of the covering of ash. 'If the body's female you can often tell the age from the pelvis. In a teenager the pubic bone is almost corrugated. As a woman gets older it starts to flatten out and then erode. This one's pretty flat, but without any real wear and tear. Which puts her in her late twenties, thirty at the most.' I pointed at one of the long thigh bones. 'You can use the femur to get a rough idea of height. There's a formula that gives you the exact ratio, but I won't bore you with the details. As for race, I've measured various skull features, which indicate that she was white or Asian, not black. But—'

'But there aren't many Asians in the Outer Hebrides,' Duncan finished.

'That's right. So we're probably looking at a white woman in her twenties, about five seven and big-boned. And I found metal buttons, along with what was left of a zip and bra hook in the ash. So she wasn't naked.'

Duncan nodded, understanding what that meant. The fact she'd been dressed wasn't conclusive, but if she'd been naked then the likelihood was that we'd have been looking at sexual assault. And therefore murder.

'Looks like it was definitely an accident, then, eh? She just got too close to the fire, something like that?' He sounded faintly disappointed.

'That's how it looks.'

The light coming through the dirty windowpane was already beginning to dim, and I still had a lot to do. I'd delayed long enough.

I drained my mug and handed it back to him. 'Right, I need to get on.'

Now that I'd cleared away most of the covering layer of ash, I could start to remove the surviving bones, bagging them for proper examination later. So far I'd found nothing that pointed to this being a suspicious death. No knife marks on the bone, no other sign of skeletal trauma or injury.

So why did I still feel I was missing something?

A wayward gust of wind from the holes in the roof chilled me as I stood looking down at the remains. I went to where the skull lay canted on the floor, crazed with heat fractures. The blowout had left a hole in the cranium nearly the size of a fist. Small fragments of bone lay on the floor around it, blown there when the hot gases had made their explosive exit. That was another indication that the damage had happened in the fire—if the hole had been caused by an impact the fragments would have been driven inwards, into the skull cavity.

Yet something about the skull bothered me, a sort of nagging neural itch.

I moved the floodlight, but it still wasn't bright enough for what I wanted. Taking out my torch, I shone it onto the gaping skull cavity.

Light spilled eerily from the empty eye sockets as I turned my attention to the shards of bone that lay on the floor. Most were tiny, no bigger than my thumbnail. I'd already recorded their positions on the graph paper, so I began piecing the fragments together, like a ghoulish jigsaw puzzle. Eventually, despite my cold-numbed fingers, I had completed a sizable section.

And then I saw it. The fragments had joined together to reveal a ragged spider web of cracks. Distinctive zigzag lines that could only have been caused by a heavy impact, one that was strong enough to fracture the bone without actually breaking it.

The skull had burst in the fire, all right, but in an area where it had been already weakened. Brody had been right all along. This was no accident.

The woman had been murdered.

I BARELY NOTICED the wind and rain as I went back to the camper van. It was pitch-dark outside, and the light from its window shone out like a beacon. There was a sour taste in my mouth. Someone had killed a young woman and then set fire to her body. Whether Wallace liked it or not, he hadn't any choice now but to escalate this to a full-scale murder inquiry.

And there was something else to consider. It would be a mistake to assume that, just because the dead woman wasn't local, her killer wasn't either. According to Brody, few outsiders came here at this time of year. So the likelihood was that the victim had either come over with, or to see, someone who lived here.

Which meant that her killer was still on the island.

That thought stayed with me as I hurried to the camper van. It was almost stiflingly warm after the icy cottage, the air heavy with the fumes from the paraffin heater.

'How's it going?' Duncan asked, getting to his feet.

'I need to talk to Wallace. Can I use your radio?'

'Uh, sure,' he said, surprised. He handed it across, then stepped outside.

Wallace didn't answer any of his numbers. I left messages telling him to call me and started struggling out of my overalls.

'Everything all right?' Duncan asked, coming back in.

'Fine.' He would find out soon enough, but I wanted to speak to Wallace before I told anyone else. 'I'm going back to the village. Look, keep an eye out, OK? Anything suspicious, call Fraser straight away.'

He looked puzzled and a little offended. 'Aye, of course.'

I went out to the car. It was raining heavily now, and the old VW's windows fogged as soon as I got in. I turned the heater on to clear them, then bumped down the track to the road, peering through the steamed glass.

I'd been driving for only a few minutes when a pale shape suddenly darted into the road in front of me. There was just time to see the reflective eyes of a dog gleam in the headlights as I stamped on the brake, then the car slewed crazily, flinging me against the seat belt as it lurched to a halt.

The impact took my breath away. I sat back, shaken, rubbing my chest where the seat belt had bruised it. The VW had run off the road and was angled down into a ditch, its headlights shining onto thick hummocks of grass.

At least I hadn't hit the dog. I'd seen it bounding off. It was a golden retriever, so unless there were two on Runa it must have been Strachan's.

I put the gears into reverse and tried to back up onto the road. The wheels churned and skidded, but the car didn't move. I shifted into first and tried to go forward, with the same result.

I switched off the engine and got out to take a look. The rear wheels were bogged down in muddy ruts. I got back in the car and considered my options, the rain glistening like white wires in the headlights. I guessed I was about halfway to the village, so there was no point going back to the camper van. If I stayed with the car until someone came along, I might have to wait for hours. If I walked the rest of the way, at least it would keep me warm.

I swore as I realised that I'd left my torch in my flight case back at the camper van. I turned off the headlights and waited for my eyes to adjust to the sudden dark. As I got out of the car, the moon appeared through a break in the clouds, picking out the road with a silvery illumination. My spirits rose as I started walking. *Not so bad after all.* And just as I thought that, clouds shrouded the moon again, and the light was abruptly cut off.

The utter blackness shocked me. Runa was a tiny island, miles from the mainland, with no towns or cities to cast even a distant glow, and the darkness was absolute. Only the sound of my footsteps told me I was still on the road. But provided I didn't stray from the road, there was nothing to worry about. Sooner or later it would lead me back to the village.

The rain was freezing and the wind whittled away at my body heat, making me virtually deaf as well as blind in the blackness.

But not so deaf that I didn't hear a scuff on the road behind me.

I spun round, heart thumping. *Probably just a sheep. Or Strachan's bloody dog.* Turning my back on it, I started walking again. But all my senses were attuned to what might be out there with me, and I was still straining to hear it when I suddenly stepped out into nothing.

I pitched forward, arms windmilling before the ground smacked into me. I tumbled downhill, all sense of up or down lost. Rough grass scratched at my face, and then I jolted to a stop.

Dazed and winded, I lay in the muddy grass, rain bouncing on my face. *Idiot!* I'd walked off the edge of the road into a gully. I started to push myself upright, and cried out as pain exploded in my left shoulder.

When it had subsided to a dull ache, I gingerly moved my arm again. The pain lanced back, but there was no sensation of grating bone. I hoped that meant nothing was broken. Swallowing back the bile that had risen in my throat, I felt the joint with my other hand. There was a bulge where there shouldn't have been, and as my fingers traced its outline I felt a strong wave of nausea. I'd dislocated my shoulder. Badly.

I told myself not to panic. *Deep breaths. Take it one step at a time.* Before I could use my arm again I knew the joint would have to be shot back into place. I reached round with my other hand as far as I could, probing with my fingers to feel where the ball of the humerus had popped out of its socket. I paused, gritting my teeth, then pushed back against it.

The pain almost made me black out. I yelled as starbursts wheeled across my vision. When they faded I was lying on my back once more, weak and shaking, sweat and rain mingling on my face.

I didn't bother feeling the shoulder again. It was throbbing relentlessly, and I knew it was still out of joint. I sat up weakly. My head spun as I slowly got to my feet. There was no question of walking to the village now. I would have to try to find the car and sit it out, hoping that Fraser or Duncan would come looking for me sooner rather than later.

Climbing back up the slippery bank was hard work. I could only use one hand to help drag myself up, and I had to keep resting. By the time the slope began to level out I was exhausted, and my shoulder continued to throb. But relief at having made it back to the top swamped out everything else. Then I realised something was wrong.

The road wasn't there.

My relief vanished. I took a few more cautious steps, hoping to feel tarmac under my boots. But there was only turf and uneven ground. Instead of climbing back up to the road, I'd clawed my way up another hummock.

I forced myself to stay calm. The road had to be opposite me. All I had to do was retrace my steps, then go up the other side.

I made my way down the muddy slope, slithering the last few feet on my backside. I groped around in the dark, trying to locate the slope I'd fallen down. I couldn't find it. *Come on, it has to be here.* But the terrain was a maze of hummocks and gullies. I knew I couldn't be far from the road, but I had no way of telling which way it was.

I'd started shivering, from shock as well as cold, and I knew I could sink into hypothermia if I didn't find shelter. *Come on, think! Which way?* I made my decision and started walking. Even if it was the wrong direction, the exertion would help keep me warm.

The ground was a treacherous mix of heather and grass, threatening to turn an ankle at every step. Soon the turf underfoot became wetter and more broken, and my teeth were chattering as I splashed noisily across the boggy ground. My shoulder was on fire, lancing me with white heat at every step. I'd lost track of time but I was tiring quickly, becoming careless with fatigue. A rustling noise came from off to one side, the sound of something moving through the grass. Straining to hear against the gusting of the wind, I spun towards it and went crashing down. Agony flared through my shoulder.

I must have passed out. When I came round I was lying face down, the rain pattering hypnotically on my coat. I spat the peat out of my mouth and tried to push myself up, but the effort was too much. Water had seeped inside my coat, chilling me to the bone. I collapsed back into the mud. *Of all the bloody stupid ways to die.* It was so absurd it was almost funny.

It was then, when it could have gone either way, that I saw the light.

At first I thought I was imagining it. It was only a spark of yellow, dancing in the blackness ahead. I shut my eyes, opened them. The light was still there. I felt a surge of hope as I remembered Strachan's house. That was closer than the village. Perhaps I'd wandered in the right direction after all.

How far away it was I couldn't tell. It didn't matter. It was something to aim for. Without even thinking about it, I crawled to my feet and began to stagger towards it. The yellow glow was the only thing in the universe, drawing me like a moth. It steadily grew larger. The ground started to rise up to it, becoming steeper. I was using my one good arm to help pull me uphill, sometimes sinking to a crawl on my knees. But I fixed on the light, shutting out everything else.

Then it was right in front of me. Not a house, just a small, untended fire in front of a ruined stone hut. As disappointment started to filter through, I began to take in what the firelight revealed. All around me were untidy mounds of rocks. They weren't natural formations, I realised.

They were burial cairns.

Both Brody and Strachan had mentioned them. And, remembering that, I knew I'd wandered all the way out to the mountain.

I swayed on my feet, the last of my reserves gone. As my vision swam, I became aware of movement from the mouth of the ruined hut. I stared, too exhausted to move, as a hooded figure emerged into the firelight.

Then the fire seemed to stutter, and the night spun me off into darkness.

CHAPTER 4

There was no wind. That was the first thought that came to me. No wind, no drumming of rain.

Just silence.

I opened my eyes. I was in a bed. Muted daylight filtered through pale curtains, revealing a large, white room. White walls, white ceiling, white sheets. My first thought was that it was a hospital, but then I realised most hospitals didn't run to duvets and double beds.

The bed was warm and soft and I lay there for a while, my mind running back over the last events I could remember. The cottage. Abandoning the car. Falling in the dark, then heading for the distant fire.

That was where it grew hazy. Memories of stumbling up the mountainside and finding myself at the ancient burial cairns, and of the figure that had emerged from the hut, had the surreal quality of a dream. I had disjointed images of being carried along in pitch-blackness, crying out as my shoulder was jolted.

My shoulder . . . I drew back the duvet, registering that I was naked but more concerned with the sling that strapped my left arm to my chest. I cautiously flexed the shoulder and winced as bruised ligaments protested. It hurt like hell, but I could tell it was no longer dislocated.

I looked at my wrist and saw that my watch was missing. I'd no idea what time it was, but it was daylight outside. I felt a growing sense of alarm. I'd still not told Wallace that we were dealing with a murder. I had to get back. I threw aside the duvet and was looking around for my clothes when the door opened and Grace Strachan came in.

She was even more striking than I remembered, dark hair tied back to reveal the perfect oval of her face, fitted black trousers and cream sweater revealing a figure that was slim but sensuous. When she saw me she smiled.

'Hello, Dr Hunter. I was just coming to check if you were awake.'

It was only when her eyes flicked down that I remembered that I was naked. I hurriedly covered myself with the duvet.

The dark eyes were amused. 'How are you feeling?'

'Confused. How did I get here?'

'Michael brought you back last night. He found you on the mountain. Or, rather, you found him.'

So it had been Strachan who'd rescued me. I remembered the figure emerging into the firelight. 'That was your husband I saw out there?'

She gave a smile. 'One of his little hobbies, I'm afraid.'

'What time is it?'

'Nearly half past three.'

The day was more than half gone. I cursed silently. 'Can I use your phone? I need to let people know what's happened.'

'Already done. Michael called the hotel and spoke to Sergeant Fraser. He told him you'd had an accident but that you were in one piece.'

I still needed to get hold of Wallace. And Jenny, to let her know I was all right. If she was speaking to me.

'Even so, I'd like to use the phone, if that's OK.'

'Of course. I'll let Michael know you're awake. He can bring it up.' Grace arched an eyebrow. 'I'll tell him to bring your clothes, as well.'

With that she went out. I lay in bed impatiently, chafed by the thought of the lost hours. But before long there was a rap on the door.

Michael Strachan came in, carrying my washed and pressed clothes. My wallet, watch and mobile were stacked neatly on top of them. 'Grace said you might be needing these,' he said, grinning as he set my things on the bed. He reached into his pocket for a cordless phone. 'And this, too.'

'Thanks. And thank you for what you did last night.'

'Forget it. I was glad to help. Although I must admit you scared me half to death when you suddenly appeared like that.'

'It was mutual,' I said drily. 'How did you get me back?'

He shrugged. 'I managed to prop you upright most of the way down, but for the last leg I'm afraid it was a fireman's lift.'

'You carried me?'

'Only as far as the car.' He said it dismissively, as if carrying a grown man even a short distance was nothing. 'So how's the shoulder now?'

I flexed it warily. 'Better than it was.'

'Bruce had the devil of a job popping it back. If not for him, we'd probably have had you airlifted to a hospital.'

'Bruce . . .?'

'Bruce Cameron. He's the schoolteacher, but he's also a trained nurse. Looks after the medical clinic.'

'Sounds like a useful combination.'

A look I couldn't quite read crossed his face. 'He has his moments. You'll meet him in a while yourself. Grace called him to say you were awake, so he offered to come out to see how you were. Oh, and your colleagues found Ellen's car this morning and got it back on the road. It isn't damaged, you'll be glad to hear. What happened? Swerve to miss a sheep?'

'Not a sheep, no. A golden retriever.'

Strachan's face fell. 'Oscar? Oh, you're joking! I'd taken him out with me, but he'd wandered off. I'm really sorry.'

'Don't worry about it. I'm just glad I didn't hit him. Look, don't think I'm not grateful, but . . . what the hell were you doing up there?'

He smiled, a little shamefaced. 'I camp there every now and then. When I was a kid back in South Africa, my father used to take me out on safari. You get the same sense of space and isolation on the mountain that I remember from that. I'm not religious or anything, but there's something . . . almost spiritual about it. The broch's a good place to think.'

'Broch?'

'The stone hut I was in. It's an old watchtower. I love the idea that someone would have been sitting up there by a fire two thousand years ago. And those cairns are even older. Puts things in perspective, don't you think?'

Abruptly, he grew embarrassed. 'Anyhow, so much for my dark secrets. Let me know if there's anything else you need.'

'Thanks,' I said. 'Actually, could you give me a lift back to the village?'

'Of course, whenever you're ready.' He paused. 'Is everything all right?'

'Fine. I just need to get back.'

He nodded, but didn't seem convinced. I waited until he'd gone, then grabbed the phone. Wallace's number was logged in my mobile. I retrieved it and dialled it on the land line.

'Yes, Dr Hunter?' he said, with the air of someone with better things to do. I kept it short. 'She was murdered.'

There was a beat while that registered. Then he swore. 'You're certain?'

'She'd been hit hard enough for the back of her skull to be cracked.'

'Could it have been caused by a fall? Panicking when she caught fire?'

'A fall could have caused it, but an injury like that would have killed her outright or at the very least left her unconscious. In which case the body would still be lying on its back, not face down like hers is.'

There was a pause. I could almost hear him thinking through the logistics of pulling teams away from the train crash and getting them out here.

'All right,' he said, all businesslike now, 'I'll have a support team and SOC out with you first thing tomorrow morning.'

After Wallace had tersely ended the call, I dialled Jenny's mobile. It went straight to voicemail. I left a message telling her I was sorry for not calling, that I was all right and I'd call her again later. It seemed inadequate.

Getting dressed with only one hand was harder than I thought. The sling was semi-rigid, made from Velcro, foam and plastic. By the time I'd pulled on my thick sweater I felt as though I'd had a hard workout at the gym.

I went out onto the landing. The white walls looked freshly plastered, the floor laid with new carpet. At the top of the stairs, a large picture window looked down onto a small sandy cove. It was flanked by cliffs, and steps ran down to where a sleek yacht was moored at the end of a wooden jetty. In the failing light I made out two figures standing on the jetty. One of them was pointing out into the cove, the black coat identifying him as Strachan. I guessed the other must be Bruce, the nurse-turned-schoolteacher.

Downstairs, a huge Turkish rug covered most of the hall floor. On the back wall was a large abstract oil painting, a swirl of purples and blues shot through with indigo slashes that was both striking and subtly unsettling. I noticed that the name at the bottom corner was Grace Strachan's.

Strains of Spanish guitar music were coming from a room at the far end. I went in and found myself in a bright and airy kitchen. Copper pans hung from the ceiling, while others bubbled on a black Aga. Grace was next to it, chopping vegetables. She gave me a smile over her shoulder.

'I see you managed to dress OK.'

'Eventually.'

'Michael's just taken Bruce down to the cove to show him his latest project. Bruce who mended your arm?' she said, making it a question.

'Yes, your husband told me. He did a good job.'

'He's a gem. Can I get you a drink, or something to eat?'

It was only then that I realised I hadn't eaten since the previous day.

Grace seized on my hesitation. 'How about a sandwich? Or an omelette?'

'Really, I don't—'

'An omelette it is, then.' She deftly broke three eggs into a bowl. 'Michael says you're from London,' she said, beating them briskly.

'That's right.'

'I haven't been there in ages. I keep trying to get Michael to go, but he's a terrible stick-in-the-mud. Hates being prised off the island.'

'How long have you been here?' I asked.

'Oh, four years, now? No, five. God!' She shook her head, amazed at the swiftness of time, as she put a knob of butter into a frying pan.

'Must have taken some getting used to. Living on an island, I mean.'

'Not really. You'd think we'd be bored, but we never are. Michael's always busy, and I help out in the school—art classes, mainly.'

'I saw the painting outside. Very striking.'

She gave a dismissive shrug, but looked pleased. 'Oh, it's just a hobby. But that's how we know Bruce so well, through me helping at the school. I love children, so it's great being able to work with them.'

A wistfulness briefly touched her face, and then was gone. I looked away, feeling uncomfortably as though I'd had a glimpse of something private. I'd already surmised that she and Strachan didn't have children of their own.

'I saw the yacht in the cove,' I said, hoping to steer back to safer territory. 'Nice boat.'

'She's lovely, isn't she?' Grace beamed as she tipped the eggs into the pan. 'Only a forty-two footer, but the cove isn't deep enough for anything bigger. And that size, one person can handle her on their own. Michael sometimes takes her to Stornoway, when he has to go over on business.'

'So how did the two of you meet?' I asked.

'Oh God, we've known each other practically for ever.'

'You mean, as in childhood sweethearts?'

She laughed. 'I know, it's a terrible cliché, but it's true. We grew up near Johannesburg. Michael's older than me, and when I was little I used to follow him around. Perhaps that's why I enjoy it out here. I like to be able to keep him to myself.'

I found myself envying Strachan and his marriage. It made me uncomfortably aware of how much Jenny and I had been drifting apart lately.

'Here you go,' she said, sliding the omelette onto a plate.

I sat down and started to eat. The omelette was delicious, and I'd just finished the last mouthful when the kitchen door opened, letting in a blast of wind and rain. The golden retriever shot in, dripping water, and bounded excitedly over to me. I tried to fend him off one-handed.

'No, Oscar!' Grace ordered. 'Michael, I'm sure David doesn't want muddy paw prints all over him.'

Strachan had followed the dog inside. With him was a man in an army-surplus peaked cap.

'Oscar, behave yourself. You've blotted your copybook with Dr Hunter enough as it is.' Strachan pulled the dog from me and gave me a grin. 'Glad to see you're up and about, David. This is Bruce Cameron.'

The other man had taken off his hat, revealing a shaved head of ginger stubble in the classic shape of male pattern baldness. He was short and slight, with a very prominent Adam's apple. He had been watching Grace since they'd come in. Now he looked at me with the palest eyes I'd ever seen. They were an indefinable non-colour, with the whites visible all the way round, so that he seemed to have a permanent stare.

'Thanks for taking care of my shoulder last night,' I said, offering my hand. There was no return pressure when we shook.

'I was glad to help.' The voice was a surprise, deep and booming. 'I gather you're out here to take a look at the body that's been found.'

'Don't bother asking him anything about that,' Strachan cut in easily. 'I've already had my wrist slapped once for quizzing him.'

Cameron looked as though he didn't appreciate the advice. 'How's the shoulder feeling?' he asked, but without any real interest.

'Better than it was.'

He nodded. 'You'll need to have it X-rayed when you get back to the mainland, but I don't think there's any serious ligament damage.'

He made it sound as though I'd only have myself to blame if there were.

'I've been showing Bruce where the pens are going to be for my new project. Runa's first fish farm,' Strachan said. 'Atlantic cod. Eco-friendly, and it'll create at least six jobs. More, if it takes off.' His enthusiasm was almost boyish. 'Could be a real boost for the island's economy.'

Grace had started to bone a chicken. 'I'm still not sure I'm keen on having a fish farm at the bottom of the garden.'

'I've told you, darling, there's nowhere else sheltered enough on the island. And we've got the sea at the bottom of the garden anyway. It's full of fish.'

The rap of the door knocker came from the hallway.

'I'll get it.' Strachan said.

'Perhaps it's one of your policeman friends,' Grace said to me, as voices carried from the hall.

I hoped so. But instead of Duncan or Fraser it was Maggie Cassidy, whom Strachan had in tow when he returned.

'Look who's turned up,' he said with the faintest touch of irony. 'You know Maggie, Rose Cassidy's granddaughter, don't you, Grace?'

'Of course.' Grace smiled. 'How is your grandmother?'

'Oh, muddling along, thanks. Hello, Bruce,' Maggie said, receiving a grudging nod in return. She turned to me with a grin. 'Nice to see you still in one piece, Dr Hunter. I heard about your adventure last night. You were quite the talk of the bar.'

I bet I was, I thought ruefully.

'So what brings you out here, Maggie?' Strachan asked. 'Hoping for an exclusive with Dr Hunter?'

'Actually, it was you I wanted to see. And Mrs Strachan as well, obviously,' Maggie added smoothly. She was looking at him with open-eyed candour, the picture of sincerity. 'I'd like to write a feature on you for the *Lewis Gazette*. We can talk about what you've done for the island, take a few photos of you both at home. It'll make a great spread.'

Strachan's good humour had faded. 'Sorry. I take a lousy photo.'

'Oh, come on, darling,' Grace cajoled. 'Sounds like fun.'

Maggie gave Strachan the full wattage of her smile. 'And I'll bet you take a great photograph.'

I noticed Grace's eyebrow go up at the reporter's blatant flirting. Although Maggie wasn't conventionally pretty, there was an energy about her that was undeniably attractive.

But Strachan seemed immune. 'No, I don't think so.' There was no doubting the finality in his voice. 'Was there anything else?'

Maggie did her best to hide her disappointment. 'Uh . . . no. That was all. Sorry to have bothered you.'

'It's no bother,' he said. 'In fact, could I ask a favour?'

Her face brightened. 'Sure, of course.'

'Dr Hunter needs a lift back to the hotel. It'd save me turning out again if you could take him. Is that OK, David?'

I wasn't delighted at the thought of sharing a car with a reporter who'd already played me for a fool once, but since she was going back to the village it made sense. And I was indebted enough to the Strachans already.

'If Maggie doesn't mind,' I said.

She gave him a look. 'I'd love to.'

'You must come out again before you go back,' Grace said, kissing my cheek. Up close her perfume was a dizzying musk.

As she stepped back I looked across to find Cameron staring at me with barely concealed jealousy.

Strachan showed us into the hall. When he opened the front door a blast of freezing wind and rain greeted us. Outside, a mud-spattered mountain bike was propped against the wall by the door.

'Tell me Bruce didn't ride out here in this weather?' Maggie said.

Strachan smiled. 'He says it keeps him fit.'

'Bloody masochist,' she snorted. She held out her hand to Strachan. 'Pleasure to meet you again, Michael. If you change your mind . . .'

'I won't.' He smiled to soften the rejection.

Maggie and I forged against the wind to where a rust-smeared old Mini was parked, looking like a poor relation next to Strachan's Saab and a black Porsche Cayenne I took to be Grace's.

Maggie was struggling out of her oversized red coat as I climbed into the car. 'The heater's stuck on full, so you'll cook if you keep your coat on,' she said, unceremoniously dumping hers onto the back seat.

I kept mine on. It had taken long enough for me to get it over my sling.

Maggie scowled as she tried to start the car, tugging on the old-fashioned choke. 'Come on, you heap of junk,' she grumbled as the engine coughed and whined. 'It's my gran's car, but she never uses it any more.'

The car chugged into life. She scraped into gear and set off down the drive towards the road. I stared through the window at the windswept moors.

'Well, aren't you going to say it?' she said suddenly.

'Say what?'

'That I lied on the ferry. When I told you I was a novelist.'

It took me a moment to realise what she was talking about. The pause seemed to make Maggie even more defensive.

'I'm a reporter, I was just doing my job. I don't have to apologise for it.'

'I didn't ask you to.'

She gave me an uncertain look. 'No hard feelings, then?'

I sighed. Under the brash act there was an appealing vulnerability. 'No hard feelings.'

The look of innocence I had doubted once before spread over her features. 'So, off the record, what do you think happened out at the cottage?'

I laughed despite myself. 'You don't give up, do you?'

She grinned sheepishly. 'I was only asking. It was worth a try.'

AFTER MAGGIE dropped me at the hotel, I went looking for Ellen to apologise for running her car off the road. She waved away my apologies.

'Don't worry about that. The main thing is you're all right. More or less,' she added with a smile as she looked at my sling. 'Not everyone who gets lost out on these islands is so lucky.'

I didn't feel lucky as I flopped down on my bed. I felt tired and bruised, and my shoulder throbbed like toothache. I tried to call Jenny on the hotel phone. There was still no answer from either her mobile or her flat.

I left messages on both, giving her the hotel number and asking her to call me. Feeling flat and out of sorts, I went online to check my emails. I'd just finished replying to the last one when there was a knock on the door.

It was Fraser. He eyed my sling unsympathetically.

'Made it back all right this time, eh?'

There didn't seem much I could say to that. 'Have you spoken to Wallace?' I asked.

He gave a snort. 'The likes of me don't get to speak to superintendents. But he's passed word down the line, let's put it that way.' He regarded me sourly. 'So you're saying it's murder?'

'That's how it looks. Are the remains OK?' I asked.

'Oh, aye, they're peachy,' Fraser grumbled. 'I've had the station radioing every five minutes, yelling for me to make sure the site is properly secured. You'd think we were guarding the crown jewels.'

His carping was wearing thin. 'There've been enough mistakes already.'

'Not made by me,' he retorted. 'I just follow orders. Speaking of which, Wallace wants this kept quiet until the SOC team gets here. That means Mr-ex-DI-Brody'll have to be kept in the dark along with everyone else.'

There was a mean satisfaction in his voice. I didn't think there would have been any harm in letting Brody know, but that wasn't my decision. And I supposed everyone would find out soon enough.

Fraser bad-temperedly stomped off to take Duncan's supper out to the camper van, and I went back to my laptop, hoping to distract myself with work. But my heart wasn't in it and the dresser made a poor desk.

Closing my laptop with a snap, I took it downstairs to the bar. There was no point sitting around waiting for Jenny to call.

The two old domino players sat at their customary table. '*Oidhche mhath*,' one of them said politely as I went in.

I said good evening in return, and they went back to their game. The only other person there was Sean Guthrie, the big ex-fisherman who Brody had told me was the island's odd-job man and Kinross's occasional helper on the ferry. He was slumped at the bar, staring morosely into his almost empty beer glass. He gave me a baleful glance as I chalked up a whisky on the slate, then went back to staring into his glass.

I took my drink over to the table by the fire, and opened my laptop. Positioning it so no one else could see the screen, I called up the Missing Persons files that Wallace had sent me. Though I doubted I'd find anything useful, I'd nothing better to do right then.

Trails of smoke flowed sinuously across the peat slab in the hearth. Its dark surface glowed, giving off a spiced, earthy fragrance. The heat made me drowsy. I rubbed my eyes and tried to focus my thoughts. But as I was about to open the first file, a shadow fell across the table.

I looked up to find the hulking figure of Guthrie looming over me.

''S that you got there?' he slurred. His face was slackened by alcohol. He gave off an odour of solder, oil and old sweat.

I closed the laptop. 'Just work.'

He blinked slowly, processing that. I remembered Brody telling me it was best to avoid him when he was drunk. *Too late.*

'Work?' he spat, flecking the table with spittle. He glared disdainfully at the laptop. 'That's not work. Work's what you do with these.'

He held up a balled fist in front of my face. It was the size of a baby's head, the fingers thickened with scar tissue.

'Work's getting your hands dirty. You ever get your hands dirty?'

I thought about sifting through the ashes of an incinerated body, or trying to exhume a corpse from frozen moorland. 'Sometimes.'

His lip curled. 'You don't know what work means. Like those bastards at the bank who took my boat. Never done a fucking day's work in their lives!'

'Why don't you sit down, Sean?' one of the domino players said gently.

'I'm just talking. Get back to your game,' Guthrie muttered sullenly. He glared down at me, swaying slightly. 'So what's on this, then?' he said, reaching for my laptop.

I put my own hand on top of it. My pulse had started to pound.

'Sorry, it's private,' I said. I kept hold of the laptop. Guthrie was easily strong enough to take it from me, but he hadn't quite got to that point. Even so, I could see his drink-addled mind turning over the possibility.

'I just want to take a look,' he said.

Even if I'd been fully fit I wouldn't have been any match for him. But I was past caring. I pulled the laptop from his hand. 'I said no.'

My voice was unsteady, but it was from anger more than anything else. Guthrie balled his fists, and I felt my stomach tighten, knowing there was nothing I could do or say that would head off what was about to happen.

'Hey, you big lump, you causing trouble again?'

Maggie Cassidy had appeared in the doorway, and was heading straight for Guthrie. I was alarmed at how small she looked against his bulk.

His face split in a huge grin. 'Maggie! Heard you were back!'

He enveloped her in a bear hug. She looked smaller than ever.

'Aye, well, I thought I'd better look in and see how you were doing. Come on, put me down, you great oaf.'

They were both grinning now. Guthrie had forgotten about me already. Maggie prodded his bulging stomach, shaking her head with mock regret.

'You been on a diet, Sean? You're practically wasting away.'

He roared with laughter. 'Pining for you, Mags. Will you have a drink?'

'Thought you'd never ask.'

Maggie gave me a quick wink as she led him to the bar. My hand trembled slightly as I raised the whisky glass, the adrenaline rush slowly fading.

The place was beginning to fill up now. Kinross and his eighteen-year-old son came in, joining Maggie and Guthrie at the bar. There were more friendly gibes and laughter. I watched how the cruel bumps of acne flared red on Kevin Kinross's face whenever Maggie spoke to him. He hardly took his eyes off her as she chatted to his father.

Watching them all, warmly at ease with each other, I was suddenly acutely aware that I didn't belong. These were people who had been born and raised here, who would probably die within this same closed community. They shared an identity and kinship that overrode other ties.

I didn't feel like staying downstairs any longer. But as I was about to go to my room, Maggie caught my eye and excused herself from the group at the bar. Kevin Kinross watched furtively as she came over to my table.

'You and Sean getting acquainted earlier, were you?' she said, plonking herself down.

'That's one way of putting it.'

'He's harmless enough. You must have rubbed him up the wrong way.'

I stared at her. 'How exactly did I do that?'

She counted on her fingers. 'You're a stranger, you're English, and you're sitting in the bar with a hi-tech laptop. If you wanted to blend into the woodwork you're going the wrong way about it, if you don't mind my saying.'

I gave a laugh. 'And here's me thinking I was minding my own business.'

Maggie smiled. 'Aye, well, Sean has been known to get a little tetchy when he's in his cups. But you can't altogether blame him. He used to be a good fisherman until the bank claimed back the loan on his boat. Now he's reduced to odd jobs and trying to fix up some old hulk he salvaged.' She sighed. 'Don't think too badly of him, that's all I'm saying.' She glanced at her watch. 'I'd best make myself scarce before Sergeant Fraser shows up.'

She obviously wanted me to ask. And I'd been curious anyway, ever since their exchange on the ferry.

'So what is it between you two? Not an ex-boyfriend, I take it?'

'I'll pretend I didn't hear that,' she said, grimacing. 'Let's say there's a bit of a history between us. A couple of years ago the good sergeant was suspended for assaulting a woman suspect when he was drunk. The charges were dropped, but he was lucky not to be demoted. The *Gazette* found out and ran the story.' She shrugged. 'It was my first big story for the paper. So as you can imagine, I'm not exactly top of Fraser's Christmas card list.'

Her smile was part rueful, part proud as she went to rejoin Guthrie and

Kinross. As she made her goodbyes, I left the bar and headed up to my room. I felt bone-weary. This trip had been a disaster from start to finish, but I consoled myself that it was about to get back on track. Tomorrow, SOC would be here, and the full machinery of a murder investigation would belatedly get under way. And I'd be on my way home.

But I should have known then not to take anything for granted.

THE STORM REACHED Runa just after midnight. Later, I would find out that it was two fronts that had collided off the coast of Iceland, playing out their battle as they swept down the North Atlantic from the Arctic. Their assault would be credited as one of the worst the Western Isles had experienced in over fifty years, creating gale-force winds that left a trail of roofless houses and flooded roads before battering themselves out against the mainland.

I was in my room when the storm hit. Tired as I was, I'd found it hard to sleep. Jenny hadn't called, and there was still no answer from either her flat or her mobile. That wasn't like her. I was starting to feel a gnawing anxiety. To make sleep even harder, the wind was booming outside, rattling the window angrily, and my shoulder was aching. I was considering whether I should get up and try to work when the bedside phone rang.

I snatched up the receiver. 'Hello?' I said, the word rushing out.

'It's me.'

Tension drained from me at the sound of Jenny's voice.

'Hi,' I said, switching on the bedside light. 'I've been calling you all day.'

'I know. I got your messages.' She sounded subdued. 'I went out with Suzy and a few of the others from work. I turned my mobile off.'

'Why?'

'I didn't want to speak to you.'

I waited, unsure what to say. A gust of wind wrapped itself round the house, its moan rising in pitch.

'I was worried when you didn't call last night,' Jenny said after a moment. 'I didn't even know where you were staying. When I got your message this afternoon . . . I just felt angry. So I switched off my phone and went out. But then I came in just now and I really wanted to talk to you.'

'I'm sorry, I didn't mean to—'

'I don't want you to apologise! I want you here, not out on some bloody island! And I've had too much to drink and that's your fault as well.'

I could hear a grudging smile in her voice.

'I'm glad you called,' I told her.

'So am I. But I'm still pissed off with you. I'm missing you and I've no idea when you're coming back.'

'I'm missing you too,' I said.

The silence on the line seemed hollow, broken only by static whispers. 'You're not responsible for everyone, David,' Jenny said at last. 'You can't solve everyone's problems.'

'I don't try to.'

'Don't you? Seems like you do, sometimes. Other people's anyway.' She sighed. 'I think we need to talk when you get back.'

'What about?' I said, feeling something cold brush against my heart.

A crackle of static cut out her answer. It faded, but not completely.

'. . . still hear me?' I heard her say through it.

'Only just. Jenny? You still there?'

There was no answer. I cut the connection and tried calling her back, but there was no dialling tone. The line was dead.

As though that had been its cue, the bedside lamp suddenly flickered. It steadied after a few seconds, but its light was dimmer than before.

Feeling leaden and frustrated, I put the receiver down. Outside, the wind was flinging rain in reckless bursts against the window. I made my way over to it and looked out. The street lamp outside was shaking in the wind.

A girl was standing underneath it.

She seemed frozen, as though the fluctuating power had taken her unawares. Her face tilted up when I appeared in the window, and for a second or two we stared at each other. She looked in her teens and was wearing only a thin coat over what looked like a pale nightgown. She was blinking the rain from her eyes as she stared up at me.

Then she darted into the shadows beyond the streetlight, heading into the village, and was gone.

ANY HOPE I might have had that the storm would have passed by morning was snuffed out as soon as I woke. The wind shook the window, rain beating against the panes of glass as though frustrated at not being able to break it.

The phone was still dead when I checked it. But at least the power was still on, although the fitful way the lights were flickering suggested it might not remain so for much longer.

'One of the joys of living on an island, I'm afraid,' Ellen said, when I went down for breakfast. Anna was eating a bowl of cereal at the kitchen table. 'The phones are always likely to go off when we get a real storm. Electricity too, if it's a bad one.'

'How long are they usually off for?'

'A day or two, sometimes longer.' She smiled at my expression. 'Don't worry; the hotel's got its own back-up generator. We won't starve or freeze.'

When I went into the bar, Fraser was already devouring a huge plate of fried eggs, bacon and sausage.

'Have you spoken to Duncan yet?' I asked as I sat down. I'd been worried about how the camper van was holding up in this wind.

'Aye, he's fine,' he grunted. He slid his radio across to me. 'The superintendent wants you to call him.'

I felt my spirits sink, suddenly certain it wouldn't be good news. It wasn't.

'The storm's buggered everything,' Wallace said bluntly. The radio connection was so bad it sounded as though he were calling from the other side of the world. 'We're not going to be able to get SOC out to you in this.'

Even though I'd half expected it, the news was a blow. 'How long before you can?'

'I don't know. Flights and ferries to Stornoway are cancelled until further notice, and the weather report's not good for the next few days. I daren't risk sending a helicopter in these conditions. Sorry, but for the time being you're just going to have to sit tight.'

I massaged my temples, trying to ease the nagging headache that had started. A buzz of static drowned out Wallace's next words.

'. . . decided to bring Andrew Brody in on this. I know he's retired, but he was SIO on two murder investigations. Until we can get more men out there, his experience is going to be useful. Do you understand what I'm saying?'

It was clear enough. I wouldn't have wanted Fraser left in charge either. I tried not to look across at the police sergeant as I handed him the radio.

He'd obviously already been told the news. He glowered at me as he stuffed the radio away, as if it were somehow my fault.

'Have you spoken to Brody yet?' I asked him.

Fraser stabbed his fork into a piece of bacon angrily. 'It can wait till I've finished breakfast. And taken Duncan his.'

'I'll go and tell him.'

'Please yourself,' Fraser said, slicing through his egg.

He was still eating when I finished my own breakfast. Leaving him to his sulk, I asked Ellen for directions to Brody's house and set off.

I staggered against the wind as soon as I stepped outside. There seemed an almost hysterical quality to it as it shrieked and gusted, and by the time I reached the seafront my shoulder was hurting from the constant need to brace against it. Keeping as far away as I could from the stinging spray, I made my away across the seafront. Brody lived at the other side of the harbour, in a neat bungalow that had somehow avoided the uPVC modifications of its neighbours. I wondered if his dislike of Strachan had made him refuse the chance to have it renovated along with the rest.

Brody opened the door as if expecting me. 'Come in.'

The house was small and tidy, with a bachelor's lack of ornament. A gas fire hissed in the lounge's tiled fireplace. A photograph of a woman and girl took centre place on the mantelpiece.

The border collie looked up from her basket and wagged her tail when we walked in, then settled down to sleep again.

'Cup of tea?' Brody asked.

'No, thanks. Sorry to call round like this, but the phones are out.'

'Aye, I know.'

'You were right. It was murder,' I said.

He took the news in his stride. 'You sure you should be telling me this?'

'Wallace wanted you to know.' I explained what I'd found, and what the superintendent had said.

Brody smiled. 'Bet that went down well with Fraser.' But he quickly grew serious again. 'I suppose there's a chance that the killer isn't from the island, but it's pretty remote. The victim had to have had a reason for being here, and my guess is he was it. I think for the moment we've got to assume the killer's local, and that the victim knew him.'

I'd already reached the same conclusion myself. 'I still don't understand why he burned the body and left it at the cottage instead of burying it or getting rid of it at sea,' I said.

'Laziness or arrogance, perhaps. Or nerves. It takes a lot of guts to go back to a crime scene.' Brody shook his head in frustration. 'I do wish Wallace had sent a full team out here when he had the chance. We might have had an ID on the victim by now. Finding out who killed her would be a lot easier if we knew who she was.'

'Isn't there anything we can do?'

He sighed. 'Just wait for the storm to lift, and hope we can keep a lid on this until then. The last thing we want is people finding out this is a murder inquiry before the mainland boys get here. The killer still thinks it's being written off as an accidental death. If he finds out otherwise, all bets are off.'

'You think he might be dangerous?'

Brody looked grim. 'Let's just say that people are unpredictable when they're cornered.' He absently patted the pockets of his cardigan.

'They're on the mantelpiece,' I told him.

He gave a shamefaced smile as he picked up the packet of cigarettes. 'I try not to smoke in the house. My wife used to hate it.'

'Is that her and your daughter?' I asked, indicating the photograph.

He looked at it, turning a cigarette in his fingers. 'Aye, that's Ginny and Rebecca. Becky would be . . . oh, about ten there. Me and her mother split up a year or so later. She ended up marrying an insurance broker.'

'What about your daughter?' I asked.

Brody didn't say anything for a moment. 'She's dead.'

The words were like a punch in the stomach.

'I'm sorry. I didn't know,' I said awkwardly.

'No reason why you should. I don't have any proof myself. But I know she is. I can feel it.'

'What happened?' I asked.

He looked down at the cigarette in his hand, then put it back in the packet. 'We didn't get on. Becky always was rebellious. Headstrong. Like me, I suppose. I lost touch with her after her mother died. When I took early retirement I started searching for her. Not that it did any good. I used to be a policeman. I know how easy it is for someone to disappear. And there comes a point when you know they aren't going to be found. Not alive, at least.'

'I'm sorry.'

'It happens.' Any emotion he felt was blanked from his face.

'Look, this might sound a bit . . . strange,' I began. 'But last night I saw a girl outside my hotel room. Must have been after midnight. Early or mid-teens, soaking wet, and just wearing a thin coat.'

Brody smiled. 'That'd be Mary Tait, Karen's daughter. You know, the loud-mouthed woman from the bar? I think I mentioned her girl's a bit . . . Well, in the old days we'd say "retarded". Her mother lets her run wild. You see her out all times of the day and night, wandering all over the island.'

'And nobody says anything?'

'She's harmless enough.'

'That wasn't what I meant.'

'Oh, I don't think anyone on Runa would hurt her.'

I thought about the body at the cottage. 'Are you sure about that?'

Brody inclined his head. 'Fair point. Perhaps I'd better—'

He broke off as there was a knock on the door. The old border collie pricked up its ears and gave a low growl.

'Shush, Bess,' he said, going to answer it.

There were voices. A moment later Brody returned. With him was Fraser, looking wet and unhappy. The sergeant shook water off his arms.

'We've got a problem.'

DUNCAN WAS WAITING anxiously outside the camper van when we arrived. He hurried over to the car as we climbed out. The wind threatened to snatch the car door from my hand when I opened it.

'I radioed as soon as it happened,' he said, having to almost shout to make himself heard. 'I heard it go about half an hour ago.'

By that time we could see for ourselves. The gale had ripped a section of the cottage roof clean off. What was left was hanging precariously, creaking and shifting as the wind tried to finish the job. If the woman's remains were still intact inside, they wouldn't be for much longer.

'I'm sorry,' Duncan shouted, as though he'd let us down.

'Not your fault, son,' Brody told him, giving his shoulder a pat.

We headed for the cottage. The door lay on the floor of what had been the kitchen. Shattered roof tiles were scattered everywhere, and rain fell freely through a gaping hole. We all ducked as another tile was ripped away.

Brody looked at the mess inside the cottage. Rain ran unheeded down his face as he turned to me. 'We don't have any choice, do we?'

'No,' I said.

He strode forward and began tearing the incident tape from the doorway.

'What the hell are you doing?' Fraser demanded.

'Getting the remains out before the roof comes down.'

'This is a crime scene!' Fraser protested. 'You can't do that without clearance! I'm not taking responsibility for this!'

'Nobody asked you to,' Brody said, striding through the doorway.

I went after him, picking my way across the broken tiles that littered the kitchen floor. In the room where the remains lay, almost half of the roof had fallen in. Rain had turned the ashes on the floor to a puddle of slurry. The evidence bags of ash and bones I'd collected were sitting in pools of water.

'Let's get the bags out of here,' I told Brody. 'I'll need my flight case from the camper van.'

There was no sign of Fraser.

'I'll get it,' Duncan offered from the doorway.

As he and Brody took the evidence bags out to the camper van, I turned my attention to the remains that were about to be sluiced away by the elements. At least the photographs I'd taken when I'd first arrived would provide a visual record. It wasn't much, but it was better than nothing.

When Duncan returned with my flight case I wrestled a pair of overalls on over my sling, then pulled on a surgical glove and hurried over to the body. I quickly put the skull and jawbone into evidence bags and began collecting up the fragments of cranium and loose teeth from the floor.

I'd only just finished when the roof gave a groan. A tile fell to shatter on the floor only a few feet from me.

All at once the wind seemed to still. A sudden quiet descended, broken only by the cascade of rain onto the floor.

'Sounds like it's easing,' Duncan said hopefully.

But Brody had his head cocked to listen. There was a distant rushing sound, like a train roaring towards us.

'No. It's changed direction,' he said, and then the wind slammed into the cottage again.

I was sprayed with ash and black slurry as it seemed to descend right into the room. Above us, the roof responded with a groan of protesting timbers, sending tiles tumbling to the floor.

'Let's go!' Brody shouted above the din, shoving Duncan to the door.

'Not yet!' I yelled. I still hadn't bagged the surviving hand or feet, and we needed those for fingerprint and soft-tissue analysis. But before I could do anything there was a loud bang as the roof began to rip free.

'Move!' Brody shouted. I grabbed the hand as he pulled me to my feet.

'The flight case!' I yelled.

Brody snatched it up without stopping. Debris rained down around us as we ran back through the kitchen. From behind there was an almighty crash. Then we were outside and in the clear.

Breathless, we turned and looked back. The whole of the cottage roof had gone. Part of it had been torn clean off, while the rest had fallen in, bringing down most of one wall as well. The room where we'd been standing only seconds before was now buried under rubble.

Along with the rest of the dead woman's remains.

Fraser and Duncan were standing nearby, their faces shocked.

'Jesus Christ,' breathed Fraser, staring at me.

I looked down at myself. My white overalls were splashed and covered with wet ash. But it wasn't the ash he'd been staring at.

Still clutched in my fist, like part of a showroom dummy, was the dead woman's hand.

CHAPTER 5

We decided to take the evidence bags back to the village. The woman's hand needed to be kept at a low temperature to preserve the decaying tissue. And the camper van didn't have a fridge.

It was Duncan who thought of the medical clinic. We would have to clear it with Bruce Cameron, but it was the obvious place to take the remains.

Fraser was still grumbling. 'I didn't say you could do this,' he reminded us, as we loaded the evidence bags into the Range Rover. 'This was your call.'

'You'd rather we'd left them in there then, would you?' Brody asked, jerking his head towards the roofless cottage. 'Explain to SOC that we'd stood by and watched the body be buried under the rubble?'

'I'm just letting you know I'm not taking the blame for it. You can tell Wallace yourself.'

'Oh, don't worry. I will.' Brody spoke mildly enough, yet somehow managed to make his contempt plain. 'And seeing how you're washing your hands of it, you might as well relieve Duncan out here. He can clean himself up at my place after he's helped take the bags to the clinic.'

'Stay out here?' Fraser exclaimed. 'What for? There's nothing left!'

Brody shrugged. 'It's still a crime scene. It shouldn't be left unattended.'

The expression on Fraser's face was poisonous as he stalked off to the camper van. Brody gave the worried-looking Duncan a smile.

'Come on, son. You could do with a shower, if you don't mind my saying.'

I went in the Range Rover with Duncan, while Brody followed in his own car. It was a relief to get out of the wind and rain. I put my head back and closed my eyes, and the next thing I knew Duncan was waking me.

'Dr Hunter? Should I stop for her?'

I sat up, blinking. Ahead of us the Porsche Cayenne I'd seen at Strachan's house was pulled to the side of the road. Flagging us down from beside it, unmistakable in her white parka, was Grace.

'Yes, you'd better,' I told Duncan.

We pulled up alongside and I wound down my window.

'David, thank heavens!' she said, giving me a beaming smile. 'The bloody car's run out of petrol. Would you mind giving me a lift to the village?'

I hesitated, thinking about the evidence bags visible behind the rear seat.

'If it's a problem, I'll walk,' Grace said, her smile fading.

'It's no problem,' I said, and turned to Duncan. 'Is that OK by you?'

'Aye, great,' he said, grinning. It was the first time he'd seen Strachan's wife. 'I mean, sure, no problem.'

I went to sit in the back, letting Grace have the front seat despite her protests. The delicate musk of her perfume filled the car, and I tried not to smile when I saw that Duncan was sitting noticeably straighter.

Grace turned to talk to me as Duncan tried to concentrate on driving.

'Thanks for stopping. I feel so stupid, running out of petrol. There's no garage on the island, so we have to top up from containers. But I'm sure Michael said he'd filled up the cars last week.' She puzzled over it for a second. 'Oh, well. Teach me to check the gauge in future, I suppose.'

'Where would you like us to drop you?' I asked.

'At the school, if that's OK. I'm taking a painting class this morning.'

'Will Bruce Cameron be there?'

'I should think so. Why?'

Without going into details, I explained what had happened at the cottage, and why we needed to use the clinic.

'God, how grim,' Grace said. 'Still, I'm sure Bruce won't mind.'

When we reached the school Grace hurried inside, while I left Duncan guarding the remains and went to tell Brody what was happening.

'This should be interesting,' he said, climbing out of the car.

We went up the path to the school. It was a new building, small and flat-roofed. The door opened straight into a classroom. Computer monitors lined one wall, and desks were arranged in neat lines facing a board at the front.

The pupils were all gathered round a large table at the back, busying themselves with pots of paint, brushes and water. There were about a dozen in all, their ages ranging from between four to nine or ten.

Grace was already busy organising her class. 'I hope we're not going to have another water-spilling crisis this week, are we, Adam?'

'No, Mrs Strachan,' a young boy with a shock of ginger hair said.

'Good. Because if anyone misbehaves, they'll have to have their face painted and we wouldn't want to have to explain that to your parents.'

There were delighted giggles.

Grace looked animated and alive. Cheeks flushed, she turned to us with a smile, motioning with her head to a door at the far side.

'Go on through. I've told Bruce you wanted a word.'

The office door was closed, and when I knocked on it Cameron's bass voice peremptorily drawled a command. 'Come.'

I opened the door and we went in. Cameron was standing with his back to us, staring out of the window. He turned and gave us an unfriendly look. 'Yes?'

I reminded myself this would be easier if we had his cooperation. 'We need to use the medical clinic. The storm brought down the cottage roof, and we need somewhere to store the remains we salvaged.'

The bulbous eyes considered us coldly. 'You mean you want to keep human remains in there?'

'Only until they can be taken to the mainland.'

'And in the meantime, what about my patients?'

Brody spoke up. 'Come on, Bruce. Your next clinic isn't for another two days. We should be out of the way long before then.'

Cameron wasn't appeased. 'What if there's an emergency?'

'This *is* an emergency,' Brody snapped. 'We're not here from choice.'

The teacher's Adam's apple bobbed angrily. 'It's a medical clinic, not a morgue. And I don't think you have any right to commandeer it!'

As I opened my mouth to object, Grace's voice came from behind us. 'Is there a problem?' She stood in the doorway, an eyebrow cocked quizzically.

'I was just telling them—'

'Yes, I heard you, Bruce. So did the rest of the class.'

Cameron blushed. 'I'm sorry. But I don't really think the medical clinic should be used for something like this.'

'Why ever not?'

'Well . . .' Cameron gave her an ingratiating smile. 'I am the nurse after all, Grace. I ought to be able to decide what happens in my own clinic.'

'Actually, Bruce, it belongs to the island,' she said coolly, 'and unless you can suggest somewhere else they can use, I don't see there's an alternative.'

Cameron made an effort to hold on to his tattered dignity. 'Well . . . in that case, I suppose . . .'

'Good. That's settled, then.' Grace gave him a smile. 'Now why don't you go and show them where everything is? I'll look after things here.'

White-faced, Cameron stared down at his desk as she went back to her class. Grace might help him out at the school, but he'd just had a public reminder that it was her husband's money that paid his wages. Wordlessly, he snatched his coat down from where it was hanging and walked out.

'I'd have paid to see that,' Brody said in a low voice as we went after him.

The medical clinic was a short distance from the school. It was little more than a small extension tacked onto one end of the community centre, with no external door of its own. Cameron had ridden there on his mountain bike, forging against the wind. By the time we arrived he was already inside the community centre. Leaving Duncan in the car with the evidence bags, Brody and I followed Cameron into a large hall. Posters advertising dances and the now-past Christmas pantomime were pinned to the walls.

Cameron had stopped by a new-looking door and was searching irritably through a jangling keyring. While we waited, I went to a scuffed upright piano that stood nearby. When I pressed a key, a deep, broken note rang out.

'Would you mind not doing that?' Cameron said waspishly, unlocking the door and going into the clinic. It was small, with pristine white walls, a well-stocked medicine cabinet, a fridge, and shiny steel cabinets.

Cameron had gone to a desk and was making a point of checking that its drawers were locked. Then, with ill-concealed dislike, he said, 'I expect you to leave everything exactly as you found it.'

Without waiting for us to answer he started to leave.

'We'll need the key,' Brody said.

Tightlipped, Cameron unhooked one and slapped it down on the desk.

'What about one for the community centre?' I asked.

'We don't keep it locked,' he responded primly. 'And if there is a key I've no idea where it is.'

Brody watched him go out. 'That man is a royal pain in the arse.'

I'd been thinking along much the same lines myself. 'Come on, let's get the evidence bags inside,' I said.

I HAD AN UNPLEASANT conversation with Wallace while Brody and Duncan carried the evidence bags into the clinic. Word had reached the detective superintendent that we'd been trying to contact him. Unfortunately, he'd called Fraser, and the sergeant had lost no time in giving his version of events. Consequently, Wallace was incandescent, demanding to know why we'd violated a crime scene without his permission. I angrily pointed out that none of this would have happened if he'd sent SOC in the first place.

It was Brody who calmed things down, taking the radio to talk to Wallace out of earshot. When he handed it back to me, the superintendent was grudgingly apologetic. He told me to go ahead and examine the remains.

When I returned to the clinic, Duncan was gingerly putting the dead woman's hand into the fridge, holding it at arm's length.

'Still can't get my head round how this happened,' he said, closing the fridge door with relief. 'Just doesn't seem natural.'

'Oh, it was natural, right enough,' I said. I'd known almost from the moment I'd set eyes on the remains. 'Have either of you heard of something called the "wick effect"?'

Both Duncan and Brody looked blank.

'There are two ways to reduce a human body to ash. You either incinerate it at a very high temperature, which didn't happen here or the entire cottage would have burned down. Or you burn it at a lower temperature, for longer, so the fire's intense enough to consume the body, but not ignite anything else. We've all got a layer of fat just under the skin, and fat burns. In certain conditions, the human body effectively becomes a giant candle.'

'You're joking,' Brody said. For once the ex-policeman seemed rattled.

'No. The fat liquefies in the heat, and the victim's clothes soak it up and act as a wick, especially if they're made from flammable fabric. The melted fat also gets carried in the smoke. Judging from how much fat was on the ceiling at the cottage, the dead woman had quite a lot.'

'So she was overweight?' Duncan asked.

'I'd say so, yes.'

Duncan pondered that. 'Aye, but why didn't all the body burn up?'

I held out my hand, pulling back my sleeve to expose my wrist. 'Hands and feet are mainly skin and bone. There's hardly any fat on them. And they're generally not covered by fabric so there's nothing to act as a wick. The feet and sometimes the shins are often far enough from the fire to survive, like they were here. She was lying on one hand, so it got burnt along with the rest. But the other hand was flung out, so it survived.'

Brody rubbed his chin thoughtfully. 'You think this "wick effect" was intentional? That somebody did it deliberately?'

'I doubt it. It's not something you can easily stage. No, I think whoever did this probably used a small amount of petrol or some other accelerant to start the fire, then dropped a match onto the body and got out.'

The furrows on Brody's forehead had deepened. 'Why didn't the killer torch the entire cottage?'

'No idea. Perhaps he hoped it would look more like an accident this way.'

They were silent as they considered that. Finally Duncan spoke.

'Was she dead?'

I'd spent time wondering about that myself. The blow that had cracked her skull would at the very least have left her unconscious. But dead?

'I don't know,' I said.

THE WALLS OF THE CLINIC shook under the gale's onslaught. Somehow the sound seemed only to heighten the silence after Brody and Duncan had gone. I pulled on one of my last remaining pairs of surgical gloves.

There wasn't much I could do without proper facilities, but now that Wallace had given me permission to examine the remains we'd salvaged there was one thing I wanted to try.

Brody had put his finger on it when he'd said the inquiry was hamstrung until the victim had been identified. I hoped I might be able to do something about that. And with luck, the teeth provided the key.

I took the skull and the lower jawbone from their evidence bags and gently laid them side by side on a stainless-steel trolley.

For a forensic anthropologist, teeth are a repository of information. They form a record of an individual's life, revealing age, diet, habits and class.

Not that I was overly optimistic. While a few back molars remained stubbornly in place in the jawbones, most of the teeth had fallen out when the fire had burnt away the gums and desiccated their roots. The ones I'd snatched up before the cottage roof collapsed were grey and cracked.

Even with my arm in the sling, I could still use my left hand to hold or support things. I spread a sheet of paper on the table and began arranging the teeth in two parallel rows in the order they would have been in the jaws.

Everything outside the clinic ceased to exist as I worked, the world shrinking down to the circle of light from the halogen lamp. Under normal circumstances I would have taken X-rays of the teeth and jaws so that they could be compared with dental records of potential victims. That wasn't an option now. So I began to fit the teeth back into the empty sockets.

It was slow work, and I had lost track of how much time had passed when the lamp began flickering. I straightened, groaning as my back muscles protested. The wall clock told me it was almost five o'clock. It had grown dark outside, I saw. Massaging my back, I looked at the skull and jawbone as they lay on the steel table. After a few false starts, I'd fitted most of the teeth back into them. I was reaching out to turn off the lamp when I heard a noise from the community centre.

The creak of a floorboard.

'Hello?' I called.

My voice echoed in the cold air. I waited but there was no answer. I went to the door but I didn't open it.

Suddenly, I felt certain someone was on the other side.

The door had a round window set in it, like a porthole. There was a blind on my side, but I'd hadn't bothered to lower it. Anyone in the dark hall would be able to see into the clinic, but on my side the window was a black circle of glass. I felt the hair on the back of my neck prickle.

There was a heavy glass paperweight on the desk. I picked it up, and stooped down to grab the door handle with my strapped hand. *Ready* . . .

I threw open the door and pawed for the light switch. I couldn't find it, but then there was a *click* and the lights came on.

The empty hall mocked me. The doors to the hall, and the entrance porch beyond it, were still closed. The noise must have been the building creaking in the wind. *You're turning into a nervous wreck.* I was about to go back into the clinic when I looked down at the floor.

Tracking across it was a trail of wet footprints.

'YOU'RE SURE you didn't make them?'

Brody was considering the slowly drying puddles on the worn floorboards. The water had run too much to gauge what size shoe or boot had made them, but their path across the hall floor was clear enough.

'Certain. I hadn't been outside since I got here,' I told him.

Brody and Duncan had arrived while I'd still been debating what to do about the tracks, the young PC looking fresh-faced after a shave and shower. Now Brody followed the trail to where it had pooled at the clinic door.

'Somebody got a good look at what you were doing,' he said.

'Cameron, perhaps? Or Maggie Cassidy?'

'It's possible, but I can't see it.'

'You think it was the killer?'

Brody nodded slowly. 'It's something we have to consider. I'll feel happier if we could lock the community centre tonight anyway. The general store probably sells padlocks.' He nodded towards where the skull was lying on the steel table. 'Intruders aside, how have you been getting on?'

'I've been trying to find some clue as to who she is.' I went over to where the cranium lay on the trolley. 'The condition of her teeth is interesting. She obviously hadn't been to a dentist for years, which suggests she was from a poor social background. And some of her teeth were almost eroded down to the gum. In someone this young, that's a strong sign of heavy drug use.'

'You think she was an addict?' Brody asked.

'I'd say so.'

Duncan looked up at me. 'I thought most addicts were skinny. Didn't you say this wick effect meant she was overweight?'

It was an astute comment. 'A lot depends on metabolism and how heavily she was using. It doesn't mean she didn't have a drug habit. But do you remember why I said her feet hadn't burned?'

'Not enough flesh on them?' Duncan offered.

'And no fabric to act as a wick. She had on training shoes, but no stockings or tights. I'd guess she was wearing something like a skirt and jacket. Probably cheap, flammable fabric that would make a good wick.' I looked at the remains of the skull, suddenly saddened by the brutal way we were dissecting a life. 'So,' I went on, 'we've got a young woman who was a serious drug user, who'd let her teeth rot, and who was skimpily dressed and barelegged in February. What does that suggest about her lifestyle?'

'She was a prostitute,' Duncan said, this time with more conviction.

Brody rubbed his chin. 'If she came out here to see a client, it'd explain why no one seems to have known she was on the island. Men who pay for sex don't usually advertise the fact.'

'But why risk bringing a prostitute out to Runa if you were worried about people finding out?' I asked. 'It would make more sense to go to her.'

Brody looked thoughtful. 'There's another possibility. She wouldn't be the first prostitute to blackmail a client. Given her drug habit, she might have thought it was worth the trip if there was money to be made out of it.'

It was a plausible theory, but I was too tired to try and make sense of it any more. 'We don't really know enough to speculate at this stage.'

'Aye, you're right,' Brody agreed. 'But I'll lay odds that when we find out who she came out here to see—and why—we'll have found her killer.'

Looking at the wet footprints drying on the floor, I wondered if the killer hadn't already found us.

BRODY VOLUNTEERED to stay at the clinic while I went back to the hotel for something to eat, and to buy a padlock and chain from the village store. The rain had stopped but the wind still rocked the car as Duncan drove through the village. Brody had told me the phones were still off, so I'd borrowed Duncan's radio to try to call Jenny. Digital or not, the signal was still patchy, and when I finally got through I reached her voicemail yet again.

A light was still burning inside the store when Duncan dropped me off. I told him I'd walk back to the hotel, and he went off to relieve Fraser.

'With you in a second,' came a woman's voice when the tinkling of bells announced my entry. Behind the worn wooden counter a woman was bending over to unpack tins of soup from a box. As she straightened I recognised Karen Tait. Without the flush of alcohol she looked more worn down than ever, with only a ghost of a lost prettiness remaining· in her puffy features. Her smile faded when she saw who her customer was.

'Do you have any padlocks?' I asked.

She jerked her chin towards a shelf on the back wall, where there was a selection of ironmongery stacked haphazardly in boxes.

I felt her hostile gaze on me as I sifted through the boxes. But I found what I was looking for: a heavy-duty padlock, and a spool of chain.

'I'll take a metre of this, too, please.'

'The cutters are there as well.'

I wasn't sure I'd be able to cut the chain one-handed, but I wasn't going to give her the satisfaction of asking for help. I found the bolt-cutters, measured out the chain, then cut it by bracing one handle of the cutters on my thigh. I took the length of chain and the padlock over to the counter.

'I'll take this as well,' I said, selecting a bar of chocolate from the display.

She rang the items into the till in silence. I paid, picked up my buys and went out, resisted the temptation to slam the door behind me.

The walk back to the hotel did me good. The air was cold and fresh, and by the time I made my way up the side street towards the hotel my temper had subsided. Light shone welcomingly from its windows, and the smell of fresh bread greeted me when I stepped inside. The bar was untended, but there were low voices coming from the kitchen. Ellen's and a man's.

I knocked on the door and the voices stopped.

'Just a minute,' Ellen called. After a few moments she opened the door. The yeasty scent of warm bread enveloped me. 'Sorry. Just getting the loaves out of the oven.'

She was alone in the kitchen. Whoever she'd been talking to must have left through the back door. Ellen busied herself turning out the bread from the tins, but not before I'd seen that she'd been crying.

'Is everything all right?' I asked.

'Fine.' But she kept her back to me as she spoke.

I hesitated, then held up the chocolate bar. 'I brought this along for Anna.'

She smiled, sniffing away the last of her tears. 'That's very good of you.'

'Look, are you . . .?'

'I'm fine. Really.' She gave me another smile, stronger this time.

I came away. I didn't know her well enough to do anything else. Although I couldn't help but wonder who Ellen's secret visitor had been.

Or what he'd done to make her cry.

I FELT BETTER after a hot shower and a change of clothes, although my shoulder still hurt. I went downstairs to get something to eat.

I pushed open the door to the bar. The weather seemed to have thinned out some of the customers. Guthrie and Karen Tait were nowhere to be seen, I was relieved to see, and only one of the domino players had turned up. He sat forlornly at their table, the box of dominoes waiting in front of him.

But Kinross was there, staring silently into his pint while his son hunched self-consciously on a bar stool next to him. Fraser was there too, sitting at a table by himself as he attacked a plate piled with sausages and mashed vegetables. He obviously hadn't wasted any time in getting back once Duncan had relieved him at the camper van. A glass of whisky stood next to his plate, announcing that he considered himself off duty.

'Christ, I'm starving,' he said, shovelling up a forkful of potato as I sat down at his table. 'First I've had to eat all day. No joke being out in that camper van this bloody weather, I can tell you.'

He hadn't seemed so bothered when it had been Duncan out there, I thought wryly.

'Did Duncan tell you we had an intruder?' I said, keeping my voice down.

'Aye.' He waved his fork dismissively. 'Bloody kids, probably. Duncan says you think the dead woman was a whore from Stornoway. That right?'

I glanced around to make sure no one could hear. 'I don't know where she's from. But I think she was probably a prostitute, yes.'

'And a junkie, by the sound of it.' He washed down his food with a gulp of whisky. 'You ask me, she'll have come out here to service the contractors, and one of them got too rough. No great mystery about it.'

'There weren't any contractors out here four or five weeks ago when she was killed,' I reminded him.

He wagged his knife at me. 'You mark my words, whoever killed her'll be back on either Lewis or the mainland by now.'

I wasn't going to argue. He'd made up his mind, and nothing inconvenient like the facts would change it. I was considering asking Ellen for some sandwiches to take to my room when the peat slab in the hearth flared from a sudden blast of cold air. A moment later Guthrie stamped into the bar.

I knew something was wrong. He glared at Fraser and me before going to whisper to Kinross. The ferry captain's expression darkened. As his son watched apprehensively, he and Guthrie came over to our table.

Fraser looked up from his food irritably. 'Aye?' he snapped, still chewing.

Kinross regarded him in much the same way he might have looked at something unsavoury caught in a net. 'What do you need a padlock for?'

I kicked myself for not anticipating this.

Fraser frowned. 'Padlock? What the hell are you talking about?'

'I bought one earlier,' I told him. 'For the community centre.'

For a moment he looked aggrieved at not being told sooner, but the lure of food overcame it. He gestured towards me as he went back to his meal. 'There you go. So now you know.'

Guthrie folded his beefy arms on the shelf of his stomach. 'And who says you can shut us out of our own fucking community centre?'

Fraser lowered his knife and fork and glowered at him. 'I do. We had an intruder in there earlier, so now we're locking it. Any objection?'

Guthrie lowered his arms threateningly. 'Aye, you're dead right we do.'

'So write a letter of complaint,' Fraser retorted. 'The centre's being used on police business. Which means its off limits until we say so.'

Kinross's eyes glittered. 'That's *our* community centre, not yours. And if you think you can come here and lock us out of our own buildings—'

I broke in before things got out of hand. 'Nobody wants to lock anyone out, but it won't be for long. And we did check with Grace Strachan first.'

Grace's name had the effect I'd hoped. Kinross and Guthrie glanced at each other, uncertainty replacing belligerence.

Kinross rubbed his neck. 'Well, if Mrs Strachan said it was OK . . .'

Thank God for that. But my relief was premature. Perhaps it was the whisky, or perhaps he felt his authority had been undermined enough by Brody, but for whatever reason Fraser decided to have the last word.

'You can consider this a warning,' he growled, levelling a fat finger at Kinross. 'This is a murder inquiry now, and if you try to interfere again then believe me, you'll wish you'd stayed on your bloody ferry!'

The entire bar had fallen quiet. Everyone in the room was staring at us. I tried to keep the dismay off my face. *You bloody idiot!*

Kinross looked startled. 'A murder inquiry? Since when?'

Belatedly, Fraser realised what he'd done. 'That's none of your business,' he blustered. 'Now, if you don't mind, I'd like to finish my supper.' He bent over his plate again, but couldn't stop the flush climbing up the back of his neck.

Kinross looked down at him, biting his lip in thought. He jerked his head at Guthrie. 'Come on, Sean.'

They moved back to the bar. I stared at Fraser, but he busied himself with his food and refused to meet my eye. Finally, he gave me a sullen glare.

'What? They'll know soon enough when SOC get out here.'

I was too angry to say anything. It was the one thing we'd hoped to keep quiet. I stood up, not wanting to stay in his company any longer.

'I'd better go and relieve Brody,' I said, and went to ask Ellen to make me some sandwiches.

BRODY WAS STILL SITTING in the hall where I'd left him, guarding the door to the clinic. He sat forward when I went in, but relaxed when he saw it was me.

'You've not been long,' he said, getting to his feet and stretching.

'I thought I'd eat down here.'

I'd brought my laptop with me from the hotel. I set it down and took the padlock and chain from my coat pocket. I handed him the spare key.

'Here. You might as well have this.'

He gave me a questioning look. 'Shouldn't you give it to Fraser?'

'Not after what he's just done.'

Brody's mouth tightened as I described what had just happened in the hotel bar. 'Bloody fool. That's just what we didn't need.' He thought for a moment. 'Look, do you want me to stick around for a while?'

'I'll be fine. You might as well go and get something to eat.'

When he'd gone, I wrapped the chain through the handles of the community centre's double doors, then slid the hasp of the padlock through the links and snapped it shut.

Satisfied that the hall was as secure as I could make it, I sat and ate the sandwiches Ellen had made. She'd also given me a Thermos of black coffee, and when I'd eaten I sipped at the scalding liquid, listening to the wind booming outside. The overhead light dimmed and buzzed indecisively before brightening to life once more. *Time to make a start.*

The skull and jawbone were as I'd left them. Once the laptop had booted up, I opened the missing persons files that Wallace had sent. There were five in all: young women between eighteen and thirty who'd disappeared from the Western Isles or west coast of Scotland in the last few months. Each file contained a detailed physical description and a photograph of a missing woman.

From a quick glance at the descriptions, one was black, while another was too short to be the young woman in the cottage. The other three, though, all matched the physical profile of the dead woman.

My laptop had a sophisticated digital imaging program, and I used it to zoom in on the mouth of the first image. When it was as large and sharp as I could make it, I began to compare it to those I'd taken of the skeletal grin.

Unlike fingerprints, which need a minimum number of matching features, a single tooth can be enough to provide a positive ID. Sometimes a distinctive shape, a certain break, is all it takes to reveal an entire identity.

The teeth I'd replaced in the skull were crooked and chipped. If none of the women in the photographs showed similar dental flaws, then it would at least rule them out as possible candidates. I knew it wasn't going to be easy, though. Even magnified and cleaned up, the photographs were only snapshots, hardly intended for the grim purpose I had in mind.

After a couple of hours poring over them, I felt as though I'd had sand rubbed into my eyes. I poured myself another coffee, massaged the kinks from my neck, then wearily went back to the original images. One in particular drew me, though I couldn't have said why. The young woman was standing in front of a shop window. Her face was attractive but hard, with a wariness around the eyes and mouth, even though she was smiling.

I studied her photograph more closely. Only the incisors and the upper canines were revealed by her smile. They were every bit as crooked as those I'd replaced in the skull, but none of their characteristics matched. The dead woman's upper left incisor had a distinctive V-shaped chip in it; the one on my laptop was unmarked. But there was still something about the picture I couldn't put my finger on.

And then I saw it. 'Oh, you've got to be joking,' I said out loud.

I clicked on a simple command. The young woman on my screen vanished and then reappeared, subtly altered. Behind her, the words on the shop sign could now be made out: STORNOWAY STORE & NEWSAG. I could read them now they were no longer back to front.

I'd been looking at a mirror image. At some point, probably when it had been scanned from the negative, the picture had been inverted.

With growing excitement, I magnified the teeth of the young woman in the photograph again. Now her upper left incisor had a V-shaped notch that exactly matched the chip in the skull's. And both lower right canines were crooked, overlapping the tooth next to them to an identical degree.

I'd found a match.

I read the description that accompanied the photograph. The young woman's name was Janice Donaldson. She was twenty-six, a prostitute and drug addict who had gone missing from Stornoway five weeks ago.

I looked at her picture again. She was full-faced, with round cheeks and the beginnings of a double chin. Even given her drug addiction, she was a young woman who was always going to be plump. I didn't have any doubts that I'd found the murdered woman.

'Hello, Janice,' I said.

CHAPTER 6

I was sitting at the desk in the clinic. A dusty twilight seemed to cover everything. The blinds on the window and door were drawn and the skull and jawbone still sat on the steel trolley. On the desk in front of me was my laptop, its screen dark and dead. The halogen examination lamp was poised over the table where I'd placed it, but now it was unlit.

There wasn't a sound. I looked around, taking in my surroundings. And, with the lack of surprise that sometimes accompanies such moments, I knew without thinking about it that I was asleep.

I felt the presence in the corner of the room before I saw it. The figure was lost in shadow, but I could still see her. A woman, heavy-boned and fleshy. A round, attractive face marred by an underlying hardness.

She looked at me and opened her mouth. I waited for her to speak, but instead of words smoke began streaming from her lips, from her eyes and nose. I could smell her burning. I knew I had to try to help her.

You can't. She's already dead.

The smoke was getting thicker, starting to choke me. I could no longer see the woman, no longer see anything. I lurched towards her . . .

And woke up. I was still in the clinic, sitting at the desk where I'd fallen asleep. Now, though, the room was in darkness. A faint glow came from my laptop, where an infinity of stars raced into oblivion. The screensaver had turned itself on, which meant I'd been sleeping for at least fifteen minutes.

The gale thrashed outside as I tried to shake off the effects of the dream. I felt short of breath, and my vision was blurred. And I could still smell the acrid stink of smoke.

I took a deep breath, and immediately started to cough. Now I could taste smoke as well as smell it. I tried the switch for the desk lamp. Nothing happened. The storm must have finally succeeded in cutting off Runa's electricity. I realised I hadn't just been dreaming after all.

The room was full of smoke.

Coughing, I jumped up and lunged for the door. I grabbed hold of the handle, but immediately snatched my hand away.

It was hot.

I'd lowered the blind over the glass panel in the door after the intruder's visit that afternoon, but now I yanked it open. The hall beyond was swirling with a sulphurous orange light. The community centre was on fire.

I backed away from the door and quickly looked around the clinic. The only other way out was the small window set high up in one wall. If I stood on a chair I should be able to squeeze through. I tried to open it, but it wouldn't budge. I snatched up the desk lamp to break the glass, but stopped myself at the last second. Even opened, the window would be only just big enough for me to crawl through. If I broke it I'd never fit through the smaller gap. And although the clinic door was shut, the rush of oxygen-rich air from outside might still cause the fire to expand explosively. I daren't risk that.

The smoke had already grown thicker in the room, making it hard to breath. *Come on! Think!* I snatched my coat off the wall hook, ran to the washbasin and turned the tap on full. I plunged my head underneath the cold water, then did the same with my scarf and glove. I struggled into my coat, wound the wet scarf round my nose and mouth and wriggled my free hand into my glove. Then I pulled the coat's hood up round my face.

As I snatched up my laptop, I spared a glance at the skull and jawbone lying on the steel trolley. *I'm sorry, Janice.*

And at that moment the glass porthole exploded.

The fact that my face was averted meant my hood and scarf protected me from most of the flying shards. I felt a few sting my exposed skin, but the sensation was dwarfed by the sudden blast of heat. I staggered back as smoke and flame billowed into the clinic.

Hacking and coughing, I hunched my back against the heat coming through the shattered porthole and grabbed hold of the door handle. The water on my glove steamed, the heat striking right though the thick fabric, but I yanked the door open and dashed through.

It was like running into a wall of heat and noise. The piano was burning like a torch, discordant notes clamouring out a madman's music as the fire plucked and snapped at its wires. But now I saw that the community centre wasn't completely ablaze. One half was engulfed in flames, but the side where the exit was located hadn't yet caught.

Eyes streaming, I stumbled through the smoke. Almost immediately I was lost and blind. Heart pounding from fear and lack of oxygen, I didn't see the stack of chairs until I fell over them.

Pain lanced through my shoulder and the laptop flew from my hands as I tumbled to the floor. But it was falling that saved me. There was a band of relatively clear air trapped against the floorboards. *Stupid! Should have realised!* I was panicking, not thinking clearly. Keeping my face pressed to the floor, I gulped in greedy breaths as I pawed around for the laptop. I couldn't find it. *Leave it! Get out!* I began crawling towards the exit. An eddy in the smoke revealed the double doors right in front of me. Taking a last deep breath, I hauled myself to my feet and tugged at the handles.

And heard the rattle of the padlocked chain.

Shock and fear paralysed me. I'd forgotten all about the padlock. *The key. Where's the key?* Brody had the spare but where was mine? I frantically searched my pockets. Nothing. *Oh Christ, it's still in the clinic.*

Then I felt the thin metal shape in my back pocket. *Thank God!* I fumbled it out. My chest heaved as I tried to fit the key into the padlock, but I daren't take a breath. If I did I'd be inhaling smoke, not air, and the heat would sear my lungs. My hand was clumsy, the lock stubbornly resistant.

Then there was a *snick* and the hasp slid open.

The chain rasped on the handles as I tore it free. I wrenched open the doors, hoping the porch would act like an air lock, allowing me to get out before the fresh air fed the fire. It did, but only partly. There was an instant's touch of cold against my face, then I stumbled out in a rush of heat and smoke.

I'd no idea how far I'd gone before I collapsed. But this time it was onto blessedly cold, wet grass. I sucked in one breath after another, tasting cool air that was tainted by smoke, but air, all the same.

There were hands on me now, dragging me away from the centre. I recognised Brody's voice saying, 'It's all right, we've got you.'

I looked up, coughing and wiping the tears from my eyes. He was supporting me on one side, the even bigger figure of Guthrie on the other. There were people all around, their stunned faces lit by the flames. Someone was shouting for water; a moment later a mug was thrust into my hands. I drank thirstily, the coldness of it wonderfully soothing.

'Are you OK?' Brody was saying.

I nodded, turning round to look back at the community centre. The whole building was ablaze, including the clinic extension.

'What happened?'

I tried to speak, but a coughing spasm seized me.

'All right, take it easy,' Brody said, urging me to drink again.

Another figure was barging towards us through the gathering crowd. It was Cameron, staring with open-mouthed disbelief at the burning centre.

'What have you done?' he demanded, bass voice quivering with rage.

'For God's sake, give him a chance, can't you?' Brody said.

Cameron's Adam's apple jerked under the skin of his throat like a trapped mouse. 'Give him a *chance*? That's my clinic going up in flames!'

I tried to control my coughing. 'I'm sorry . . .' I croaked.

'You're *sorry*? Look at it! What the hell did you do?'

I forced myself to stand, wiping my streaming eyes. 'I didn't do anything.' My throat felt full of gravel. 'I must have fallen asleep, and when I woke up the hall was on fire. It started in there, not the clinic.'

Cameron wasn't about to back down. 'Oh, so it started by itself, did it?'

'Leave him alone, he only just made it out himself,' Brody warned.

A harsh laugh came from nearby. It was Kinross, standing at the front of the crowd. 'Aye, made sure he was all right, didn't he?'

'Would you rather he'd still been in there?' Brody snapped.

'Do we get a choice?'

I glanced round and saw that islanders were gathered in a circle round us, their faces harsh and unforgiving in the flames.

'It didn't just burn down by itself,' one man muttered.

Others wanted to know why we'd used the centre, who would pay for it to be replaced. I could feel the mood shifting from shock to anger.

Then the crowd began to part, making way for a tall figure. With relief I saw it was Strachan. And just like that, the tension subsided.

He strode up to us. 'Christ! Was anyone inside?'

I shook my head, trying to stifle the coughs. 'Only me.'

And Janice Donaldson. There was no way her remains would survive this second burning.

Strachan took the empty mug from me. 'Some more water here, please.'

He held it out. Almost immediately the mug was refilled and pressed back into my hand. I gulped at the icy water gratefully.

'Any idea how it started?'

Cameron had been watching with barely concealed anger. 'Isn't it obvious? He was the only person in there!'

'Don't talk rubbish, Bruce,' Strachan told him impatiently. 'Why don't we wait until we know what caused it before we start blaming anyone?' Turning his back on Cameron, he addressed the gathered islanders. 'I promise we'll find out what happened. And we'll build a new and better clinic and community centre, you have my word. But everyone should go on home now.'

Nobody moved. Then, as if on cue, what was left of the hall suddenly collapsed in a shower of sparks and flame. Gradually the crowd began to break up, the men grim-faced, many of the women wiping their eyes.

Strachan spoke to Kinross and Guthrie. 'Iain, Sean, will you get a few men together and stay for a while? I can't see that it'll spread, but I'd appreciate your keeping an eye on things.'

It was a deft way of defusing the remaining tension. Kinross and Guthrie looked taken aback, but flattered to have been asked.

'I still say we should—' Cameron began, but Strachan spoke over him.

'No need for you to stay, Bruce. You're teaching in a few hours.'

His tone didn't brook any argument. Cameron stalked off, his expression thunderous. Strachan watched him go, then turned to me.

'OK, so what happened?'

I took another drink of water. 'I must have dozed off. When I woke up the lights were off and the clinic was full of smoke.'

He nodded. 'The power went off all over the island about an hour ago. The blackout must have caused some sort of short.'

For the first time I noticed that the village was in darkness beyond the yellow glow of the flames. The storm had finally succeeded in leaving Runa without electricity as well as phones.

'It's been a hell of a night. Still, it could have been a lot worse.' Strachan paused, his manner changing subtly. 'I heard a rumour that the police are treating the body that was found as murder. Know anything about that?'

Brody spoke before I could answer. 'Take no notice of rumours.'

'Right. Well, I'll say good night, then. I'm glad you're all right, David.'

Brody waited until he was turning away. 'I'm curious. You can't see the village from your house. So how did you know about the fire?'

Strachan's expression was controlled, but I could see the anger under it.

'There was a glow in the sky. And I'm a poor sleeper.'

The two of them held each other's stare, neither of them giving an inch. Then, with a final nod in my direction, Strachan walked off into the dark.

BRODY DROVE ME BACK to the hotel. Since his house was down by the harbour, he'd rushed up to the community centre in his car when he saw the blaze from his bedroom window. As we drove through the blacked-out streets, I resisted the urge to lean back against the headrest and shut my eyes. The cuts and burns I hadn't noticed before had begun to make themselves felt, and the stink of smoke clogged my nose and throat.

'So how do you think it started?' Brody asked after a while.

'I suppose Strachan could be right.' My voice was still hoarse from smoke. 'The power cut could have caused an electrical short or surge.'

'Just a few hours after Fraser let slip this was a murder inquiry?'

I felt too shattered to think clearly. 'I don't know.'

He didn't push the point. 'Did we lose everything?'

As well as Janice Donaldson's remains, my flight case and equipment, my camera, my laptop containing my notes, had all gone up in smoke.

But even as I was thinking that, I was already feeling in my pockets.

'Not quite,' I said, pulling out the USB stick. 'I backed up my hard drive earlier. Force of habit. So at least we've still got a photographic record.'

'Better than nothing, I suppose.' Brody sighed.

'There's something else,' I said. 'I know who she was.'

I told him how the flaws in the skull's teeth had matched those in the photograph of Janice Donaldson, the missing prostitute from Stornoway.

Brody gave the steering wheel a little punch of satisfaction. 'Well done.'

'With luck, Forensics might be able to salvage enough undamaged soft tissue from the cottage to try for a DNA match.'

We were coming to the hotel now. A light on in the hallway told us that Ellen was still up, and that the back-up generator was doing its job.

She looked horrified when she saw me. 'Oh my God, are you all right?'

'I've had better nights,' I admitted. I nodded at the light bulb, slightly dimmer than usual but still working. 'That's a welcome sight.'

'Aye. Provided we're careful, we've enough oil to keep the generator running for three, perhaps four days.'

While Brody went to rouse Fraser, she ushered me into the kitchen and helped me off with my coat. It stank of smoke and was badly scorched.

Her nose wrinkled. 'Shame it wasn't fireproof as well as waterproof.'

I looked at the charred fabric on the hood and shoulders. I could feel a corresponding sting on my own flesh, but nothing serious.

'I'm not complaining,' I said.

Brody returned a few minutes later with a sleep-bleared Fraser, whisky-breathed and still buttoning his shirt. He made reluctant noises about going to examine the community centre, but there was no real point until the fire had died down. After taking a brief statement from me, he went back to bed.

Ellen began ushering Brody out as well. 'Go and get some sleep. You look nearly as bad as David,' she scolded.

She was right. He was haggard.

He managed a weak smile. 'I'm not sure which of us should be most insulted. But perhaps I will go. It's been a long day.'

'We've another tomorrow,' I told him.

After he'd gone, Ellen filled a basin with hot water, brought out antiseptic and cotton wool, and began to clean the cuts and grazes on my face. 'Are you always as accident-prone as this?' she asked.

'Not usually. Must be this place.'

'Aye, I can believe it.'

I'd been wondering what a young woman like her was doing in a backwater like Runa. 'So what about you? Do you like it out here?'

She suddenly became preoccupied with a cut. 'It's not so bad. You should be here in summer. The nights are glorious.'

'But . . .' I prompted.

'But it's a small island. You see the same faces all the time. And financially, it's a struggle. Sometimes I wish . . . Ah, well, it doesn't matter.'

'Go on.'

Unguarded, her face showed the sadness I guessed she normally kept in check. 'I wish I could leave this place behind, and take Anna and just go. Somewhere where there are decent schools, and shops, and restaurants, and people who don't know you and your business.'

'So why don't you?'

There was defeat in the way she shook her head. 'What would I do?'

'Andrew Brody told me you'd been to college on the mainland. Isn't that something you could use?'

'I spent a couple of years at catering college in Dundee, but when my father took ill, I came back. Only temporarily, I thought. Then I found myself with a child to support, so when he died I carried on running this place.'

She raised an eyebrow at me. 'Aren't you going to ask?'

'Ask what?'

'About Anna's father.'

'Not when you're putting antiseptic on my cuts, no.'

'Good. Just so you know, let's just say there was never any future there.' Her tone made it clear the subject was closed. She went back to her swabbing. 'So what else did Andrew Brody tell you?'

'Not much. I'd hate to get him barred from the hotel.'

'Not much danger of that.' She laughed. 'Anna and I are too fond of him.' She paused. 'Do you know about his daughter?' she asked.

'He told me.'

'He must like you. It isn't something he talks about as a rule. The girl was a bit wild, from what I gather. Still, I can't imagine what it must be like for him, not knowing what happened to her.'

She dropped the bloodied cotton wool into a bowl. 'There you go. Best thing you can do now is have a hot shower and get some sleep.'

A sudden gust of wind struck the hotel, making the entire structure vibrate. Ellen cocked her head, listening. 'Storm's getting up,' she said.

BRODY, FRASER AND I went out to the community centre as soon as it was light. I felt exhausted. I'd had less than four hours' sleep and I ached all over. I'd hardly recognised myself in the shaving mirror that morning. The skin of my face felt sunburnt, peppered with small gashes from the flying glass. My eyebrows had been singed off, giving me a strange, startled expression. Still, as Strachan had said, it could have been much worse.

Brody and Fraser stood behind me as I studied the smoking wreckage. All that remained now was an uneven mound of grey and black ash. The rain was coming down in sheets, but the debris was still smouldering.

'Do you think anything could still be intact?' Brody asked.

'Not really.'

Fraser gave an irritable sigh. 'So why bother looking?'

'To make sure.'

I could make out one blackened corner of my flight case, protruding from the ashes of what had been the clinic. It was open, its contents charred. Beyond it was the trolley where I'd worked on Janice Donaldson's cranium, lying half buried under the remains of the roof. The skull and jawbone were nowhere to be seen, undoubtedly shattered to powder by the impact.

I'm sorry, Janice. As I brushed a piece of wind-blown ash from my face, a square shape hidden under a pile of panelling caught my eye.

Brody moved closer to look. 'What's that?'

'It's the fridge.'

I edged forward, carefully picking my way through the still-hot ash. The dead woman's hand had been inside the fridge, so there was a chance the insulation had protected it. That hope quickly died when I cleared away the covering of debris. The fridge's rubber seal had melted, letting the door swing open to expose the contents to the flames. Of Janice Donaldson's hand, all that was left were bones, cooked to a dark caramel. I picked them out, allowing them to cool a little before bagging them in freezer bags I'd brought from the hotel, then rejoined Brody and Fraser.

Fraser squinted at the bag. 'That it? Hardly worth bothering with.'

Ignoring him, I went to where an upright section of charred timber still stood in the ruins. Attached to wooden post were bright copper strands, all that remained of the centre's electrical wiring. Judging from their position, they would have fed the light switch by the entrance. Seeing them, an idea began to form, too faint even to call suspicion. I'd only managed to escape from the burning hall because the fire hadn't spread as far as the doors. So it must have started at the far side, opposite where I now stood.

I started to circle the remains of the centre, scanning the ashes where the back wall had been. Then something caught my eye. Crouching down, I gently brushed away the ash to reveal what I'd hoped I wouldn't find.

Small metal puddles, gleaming against the charred wood.

The sight sent a chill through me. I'd attended enough fire scenes to know only too well what they meant. This was no accident.

Gripped by a new sense of urgency, I hurried back to where Brody and Fraser waited. 'Have you spoken to Duncan this morning?' I asked Fraser.

'Duncan? No, not yet,' he said defensively. 'He hasn't called in yet. But, you know, I was going to take him out some breakfast later . . .'

'Try him now.'

He gave me a dirty look but reached for his radio. 'Can't get through,' he said, frowning.

'All right, get in the car. We're going out there.'

Brody had been watching with a worried expression, but said nothing until we were in the car and Fraser was pulling away. 'What did you find?'

I was staring anxiously through the windscreen as we left the village. 'I checked the wiring at the community centre. A fire caused by an electrical fault wouldn't have been hot enough to melt the copper core. But there's an area round the back where the wires were melted.'

'It means the fire was hotter there,' Brody said slowly. 'Oh Christ.'

'So what?' Fraser asked impatiently.

'It was hotter there because an accelerant was used to start it,' I told him. 'The fire wasn't caused by a short. Somebody set it deliberately.'

He was still trying to work it out. 'What's that got to do with Duncan?'

It was Brody who answered. 'Because if someone wanted to get rid of the evidence, it might not only have been the clinic that was torched.'

I could see from Fraser's face that he finally understood. But even if he hadn't there was no need to explain further.

Smeared across the sky directly ahead was a black trail of smoke.

THE MEANDERING TERRAIN prevented us from seeing the source of the smoke. Fraser put his foot down, tearing along the narrow road much faster than was safe in the atrocious conditions. No one complained.

Then we rounded one final bend, and the old cottage was revealed in front of us. So, too, was the camper van. What was left of it.

'Oh, no,' Fraser said.

Most of the smoke we'd seen was coming from the ruined cottage, but it was the sight of Brody's camper van that transfixed us. It had been reduced to a burnt-out shell, tyres melted to misshapen lumps of rubber, the roof blown off when either the gas cylinder or petrol tank had exploded.

There was no sign of Duncan.

Fraser didn't slow as he went off the road and onto the track, the heavy car slewing on the muddy surface as he stamped on the brakes. He jumped out of the car and ran towards the camper van.

'Duncan? *Duncan!*' he bellowed, charging across the grass.

Brody and I ran behind him, rain whipping into our faces. Fraser lurched to a halt in front of the camper van.

'Oh Jesus Christ! Where is he? Where the fuck is he?' He stared round wildly, as though hoping the young PC would suddenly come strolling up.

'He's here,' I said quietly.

Fraser followed my gaze. A boot was sticking out from under a piece of heat-buckled roof, the leather burnt away to reveal charred flesh and bone.

He took a step towards the camper van. 'Ah, no . . .' He grabbed hold of the panel and started trying to heave it off.

'Don't,' I began, but as I started forward a hand fell on my shoulder. I looked round at Brody.

He shook his head. 'Leave him.'

Fraser wrenched the panel free, letting the wind carry it away. Even from where I stood, the smell of burnt meat was overpowering. Fraser continued to tear at the rest of the wreckage like a madman.

Then he stopped, staring at what he'd uncovered. He stumbled back, as uncoordinated as a broken puppet.

'Oh Christ. That's not him. Tell me that's not him!'

The body lay in the centre of the camper van. Its limbs had drawn up, so that it was curled in a foetal position, pathetically vulnerable. Cooked into the flesh round its middle was a charred police utility belt, fire-blackened handcuffs still attached to it.

Fraser was weeping. 'Why the fuck didn't he get out?'

I took hold of his arm. 'Come on.'

'Get off me!' he snarled, jerking free. Then all at once he seemed to sag. 'He was twenty-one,' he mumbled. 'What am I going to tell everyone?'

'Tell them he was murdered,' Brody said brutally. 'Tell them we've got a killer loose. And tell them if Wallace had sent out a proper inquiry team, your twenty-one-year-old PC might still been alive!'

There was rare emotion in his voice. And we all knew what he'd left unsaid: that it had been Fraser's slip that had shown our hand about the woman's murder, and perhaps panicked her killer into action.

'Take it easy,' I told Brody.

He took a long breath, then nodded, in control of himself again. 'We need to let the mainland know what's happened.'

Red-eyed, Fraser took out his radio, turning his back to the wind and rain as he stabbed a number into its keypad. He listened, then tried again.

'Come on, come *on*!'

'What's wrong?' Brody asked.

'It's not working. There's no bloody signal!' He thrust it at Brody.

Brody tried it, then shook his head. 'Dead. The gale must have taken out a mast. The whole comms network for the islands could be down.'

I took in the empty, windswept landscape that surrounded us. The low, dark clouds that squatted over the island seemed to shut us in even more.

'So now what do we do?' I asked.

For once even Brody seemed at a loss. 'We keep trying. Sooner or later we'll get the radios or the land lines back. Until then, we're on our own.'

I VOLUNTEERED to stay at the croft while Brody and Fraser drove back to the village to find stakes and a hammer. We needed to tape off the camper van, but there wasn't enough of it left to fix the tape to. This time I was determined to preserve the crime scene as we'd found it.

And none of us doubted that it was just that—a crime scene. Someone had torched this deliberately, just as they had the medical clinic. Except Duncan hadn't managed to escape.

Before he and Fraser left, Brody and I stood huddled on the track, bracing ourselves against the gale while the police sergeant tried once more to raise the mainland on the radio.

'You think this was done before or after the community centre?' I asked.

Brody considered the van's blackened shell. 'Before, I'd say. No point in starting a fire that would alert the entire village until he'd taken care of this.'

I felt anger as well as shock at the senselessness of it. 'Why leave the remains out here for weeks, then suddenly do this? It doesn't make sense.'

Brody wiped the rain from his face. 'Whoever did this, he's panicking.

He knows he made a mistake leaving the body here, and now he's trying to rectify it. He's determined to destroy anything that might tie him to it. Even if that means killing again.' He paused, giving me a level look. 'You sure you'll be all right by yourself?'

'I'll be fine,' I said.

'Anybody shows up, anyone at all, be bloody careful,' Brody warned.

He didn't have to tell me. But I didn't think I'd be in any danger. There was no reason for the killer to come back here now, not any more.

Besides, there were things I needed to do.

I watched the Range Rover bump down the track, then walked back to the burnt-out camper van, and Duncan's body.

The remains I deal with are usually those of strangers. I know them only through their death, not their life. This was different, and it was hard to reconcile my memory of the young constable with the thing of charred flesh and bone that was in front of me.

Rain dripped from my hood as I stared down at the corpse, letting my mind clear of thoughts of who it had been. *You want to catch whoever did this? Forget Duncan. Put aside the person.*

Look at the puzzle.

The body was lying face down. The clothes had been burned from it, as had most of the skin and soft tissue. The arms were bent at the elbows, pulled up as their tendons had contracted. The legs were similarly contorted, throwing the hips and lower body slightly out to one side as they had drawn up in the heat. Part of what remained of the tabletop was visible underneath the body. The feet were nearer the door, the head turned slightly to the right and pointing towards where the small couch had been. There was nothing left of the couch but a few blackened springs. Something else was lying among them. Leaning forward, I recognised the steel cylinder of Duncan's Maglite, blistered and dulled by the fire.

My camera had been destroyed in the clinic along with the rest of my equipment, so I made do with sketching the body's position on a notepad I'd borrowed from the Range Rover. The sling made drawing difficult, and I had to shield the pad from the rain. But I did the best I could.

Then I tried to study the body in more detail. Careful not to disturb anything, I leaned as close as I could, until I saw what I'd been looking for.

A gaping hole in the skull, the size of a man's fist.

The sound of a car coming down the track disturbed my thoughts. I looked round, surprised that Brody and Fraser were back so soon. But it wasn't the Range Rover. It was Strachan's silver-grey Saab.

Brody's warning sprang uncomfortably to mind. *Anybody shows up, anyone at all, be bloody careful.* I climbed to my feet, slipping my notepad away, and went to meet him as the car pulled up. He climbed out, staring past me at the camper van, too shocked to raise the hood of his coat.

'Christ! This burned down as *well*?'

'You shouldn't be here.'

But Strachan wasn't listening. His eyes widened as he saw what was lying in the wreckage. 'Oh my God!'

Abruptly, he twisted away, doubling up as he vomited. He slowly straightened, fumbling in his pocket for something to wipe his mouth.

'Are you all right?' I asked.

He nodded, white-faced. 'Sorry,' he mumbled. 'Who . . . who is it? The young policeman?'

'Brody and Fraser are going to be back any time,' I said, by way of answer. 'You shouldn't let them find you here.'

'To hell with them! This is my *home*! I've spent the past five *years* getting this place back on its feet, and now . . .' He broke off, running his hand through his rain-flattened hair. 'Who the hell's *doing* this?'

I didn't say anything. Strachan was recovering from the shock now. He lifted his face to the clouded sky, oblivious to the wind and rain.

'The police won't be able to get out here in this weather. And you're not going to be able to keep this quiet. There are going to be a lot of frightened people wanting answers. You've got to let me help. They'll listen to me more than your police sergeant. Or Brody, come to that.'

It was tempting. I knew from bitter experience how ugly the mood could turn in a small community like this. The question was, how far we could afford to trust anyone? Even Strachan?

Still, there was one way he could help. 'We lost one of our radios in the fire,' I said. 'Could we use the radio on your yacht, if necessary?' I didn't want to tell him we didn't have any form of communications at all.

He looked surprised. 'My yacht? Yes, of course.' He stared again at the camper van. 'Poor devil,' he said softly. He turned to me. 'Remember. Anything you need, anything at all.'

He returned to his car and set off back down the track. As the Saab neared the road, I saw the distinctive shape of the police Range Rover heading towards it. The road's narrowness forced the two cars to slow as they skirted each other, like two dogs warily circling before a fight.

I waited for the Range Rover to pull up. While Fraser went to open the back, Brody came over, staring at the disappearing fleck of Strachan's car.

'What was he doing here?'

'He came to offer his help.' I told him my idea of using the yacht's radio.

Brody sighed. 'I should have thought of that. But we don't need Strachan's yacht. Any boat in the harbour will have ship-to-shore. We can use the ferry's.'

'The yacht's nearer,' I pointed out.

As much as he might dislike the idea of asking Strachan for a favour, Brody knew it made sense. 'Aye, you're right,' he said.

Fraser came over, clutching an armful of rusted steel reinforcing rods and a roll of tape. He let the rods fall onto the grass, his eyes red-rimmed. 'This still doesn't sit right with me. Just leaving him out here . . .'

'If you can think of an alternative, tell us,' Brody said, but not unkindly.

The sergeant nodded miserably. He strode ahead of us to the remains of the camper van, his posture rigid and determined. But at the sight of Duncan's body, he faltered. 'Oh Jesus . . .'

'If it's any consolation, he wouldn't have felt any of this,' I told him.

He glared at me. 'Aye? And how would you know?'

I took a deep breath. 'Because he was already dead when the fire started.'

The angry light died from the sergeant's eyes.

'You sure?' Brody asked.

I led them through the wet grass until we had a better view of the skull. I felt myself falter. *The puzzle, not the person.* I pointed to the jagged hole on the left side of the skull that looked like the entrance to a dark cave.

Fraser glanced, then looked away.

Brody cleared his throat before he spoke. 'Couldn't that have happened in the fire, like you thought Janice Donaldson's had?'

I shook my head. 'Duncan was hit a hell of a lot harder than Janice Donaldson. You can see even from here that pieces of bone have been pushed into the skull cavity. And from the position of the arms, it looks like he just went straight down. He literally didn't know what hit him.'

There was a silence. 'And what did hit him?' Brody asked.

'From what I can see so far it looks like some sort of club.'

Like a Maglite, I thought. The steel case of Duncan's torch was poking through the ashes near his body. It was the right size and shape.

Fraser had his fists balled, his eyes drawn to the body despite himself. 'He was a fit lad. He wouldn't have given in without a fight.'

I spoke carefully. 'Perhaps not, but . . . well, it looks like he was hit from behind. The body's lying face down, feet towards the door. So he was facing away from it and pitched forward. I think the killer must have been standing behind Duncan, between him and the door. That points to him being left-handed, because the impact is to the left-hand side of the skull.'

The rain squalled around us as they stared down at Duncan's body. I waited, wondering which one of them would say it first. It was Fraser.

'So he let them in? And then turned his back?'

'That's how it looks.'

Duncan hadn't thought he was in any danger when he let his killer in.

Brody reached out and took the tape from Fraser. 'Let's get this over with.'

Once the flimsy barricade of police tape had been secured, our priority was to let the mainland know what had happened. While Wallace still wouldn't be able to send any support until the storm eased, the murder of a police officer would escalate this to a whole new level.

Taking one last look at the camper van behind its symbolic barrier, we headed back to the Range Rover. Fraser trudged ahead, shoulders slumped.

Beside me, Brody suddenly stopped walking. 'Have you got any bags left?'

He was looking down at a tuft of wiry grass, rippling and bent in the wind. Something dark was snagged against it. I reached in my pocket for one of the freezer bags I'd brought from the hotel and passed it to him.

Putting his hand into the bag, Brody bent down and picked up the object. Then, reversing the bag so it was inside, he held it up to show me.

It was a large, black plastic screw cap. A thin strap that would once have fastened it to a container stuck out from it, snapped clean after an inch or so.

He put his nose to the open top of the bag. 'Petrol.'

Fraser had joined us. He took the bag from Brody and sniffed it himself. 'You think the bastard dropped this last night?'

'I'd say it's a fair bet. Wasn't here yesterday, or we'd have seen it.'

Fraser's expression was furious as he tucked it into his coat pocket.

The drive to Strachan's house passed in subdued silence. When we turned up the long driveway leading to the house we saw that Grace's Porsche Cayenne had gone, but Strachan's Saab was parked outside.

I couldn't see Strachan's house being without its own generator, but despite the day's gloom, there were no lights on. Rain dripped from Fraser's fist as he banged the door knocker. We could hear Strachan's dog barking inside, but there was no other sign of life. Fraser gave the door a thump.

'Come on, where the fuck are you?' he snarled.

'Probably off on one of his walkabouts,' Brody said, standing back to look up at the house. 'I suppose we could always just go down to the yacht ourselves. It's an emergency.'

'Aye, and what if it's locked?' Fraser asked. 'We can't just break in.'

'Then let's go and find Kinross,' Brody said. 'We'll use the ferry's radio.'

Kinross lived by the harbour. When we reached the outskirts of the village, Brody told Fraser to take a short cut down a narrow cobbled street to the ferry captain's home, a run-down bungalow with an overgrown garden strewn with rusting boat parts. Brody had told me Kinross was a widower who lived alone with his son. It showed.

Brody and I left Fraser brooding in the car while we went up the path. The doorbell chimed with a cheery electronic melody. Muted sounds of movement came from inside, then the door was opened. Kevin, Kinross's teenage son, stood in the hallway, eyes briefly making contact. The angry red mounds of acne scarred his face in a cruel topography.

'Is your father in?' Brody asked.

The teenager gave a shake of his head, not looking at us. 'He's down at the boatyard,' he mumbled. 'In the workshop.'

The door snicked shut.

We went back to the car, and Fraser drove down to a corrugated shack on the seafront, set close to the foot of the cliffs.

'The yard's communal,' Brody said as we climbed out of the car and hurried over, having to fight against the wind. 'Everybody with a boat chips in to the running costs, and if they need repairs everyone pitches in.'

'Is that Guthrie's?' I asked, indicating a dilapidated fishing boat hauled up on blocks. Half its timber hull was missing, giving it a skeletal look.

'Aye. Supposed to be making it seaworthy again, but he doesn't seem in any hurry.' Brody shook his head. 'Rather spend his money in the bar.'

We hurried to the workshop entrance. Inside, it was stiflingly hot, thick with the smell of machine oil and sawdust. The walls were lined with shelves of tools, and lathes, welding torches and cutting gear littered the floor. A radio was playing, the tinny melody fighting against the chug of a generator.

About half a dozen men were in the workshop. Guthrie was crouched over a dismembered engine spread out on the concrete floor. Kinross and the others were playing cards at an old Formica table. They all broke off what they were doing to stare at us. Their expressions weren't friendly.

Brody stopped in front of Kinross. 'Can we have a word in private, Iain?'

'It's private enough here.'

Brody didn't bother to argue. 'We need to use the ferry's radio.'

Kinross nodded towards Fraser. 'What's wrong with his? Don't the police have radios these days?'

Fraser started forward angrily but Brody laid a restraining hand on his shoulder and said, 'We're asking for your help. We need to get in touch with the mainland. It's important, or we wouldn't ask.'

Kinross unhurriedly lit a cigarette. He shook out the match and tossed it into an ashtray, considering Brody through a plume of blue smoke.

'You can try, for what it's worth. But you won't be able to transmit from the harbour. The radio's VHF. Has to have line-of-sight, and the cliffs block the signal to the mainland. It's the same for the other boats.'

'What if you need to send a mayday?' Brody asked, incredulous.

Kinross shrugged. 'If you're in the harbour, you wouldn't need to.'

Fraser had bunched his fists. 'So take the bloody boat out to sea, where you can transmit.'

'You want to try going out in this, go ahead. But not on my ferry.'

Brody kneaded the bridge of his nose.

'There's Mr Strachan's yacht,' one of the card players suggested.

Guthrie laughed. 'Aye, that's got communications coming out of its arse.'

I saw Brody's face close down. 'Look, can we try the ferry anyway?'

'If you want to waste your time, it's up to you.' Kinross threw in his cards and rose to his feet. 'Sorry, lads.'

He pulled on an oilskin and went out, letting the doors swing back on us as we followed. Rain and spray filled the air with an iodine tang as he strode along the harbour to the jetty. The ferry was bucking against its moorings, but he walked up the gangplank without hesitation. The rest of us were more cautious, holding on to the rail as the gangplank tipped and swayed.

Kinross was already fiddling with the radio set when we crammed into the claustrophobic bridge. A medley of discordant hums and squeaks came out as he spoke into its handset, then waited vainly for a response.

'Who are you calling?' Brody asked.

Kinross answered without turning round. 'Coastguard. They've got the biggest radio mast on Lewis. If they can't hear us then no one else will.'

Fraser watched the ferry captain with an expression of sullen dislike. Suddenly he said, 'You remember bringing any strangers across on the ferry about four or five weeks ago?'

Brody gave him an angry look, but he took no notice.

Kinross turned to stare at Fraser. 'This to do with the murder?'

'Just answer the question.'

Kinross's smile threatened violence. 'And if I don't?'

Brody cut in before Fraser could respond. 'Take it easy, Iain. No one's accusing you of anything. We just came out here to use the radio.'

Deliberately, Kinross lowered the handset. 'This is my ferry and my radio. You want to use it, you can tell me what's so urgent.'

'We can't yet, Iain. But it's important. Trust me on that.'

Kinross stared at him, his expression giving nothing away. Then he got up and headed for the door.

'Where are you going?' Brody asked.

'You wanted me to try the radio, I have. You want to waste your time pissing in the wind, that's up to you, but you can do it by yourselves.'

With that he walked out. The door banged shut behind him.

Brody took a deep breath. 'Kinross is right. There's no point wasting any more time here when Strachan's yacht has a satellite comms system. We can call into the school on the way and see if Grace is there.'

We drove up through the village from the harbour, but when we reached the school, Grace's car wasn't outside and the building was empty.

'They must have sent the kids home early because of the power cut,' Brody said, his frustration evident.

There was nothing to do but head for Strachan's house and hope one of them was back. Fraser drove in moody silence. I couldn't help but feel sorry for him. Duncan's death had hit him hard. And he'd been out of his depth even before his colleague was murdered.

We were approaching the big house when the sergeant suddenly tensed. 'What the hell's he doing?'

Strachan's Saab was tearing down the road towards us. Fraser swore and swerved into the side, stamping on the brake as the Saab skidded to a halt.

'Bloody idiot!' Fraser cursed.

Strachan had jumped out and was running towards us. Fraser angrily wound down the window and yelled at him.

'What the hell are you playing at?'

Strachan didn't seem to hear. His eyes were wide and scared as he bent to the open window. 'Grace is missing!' he gasped. 'We have to find her!'

Brody had climbed out of the Range Rover. 'Slow down and tell us what's happened.'

Strachan made an effort to compose himself. 'I got back a few minutes ago. Grace's car was here, and there were lights on and music playing. She'd left a cup of coffee going cold in the kitchen, but when I called she didn't answer. I looked in every room, but there's no sign of her!'

Brody turned to Fraser, assuming command. 'We need to organise a search. Return to the village and bring as many people back as you can.'

'What about you?' Fraser asked, not liking being told what to do.

'I'm going to go up to the house and take a look.'

'I've told you, she isn't there!' Strachan almost yelled.

'We'll take a look anyway. Dr Hunter, do you want to come with me?'

We hurried over to the Saab as Fraser drove off in the Range Rover.

'What do you think?' I asked Brody in a low voice.

He just shook his head, his expression grim.

Strachan had left the Saab's engine running. He barely waited for us to get in before he set off, reversing back up the road and up the driveway. He screeched to a halt next to Grace's Porsche. We followed him as he ran inside, shouting her name. The only response was a frenzied barking from the dog.

'See, she's not here!' he shouted.

Brody remained calm as we carried out a quick search of the house and the barn. There was no sign of Grace.

'We're just wasting time!' Strachan said, his panic nearing the surface.

'What about the cove?' Brody asked. 'Did you look there?'

'I . . . No, but Grace never goes down there, not without me.'

'Let's take a look anyway, shall we?'

Strachan led us into the kitchen. A half-drunk cup of coffee stood on the table, as though Grace had merely stepped out for a moment. Strachan led us through the back door and down the steps to the cove.

Except for the yacht moored at the short jetty, the cove was empty. It was a beautiful boat, its hull squeaking against the rubber fenders as the sea threw it about, setting the tall mast swinging back and forth.

Strachan hurried along the jetty towards it. He bounded up the gangplank and ran to the cockpit. I was slower to board, struggling for balance. As I stepped onto the deck, Strachan threw back the cockpit hatch and froze.

When I reached him I saw why.

Like the rest of the yacht, the cockpit was beautifully equipped: teak panels, stainless-steel fittings, and an elaborate instrument console. Or what was left of it. The radio and satcom had been smashed to pieces.

Strachan stared at it for a moment, then rushed through the cockpit to the main cabin. 'Grace? Oh God, *Grace*!'

She lay on the cabin's floor, curled on her side, arms pulled behind her and tied behind her back. Her head and shoulders were covered with a sack. From the waist down she was almost naked. Her jeans had been left pulled down round her ankles and her pants were round her knees, as though her attacker had been interrupted in the act of removing them.

She looked obscenely vulnerable lying there, her long legs bare and blue-white with the cold. She wasn't moving. I thought we were too late, but then Strachan touched her and she suddenly began to thrash around.

'It's all right, Grace, it's me! It's me!' Strachan said, yanking the sacking from her head.

A piece of dirty cloth had been crammed into her mouth. Her eyes were wide and terrified, then they fixed on Strachan and she stopped struggling.

'It's all right, I'm here, it's all right!' He eased the gag from her mouth.

She sucked in a breath, sobbing. '*Michael. Oh, thank God, Michael!*'

Her right cheek was discoloured by a livid bruise, and her mouth was swollen and bloody. But other than that there were no obvious injuries.

'Are you hurt?' he was asking her, his voice cracked.

'No, I . . . I don't think so.'

Tears were running down Strachan's face as he tenderly brushed the hair from his wife's face. 'Who did it? Did you see him?'

'I don't know, I . . . I . . .'

'Shh, it's all right, it's over now. It's over.'

Brody and I gave them as much privacy as we could while Strachan drew up Grace's underwear and jeans. Brody searched for a knife to cut the rope binding her wrists, then we stood back as Strachan helped her to her feet.

'Help me carry her,' he said to Brody.

'I'm all right. I can walk,' Grace said firmly, but she huddled against her husband as he supported her along the jetty.

Brody and I kept a discreet distance behind as they climbed the steps from the cove, the gulls' lonely cries sounded like mocking laughter on the wind.

CHAPTER 7

Fraser arrived with a convoy of cars from the village shortly after we got back to the house. Strachan objected to his wife being questioned so soon, but I suggested that it was best to get it over with. Not only was it better for her to describe what had happened while the memory was still fresh, but I'd also be able to make sure Fraser didn't push her too hard. Somehow I didn't think he'd be the most sensitive of interviewers.

Strachan sent everyone who'd come to help search for Grace back home again, after he'd distractedly thanked them and reassured them that she wasn't badly hurt. Shock and anger was visible on all their faces. Even though news of Duncan's death hadn't yet spread, by now everyone had heard that the body found at the cottage had been murdered. As shocking as that might be, what had happened to the well-liked wife of Runa's benefactor was at that moment even more so.

Given his infatuation with Grace, it was no surprise that Cameron had also rushed out to help with the search. He was the last to leave, and his voice carried from the hallway into the kitchen where Fraser and Brody waited as I cleaned Grace's wounds.

'If she's been injured, I need to examine her,' Cameron boomed.

Strachan's voice was unmoved. 'There's no need. David's doing that.'

'Hunter?' Cameron fairly spat the word. 'With all due respect, Michael, if anyone's going to treat Grace it should be me, not some . . . some ex-GP!'

'I'll decide who's going to look after my wife!' snapped Strachan, then he added more gently, 'Go home, Bruce. If I need you, I'll let you know.'

When Strachan rejoined us in the kitchen his chiselled features were drawn. Fraser was waiting with his notebook, ready to take Grace's statement, while Brody sat staring into his cooling mug of tea with a faint frown. The old DI had been unusually quiet since we'd come back to the house.

Strachan sat holding Grace's hand as I dabbed antiseptic on her wounds. None was serious, the worst being the bruise on her face. It was on her right cheek, which meant whoever had struck her was probably left-handed.

The same as Duncan's killer.

Grace started telling Fraser what she could remember. Her hand trembled as she held the glass of brandy and water I'd given her in lieu of any other sedative.

'I'd not been back from school long. I'd just made myself a coffee.'

'When was this?' Fraser asked, writing ponderously in his notebook.

'I don't know . . . about two, two thirty, I think. Bruce decided to close the school early because of the power cut.' She broke off to take a sip of brandy. 'Oscar was barking at the kitchen door, and as soon as I opened it he shot off for the cove. I went after him. When I got down there he was barking like a mad thing at the yacht, and I saw that the hatch was open. I thought Michael must have forgotten to close it. I started to go into the cockpit, but there was no light on and I couldn't see. Then . . . then something hit me.'

She faltered, her hand going to the bruise on her right cheek.

'You don't have to talk about it if you don't want to,' Strachan told her.

'I'm fine. Really.' Grace gave him a small smile. 'Everything got a bit blurry then. I was on the floor and my hands had been tied behind me. There was something over my head, as well. I thought I was going to suffocate. The sack or whatever it was stank of fish and oil, and a horrible piece of cloth had been stuffed in my mouth. I tried to yell or kick out, but I couldn't. Then I felt . . . I felt my pants being pulled down . . .'

She broke off, her control slipping. 'I just can't believe it must have been someone I *know!*'

Strachan turned angrily to Fraser. 'Can't you see this is upsetting her?'

'It's all right, really. I'd rather finish.' Grace wiped her eyes. 'There's not much more to tell anyway. I sort of passed out again after that.'

'But you weren't raped?' Fraser asked tactlessly.

She looked at him levelly. 'No. I can remember that much.'

'Thank God,' Strachan said fervently. 'The bastard must have heard us shouting for you and cleared out.'

Fraser made notes. 'Can you remember anything about your attacker? Was there any sort of smell about him? Aftershave, anything like that?'

Grace thought for a while, then shook her head. 'Not really. I'm afraid all I could smell was rotting fish and oil from the sack.'

'Is there another way out of the cove?' I asked.

'Apart from the sea, you mean?' Strachan shrugged. 'There's a path from the shingle beach beyond the rocks up to the cliff top. It would be a bit hairy in this weather, but not impossible.'

Fraser had no more questions after that. I thought Brody might want to ask something, but the old DI remained silent as Grace excused herself. Strachan wanted to run a bath for her, but she would hear none of it.

'I'm not an invalid,' she said, smiling but with a touch of exasperation. She came and kissed my cheek, the musk of her perfume distinctive even under the reek of antiseptic. 'Thank you, David.'

'Glad to help.'

There was a haunted look in Strachan's eyes as he watched her go out.

Brody spoke for the first time since bringing Grace into the house. 'Tell me again what happened.'

Strachan was taken aback. 'I told you, I came home and she wasn't here.'

'And where had you been, exactly?' His tone wasn't quite accusatory, but it didn't leave much doubt why he was asking.

Strachan regarded him with growing anger. 'I'd gone for a walk up to the cairns. I came home after I'd seen David at the cottage, but I was still upset over what had happened to the young constable. Grace was at the school, so I left the car here and went out again.'

'To the mountain.'

'Yes, to the mountain,' Strachan said, his temper barely in check. 'And believe me, I wish to Christ I hadn't! So if that's all, Andrew, thanks for your help, but I think it's time you went now!'

The atmosphere in the kitchen fairly crackled. I was surprised at Brody myself. Even though there was no love lost between the two of them, that was no reason to imply that Strachan might have attacked his own wife.

Getting to my feet, I broke the silence. 'Perhaps we should all be going.'

Strachan still looked angry, but he hesitated. 'Actually . . . I'd appreciate it if you'd stay for a while, David. To make sure Grace is all right later.'

I glanced at Brody. He gave an almost imperceptible nod.

'There's nothing for you to do back at the village. We can meet up at my place later to talk things through.'

I waited in the kitchen as Strachan showed Brody and Fraser out. The front door closed. When he came back he seemed ill at ease.

'Thanks for staying. Just for an hour or so, until Grace goes to bed, then I'll run you back to the hotel. Can I get you a drink? I've a bottle of twenty-year-old malt waiting to be opened.'

'Don't open it on my account.'

He grinned. 'It's the least I can do. Come on, let's go into the other room.'

He led me out across the hallway into a large sitting room. Two black leather sofas faced each other across a smoked-glass coffee table, and the parquet floor was covered with thick rugs. A glass case of flint tools and arrowheads stood against one wall, and other archaeological artefacts—fragments of ancient pottery, stone carvings—were placed around the room.

I browsed the bookshelves while Strachan opened a drinks cabinet. Most of the titles were nonfiction, biographies and books on archaeology and anthropology. Strachan set a bottle of malt on the coffee table with two thick tumblers and sat down on one of the leather sofas.

'I didn't think you drank,' I said, sitting on the other sofa.

'I don't. But right now I feel like breaking my rule.' He poured the whiskies and handed one to me. '*Slàinte.*'

The malt was peaty but mellow. Strachan took a long drink, then put his head back on the sofa, resting the nearly empty glass on his chest.

'My father always used to say that it's the things you never see coming you have to watch out for.' He gave a rueful smile. 'Now I know what he meant. You think you're finally in control of your life, and then—bam!'

'That's just life. You can't guard against everything.'

'No, I suppose not.' He stared broodingly into his glass. 'This assault . . . do you think Grace'll be all right? I don't mean physically. Do you think there'll be any . . . I don't know. Psychological scars?'

I chose my words carefully. 'I'm not a psychologist. But I'd say she's handling it pretty well so far. And she strikes me as being pretty resilient.'

He still seemed troubled. 'I hope you're right. It's just that . . . Well, a few years ago Grace had a breakdown. She'd been pregnant, and she miscarried. The doctors told her she couldn't have any children. It hit her hard.'

'I'm sorry.' I thought of the wistfulness I'd seen on his wife's face when she'd talked about children the other day. 'Did you ever consider adopting?'

Strachan gave a quick shake of his head and took another drink of whisky. 'It wouldn't be right for us. It's fine, though, really. She's OK. But that's why we left South Africa. We wanted a fresh start. Runa seemed like a sort of . . . of sanctuary. Somewhere we could feel safe.' He was slurring his words slightly, fatigue and reaction compounding the effect of the alcohol. He drained his glass and reached for the bottle. 'Another?'

'No, thanks.'

I was starting to think that I should be going. He needed to be with his wife, not down here getting drunk with me. I was saved from having to say anything by the sound of someone hammering on the front door.

Strachan frowned and put the bottle back down. 'Who the hell's that?' He stood up, swaying. 'Now I remember why I don't drink.'

'Shall I see who it is?' I offered.

'No, I'll go.'

Still, he didn't object when I went with him into the hallway. I hung back as he opened the door, and I recognised Maggie Cassidy's red coat.

Strachan wasn't pleased to see her. 'What do you want?' he asked without inviting her in.

The rain blustered through the open doorway as Maggie stood framed in it. Her elfin face looked tiny inside the hood of her oversized coat. She gave me a glance that was almost furtive, then addressed Strachan.

'Sorry to disturb you, but I heard about what happened. I just wanted to see how your wife was. I . . . I brought this.' She held up a cloth-covered basin. 'It's chicken soup. My gran's speciality.'

That obviously wasn't what Strachan expected. 'Oh. Well . . . thank you.'

Maggie smiled as she held out the soup. It reminded me of the way she'd smiled at Duncan just before she'd tricked him by dropping her shoulder bag, and I suddenly knew what was about to happen. As Strachan started to take it from her, the basin slipped between their hands. Soup and broken crockery went everywhere as it shattered on the floor.

'Oh God, I'm sorry . . .' Maggie stammered. She avoided looking at me as she fumbled in her pocket for a tissue. Pale splashes of soup dotted the bright red of her coat as well as Strachan's clothes.

'Leave it, it doesn't matter,' he said irritably.

'No, please, let me clean it up . . .'

Strachan crossly took hold of her wrists as she began dabbing ineffectively at the front of his shirt.

'Michael? I heard something breaking.'

Grace was coming downstairs, wrapped in a thick white towelling bathrobe. Her damp hair was piled loosely on top of her head.

Deliberately pushing Maggie's hands away, Strachan stepped back from her. 'It's all right, darling.' He gestured ironically at the mess. 'Miss Cassidy here just brought you some soup.'

Grace gave a wry smile. 'So I see. Well, don't keep her standing outside.'

Reluctantly, Strachan moved aside to let Maggie in. As he closed the door behind her, she finally acknowledged me.

'Hello, Dr Hunter,' she said with a look of studied innocence, before turning back to Grace. 'I'm sorry, Mrs Strachan. I didn't mean to bother you.'

'It's no bother. Come on through into the kitchen while I get a cloth for the mess. Michael, darling, why don't you see to Maggie's coat? There's a sponge you can use in the utility room.'

Maggie shrugged out of her coat and gave it to Strachan. Without its bulk she looked even tinier than before. She didn't look at me as we went into the kitchen. Grace started to fill the kettle.

'I feel really bad about this,' Maggie said to her. 'Especially at a time like this. Being attacked like that . . . it must have been awful for you.'

It was time I intervened. 'Grace, you really should be taking it easy. Maggie and I will be fine by ourselves for a few minutes. Won't we, Maggie?'

Maggie looked daggers at me. 'Well . . .'

'Actually, I do feel washed out,' Grace said with a wan smile. 'If you're sure you don't mind keeping Maggie company, David, I think I'll go to bed.'

I told her I didn't mind at all.

Maggie watched her go, then her shoulders slumped. 'Bollocks. Now look what you've done.'

I went to the sink and pulled a sheet of kitchen paper from a roll. 'You've got soup on your jeans,' I said, handing it to her. 'Your gran's name isn't Campbell, by any chance?'

'Campbell? No, she's a Cassidy, same as . . .' Her face fell.

'I practically lived on the stuff when I was a student,' I told her. 'Cream of chicken was my favourite. It's the sort of smell you never forget.'

'All right, my gran didn't make it. So what? It's the thought that counts.'

Her defiance was wafer-thin, but before either of us could say anything we heard Grace scream. I ran out to find Strachan staring through the open front door, while Grace stood in the hallway, anxiously hugging herself.

'It's all right,' Strachan said, closing the door. 'False alarm.'

Grace wiped her eyes and gave a tremulous smile. 'Sorry. I thought I heard someone outside. I'm jumping at my own shadow.'

'Can I do anything?' I asked.

Strachan had put his arms round his wife. 'No. I'll be with you in a minute.'

'Actually, we were just leaving,' I said. 'Maggie's offered to drive me back to the hotel. Haven't you, Maggie?'

The reporter managed a strained smile. 'Aye. I'm a regular bus service.'

Neither of us spoke as Strachan helped Grace upstairs, then came back down and collected Maggie's coat from the utility room.

'Thank you,' Maggie said in a small voice. 'I'm sorry about the mess. And I'm really glad your wife is all right.'

Strachan gave her a cold nod. I told him I'd come the next day to check on Grace, and ushered Maggie outside. Night had fallen as we hurried to the Mini, leaning into the wind as the rain was driven against us in sheets.

I slammed the car door and turned to her angrily. 'So are you going to tell me what you were doing back there?'

Maggie rammed the car into gear and headed for the road. 'Nothing! I told you, I just came out to—'

'I know why you came. Christ, Grace might have been *killed*, and you pull a trick like that! Just to get your name on the front page?'

'OK, so I'm a cow! But I can't just sit at my gran's pretending nothing's happening.' She was on the verge of tears. 'Whatever's going on, a story like this could be a big deal for me! All I want is a few words from one of them.'

'Is that all this is? Just a career opportunity?'

'No, of course it isn't! I was born here. I know these people!'

Her small face was pinched and intense. I still didn't like what she'd done, but her need to be believed seemed genuine. The wind shook the Mini as I debated if I could trust her. *What do your instincts say?*

I just hoped I could trust them, as well.

'This is strictly off the record, Maggie. OK? People's lives are at stake.'

She nodded earnestly. 'Aye, of course. And I know I shouldn't have come out to see Grace—'

'This isn't just about Grace . . .' I paused, uncertain even now. But it was going to come out soon, anyway. Better to tell her now than have her keep snooping around. And perhaps getting herself hurt because of it.

'Duncan, the young PC, was killed last night.'

Her hand went to her mouth. 'Oh my God!' She stared through the windscreen as it sank in. 'I can't believe it. I mean, he was . . . What the hell's going on? This is *Runa*, for God's sake, things like that don't happen here!'

'Apparently they do. Which is why you need to stop pulling stunts like this. Two people have been killed already. This afternoon it could easily have been three. Whoever's doing this, they're not playing games, Maggie.'

She nodded. 'Does anyone else know? About Duncan, I mean?'

'Not yet. Brody or Fraser will probably have to tell people before much longer. But until they do, I'd appreciate it if you kept it to yourself.'

'I won't say anything, I promise.'

WRITTEN IN BONE | 265

I believed her. For one thing, she couldn't get word out to her newspaper. For another, Maggie looked stunned. She still seemed shell-shocked as the headlights picked out a shape on the side of the road ahead of us. It was blurred by the squeaking windscreen wipers, then resolved into a figure crouched in a reflective yellow rain cape.

'Look's like Bruce has had an accident,' Maggie said.

As she slowed I could see it was Cameron, white face caught in the head-lights as he worked over the chain of his mountain bike.

'Don't tell me he cycled out here in this?' I said, realising that he must still be on his way back from Strachan's house.

'Aye. I passed him on the way out. Prides himself on being out in all weather. Bloody *amadan*.'

I didn't have to understand Gaelic to know an insult when I heard one. Cameron shielded his eyes against the car's lights as we pulled up, a spanner still clutched in his hand. Maggie wound down the window.

'You want a lift, Bruce?' she called.

The cape thrashed around him in the wind, moulding to his skinny frame like a live thing and threatening to blow him off balance. He looked frozen and soaked, but when he saw me in the car his expression hardened.

'I can manage.'

'Suit yourself,' Maggie muttered. She closed the window and pulled away. 'God, he gets up my nose. Got all snotty the other day when I asked to do a story about him being a teacher and male nurse. I wouldn't have minded, but he could hardly keep his eyes off my boobs. Randy bugger.'

Cameron's feelings for Grace Strachan evidently didn't stop him ogling other women, I thought. And then I realised something else.

He'd been using the spanner with his left hand.

I turned to look back through the rear window. But the darkness and rain had swallowed him up.

'CAMERON'S AN AWKWARD SOD. But I don't see him as a killer,' Brody said, putting the kettle on the cooker and lighting the gas under it.

We were in his small kitchen, sitting at his spotless table while he made tea. I'd had Maggie drop me off at the hotel, but only stayed long enough to collect Fraser. I'd expected to find him in the bar. Instead he'd been in his room, and when I'd knocked I could hear him blowing his nose before he came to the door. When he opened it, his face was blotched and red. But his manner was as gruff as ever as I told him we needed to talk with Brody.

'I'm not saying he is,' I said, as the old DI shook out the match he'd used to light the gas. 'But he was using the bike spanner with his left hand. We know that whoever killed Duncan was left-handed. And Grace was hit on her right cheek, which suggests the same thing about her attacker.'

Fraser sniffed dismissively. 'Cameron's a prick, I'll grant you that. But I can't see a runt like him getting the better of Duncan.'

'Duncan was hit from behind. He didn't get a chance to defend himself,' I reminded him. 'We already know that Cameron's got a thing about Grace. He's the schoolteacher, so he'd hardly want it known he was using a prostitute. If Janice Donaldson threatened to tell, he might have killed her.'

The kettle set up a mournful whistling and Brody poured the boiling water into a teapot. With his right hand, I noticed.

I was getting obsessive.

He brought the teapot and three mugs over to the table. 'It's possible,' he said, setting them down in front of us. 'But let's forget Cameron for now and look at what else we've got. The body of a murdered prostitute turns up, badly burned. Whoever killed her was apparently unconcerned about it being found, until word gets out it's being treated as a murder inquiry.'

He didn't look at Fraser as he spoke, but he didn't have to.

'The killer panics and decides to get rid of the remains, as well as whatever other evidence might be left. In the process he kills a police officer, and very nearly the forensic expert as well.'

'We're missing something here,' I insisted. 'Why was Janice Donaldson's body left in the cottage instead of being buried or thrown off a cliff? Chances are it would never have been found then.'

Brody looked thoughtful as he poured the tea. 'Let's go back to the attack on Grace. My feeling is that it was opportunistic. That she walked in on somebody as they were smashing the yacht's comms system. So whoever it was, it had to be someone who knew we can't use the police radios.'

'That rules out Cameron,' Fraser said. 'Had to be someone from the boatyard, if you ask me. They all knew our radios weren't working. One of them could have legged it up to the yacht while we were on the ferry.'

'Could be,' Brody said. 'But let's not forget there's someone else who knew we wanted to use the yacht's radio.'

I could guess what was coming. 'You mean Strachan?'

He nodded. 'You asked him about it when he came out to the cottage.'

I'd come to respect Brody's instincts, but I was starting to think he was letting his animosity cloud his judgment where Strachan was concerned. I'd seen the man's reaction when he'd realised Duncan was dead. Even if his shock had been feigned, I didn't think anyone could make themselves throw up to order, no matter how good an actor they were.

Fraser obviously shared my doubts. 'Why the hell would he attack his own wife and then come running for help? Doesn't make sense.'

'It does if he wanted to divert suspicion away from himself,' Brody said mildly. Then he shrugged. 'But you could be right. I just don't think we can afford to rule anyone out at the moment, that's all.'

He was right, I realised. Duncan had already died because too much had been taken for granted.

'I still don't understand what was gained by smashing the yacht's radio anyway,' I said. 'Even if we could contact the mainland, no one can get out to us until the weather improves. So what was the point?'

Brody took a drink of tea and placed his mug carefully back on the table. 'Time, perhaps. If the mainland knew that a police officer had been killed, there'd be a helicopter ready to lift off the minute the weather permits. But as things stand, they'll wait till it clears before they start things moving, giving the killer a clear window to get off the island.'

'So what do we do about it?' Fraser demanded.

Brody gave a shrug. 'Watch our backs. And hope the weather clears.'

It was a depressing thought.

The three of us took the Range Rover back to the hotel shortly afterwards. The gale showed no sign of abating, and the unlit streets seemed eerily deserted as we drove up the steep hill to the hotel. It was only when we got out of the car that we became aware of the hubbub coming from inside.

Brody frowned. 'Something's up.'

The small bar was packed to overflowing, people crowding the hallway around its doorway. Heads turned towards us, the conversations abruptly dying to silence as word spread that we'd arrived.

'Now what?' Fraser muttered.

Kinross emerged from the bar, the hulking figure of Guthrie just behind him. His ice-chip eyes brushed on Fraser and me before fixing on Brody.

'We want some answers.'

Fraser drew himself up, shoulders bunched, but Brody cut him off.

'Aye, I dare say you do. Just give us a minute here, will you?'

Kinross gave a short nod. 'You can have two.'

He and Guthrie went back into the bar. Fraser turned on Brody angrily. The shock of Duncan's death had been building up all day. Now he was looking for somewhere to vent it.

'You've no authority to tell them anything!' he said.

Brody kept his voice level. 'They've a right to know. Two people are dead. You want to risk anyone else being killed because you didn't warn them?'

'He's right,' I said. 'You've got to tell them what we're dealing with. If not you're putting more lives at risk.'

Fraser had a cornered look about him, but he wasn't giving in. 'I'm not telling anybody anything without proper orders, and nor is anyone else!'

'No?' A muscle was ticking in Brody's jaw. 'And what are you going to do? Arrest me?' He looked at the police sergeant disdainfully.

Fraser dropped his gaze. 'I'm not having anything to do with this.'

'Then don't,' Brody said, and started towards the bar.

I went with him, leaving Fraser in the hallway. We had to ease through the crush in the small room. Ellen was serving behind the bar, looking flustered. Cameron was standing by himself in a corner. Maggie was there too, standing with Kinross, a look of anticipation on her face.

Brody made his way to the fireplace and calmly surveyed the room.

'By now I'm sure you're all aware that Grace Strachan was attacked this afternoon,' he said, his voice carrying without effort. 'Most of you will also have heard that the police are treating the body found in the old cottage near Beinn Tuiridh as a suspicious death.'

He paused, looking round the room. I noticed that Fraser had come into the bar. He stood in the doorway, listening sullenly.

'What you don't know is that, sometime last night, the police officer who was on duty there was murdered. Whoever killed him also torched the community centre and medical clinic, and almost killed Dr Hunter here.'

His words provoked an uproar. Brody raised his hands for quiet, but no one took any notice. I could see Ellen looking nervous behind the bar. Then a voice was bellowing above the rest.

'Quiet, everyone! *I said QUIET!*'

The clamour died down. It was Kinross who'd shouted. In the silence that followed, the ferry captain stared across at Brody.

'Are you saying it was somebody from the island? One of us?'

Brody stared back without flinching. 'That's exactly what I'm saying. I don't like it any more than you do. But the fact is that somebody on this island has killed two people and assaulted another.'

'No.' Kinross shook his head. 'No way. If there was a killer here, don't you think we'd know it?'

There were murmurs of agreement. As Brody tried to make himself heard above the rising volume, Maggie squirmed her way to the front. She thrust out her voice recorder, as though this were a press conference.

'The body that was found at the cottage. Do you know who it is?'

Brody paused. I knew he was judging how much he should say.

'It hasn't been formally identified yet. But we think it might be a missing prostitute from Stornoway.'

I was watching Cameron as Brody spoke. But if the news meant anything to him, he didn't show it.

'What the hell was a tart from Lewis doing here?' Karen Tait called out.

Guthrie grinned. 'Take a guess.'

No one laughed. But I was more interested in another reaction. Kinross's son, Kevin, had given a start at the mention of the dead woman. His mouth opened in a shocked 'O' before he noticed I was watching him.

Everyone else's attention was still on Brody. 'The police are going to be sending teams out here as soon as the weather allows. I'll ask you all to cooperate with them when they arrive. The cottage is a crime scene now, so please keep away from it. And if any of you think you might have any information, you need to tell Sergeant Fraser over there.'

It was a clever touch from Brody, a way of handing some self-respect back to Fraser, while reminding the islanders that there already was a police presence on Runa. One by one, people turned away. Maggie lowered her voice recorder and gave me a troubled look before making her way from the bar.

I looked over to where Kevin Kinross had been standing. But at some point the teenager had slipped away too.

WE FOUND an empty table when the bar started to thin out. Fraser insisted on buying malts for himself and me and a tomato juice for Brody.

He raised his glass. 'To Duncan. And to the bastard who killed him.'

Solemnly, we toasted. Then I told them about Kevin Kinross's reaction to the news that the murdered woman was a prostitute from Stornoway.

'Worth following up,' Brody mused. 'Perhaps we should have a word with him tomorrow, if the support team still aren't here.'

Fraser looked morosely into his glass. 'I hope to Christ they are.'

So do I, I thought. *So do I.*

I made my excuses not long after that. I'd eaten nothing, and on an empty stomach the alcohol had made me feel light-headed. All at once, everything seemed to catch up on me, and I could hardly keep my eyes open.

Ellen was still serving behind the bar as I made my way out. I didn't think she'd seen me, but then I heard her call as I started up the stairs.

'David?' She hurried out of the bar. 'I'm really sorry, I've not had a chance to get you anything to eat. Do you want me to bring something up?'

'I'm fine, really. I'm going to get some sleep.'

There was a creak on the landing above us. We looked up to see Anna. She was in her nightdress, and her face was pale and bleary with sleep.

'What have I told you about coming downstairs?' Ellen scolded, as her daughter came down the rest of the way.

'I had a bad dream.'

Ellen cuddled her. 'It was just a dream and it's gone now. Did you thank Dr Hunter for the chocolate he brought you the other day?'

Anna considered, then shook her head. 'Thank you,' she said sleepily.

'That's better. Now come on, young lady. Back to bed.'

The little girl slumped against her mother's legs. 'I can't walk.'

'And I can't carry you. You're too heavy.'

Anna lifted her head enough to regard me with a sleepy eye. 'He can.'

'No he can't, madam. He's got a poorly arm.'

'It's OK. I can manage,' I said.

Ellen looked doubtfully at my sling.

'I'd be happy to. Really.' I hoisted Anna up and she snuggled down against my shoulder, just as my own daughter used to. The small, solid weight of her was upsetting and comforting at the same time.

I followed Ellen to the attic floor, where there were two small private rooms. Anna barely stirred as I lowered her into her bed. Then we crept out and went back downstairs.

Ellen paused when we reached my floor. 'Are you OK?'

She didn't have to say what she meant. I smiled. 'I'm fine.'

Ellen knew enough not to push. With a final good night she went back down to the bar. I went into my room and sank heavily onto the mattress. I could still feel the phantom weight of Anna. If I closed my eyes I could almost pretend it was Alice's. I sat there, thinking about my dead family as the wind howled outside. More than ever, I wished I could call Jenny.

But that was something else I couldn't do anything about.

My head jerked up as there was a rap on the door.

'Just a second.' I'd started to drift off, I realised.

Rubbing my eyes, I went to the door. I thought it might be Ellen, determined to feed me after all. But when I opened it I found Maggie Cassidy.

She was holding a tray, on which was a bowl of soup and two chunks of bread. 'Ellen said if I was coming up anyway I had to bring you this. Said to tell you that you'd got to eat something.'

I took the tray and stepped back to let her in. 'Thanks.'

She smiled hesitantly. 'Soup again. Been quite a day for it, eh?'

'At least you didn't drop it this time.'

I set the tray down on the cabinet. Maggie sat on the room's only chair, and gestured to the tray.

'Go ahead, you might as well start. Ellen'll kill me if you let it get cold.'

I didn't have the energy to argue. I was still too tired to feel hungry, but the first mouthful changed that. Suddenly I was famished.

Maggie toyed with the edge of the chair as I tore off a hunk of bread. 'There's something I want to ask you,' she said eventually.

'You know I can't tell you anything.'

She held up a finger. 'One question, that's all. And strictly off the record.'

'Where's your voice recorder?'

'God, you're a suspicious bugger, aren't you?' She reached into her bag and took out her recorder. 'Turned off. See?'

I sighed. 'All right, one question. But I'm not promising anything.'

'That's all I ask,' she said. She seemed nervous. 'Brody said the dead woman was a prostitute from Stornoway. Do you know her name?'

'Come on, Maggie, I can't tell you that.'

'I'm not asking what it is. Just if you know it.'

I tried to see the trap. 'Not officially.'

'But you've a pretty good idea who she is, right?'

I let my silence answer that.

Maggie bit her lip. 'Her first name . . . It wouldn't be Janice, would it?'

My face must have been confirmation enough. 'Why do you say that?'

'Sorry, I can't reveal sources.'

'This isn't a game, Maggie! If you know something, tell the police.'

'I'm doing my job!' she flashed back.

'And what if someone else gets killed? Chalk it up as another exclusive?'
That hit home. Maggie looked away.

'You're from Runa,' I pushed. 'Don't you care what happens here?'

'Of course I bloody do!'

'Then tell me where you got the name from.'

I could see conflicting emotions warring in her. 'Look, it's not like it
sounds. The person who told me . . . they're not involved.'

'How do you know?'

'Because I *do*.' She stood up. 'Look, give me till tomorrow. I promise I'll
tell either you or Brody then.'

'Don't do this, Maggie. You can't just walk away.'

But she was already heading out of the door.

THREE O'CLOCK in the morning is the dead time. It's the time when the body
is at its lowest ebb, physically and mentally. The time when defences are
lowest, when the worst imaginings seem inescapable.

I surfaced from unconsciousness reluctantly, knowing that I would find it
hard to sleep again once I was fully awake. The bed springs squeaked under
me as I looked at the clock. *Just after three.* I could hear sinister creaks and
groans as the old hotel shifted and settled, like an arthritic old man. Outside,
the wind still blustered. I lay staring up at the ceiling, feeling sleep retreat
further. Then I realised something was different.

I could see the ceiling.

The room wasn't dark. A faint glow was coming through the curtain. My
first thought was that it was from the street lamp outside the hotel, that the
power must be back on. But the light coming through the window wasn't
constant. It had a febrile, flickering quality.

I hurried to the window and pulled back the curtain. The rain had stopped,
but the street lamp outside was dead and dark, quivering in the wind like a
limbless tree. The light I'd seen was coming from the harbour, a sickly
yellow glow that reflected from the wet rooftops of the houses.

Something was on fire.

I quickly pulled on my clothes, wincing as my injured shoulder complained. I hurried down the hall and banged on Fraser's door.

'*Fraser!* Wake up!'

There was no answer. If he'd stayed in the bar all night, trying to drown
his guilt and grief over Duncan, there was no way I'd raise him.

I ran downstairs. There was no sign of Ellen. The wind tried to rip my coat from me as I rushed outside, struggling to fasten it over my arm. Further down the hill people were emerging from houses, their voices calling urgently to each other as they hurried towards the harbour.

As I passed the lane that ran behind the hotel, I noticed that Ellen's old Beetle wasn't there. I guessed she'd already gone to investigate the blaze. The glow in the sky was brighter now, shining on the rain-slick street. I thought it might be the ferry that was burning, but when I reached the quayside I saw it was still moored safely out on the jetty.

The fire was in the boatyard.

Guthrie's derelict fishing boat was ablaze. Its stern was already engulfed, the wheelhouse on its deck burning fiercely. As flames flowed over its half-timbered hull with a sinuous grace, figures scurried about, snatching up buckets. Guthrie was bellowing frantic instructions, and I saw Kinross with a heavy extinguisher, venturing as close to the flames as he could.

A hand fell on my shoulder. I turned and saw Brody, face jaundiced by the yellow light.

'What happened?' I asked.

'No idea.'

It seemed like most of the village was there now, passing buckets along a line. They couldn't save the boat, but they could stop the fire from spreading.

Across the yard, I caught a glimpse of Maggie's distinctive red coat as she stood with a group of onlookers. Cameron was standing by himself, his face shadowed as he stared at the flames. I looked around for Ellen. I'd assumed she'd come down to the harbour, but now I thought about it, it seemed odd that she hadn't woken Fraser or me first.

Brody saw me looking around. 'What's wrong?'

'Ellen's car wasn't at the hotel. I thought she must have come down here.'

'She wouldn't have left Anna,' Brody said, scanning the crowd. There was a note of anxiety in his voice.

I became aware of a sudden tension in the air. It was like a ripple of communal unease, spreading as quickly as the flames. Then the wind gusted, lifting the veil of smoke to reveal something moving inside the blazing boat.

Cocooned in fire, a human arm was slowly lifting, as though in salute.

'Jesus Christ,' Brody breathed.

Then, with a flurry of sparks, the deck collapsed and buried the awful sight from view.

Pandemonium broke out. People were crying and yelling instructions, shouting, for someone to do something. I felt a sudden grip on my shoulder. Brody was staring at me, his face etched with an unforgettable expression.

He uttered just one word, but it was enough. 'Ellen.'

Then he was barging people aside as he ran towards the burning boat.

'Brody!' I yelled, going after him.

The flames beat him back. I grabbed hold of him. We were close enough now for our coats to steam. If the boat collapsed we'd be caught in it.

'Come on, get back!'

'She was moving!' He pulled away from me, staring into the flames as though trying to find a route into them. I grabbed him again.

'It was only a reflex! Whoever it is, they're dead! You can't do anything!' What we'd seen wasn't a sign of life. It was the opposite.

Brody finally allowed me to pull him away, stumbling like a man caught in a nightmare. What was left of the boat looked as though it could collapse any second. I ran to where Kinross was still futilely spraying the fire extinguisher onto the flames.

'We need to get the body out!' I shouted.

'Get the fuck out of my way!' he said savagely.

I grabbed his arm. 'You can't put it out! We need to get the body out before the fire destroys any evidence that's left. Get some poles! Now!'

He wrenched free, and I thought he might take a swing at me. Then he shouted to the other men battling the fire to fetch scaffolding poles and long pieces of timber from the building supplies stacked nearby.

Feeling helpless, I could only stand with Brody and watch as they began using the poles to try and snag the body from the flames.

Brody's face was haggard. *It can't be Ellen*, I told myself, feeling an awful hollowness. I tried to think of where she could be, for another reason for her car to be missing. *Dear God, what about Anna? Where's she?*

Across the other side of the yard I caught a glimpse of Maggie's bright red coat, and I felt my anger start to rise. Whatever she'd kept from me earlier might have been able to prevent this.

Skirting the burning boat, I started across the yard, and as I did I almost bumped into someone coming the other way.

It was Ellen. She was carrying Anna on one shoulder. The little girl was half asleep as she stared at the flames.

'What happened?' Ellen asked, staring past me to the fire.

Before I could answer Brody came running over. 'Thank God you're all right!' He seemed about to hug her but stopped, suddenly embarrassed.

Ellen was looking bewildered. 'Why wouldn't I be? I've been at Rose Cassidy's. What's going on?'

'You were at Maggie's grandmother's?' I asked, recognising the name.

'Aye, she had a fall, so one of her neighbours came to fetch me. Rose isn't fond of Bruce Cameron,' she added wryly. 'Poor woman's worried more than anything. Maggie went out earlier and hasn't come back.'

'I just saw her, she's down here,' I said, looking round.

Maggie was still where I'd last seen her, watching the boat burn with Karen Tait. She had her back to me, a familiar, diminutive figure in her oversized coat. I went across, driven by an apprehension I couldn't name.

'Maggie?' I said.

But at that moment a cry went up from the boat. '*Over here. We've got it.*'

I looked over, saw that the men had succeeded in dislodging a blackened object from the fire and were trying to drag it further away from the flames.

I'd actually started to go over when Maggie turned round, and shock rooted me to the spot.

The face gazing back at me from inside the red hood wasn't Maggie's. It was a teenage girl's, blank and uncomprehending.

Mary Tait. The girl I'd seen outside my window.

CHAPTER 8

An eerie silence had descended in the boatyard as people saw what had been pulled from the blaze. Then a fresh clamour erupted as they jostled either to get away from the sight, or to get a better look.

But I was still struggling to recover from the shock of seeing Karen Tait's daughter wearing Maggie's coat.

Karen had turned to glare at me, but by now Brody had followed me over. 'What's wrong?' he asked.

I found my voice. 'That's Maggie's coat.'

Karen Tait bridled drunkenly. 'He's lying!'

Kinross had broken away from the group of men by the fire and was pushing his way towards us. He was blackened and stinking of smoke, still clutching the charred pole he'd used to drag the body from the fire.

'We've got it out, like you asked.' He looked from me to Karen Tait. 'What's going on here?'

'It's them. They're calling Mary a thief!' Karen cried.

'That's Maggie's coat Mary's wearing,' Brody said calmly.

Karen's face contorted. 'That's a lie! Don't believe him!'

But Kinross was staring at the girl's coat with recognition. I remembered how he and Maggie had bantered on the ferry. There had been real affection there. He looked back at the smouldering body, and I saw him make the same connection that I already had.

'Where is Maggie?' he asked sharply.

No one answered. Something in Kinross's expression closed down. He swivelled his gaze back towards Karen Tait.

'We don't have time for this now,' I said quickly, trying to ignore my own fears for Maggie. 'We need to get the body somewhere safe.'

Kinross levelled a finger at Karen. 'We haven't finished,' he warned. Then, turning his back, he began yelling instructions to clear the yard.

Leaving Brody to watch Mary Tait and her mother, I pushed my way over to the body. It lay charred and twisted on the dirty concrete floor of the yard, a sight both pitiful and horrific. *Please, let me be wrong.*

I turned to Guthrie as he went past, ushering a huddle of people from the yard. 'Can I have a sheet of plastic or tarpaulin?'

I thought he either hadn't heard or was ignoring me. But a few moments later the big man returned with a bundled-up piece of dirty canvas.

He thrust it out at me. 'Here.'

I started to open it out, struggling in the high wind with only one arm. To my surprise, Guthrie helped me to spread it over the blackened form.

'Who do you think it is?' he asked, an almost fearful note in his voice.

I just shook my head as we hid the body from sight. But the heaviness in my heart told me that Maggie finally had her front-page story.

THE FIRE HAD ALL but burned itself out, and most of the islanders had gone home. What had once been a boat was now a mound of glowing ash and embers, still guttering fitfully with flame.

We'd eventually decided on taking the body into the workshop. There was still no way of knowing when SOC would arrive, and the protocol that said a crime scene should be left undisturbed hardly seemed to apply here.

The body was far too badly burnt to be recognisable, but I don't think anyone really doubted who it was. There had still been no sign of Maggie. Once Guthrie and Kinross had carried the body inside, using the tarpaulin as a stretcher, Guthrie went home, but Kinross refused to leave.

'Not until I've heard what she's got to say,' he declared, jerking his chin towards where Karen Tait waited miserably with her daughter.

Mother and daughter were sitting at the same table where the men had been playing cards yesterday afternoon. Later, Mary would have to be persuaded to take off Maggie's coat so that Forensics could examine it for trace evidence, but for now Brody let her keep it on, as proof against the cold.

Karen Tait stared resolutely down at the table's cigarette-burnt Formica, refusing to look at any of us. Brody took the chair opposite her, and I noticed that Fraser no longer made any objection to him taking over.

'All right, Karen. Where did Mary get Maggie's coat?'

'I told you, it's hers,' she said dully, and flinched as Kinross suddenly slammed his hand down on the table.

'Don't lie! We've all seen Maggie wearing it! For Christ's sake, tell us where she got the coat!' Kinross's voice held part warning, part entreaty.

'It's hers, Iain, honestly!'

'Don't fucking lie to me!'

Karen's resistance abruptly collapsed. 'I don't know! I only saw it tonight! That's the God's honest truth! She must have found it.'

'Where?'

'How should I know? You know what she's like, she wanders all over the island. She could have got it anywhere!'

'Jesus, Karen,' Kinross said in disgust.

'Don't you look at me like that, Iain Kinross! You never worried about Mary being out on the nights you've wanted to come round!'

Kinross started towards her, but Brody put out a restraining arm.

'Calm down. We need to find out where she found it.' He turned back to Karen. 'What time did Mary go out?'

She gave a sullen shrug. 'I don't know. She was out when I got back from the hotel at about twelve o'clock.'

'And what time did she get in?'

'How should I know?' Karen said again. 'I fell asleep. I didn't see her until the commotion with the fire woke me up.'

'And she had the coat then?'

'Yes, I've already told you!'

If he felt any contempt for the woman, Brody didn't show it as he switched his attention to her daughter.

'Hello, Mary. You know who I am, don't you?'

She looked at Brody without comprehension, then went back to the torch she'd been playing with. It was a child's, plastic and brightly coloured.

'You're wasting your time,' Kinross said. Despite his words, his tone wasn't unkind. 'She probably doesn't remember where she got it herself.'

'No harm in trying. Look at me, Mary.'

Brody spoke gently. Finally, she seemed to notice him.

He gave her a smile. 'That's a nice coat you've got on.'

Nothing. Then, suddenly, a shy smile lit her face.

'It's pretty.' Her voice was soft, like a little girl's.

'Yes, it's very pretty. Where did you get it?'

'From the man.'

I felt rather than saw Brody stiffen. 'Which man? Is he here now?'

She laughed. 'No!'

'Can you tell me who he is?'

'The *man*.' She said it as though it were obvious.

'This man . . . Will you show me where he gave you the coat?'

'He didn't *give* it to me.'

'You mean you found it?'

She nodded absently. 'When they ran off. After all the noise.'

'Who ran off? What noise, Mary?'

But he'd lost her. Brody continued to try for a while, but it was obvious he was wasting his time. Mary had told us as much as she was going to. He told Fraser to drive them home, and then come straight back. Kinross also left now, but before he did he gave one last look towards the back of the workshop, where he and Guthrie had laid the body.

'She always was one for getting into trouble,' he said sadly. Then he went out, letting the workshop door bang shut behind him.

Outside, the wind's banshee wail seemed louder than ever. The rain had started again, and was thundering against the corrugated roof. Brody and I went over to the body. It lay on the concrete floor, covered by the tarpaulin.

'You think it's her?' Brody asked.

I'd told him about Maggie's visit to my room earlier that night. How she'd known Janice Donaldson's first name, but wouldn't say who had told her.

I nodded. 'Don't you?'

Brody sighed. 'Aye. But let's see if we can be more sure.' He glanced at me. 'You ready?'

The honest answer would have been no. You never can be, not when it's someone you know. But I just nodded and pulled back the tarpaulin. A waft of warm air greeted me, carrying with it an odour of overcooked meat.

I crouched down beside the body. Shrunken by the fire, it looked pitifully small. Whatever clothing it had worn had burned away, as well as most of the soft tissue. The flames had twisted and warped it, exposing bone and tendons, drawing up the limbs into a characteristic boxer's crouch.

It was a sight that was becoming sickeningly familiar.

'So what do you think?' Brody asked.

An image of Maggie's gamine grin rose up in my mind. Almost angrily, I pushed it away. *Compartmentalise. This is work. Save the rest for later.*

'It's female. The cranium's too small to be a man's. Also, the chin's pointed, and the forehead and eyebrow ridge are smooth. A man's would be much heavier, more pronounced.' I took a deep breath. 'Then there's the height.' I indicated where the thigh bone was showing through the burnt muscle tissue, aware of the awful intimacy of what we were doing. 'Judging by the length of the femur, she was quite short. Five foot, perhaps a little less.'

'Could it be a child?' Brody asked.

I peered into the silent scream of the mouth. 'The wisdom teeth have broken through. So she was at least eighteen or nineteen. Probably older.'

'Maggie would have been what? Twenty-three, twenty-four?'

'About that, I expect.'

Brody sighed. 'Right height, right age, right sex. There's not much doubt, is there?'

I found it hard to speak. 'No.' Somehow, admitting it made it seem worse, as though I were letting Maggie down in some way.

Brody pursed his lips. 'Any idea about cause of death?' he asked.

'Well, from what I can see there's no sign of any head injury as there was with both Janice Donaldson and Duncan. Although . . .'

I bent forward for a closer look. The fire had stripped away the skin and muscle of the throat to expose burnt cartilage and tendon. The soft tissue was charred enough to disguise the signs, but not hide them altogether.

'What is it?' Brody prompted.

I pointed to the throat. 'See here? The tendon on the left-hand side of the throat's been severed. Both ends have contracted away from each other.'

'You mean someone slit her throat?'

'I can't be sure without carrying out a proper examination, but that's how it looks. There are what look like other puncture wounds as well. Here, on the shoulder, and the chest and stomach.'

'So she was stabbed to death?' Brody asked.

'She was certainly attacked with a bladed weapon. I'll need to examine the cuts to the bones in a lab before I can say for sure what type. But it's more complicated than that.'

'Complicated how?'

'Her neck's broken.'

I kneaded my eyes as a wave of tiredness washed over me. Tired or not, though, there was no doubt about what I'd seen.

'Look at the angle of her head. The third and fourth vertebrae are splintered. And the left arm and right shin are broken as well. They look like compression fractures, so they were probably caused by an impact . . .'

I stopped, then went to the grubby window. It was too dark to see much, but in the dying light from the burning boat I could just make out the dark cliff face, rising up only ten or twenty yards away.

'That's how he got her body down here. He threw her off the cliff.'

'You sure?'

'It would explain the fractures. She was attacked with a knife, and either fell or was thrown off the top. Then her killer came down and dragged the body from the foot of the cliff into the yard.'

Brody was nodding. 'There are steps at the end of the harbour that lead to the cliff top. With a torch you could just about manage them in the dark.'

That didn't explain why Maggie was up there in the first place. But at least a picture was forming of what had happened, if not why.

Brody rubbed his face wearily, his hand rasping on the grey stubble silvering his chin. 'Do you think she was alive when she went over?'

'I doubt it. Fall victims almost always have what are called Colles' fractures in their wrists, where they've put out their arms to stop themselves. There's nothing like that here. Only one arm's been broken, above the elbow, which suggests she was either dead or unconscious when she fell.'

Brody glanced out of the workshop window. 'Soon as it's light we'll go up and take a look. In the meantime—'

He broke off at a sudden commotion outside. There was a yell, then we heard the unmistakable sounds of a struggle. Brody jumped up and ran for the door, but before he reached it a blast of icy wind roared into the workshop as Fraser burst in, dragging someone with him.

'Look who I found snooping at the window!' he panted, thrusting the intruder ahead of him.

The figure stumbled into the centre of the workshop. Shocked and pale, the acne-scarred face of Kevin Kinross stared at us fearfully.

THE TEENAGER STOOD in the workshop, dripping water on the concrete. He was shivering, his eyes downcast, shoulders hunched in abject misery.

'I'm only going to ask you once more,' Fraser warned. 'What were you doing out there? Trying to listen in, is that it?'

Kevin didn't answer. I'd covered the body with the tarpaulin again, but not before he'd had a chance to see it lying on the floor. He'd immediately jerked his gaze away as though scalded.

'Can I have a word with him?' Brody asked.

Fraser flashed him an irritated look, but gave a terse nod. Brody went and fetched a stool from the table, and set it down next to Kevin.

'Here, sit down.' He perched himself on the corner of a workbench.

Kevin hesitated, then slowly lowered himself onto the stool.

'So what have you got to tell us, Kevin?'

The teenager swallowed. 'I . . . Nothing.'

Brody crossed his legs, as though the two of them were having a friendly conversation. 'I'm pretty sure you haven't done anything wrong, except for sneaking around outside. And I'm sure we can persuade Sergeant Fraser here to overlook that. Provided you tell us exactly why you were doing it.'

Kevin's eyes went to the tarpaulin-covered body. 'Is it right? What everyone says?' He sounded agonised.

'What are they saying?'

'That that's . . .' He darted another look at the body. 'That that's Maggie.'

Brody paused, but then answered, 'We think it might be, yes.'

Kevin started to cry. I remembered the way he'd behaved around Maggie, how he'd blushed whenever she'd acknowledged him. His crush had been painfully apparent, and I felt more sorry for him than ever.

Brody fished in his pocket for a handkerchief and gave it to him. 'What can you tell us about it, Kevin?' he said.

The youth was sobbing. 'I killed her!'

The statement seemed to charge the air with an electric current. In the silence that followed, the workshop's walls reverberated under the gale's assault, rain clattering like tintacks against the corrugated roof.

'What do you mean, you killed her?' Brody asked, almost gently.

Kevin wiped his eyes. 'Because if not for me she wouldn't be dead.'

'Go on, we're listening.'

Having come this far, though, now Kevin seemed to baulk. But I was thinking about his reaction when Brody had revealed that the body found in the crofter's cottage belonged to a prostitute from Stornoway. Not just shocked. Stunned. What was it Maggie had said about her source? *It's not like it sounds. The person who told me . . . they're not involved.*

'You told Maggie the dead woman's name, didn't you?' I said.

Kevin stared at me open-mouthed. He seemed to search for a way to deny it, then his will buckled. He nodded.

'How did you know her name, Kevin?' Brody asked, taking over.

'I . . . I can't tell you.'

'You want to spend time in a cell, lad?' Fraser cut in, oblivious to the angry look Brody shot him.

'Come on, Kevin,' Brody coaxed. 'Tell us. Where did you get the name from? Did someone tell you? Or do you know someone who knew her?'

Kinross's son hung his head. He mumbled something none of us could hear.

'Speak up!' Fraser barked.

Kevin's head jerked up angrily. 'My dad!'

The cry rang out in the confines of the workshop. Brody's face had stilled to immobility, masking any emotion.

'Why don't you start at the beginning?'

Kevin hugged himself. 'It was last summer. We'd taken the ferry across to Stornoway. My dad said he had some business to see to, so I walked into town. I thought I might go and see a film, so I cut through some backstreets and close by the cinema I saw my dad standing outside a house. I was going to go over to him, but then this . . . this woman opened the door. She was just wearing a bathrobe. You could see nearly everything. She gave my dad sort of a dirty smile. And then he went inside with her.'

Brody nodded patiently. 'What did she look like?'

'Well . . . like she was a . . . you know . . .'

'A prostitute?'

That earned a shamed nod.

'Can you describe her?'

'I don't know . . . Tall. Dark hair. Not fat, but not skinny. Older than me, but not that old. Pretty, but . . . she didn't look after herself.'

'So how did you know what she was called?' Brody asked.

The teenager's face flamed. 'After he'd gone in, I . . . I went over to the doorway. I'd seen he'd pressed the top buzzer. It just said "Janice".'

'Did your dad ever know that you'd seen him?'

Kevin looked appalled. He shook his head.

'So did he go to see her again?' Brody asked.

'I think so . . . Every few weeks he'd say he'd got some business to see to, so I . . . I guessed that was where he was going.'

'And did she ever come to see him here? On the island?'

The question was met with another quick shake of the head.

'How much of this did you tell Maggie?'

'Only the woman's name. I didn't want Maggie knowing my dad went with . . . you know. I just thought . . . her being a reporter, she'd be able to write a story saying who the dead woman was. I thought I was doing her a favour. I didn't know it would end up like this!'

Brody patted the youth's shoulder as he started crying again.

'Can I go now?' Kevin asked, wiping his eyes.

'Just a couple more questions. Do you have any idea how Mary Tait might have got Maggie's coat?'

Kevin lowered his head, avoiding anyone's eyes. 'No.'

The denial was too rushed. Brody regarded him expressionlessly.

'Mary's a pretty girl, isn't she, Kevin?'

'I don't know. I suppose.'

Brody waited until Kevin had started to shift uncomfortably before asking, 'So how long have you been seeing her?'

'I haven't!'

Brody just looked at him. Kevin dropped his gaze again.

'We just . . . meet up. We haven't . . . you know . . .'

Brody sighed. 'So where do you "meet up"?'

The teenager's embarrassment was painful. 'On the ferry, sometimes. The kirk ruins, if it's dark. Or . . . at the old cottage out at the croft.'

Brody looked surprised. 'You mean where the body was found?'

'Yes, but we haven't been there for ages. Honest! Not since summer!'

I thought about the empty cans and bottles we'd found. Nothing to do with the murdered prostitute after all, only the detritus of sneaked encounters between a handicapped girl and a scarred and frustrated boy.

'Is that where Mary goes when she wanders off? To meet you?'

Kevin stared down at his hands. 'Sometimes.'

'And how about tonight? Did you meet her then, as well?'

'No! I . . . I don't know where she went! Honest!'

He seemed on the verge of tears again. Brody considered him for a few seconds, then gave a short nod. 'You'd better get on home.'

'Now, just wait a second . . .!' Fraser objected.

But Brody had anticipated him. 'It's all right. Kevin's not going to say anything about what he's told us. Are you, Kevin?'

The youth shook his head. 'I won't. I promise.' He hurried to the door, then stopped. 'My dad wouldn't have hurt Maggie. Or the other woman. I don't want to get him into trouble.'

Brody didn't respond. But then there wasn't much he could say. There was a glimpse of lashing rain as Kevin went out, then the door swung shut.

Brody went over to the table and pulled back a chair to sit down. He looked drained. 'Christ, what a night.'

'You think we can trust the lad to keep quiet?' Fraser asked doubtfully.

The former detective passed his hand across his face. 'I can't see him running home to confess this to his father, can you?'

'So what now?' Fraser said. 'Arrest the bastard?'

Brody was silent. 'Not yet,' he said at last. 'All we have against Kinross is the fact he knew Janice Donaldson. If we arrested him we'd only be giving him time to prepare his story before Wallace's team get here.'

'We can't just sit on our arses! We've got to do something.'

'And we will.' Brody looked across at the tarpaulin-covered shape, thinking. 'David, do you still believe Maggie's body was thrown off the cliff?'

'I'm sure of it,' I said.

He looked at his watch. 'It'll be light in a couple of hours. As soon as it is, I say we take a look up there. In the meantime, I suggest you two go back to the hotel and try to get some sleep.'

'What about you?' I asked.

'I don't sleep much. I'll stay here and keep Maggie company.' He gave a smile, but his eyes looked haunted. 'I couldn't stop her from getting killed. Seems the least I can do for her now.'

I WOKE THE NEXT MORNING to the moaning of the gale. Feeling more tired than I could remember ever being, I plunged my head into cold water to wake myself up, then knocked on Fraser's door and went down to the kitchen.

Ellen insisted on cooking a full breakfast—a steaming plateful of eggs, bacon and toast, and sweet, scalding tea. I ate ravenously, feeling energy seep back into my limbs. Fraser came downstairs and sat opposite me.

'Radio's still out,' he grunted, without being asked.

I'd not expected otherwise. I was long past optimism or disappointment. Now all I wanted to do was see this through.

Dawn had broken and the sky was lightening imperceptibly as we drove back down to the boatyard. The storm had gained in intensity, buffeting the Range Rover and flinging rain against the windscreen in torrents.

Inside the workshop, Brody was sitting with a crowbar on his lap, coat collar turned up against the chill. Behind him, Maggie's tarpaulin-shrouded body looked childlike and pathetic on the concrete floor.

He smiled wanly when Fraser and I went in. 'Morning.'

He seemed to have aged overnight. His face was haggard, the flesh more tightly stretched over the bones.

'Any problems?' I asked.

'No. It's been quiet enough.'

He gave a sigh of appreciation as he took a bite from the bacon sandwich that Ellen had sent for him. When he'd finished eating he stood up and dusted crumbs from his fingers.

'Right, let's lock up here and take a look at the cliffs.'

We secured the doors with an oil-smeared padlock that Brody had found in one of the drawers, then set off for the cliffs. At their closest point, they lay only thirty or forty yards from the boatyard, but the rain battered us relentlessly as we crossed the open ground.

'Christ on a bicycle!' Fraser exclaimed, hunching against it.

The cliffs themselves afforded some protection once we reached them. A strip of shingle ran along their base, and we made our way, treading carefully as we scanned the rain-slick pebbles.

After a few yards, Brody stopped. 'Here.'

He pointed to a jagged rock protruding from the shingle. It had been sluiced almost clean by the rain, but a smear of something dark clung to it. I crouched down. It was a clot of bloodied tissue. The shingle around it was disturbed, a depression that could have been left by the impact of something heavy. What might have been drag marks ran from it towards the boatyard, disappearing where the shingle gave way to firmer ground.

I'd brought more freezer bags from the hotel to use as evidence bags. Taking one from my pocket, I used the blade of my penknife to scrape up a sample of bloody tissue.

Brody was looking up at the top of the cliff, about a hundred feet above us. 'No point all three of us climbing up.' He turned to Fraser. 'Makes more sense for you to take the car and meet us at the top of the steps.'

'Aye, you're right,' Fraser hurriedly agreed.

I gave him the plastic bag to take back to the Range Rover, then Brody and I crunched along the shingle to steep and winding steps cut into the cliff face. There was an old handrail, but it didn't inspire confidence.

Brody regarded them, then looked at my sling. 'Sure you're up to it?'

I nodded. I wasn't going to back out now.

Brody went first, leaving me to follow at my own pace. The steps were slippery with rain. Sea birds huddled against the cliff, feathers ruffling in the wind. The higher we climbed, the more it shrieked and flailed at us, as though wilfully trying to fling us off the cliff face.

Suddenly I noticed something on the rocky surface a few yards away.

'Brody,' I called.

When he turned, I pointed to where another dark smear tufted a bulging outcrop on the cliff face. It was too far out of reach for me to get a sample, but I could guess how it got there.

This was where Maggie's body had struck the rock on its way down.

We reached the top of the cliff a few minutes later. As we emerged onto it, the gale filled our coats like kites, threatening to fling us back over the edge.

'Bloody hell!' Brody exclaimed, bracing himself against it.

Below us, Runa's harbour was revealed as a shallow horseshoe of churning water, hemmed in by cliffs. A hundred yards away, Bodach Runa, the island's standing stone, rose from the turf like a crooked finger. Other than that, all there was to see was the treeless moor.

'Over there,' Brody said, pointing.

A couple of yards in front of us the turf was flattened and torn, and when I looked more closely I could see gouts of viscous black clotting the grass.

Even after all the rain, there was a lot of it.

'This is where she was killed,' Brody said, wiping rain from his face. He scanned the ground around us. 'There's more over there. And there.'

The patches, already almost washed away, formed a trail of blood that led away from or, more likely, towards the drop.

'She was running away,' I said. 'She was already injured before she got to the edge.'

'Could have been trying to reach the steps. Or just running blindly.' He gave me a look. 'You thinking what I'm thinking?'

'About what Mary Tait said?' I nodded.

They ran off. After all the noise. Perhaps the people she'd seen hadn't just run off. Perhaps one of them had been chasing the other.

But where had they come from?

Brody looked around the empty cliff top, shaking his head in frustration. 'Where the hell's her car? It's got to be around here somewhere.'

I considered the windswept cliff top. 'Remember when you asked Mary where she'd got the coat? What did she say, exactly?'

Brody gave me a puzzled look. 'That she got it from a man. Why?'

'No, she didn't say *a* man. She said *the* man.' I pointed at the standing stone, now no more than fifty yards away. 'You told me Bodach Runa meant "The Old Man of Runa". Perhaps that's the man she meant. Mary had a torch. She could have got up here using the steps, the same as us.'

Brody stared off at the standing stone. 'Let's take a look, shall we?'

The police Range Rover was visible perhaps a quarter of a mile away, snaking its way towards us as we set off. Fraser would be able to see where we were heading and meet us at the stone.

Brody walked at a fast pace across the uneven terrain. Shivering from the cold and rain, I was hard pushed to keep up with him. The ground rose up in a ridge between us and the standing stone, so that we could only see its upper half, but as we drew nearer I could make out something in a dip behind it. Gradually, the roof of a car came into view.

Maggie's old Mini.

It was parked in a hollow just beyond the stone. Brody and I slithered down the grassy bank towards it. A few moments later the Range Rover came bumping along the track.

Fraser parked beside the Mini and climbed out. 'That hers?'

'Aye,' Brody told him. 'That's Maggie's.'

Both doors hung open, swinging slightly as the wind pushed them back against their hinges. Splashes and smears of blood dappled the windscreen as though flung there by a mad artist.

'Jesus,' Fraser breathed.

Brody peered through the open driver's door at the blood-spattered interior. 'Looks like she was attacked from her side and she managed to scramble out of the passenger door. What do you think, a knife or axe?'

I approached closer. 'Knife, I'd say. Not enough room to swing an axe inside the car, not without leaving marks.'

I looked around the hollow. At night, beyond the arc of a car's headlights, it would have been impenetrably dark. Dark enough for Mary Tait to watch, unobserved. And to hear.

Fraser was looking behind the car. 'There's more tyre tracks back here. Don't look like they're from the Mini.'

Brody clicked his tongue, exasperated. I knew he was thinking that rain would churn the tracks into mud before SOC got here to take casts.

'Maggie must have come to meet someone up here. Mary must have been here already and close enough nearby to hear the commotion.' He frowned, staring at the car. 'I still can't see how she came by the coat. How come Maggie wasn't wearing it on a night like that?'

'Perhaps she took it off for Kinross,' Fraser suggested. 'Along with a few other things, if you get my drift. No other reason for them to meet up here. Then they had a lovers' tiff, or whatever, and Kinross lost his rag.'

'Maggie was an ambitious young woman,' Brody snapped. 'She'd have set her sights higher than a ferry captain. And until we can prove it was Kinross she met last night, I'd try not to jump to conclusions.'

Fraser coloured up at the rebuke.

'He's probably right about Maggie taking off her coat,' I said. I told them about the car heater being broken and stuck on full. 'When Maggie gave me a lift, she put it on the back seat.'

Brody was trying to see into the back of the car. 'Could be. There's hardly any spatter back there. After Maggie tried to get away, Mary could have just walked up and looked inside. Even if she noticed the blood in the front I doubt she'd realise what it was.'

He began to circle the Mini. When he got to the other side he stopped.

'There's something under the car.' There was a new excitement in his voice. 'Looks like her voice recorder.'

Brody could barely contain his impatience as I peeled off another plastic bag. 'Don't worry, I'll tell Wallace this was my decision,' he said, giving Fraser a shrewd glance.

For once, the police sergeant didn't argue. Evidence as potentially important—and vulnerable—as this could hardly be left until SOC arrived.

Putting his hand into the plastic bag, Brody picked up the voice recorder, then reversed the bag so the machine was enclosed in it.

'Wonder how long the batteries last on these things?' he mused.

'Long enough,' I told him. 'It's still recording.'

'What?' He stared at it. 'You're joking.'

'It started when you spoke. Must be voice activated.'

Brody studied the LCD display. 'So this could have been running when Maggie was killed.'

The wind wailed around us as we all considered that. I knew what Brody was going to say next.

'How do I play it?'

THE POLICE RANGE ROVER rocked in the wind, rain beating a tattoo on its roof. We'd retreated back to its warmth to play Maggie's voice recorder. Her entries were ordered by date. About a dozen of them had been made since Maggie had arrived on Runa.

Brody selected the most recent. According to the logged time and date, it had been made just before midnight.

'Here goes,' Brody said, pressing the PLAY button through the plastic bag. Maggie's voice issued eerily from the speaker.

'. . . Well, this is it. No sign of him yet, but I'm a few minutes early. Just hope he turns up after all this . . .'

'Hope who turns up? Come on, tell us the bastard's name,' Fraser muttered. But Maggie had other things on her mind.

'God, what am I doing here? Why the hell did Kevin have to tell me the woman's name? How did he know it anyway? And that stupid stunt with David Hunter. "Is the victim called Janice?" Really slick, Mags. Now he thinks I'm withholding information. But I can't just drop Kevin in it.'

There was a sound it took me a moment to place—Maggie was drumming her fingers on the steering wheel. She gave a sigh.

'Christ, this car's still like a bloody oven . . .' There was a rustling noise: she was taking off her coat. 'Must admit, I'm starting to feel a bit spooked. I mean, there's a killer loose on the island, for Christ's sake! If I heard about anyone else doing this I'd . . . Hang on, what was that?'

There was a long pause. The only sound was Maggie's breathing.

'I'm getting jumpy. Can't see anything now. Looked like a flash, like a torch. Probably a shooting star, or something. I'll give him five more minutes, and if he's not here then—Shit!'

Her breathing had become fast and ragged.

'There's that flash again. Somebody's out there! That's it, I'm going . . .'

There was a coughing whine as the car's engine turned over but wouldn't start. Over it we could hear Maggie's voice.

'Come on, come on! Oh, don't do this! You heap of junk, come on!'

Then she gave a laugh of pure relief.

'Oh, thank Christ! There's headlights. He's here. Bloody late, but I'll forgive him that! Shit, I can't see a bloody thing for his headlights. Right, let's hide this thing out of the way . . .'

We heard more rustling as she moved the voice recorder out of sight. There was the creak of a door opening.

'Hi. Thought you said midnight? Look, how about turning off the headlights? I can't see a . . . Hey, what are you . . .? Oh Jesus! JESUS!'

I bowed my head as Maggie's screams began to shrill out of the speaker. The machine had dutifully recorded a soundtrack of Maggie's murder.

The confusion of cries and scrambling reached a climax, then there was a sudden silence. The voice recorder had been knocked from the car as Maggie made her short-lived escape. With nothing louder to activate it, the machine soon shut off. There was a brief lull, then Brody's voice emerged.

'Wonder how long the batteries last on these—'

Brody stopped it there.

None of us looked at each other. It was as though, by listening to the recording of Maggie's killing, we'd colluded in something shameful.

'Why couldn't she have just said the bastard's name?' Fraser said.

I stirred. 'She'd no reason to. The recording was for her own benefit. Whoever it was, she didn't think she was in any danger from him.'

'Got it wrong, didn't she?' Fraser said. 'What's the betting he left the headlights on to dazzle her, so she wouldn't see he'd got a knife?'

Brody had been listening without comment. 'What about the flash she saw before the car arrived?'

'Mary Tait,' I said.

He nodded, his face a mask of fatigue. 'Wandering around with that toy torch of hers. If it wasn't so bloody tragic, it'd be funny. Maggie gets spooked by a harmless teenager, and opens her car door to a killer.'

'Aye, but who the hell was it?' Fraser said frustratedly.

Brody turned his attention back to the voice recorder. 'Let's see if there's anything else on here that might tell us.'

Brody went back to the start and played the entries in order.

'*Well, this is turning out to be a better trip than I expected. Just wish my gran had access to the Internet. Have to get someone at the newsroom to do a search on David Hunter. What's an expert from London doing out here, and with Sergeant bloody Neil Fraser? Of all the bloody cops to run into! Got a real bruise on my arm where he threw me out of the cottage. Too shocked to do much when it happened, though. God, the state of that body! I'd love to get a better look. Perhaps I should take a trip out there tonight. Fraser's bound to be in the bar by then . . .*'

The back of Fraser's neck was burning crimson. Brody kept his face impassive as he played the next entry.

Maggie sounded bad-tempered and out of breath. '*Well, a right waste of time that was. I still didn't manage to get a proper look at the body. That young PC's a keen bugger! What was his name? Duncan, I think they called him. Still, at least he seemed human. Cute, too, come to think of it . . .*'

The following four entries were mainly personal musings on family and work. Brody skipped through to the next. I felt a jolt of recognition when I realised what it was about.

'*Bit of a turnup for the books this afternoon. Took a short cut to my gran's down the alleyway behind the hotel, and who should come rushing out of the back door but Michael Strachan. Looked guilty as hell when I said hello. Never even occurred to me there might be anything between those two. I mean, Ellen's attractive, but the man's married to a goddess, for God's sake! But there's definitely something going on there . . .*'

So that had been who Ellen's anonymous visitor had been, when I'd discovered her crying in the kitchen. I glanced uneasily at Brody, but he made no comment as he played the next entry.

'*Well, here's me thinking I'm the seasoned reporter, unearthing some big secret, and it turns out to be old news. 'Course, my gran's sworn me to secrecy anyway.*' She gave a cynical laugh. '*The thing is, it's obvious once you look for it. The little girl's got Ellen's lovely red hair, but if you ignore that you can see that Strachan's her father . . .*'

Oh hell, I thought. Fraser gave a low whistle. 'So Strachan's been playing away from home? Some people are never satisfied.'

Brody looked startled, then his face hardened. Tightlipped, he stabbed at the machine with a blunt finger to play the next entry. It was Maggie recounting her futile visit to the Strachans' after Grace had been attacked, when she dropped the soup. The entry after that recorded the meeting at the hotel. Then came the last one. This time Maggie's voice sounded upbeat.

'*Finally, some good news! Almost missed it, too. I'd no idea the note was there, it was stuffed so far down in my coat pocket. Why he wants to meet me at midnight, and out at Bodach Runa, I don't know. Man's got a sense of the dramatic, I'll give him that. Anyone else but him, I might have second thoughts, but I dare say he just wants to wait till his wife's asleep. Well, if Michael Strachan wants to keep it private, I'm not going to argue.*'

The recording finished. The only sound was the drumming of the rain on the car roof, and the mournful bluster of wind.

CHAPTER 9

Fraser was the first to find his voice. 'Jesus Christ! She went to meet *Strachan*? But it doesn't make any sense! Why would Strachan kill her? And the others?'

Brody slowly shook his head. 'I didn't see this coming either, but Strachan makes more sense than Kinross. We thought Janice Donaldson might have been killed because she tried to blackmail a client, and who'd make the best target? A widowed ferry captain, or a wealthy married man who's the pillar of his community?'

'Aye, but . . . why would Strachan bother with a low-rent tart like Janice Donaldson when he's got a wife like that?'

Brody gave a weary shrug. 'For some men it's the sordidness that provides the kicks.'

It made an awful sort of sense. First Janice Donaldson, then Duncan had been killed as Strachan tried to cover his tracks. And even though Maggie's persistence in trying to interview him was innocent, to a killer who wasn't prepared to take any chances it would have appeared in a very different light.

'He planted the note yesterday,' I said slowly. 'While I was out there. He left Grace and Maggie with me while he went to clean her coat.'

Even the prowler that Grace thought she'd seen had no doubt been engineered by Strachan, a distraction so he could slip a note into Maggie's coat pocket. I felt shock give way to anger; outrage at the extent of Strachan's crimes. His betrayal of everyone who'd trusted him. Including me.

'So what do we do now?' Fraser asked.

Brody slowly opened the glove compartment and put the voice recorder inside. He closed the door again, pressing it shut with a deliberate *click*.

'We can't afford to wait any longer for the mainland team. We need to bring Strachan in. Or he'll be off on his yacht the second the weather clears.'

'We don't know for sure he'll run,' Fraser countered, but he didn't sound as if he believed it himself.

'He's killed three people, including a policeman,' Brody said implacably. 'He's losing it, getting desperate. We give him the chance, he'll run. Or kill somebody else. You think Wallace will thank you if that happens?'

Fraser gave a reluctant nod. 'Aye. Aye, you're right.'

Brody turned to me as the police sergeant started the car. 'What about you, David? I can't ask you to come with us, but I'd appreciate it.' His mouth twitched in an attempted smile. 'We need all the help we can get.'

I nodded. I'd come this far. Now I wanted to see it through.

Strachan's Saab and Grace's Porsche SUV were parked outside the house. Fraser pulled up behind them—blocking them both in, I noticed. The wind clubbed at us as we climbed out of the Range Rover. Brody paused by the Saab, bending to examine its tyres. They were thickly caked with mud.

He stood back, letting Fraser take the lead. Seizing the iron knocker, the burly sergeant began pounding on the front door.

From inside we could hear the dog barking, then the door was opened.

Grace looked out at us from behind a security chain. She smiled, relieved when she saw who it was. 'Just a second.' She slipped off the chain and stood back so we could enter. 'Sorry about that. But after yesterday . . .'

The bruising on her cheek somehow only accentuated her beauty. But there were shadows under her eyes that hadn't been there before the attack. An attack carried out by her husband to divert attention from himself.

'Is your husband in?' Fraser asked.

'No, afraid not. Gone off on one of his jaunts again.'

'Do you know where he is?'

Grace looked startled by his brusqueness. 'No, I'm sorry. Look, would you mind telling me what's going on? Why do you want to speak to Michael?'

Fraser ignored the question. 'Do you mind if we look around the house?'

Her eyes flashed at his tone, and for a moment I thought she would refuse. Then she gave an angry toss of her head. 'If you must.'

'I'll look in here,' Brody told Fraser. 'You check the barn.'

Grace watched them go, still angry but also bewildered. 'David, why are they looking for Michael? What's wrong?'

My hesitation must have been answer enough.

'Is this something to do with the murders?'

'I can't say. I'm sorry,' I said, hating the fact that her world was about to be shattered.

The dog was becoming hysterical at the sound of our voices. 'Oscar, be quiet!' Grace said, impatiently opening the kitchen door and pushing the retriever in. 'Come on! Outside!' She tugged him towards the back door.

Brody came back downstairs. He gave a quick shake of his head.

'Not there. Where's Grace?'

'Quietening the dog. I think she's started to guess why we're here.'

He sighed. 'Strachan's got a lot to answer for. Bad enough finding out your husband's a murderer, let alone got a child by another woman. What the hell was Ellen thinking of . . .?'

'Brody—' I said quickly, but it was too late.

Grace stood frozen in the kitchen doorway.

'I don't believe you . . .' she whispered. She'd gone white.

'I'm very sorry,' Brody began. 'You shouldn't have had to hear like that.'

'Get out! Get *out*!' It was more a sob than a shout.

'Come on, let's go,' Brody said quietly.

I didn't like leaving her like that, but there was nothing I could do or say that would make any difference now to Grace.

As we went outside, her perfect face was a stricken mask.

Brody closed the door behind us. 'Christ. I didn't mean that to happen.'

'Well, it has.' I felt unaccountably angry. 'Let's find Fraser.'

I pulled my coat hood tight against the cold as we made our way towards the barn. Fraser was just emerging.

'Find anything?' Brody asked.

'You'd better see for yourselves.'

Fraser led us back into the barn and went to where a petrol-driven lawn-mower stood in the far corner. Behind it was a large petrol container. There was no lid, only a broken plastic strap to show where one had been attached.

'What's the betting that the top we found near the camper van is from that?' Fraser said. 'Remember when Strachan's wife's car ran out of petrol? I'd put money that's where he got his accelerant from to start the fires.'

Brody looked down at the container. 'Let's check the boat.'

The yacht was unlocked. It was as we'd left it, the shattered remains of its comms still lying on the floor. But Strachan wasn't on board.

'So where the hell is he?' Fraser asked savagely.

But even as he said it I knew there was only one place Strachan would have gone. Looking across at Brody, I saw that he'd realised too.

He was on the mountain. At the burial cairns.

THE STORM HAD REACHED its peak on Runa, building into a frenzy as though determined to wrench the tiny island from the sea. As we clambered up the exposed slopes of Beinn Tuiridh, the wind seemed to have doubled its intensity. And the temperature had plummeted. The icy rain had turned to hail, white stones that bounced and skidded underfoot.

It was still light, but visibility was poor and there was another hour, two at most, before the first dimming of twilight. To make matters worse, we'd only a vague idea of where the cairns were.

'Never been up here before,' Brody panted. 'But I don't think the cairns are very far. If we head straight up we're bound to come to them.'

I wasn't so sure. The slope was treacherous with loose stone and scree, and there was nothing resembling any sort of path. We'd started out close together, but as the steep gradient took its toll we'd become strung out. Brody forged on resolutely, but with my balance impaired by my strapped arm I was finding the going harder. Overweight and unfit, Fraser was wheezing for breath and falling further behind with every step.

I was considering calling for a rest when there was a clatter from behind me. Looking back I saw that Fraser had fallen. Loose rocks formed a mini-avalanche around him as he slid backwards. He gulped air through his open mouth, too exhausted to get up. Ahead of us, Brody was carrying on, unaware.

'Brody! Wait!' I called, but the wind threw my words back at me.

I hurried back down to Fraser. I got my hand under his arm and tried to pull him to his feet. He was a solid, dead weight.

'Give me a minute . . .' he gasped.

But I could see there was no way he could go any further. I looked up for Brody again and saw him almost lost in the hail.

'Can you make it back to the car?' I asked, putting my mouth close to his ear so he could hear me over the wind.

He nodded, chest heaving, and waved me on irritably. I left him to it and hurried after Brody. I couldn't see him at all now. My breathing became ragged as I tried to catch up. I kept my head down to protect my face from the wind's bite, and stared at the ground directly in front of me.

A stone skidded from under my foot, sending me down onto one knee. 'Brody!' I shouted, but the only answer was the shriek of the gale.

I clambered to my feet again. It was too exposed to stay where I was. I had to decide whether to carry on or follow Fraser back down, and as I stood there I realised that the tumbles of rock nearby were oddly symmetrical. I was standing among the burial cairns.

But there was no sign of Brody. As I looked round for him, an eddy in the wind created a gap in the swirling hail. It only lasted for a moment, but while it did I saw a larger stone structure further off along the slope.

I went to take a closer look. The structure was like a round stone hut, partially caved in. Just outside it were the remains of a campfire. I remembered the hooded figure emerging into the firelight the night I'd been lost. Strachan's words came back to me. *The broch's a good place to think . . .*

I edged closer to the entrance and peered into it, trying to sense if anyone was inside. All I saw was blackness. Crouching down, I ducked through the low opening. Silence draped around me like a blanket. It was pitch-black, the air heavy with loam and age. As my eyes acclimatised, I made out cold stone walls and bare soil underfoot.

Then, from the corner of my eye, I noticed a small, pale blur. I bent down to examine it. Some of the stones had tumbled from the inner wall, forming a small hollow. Inside was a half-melted candle stub, surrounded by dirty yellow pools of solidified wax from countless predecessors.

I'd found Strachan's hide. But where was Strachan?

I straightened, and as I did the grey light coming from the entrance suddenly dimmed. I spun round as a shape rose from the shadows behind me.

'Hello, David,' Strachan said.

STRACHAN TOOK another step away from the wall, so he was silhouetted in the entrance. He held a knife down by his side, its blade catching the light from behind him.

'Found your way up here again, eh? Told you you'd find it interesting.'

He didn't come any closer, but he was between me and the only way out. I tried not to look at the knife.

He tilted his head, listening to the wind howling outside. 'Do you know what Beinn Tuiridh means? It's Gaelic for "Moaning Mountain". Pretty apt, I always thought.' His tone was conversational, as though he'd come here for a stroll.

I found my voice. 'Maggie Cassidy's dead.'

He was studying the hard stones. 'I know.'

'Did you kill her?'

Strachan stood poised for a moment with his hand on the wall. He dropped it with a sigh. 'Yes.'

'And Duncan? And Janice Donaldson?'

There was no surprise at hearing the prostitute's name. He just nodded. '*Why?*'

'Does it matter? They're dead. You can't bring them back.'

He seemed shrunken. I'd expected to hate him, but I felt more confused than anything.

'You must have had a *reason*!'

'You wouldn't understand.'

'Did Janice blackmail you? Was she threatening to tell Grace?'

'Leave Grace out of this,' he warned, his voice grown suddenly hard.

'Then tell me.'

'All right, she was blackmailing me. I'd been fucking her, and when she realised who I was she got greedy. So I killed her.' He sounded listless, as though none of this had any real bearing on him.

'And what about Duncan and Maggie?'

'They got in the way. I butchered them all like pigs, and I got a thrill out of it! Because I'm a sick, twisted bastard! Is that what you wanted to hear?'

I tried to keep my voice steady. 'So now what?'

He was backlit by the light from the entrance, half in shadow as he answered. 'Well, that's the question, isn't it?'

'Don't make this any worse for yourself than it is already,' I said, with a confidence I didn't feel. 'Think about Grace.'

He took a step towards me. 'I told you to leave her out of this!'

I made myself stay where I was, resisting the impulse to back away. 'Why? You *attacked* her! Your own wife!'

There was real pain in his voice. 'She took me by surprise. I only wanted to stop you using the yacht's radio. But the bloody dog knew I was down there, and when I heard Grace coming into the cockpit, I . . . I just spun round and backhanded her. I didn't mean to hit her so hard, but I couldn't let her see it was me!'

'So then you staged everything? Put her through all that?'

'I did what I had to do!'

But he sounded shamed. I pushed on, sensing an advantage.

'You're not going to get off the island, you know that, don't you?'

'Probably not.' He had an odd smile on his face. Seeing it, I felt suddenly cold. 'But I'm not going to give myself up, either.'

He lifted the knife. Its blade glinted silver as he held it up, considering it.

'Do you want to know why I came up here?' he began.

I never heard his answer.

A bulky shape flew into him from behind. There was a clatter as Strachan's knife flew from his hand, then I was knocked against the wall. Pain burst in my shoulder. Everything was shadow and confusion as Strachan and another figure struggled on the floor. In the half-light I made out Brody's features. Strachan was younger and fitter, but the older man had size on his side. Using his weight to pin him, he smashed his fist into Strachan's face, then hit him again. Strachan went limp even before Brody hit him a third time.

'Brody!' I caught hold of his arm. 'You'll kill him!'

He shrugged me off. In the light from the entrance I could see the grim intent in his face and knew he was beyond reasoning. I pushed myself off the wall, driving into him to knock him off the unmoving Strachan.

Fire lanced through my injured shoulder. Brody tried to push me aside, but the pain maddened me. I shoved him back.

'No!'

The rage seemed to drain from him. Panting, he slumped against the wall. I knelt down next to Strachan. He was bloody and dazed, but alive.

'How is he?' Brody asked breathlessly.

'He'll live.'

'More than the bastard deserves. Where's Fraser?'

'Back at the car. He couldn't make it up.'

I found the knife lying by the wall and used a freezer bag to pick it up. It was a folding fishing knife, its blade five inches long. But as I looked at it something stirred at the back of my mind. *What is it? What's wrong?*

There was a groan from Strachan.

'Help me get him up,' I said.

'I can manage,' Strachan gasped.

His nose was broken, making his voice sound hollow. Brody wrenched Strachan's arms behind his back and produced a pair of handcuffs.

'What are you doing?' I exclaimed.

'Souvenir from when I retired. Call it a citizen's arrest.' He snapped the cuffs onto Strachan and roughly pulled him to his feet. 'Aren't you going to plead innocence, Strachan? Insist you didn't kill anyone?'

'Would it make any difference?' he asked dully.

Brody looked surprised. 'No.' He pushed him outside.

I ducked through after them, blinking as I emerged into the daylight. The freezing wind took my breath away as I went to examine Strachan. Blood and mucus smeared his face and one of his eyes was puffed almost shut.

'Can you make it down?' I asked him.

'Do I have any choice?'

None of us did. Strachan wasn't the only one in bad shape. The climb and fight had taken its toll on Brody. His face was grey and I doubted I looked any better. We all needed to get off the exposed mountainside, fast.

Brody gave Strachan a shove. 'Move.'

'Take it easy,' I told him, as Strachan almost fell.

'Don't waste your sympathy. He would have killed you back there.'

Strachan looked over his shoulder at me. 'You were never in danger from me. I came up here to kill myself, not anybody else.'

'Save it, Strachan,' Brody told him roughly, steering him down the slope.

But the feeling that I was missing something was stronger than ever.

'You've murdered three people,' I said. 'Why kill yourself now?'

The desolation on his face seemed genuine. 'Because enough people have died. I wanted to be the last.'

Brody's next shove sent him to his knees. 'You lying bastard! All the blood on your hands, the lives you've ruined. Ellen's as well . . . I ought to—'

'Brody!' I quickly moved in between them. 'Let the police handle it now.'

Brody drew in a long, shaky breath, reluctantly nodding assent.

But Strachan was still staring at him. 'What about Ellen?'

'Don't bother denying it,' Brody said bitterly. 'We know you're Anna's father, God help her.'

Strachan scrambled to his feet. 'How did you find out? Who told you?'

'Maggie Cassidy. Seems like everyone on the island knew about it.'

'What about Grace? Does she know?'

'That's the least of your worries. After this—'

'*Does she know?*' His vehemence was startling.

I answered, feeling an awful apprehension start to bloom. 'It was an accident. She overheard.'

Strachan looked as if he'd been struck. 'We have to get back to the village.' Brody grabbed hold of him. 'You're not going anywhere.'

Strachan shook him off. 'Let me go, you bloody idiot! Christ, you've no idea what you've done!'

It wasn't his anger that convinced me. It was the fear in his eyes.

All at once I realised what had been bothering me. Why the sight of the knife had sparked it. It had been what Strachan had said: *I butchered them all like pigs!* It had been a sickening, distracting image, especially after seeing the vicious slashes on Maggie's body. But although Maggie had been killed with a knife, none of the other victims had. So either Strachan hadn't meant what he'd said, or . . .

Oh my God. What had we done . . .?

I fought to keep my voice steady. 'Take his handcuffs off.'

Brody stared at me as if I were mad. 'What? I'm not going to—'

'We need to get back!' Strachan broke in. '*Now!*'

'Why, for God's sake?' Brody demanded.

'He didn't kill them,' I said. The enormity of our mistake was starting to dawn. 'It was Grace. He's just been protecting her.'

'Grace?' Brody echoed incredulously. 'His *wife*?'

A look of self-loathing crossed Strachan's battered face.

'Grace isn't my wife. She's my sister.'

CHAPTER 10

Hindsight is the cruellest luxury. We'd been right, and yet hideously wrong. The intruder at the clinic, the wrecked yacht radio and attack on Grace, that had all been Strachan. He'd been stalking us, sabotaging us from the first day we'd arrived on the island to protect his sister, not himself. He wasn't the killer.

She was.

We didn't talk on the way down. We didn't have the time, or the breath. The hail had stopped, but the mountainside was littered with pellets of ice, and the wind chased us down. Once we reached more level ground we broke into a stumbling jog, silent except for the laboured rasp of our breathing.

Fraser was waiting in the Range Rover, engine running and the heater pumping out blessed hot air.

'Get us back to the hotel. Fast,' Brody gasped, hauling himself into the front passenger seat. 'We need to find Ellen.'

'Why? What—'

'Just drive!'

Still breathless, Brody turned round to confront Strachan as Fraser banged the Range Rover into gear. 'Talk.'

Strachan's broken nose was flattened, and his cheek was dark and swollen. He must have been in considerable pain, yet he gave no sign.

'Grace is ill. It's my fault, not hers,' he said dully. 'That's why I wasn't planning on coming back down the mountain. With me dead, she wouldn't be a threat any more.'

'Why is she a threat anyway?' Brody demanded. 'You're her brother, for Christ's sake. Why's she doing this?'

'Her *brother*?' Fraser exclaimed, swerving into a bend.

Strachan looked like a man staring into an abyss of his own making. 'Because she's jealous.'

The barren landscape flashed by outside. I found my voice first.

'She killed Maggie because she was *jealous*?' I said incredulously.

Strachan's bloodied mouth twitched involuntarily. 'I didn't know what she'd done until she came back, covered in blood. But Maggie had called to the house twice to see me. Grace might have overlooked the first time, but not the second. She pretended she'd seen a prowler to get me out of the way, then slipped a note into Maggie's coat arranging a meeting.'

So the prowler had been a distraction, after all, I thought. Except it had been Grace's own, not Strachan's.

'You've got to understand how it was,' Strachan said, and for the first time a hint of pleading had entered his voice. 'When we were growing up, there was just the two of us. Our mother died when we were young, and our father was away most of the time on trips. We lived on an isolated estate, with security guards and private tutors. All we knew was each other.'

'Get on with it,' Brody told him.

Strachan lowered his head. 'When I was sixteen I got drunk one night, and went to Grace's room. It was wrong, and it was my fault. But neither of us wanted to stop it. It became . . . normal. As I got older I thought about ending it, but then . . . Grace got pregnant.'

'The miscarriage,' I said, remembering what he'd told me in his sitting room. It seemed an age ago now.

'It wasn't a miscarriage. I made her have an abortion.' Now there was no mistaking there was pain as well as shame in his voice. 'There were complications. Grace almost died. They told her she could never have more children. She was changed after that. Unstable. She'd always been possessive, but now . . . I tried to finish it between us. I told Grace it was over and started seeing another girl. She went to the girl's flat and stabbed her to death.'

'Jesus,' Fraser said. The tyres skidded on the wet surface as he threw the car into another bend.

Strachan passed a hand over his face, oblivious to his injuries. 'No one suspected Grace, but she didn't even try to deny it to me. She told me she didn't want me to see anyone else. Ever.'

'Why didn't you tell the police?' I asked.

'And let everyone know what had been going on?' Strachan shook his head. 'It was my fault Grace was like she was. I couldn't just abandon her. We left South Africa, travelled around the world to places where nobody knew us. Where everyone would assume we were married. I tried to limit the . . . physical aspect between us. I'd still see other women. Prostitutes, mainly.' The self-loathing was plain in his voice. 'But Grace always seemed to find out, and when she did . . .'

He didn't need to finish. I willed Fraser to go faster.

'Each time it happened, we'd move somewhere else,' Strachan continued. 'And each time she got that bit worse. That's why we came here, to Runa. I liked this area, its wildness, and on an island like this Grace wouldn't be able to just come and go. We started to feel we were really part of something here. I found myself really wanting to *make* something of the island!'

Brody regarded him with contempt. 'So where did Janice Donaldson fit into your little paradise?'

A spasm of pain etched itself onto Strachan's face. 'She blackmailed me. I'd been seeing her for a while, but hadn't told her my real name. Then one day Iain Kinross showed up at her flat while I was there. He didn't see me, but my reaction tipped Janice off. She found out who I was. The next time I went she threatened to tell Grace. I paid her off. It can't have been enough.'

'Did you know all along your sister had killed her?' Brody asked.

'Of course not! I'd no idea she'd come to Runa. Even when I heard a body had been found, I didn't know it was anything to do with Grace. The whole burning thing, the fires, that was new. But when the constable was killed . . . I couldn't kid myself any longer.'

I thought about his reaction when he'd seen Duncan's body. It had been genuine after all. But it hadn't been the shock of seeing a body; it had been the realisation that his sister had started killing again.

'Why did she kill him?' Fraser demanded, his voice cracked. He was slewing the car round the bends, throwing us from side to side.

'I don't know. When she realised there was going to be a murder investigation she must have panicked and tried to get rid of anything that might incriminate her. Duncan must have just been in the way.'

'In the fucking *way*?' Fraser snarled, the car swerving as he started to turn round.

'Easy,' Brody warned him. His face was like stone as he turned back to Strachan. 'How many people has she killed?'

Strachan shook his head. 'I don't know. Four or five before this, perhaps.'

'Tell me about Ellen,' Brody grated.

Strachan closed his eyes. 'Ellen was a mistake. There always was that . . . *tension* between us. I tried to avoid her. But a few months after we'd arrived here, I found out Ellen was going to visit college friends in Dundee. So I made an excuse to be there as well. It only happened that once, Ellen insisted on that. When I found out she was pregnant, I tried to pay her to go away somewhere. Somewhere safe. But she refused. I've lain awake at night, terrified what would happen if Grace found out. And now she has . . .'

He tailed off. Now his house was visible up ahead. Both cars were still outside, and the lights still burned in the window.

'Should we see if she's still there?' Fraser asked.

'She won't be,' Strachan said with certainty.

'What's that on the drive?' I asked. A pale yellow shape was lying motionless in the driveway. I felt cold as I realised what it was.

The body of Oscar, Strachan's retriever.

'She killed his *dog*?' Fraser exclaimed. 'Why the hell would she do that?'

No one answered. Strachan's face was bleak as we left the house behind.

'Drive faster,' Brody told Fraser.

The light was fading as we entered the village. Fraser barely slowed as he flung the Range Rover into the side road leading up to the hotel.

The front door stood open.

Strachan leapt out of the car even before it had stopped moving. He ran up the hotel's steps to the entrance, but then stopped dead.

'Oh Christ,' Brody breathed, staring inside.

The hotel had been wrecked. Broken furniture littered the hall. The grandfather clock lay face down and smashed, the mirror shattered into crazed shards of glass. But that wasn't what had stopped Strachan.

The hallway was covered with blood.

The metallic stink of it thickened the air with a slaughterhouse taint. It was pooled on the floorboards and spattered across the panelled walls. It formed a trail, big round splashes at first, then smeared tracks as its source had stumbled down the hallway.

The trail disappeared into the bar.

'Oh, no . . .' Strachan whispered. 'Oh, please no . . .'

Both Strachan and Brody seemed paralysed by the sight of the blood. I forced myself to go past them down the hall. A bloody handmark stood out on the white door frame, where someone had clutched it for support. It was too smudged to say how big or small the hand had been, but it was low down on the frame, as though whoever had made it had been crawling.

Or a child.

I took a breath, trying to prepare myself, and stepped into the bar.

Chairs and tables had been tipped over and smashed, curtains slashed, bottles and glasses shattered in a frenzy. In the middle of it all, slumped against the bar, was Cameron, a wide gash sliced across his trachea. The teacher's eyes were wide with shock, as though unable to believe what Grace had done to him.

The air was a nauseous cocktail of alcohol and blood. There was another odour as well, but even as my stunned senses began to recognise it, a sudden sound tore through the silence.

A child's scream.

It came from the kitchen. Strachan was running even before it had died. Brody and I were just behind him as he burst through the kitchen's swing door, but the scene inside halted us all in our tracks.

Broken crockery crunched underfoot. The kitchen table had been upended and its chairs smashed, the tall pine dresser pushed over onto the floor. Even the ancient cooker had been wrenched away from the wall.

But right then none of that really registered.

Ellen was backed into a corner, terrified and bloodied, but alive. She clutched a heavy saucepan, gripping it white-knuckled in both hands.

Standing between her and the door was Grace. She clutched Anna tightly to her, one hand clamped over the little girl's mouth.

The other held a kitchen knife to her throat.

'*Get back! Don't go near her!*' Ellen screamed.

We didn't. Grace's clothes were mud-spattered and wet. Her raven hair was wild, her face streaked with tears. Even dishevelled as she was, she was still beautiful. But now her madness was all too apparent.

So, too, was something else. The smell I'd noticed in the bar was instantly identifiable in here, thick enough to clog the throat.

Gas.

I looked again at how the cooker had been pulled away from the wall, and glanced at Brody. He gave a barely perceptible nod.

'The cylinders are round the back,' he murmured to Fraser, not taking his eyes from Grace. 'There should be a valve. Go and turn it off.'

Fraser slowly backed out, then disappeared down the hallway.

'She was waiting when we got back from Rose Cassidy's,' Ellen sobbed. 'Bruce came in with us, and when he tried to talk to her she . . .'

'I know,' Strachan said calmly. He took a step closer. 'Put the knife down, Grace. Let the girl go.'

Grace's face grew ugly. 'Don't you mean your *daughter*?'

'She's done nothing to you, Grace. You've always liked Anna. I know you don't want to hurt her.'

'Is it true?' Grace was crying. 'Tell me they were lying! Please, Michael!'

Tell her what she wants, I thought. But Strachan hesitated for too long.

Grace's face creased up. 'No!' she moaned.

'Grace . . .'

'*Shut up!*' she screamed, the tendons in her neck standing out like cords. 'You fucked this *bitch*, you chose her over *me*? How *could* you?'

The smell of gas was growing stronger. What the hell was Fraser doing? Brody began edging nearer to Grace.

'Put the knife down, Grace. No one's going to—'

'Don't come near me!' she screamed.

Brody slowly backed off. Grace glared at us, her face contorted.

The silence was broken by a metallic clatter. Ellen had let the saucepan drop. As it bounced on the floor, she stepped slowly towards Grace.

'Ellen, don't!' Strachan ordered, but there was more fear than authority in his voice.

She ignored him. 'It's me you want, isn't it? All right, I'm here. Do what you like to me, but please don't hurt my daughter.'

Grace had turned to face her, a tick working one corner of her mouth.

Strachan broke in desperately. 'Forget her, Grace. She's not important.' He took one pace forward, then another. He held out his hands as if he were trying to soothe a wild animal. 'You're all that matters to me, Grace. You know that. Let Anna go, and then we'll get away from this place, start again. Just me and you.'

Grace was staring at him with such naked yearning it felt obscene to see it.

'Put the knife down,' he told her softly.

Some of the tension seemed to drain out of her.

Then Anna chose that moment to wriggle free of Grace's hand.

'*Mummy, she's hurting—*'

Grace slapped her palm back over Anna's mouth. 'You shouldn't have lied, Michael,' she said, and pulled back Anna's head.

'*No!*' Strachan cried, flinging himself at her as the knife swept down.

Brody and I lunged forward as Strachan struggled with his sister, but Ellen was faster than either of us. She snatched Anna away as Grace screamed, a cry of pure fury. Leaving Brody to help Strachan, I rushed to where Ellen was clutching her daughter, both of them weeping hysterically.

Ellen wouldn't let go. But I could see that the little girl wasn't hurt. As I sagged with relief, Brody's voice came from behind me.

'David.'

He sounded odd. He had pinned Grace's arms behind her back, but she wasn't struggling any more. They were both staring at Strachan. He stood looking down at himself with a faintly surprised expression.

The knife handle was jutting from his stomach.

'Michael . . .?' Grace said in a small voice.

'It's all right,' he told her, but then his legs gave way.

'*Michael!*' Grace screamed.

Brody held her back as she tried to go to Strachan. I managed to reach him, trying to take his weight on my good shoulder as he sank to the floor.

'Get Anna outside. Take her to a neighbour's,' I told Ellen.

'Is he . . .?'

'Just take her, Ellen.'

I wanted them well away from here. The stink of gas had become so thick it was nauseating. I wondered again what was taking Fraser so long.

I knelt by Strachan. His face had gone shockingly white.

'You can let go of my sister now,' he said, voice hoarse with pain. 'She's not going anywhere.'

I gave Brody a nod when he hesitated. As soon as he released her, Grace dropped down beside Strachan.

'Oh God, Michael . . .!' Her face was a mask of anguish as she turned to me. 'Do something! *Help* him!'

He tried to smile as he took hold of her hand. 'Don't worry, everything'll be all right. I promise.'

I started to examine his wound. The knife blade was fully lodged in his stomach. I couldn't guess what internal damage it had caused.

'I'm going to help you lie down flat,' I said. 'Try not to move the knife.'

Its blade was the only thing preventing him from bleeding to death.

Grace was weeping quietly now, the violence drained from her as she cradled her brother's head on her lap. I ran through my options. There weren't many. There were none of the facilities here that Strachan needed, and the only nurse on the island was lying dead in the other room. Unless we could get him evacuated, and soon, he was going to die whatever I did.

Fraser rushed back in, skidding on the broken crockery.

'Jesus!' he panted, seeing Strachan, then gathered himself. 'The gas canisters are locked in a cage. I can't open it.'

'The keys for the cage must be here somewhere,' Brody said, staring round the wrecked kitchen. 'But we don't have time to look. Let's get everybody out while we break into the cage to turn off the gas.'

There was no way Strachan should be moved, but the gas left us no choice. It was so thick I could taste it.

I gave a quick nod. 'We can use the table to carry him.'

Strachan had been watching us in silence. He seemed remarkably calm. Almost peaceful. 'Just leave me here,' he said, his voice already weakening.

Grace was keening, an almost animal sound of grief as she stroked his face. 'I'm sorry, I'm so sorry . . .'

'Shh. Everything's going to be fine, I promise.'

While Fraser and Brody struggled to right the heavy table, I went to the kitchen's small window. Even a little ventilation would be better than nothing. But I'd only taken a few steps when I saw Strachan grope for something lying in the broken crockery nearby.

'Get away from there, David,' he said, holding it up.

It was the lighter for the gas range.

He had his thumb poised on the ignition button. 'Sorry, but I'm not going anywhere . . .'

'Put it down, Michael,' I said, trying for an assurance I didn't feel. There was so much gas in the kitchen that one spark would set it off.

'I don't think so . . .' Strachan's pallid face shone with sweat. 'Go on, get out. All of you.'

'Don't be bloody stupid,' Brody snapped.

Strachan raised the lighter. 'One more word from you, and I swear I'll press it right now.'

'What about Grace?' I said, stalling for time.

'Grace and I stay together. Don't we, Grace?'

She was blinking through her tears, as though only now becoming aware of what was going on. 'Michael, what are you going to do . . .?'

He smiled at her. 'Trust me.'

Then, before anyone could stop him, Strachan wrenched the knife from his stomach.

He screamed, seizing Grace's arm as blood gushed from the wound. I started forward, but he saw me and raised the lighter.

'Get *out*! *Now!*' he hissed through clenched teeth. 'Oh, *Jesus!*'

Brody grabbed hold of me. 'Move.'

Fraser was already running for the door. I took one last look at where Strachan lay, teeth gritted in agony as he held the lighter raised in one hand and gripped his sister's hand with the other. Grace's expression was one of dawning incredulity. She looked across at me, her mouth opening to speak.

Brody hustled me into the hall. 'Just run!' he bellowed, shoving me outside.

There was an old stone wall nearby. Brody half dragged me behind it, and Fraser threw himself down beside us a moment later.

We waited, panting. Nothing happened.

I looked back at the hotel. It seemed familiar and mundane in the twilight, its front door banging forlornly in the wind.

'Been more than ten seconds,' Fraser muttered.

I stood up.

'What the hell are you doing?' Brody demanded.

I shook him off. 'I'm going to—' I began, and then the hotel exploded.

There was a flash, and a wall of noise almost knocked me off my feet. I ducked, covering my head as pieces of slate and brick rained down. As the thuds petered out, I risked a look back up the hill.

Dust and smoke swirled around the hotel like a gauze veil. Its roof had been blown off, and bright yellow flickers were already visible through the shattered windows as the fire took hold.

I turned on Brody angrily. 'I could have stopped him!'

'He was a dead man as soon as he pulled out the knife,' he said tiredly.

I looked away, knowing he was right. The hotel was an inferno now, its timbered floors and walls so much kindling.

'What about Grace?' I asked.

Brody's face was shadowed as he stared into the flames.

'What about her?'

TWO DAYS LATER, the sky dawned bright and clear over Runa. It was approaching midday when Brody and I left his car on the road above the harbour and walked up to the cliff top overlooking Stac Ross. Sea birds soared around the tall black tower, while waves shattered against the rock's base, flinging sheets of spray high into the air. I breathed in the fresh salt air, savouring the thin warmth of the sun on my face.

I was going home.

The police had arrived on Runa the previous morning by coastguard helicopter. The storm had blown itself out within hours of the hotel burning down, and before the night was out, while the hotel ruins still smoked and smouldered, the phone lines had started working again. We'd finally been able to get word out to Wallace and the mainland.

There was no reason for me to remain on Runa any longer. I'd said what few goodbyes I had to make, shared an awkward handshake with Fraser, then called to see Ellen and Anna. They were staying with neighbours for now, bearing up surprisingly well after what they'd been through.

Another coastguard helicopter was due within the hour, and once it had discharged its cargo of police officers it would take me back to Stornoway. From there I'd fly to Glasgow and then London, finally completing the journey I'd started just over a week ago.

I was looking forward to seeing Jenny, yet I felt oddly flat as Brody and I walked up to the cliff where the helicopter would put down. Brody, too, was silent and lost in his thoughts. I'd not seen much of him since the police teams had arrived. Ex-inspector or not, he was a civilian now, and he'd been politely excluded from the investigation.

When we reached the cliff top, we rested. The stone monolith of Bodach Runa stood some distance away, the Old Man of Runa still keeping his lonely vigil for a lost child. Gulls and gannets wheeled and cried in the bright winter sunlight as wisps of cloud skated serenely across the sky.

'This is one of my favourite views,' Brody said. The wind ruffled his grey hair, mirroring the movement of the waves two hundred feet below. He reached down to stroke his dog's head. 'Been a while since Bess has had a chance to stretch her legs up here.'

'What do you think will happen now . . . to Runa?' I asked.

Brody turned down his mouth. 'God knows. Might keep going for a while. But the fish farm, the new jobs, the investment, all that's gone. Can't see it surviving without them.'

'Will you stay?'

Brody shrugged. 'We'll see. I've no reason to go anywhere else.'

The border collie had crouched at his feet, head down on her paws as she stared up at him intently. Smiling, he took an old tennis ball from his pocket and tossed it for the dog.

'I just wish we'd had a chance to talk to Grace, find out why she did what she did,' I said.

'Jealousy, like Strachan said. And hate, I expect.'

'That still doesn't explain everything. Like why she clubbed Janice Donaldson and Duncan, but used a knife on Maggie and Cameron.'

'Means and opportunity, I expect. I don't think she really planned anything, just acted when she got the urge. Duncan's Maglite was probably lying to hand, and I dare say something similar happened with Donaldson.'

The collie had dropped the ball at his feet. Brody picked it up and threw it again, then gave me a rueful smile.

'There aren't always answers to everything, no matter how hard we look.'

He took out his cigarettes and lit one, drawing on it with satisfaction. I watched as he put the pack away.

'I didn't know you were left-handed,' I said.

'Sorry?'

'You threw the ball with your left hand just now.'

'Did I? I didn't notice.'

My heart was thumping. 'A few days ago in your kitchen, you used your right hand. When I told you that whoever killed Duncan was left-handed.'

He turned to look at me, quizzical and a little exasperated. 'Where are you going with this, David?'

My mouth had dried. 'Grace was right-handed.'

Brody considered that. 'How do you know?'

'When she had hold of Anna, the knife was in her right hand. I'd forgotten about it till I saw you just now. And when I saw Grace preparing food earlier she used her right hand.'

'Perhaps your memory's playing tricks.'

'No,' I said, with something like regret. 'But even if it was, we can check to see which hand the fingerprints on her paintbrushes are from.'

He took a long draw on his cigarette. 'You saw what Grace was like. You can't seriously think Strachan was lying?'

'No. I don't doubt she murdered Maggie, and God knows how many others before they came here. But Strachan just assumed she'd killed Janice Donaldson and Duncan as well. He might have been wrong.'

Brody sighed. 'You've been here too long, David. You're looking for things that aren't there.'

I had to moisten my mouth before I could get the next words out. 'How did you know Duncan was killed with his own Maglite?'

Brody frowned. 'Wasn't he? I thought that's what you said.'

'No, I didn't say anything about the Maglite until SOC got here.'

'Well, I must have heard it from one of them.'

'They only removed the torch during the night. And no one's going to know for sure that's what killed him until lab tests have been carried out. They wouldn't have said anything.'

Brody stared out across the sea at the black pinnacle of Stac Ross.

'Let it go, David,' he said softly.

But I couldn't. My heart was banging so hard now I could hear it.

'Grace didn't kill Duncan, did she? Or Janice Donaldson.'

The only answer was the crying of gulls, and the distant crashing of the waves below the cliffs. *Say something. Deny it.* But Brody might have been carved from the same stone as Bodach Runa, silent and implacable.

I found my voice. 'Why? Why did you do it?'

He dropped the cigarette to the ground and crushed it out with his foot. 'Because of Rebecca.'

It took a moment for the name to register. Rebecca, the estranged daughter who had gone missing. Whom Brody had spent years trying to find. Suddenly everything sprang into focus.

'You thought Strachan had murdered your daughter,' I said. 'You killed Janice Donaldson to try and frame him.'

The pain in his eyes was confirmation enough.

'It was an accident. I'd been trying to put together evidence against Strachan for years. That's the only reason I moved out to this godforsaken island, so I'd be close to him.'

Standing there in the cold winter sun, I felt a rush of unreality, like plunging too fast in a lift. 'You *knew* there'd been other deaths?'

'I had a good idea. I'd been able to follow Becky's trail so far, but then it just stopped. So when I heard rumours about her seeing some rich South African before she'd vanished, I started digging. I found out that Strachan had lived in different countries but always for short periods of time. So I looked at newspaper archives of places where he'd settled. I found reports of girls being murdered or disappearing around the same time, too many to be coincidence. And the more I looked, the more convinced I was that Becky was one of his victims. Everything fitted.'

'And you didn't tell the police? You used to be a detective inspector, for God's sake! They'd have listened to you!'

'Not without proof. I'd pulled in every favour I could when I was looking for Becky. A lot of people thought I'd lost the plot as it was. And if I'd confronted Strachan he'd have just gone to ground. But Rebecca had been using her stepfather's name. There was no way he could connect us. So I decided to play the long game and came here, hoping he'd slip up.'

'What happened? Did you get tired of waiting?' I asked, surprising myself with my own anger.

'No. Janice Donaldson happened.'

His face was unreadable as he told me how he'd followed Strachan on his trips to Stornoway, inventing business of his own, taking the ferry to arrive first whenever Strachan had gone on the yacht. To begin with he'd been worried that Strachan had been preparing to select another victim. But nothing happened to any of the women he spent time with.

Finally, Brody had approached Janice Donaldson in Stornoway one night after she'd left a pub, offering to pay her for information about Strachan. It had been the first time he'd shown his hand against his enemy, but he reasoned it was worth the risk. It wasn't as if Donaldson knew who he was.

Or so he'd thought.

'She recognised me,' Brody said. 'Turned out she used to live in Glasgow, and I'd been pointed out to her when I'd been searching for Becky. Donaldson had known her. She'd been thinking about claiming the reward I was offering for information, but she'd been picked up for soliciting before she had the chance. So she offered to sell it to me now.'

He lit another cigarette, drew down a lungful of smoke and blew it out again for the wind to take away.

'She told me Becky had been a prostitute. I suppose on some level I'd already guessed, but actually being told it . . . When I refused to pay her, she threatened to tell Strachan that I'd been asking questions. Then she started saying things about Rebecca no father wants to hear. So I hit her.'

Brody held out his hand, considering it. I remembered how easily he had battered Strachan senseless in the broch. It took a conscious effort not to look at the cliff's edge only a few yards away, or to step away from him.

'I always had a temper,' he went on, almost mildly. 'That's why my wife left. That and the drinking. But I thought I'd got it under control. I didn't even hit Janice very hard, but she was drunk. We were down at the docks, and she fell backwards, cracked her head on a stanchion.'

'If it was an accident, why didn't you turn yourself in?'

'And be sent down for manslaughter, when that murdering bastard was still free? I don't think so. Not when there was another way.'

'You mean frame him.'

'If you like.'

It made a twisted sort of sense. There was no link between Brody and Janice Donaldson, but Strachan was a different matter. If she was found dead on Runa, when it emerged that he was one of her clients—and Brody would have made sure that it did—then suspicion would quickly focus on him. It would have been a justice of sorts.

For Brody that was better than nothing.

So Brody had gone ahead as planned. He'd put Janice in the car boot and brought her over on the ferry. Then he'd planted evidence at the crofter's cottage that would further incriminate Strachan: dog hairs from his retriever, an imprint from one of Strachan's Wellingtons that Brody had taken from their barn one night, and which he'd then hidden back there for the police to find. He'd set fire to the body to hide the fact that Janice hadn't died in the cottage, as an examination would otherwise have found. He'd even traded in his car, because he knew there would be microscopic evidence left in the boot, no matter how well he cleaned it. Using all his experience as a police officer, Brody had tried to anticipate everything,

But with murder, as with life, that's never possible.

His cheeks hollowed as he drew on the cigarette. 'I was going to let someone else find the body. But after a month of waiting, knowing it was just lying there, I couldn't stand it any longer.' He shook his head mutely. 'I'd not used much petrol, just enough to make it look like a botched attempt to torch the body. I *wanted* it to be identified; that was the whole point. But all I could do then was report it and hope that SOC did their job.'

But instead of SOC, he'd got a drunken police sergeant and an inexperienced constable. And me.

I felt physically sick at the extent of his betrayal. He'd used us all, playing on our trust as he'd steadily pointed us towards Strachan.

'What about Duncan?' I asked, too angry to care about provoking him. 'What was he, collateral damage?'

Brody accepted the accusation without flinching. 'I made a mistake. When the cottage collapsed, it wiped out all the evidence I'd planted. I was starting to worry that there wasn't enough to incriminate Strachan. I'd been sounding out Duncan, knew he was a smart lad. So I decided to use him.'

He shook his head, annoyed with himself.

'Stupid. Should have known better. I didn't say much, only that I'd got my suspicions about Strachan. I thought I could steer bits of information his way, let him take the credit for it. And then I cocked up. I told him that Strachan had been visiting prostitutes in Stornoway.'

Brody studied the glowing tip of his cigarette.

'First thing he asked was how I knew. I told him it was just gossip, but I knew that wouldn't hold up. No one else on Runa had any idea. I could see Duncan starting to wonder how I'd known. I couldn't risk it.'

He sighed regretfully. 'It's the little things that trip you up. Like that bloody Maglite. I'd got a crowbar under my coat, but when Duncan let me in he put the torch down and turned his back. So I picked it up and hit him with that instead.' He gave a shrug. 'Seemed the thing to do at the time.'

The disgust I felt only fuelled my anger. I tried to control both. 'The fires were just a distraction, weren't they? Torching the community centre and the camper van, it wasn't to destroy forensic evidence. You just wanted us to think it was, so Duncan's death would look incidental. And you could incriminate Strachan at the same time, planting the petrol cap—'

I broke off, staring at him as another missing piece fell into place. 'That's why Grace's car ran out of petrol. You siphoned it off to use to start the fires.'

'I had to get it from somewhere.' Brody had been gazing out at the horizon, but now he turned to me. 'For the record, I didn't realise you were still in the medical centre when I started the fire.'

'Would it have made any difference?'

He flicked ash from his cigarette. 'Probably not.'

'Jesus Christ, didn't you ever think that there was something else going on? What about when Grace was attacked? Didn't you wonder *why* Strachan would do something like that when he hadn't killed anybody?'

'Anybody *here*, perhaps,' he said, and for the first time there was an edge to his voice. 'I assumed he was panicking. I thought he wanted to get off the island before the police started looking into his past.'

'But it wasn't *his* past that was the problem, was it? It was his sister's. You picked the wrong Strachan!'

He sighed, looking out at the horizon again. 'Aye.'

There was an appalling irony to it. Because of Brody's attempts to frame her brother, Grace had believed along with everyone else that there was a killer loose on Runa. So she'd taken advantage of the situation, murdering Maggie and burning her body so it would appear that the killer of Duncan and Janice Donaldson had claimed another life.

'Was it worth it?' I asked quietly. 'Was it worth all those lives?'

Outlined against the cold blue sky, Brody's hewn features were unreadable. 'You used to have a daughter yourself. You tell me.'

I had no answer to that. The heat was ebbing from me now, leaving in its wake a leaden feeling of sadness. And a chilling awareness of my own situation. Even if I'd had both arms free, Brody was bigger and stronger than me. He'd already killed twice. I couldn't see him baulking at a third time.

I took a quick look at the cliff edge, only yards away. *You won't be leaving Runa today after all*, I thought numbly.

A dark fleck had appeared on the horizon. The coastguard helicopter was early, I realised, but the surge of hope quickly died. It would take it another ten or fifteen minutes to get here. Too long.

Brody had seen it too. The wind ruffled his grey hair as he stared at the approaching speck. His cigarette had burned almost down to his fingers.

'I used to be a good policeman,' he said casually. 'A lousy husband and father, but a good policeman. You start off on the side of the angels, and suddenly you find out you've become what you hate. How does that happen?'

I glanced desperately at the helicopter. It didn't seem to have grown any bigger. 'So what now?' I asked, trying to sound calm.

Something like a dry smile touched his mouth. 'Good question.'

'Janice Donaldson was an accident. And what happened to Rebecca will be taken into account.'

Brody took one last draw on his cigarette, then ground it out with the sole of his boot. 'I'm not going to prison. But, for what it counts, I'm sorry.'

My heart was thudding as he reached down to stroke the old collie.

'Good girl. Stay.'

I took an involuntary step back as he straightened. He turned his face up to the sun, closing his eyes for a moment.

Then, before I realised what he was doing, he ran at the cliff edge.

'Brody, no!' I yelled.

My words were carried away. Without slowing, Brody reached the edge and flung himself off into space. For an instant he seemed to hang there, borne up by the wind. Then he'd gone.

I stared at the empty air where he'd been a moment before. Only the cry of the gulls filled it, and the sound of the waves crashing below.

EPILOGUE

By summer, the events that had taken place on Runa had started to recede, blunted by fading memory. The post-mortem into what had happened had produced little else that wasn't already known.

A search of Brody's house turned up the file that he'd put together on Strachan. It was a good, solid piece of police work, but he hadn't dug quite far enough. Like everyone else, Brody had never considered that Grace might not be Strachan's wife. But the file still provided a chilling roll call of victims, although there was no way of knowing how many Brody—like

Strachan—might have missed. It was probable that the fate of some of Grace's victims would never be known.

Like Rebecca Brody.

Her father's body had been recovered from the sea by a fishing boat a week after he'd thrown himself from the cliff.

Not everything had such a neat resolution. The fire had razed the hotel to the ground. A few charred pieces of bone, too damaged by the heat to yield any DNA, were identified as Cameron's because of their location in the bar. But Grace and Michael Strachan had died together in the kitchen. What few calcined bone fragments were recovered were impossible to differentiate.

Even in death Strachan hadn't been able to escape his sister.

I'd met Ellen again at the inquest into Brody's suicide. She carried herself with the same dignity I remembered, but there was a new optimism. She and Anna had moved to Edinburgh, and were living in a small house paid for by the hotel's insurance. Though there was talk of rebuilding the hotel, Ellen wouldn't be running it. Both Strachan and Brody had left her well cared for in their wills, but she put everything they left her into a fund to help rebuild the island. It was blood money, she'd said, with a flash of her old fierceness. She wanted nothing to do with it.

But there was one thing they had brought with them from Runa: Brody's old border collie. I thought Brody would have been grateful for that.

As for me, it was surprising how quickly life slid back to normal. But there were days when I'd wonder how many people would still be alive if I'd never gone to Runa, if Janice Donaldson's murder had been dismissed as an accident. And it weighed heavily on my conscience.

One night as I lay awake thinking about it, Jenny had woken and asked what was wrong. I wanted to tell her, wanted to exorcise the ghosts that had followed me back from the island. Yet somehow I couldn't.

'Nothing.' I'd smiled to reassure her. 'I just can't sleep.'

Things had been tense enough between us anyway after my return. What had happened on Runa had only served to reinforce her dislike of my profession. I knew she thought it was too much of a link to the past, that it tied me to my own dead in a way she mistrusted.

But as the weeks passed, the friction between us smoothed away. Summer came, bringing hot days and balmy nights, making the events on Runa seem ever more distant.

Then, late one Saturday afternoon, the past caught up with us.

We were at my ground-floor flat rather than Jenny's, because it had a small terrace at the back. It was a warm, sunny evening, and we'd invited friends round for a barbecue. They weren't due to arrive for another half-hour, but I'd already started the fire. Jenny had brought out bowls of salad, and was feeding me an olive when the phone rang.

'I'll get it,' she said, when I started to put down the tongs and spatula. 'You're not getting off cooking that easily.'

Smiling, I watched her go inside. She'd grown her blonde hair longer in the two years since we'd met and it suited her. Contentedly, I took a drink of beer and turned my attention back to the charcoal bricks. I was squirting lighter fuel onto them when Jenny came back out.

'Some young woman for you,' she said, arching an eyebrow. 'Said her name was Rebecca Brody.'

I stared at her.

It had been months since Runa. Knowing she wouldn't want to know such details, I'd never told her the name of Brody's daughter.

'What else did she say?'

'She wanted to know if you were in, and said she'd like to call round. I probably didn't sound very enthusiastic, but she said it would only take a few minutes. Are you OK? You look like you've seen a ghost.'

I gave an uncertain laugh. 'Funny you should say that.'

Jenny's face fell when I told her who the caller was.

'I'm sorry,' I said when I'd finished. 'I thought she was dead. God knows what she wants. Or how she found out where I live.'

The door buzzer sounded from the hallway. I hesitated, looking at Jenny.

She smiled, then leaned forward and kissed me. 'Go on. I'll leave you in peace while you talk to her. Ask her to stay for something to eat, if you like.'

'Thanks,' I said, kissing her before going inside.

I was glad Jenny had taken it so well, but I wasn't sure I wanted Brody's daughter as a guest. I couldn't deny I was curious, but her father had died believing she was dead. And five other people had died because of it.

But she could hardly be blamed for that, I reminded myself. I took a deep breath and opened the door.

A red-haired young woman stood on the doorstep. She was slim and tanned, a pair of dark sunglasses perched on her nose. But neither they, nor the unflattering loose dress she wore, could hide the fact that she was startlingly attractive.

'Hi,' I said, smiling.

There was something familiar about her. I was trying to place it, looking for something of Brody in her without being able to find it. Then I smelt the musky scent she was wearing and the smile froze on my face.

'Hello, Dr Hunter,' Grace Strachan said.

Everything suddenly seemed both slowed down and pinprick sharp. Then Grace's hand was emerging from her shoulder bag with the knife.

The sight of it freed me from my shock. I started to react as she lunged at me, but it was always going to be too late. I grabbed at the blade, but it slid through my hand, slicing my palm and fingers to the bone. The pain of that hadn't had time to register when the knife went into my stomach.

There wasn't any pain, just a coldness and a sense of shock. *This isn't happening.* But it was. I sucked in air to shout or scream, but managed only a choked gasp. I clutched hold of the knife's handle, feeling the hot sticky wetness of my blood smearing both our hands, gripping it as tightly as I could as Grace tried to pull it out. I held on even as my legs sagged under me. *Keep hold or you're dead.*

And so is Jenny.

Grace was grunting as she tried to tug the knife free, following me to the floor as I slid down the wall. Then, with a last frustrated gasp, she gave up. She stood over me, panting, her mouth contorted.

'He let me go!' she spat, and I saw the tears running in parallel tracks down her cheeks. 'He killed himself but he let me go!'

I tried to say something, anything, but no words would form. Her face hung above me for a moment longer, ugly and twisted, and then it was gone. The doorway was empty, the sound of running feet a fading echo.

I looked down at my stomach. The knife handle protruded from it obscenely. My shirt was soaked through with blood. I could feel it under me, pooling on the tiled floor. *Get up. Move.* But I no longer had any strength.

I tried to shout out. All that emerged was a croak. And now it was growing dark. Dark and cold. *Already? But it's summer.* From a nearby street, the chime of an ice-cream van drifted cheerfully on the air. I could hear Jenny moving around on the terrace, the tinkle of glasses. It sounded friendly and inviting. Everything was growing hazy. All I could remember was that I couldn't let go of the knife. I didn't know why any more.

Only that it was very important.

SIMON BECKETT

Born: Sheffield, April 20, 1960
Profession: writer and freelance journalist
Website: www.simonbeckett.com

RD: Can you tell us about your origins?

SB: I grew up—and still live—in Sheffield. I had a fairly ordinary working-class background, at a time when the city was still dominated by the steel industry. I've lived in other places but always gravitated back here. Sheffield tends to get a lot of bad press, but it's a good place to live, and a lot greener than most people give it credit for—I mean that in the sense of trees and countryside rather than in the ecological sense.

RD: Where did you study, and did you enjoy those years?

SB: I took my degree in English at Sheffield Polytechnic (now Hallam University), and then an MA at Newcastle University. Yes, I did enjoy being a student, especially at Newcastle—it's a great place.

RD: And you became interested in music at that time?

SB: Yes. A bunch of us decided to form a band after university, and I ended up with the bongos. I played regularly until fairly recently, but the bongos are mothballed for now.

RD: What did you do after graduation?

SB: I ended up doing property repairs for several years. Not much fun in winter, believe me. That was followed by a stint teaching English in Spain, and then I came back to the UK and played percussion in various bands. None of the bands came to anything, but several musician friends became successful after I'd left, which probably says it all. At more or less the same time, I started writing feature articles for the national broadsheets and colour supplements. I don't have any formal training as a journalist, but I've always found it complements writing novels fairly well. It forces you to be disciplined and gets you away from your desk, which is no bad thing. And if it were not for the journalism, I would never have visited the Body Farm in Tennessee and got the inspiration for my first novel, *The Chemistry of Death*.

RD: What is the Body Farm?

SB: The Body Farm is the nickname given to the Outdoor Anthropology Research Facility in Tennessee, which was set up in 1980 to find ways of establishing the all-important time-since-death of human remains. I visited it in 2002 when I wrote an article for the *Daily Telegraph Magazine* on the National Forensic Academy, which delivers training for police officers and crime-scene investigators that's as close to the real thing as possible. As part of the course, the students go to the Body Farm so that they can use actual corpses to reconstruct crime scenes. You can read the article on my website.

RD: Have you always wanted to write a book?

SB: It was something I'd been interested in for ages, but I only started to think of writing as a potential career when I was teaching in Spain. I worked in the evenings, so I used to write during the day. It was six years before I was published, though. I didn't have an agent, so I started touting my manuscript around publishers myself. After countless rejection slips it was picked out of the slush-pile, and within 48 hours I'd got myself both a book deal and an agent. That was a real watershed moment.

RD: Is there a particular reason for your choice of backdrops—Norfolk for *The Chemistry of Death*, the Hebrides for *Written in Bone*?

SB: I picked settings that were very atmospheric, with plenty of lonely, isolated spots. Norfolk's marshes and Broads were ideal, and it was the same with the Hebrides— the setting fits what I want to write about.

RD: Did you have to do a lot of research into spontaneous human combustion for your latest plot?

SB: Yes. I like to get the facts as accurate as possible. Luckily, I found an extremely helpful forensic anthropologist who specialises in fire deaths.

RD: Do you include the forensics because it's popular in crime writing today?

SB: I think I'd find it hard to write about it if I didn't find it interesting. But I'm just as interested in the psychological aspects, so I try to balance the two.

RD: You said in an interview once that your ideas 'tend more towards the darker aspects of life'. Could you say a bit more about that?

SB: I suppose there's a fascination with how thin the line can be between normal life and catastrophe. It's better to read about this phenomenon than experience it, and books like mine deal with what happens when the line is crossed.

RD: How real do the characters become to you?

SB: They're obviously inventions, but as the book progresses they tend to become more and more real. You begin to know what they would and wouldn't do, how they talk, and so on.

RD: Can you give any clues as to what might be ahead for Dr David Hunter?

SB: I don't like to say too much about work in progress. But I can reveal that I plan to take him back to his roots in the near future.

WHITE CITY

GROWING UP IN WAR AND PEACE

DONALD JAMES WHEAL

In 1944, just months after losing their home

in a Luftwaffe raid on London's World's End,

the Wheal family stepped into their new house in

the anonymous, sprawling suburb of White City.

For twelve-year-old Donald Wheal, the move

was a turning point: the ties that bound him

to the past were broken, and a whole new world

of exciting adventures beckoned.

ONE

One Saturday evening in the winter of 1930 two young working people left the 22 bus at the World's End, Chelsea, and walked down Blantyre Street to the river. The tide was on the turn lapping a wide, glistening mud bank pockmarked with pieces of broken machinery and peppered by the tracks of rats and sea birds. It was the second evening the couple had been out together and they had already put flirtatious banter behind them. Leaning on the embankment wall with the shouts and Saturday night songs of the King's Arms pub behind them, watching the navigation lights of the coalers heading upriver for Lots Road Power Station, she asked him what he really wanted out of life.

He didn't hesitate. 'I want to marry you and have two sons.'

'Then,' she said, completely unruffled, 'I'll have to see what I can do.' She lifted her eyebrows, smiling. 'Anything else?'

'Yes. I want us to get out of the World's End. Find our own place. Bring the boys up somewhere different. Somewhere where a Saturday night in the King's Arms'—he tipped his head towards the pub behind them—'isn't all they have to look forward to each week.'

'Our own place?' Nobody she knew owned their own place. 'And where will the money come from for that?'

'I don't know yet. Will you leave that to me?'

'I'll have to,' she said. 'After all, I'm going to be busy with the two boys.'

MY PARENTS had known each other for most of their lives. In their late-teenage years they used to go to the same youth club and had begun occasionally to dance together on music nights before my father formally asked my mother to go to the pictures with him. He was a plumber by trade, a strongly built young man of no more than average height, but determined, direct in his approach to his world's challenges. She was an unusually tall young woman who attracted a lot of interest among the local boys. My father often tactlessly outspoken, my mother a natural diplomat, they were a perfectly balanced pair.

My brother and I were lucky.

IN THE THIRTIES and wartime forties when I grew up there, the World's End was an area of mostly mean streets showered by dust and grit from the coal-burning Lots Road Power Station. King's Road linked us to Sloane Square and Belgravia a mile away, or a world away, however you chose to look at it.

The World's End's cheap purpose-built tenements, though only fifty years old, were already mouldering with damp and often rat-ridden. Bathrooms were unknown, lavatories were one between every two or three flats. Haphazardly among these slums were streets of houses that still retained a suggestion of Victorian elegance, unpainted, broken-windowed and crowded with several families as many of them were. They pointed back to a more prosperous period in the history of the area.

On Saturday evenings, the World's End throbbed with life. On summer nights there would often be accordion music and dancing outside the World's End pub from which the area took its name. A crowd would be gathered outside Thwaite's, the brightly gas-lit butcher's where the Saturday night meat auction took place. With no refrigeration, butchers were obliged to sell off the week's unsold cuts in an auction conducted with less than Sotheby's decorum. Mr Thwaite would be standing in blood-stained apron and straw boater on a heavy chopping table. Pieces of dripping, unwrapped meat were waved about above the heads of men and women jostling for a better view. My maternal grandmother, Eliza Toop, looked after my younger brother Kit and myself, while my mother worked in a local shop, and would often be charged with buying the Sunday joint. She was a tall woman, good with her elbows, and I fancy usually got the joint she was aiming for.

On really exciting nights in the late 1930s there were big political meetings. Union Jacks and party flags flying, Oswald Mosley and William Joyce (the man later notorious as Lord Haw-Haw) would march down King's Road at the head of a chanting column of Black Shirts from Mosley's headquarters in nearby Sloane Square. The Communist Party would often filter through the side streets to confront the Fascists and my grandmother would hurry us back through the surging, menacing crowd before the serious fighting broke out.

Once or twice we were caught in the fray. Mounted police would be fighting to control the crowds and my grandmother, leg of lamb wrapped in bloodied paper in one pocket, twist of snuff and a bottle in the other, would guide my brother and me away among the bucketloads of flying marbles hurled by Fascist and Communist alike underneath the police horses' hooves in an attempt to make them lose their footing.

IN ITS NINETEENTH-CENTURY PAST the World's End had been an area of prosperous prostitution centred on the open-air cafés and dance-rooms of the notorious Cremorne Pleasure Gardens, which ran from King's Road down to the river. After the gardens were closed, the houses of ill repute lingered on along Lamont Road, Blantyre Street and Seaton Street for another generation or two. By the time I was growing up this source of income was no longer significant in the local economy, though I suspect casual or occasional prostitution was a last resort of more working-class women than is generally recognised. Indeed, my own grandmother had been on the fringe of this life for much of her youth, working as a 'waitress' in places like Dirty Dick's in Spitalfields. The morality of such matters looks different when it's a straight choice between the workhouse, with inevitable separation from your child, and doing what you can to keep a roof over your family's head.

OUR IMMEDIATE FAMILY consisted of my mother and father, my brother and myself, and my grandmother Eliza. On my father's side, too, we had grandparents living in the World's End: Henry James Wheal, my quiet, sharp-eyed grandfather, a First World War conscientious objector who had survived four years of the Flanders battlefields as a volunteer ambulance driver; and his wife, Minnie, a hard, aggressive woman. There were also a number of uncles, aunts and cousins. We were much closer to my mother's side of the family: her sister, our Aunt May, and her six children lived a few yards from us. My grandmother Eliza, ever broke, overgenerous, and full of wildly inappropriate stories about her early life, felt part of our family. Not so my other grandmother, Minnie. I have no idea why my grandfather married her. She ruled her family and a good many other families in her street.

She was squarely built, loud, and from the age of about twenty-eight, toothlessly ugly. Notorious for physically intervening in other families' disputes, Minnie was prepared to fight if the cause, as *she* judged it, was right.

From the time I was born we lived in one room in Seaton Street. The house had once been a brothel, but had since sunk low. The gas stove, lavatory and sink were on the floor below. But my mother already had her sights locked on to a different form of accommodation.

In the twenties and thirties poverty-stricken Victorian dwellings around Sloane Square were being erased and people resettled in blocks built by charitable institutions like the Peabody, Lewis and Guinness Trusts. These blocks were titled Dwellings or Buildings, to distinguish them from the blocks of expensive flats that were also being erected.

The day the Buildings were opened for occupation was an event. Of course no one could afford the hire of a van. Instead, a convoy of pony-drawn carts and costermongers' barrows piled high with chairs, brass beds and mattresses, swaying like a camel train, made its way down King's Road.

The new tenement blocks were designed to be a cheaper version of the established Guinness style of working-class dwellings, having fewer frills and amenities (white-tiled entrances for easy cleaning, gaslight only, no electricity, no bathroom and an outside 'balcony' lavatory), so that low-paid workers could afford the very modest rents. Shortly after my younger brother was born, my mother, father, our newly widowed grandmother Eliza, Kit and myself moved into a one-bedroomed flat at number 3, Guinness Trust Buildings, Chelsea, London SW10.

THE LUFTWAFFE RAID on London during the night of February 23, 1944 had Chelsea Power Station as its principal target. The power station survived but bombs were scattered across the World's End. The morning following the raid we were homeless. We were not alone. Hundreds of people were sifting through the wreckage for their possessions, wondering where they would sleep that night. Hundreds of others were lying injured in hospitals. The bodies of a further seventy-seven men, women and children, some school friends of ours, almost all nodding acquaintances at the very least, filled makeshift mortuaries. A few, nobody knew how many, some still living, some dead, remained buried under the rubble.

I was still several months off my thirteenth birthday, Kit a little younger; my mother and father were a few years into their thirties. The World's End was an area that my brother and I loved. It offered freedom, plentiful friends, bombed houses to explore, the excitements of the muddy foreshore of the Thames . . . For my parents, it was different. They were aware of the stigma attached to being from the World's End and to living in Guinness Trust. They were determined it was not going to attach to my brother and myself. For my mother, there was some regret at leaving the warmth and familiarity which comes from having lived in one place all your life; for my father a move away from the World's End was part of his young life's ambition. I believe they were both ready to go.

Yet on the morning of February 24, 1944 our thoughts were all for the catastrophe around us. We had escaped from our flat but as we returned we could see by shocking daylight what had really happened in the night's air raid: fires still burning, our part of King's Road totally demolished, half Guinness Trust Buildings torn down, and damage in the streets all around us. It was clear to us all we could no longer live in the World's End. Whichever way you looked at it, it was the beginning of a new life for us.

TWO

Our first refuge was with our Aunt May, who had taken her large family from the World's End at the beginning of the war and was now billeted in the disused wing of a rectory a few miles outside Windsor. As ever we received a warm welcome from my aunt and her family, the Easts. Indeed we received a warm welcome from everybody except the Vicar of Braywood.

The Reverend Daniels looked with disdain at Kit's soot-embedded face and myself, dust-covered from rummaging through the remains of our flat. 'Out of the question,' he said when my mother's sister asked if we could rent two unused rooms in the rectory. 'Storage. I've plans to move some of the church draperies to a dryer place. Those two rooms will be ideal.'

'My sister's family have just been bombed out,' my aunt told him. 'They've nowhere to live.'

'Then she'll need to see the local billeting officer in Windsor. I can't sacrifice any more space. No one could deny that I've done my bit.'

We were allowed a few days but no longer. Charity was simply not a word in the Reverend Daniels's vocabulary.

My mother faced a difficult choice. She might have tried to find somewhere to live with a few creature comforts, that's to say with electricity and perhaps an indoor plumbed lavatory. Or equally she might have thought that to return to people we knew, even in conditions that were far from perfect, would be better for all of us.

This was not our first stay in the area. We had been evacuated to Windsor at the end of the first London Blitz and already knew one couple here. We had stayed several months with Joe the Poacher and his wife Jinny, champion Brussels sprout picker, world's worst cook, and the kindest-hearted Gipsy woman you could hope to find.

I can still see Joe walking down the lane: broad, weighty, cap pulled to one side, red face grinning with pleasure at seeing us all again. He walked as always when he came back from a poach, hands pushed deep in trouser pockets, elbows steadying the shotgun hinged to fit in the special poacher's pocket my mother had sewn into his jacket.

And Jinny, small, dark-skinned, black-eyed, in the rear room of the two-up, two-down cottage, the back-house or 'backus' as we all knew it, her nut-brown hands and arms smeared with blood as she tore the skins from the half-dozen rabbits that Joe had snared with the help of his ferrets.

Joe was quick, cunning, sly and generous. Unless you lived with him, it would have been difficult to tell that he was unable to read or write. Jinny could write a letter with her own colourful phonetic spelling, Elizabethan in tone. Asked where they were born, Joe would vaguely claim Langley in Buckinghamshire, though I believe that was simply the farm on which he and Jinny had first met. They were probably in their late thirties, although I doubt whether either of them would have been sure of their age. Neither of them ever once mentioned parents. Neither seemed to have a past.

Uncomfortable, even unsavoury, as Water Oakley Cottages were, my mother decided the advantages of living with old friends prevailed. By the end of March 1944 we were reinstated in the upstairs two rooms of Joe and Jinny's farmworker's cottage.

The cottages, a row of five, stood on the Windsor Road not far from the village of Bray. Unknown to us then, Bray Film Studios stood on the river bank 100 yards away. Joe and Jinny were unable to tell us that we lived cheek by jowl with a film studio since they were totally unaware of what a film studio was, having never seen a film in their lives. Kit and I were left to imagine that the studio was the secret headquarters of some covert wartime activity because there were occasionally guards on the gate. This was, in fact, because the studio shared an entrance drive with the abandoned stately home next door, where Winston Churchill had temporarily installed General de Gaulle, exiled from London. Oakley Court was the postwar HQ for Hammer Horror films. From our tree house in the copse beside the cottages we had often seen a big official car leave the driveway, a long-necked unknown man in foreign uniform sitting alone in the back.

These were days of intense excitement. Nobody could miss the vast preparations being made in southern England for the invasion of Europe. Everywhere there were marching soldiers—British, American, Canadian, Polish; everywhere tented camps had sprung up; on every road huge convoys of military vehicles thundered by, day and night.

But our world revolved around the row of cottages and their farmworker inhabitants, every man, woman and child there looking up to Joe as ratcatcher, weather-man, poacher, unofficial farm manager, and commentator on the probable course of the war.

Joe had changed since our last stay at Water Oakley. Now, for instance, he wore under his jacket a dark green US Army sweater; he had never possessed a sweater before. He would also, on occasion, pull out a packet of Lucky Strike cigarettes and offer them to anyone he was talking to, though he never smoked himself. Most remarkable was the fact that he had begun to move his lips when he stared at the *Daily Mirror* headlines.

Jinny was touchingly proud of these developments. 'It's they there Yanks,' she said. 'Joe's friend the colonel, he bin and told Joe to go on a course they have up at Holyport. Lots of they young Yanks can't read properly. 'Course Joe can, but he's been a bit lazy with his reading these last few years.'

My mother, perfectly straight-faced, said she'd never guessed. Good for Joe if he were polishing up his reading.

'They Yanks are different,' Jinny said. 'They don't take no for an answer. They just laugh and say "move your bum", though they use a different word for it.' Her eyes sparkled. 'Joe said he's going to take me to Lunnon after the war. See the sights. And we'll come and see you and the boys. We'll bring a couple'a rabbits with us and a bit of old Drakey's pork fat to fry them in.'

My mother smiled. 'When we find a house, you'll be the first on the list, Jin.'

OUR WORLD WAS ONE of a great deal of warmth and friendliness, but the nearby bluebell glade offered no challenge to the cottages' stench of over-flowing privies, the hideous reek of Joe's caged ferrets, the nauseating sweet-sour smell of a cupboardful of dead rabbits, or the high stink of three-hour-long cooked cabbage, Jinny's *specialité de la maison*.

Yet we felt lucky. We had survived the bombing. Every time my father came to Windsor for a weekend (he worked as a porter in Whitelands House, a very upmarket block of flats just short of Sloane Square), he brought with him news of other families, who had died or been injured. We felt lucky, too, to be with people like Joe and Jinny who had become some-thing more than friends. But we had lost the anchor that the World's End had always provided.

I remember the weekend my father told us that he had just discovered that La-di-dah had been killed. He was a madly eccentric newspaper seller, small, emaciated, epileptic, invariably dressed in a flat cap and an overlong raincoat. He was known as La-di-dah from the garbled way he screeched his wares: '*News, Star, Standard!*' When we were younger we were all a little afraid of him. Later, 'La-di's 'ad a fit again,' from some passer-by was enough to get a dozen callous, thrill-seeking kids racing down Dartrey Road to see for themselves. Kit and I would certainly be among them.

News of his death was yet another reminder of the permanent change that had taken place in our lives. Playing down by the river at the bottom of the lane, Kit and I talked about it.

'I wonder who'll be there when we go back?' I said.

We were trying to lure a duck close enough to be captured for dinner. We'd never succeeded yet.

Tears welled up in Kit's eyes. Perhaps he was thinking, like me, of the last time we had seen our flat. We'd picked our way through the suddenly unfamiliar rooms, silenced by the thought that all this destruction had taken place around us yet the four of us had scrambled from it uninjured. We stared at shattered walls, window frames ripped from their setting, broken furniture, doors torn off hinges. Smoke drifted through it from fires still burning in King's Road. Outside, I watched my school friend, Ted Simon, picking his way over a huge mound of rubble. He was holding high a badly bent cage with a dusty yellow canary, still alive, fluttering about inside.

We forgot about the duck. We didn't feel like murder any longer. 'Let's go back home,' Kit said. 'I mean, back to Joe and Jinny's.'

We stood on the river bank and gulped at each other. We no longer had a place we could talk about as home. We still used the word, and it still referred to number 3, Guinness Trust Buildings. But it was like talking of the dead. They are both with you and irretrievably lost to you at the same time.

MY FATHER was a dominant personality. But except perhaps in his desire to execute a decision immediately, to 'get cracking', he was not overbearing. He would not, in any case, have succeeded in being overbearing with my mother, who exuded a quiet authority. She was tall and good-looking, but there was more to her than that. She was not educated—like everybody of that World's End generation she had left school at thirteen or fourteen—but I never met anyone who knew her who was not impressed by her good sense and balanced view of the world around her.

Together they made a formidable marital team. Different as they were, Kit and I never once saw an argument between them. Talents they certainly had, but they lived in an age that wasted such talent in the working class with an insouciant profligacy. My mother's talent for diplomacy was to be confined to her family, friends, and to schmoozing the authorities into improving our lot. Against all competition she had got us our flat at Guinness Trust; in 1939 she had talked herself into a job as a London County Council auxiliary in order to stay with Kit and myself when we were evacuated. My father's talent for organisation was expended on rising from journeyman plumber to manager of Whitelands House.

Whitelands occupied an important place in our lives. Its tenants and their wealthy way of life were the subject of endless talk and a good deal of laughter between our parents. Whitelands was where we slept in the heat and coke dust of the huge furnace-room during the 1940 Blitz. It was where we stumbled to the night we were ourselves bombed in 1944. It was the source of good things from a variety of tenants, from German U-boat captain's boots to, one Christmas, mysterious hard, cold green peas, from an American tenant: the first frozen peas we had seen in our lives. By 1944 my father had long emerged from the boiler room where he had begun as stoker, though he continued for many more years to stoke its great furnaces if the regular stoker were absent. He had been promoted to porter among the six or so (unfit for military service) who serviced the one hundred flats.

Kit at this time was an eleven-year-old, still wrapped in dreams of sporting success. I had emerged from the World's End a twelve-year-old boy with a hyperactive imagination, much of this inherited from my grand-mother Eliza with her stories of her early life. She had died just four months before, a last link with a Victorian world of sentimental song and unsentimental story where poverty made up the trappings and not the point of the tale. From my father came the lesson that you had best learn to fight your own battles. My mother's philosophy made for a sturdy sense of independence but was not competitive. My father's was. He once told Kit that he believed he would have been a rich man 'if it hadn't been for your mother'. There was, however, Kit says, no regret in his voice.

THE WINTER had turned from mild to a cutting cold. There was thin snow on the ground and ice on the puddles of urine and excrement leaking from the outside bucket lavatories. At least it meant that the little girl in the next-door cottage was no longer playing in it.

Kit and I found plenty of things to grumble about. As the temperature dropped, our bedroom froze. All three of us slept on the floor and there weren't enough blankets to go round. We loved Jinny but we hated her food. We missed the World's End.

For my mother, life was impossibly difficult. The water supply to the cottage was one communal tap, sometimes frozen, situated in the backus. There was no electricity on our floor, although my mother had confronted the farmer landlord and a single electric light was provided for the ground-floor front room. Water was heated on the iron stove in the front room, which was also Joe and Jinny's bedroom. Our washbasin was a bowl with a splash of warm water in it from the kettle if there was any left to cut the cold. A pee in the night was into a bucket on the landing. A bath was, of course, unknown to anybody who lived in Water Oakley Cottages.

Then came a further blow. Kit and I had passed a certain bureaucratic marker since we were last living in Windsor. My mother was thus no longer recognised as having small children and therefore became eligible for conscription. She was issued with call-up papers for work as a farm labourer. Somehow she took this cheerfully, joking with Joe and Jinny about how well equipped she was for land-work. They and others at the cottages helped her all they could. But it was bitterly hard work in this raw weather, digging out potatoes, shredding Brussels sprouts from the vine, bagging them up in heavy, mud-sodden sacks and lugging them to distant tractor points in the fields.

When he came down the weekend after she had started, my father took my mother off to the pub. They seemed to us to be away a long time. When they came back he gave a brisk nod, meaning that he wanted to speak to Kit and me upstairs. My mother said: 'Go easy on them. It's not their fault.' We didn't like the sound of that.

Upstairs, my father forcibly pointed out how much rested on our mother's shoulders these days, and how much any grumbling by us could increase the weight on her. She bore enough already, trying to organise schools, new ration books, replacement Identity Cards, furniture for these two rooms here at Joe and Jinny's . . . None of it was easy for her, four months since her mother had died, and now she had to spend most of her day in the fields while we sat in warm classrooms. 'Stone the crows!' he said. 'You boys have it easy, and don't forget it.'

The message was more than clear: pitch in and help, and no complaints.

AFTER MY FATHER'S robust lecture Kit and I tried to keep our grumbles from my mother but she was aware that we were both deeply unsettled, particularly by the fact that we would now be going to different schools. These were not schools that backed onto each other as at the World's End where we could shout to each other across the dividing fence, but buildings five miles apart. Kit was to go back to Braywood, the village school we'd both attended when we were first evacuated, and I to the local grammar, Windsor County Boys' School.

At Braywood Kit was faced with the familiar attempts at bullying from the local boys. But we had grown up in my father's credo that there was nothing to be expected but misery for anyone who was not prepared to fight the bully. In London we had practised with him, swinging ill-aimed punches and receiving a poke in the ribs to show us that no fight was all one-sided. In our teens, we would take turns to fight my father bare-fisted but under strict rules—no punching above the throat. Not the sort of upbringing that would be much approved of today. But the result so far had been a happy school life for us both in a culture where bullying was rife. There were by then a few more Londoners at the Braywood school than there had been during our previous stay. Kit quickly became the Londoners' champion and he and his friend Freddie Coco organised them into a highly effective defence group.

At Windsor County my problems were of a very different order. First, it

336 DONALD JAMES WHEAL

was made clear to me that boys should arrive on time. A minute or two late and you were punished. When I first heard this I was deeply shocked. In London, I had attended the West London Emergency Secondary School for Boys where it was accepted that a high proportion of the pupils would be late, especially after a night of heavy raids. So a five-mile bike ride in the mornings tested my unpractised punctuality to the limit.

Secondly, I quickly realised how far behind I was academically. The West London School for Boys was a makeshift amalgamation of the remnants of six grammar schools that had been evacuated at the beginning of the war, housed in Sloane School. We spent much of our time playing cards in the shelter and calling out to the girls next door in Carlyle School. From time to time we'd indulged in a very modest amount of school work. To my horror I found the boys at Windsor were under the whip from nine to four. Homework was given, and even expected to be completed!

I made nervous enquiries about progress in History and French, my strongest subjects. A boy named Grant-Smith (there were quite a few double-barrelled names), or Granny Smith as he was known (a rural joke I never got until years later), told me that they were studying Magna Carta— some of it in Latin. I had heard of Magna Carta—but in Latin! And they were doing the Future, he said, in French.

I stared at him in astonishment.

'If you know the Future,' Granny Smith said loftily, 'there are so many more things you can do.'

I knew that I had not understood but I wasn't at all sure what it was I hadn't understood. My grandmother had regularly used tea leaves to tell our fortunes, but if we were to be studying the Future, why do it in French? I asked Joe.

'They there Frenchies,' he said, 'they don't really have a future till we kick out they Jerries.'

In my first minutes at Windsor County I had identified my most alarming problem as being the school uniform. At the West London School for Boys we'd had six different ones. Uniformity was, in the nature of things, out of the question. Even tidiness was difficult to impose. We pleaded shortage of clothes coupons, mothers on war work unable to spare the time for repairs. Some boys (sometimes genuinely) pleaded narrow escapes from the bombing that week. Our masters just shrugged. They were mostly long past retirement age, recalled to replace staff serving in the forces.

At Windsor, the masters were very keen on turn-out. The school uniform was grey shorts until the age of fourteen, green school jacket with red piping and school badge sewn on breast pocket, green cap with roundels of red tape. Every boy came to school looking like an immaculate 'Just William'. In screeching contrast I had presented myself on my first day perfectly turned out, or so I imagined, in the only clothes I had: items supplied by the Lord Mayor of London's Air Raid Relief Fund, all donated via the unending generosity of the American people. Not surprisingly, my outfit caused a stir among boys and staff. I was dressed in a wide-shouldered, dark grey, generously orange-checked Californian cashmere jacket and palest zoot-suit gabardine trousers. Hair flopping over the eyes, I felt I only needed a clarinet to step up with the band and swing to 'American Patrol'.

In the classroom I met for the first time the cold eyes of my new form master. I introduced myself.

He drew himself up straight-backed. 'What are you wearing, boy?'

I knew that to respond, 'A jacket and trousers, sir,' would be unwise.

I stumbled over my reply: 'I, sir . . . Well, sir . . . It's all I've got, sir.'

'At Windsor County we have a school uniform. In case it has escaped your notice, boy, it is forest green in colour. With red piping to the jacket.' He leaned forward to inspect me. 'I see no forest green. I see no red piping.' He raised his eyebrows, inviting an explanation. When I clearly had none to offer, he began again. 'Where did this come from?'

'It's from the Lord Mayor, sir,' I stuttered.

'The Lord Mayor's Show?' he enquired silkily, infinitely pleased with his *bon mot* and the burst of laughter from the class.

'The Lord Mayor's Fund, sir.' I was getting angry. Bullies come in all shapes and sizes, but this one I couldn't challenge to a playground fight.

As I explained our recent difficulties, he frowned in an exasperated, superior manner. A cockney oik in tasteless American hand-me-downs, I suppose he was thinking. He looked down at his school register, bored with the game.

My American outfit was not without its impact on my acquisition of status. I was the only boy in the second form wearing long trousers. I also had the distinction of having been bombed out by the Luftwaffe. I even let it be known that I sometimes wore a captured U-boat captain's soft leather boots. When I felt like it, I added casually. Life became more tolerable as I was seen as something of an early well-dressed rebel-without-a-cause.

THERE WAS A GIRL we used to play with down at Monkey Island Lane during our earlier stay at Water Oakley: a bold, red-haired tomboy a year or two older than me, named Shirley. She lived with her farm-labourer parents about a mile down the road from us. I remember seeing her again shortly after we arrived for the second time. She got off the bus from Windsor, hair flowing, fourteen maybe just touching fifteen, a big girl, the sort of girl I was very much beginning to notice.

She recognised me. Her lipsticked lip curled for a moment, then she looked the other way and crossed the road, swinging her handbag. But as she passed, barely turning her head towards me, she said: 'Flash jacket.'

I couldn't think what to say. She was past me before I got out the words. 'It's American,' I called to the back of her bobbing auburn head.

She didn't stop, just continued walking over to where two older girls were standing on the street. Within moments they were laughing together, one of them, a girl of about sixteen, occasionally turning and making it clear that they were laughing at me.

IT WAS LATE MAY. By now there was no other subject of conversation in the barracks, pubs, clubs, schools and hospitals, but *invasion*. This time we weren't talking about the Germans invading *us*. Our armies—British, American, Canadian and Polish—were poised to invade *them*. Where exactly on the coast of France we didn't know. The choice was wide: the Pas de Calais, Normandy, Brittany. More important than where, however, was when, and on that we speculated endlessly.

Invasion activity was all around us. Army trucks rumbled through the night; American signals specialists, mostly black, worked at the top of telephone poles to keep the overloaded system operating.

Joe went out, sniffed the air and said, 'Weather looks rough.'

This was deeply worrying. It meant no invasion of Europe this week. Did Joe agree?

'Mebbe so, Raz D.' He often, mysteriously, prefaced my initial with this Arab honorific. Kit similarly was usually Raz K. 'Tell you what,' said Joe, who had developed a close if unlikely relationship with a very upright West Point colonel at the Hare and Hounds, 'you watch out for they Yankees to leave Holyport.' Holyport was the huge American army camp just down the road to Maidenhead. 'The day they Yankees be gone, the next morning you'll have your invasion.'

'Did the colonel tell you they were in the first wave?' I probed. 'Did he say where his beaches were? I won't tell a soul.'

Joe grinned. 'You arse too many questions, Raz D, you know that? Me and the ole colonel just talks about how you outwit they there hares.'

Poachers have a special tight-lipped quality. People knew instinctively that they could trust Joe. I wonder now how much he really knew about the exact date the Americans were to move down to the assembly areas on the south coast.

THESE SIX MONTHS in the country were, for me, a watershed in a dozen ways, but most particularly in the way that I thought about the opposite sex. In the blackout I had played touch-and-kiss games with the girls from Guinness Trust. There'd been excitement then—especially when I became aware that the girl I most favoured was not running off into the darkness as speedily as she might have—but as much as anything else, curiosity. I could understand well enough why I should be interested in kissing her, but I couldn't really understand why she should be interested in kissing *me*.

When we went to the country I had already started my journey through puberty. Now it seemed I was developing a different cast of mind as well. I spent much more time alone, usually riding my bike down to the village. In the newsagent's there I would buy a comic and hang around covertly looking at the covers of *Woman* and *Woman's Own*, studying the bright-eyed young housewives depicted there.

I found such changes alarming. Hitherto I'd always been clear about what was right and wrong. Suddenly there was something at least as powerful as the wish to do the right thing. There was, ill-defined as it might have been, desire. Or rather, lust.

At this time it centred on Shirley. Despite the humiliation of my last meeting with her, I wanted to talk to her again. At just fifteen she was already shapely. I couldn't say I liked her, she had an acid tongue, but I liked looking at her. I used to look out for her when I was down in the village, even timing my visits to coincide with the bus that brought her from her work in Windsor. She knew I was interested. I could tell that by the way she swung her bag, and her hips, as she passed me. Sometimes she'd stop to say a few words in a flip, jeering manner, sometimes she ignored me.

But one day she confirmed her liking for my cashmere jacket.

'Where d'you get 'un, then? Soft, annit?' laying a hand on my arm.

'I told you, it's from America.'

'That's true, that is? Come all the way from America?' Her face lit up.

The next few times I saw her she'd always mention the jacket. If I was wearing a pullover instead, she'd stop. 'Where is it, then?'

'The jacket? At home.'

'You ought to wear it all the time. I told you, it's really flash.'

A few days later it was a hot day and I had taken off my cashmere jacket and strapped it to the rack above the back wheel of my bike. I arrived home to find that it had slipped off. I rode all the way back to Windsor but there was no sign of my cashmere jacket.

When I next saw Shirley I was wearing a secondhand Windsor County green and red-edged blazer. A size too small.

She stopped and stared at me. 'Where is it then, that Yankee jacket?'

I shrugged uncomfortably.

'What you be wearing *that* for?' She plucked contemptuously at my blazer.

'I have to. For school. Windsor County,' I added, hoping that might impress her.

Her lip curled and she walked on, swinging her handbag.

To me this was a catastrophe. In a rural world of open identities, known faces, I was beginning to need anonymity. I think now of this need as one of the most important stages in puberty. My cashmere jacket was a disguise.

My jacket was gone, but I still had the pale grey trousers. Worn with a white open-necked shirt, I thought they had a sporty air. Man of the world *en relaxe*. I would have to get Shirley's reaction.

I rode down to the village that week. I was in good time, well placed when the bus rolled in. She was not among the villagers who alighted. I was about to turn back when I saw her auburn hair in the front seat. I wanted to drop my bike, run along beside the bus, rap on the window, warn her that she was going to miss her stop, but the bus drew away. I cycled after it.

I was soon far behind the square-ended green bus. In minutes it had disappeared altogether along the twisting country road, arched over with the new leaf of early-summer trees. I wasn't going to ride all the way into Maidenhead. Perhaps, I thought, I'd go to Holyport to watch the Americans playing baseball instead.

As I approached the camp I saw an American soldier at the gate talking to two girls. It was impossible to miss Shirley's bright hair. Or the tight white sweater and the bow of bright lipstick. She looked like Betty Grable.

I was consumed by love. Or something.

A Jeep came through the camp gates. The GI driver stopped. The soldier talking to Shirley and her friend swung himself into the front, the two girls got into the back. With a lot of whooping from the two GIs, the four of them drove off together.

I felt half a dozen emotions. Suddenly, I now knew so much more about Shirley. I knew in theory what some girls were supposed to allow American soldiers to do to them for cigarettes or money. I had seen the condoms on grassy banks at bus stops, although I didn't imagine that Shirley went that far. I felt sick with unrequited lust.

I CYCLED DOWN to the village early one Saturday evening as spring was turning to summer. As I passed the bottom of Monkey Island Lane I saw a small group of people. Another few yards and I heard voices, a man's and a girl's. Shirley was struggling with her father. She wore her white Betty Grable sweater and a wide belt, bright red like her lipstick. Her father was a small, wiry man. His cap was off, lying a few yards away, the few strands of hair normally brushed across his crown now hanging down by his temple.

'I'm not letting you on that bus,' he was shouting as he tried to take a grip on her arm.

'I'll go where I like,' Shirley was shouting back, pushing him.

'You going with that there Martha girl,' he said, his voice loud enough for the people around them to hear. 'I know what you're doing.'

He loosed his grip and Shirley was big and strong enough to take advantage. The bus was drawing up now, a few yards from them. Turning, she ran. In a desperate attempt to stop her, he snatched at the side of her white sweater. With his free hand he was hitting her across the back of the head.

'Let go my sweater,' she screamed. 'Stop that . . . stop hitting me!'

'Prostituting for they Yanks,' he shouted, purple with rage and humiliation. 'You and Martha, common prostitutes, the pair of you!'

She turned and slapped him hard, high on his cheek. He reeled back, releasing his grip on the sweater. The bus was just pulling away behind Shirley but she twisted back quickly, leapt for the platform and was gone.

People stood silently watching her father as he stared after the disappearing bus. Then he slowly bent to retrieve his cap. Pushing his hair back over his bald head, he fitted his cap over it. The onlookers were drifting away.

'And you get going.' He turned on me. 'Go on, before I give you one.'

WITHIN DAYS, it seemed, I heard them all talking about Shirley.

'Youse heard she goes with they Yankees?'

'If you're short of fags,' Dimple Soden from the cottage next door said, 'ask that there Shirley. She'll sell you a packet.'

'*Give* you a packet, more like.' I didn't understand the men's laughter at the time.

And from the women: 'Always said she'd turn out a bad lot, din't I?'

I met Shirley in the village a week or so later. She asked me when we were going back to London.

'Soon as we can find a flat,' I said. 'They're not easy to find.'

'Yeah?' Her thoughts were clearly somewhere else. She swung her bag idly around. 'I'd like to go to Lunnon myself. What's it like?'

'Well . . .' I was at a complete loss, mouth dry with anxiety to say something she'd like to hear. I shrugged as if I used to be up in Piccadilly every night. 'There's always something going on.'

She nodded. 'Lunnon's big, annit? Like twice as big as Windsor?'

'Twenty times at least.'

'Never. Where did you live in Lunnon, then? Anywhere near Rainbow Corner?'

'Rainbow Corner, the Yanks' club?'

'You been there?' she asked.

I shrugged in a way that might have meant yes. 'We're not far from there.' Well, we used to be just a 22 bus ride away. 'Why d'you want to know?'

'Somebody asked me if I wanted to go there, that's all. Dancing.'

'Round Piccadilly it can get rough,' I said. 'You're better off here.'

She flicked her hair. 'It's all right for you, from Lunnon. But who'd want to live in a dump like this for the rest of their lives?'

I felt grown up talking to a girl like that, a girl wearing platform heels and make-up. I didn't share in the condemnation that surrounded Shirley. My own secret desires predisposed me to her defence. I knew also that her father had never been reluctant to take his belt to her and that she lived in the sort of squalor we were now familiar with. I wasn't too surprised that young, clean-cut GIs wanting to 'feel your top' seemed to offer a road out.

A week or two later the village gossip was that Shirley had left home (thrown out more like, the women said) and had gone to live in London. When we finally arrived back there I used to scan passing groups of girls hoping to see her. Or I did for a week or so.

BY THE BEGINNING of June, Kit and I had taken to leaping out of bed to go down to the front room to catch the early news. Joe and Jinny were already in the fields. My mother was allowed an extra half-hour to get our breakfast. We held our breaths for the announcement of the invasion. Now the roads outside Water Oakley Cottages were crammed with marching American troops and long convoys rumbled past. We knew from the number of units around us that our area was an American staging point. Each day we cycled up to the Holyport camp but there seemed to be no change there. Baseball games flourished on the huge dusty diamond in the centre of the hundreds of neatly aligned bell-tents. A half-dozen girls waited with exaggerated nonchalance at the gate.

Then, one day, we arrived back from school to the rumour that the Americans had gone. Kit and I looked at each other. We had heard the rumbling of heavy trucks passing the cottages before we went to sleep, but it never occurred to us that they were *our* Yanks on the move.

We jumped on our bikes. Holyport was a desolate sight: a field of churned earth and flattened grass. The prefabricated sentry post had been demolished. Scattered condom packets around the unguarded gate, Wrigley's Chewing Gum wrappers, and a few shocked girls in heavy make-up were all that was left of 20,000 men, their equipment and vehicles, all now heading for the south coast. Then, as we rode back to Water Oakley, in the skies above, hundreds of aircraft, British and American, passing in massed squadron formations overhead. Kit and I stopped. For a few moments we stared up at the sky, then we jumped on our bikes and dashed back home with the news. We could not be more than days, hours even, from the cross-Channel invasion.

The real news burst upon us on June 6. Allied troops had landed on the coast of France. Of the five beach-heads (three Anglo-Canadian and two American), landings on four had gone according to plan. The fifth beach, code-named Omaha, was yet to gain its tragic reputation. Kit was smiling smugly throughout the day. He had won the sweepstake that my mother had organised along the cottages. The kitty was five shillings. He had never in his life had so much money.

SIX DAYS LATER, early-shift workers living just beyond the railway bridge at Grave Road, Bethnal Green, in the East End of London, pulled back the blackout curtains to hear the sound of a loud motorbike. Curiously the bike seemed to be sailing through the lightening sky above. When the noise ceased abruptly people turned back to the task in hand: shaving, tea-making, rousing others for work. The explosion that followed a moment or two later was sharper, fiercer, than any of the bombs the East End already knew well, with a blast-force powerful enough to render 266 people homeless and a number dead or injured. Grave Road had suffered from the first of Hitler's Revenge Weapons, the V-1, a ton of high-grade explosive in a stubby-winged black robot aircraft. Londoners called the new weapon the flying bomb, the buzz-bomb or the doodlebug—and tried to live with it.

A housing consultant for London Underground named Harry, another improbable friend of Joe's, worked in London and came back to his wife Molly in Windsor at weekends. She told my mother that London Underground properties (for housing their workers) were being damaged' faster now than at any time since the height of the Blitz. Londoners, Harry said, were getting weary. Fast as the V-1 sites along the Channel coast were being cleared by the Canadians, the Germans developed new launch sites.

My first sight of a V-1 was one afternoon just before the beginning of the summer holidays. Cycling back from school, I was aware of a motorbike engine somewhere behind me. I looked back and saw that the noise was in the sky, coming from a small, low-flying, black plane with a flame streaking from its tailplane. It came over Windsor Castle and the engine cut. The plane glided towards Dedworth, a mile outside the town. It tipped, hurtled down at an angle and hit a timber yard factory chimney. The explosion was terrifying. Staring in astonishment, I watched the chimney cut clean off at its base. Then it toppled and disappeared behind the line of rooftops.

I turned my bike and rode up towards Dedworth. When I arrived people were standing about in the streets talking quietly and shaking their heads. There were one or two ambulances and wardens but no Heavy Rescue people. Buildings had been laid low by the fall of the chimney. Some of the houses had been wrecked but were still standing. A fat man in overalls came running past and stopped, looked at me and said: 'Here, they say there's a baby up there in the bedroom. You want to lend a hand, son?'

As I dropped my bike and followed him, I cast a nervous glance behind me. There seemed to be only the two of us.

'They thought they got everybody out,' he shouted as he ran. 'But someone's reported hearing a baby crying in number sixteen.'

'Where's its mother?' I caught up with him and jogged along beside him.

'Unconscious,' he puffed. 'They took her off to the Aid Station.'

We stopped before the house. The outer wall facing the street had collapsed so the bedroom floor-joists had no support on that side. They sagged, stripped by blast of their ceiling plaster, the laths exposed.

We looked at it, neither at all happy about going in. We listened. Nothing. I hoped he'd say, 'That's it. No baby there.' But he didn't. He turned to me. 'OK, son?'

I nodded. I felt suddenly cold and hot—like having 'flu.

He edged through the doorway, walking across the flattened front door. I followed him in.

The dust had settled. I was looking at the ceiling and the sloping, unsupported joists. If we ducked under them we could see the staircase. It was missing almost everything: banister rail, several stairs.

I could sense his uncertainty. 'What d'you think?' he said.

Then it came to me that I'd been in far more bombed houses than he had. I was an expert at climbing around obstacles, testing the strength of a joist or the solidity of a staircase. Bombed houses were where we used to play in London. Here, we were going to have to jump from the upper usable step of the staircase to the shaky floor level about three feet below and hope it held. I looked at my overweight companion. If I stayed at the foot of the stairs, he could easily bring the whole lot down on my head. 'I'll go first,' I volunteered. He thought it was courage that inspired me.

There was a cot in one of the rooms and some baby clothes spread across the undulating carpet, but there was no baby. When I clambered back to the staircase a woman was standing just inside the doorway telling us the child was safe with his grandmother.

We all got out of the house. The woman talked, at least part of the time, directly to me. The senior warden came over and did the same, telling us there had miraculously been no deaths or serious injuries. Covered with dust, I enjoyed being a bit of a hero.

Back in Water Oakley, where the summer stench was more intolerable than ever, my mother had news. Harry, the London Underground housing manager, had somehow contrived to get a house allocated to us. A whole three-bedroomed house, just the four of us.

'Is it in London?' Kit and I asked anxiously.

'Of course it is,' my mother said. 'It's a place called White City.'

White City? Anyway, London. We were going home.

THREE

I had only heard of White City as a dog track. But then ignorance of place other than their own was an aspect of most London children's life. Before the war ended, I had never been to Piccadilly, never seen Buckingham Palace or the Houses of Parliament, although they were all fifteen minutes away (in those traffic-free days) on the 11 or 22 buses that ran down King's Road. We knew our own pockets of London well, but a mile or so away, Bayswater, Brixton, Victoria, Notting Hill Gate were no more than names on the front of buses. Indeed, for many of my very early years I had thought 'abroad' was anywhere across the other side of the Thames, because all the men I knew talked of abroad as 'over the water'. I used to stare suspiciously across the river, steeling myself for the moment when the Kaiser, probably concealed behind the Morgan Crucible Works, led his inevitable dash across Battersea Bridge to seize the World's End, understandably his primary London objective.

White City Stadium, which gave the area of our new home what fame it had, was on a strip of double carriageway called Westway, not to be confused with the modern elevated section. The houses in the small roads off Westway, of which our crescent, Primula Street, was one, were divided by strips of grass. No pubs, it's true, no shops, no street corner paper sellers, no whelk stall on Sunday morning. But well-kept grass between each block.

The area seemed strange to us. The homogeneity of the buildings was depressing. Every red-brick, Crittall-windowed two-storey house had been built in the seven or eight years straddling the twenties and early thirties. We were living on the edge of Metroland. Nothing and nowhere around seemed as homely as the variety of the World's End.

We nevertheless walked around our empty house in wonder. I felt acute excitement at the idea of having a bedroom I wasn't sharing. Kit, I know, felt the same. I've no doubt that my parents felt equally blessed. Single, my mother had slept all her life with her mother or elder sister May, often both. At his childhood home, my father had had his sleeping place under the kitchen sink. Married, they had never had a room to themselves since Kit and I were born.

Today, it's impossible to convey the pure lift it gave us to have a bathroom. Almost absurd now to think that young boys could be moved by a bathroom. But I can remember Kit and myself standing in the doorway, the sun slanting through the window onto the white bath, the fresh smell of soap from the last occupants, and the cold thrill that ran down my spine. Neither of us spoke but I would have bet money we were both thinking of Joe and Jinny's place and, for all the gratitude we felt towards them, promising ourselves we would never be forced to live like that again.

There was a garden outside with red Underground trains running along the embankment at the end. In the middle was an Anderson shelter, a hump of earth planted with a few dahlias. Most gardens along the railway line had one. The base, sunk about three feet into the ground, was lined with six inches of concrete. Into this was set a curving roof of galvanised steel, the whole covered with a foot or two of earth. A small opening, three foot high and two foot wide, was the entrance, easy enough for teenage boys, much more difficult for adults to clamber into. Across the railway was the main gate of Wormwood Scrubs Prison, sombre and menacing.

This was our new home. We were breathless with excitement. But where was it? In the Borough of Hammersmith my father told us, but neither completely Shepherd's Bush nor East Acton. That sounded to me on the very lip of the world. The district, he said, was known as White City from the bright white concrete stadium. In the World's End we were aware of living somewhere that went back for centuries. My mother's mother told stories about her childhood when Cremorne Gardens attracted all the young toffs and the ladies of the town, and I knew that we lived no distance from writers and painters. My other grandmother, the ever aggressive Minnie, used to clean for the director of the Tate Gallery at his house on King's Road. Painters and sculptors from Augustus John to Henry Moore came to tea there. At school and on the wireless we heard references to Chelsea artists, writers, Chelsea Pensioners or Chelsea's football team. Much of our attachment to the World's End was undoubtedly that sense of living in a long-established, well-known part of London. White City, by contrast, had no history.

My mother set out to get to know our immediate neighbours. She could always sense when a little good public relations were necessary. What story she told them to account for the fact that we were renting a London Underground house, I don't know. But her way of just getting to the heart of people was remarkable. In no time Mrs Fribbins next door was smiling at us over the back fence. Later, when she decided she must leave her husband, it was my mother she turned to for advice and support. When young Mrs Sandom on the other side suffered a fatal heart attack, it was my mother and Kit who carried her body downstairs in the middle of the night so that her young son would not see it.

In furnishing the new house my father's formidable energy came into play. Enough carpet to lay on the stairs, a bedroom or two, and in the sitting room, a pair of comfortable armchairs and a kitchen table, all came from Whitelands House where he had been storing them in the boiler room against the day, which he never doubted would arrive, when we moved. Where did they originally come from? God knows.

The carpet was thick with dust. Somehow he manhandled it into the Whitelands service lift and up to the roof of the building where he, Kit and myself hurled buckets of soapy water at it and scrubbed it with bristle brooms. In the feeble London summer of 1944 we waited for it to dry, watching for the next shower as anxiously as we watched for the next flying bomb, our carpet poised perilously between drying and rotting. Finally a great damp pink roll was conveyed by Mayfair laundry van for half a crown to the driver and before long we had wall-to-wall carpet, an incredible luxury, albeit a luxury with a damp smell for the first month or two.

A bombed families furniture grant provided our beds and curtaining. Blackout material, I seem to remember, was available off-ration. In fact we had passed the period when a blackout was necessary. The *Operation Steinbock* Blitz of early 1944 was pretty much the last time German bombers penetrated as far as London. Our problem now was the pilotless V-1.

KIT AND I might have chosen to go to Clement Danes, the grammar school backing onto Wormwood Scrubs, a few minutes' walk from where we now lived. In fact we both preferred to make the journey of nearly an hour back to the West London Emergency Secondary School for Boys—or Sloane School as we all called it. For me it would be a return to old friends, to Kit it would be a new school but there were plenty of boys from the World's End he already knew. I think we both had no doubts it was worth a long bus ride. We were reluctant to cut all ties with the World's End. If we chose Sloane School we would be returning to a place of familiar warmth.

There was no denying the air of desolation that marked the World's End. Chelsea Council had acted firmly in requisitioning empty flats and houses in the expensive part of the borough. Many of the survivors of the Guinness Trust bombing would finally move back to the rebuilt blocks on the old site, but when we returned to Sloane in the late summer of 1944 it hadn't yet happened, the community was scattered. The dangerous buildings had been demolished but dozens of houses stood like cardboard cartons, roofless, and with huge holes torn in the walls where there had once been windows. And the area smelt different. The power station still dominated, but along the streets when it rained you could smell nothing but charred beams and joists, or the wet dust of a million crushed bricks and tiles.

ONCE AT SCHOOL we spent a great deal of time in the cloakrooms, which had been strengthened to provide shelters. These would certainly not have saved the lives of all the masters and boys in the case of a direct hit but lottery was what everybody in London lived with during the days of the V-1. Between seventy and 200 flying bombs daily were now being launched at the city. Explosions punctuated our days.

On clear days and even nights a good proportion of the V-1s were shot down by flak or fighters; on misty mornings or foggy nights the majority would probably get through, although even then much reduced in number by RAF 11 Group with its crack 456 Royal Australian Air Force night-fighter squadron. Alerts were sounded day and night until finally they became largely ignored. At school it was different. Air raid warnings had to be observed and the shuffle of gabbling, grubby boys down the two stair-cases and into the cloakrooms seemed to take up much of our day. Once there we sat tightly packed on wooden benches. Card games were renewed from where they'd been left off twenty minutes before. Comics were swapped from boy to boy and then from form to form, and tall tales were told about girls from the school next door. Teachers read, chatted among themselves or went out for a smoke.

We did less work than we had done in any period since the Blitz. But some understanding of the world at war was something to which even a young boy could aspire. What gave it total relevance, of course, was the fact that some of it was happening to us. We knew that advances along the north European coastlines meant fewer flying bombs. The number of miles advanced per day occupied the headlines so that every schoolboy was aware of progress towards the final defeat of Hitler. We concentrated on battles, mostly won at this time, or at least, like Arnhem, failure depicted as victory.

With glee we studied newspaper maps illustrating the developing strangle-hold on Germany.

Through my father, there was an awareness of something else: that the fighting in the last months had been directed by Churchill, Roosevelt and Stalin, each with one careful eye cocked on the postwar future. As a porter standing in the entrance hall of Whitelands House, or taking tenants up in the lift, my father seized every opportunity to ask questions. If it was an American admiral he would ask about the war in the Pacific; a Frenchman would be questioned about Marshal Pétain and the Vichy government; a Polish diplomat would be quizzed about the postwar Polish frontiers. I think almost everybody at that time believed that the Russian influence in the new world would be both significant and beneficial.

But at this stage none of us could look beyond the defeat of Germany. After six years, war was really all we could remember. It had to end for new thoughts to germinate.

At the West London School the days were tolerable, even in some ways enjoyable. We felt that we (with Adolf's help) were putting one over on the school system, as we spent our days playing cards in the cloakrooms.

The nights, however, were different. When a V-1 chugged across the night sky in your direction there was no companionable bravado to warm the chilling blood. When the engine cut and you heard the V-1 singing across the rooftops, your breathing stopped until, perhaps only fifty foot above your head, it swished over and exploded with a great powerful crack on the houses of some unfortunates a few streets over.

In August, at the height of the V-1 attack, Churchill told Parliament that 180,000 houses had so far been destroyed and 800,000 damaged by the new weapon. On September 7, Duncan Sandys, junior air minister in charge of the Revenge Weapon problem, made a statement to the press in a somewhat different tone: 'Except for a few last shots, the Battle for London is over.'

ON THE SAME DAY, across the North Sea in Holland, an SS unit was clearing all Dutch civilians from a suburb in The Hague. Muted blue lighting was set up in the main square. During the night a special convoy of unusually long, tarpaulin-covered trucks arrived. They carried the new Revenge Weapon, the V-2, forty-five-foot long, loaded with one ton of high explosive, and set to descend on London at over three times the speed of sound. Far too fast to be shot down by antiaircraft fire, untouchable by even the most modern

WHITE CITY | 351

mark of Spitfire. That morning Hitler's second Revenge Weapon was hoisted vertical on its launch pad in the square.

Just before 6.40 p.m. on September 8, 1944, the first rocket thrust into the sky above Holland. Travelling at 3,000 mph, it burst through the atmosphere, turned an arc in space and hurtled down towards London. It was in the air for less than four minutes.

In White City we were just about to have tea, our evening meal. That night it was late because my father had been delayed. The sequence of events was an almost simultaneous flash and thunderous explosion, not sharp like a V-1 explosion, more muffled but menacingly powerful. I looked at my mother. Her face was set.

'I didn't hear the engine cut,' my mother said.

My father said nothing.

I think we all knew this was something different even before the next stage, a totally strange, deep rumble that seemed to move round the horizon for perhaps ten or fifteen seconds. We had been listening to the first stratospheric rocket attack in history.

We went out into the street. A pall of smoke and crushed debris rose above the roofline not far from us, a low distorted mushroom cloud slowly drifting across the rooftops. There were other people on the street, women in what had become the classic Londoner's pose, arms folded in front of them. A few words were exchanged before they went back in. The men and boys remained to exchange opinions. What the dickens was that? the men asked themselves.

The government, in order to give German scientists no information on which to adjust their target settings, made no public announcement. The local press carried a story about a gas main explosion in Staveley Road, Chiswick. My father smiled and told me that a lot of people were talking about a *flying* gas main.

I didn't understand. 'How can you have a flying gas main?'

'Let's say you can bet your life it's not some secret weapon developed by the Gaslight and Coke Company,' he said.

'What then?'

He shook his head. 'I don't know, Dee. Nor does anybody else outside the government. But you can be sure we're not going to like it.'

How right he was.

Our life as a family now took on a truly bizarre quality. Rockets were rumbling round the horizon, not many, perhaps an average of ten a day, but the peculiarities of the sound barrier meant that a rocket explosion could seem close by to someone up to six miles away. There were no sirens that could alert us to this danger, though of course the siren system continued to give constant warnings of the approach of flying bombs.

Everyone had their personal blast stories, of banknotes blown helter-skelter down the high street or crated geese released in their hundreds. One night on the railway line that separated us from Wormwood Scrubs Prison our blast story was delivered when a flying bomb came down, derailing a lengthy milk train. Huge steel containers were split open by the blast or burst as they toppled from their wagons to roll, gushing milk, down the embankment. Gallons of it washed in a white flood along the gutters past the prison. After a day or so the sourness in the air was almost unbearable.

By now we were all beginning to feel seriously short of sleep. We weren't alone, of course. Fatigue was visible in the faces of people on buses, women in food queues, and boys at school where it was not uncommon to see someone fall asleep at his desk. They were usually left sleeping by all but the more sadistic of the staff. The whole of London looked tired.

SOMETHING HAD TO BE DONE. The first decision was that while my father was on fire-watching duty at Whitelands House, my mother, Kit and myself would sleep in one of the Underground stations. Lancaster Gate was chosen, just along the Central Line that ran past the back of our garden.

The new routine would begin as soon as Kit and I were back from school. We'd do our homework, set to maintain the practice rather than to exercise us in any way. When my father arrived home at about six we had tea. This was always taken with the back door open, however cool the autumn evenings were becoming. We had discovered that we had a special alarm system all our own. After tea our parents took this rare opportunity to be alone together, Kit and I sat on the back step completing our homework and listening for warning signals from the prison.

These took the form of a loud klaxon placed somewhere above the Victorian prison gate. It was directly connected to radar stations on the Kent coast and to V-1 watch stations in southeast London. One blast signalled a flying bomb approaching London, on course for Wormwood Scrubs. We would shout out to our parents and they might join us at the door. Inside the prison the warders would rouse the prisoners from their bunks and get them out onto the landings outside their cells. Two blasts on the klaxon meant there was a V-1 directly on course for the Scrubs. The prisoners would be brought down from the top landings. Three blasts, continuously replayed, conveyed a sense of extreme urgency: V-1 less than ten miles distant. I suppose the prisoners were assembled somewhere relatively safe on the ground floor.

For us that urgent three-blast klaxon meant a quick retreat to the Anderson shelter in the garden. There, we'd crouch inside this (barely) underground block of damp concrete listening for the *phut-phut* of the pulse-jet engine of the flying bomb. Most times it would pass over without the engine cutting. A sigh of relief would go up and a great deal of laborious clambering began as my parents got out of the Anderson. And they were young. I can't imagine a sixty-five-year-old man or woman getting in and out of that entrance hole.

This would be the beginning of the evening. In the interlude we might hear two or three rockets and speculate about where they had struck. Part two of our evening began with my father leaving as it began to get dark, by bus or bike for Chelsea, and my mother, Kit and I making for East Acton tube station from where we would take the train to our second home on the platform at Lancaster Gate.

A nightly journey down to Lancaster Gate was hard work. Three suitcases contained blankets and a pillow each. The rushing air from the passing tube trains was notably dry so bottles of tap water were necessary. Add a book or two for a final brief, hopeless scribble at the ever-neglected homework and sandwiches for our late supper at perhaps ten o'clock, and you had a heavy suitcase. Other family groups, usually without men, would be making their way to the station, small children struggling with suitcases, occasionally stopping to rest, mothers casting apprehensive glances at the sky as they hurried them on.

Our places below were reserved for us in a system I no longer remember. We were among 73,000 Londoners sleeping in the tube at this time, occupying the same station every night. On busy nights we stepped into a Hieronymus Bosch scene. Pallid arms and legs, toothless men, half-dressed old women, were all around. The lights were blue and low. Some people slept and snored, others read or shouted out to acquaintances. One of our neighbours, who always settled down early, produced something approaching a soap opera in his sleep. 'Elsie' was the star.

'Elsie told me,' he would yell, startling everybody around him. People would rise on one elbow in anticipation of another instalment. 'Elsie's off with Billy,' he would confide in a slurred voice to the people around him. 'Slips round Billy's place . . . first chance she gets.' A belch would roll along the platform, carrying the sourness of half-digested beer. 'Her dad won't have it, you know. Not with her husband overseas and all. Oh, no.' By now he was wide awake. He'd rub his eyes, pass his hand over the few wisps of grey hair on his bald head, shrug with what might have been embarrass-ment or, equally, indifference, then turn over and go back to sleep.

Our sleep-talker was only one among many night-time performers. Most of them were wide awake, however, as they sang or mumbled through the night. They were never short of an audience. Sometimes, as we settled down for the night, a woman would start softly singing one of the popular songs of the day: 'As Time Goes By', or 'A Nightingale Sang in Berkeley Square'. Other women might join in, all singing equally softly. I remember the undercurrent of sadness.

The preacher who paid us a visit every few nights was given short shrift. 'Put a sock in it,' someone would yell at the first blast of fire and brimstone—and, if enough dissenting voices joined in, the man would succumb, haughtily packing his 'Jesus Saves' stand and stepping through the open doors of the next train. 'At Marble Arch they'll listen,' he'd shout defiantly over his shoulder as the doors were closing. 'Marble Arch will not reject the Word of God.' And he'd wave his fist as the train pulled away.

As late-comers we slept on the platform a few feet from the incoming trains, Kit and I on either side of my mother. The air was foetid and insuffi-cient until another train arrived and dragged with it coolness from the tun-nels. It made for disturbed nights. Women, I noticed, cried out often. Maybe they had succumbed to the same temptations as Elsie. Or perhaps they were just desperately worried about their husbands or boyfriends in Normandy or Italy, in Burma, in the skies over Germany or out on the Atlantic.

But for youngsters like us it wasn't all bad. During the evening Kit and I hopped on the trains to go up to Marble Arch, the next station on the West End side. Taking orders for a mug of tea or a sandwich from the NAAFI can-teen there, we would sometimes make as much as sixpence a night in tips.

Most fortunate about the choice of Lancaster Gate station for us was that the American Army had an Enlisted Men's Club pretty much directly above us. It made for a constant flow of GIs, dispensing gum and Hershey bars as they passed through on their way to Oxford Circus, Soho, and the huge

American club at Rainbow Corner. On an exceptionally good night one of the GIs would leave a copy of *Yank*, the soldier's magazine, which always carried at least one really worthwhile pin-up.

Morning was not a pretty sight at Lancaster Gate. Even in the worst conditions of waking, there is usually the compensation of a little daylight, a few streaks of dawn across the sky. Not in the depths of Lancaster Gate tube. There were always a few early risers stepping carefully over others in an attempt not to wake their neighbours. But at about six thirty the denizens of Lancaster Gate rose, stretching and snorting, yawning and coughing. A thousand arms and legs were pulled and pushed through garments, some to remove the shirt they'd slept in, others to get into warmer clothes in expectation of a chilly morning 'upstairs'. It was a seminal Second World War scene, repeated in camps and bomb shelters all over Europe. The chain-link wooden bunks, the overcrowding, the dim lights and deep shadows, the utter lack of anything approaching privacy . . .

We would take the train back from the neighbouring tunnel, sitting dirty and sleepy, not speaking too much except to wonder how the night had been upstairs, especially in Chelsea where my father was fire-watching. Then we would emerge, often into brilliant sunshine, and the world would take on its usual shape again. Perhaps a rocket or two rumbling round the horizon, before tea and fried bread and dried egg for breakfast. My mother would always go out to phone Whitelands House from the call box at the bottom of the street to see my father was all right before she made her own breakfast.

Then, for Kit and me, a quick wash before we went off to school.

AT ABOUT THIS TIME it was decided that I should spend the nights in Chelsea with my father. Technically he was on fire-watching duty. In fact, by this stage of the war any fire was likely to be the result of a V-1 or V-2 rocket explosion, which would bring the Fire Brigade on the scene immediately. In effect this meant the fire-watch system was no longer needed. My father, however, had other reasons for needing to be in Chelsea every night.

These revolved around the recent difficulties with the law of the local World's End bookmaker, Alf Gordon. My father was well known to Alf, having worked for him on Saturday evenings for the last year as bookmaker's clerk at Stamford Bridge dog track. On occasion I had been called in to do some general running, a few times even calling the odds as tick-tack man, with the hand signals then used at race tracks.

Alf's problems began when a new police inspector arrived on the World's End scene to police the illegal practice of street bookmaking, which was a large part of Alf's business. The system was that his two runners, Fatty and Darkie, strolled through the streets collecting betting 'slips' which carried the scrawled details of the bet and wrapped the sixpence or shilling to be gambled. There would be a twice-daily visit to the King's Arms, the Riley Arms and the World's End pub. If a copper were seen to take an interest in them, Darkie, who would carry all the slips, would run for World's End Passage from where he had a choice of back doors to escape through. Fatty, who was incapable of running, would feign well-worn surprise at the extraordinary behaviour of his friend. Mostly the police didn't lean too hard. Fatty allowed himself to be found with the occasional betting slip in his pocket and the inspector at Chelsea Station was content that his men were doing their bit. Everybody played by the rules. But a new inspector was an obvious problem. What would his rules be?

One evening, over a drink with the new inspector, Alf thought he heard a discreet invitation. He therefore offered the inspector the occasional pony (£25) not to press too hard on his runners. The inspector agreed but refused to take the money from Alf in the crowded pub. He'd meet him on Albert Bridge, he said, later that evening.

In the blackout Alf Gordon ambled along the embankment to Albert Bridge. He was, I suppose, a man of about forty-five, rather overweight, wearing a suit and Homburg hat. He crossed to a halfway point between the ornate Victorian suspension towers and leaned on the rail. Below him, no doubt, the moon metalled the dark water. I can almost hear the zither music.

Then the new inspector appears out of the darkness. Cigarettes and pleasantries are exchanged. But barely has the pony been slipped into the inspector's inside pocket when there's a shout from the Battersea side of the bridge. Blue-masked torches bob towards them.

'You bastard!' Alf turns to run but there's another bobbing blue light on the Chelsea side. He is trapped.

'Just my job, Alf. You'll go down for this, you know. Bribing a police inspector.' He shakes his head sadly.

Most small bookmakers at this time started out with an illegal street-bookmaking business before graduating to a licensed pitch at one of the big dog tracks. With Alf *hors de combat* there was a clear, if dangerous, opportunity for my father to take over the illicit part of the business, at least temporarily. Alf himself approved the idea; Fatty and Darkie said they'd be happy to work for my father.

My father talked to my mother. Moving up from clerk, where you bore no part in the losses, to being bookmaker and sole loss-taker, took courage. To operate where the local inspector was known not to turn a blind eye involved serious risk. But the decision involved more than bookmaking, the infinite calculations of which my father loved. It was for him another step up a ladder he had set himself to climb.

He was clear-eyed about the risks involved. His savings (which were probably less than £150) could go in a couple of bad weeks. His job at Whitelands House would undoubtedly go too, if he were prosecuted.

'What do you really think?' he asked my mother.

She was silent for a moment. 'It's what you want to do,' she said. 'We're with you.'

My father became an illegal street bookmaker.

Each evening, he would collect the bets, calculate the winners and losers, and pay out through Fatty and Darkie. All this normally took place in a discreet corner of the World's End pub. Sometimes Darkie or Fatty would be delayed at one of the pubs. In that case I would be sent down to pick up the betting slips and deliver them back to where my father was calculating the odds. The winnings or losses would usually amount to a few pounds. I seem to remember that more often than not it was a few pounds of winnings, even after the two runners had been paid. This amounted to good money.

By ten o'clock most nights we would be finished, the slips recorded, the winners paid out. Then, for us, my father and I, the number 11 bus up King's Road to Sloane Square, to Whitelands House.

Whitelands House was made up of 100 rented flats whose tenants ranged through generals and ambassadors to writers like Daphne Du Maurier. There was the usual sprinkling of barristers, surgeons and wealthy unemployed. Many were notably civil and considerate. Others were not. Frequently, in their overbearing manner and their shockingly bad manners, they were typical of that dissolution of the sense of responsibility that had begun to undermine many of the upper class before the war. My father liked and respected many, like General 'Boy' Browning who planned Arnhem, or the daughter of John Galsworthy, but he disliked others who seemed to believe they somehow deserved to live in a world where cleaning, sweeping, carrying parcels and opening lift doors was done by invisible hands.

Nevertheless, as my mother was always quick to remind us, Whitelands served us well. It provided a job for my father, a cover for his bookmaking, as well as a barely furnished bedroom to sleep in. It had provided us with an underground shelter in the furnace basement during the Blitz, and in the autumn of 1944 it was about to offer a new type of shelter.

My father explained. 'The V-1 approaches from the Kent or Essex coast. Always from the south or east. That's why I've been sleeping in a room on the King's Road side, the north face of Whitelands. Flying bombs have a fixed guidance system—if the building gets hit it'll be on the river side.'

Seemed sensible.

He grimaced. 'Except, I was wrong. Your uncle George was outside the King's Arms yesterday watching one. The engine cut as it crossed the river. He watched it glide towards King's Road, when suddenly it banked and started diving straight at him. He said it chased him down to Lots Road Power Station. The point is, it changed direction.'

Which meant his room on the north side of the building was no longer as safe as he thought. 'So where do we sleep?' I asked him.

'Same place, but we've got to be quick about getting out if we hear one.'

'We wouldn't have time,' I said. I was a heavy sleeper. I was thinking of how I'd have to struggle awake every night. 'And where would we go?'

'To the one place a flying bomb could never hit. The central well.'

Whitelands had been constructed round a central light well. Corridors and some servants' rooms overlooked the well. My father's room was a twenty-yard sprint away from safety.

The logic seemed impeccable. If we could get there in time.

I had a lot of confidence in my father's wartime arrangements. He had bought huge catering tins of Spam before full rationing set in, rice and pepper the day after Pearl Harbor. He'd built a shelter in the bedroom at our flat in Guinness Trust. But any arrangement that depended on me waking and leaping out of bed within four to five seconds filled me with horror.

'There's one problem,' I said, hoping to undermine the whole scheme.

'What's that?'

'The Ghost.'

His lips twisted in frustration. 'Ah,' he said. 'Yes, the Ghost.'

The Ghost was an older man to whom my father had given a cleaning job at Whitelands. The mystery was, why? The Ghost was everything my father disliked: dirty, lazy, sly and usually drunk.

His name was Albert, his surname never mentioned. He was probably in his fifties but drink had added a good ten years to his appearance. He was bent, with wispy grey hair and a lined face. He wore a stained double-breasted suit, a shirt with a stud at the throat and no collar. Bent forward as he was habitually, he would look up at you slyly with clear blue eyes.

The Ghost plagued my father's existence. He could be drunk on cider at any time of the day or night. He would begin drinking in his room or in one of the staff lavatories and would disappear when he was needed for some task. At his most relaxed he would take his quart of cider and stroll down the carpeted corridors, mumbling incoherently to the tune of 'Nellie Dean'. Then a call would come down to the porter's lodge from Captain Fitzgerald ('of the Guards') or perhaps Daphne Du Maurier, that there was an inert creature outside their flat, and my father would go up and drag the Ghost down to his room to sober up, claiming to whichever tenant had complained that it was an outside intruder. The story just about stood up because few people living in Whitelands had ever seen the Ghost, whose nickname derived from the way he went about his duties (when sober), slipping from corridor to corridor, never presenting more than a disappearing back.

The Ghost's room was next door to my father's. This was our problem.

My father and I slept in our shirts and underpants in the one single bed in the narrow, cell-like room. In that first week there were Alerts every night but only one evacuation of the room was attempted. I was woken by an elbow hitting my ribs with some force. A second later the blankets were ripped from me. 'Run,' my father ordered. I got my feet down onto the floor and sat yawning as overhead the V-1 cut. 'Albert, get down,' he yelled at the dividing wall, pulling me to the floor. We rolled under the bed. There was a long, long pause. The ensuing explosion was somewhere in Knightsbridge.

At that moment the door opened and the Ghost stood in the doorway. He wore a long nightshirt and carried his bottle of cider in one hand. 'What was you shouting about?' he said.

We peered up at him from under the bed, then looked at each other, finding it impossible not to laugh. 'Up you get, son,' my father said finally. 'The next one may be closer.' He looked at Albert's wobbling legs. 'Stiffen the Prussian Guards!' he said. 'Go and get some sleep.'

I got a little better at it, a little quicker. But the task of getting a drunken Ghost to his feet equalled the problem of getting me moving in the middle of the night. There would be shouting and mad scrambling, the Ghost being pushed or kicked down the corridor, the three of us rolling on the thick Whitelands carpets. And the sick realisation that the V-1 had passed overhead seconds ago.

On the dozen nights we executed this mad routine, I never heard, after that first night, an engine cut above us. My father would wake at the approach of a V-1. As we scrambled for safety it would pass overhead with its chilling, popping sound to strike somewhere in north London. Three or four times I heard an uncomfortably close explosion. Soon even my father, concerned as he was for my safety, had to recognise that this procedure was a dud.

All our antics really achieved was to forge a sort of bond between the Ghost and myself, though he volunteered almost nothing about himself. He was always telling me what a good father I had. To which I agreed. He liked to say that if I 'watched it', I'd be a chip off the old block.

Then one evening, when my father was busy downstairs, the Ghost brought me a present, putting it on the table and flitting away with a faint smile. I saw it immediately as further evidence of his eccentricity. He had 'given' me my father's 'John Bull' English Dictionary.

I showed it to my father when he came upstairs. 'Stone the crows!' he said quietly. It was one of his favourite exclamations. 'Steady the Buffs!' and 'Snakes Alive!' all found their way into his daily vocabulary. He picked up the dictionary. 'I got this for six Persil packets,' he said. He flicked it open. On the blank opposite the title page my father had many years ago drawn up a family tree in red ink.

I saw him react and looked over his shoulder. There was an additional scribble in black ink on the page. I had no time to read it before my father snapped the dictionary closed. 'Bloody Ghost,' he said. He swore almost never. It was a measure of his anger.

When I next saw the book, at home, that page was missing.

I stopped sleeping at Whitelands shortly after that. I don't know how much I thought about what the Ghost had done, but recently I've wondered about that scrawl across the page.

My mother's hint at some sort of distant relationship to my father to explain his tolerance of the Ghost comes back to me now. A cousin was, I suppose, a distinct possibility. An elder brother was not out of the question, given my paternal grandmother Minnie's nature. An illegitimate child when she was sixteen or seventeen would have roughly fitted with the Ghost's age. Giving the child away would definitely have fitted with Minnie's hard view of the world, and determination never to be in the wrong. Against his will, she had organised a similar disposal of my uncle's illegitimate son when a magistrate, finding him guilty of the theft of some building materials, had sent him to sea in the Merchant Navy as an alternative to prison. Though I felt I could ask my father most things I found myself reluctant to ask him if the Ghost was his half-brother. His view of his mother was, I think, complicated. He believed in family and family ties, yet Minnie had on so many occasions betrayed her family by her reckless arrogance. When she died he paid for her funeral and barely mentioned her thereafter.

I don't know what happened to Albert the Ghost. When I next remember asking my father about him, he said, abruptly for him, 'Moved on.' And after a pause, 'High time.'

FOUR

On the one hand everybody in Britain was convinced that Germany was on the edge of defeat. In the east the Soviet Armies were rolling across Poland. Allied troops were at the Westwall, Germany's Siegfried Line. Yet civilians in London and other parts of the country were still under attack from the air by the V-1s and V-2s. We ourselves came closest to a direct hit when a rocket struck the White City flats behind the Stadium, 100 yards away. The flash was blinding, the explosion terrifying. Kit and I went across to the estate on our way to school the next morning. It was the first rocket crater we had ever seen, deep enough to engulf a London bus.

That rocket was certainly not the last to fall. There were many V-1s as well, some launched right up to the last few days of the war. But after the White City flats I think we had the feeling that we had turned the final corner, that by Christmas, or maybe a week or two after, it would all be over.

Meanwhile, at school there had been what we considered to be a sinister development. We regarded ourselves as Sloane School, Chelsea. We played football as Sloane. But the real Sloane School had been evacuated to Addlestone in Surrey. The headmaster was a significant and well-connected figure named Guy Boas. At least one of the school governors, an amiable old gentleman named Bowes-Lyon, was related to the Queen. So indeed was Guy Boas's wife, Pussy. In the autumn of 1944 Boas returned to the school with one or two masters for a two-week reconnaissance.

We felt his presence immediately. Speaking from the platform in hall, he said that he had observed several boys slipping into school after the bell that morning. Henceforth masters would be posted on the gate. Every boy who was one minute late the following morning would be caned.

We didn't attempt to hide our outrage. Lateness for school was accepted as one of the perks of living in London during the war. Boys weren't on the whole very late. Ten, twenty minutes, half an hour if there had been a serious hold-up. But it was not good enough for Bo. Next morning the new guard took over on the gate. We latecomers straggled in . . . Jostling in the playground finally were eighty-two miscreants.

We were lined up in alphabetical order and marched upstairs to the headmaster's study in batches of twenty-five. A surname that begins with 'W' is either good fortune or bad. This time it was good. I arrived to find a wild-eyed, exhausted headmaster slumped against his desk. His right hand, which gripped the cane, was wrapped in several handkerchiefs.

He pushed himself up to his feet. His full red face was slick with sweat. He gestured to the first boy of our column to lean on the back of a chair placed in the middle of the room. The boy leaned over. I wondered why Boas had not recruited other masters, then I realised that this was a very personal contest. For the sake of the new Sloane School, he had to win.

Glassy-eyed, he advanced on the boy. He gave him four cuts with the cane before stepping back to take a breath. His arm was shaking.

'Next,' he croaked. And I stood up to the chair. My four of the best were painful but, afterwards, I wouldn't have wanted to be without them. I believe we all rather admired him. I think that we boys would not have wanted to abandon so significant a privilege as tolerated unpunctuality without a fight. He, in turn, would not have been happy for so significant a victory simply to have fallen into his lap. By the end of the morning both sides, headmaster and boys, could feel they had acquitted themselves honourably.

Some of the masters stayed on under the new regime. The ascetic Mr Nightingale, former Franciscan monk, brilliant mathematician for the mathematically gifted but confounder of the rest, was a recognisable eccentric. Towards the end of the first term he entered the classroom with his long, dipping Groucho Marx strides, cleaned the board by ripping a strip from his gown, stared alarmingly along the rows of boys in front of him and began to record on the blackboard predictions of our eventual salary level. 'Chapman, ten thousand a year man . . . Thomas, eight thousand . . . Roberts, based on a term's unsatisfactory effort, less than a thousand . . .' It was a novel way of making an end-of-term report.

Mr Colon, heavy-shouldered and with a cat-and-mouse smile, who had failed to teach us Latin, left at the end of the war. Harry Little, overweight, fast-talking and full of energy, would continue teaching his Commando French Course. This was popular with the boys, containing as it did an introduction to French life and art. For Harry that meant the life of the low apache clubs of Place Pigalle and the art of the Folies Bergère. He would lace his lessons with tall stories. He had been wounded as an infantry offi-cer in the Great War and posted to a Paris hospital. He claimed that as he was recuperating he had been recruited by British Intelligence to sit at the boulevard cafés and retail false military information to the street girls who approached him. If it were an exceptionally important piece of misinforma-tion, he confessed, '. . . it would then behove me to accompany the young lady to her lodgings, to press the point home.' He'd shake his head and add soulfully, 'You boys can imagine how painful a patriotic duty that was to me. How potentially threatening to my cherished moral standards.' And we'd all appreciate the joke, though we didn't yet know too much about Harry's cherished moral standards.

As THE WEEKS SHORTENED things were improving all round. Everywhere German armies were retreating. The British and Canadian army groups were fighting through Holland; US forces had just taken Metz, while a French and American army group had captured Strasbourg and penned in a large German force at Colmar.

Then, ten days before Christmas, out of the freezing snow of the Ardennes, the Wehrmacht struck back. Eleven Panzer divisions overran six resting US divisions on a sixty-mile front and threatened to split the British and American forces in two. In Britain it was a massive blow to morale. Americans were fighting to prevent Hitler achieving a complete reversal of fortune on the Western front.

As Christmas passed and the US 101st Airborne's defence at Bastoigne catapulted the Battle of the Bulge into legend, we began to see that there was no prospect of Adolf Hitler holding out past the coming spring.

Yet there was still one more nightmare before it was all over. In April 1945 British Army units reached Belsen in northwest Germany. Today its horrors are well known: the unburied mounds of dead, the pits full of bodies, the barely living stumbling aimlessly from wire to hut and back again . . . Belsen was a shock on the level of 9/11. A film, rapidly put together on Churchill's orders, was given wide distribution in local cinemas. People watched it in silence, stunned by the barbarism.

We struggled to understand the full horror of what had been happening for five years in central Europe. That same month US troops liberated Buchenwald and the far bigger camp at Dachau. The Russians had already taken Auschwitz and Sobibor, true extermination camps, but at this point we had little real information about them. Even at my age, just short of fourteen, many children realised that there was a new dimension to the Nazis. The death camps, when we learned their full purpose, presented us with a baseplate for evil, a level of suffering imposed on humans by humans against which to measure all suffering. Humanity had no such measure before.

THE LIGHTS CAME BACK ON. Streetlights that we hadn't seen since I was a very young child. They seemed incredibly bright. Even more exciting were the uncurtained windows. You could walk down a street and see people inside, talking, dancing, making tea.

We spent VE night in the World's End. There was a bonfire where La-di-dah once sold newspapers. There was port and lemon for the ladies, crisps and lemonade for the children, a grand knees-up along Blantyre Street and a conga line that went down to the river and back. For all the joy, I think it was a subdued event. Women thought about their loved ones still away fighting in Burma or suffering in Japanese camps. There were memories, too, of the World's End bombing little more than a year ago and the neighbours who had lost their lives. All the same it was victory, or at least Victory in Europe.

We moved round from group to group, family to family. There were people we hadn't seen since the bombing, people who no longer lived in the World's End and had been allocated flats or houses, like the Cheeseleys who had lived opposite us in Guinness or Kit's football friend Ronnie Howes's family. It seemed all had come back for the celebration.

We left quite early. We walked past the Guinness Trust Buildings where we had once lived. By now the rubble had been removed, the ends of the building shored up with huge timbers.

We talked about the last night we had lived here. About the plaster and chimney dust blasted into Kit's face, about the glass shards that had miraculously missed us all.

'I must admit,' my father said to my mother, 'for a long time I didn't think we'd make it.'

'I thought we'd win,' she said. 'What else *could* we do?'

He smiled, pulled her to him and kissed her.

'What are you doing?' Kit said, embarrassed.

'I'm kissing your mother,' he said. 'I think you boys should, too. She brought us through, you know. Kept us together.'

Young boys don't do gratitude. I'd never thought of it like that. But Kit and I probably both had a lump in our throat as we gave her a quick, embarrassed hug.

THAT NIGHT, as a Victory treat, my father hailed a taxi to take us back to White City. For Kit and myself it was the first time we had ever been in one. I think it was the first time we had been in a car of any sort.

There were a few people in Hammersmith Broadway waving Union Jacks, and a couple of dozen dancing on Shepherd's Bush Green, but for the most part the city seemed quiet.

The next morning the newspapers showed hundreds of thousands of people in the West End and girls happily submitting to be kissed in Piccadilly. Front-page stories carried hints of unrestrained behaviour in the Royal Parks. I felt an intense longing. A terrible sense of missed opportunity.

I, AND I THINK KIT and both our parents, still felt extraordinarily privileged to be living in a house at a time when all the bombed cities of Britain were suffering an acute housing shortage. Tens of thousands of people had been obliged to move into old Nissen huts vacated by the army. Families were living in the German prisoner-of-war camp on Wormwood Scrubs. Many hundreds were living in the Underground.

By now my mother had made 55 Primula Street more comfortable than anywhere we had lived before. It was a small house but the luxury of having our own rooms, a kitchen, sitting room, bathroom, made living in White City a total contrast to our years in the World's End.

THERE WERE NO more rockets or flying bombs, so my father saw no reason why I shouldn't be freer to go out in the evening to see friends, or why I shouldn't go out on Saturdays or Sundays for walks. I was drawn by the river. I would walk down to Hammersmith and see how far I could make it along the towpaths and riverside walks. By Chelsea Embankment it was easier and I would go east as far as I could in the few hours I had, to the Tower, Shadwell, Limehouse and the Isle of Dogs. London, to me, has always been inextricably bound up with the river.

Walking soon became a regular part of my weekend, burning off energy and giving me the hours of autonomy that I craved. At the same time the idea of staying away by myself for a night or two had gripped me. I began to plan and fantasise about the adventures I might have. Of course, there was an element of nervousness, if not fear, too. But I was thirteen, quite tall for my age and growing physically more confident all the time. I thought.

When I told my father I wanted to go camping by myself he was less than happy, but it was so much a point of principle with him that if Kit or I wanted to push ourselves we should, that he didn't refuse. I'll always admire the way my mother disguised her obvious anxiety.

My father had brought back from Whitelands an abandoned souvenir from one of the tenants, a German one-man parachutist's tent. I planned to use that. On a Friday evening after school I packed the saddle bags on my bike with Heinz baked beans and mulligatawny soup, an axe to cut firewood, a paraffin stove in case it rained, a couple of candles and a box of matches. Under the back of the saddle I rolled a blanket and the separate quarters of the tent and fixed them with straps.

About ten or fifteen miles up Western Avenue a disturbing thought struck me. I had brought everything for the night. Except one thing—a tin opener. I rode on to just before Uxbridge. To the right I could see fields and a twisting cart-track which I guessed might take me a half-mile or so from civilisation. I wasn't ready for much more.

I took the track. It was uneven and here and there puddled from the rain we'd had. Close up the fields looked marshy. I rode on and chose a spot to pitch my tent. It was in a higher corner of the field, dryer than the surrounding area and just a few yards off the track.

Putting up the tent took time. When I was ready to raise the central pole it was already growing dark. And I still had to solve the problem of the tin opener. Without one I would be eating dry bread for supper. I decided to stow my saddle bags in the tent, which was almost invisible in the darkening corner of the field, then ride down to Uxbridge to find a soldier with one of those clasp knives with things on it for taking stones out of horses' hooves and a tin opener attached. In my front basket I would carry back the tins, held upright by the crumpled sheets of firelighting newspaper I had brought with me.

My bike had a headlamp which flickered feebly but I made it to the main road without much difficulty. From there into Uxbridge was no problem.

I found my soldier within five or ten minutes. He affably helped me open the tins and within no time I was on my way back to camp. Off the road it was now pitch dark. Five or six hundred yards down the lane I stopped, leaned the bike against a tree to fix my headlight to improve the angle of its beam. As I was bending over, I thought I heard a soft cackling behind me. Coughing maybe. Or a tree creaking. Nerves, I thought. Bound to have nerves. By yourself in the dark like this.

Then a soft footfall in a puddle. *Plash*. And a grunt.

Somebody walking along the lane. Nothing alarming about that. At least, not necessarily. People in the country walked down dark lanes at night, I knew that. They weren't all maniacs. But some of them could be. You only needed one. Hurriedly I got on my bike.

Almost before I began to pedal I saw him. In a sudden shaft of moonlight he was stumbling towards me, his arms flung wide. He was blocking my path. Then suddenly he *screamed*. I slowed, trying to turn back towards the main road, realised he'd be upon me by then, clawing me off the bike. There was nothing else for it. I turned the handlebars back again and pedalled straight at him. I could see him clearly now, a tramp, nearly bald, middle-aged, unshaven, drunk or mad. Both. All my nightmares.

To the left the lane appeared to meet a mound like a rising bank. I knew there was every chance of a ditch in front of it, but I had no choice. I mounted the mound, and dropped two feet as I roller-coastered over the top to sail past the tramp and go speeding into the darkness.

My heart was beating, my legs shaking, as I drove the bike through slush and puddles. Behind me now, I could hear the madman shouting. But I had got away from him. I reached my marker tree, an elm with a big broken branch hanging white at the break. The tent was well concealed. I switched off the bike's front light and stood in the darkness listening. Not a sound. I delved into the basket. The newspaper was soaked with soup. I lifted the two tins out, leaned over a low point in the hedge and placed them on the grass.

I hid the bike in the bushes and crawled inside the tent. My first move was to get out my axe and place it somewhere where I could easily reach for it. It was too dangerous to light the Primus stove. Through the camouflage material of the tent it would be possible to see a light. I lay back against the roll of blanket. My trousers were soaked from riding through the puddles. I was shivering, partly from cold, mostly from plain fear.

I could, of course, leave the tent and make for home. But if I did that, it would mean the end of my camping. Kit would laugh; my mother would say comfortingly, 'Better leave it till next year.' My father would say very little but I would know that he was disappointed.

I stuck my head out and listened. There was a touch more moon but I could see very little and hear nothing. Perhaps the madman had gone on towards Uxbridge. I pulled back into the tent. In the darkness I located a spoon and ate my soup and beans cold.

I had no watch but I guessed it was about ten or eleven o'clock. Time for bed. I rolled myself fully dressed in the blanket.

Don't dwell on the madman, think about Shirley. Think about if you met her again catching a number 11 bus at Shepherd's Bush.

She'd be dressed up, working in a shop on the Green.

'Shirley . . . you remember me?'

'Hey, of course I do. The one in that American jacket.'

'Maybe I could buy you dinner?' (American dialogue figured large in my fantasies.) 'Maybe take in a movie?'

'Sounds good to me.'

'I'll pick you up at seven.'

I drifted. I don't know how long I slept. It didn't seem long, if at all, when I woke to hear a rustling outside the tent. Within yards.

I threw off the blanket. The axe in my hand, I chose the side of the tent away from the entrance panel and slid my head under, cheek flat against the damp grass. I listened hard, then heard it again. A rustling . . . I strained into the darkness. I could make out trees and hedges but nothing human.

Wriggling forward, I got half my body out, then my legs. Slowly I lifted my head. Then panic made me gasp. A dark figure was lying in the grass about thirty feet away. There was movement too. It looked as though the figure was slithering forward. I listened. A low grunt, undoubtedly a man.

I leapt to my feet. Racing across the short distance between us, I took one

Indian leap, deadly Tomahawk poised above my head . . . and landed astride the back of an RAF man, trousers round his buttocks, a girl's face staring up at me, pop-eyed with fear. I just stopped the swing of the axe.

For a moment the couple lay paralysed on the man's uniform greatcoat.

'A tramp,' I said quickly. 'Did you see him?' I dropped my voice to a whisper. 'Bald,' I confided. 'Or almost. Completely mad.'

'It's just a kid,' the RAF man said. 'Just a bloody kid.'

The young woman was fumbling with her clothes, sobbing and glaring at me. 'Take me home, George. Now!'

The idea of them leaving struck fear into me. I didn't want them to go. 'Please don't go. You'll be all right. I'm just over there—in the bushes.'

'He thinks we're staying here? He's off his bleedin' rocker,' the RAF man said. He was standing now, pulling up his trousers. 'Come on, love, we'll find somewhere else. There's only one mad bugger around here.'

It took only a little reflection the next morning to realise that he was right.

FIVE

Three months passed. Strange months when the German war had been won but we were not yet at peace. In Britain these months were dominated by the General Election. The world saw it as a foregone conclusion: Winston Churchill would be returned as Prime Minister. But, in fact, millions of British voters who admired Churchill as a war leader simply did not associate him with any particular party. Now they were being told to look on him not as the leader of Britain but of the Conservative Party. Churchill and his party had not realised that the experience of the thirties and the war had changed Britain. There was to be no return to the days of effortless neglect favoured by too many senior Conservatives. The real innovations of the war years—the Butler Education Act and a National Health Service initiated under Churchill's leadership—came too late in the war to fix in the mind of the electorate the image of Conservative-driven reform. Churchill lost by a landslide. The Attlee government took over.

I was fascinated by all these developments. For as long as I could remember I had followed the day-to-day developments of the war as a modern youngster might follow the fortunes of Manchester United. With that war, even in the Far East, moving towards a close, my interest turned to the politics of peace.

THEN THE FIRST atomic bomb was dropped over Hiroshima; three days afterwards another at Nagasaki. A day later Japan agreed to surrender unconditionally.

The celebrations for VJ Day were different in spirit from those of VE night. Purely as celebrations of victory they were less deeply felt than the profound satisfaction we experienced as Hitler's Germany crumpled in defeat. Throughout VJ Day the rejoicing was subdued, and VJ night was, by some curious common consent, appropriated by the young.

Leave passes had been issued to the forces in the United Kingdom, and the British-based forces of all nationalities included tens of thousands of young women as well as men. All headed for the West End. The scene was set for a Night of Misrule. I went with a few friends of about my age, but I had already decided that I would not be spending the evening with them.

The crowds swirled into Piccadilly. Eros, the Lord of Misrule himself, was shuttered in his wartime green plywood enclosure in the middle of the Circus, but everybody knew he was there. Accordion music came from every corner. Loudspeakers played from the tops of buildings. The occasional American soldier held his own audience with his trumpet or trombone. In the noise and dancing, in the singing and jiving, among the endless conga lines, not without deliberation I lost my three friends.

I had no plan, I simply wanted to behave as I wanted. I was alone among this vast crowd, a crowd reaching out to embrace strangers, a crowd throbbing with something I couldn't quite understand. Yet part of me understood because I felt it myself.

Darkness fell quite quickly. The streetlights glowed all the way down Piccadilly, past the Ritz to where fireworks were exploding in Green Park. I walked through the crowds. Sailors were kissing unprotesting girls who peeled off from one embrace into the arms of an American, Pole or Canadian until they reeled back, drunk with kissing, giggling.

It seemed to me a chance that would never come my way again. A chance to kiss a grown woman, by which I meant a girl of at least seventeen. All around me they were throwing themselves into the arms of strangers, not all uniformed . . . Why not me? I chose a young-looking girl, seventeen or eighteen, dancing by herself, arms held high above her head. She smiled at me. I put my arms round her waist and she brought her body close to mine. I lunged towards her. My mouth touched her lips.

She laughed. With one hand she pushed me full in the chest. I stepped back and tripped. Her friends gathered around me, laughing. 'At his age!' 'Cheeky bugger!'

I scrambled to my feet and snaked off through the crowd. When I had regained my anonymity I leaned against a wall, trembling. I had done what I'd come here to do. I'd kissed a grown woman. Almost.

FROM THE DAY the German war ended Harry Little had his eyes set on France. As the summer holidays approached the 'onlie begetter' of the Commando French Course began to put out feelers. 'You, boy, you'd like to go to Paris, wouldn't you? All the sights. Harry Little's Commando Paris Trip.'

I assume he had made all the preparatory arrangements with the Foreign Office and the French Embassy before the Japanese surrender. Certainly he was recruiting before the end of the summer term. 'This'll be in the nature of a free trip, my boys. Or very nearly,' he'd add with a conspiratorial lift of the eyebrows that meant: Harry Little's up to something. It'll do you some good—and him even more. 'Tell your dads it won't cost more than a fiver.'

At home in White City I was ready with all sorts of proposals to help contribute to the five pounds, but they weren't necessary. On his return from work, my father agreed immediately. He thought it a great opportunity to see another country. Educational. A chance to learn some French.

My mother was horrified. 'It's a long way,' she said. 'And what will you do for food? Real food, I mean?'

'Mr Little says we'll take food with us.'

'I was wondering how he was doing it so cheap,' my father said mysteriously, as if he already knew something that I didn't.

For all my remembered life there had been a line drawn down the middle of the English Channel. Now the idea of leaving England, of seeing what was on 'the other side', was as exciting as it could get. I began to read anything I could see in my father's *News Chronicle* about France.

General De Gaulle was in power. I knew that from the newsreels of him walking down the Champs Elysées in a hail of bullets when Paris was liberated the previous year. Eastern France had only just been liberated and the

Nazi-loving Vichy government, under the oily, white-tied Laval and old Marshal Pétain, had been chased out. The marshal was going on trial for his life. I suppose that fact alone might have given me some measure of the turmoil of the France I was going to. I had one more fact, drawn from many a film featuring agents dropping by moonlight, the tumble of parachute silk, the relief that it was a fellow agent waiting and not a German patrol: the Resistance were the only Frenchmen who'd supported us. That was about all I knew. There was, of course, so much more to know.

I hurried to school the next morning to put my name down with a couple of other boys. Harry gave us a list of necessary items.

'One pound of sugar . . . on ration but I'm sure your mothers'll manage somehow. Two bars of chocolate. One packet of tea . . . six tins of Nescafé, fifty Players cigarettes. The system is we sell the goods, details arranged by Harry Little, and divide the spoils between you.'

For three days I lived in a French dreamland. I was walking down the Champs Elysées. I was looking out over Paris with the Tricolor fluttering in my face. Then the blow fell. Harry Little took me aside, a kindly, regretful expression on his face.

'Bad news, my boy,' he said. 'I'm oversubscribed. One too many for the group visa the French Embassy are letting me have. Somebody's going to have to drop out.'

'Not me, sir?'

'You're the youngest. First on the list for next year, though. Sorry, lad.'

But my father was not someone to take no for an answer if there were any possibility at all that he could do something about it. I knew he'd try hard but what chance was there of him knowing someone in France? I mooched around, trying to put a brave face on things.

The summer holiday began. Two days later my father bustled in. 'How do you fancy La Frette sur Seine?' he asked, taking out a piece of paper with an address written on it.

'What is it?'

'Near Paris, apparently. On the River Seine. Sort of suburb.'

I was beginning to get excited. 'And?'

'Someone I know'—he was as excited as I was—'her sister's just moved there. Very hard up at the moment. The sister says they'd probably like to take an English boy for a couple of weeks.'

Near Paris. It was too good to be true. Then a thought struck me.

'These people, can they speak English?'

'Well, the lady comes from Guildford and the man's French. Julien Lelong. He was a submarine commander with the Free French here during the war, so his English is pretty good . . . Do you want to go?'

I couldn't wait. Even my mother was mollified by the thought that there would be an Englishwoman doing the cooking.

My father was not an easy man to thank. Expressions of love or affection embarrassed him. Emotional communications passed from him through my mother. His was a world of practically expressed emotion. You did what you could for your family. You derived your pleasure from hearing from your son what it was like in France today.

'There's a catch,' my father said as he watched me dance around in delight. 'You'll have to become a smuggler.'

I stopped. 'What?'

'This Julien Lelong saved a few bob while he was over here and his wife's sister has it in a bank account here in London. Now he needs it.'

'How much am I going to be taking?'

'A hundred pounds. Problem is, Dee, it's illegal to take that sort of money into France. You needn't tell your mother about this. All right?'

I nodded.

A smuggler. Then that's what I would have been with Harry Little, too. But a lone smuggler, this was different. At what age were you eligible for the guillotine over there?

TODAY IT'S NOTHING, but immediately after the war the journey to Paris for a thirteen-year-old was roughly equivalent to a journey to Afghanistan today. My parents and Kit saw me off from Victoria, my mother looking strained and apprehensive. My father had given me a brand new pale pigskin Gladstone bag with heavy brass fittings (from Whitelands, no doubt). It seemed to me pure Sherlock Holmes and I was embarrassed even to carry it down the platform, but I didn't want to disappoint him.

'Watch out for anybody takes a fancy to your bag,' he warned.

I assured him I would, although I couldn't imagine any thief who'd want my Gladstone instead of the smart leatherette suitcases most of the officers getting into the first-class carriages were carrying.

I found a second-class seat, put my case up on the rack, and waved to my mother who was blinking in an effort to hold back the tears. As the train pulled away I was already thinking of France—and of the hundred pounds in big white five-pound notes bound in a bandage under my right sock.

CALAIS WAS A WRECK. As we approached, I could see the German concrete bunkers, part of the Fortress Europa that had been constructed to keep the British out. Many of the three-foot-thick concrete lids had been blown apart. The town itself was battered, the station already being rebuilt. From the boat deck I could see dozens of workmen in blue overalls and black leather caps. The first Frenchmen I had seen on French soil. Along a harbour wall white-painted graffiti called for the hanging of Laval and Pétain. Thin red distemper had been used by someone in an attempt to obliterate it. Another first, although this one I didn't appreciate, but it was, in fact, my first glimpse of the deep divide in French society.

Then, as we docked, the smells of a French port. Tobacco, acorn coffee, fish, the oily steam from the hissing locomotives . . .

I shifted about on the train's wooden seats. We were already nearly an hour late. Julien Lelong was to meet me in Paris. Say we missed each other?

I was puzzling over this when: '*Jeune homme*,' a woman's voice said sternly. She was short, heavy-breasted, and wearing a black skirt and some sort of uniform shirt. '*La douane*,' she said. Customs.

I'm sure I went pale.

'*Passeport.*'

I fumbled it out and gave it to her.

'Why you here?'

'Holiday. To learn French.'

'*Ta valise*,' the woman said, gesturing towards the Gladstone bag.

I pulled it down from the luggage rack and put it on the seat.

'*Ouvre . . . ouvre.*' Open . . . open.

She searched it, pulling out a couple of books, socks and a sweater or two. Her eyes fixed on me. 'No foodstuffs?'

'A cheese sandwich.'

She picked it up, sniffed it and sneered. 'Coffee?'

'No,' I said. 'No black-market coffee.'

She narrowed her eyes. 'Money?'

I pulled my three pounds' worth of francs from my pocket. 'I have francs,' I said.

'English money. You have English money?'

'No.'

'I think, yes. How much English pound you have?'

I was trembling. 'No English pound,' I said, suddenly aware that I was echoing her poor English.

'Give to me your coat.'

I took off my school blazer. She frowned suspiciously at the breast pocket. For a few moments she bent the Sloane badge backwards and forwards, no doubt hoping to hear the crackle of concealed five-pound notes. A second customs officer, male, had come to lean on the back of the seat opposite. He grinned while the woman searched my jacket pockets.

Disappointed, she tossed the coat on the wooden bench. She gestured me forward with a snap of her fingers. 'Come.'

I stepped forward.

'Lift your arms.' She ran her hands down my arms and back up again. Then all over my chest. Then reached round to feel down my back. 'Open legs,' she said. She dropped on to one knee and frisked me from the left ankle up to the groin. 'This part, she like,' her colleague said.

I'm not sure if I was more shocked at the intimacy or scared of what she'd find below my right ankle when she reached it.

She dropped her hands down my right leg.

Laughing, the man said something in French. She turned angrily towards him and her hands lost contact with my leg at the bottom of my calf, half an inch above the bandage and the twenty white five-pound notes.

They left and I fell back on the seat.

AT GARE SAINT LAZARE a man of about thirty, tall, thin, saturnine, wearing a dark green tweed jacket, dark glasses, a smoking Gauloise on his lip, leaned against an ornate cast-iron pillar. He carried our prearranged signal, a copy of *Figaro*.

I found Julien intimidating and I didn't understand his sardonic sense of humour. I concluded that he didn't like the British much even though he had married an English wife. Later on I would understand a little more. I think he found it near-impossible to accept that Britain had emerged into the postwar world impoverished but widely admired for her stand against Hitler, while France had emerged impoverished and with its First World War reputation in shreds.

We took the train to La Frette. It was crowded, the automatic doors held open by young men who stood in the doorways, or even, one hand gripping the mounting post, swung out over the track, smoking. Anarchy, I thought smugly. I asked Julien about the customs inspection.

He laughed. 'She was looking for coffee. She confiscates it and makes fifteen hundred francs. A small tin of Nescafé's worth more than money in France today,' he said bitterly.

We passed the football Stade de Colombes and the train slowed through an industrial suburb called Argenteuil. Julien told me that it was a place where some of the great painters of the last century had worked: Monet, Manet, Renoir, Sisley . . . had I heard of them? No.

'Have you heard of Racine?'

'Racine? No.'

'Victor Hugo?'

I shook my head, hot and embarrassed. 'Perhaps.'

He grinned, but it was to himself. 'Anyway, you've heard of Shakespeare, I suppose. That's all that matters then, *n'est-ce pas*?'

LA FRETTE ITSELF was a suburb that had been a village only yesterday. The high street was easily differentiated with its church and cafés. Several streets of villas were built to cross it, running down to the Seine. The house Julien lived in, La Maison Blanche, was rented by two other families besides his own. It gave me a deep frisson to be told that it had been Gestapo district headquarters.

I got along well with Jane, Julien's English wife. She didn't ask me about French painters. It was a little different with Julien himself. I came to think he both liked and disliked me. I realised later that he struggled with the problem of many Frenchmen, both admiring the English and envying them.

He had left England a hero, and arrived back in France a stranger to the attitudes, slang, and above all occupation experiences of his own people. He found himself in an invidious position. The French Navy had found him a job in the Ministry of Marine off Place de l'Etoile. It was far below his expectations, and the salary was pitiful. To eke it out he took home work for an entrepreneur who supplied medal ribbons to the American Army in Paris. Night after night Julien, former Légion d'Honneur submarine commander, would sit at the kitchen table, wrapping and sewing coloured ribbon round inch-long pieces of cardboard.

I was excited, intrigued, bored, fascinated, embarrassed, bewildered, and above all made homesick by my fortnight in France. I had never suffered or enjoyed such a rush of new experience. On my second morning I was sent shopping by Jane Lelong, with precise instructions. 'A dozen large eggs from the *boulangerie*. You ask for them *sans tickets*. And then on to the café for twenty Gauloise, *sans tickets.*'

'What does that mean exactly? Without tickets?'

'Off ration.'

Alarm bells. 'Black market?'

'That's it. An extra ten francs an egg.'

I went out into the August sunshine, francs in my hand. Before I was a couple of hundred yards down the street a gendarme passed by on the other side. '*Bonjour, jeune homme,*' he said, saluting smartly.

'*Bonjour, Monsieur. Il fait beau,*' I answered and felt ridiculously proud of my command of the language.

This part of the village was probably not unlike Argenteuil had been when all those painters were working there. I could see the café on the corner. A man with a fishing rod strapped to his old bicycle pedalled laboriously towards the Seine. Women stood in pairs talking on the street corners.

The bakery window was stacked with long loaves and fruit tarts. Through the window, I could see a big bowl of eggs on the counter. Inside there were two women serving and four others buying and talking. This was a problem. I wasn't going to stand in line and ask for my eggs *sans tickets* with others in the shop.

I hung about inspecting the dozens of posters on every ancient wall surface, then walked on to the butcher's a little further along and gave it a quick once over. Meat on hooks. Sausages. Meat pies. Plus sinister bits of animal I wasn't at all sure about. I turned back to the bakery. It was empty of customers. I entered. To my horror there was still another woman in the shop, feeding a long loaf into her string bag.

Bending to examine the cakes, I ignored an attempt by the assistant to ask me if she could help. I shook my head and tried to flick my eyes significantly towards the eggs. Too significantly. The assistant said: '*Des oeufs?*'

The woman with the string bag was still there. Worse, the gendarme was now looking in the window. '*Avec tickets ou sans tickets?*' the assistant said in a voice I was sure could have been heard down the river to Argenteuil. Couldn't she see the gendarme standing behind me in the doorway?

In a fluster of confusion over the number of eggs in a dozen and the additional price *sans tickets*, I bought my eggs and pocketed the change.

The gendarme no longer filled the doorway. I peered outside, left and then right. He had disappeared. Weak at the knees, I passed on down to the café to buy my black-market cigarettes.

At the bar, the gendarme was enjoying a mid-morning brandy with the *patron*, who saw me as I tried to shuffle past. '*Ah, Monsieur l'Anglais. Tu viens acheter des cigarettes pour Julien?*'

'*Oui*,' I croaked.

'*Pour des cigarettes sans tickets il faut un supplément, tu comprends?*'

A supplement. Of course. Anything you ask.

We exchanged cigarettes and money.

Reminded that he'd run out himself, the gendarme counted off the black-market sum on the counter. 'I smock too many,' he said to me. 'I 'ave no longer *tickets*.' He raised his glass. '*Vive le marché noir*.'

I WAS TOO YOUNG to understand much of the turbulence swirling around me in France. People were still being murdered in the *épuration*, or purging, which Communist and Gaullist *Résistants* were carrying out that summer. During the war so many people were involved in denunciations of Jews or of members of the Resistance that it was necessary for the Préfecture in each *département* to lock away parts of its archives to prevent the widespread revenge-taking of 1945 from becoming a national bloodletting. There were, of course, many examples of French courage in concealing Jewish families, but 75,000 Jews were transported via Paris by cattle-train for Auschwitz with the consent or connivance of Marshal Pétain's Vichy government.

A shot in the woods at night announced the disappearance for ever of many a collaborator. For some Pétainists survival meant going into hiding, sometimes for years. For others it meant buying documents. Classically it meant acquiring a little red booklet, one of the internal passports of the time. Of course some were perfectly genuine and the holder *was* indeed a former Resistance member. Inside, the red book said simply: *The under-mentioned is a man of honour*.

Later in life I married a Frenchwoman. Sometime in the 1980s, dealing with her deceased father's papers, I came across one of these little red books in his name. He had been decorated with the Croix de Guerre and the Légion d'Honneur for his courage when the Germans invaded in 1940 and he was taken prisoner. He never talked about the war after his return from Germany in 1941 beyond shrugging and saying that he had been in the Resistance.

Today I have inherited part of his library. Taking down a book on old Paris recently, a photograph fell out. It showed the glossy interior of an opulent office. Marshal Pétain's. Two men, at ease with one another, are casually discussing some issue. The white-haired marshal makes a point. My father-in-law smiles in agreement.

The savagery of the *épuration* in 1945 and the torrent of abuse against Vichy in the press rose to flood level as the *déportés* and *transportés*, the men, women and sometimes children who had somehow survived the death camps or the murderous working conditions in Germany and Poland, began to arrive in trainloads at the main Paris stations. Parisians were deeply shocked by their physical condition. Shaven heads, faces covered with sores, teeth blackened with rot, they were often too weak to lift their bundles, too confused to scan the faces of the waiting crowd for family members.

ONE DAY JULIEN CAME home from his job at the Ministry of Marine and invited me down to the café for a glass of *jus de fruit* before dinner. He had things to do in the village. He would meet me down there, he said.

Before I left, Jane called me into the kitchen. She continued preparing dinner as she talked, so that most of the time she had her back towards me. Did I know that, before the war, Julien had had another wife?

I said no, I didn't. Jane glanced over her shoulder. 'It's necessary you know. Julien has something to ask you, but first he wants me to tell you about what happened. Julien and Olivia were divorced just as the war began. They had two children, Yves and Pierre, known as Pierrot.'

She turned back to chopping carrots. As soon as Paris was liberated, she said, Julien got leave to come to La Frette to see what had happened to his children. He'd imagined his ex-wife and the boys had all stayed with his parents who lived nearby. But when he returned to the village there was no sign of his ex-wife or his sons. His parents had seen none of them since Olivia had left the village with the children some time in 1941.

'The local gossips talked and the usual stories were spread about. But then there was someone who had heard talk of Jane in Paris a year or so later. This someone reported that the two boys had been placed in an orphanage for children whose parents had died or disappeared in the war.'

'Did she do it?'

'Perhaps. Perhaps not. Nobody knows.'

She finished preparing the vegetables and turned round. 'Go down and have a *jus de fruit* with Julien. The rest of it is his to tell.'

Mystified, I walked down to the café. I was quite shaken by the idea of any mother putting her children in an orphanage.

I got to the café and Julien left the bar and came to sit at one of the tables. He smiled at me, not the sardonic smile I was by now accustomed to but a quieter smile, more friendly. '*Un jus de fruit? Ou un petit vin blanc?*'

'Wine?'

'Why not? Go on, have a glass of wine.'

He ordered and the *patron* brought two wineglasses and left us the bottle.

'Jane told you about my children?'

'She said you'd finish off telling me.' I sipped the wine. It was bitter, not at all like *jus de fruit*. 'Why did your wife put them in an orphanage?'

'I suppose she found they were in the way. She was looking for a good time, perhaps. Easier without kids. Maybe she felt it was better for them.'

I could see he didn't believe that. I drank again. I wasn't enjoying any of this, the wine, the way Julien's eyes were glistening.

'Do you know where they are now, your boys?'

'They were in a *département* still in German hands. Even after the Germans surrendered it took me nearly three months to get the paperwork sorted out.' He poured us both more wine. This glass tasted better. 'Yes, I found out where they were.' He lit a Gauloise and blew out smoke.

I wondered why he'd told me all this. 'When will the boys be back?'

'Saturday,' he said. 'Gare de l'Est in the afternoon. A special children's train.' He paused. 'I want you to come with me to meet them.'

I pushed my wine glass away. I was feeling slightly sick.

'They won't remember me,' he said. 'I'm a stranger to them. It'll help to have someone young there.'

He moved to pour me another glass. I shook my head.

'What?' He looked anxious. 'You'll come with me, won't you?'

'If it'll help,' I said. 'I'm just feeling a bit sick.'

THE FOLLOWING DAY I escaped to Paris alone. I took the train from La Frette, as excited as I could ever remember being. In wartime England the myths of Gay Paree were constantly repeated in the press, magazines and films. As the school's first visitor to the capital of vice (I left a week or two before Harry Little's Commando set sail), I could not go back without an adventure to recount. I planned to track down a real, functioning brothel of the sort we thought we knew existed. The sort Harry Little had *told* us existed.

At Saint Lazare I left the train and headed for Notre Dame. I walked miles. I got hopelessly lost searching backstreets and alleys that seemed to me suitable locations for a brothel. But nowhere did I find anything suggestive. I realised that my deep ignorance of the city meant I might have been searching in the Paris equivalent of Cricklewood. But I could not give up. After buying a vastly overpriced split baguette with a slice or two of fatty ham inside, I continued my sleazy researches into the afternoon.

As the travelling world now knows, the sign for a tobacconist in France is two red cones joined at the base and, by law, suspended over the entrance to any café or bar licensed to sell cigarettes. I had not noticed them until I found myself walking down the Boulevard Saint Michel towards the Seine.

I looked up and with a jolt in my stomach I saw it. Over the Café de la Paix, on the corner of the rue Saint Séverin, a *red light*. I stared at the *tabac* cone. At night that would no doubt be lit up to lure clients in. Yes!

The hanging fringe of the blind was inscribed with the café's name, of course, but it was flanked on either side by the words *Blondes* and *Brunes*. A choice of blondes or brunettes on offer! I was transfixed. Stunned. I looked down the boulevard. There were red-light signs over almost every café bar. Hotels too. I must be bang in the centre of the red-light district.

I sat down boldly under the canopy of the Café de la Paix, directly under the word *Blondes*, and ordered a *vin blanc*. I sipped my white wine nonchalantly, while craning my neck to see if I could see any sign of the blondes and brunettes inside. It must have been a quiet afternoon. No matter. Would I have something to tell the boys.

Unfortunately I took another step forward in my understanding of France before I had time to recount my story. At the local café in La Frette next day where, mystifyingly, I'd noticed for the first time a red cone hanging over the door, Julien ordered a beer, a *demi*. '*Blonde*,' he had added. A half-blonde? Couldn't be.

I asked him. A *demi* was a half-litre, he explained.

And why blonde?

'Bad luck, Dee,' he said as if he knew. 'Nothing to do with blondes. It's the beer, *blonde* for light beer, *brune* for dark.'

SATURDAY CAME. I had taken the train from La Frette by myself. I stared at the new-looking football stadium at Colombes, thinking with more than a touch of homesickness how much Kit would like to play there. But mostly I thought of those two small boys coming all the way from eastern France to live with a man they didn't know. Had they been well treated in the orphanage? Of course, in those days, even had I been an adult, I would never have thought of sexual abuse. But had they been bullied, shouted at, made miserable?

Julien met me at Saint Lazare and hardly said a word. I could feel his tension in the clenching of his hands, the number of cigarettes he smoked. I wanted to ask how would we know them. Did he have photographs? But his anxiety was too intimidating.

It was the usual shabby scene common to any Paris railway station in those days, a sense of stress in every encounter. Hissing steam, people lugging roughly tied parcels of food back from the country, irritable nuns shepherding groups of girls across to trains as if expecting their charges to be pounced on at any moment by white slavers. Gendarmes leaned against the wall of the ticket office, each with a cigarette pinched between thumb and finger, their manner proclaiming that anything that happened on the station forecourt was nothing to do with them. Soldiers were everywhere.

We were early and went to a café inside the station. Julien drank coffee, a small black, and a cognac. I stuck firmly to *jus de fruit*. After a few moments it seemed to me the forecourt was getting more crowded. People were all drifting towards this side of the station. Some were quite old; some of them young couples clutching each other . . . or quite often a man alone, standing apparently unmoved except that he kept glancing at the big chalked blackboard declaring: '*Train des enfants, 16.40 heures.*' A number of railway officials had appeared and were corralling the waiting adults into one corner of the concourse.

As the train pulled slowly into the station Julien got to his feet. The officials had linked arms by now and were trying to contain the waiting crowd in the corner assigned to them. Julien lit a cigarette.

No doors opened. For several minutes the people behind the barrier of officials—the parents, grandparents, uncles, aunts—stood staring at the silent train. Then the doors of the front carriage opened and officials stepped down onto the platform. I won't forget that fearful gasp from the waiting crowd as wheelchairs were wheeled up to the front carriage. Children were lifted or helped from the train into them. Parents or grandparents who knew no more than Julien about the condition of the children they hoped to meet craned their necks to see if any of the wheelchair children were their own. I could hear sobbing all around me.

Officials ordered the other children down from the train. Struggling lop-sidedly with heavy suitcases, they marched in pairs down the platform, most of them very young.

Suddenly the whole forecourt dissolved into chaos. The orderly line of children scattered under the adults' charge. Women were running forward and throwing their arms round children; others were pushing them forward, snatching at the card pinned to their jacket, bending to read then pushing them on again. Names were screeched or shouted.

I stayed close to Julien who had climbed onto a luggage cart and was glaring down on the swirling crowd, glancing every few seconds at two photographs he held in his hand. I could see very little from where I was. Suddenly Julien jumped down beside me. 'Stay put,' he said. 'Don't move from here.' And he was gone, barging his way angrily through the crowd.

TWO BOYS STOOD before me, Julien between them. The elder, Yves, was dark-skinned, very small for his age, thin, with darting eyes and uneven teeth, already smiling ingratiatingly. Pierrot was snuffling after tears, his round face streaked with dirt. Beside Yves he looked well enough fed, shy, blue-eyed, a charmer in his over-long shorts.

'*Eh bien, mes enfants*,' Julien began but couldn't continue. He pulled a packet of cigarettes from his pocket and fumbled with them.

'I'm English,' I volunteered to the boys to fill the gap. '*Je suis anglais.*'

'Like the bombers?' Yves said with a smirk.

THE BOYS WERE CLEARLY not accustomed to family life. Both were, not unnaturally, disturbed by their experiences. I never learned much about these. Julien's wife found the boys, Yves particularly, surly and rowdy by turns, difficult to deal with. The house was not big enough for us all and I think everybody was now looking forward to my return to England.

La Frette was a small enough place for most people to have known me by sight, and indeed as an English boy I was something of a curiosity. It was therefore no great surprise, shortly before I was due to return, to be told that a family living on the other side of the village, the Linquiers, wanted to meet me. Monsieur Linquier was a water standards inspector, short, lively, gesticulating. Madame Linquier, originally from the Italian–French border, was dark-eyed and laughing. They had a daughter born in the first year of the war and given the patriotic name, Marie-France—and a boy of almost exactly the same age as myself, Daniel, a tall, good-looking boy who looked on me with that very French combination of wariness and disdain.

Monsieur Linquier and his wife, both of whom I liked immediately, were proposing I should come back next Easter to stay with them. Daniel and I could make an exchange. Be friends.

Friends? I wasn't too sure about that. Nor, I think, was Daniel. I said I would have to speak to my parents.

SIX

Life back in Primula Street was comfortable even in those bleak postwar years, my father obtaining some of the good things of that life (PX rations, even a secondhand refrigerator) from the American officers and diplomats still stationed in London. But, most importantly, we retained a strong link with our roots in the World's End, through school, through my father's work at Whitelands and his Saturday evening job at Stamford Bridge. My mother would take the number 11 bus down to see my aunt May and the rest of the Easts who were back, rehoused in the repaired block of Guinness Trust, and in the process meet old neighbours. On my father's side we still had family living there, most closely his eldest brother, Fred, our favourite among his brothers and sisters. And Kit and I were getting off the bus at World's End every day in term time, of course.

This connection was so important to us, and to many others who left the World's End after the bombing. Chelsea Borough Council had an extensive requisition programme for the bombed out, which meant that most people were now more sumptuously housed than they had been before. There would have been less or none of the overcrowding that we had grown up with. But there was no replacing that special warmth that comes from growing up with the same people, knowing so much about them. A life lived almost entirely without strangers.

White City may well have been dull in comparison, but I think it no exaggeration to say that our home life in Primula Street was different from almost any other in Britain. We had a telephone. That alone was rare among people like us, but what made it really different in our case was the way in which our telephone was used. My father's street bookmaking business had flourished, but Alf Gordon had emerged from wherever he'd done his time. That meant my father was now without a territory of his own.

His solution was not to have any set territory where he might clash with the established street bookmaker. Instead he took bets from anywhere in west London where he happened to have a friend or contact. All bets would be transmitted by phone, which meant that it had to be manned day and evening (by my mother during the day, Kit and I several evenings a week), each of us taking down careful details of a long list of shilling accumulators and sixpenny each-way cross-doubles from runners or punters.

This was all illegal, of course. The result was that we lived in fear of any passing policeman. Our telephone shiftwork had to be concealed from friends at school and could never be given as an excuse for late delivery of homework. I think the need for secrecy, the sense of shared responsibility in a matter so important to the four of us, deeply influenced both Kit and myself.

IT WAS A TIME when I wandered about London a lot on Saturday afternoons. I enjoyed the back streets of Victoria, Charing Cross Road, Hammersmith Broadway, watching the passers-by, listening to the arguments outside the pubs, taking in the life on the streets.

Because of our close family background, isolation never turned to alienation and I never became a surly teenager. Kit and I dug out the concrete shelter in the back garden and sledge-hammered it to pieces small enough to have the council carry it away. I did my usual shifts at the telephone taking bets, and I went with my father to the Dogs and joked with Fatty and Darkie. But I was always anxious to get away on my own.

Perhaps my grandmother Eliza, had she still been alive, might have assured me that there was nothing freakish about what I was feeling and reassured me that there were hundreds of thousands of young people wandering around London in the same dazed, hypertensive state.

I had felt a sense of personal liberation in France. Mildly homesick though I was, I'd relished being there on my own. Relished, perhaps, trying to be an adult. Back home in London, I was happy with my schoolboy life, but it wasn't enough. I needed to move outside the circle.

It was the dog track that gave me the opportunity. Stamford Bridge Greyhound Racing was also to give me the chance to earn money. In the 1940s it was not easy for children to earn. Regular jobs were a paper or milk round, both of which Kit and I had done in our World's End days. We'd also earned money carting coke during the war, but profits were measured in pennies. At the Dogs, however, I had a skill to sell.

One day my father announced he had made a bid for a bookmaking stand at Stamford Bridge and had just heard that the bid had been accepted and the licence granted. He was now a fully fledged legal bookmaker working under the pseudonym 'Mick Burns'. At the same time he maintained his illicit phone bookmaking business. As always he involved Kit and myself immediately. He regarded all his extramural work as a family activity, carried out for the benefit of all four of us, and thus requiring our commitment.

'Mick Burns' was an enterprise that had to be kept secret from our neighbours in White City too. If it had been known by the London Underground Housing Department that my father was a licensed bookmaker we would undoubtedly have lost the house. This meant the postman had to be given a story to cover some of the envelopes he had to deliver to Mick Burns. It meant keeping the bookmaking stand and money bag, with 'Mick Burns—Turf Accountant' painted on the side, at my uncle's house in the World's End. On Saturdays, while my mother and Kit manned the phone at home for street bets, my father and I would go to Stamford Bridge, where I would earn ten shillings and sometimes half a crown more as a white-gloved tick-tack man at our stand.

By my fifteenth birthday, I sometimes made as much as fifteen shillings in a week. I spent most of this on Friday nights. At school we began to study *Macbeth* for Matriculation, and perhaps once a month I would go off by myself to the West End to see a Shakespeare or perhaps a Shaw play.

I soon discovered Soho. Narrow gaslit streets and courtyards where lights shone from foreign restaurants. Deep cream-painted doorways where a shaded red bulb lit a bell inscribed 'Model' and an arrow pointed to a narrow carpetless stairway. Up and down the streets foreign languages were spoken: Italian, Arabic, lots of French. Shady figures tried to lure you down into basement clip-joints. Drunks who might have been Francis Bacon (the painter) and his friends came staggering out of one pub and headed for another. Heavily made-up 'girls' clicked busily along the street on their high heels. I loved the sheer raffishness of the place.

There were membership-only clubs like the Gargoyle, busy pubs like the French pub, restaurants like the Gay Hussar or Leoni's. I had never been in a restaurant, as I later learned to call it, and was very curious to know what happened there, but I guessed I didn't have the money just to walk into the Gay Hussar and sit down, especially when I saw Aneurin Bevan and another Labour Minister going in. A pub was more of a possibility. I was well below the legal limit but knew I was tall for my age and, desperate as I was to shoulder my way into this Soho life, I thought it was worth the risk.

On a misty Friday night after a performance of *Julius Caesar*, I plucked up courage to push open the door of The Wheatsheaf on Wardour Street.

There were about a dozen men at the bar and three or four women. Everybody there seemed a lot older than my parents and there was a generally shabby or tattered air to the clientele. As I walked across to the bar I was terrified, certain that my own underage appearance would show up against this bunch. At the bar I stood as tall as I could, which, I was pleased to see, was taller than the man I was standing next to.

The barman raised an eyebrow as if he'd come to a decision and said, 'OK then, what's it to be?'

I had the answer already worked out. 'I'll have a glass of white wine.'

'White wine? The only wine we sell here is port wine,' he said. 'And that's red.'

'I'll have a glass then,' I said hurriedly.

'On me, Tyrone.' The man next to me pushed a half crown across the counter. I saw that he was wearing pale pink nail varnish.

'No,' I said. 'Thank you but no, I'll get it myself.'

'Independent,' he said.

I took the glass of port and paid for it. Moving away from the bar I lifted the glass to my mouth, intending to take a small sip. At that moment I caught the eye of a woman in her forties who was sketching rapidly on a pad propped on her arm. She wore a black roll-neck sweater and a man's jacket with coloured pencils sticking from the top pocket. She turned the pad so that I could see her sketch. It was of me. Or rather, a grotesque, distorted, lipsticked version of me.

She winked. I gulped. The port caught in the back of my throat, burning as it went down. I loosed a rasping cough, spluttering port wine.

The man who had offered to buy my drink was at my elbow.

'You all right, Tyrone?'

I nodded and pulled my arm away. 'I'm fine.' I put the glass down. 'My name's not Tyrone.' I turned for the door.

'Suits you,' he whispered as I pushed at the door and stepped hurriedly past him into the enveloping comfort of the mist.

THINGS WERE NOW dramatically different at Sloane. The masters who had returned from evacuation had begun to introduce us to the idea of work. Young teachers were returning from the war, in one case from a German prison camp having spent four years reading German and French literature. And an Australian master brought his own refreshing attitudes to teaching, questioning our views on the shape of the postwar world. Our intellectual somnolence of the last six years came under attack by teachers who enthusiastically accepted the challenge that such uneducated pupils presented. Before too much time had elapsed, something was stirring in our heads.

Our new History master, Leslie Berkeley, was to remain a friend of mine until the end of his life. His teaching was flawed only by an excessive modesty, a sense that some of his pupils deserved something better than a third-class degree from Oxford to instruct them. 'Mr Gorman,' he would say with reverence, 'has a double first from Cambridge.'

Latin had once been a matter of learning a few meaningless declensions for Mr Colon. It now became a life or death struggle against the determination of Isaac Gorman to reveal to us its subtleties and pleasures.

We had a long way to go. The need to catch up the largely lost years of the war rapidly sank in when the standards we were going to have to reach for Matriculation were laid out for us. In those days the core subjects—in my case English, English Literature, History, Geography, Maths and French—all had to be passed at one sitting. One failure meant total failure.

But you can't activate young people's thinking processes on one level only. As we came to appreciate a little Virgil, get a thrill from the poetry of *Macbeth* or find ourselves intrigued by the causes of the French Revolution, we also began to think about our postwar political direction. My friend Ted Simon was very definitely ahead of the pack here, a signed-up member of the Young Communist League. When one of the masters set up a mock election, Ted put himself forward as the Communist candidate. There were Labour and Conservative candidates and each was allowed a week to canvass.

I suppose the Conservative Party candidate never really had a chance although most of us continued to admire Winston Churchill. The Labour

WHITE CITY | 389

candidate had the predictable uphill struggle of any champion of a party that had already spent two grey years in office. And they *were* grey, austere years. When people today think of rationing they tend to think only of food rationing. In fact postwar rationing applied to clothes, shoes, coal, building materials like wood and glass. To a large extent rationing set the scene in postwar Britain: shabby, poorly heated, no more than adequately fed.

We were still some days off the election when Ted asked me to go with him to a meeting of the Young Communist League. Not as a Communist, he cleverly argued, simply as a sympathetic searcher after truth. We went to King Street, Covent Garden, Communist Party headquarters. I remember being impressed by the way adult members of the party treated Ted, calling him Comrade, looking out posters from the files for his election speech or explaining the party line on Soviet policies. An admissions secretary asked me if I would like to join the League. I hesitated.

On the day of the school election the three candidates delivered their speeches. The Conservative spoke fluently enough but had nothing to offer that might dent the Labour candidate's recitation of the step-by-step process by which the Welfare State was being created.

Ted's speech was by far the best prepared of the three. He stood at the lectern in the school hall, dark-eyed and intense, his great mop of black hair untamed. He was offering revolutionary policies of immediate nationalisation at home, the abolition of the monarchy and the public schools, and abroad, realignment with the Soviet Union rather than the United States. Few of us had until then seen the necessity of a choice between America and Russia. 'Good old Joe' slogans still daubed the walls of most working-class districts of London. Stalin was popular, Harry Truman unknown.

For Ted it was a landslide victory. He was duly elected Communist Member of Parliament for Sloane School, World's End, Chelsea.

Guy Boas, the headmaster, was furious. What was he to tell Pussy and our august chairman of school governors, a member of the Bowes-Lyon family and uncle of the Queen?

On our way to the Dogs that night I reported the result to my father with some glee. But I saw the look on his face when I told him I had voted for Ted. 'And were you just voting for a friend?'

'I don't know. I like a lot of the things Communists say they're going to do. And I think they mean what they say.'

'They probably do. But just watch your step, Dee. I'm not saying you're too young to make up your mind. I'm saying none of us knows enough yet about how it's all going to turn out. The world's splitting in two. Joining the Communists now could leave you stranded on the wrong side of the fence. You're certainly too young to let that happen.'

I knew that one day I was going to have to decide which camp I was in. Like the decision we all made as World's End kids about whether we were Oxford or Cambridge, it was an allegiance that would stay with most of us for the rest of our lives.

WE WERE NOT, for obvious financial reasons, in the habit of taking family holidays, although we had once had a long weekend at Margate. During our late-fourth and fifth-form year, however, a group of us spent part of our school holidays hitchhiking around the country of which we had so far seen so little. Our Geography lessons spoke of steel-making in Wales, the Yorkshire coalfields, shipbuilding in Glasgow and on the Tyne, the splendours of Durham Cathedral or Georgian Edinburgh. It was time we took a look for ourselves.

I was unaware of it then, but these journeys round the country, sometimes by Rolls-Royce, sometimes on the back of a coal lorry, were another element in forming my view of the world.

We soon found that putting up tents, laying down groundsheets and the whole process of conventional camping, was not what we wanted. It was too comfortable; the only adventure you were likely to come across camped in a field would have involved an inquisitive cow. So we abandoned our tents and chose instead to rough it at night on the streets of Birmingham, Salford, Newcastle and Glasgow. We mixed with miners coming off shift, we talked to a hundred lorry drivers in their cabs or in all-night transport cafés up and down the A-roads. Some nights we froze; some nights we sat under the shelter of a covered market and drank tea with the local police.

What struck us most on our travels was the simple goodwill of so many people we met—in Darlington a woman coming out of her house to invite us in for tea and jam butties when we sat disconsolately on the kerbside, having run out of food and money; two Glasgow police sergeants debating which doorway beside the Clyde would be likely to be more out of the way of heavy snow and scuttling rats; middle-class people driving miles out of their way simply to get us to the most favourable road for a lift; one of the Wingfield Digbys, who had been there since at least Charles I's time, spending a morning showing Ted and myself round the ruins of Sherborne Castle. Such a lack of suspicion in casual contact.

And there were unforgettable sights. A lift on a January night north from Sunderland on the open back of a lorry carrying heated oil drums (heated to stop the oil congealing in the extreme cold). We lay wrapped in our sleeping-bags, as we drove through the freezing starlit night along the Northumberland coast road and watched the dawn break over the North Sea. Or a camp pitched high above a Welsh valley as a steelworks bellowed flame and sparks into the night air. I have never lost that sense I had then of a country of great variety of landscape, accent and class but united by the same essential values.

BRITAIN WAS STRUGGLING. But the countries of western Europe were drowning. France and Italy were wracked with strikes. Germany was ravaged by warfare. Throughout Europe, East and West, there was a desperate need for American Aid. The year 1947 was the watershed. It was the year of Marshall Aid, the American offer of $17 billion to restore Europe. It seemed an act of unparalleled generosity and world statesmanship.

But Russia refused the offer. Communist Parties in the West denounced it as American Imperialism: the object of the whole exercise was to increase American markets in Europe, and when that happened the standard of living of European working men everywhere would be lowered. I was baffled. If that were the case, why was the British Labour government in favour of Marshall Aid? Why were French Socialists equally enthusiastic?

The actions of the Soviet Union itself were throwing into doubt the views of my friend Ted and the kindly men in King Street. Soviet Armies had occupied a huge area of Central Europe with as yet no sign that they were planning to pull back.

The faded 'Good old Joe' and Hammer and Sickle slogans painted on brick walls began to disappear, sometimes weathered, often rubbed out. The struggle for the hearts and minds of Western Europe hung in the balance. Then the Victor Kravchenko book, *I Chose Freedom*, struck the Western world with cyclonic force.

Kravchenko was a Soviet defector. His book was a record of Stalin's collectivisation programme in the Ukraine. It was a total challenge to the soupy sentimentality in which Stalin was enveloped. It was the first book to bring the point home that the heroism of the Russian people was divisible from the leader and the Bolshevik system. Nobody could ignore the book. Years before Solzhenitsyn, it proclaimed the existence of a savage Gulag system, the last stop for millions of innocents. It denounced the racism of Stalin's deportations, his hypocritical antisemitism, terror as an instrument of Soviet government.

I bought a copy.

I found myself struggling with astounding facts, or what were presented as facts. At least as many murders as Hitler, even more betrayal, mendacity and deceit! Could it possibly be true? The *Daily Worker*, which I read regularly in the White City public library, gave a compelling refutation. Millions murdered? Stalin's friends and colleagues silently imprisoned in the wastes of Siberia? Secret protocols in the Russo-German Pact to carve up Poland? Pure Hollywood, the *Daily Worker* maintained. Concocted by American Intelligence, the Party alleged.

On my own doorstep there was further condemnation. Decent people like Ted. And at least two of the masters at school were Communists. They all knew a great deal more about Communism than I did.

Perhaps it's easy now to say that some were simply blind to the overwhelming truth about the Soviet Union. But we came from a world that at least *thought* the facts were accessible to us in peacetime. No nation at peace had hitherto misled the world on the scale Kravchenko was asking us to believe the Soviet Union had done.

I would be sixteen in two or three months' time. At home I carried *I Chose Freedom* around. My mother was concerned about how involved I was getting with it. My father thought it good that I was trying to decide whether or not the book was true and would sometimes even play the devil's advocate. He would remind me of the social injustices in Britain, of class differences, inherited wealth, restricted opportunity; for many people, these things meant living conditions like Joe and Jinny's, small children playing in sewage, the lack of proper health care that my own grandmother had suffered all her life. It was an effective counterweight to my adolescent black-and-white-ism.

About this time Ted asked me again to go with him to the Young Communist League. This time I told him I wouldn't. I hadn't yet made my mind up about Victor Kravchenko but I had made up my mind not to commit myself to the Communist Party until I did. What if Kravchenko were telling the truth?

ONE CHRISTMAS, in I think my fifteenth year, we had a surprise visitor. She was a young airforce woman, a WAAF, the daughter of the man who had secured the house for us in White City. Bunny, as she was known, was a tall, slim, fair-haired girl of perhaps twenty, notably attractive in her blue uniform. I can no longer remember the circumstances of her coming to spend Christmas with us.

For me these were the years of high adolescence—fourteen, fifteen—in all probability the most difficult years of my life so far. My problem centred on the gulf between my sensual needs and the possibility of fulfilling them. We had a girls' school, Carlyle, next to Sloane, but the authorities had clearly plotted deep into the night to keep the two sexes apart. I can barely remember seeing a Carlyle girl out on Hortensia Road despite the fact that the main gates of both schools were no more than forty yards apart. The few girls of my own age that I did meet seemed interesting enough, but they did nothing for my fantasies. My sights were set hopelessly on young women of perhaps eighteen to twenty.

The arrival of a young WAAF to spend Christmas was therefore electrifying. Bunny was uninhibited in her talk, candid in her description of life as an attractive young woman on an airbase mostly staffed by men. She seemed happily incapable of listening to any music on the wireless without swinging her hips, fingers clicking as she kicked out her unusually long legs. 'Jive,' she said. 'It's all the rage.'

One afternoon when she and I were the only ones in the house, she began to tell me about her belief in Yoga. I would have been happy enough to have sat and listened to her expound on a recipe for mixing cement, so I nodded appreciatively and asked what I hoped were the right questions.

I suppose I had got to a broad understanding that the practice of Yoga involved invoking the power of mind over body when my fifteen-year-old scepticism prompted me to ask her what it was good for.

'What's it good for?' she said. 'Well, pain control, for instance.' She jumped up. 'Just wait a minute and I'll show you.'

She left the room and a moment or two later came back with a pin at least an inch long and a box of matches. She sat on an upright chair, crossed her legs and, to my gasping astonishment, pulled up her skirt. 'Watch this,' she said. A white suspender held her WAAF pale blue stocking in place.

She lit a match. For a moment or two she held the pin carefully in the blue part of the flame before dropping the match into an ash tray. With a practised hand she undid the exposed suspender and pushed down the stocking.

'Put your finger on my leg,' she said.

I extended my index finger and brought it to a point over her thigh. My hand was shaking slightly.

She looked up. 'You're not shy, are you?'

'No.' I really was shaking now.

'Well . . . press down. Hard.'

I did.

'That's enough.' She took my wrist and removed my fingers from her leg. 'Now watch.' In the pink indentation I had made on her thigh she brought the pin down and broke the skin. 'No pain,' she said.

I leaned forward and stared.

With one hand she held the pin upright. With the other, fist clenched, she tapped the pin deep into her thigh. 'There,' she said with an exhalation of satisfaction. 'No pain. No blood.'

I was inflamed by the sight of her long, stockinged leg.

'You want to try?'

That meant taking off my trousers. 'No,' I said. 'I can see it works.'

She laughed, pulled out the pin, put it aside and did up her suspender. 'Believe me now, do you?' she said, flicking down her skirt.

'Of course,' I said. 'I always did.'

I had four more days of her presence. Had she fallen in love with me, despite the huge age gap? Had the Yoga trick been her way of saying the unsayable?

I behaved as though nothing had happened between us. As maybe it hadn't. But I didn't believe that. She left on Boxing Day. I looked for some sign that parting from me was painful to her. With the most urgent will in the world, I saw nothing to convince me.

'Wow!' Kit said as the door closed behind her. 'Did she show you that trick with the pin in her knee?'

IN THE NEXT YEAR I was not completely without 'conquests'. As part of my attempts to extend my knowledge of France and French, I used to go to the Classic Cinema on King's Road where foreign films, mostly French, were shown. Not furthest from my mind was the possibility of meeting a slightly older French girl, in London to study English.

The Classic was one of those small, extremely comfortable cinemas and, like many other small London cinemas at that time, ran an uncomplicated programme of just one film with a five-minute break before the lights darkened and it was rerun. I was seeing *Les Enfants du Paradis* and we had trundled almost to the end when a movement to my left made me glance up. Coming towards me was a girl in a pale trench coat. I half stood to let her pass, but to my delight she indicated that she was going to sit next to me.

We settled down, my eyes fixed on the film, my mind fixed not on Arletty but on her fellow-countrywoman in the seat beside me. I was conscious of every movement. So was she. When we bumped elbows she murmured '*Pardon*' in a charming French accent. I responded: '*Pardon, ma'moiselle.*'

We drew closer as the film came to an end. Nothing too obvious, but it was nevertheless clear to both of us that we weren't just two strangers sitting next to each other in a cinema.

The end credits rolled and I took a quick glance sideways as the lights came up. Dark-haired, a rather sharp but definitely attractive nose, full lips touched with lipstick—and an Hermès scarf casually knotted. So *chic*.

How to handle this? A few words about the film? Was this the first time she had seen it? I took a deep breath—and the house lights went down.

We both felt the tension. We couldn't have got any closer to each other. The merest bump of elbows now would bring a smile and a '*Pardon*' from each of us. Tense but exciting.

The end came round a second time, the credits rolled and the lights came up. I turned to her, about to pose my question, but she beat me to it.

'You're French, aren't you?' she said in the accents of Sloane Square.

I suppose it was surprise. Shock even. To my eternal embarrassment I grunted acknowledgment in international tones. 'Aargh,' I gargled. To her it was clearly an affirmative.

She leaned over and grasped my wrist. 'Knew it,' she said triumphantly. 'I absolutely knew it. There's something about you French. It's your *savoir-faire*. I think you inherit it at birth.'

'*Possible*,' I said disarmingly in the accents of La Frette sur Seine.

She stood up. 'Are you coming? Or are you going to see the film again?'

'*Nevair*.' I stood up.

We left the cinema and walked towards the river. I was already far too committed. I felt there was no choice but to leap feet first into the accent. 'Tell me,' I said, ''ave you evair been . . . at Paris?'

'No—going next month, though. Daddy's just been appointed to some

Anglo-French committee. He and Mummy have left already. But we're keeping on the flat here in Sloane Square.'

A flat empty of parents. 'Is near 'ere?'

'Walpole Street. Just opposite Whitelands House, d'you know it?'

Whitelands House! Speech failed me. I nodded vigorously.

'Do you live in Paris?'

'Vairy close to it. La Frette sur Seine. Like your 'ome counties.'

She pulled a face. 'I love your accent. How long are you in London?'

'Regretfully, I leave tomorrow.'

She grimaced. Then lightened the look. 'Can we meet in Paris?'

'*Bien sûr*. Give me your *numéro de téléphone* and I will call you.'

We stood on Chelsea embankment. I put my arm round her shoulders and she put her arm round my waist. I felt terrible. She was a nice girl. Perhaps too upper class for me. But then that wasn't the only reason that I knew I could never phone her.

SPEAKERS' CORNER was a Hyde Park institution. On Sundays you might get six or seven speakers addressing their own little crowd of ten or fifteen people. There were some very polished speakers, like the Methodist minister Donald Soper. There were performers, people who spoke for fun, and a good sprinkling of crazies warning against visitations from Mars. Heckling was common practice. I loved the place.

I was drawn to Hyde Park on Sunday afternoons to hear the speakers but soon found that the park, as darkness fell, offered another attraction. I noticed that a young woman had taken up a spot under the trees that line the carriageway running parallel to Bayswater Road. Further along I saw two more women. Whenever a man passed, one of them would step forward to talk to him.

I didn't need telling why. My mother's father had been a ticket collector here in the days when young gentlemen hired a slatted green chair for a penny and watched young women promenading by. And some of the women, of course, especially as dusk approached, were less than 'respectable'. Perhaps my grandmother was one of them. Eliza Toop, as she became after she married my grandfather, had kept her head above water throughout her life by courage, hard work and scant concern for the stifling morality of her day. At the age of fifteen she had run away from service somewhere in the southwest and walked back to London. Afraid to go home to World's End Passage, she lay in wait for her brother and asked him to help her. He was a gold-leaf tradesman working at the time on the ceilings of the Bank of England. He had taken her up to the City with him and found her a job as a barmaid.

Later, at the end of the 1890s, after she had returned to live in World's End, by now with an illegitimate child, she began to spend time in Hyde Park. I assume her mother, a God-fearing woman with an idle drunk for a husband, looked after my mother's half-sister while Eliza was working in the park. In the end it all worked out well for Eliza and Jesse James Toop, the ex-butler turned park ticket collector whom she met there. They married a month before my mother was due and spent a happy twenty years together until Jesse James died a month before I myself was born.

I FOUND IT DIFFICULT to get the women in the park out of my mind. I told nobody at school, of course. Perhaps guilt weighed too heavily upon me. Perhaps I already knew what was going to happen.

The following Friday I left at the interval a play whose title I no longer remember and took a bus to Hyde Park corner. I walked back and forth across the park, fascinated by what I was seeing. There were, by about nine o'clock, at least thirty women walking the carriageways, gathering under the lights, exchanging banter with passing men. In their mid-twenties or less, they were at the age where my attention was keenly focused.

Fantasies came thick and fast. The women resurrected for me the memory of Shirley, the girl who had begun 'going with Americans' at Windsor. I began to believe that she could easily be one of these young women. I had no doubt that she had headed for London. With the return home of so many of the GIs, Rainbow Corner was not the place it had been. As far as I knew there were only two places for her to make a living, Soho and Hyde Park. What was so unlikely about thinking there was a chance of meeting her walking the shadows of the Bayswater carriageway?

IT WAS NOT LONG before Christmas, bitterly cold that year of the national fuel crisis, the snow cleared from the walkways but stretching like a pale lake across the open spaces of the park. There were fewer girls than usual. Those there were were bundled in heavy coats.

My search for Shirley had by now become an obsession. This was the fifth or sixth Friday night I had been looking for her in the park in the last three months. I now realised that the girls came and went on an unpredictable basis. One night, I was sure, I would see Shirley's flowing red hair as she stepped under a lamp. And then . . . what?

That night I was walking, muffled in a scarf, hands deep in my pockets, the snow drifting through the lamplight, when I saw her on Serpentine Bridge. She was leaning against the parapet smoking a cigarette. She flicked it over her shoulder onto the ice of the frozen lake and began to walk slowly away. She wore a dark coat and a scarf draped high on the back of her head. That red hair tumbling beneath the dark scarf was unmissable. I hastened my step. When I was about ten feet behind her I called her name: 'Shirley . . .'

She turned. 'Shirley?' she said in a foreign accent. She stared at me, then her face relaxed. 'I am not your Shirley.' She was a young woman in her early twenties with large wide-set eyes, her hair more fair than red.

'I'm sorry. I thought you were Shirley,' I said. 'A friend of mine.'

She didn't believe me, didn't care. 'In my country we don't have girls called Shirley. I'm Swiss.' She made no attempt to turn away. 'What does it matter if I am not Shirley? You want to come with me? You have a pound?'

I had my dog-racing earnings in my pocket. 'OK,' I said.

She took my arm, guiding me until we reached the nearest in a stand of leafless trees. I took a pound note from my pocket. She made it disappear somewhere inside her coat. The tree she had chosen was striped with driven snow. She brushed it away and rested her back against the trunk, removed her gloves and undid her topcoat.

I watched her, my mouth dry; a swishing in my ears. A large part of me wanted to turn and run.

'Come closer,' she said. 'You can't do much from there.'

Two or three minutes only passed while she clasped me to her. In these moments, urgently needed, desperately awaited, God knows what I felt. I was shivering, but at least the swishing sound had come to a stop.

'Such a young boy,' she said as I shuddered.

Should I say thank you? I said thank you, my chin on my shoulder.

'Good night, young boy,' she said. The Swiss girl broke from me and, facing away from the wind, began buttoning her coat. Without turning back to me she lifted her hand in a finger-fluttering wave then, pulling on her gloves, she strolled back to her place on the bridge.

I crossed the park to Marble Arch and bought a tube ticket back to White

City. On the journey I sat pierced by guilt. But for all the regret I felt, I realised I would not have it otherwise. It was a hurdle of my own making but it was still a hurdle cleared.

I was no longer a virgin.

SEVEN

B y now I was well established with the Linquier family whom I had met on that first visit to La Frette sur Seine. Monsieur Linquier's original plan had been for exchange visits by his son Daniel and me. It didn't entirely work out like that.

Daniel came to London once and didn't like it one bit. He found the city battered and ugly compared with Paris, and English food, except for baked beans, dull and uninteresting. All true. But his real problem was a serious Gaullist contempt for the Anglo-Saxons. We sparred throughout the time he stayed. There was no overt unfriendliness. We just didn't get on well.

Nevertheless I continued to stay with the Linquiers at La Frette. Monsieur Linquier was a man I greatly admired for his enthusiasm for French history and his honesty about the recent past. Madame Linquier was mildly amused by me, I think, as an eccentric English boy who had never seen artichokes, asparagus or courgettes. But she was kindly and an impressively good cook and, like her husband, made me feel as much at home as she possibly could. Of course she never knew that I didn't get along with her son, unless she knew it from him.

Days at La Frette were spent less and less with Daniel. Most of the time he spent with his girlfriend, Monique. By now I was accustomed to going into Paris by myself and, on a summer visit, would sometimes meet up with some of the Sloane boys on one of Harry Little's Commando Paris Trips.

Best of all was the summer when Kit was one of Harry's party. This trip had a different purpose from the others. It was essentially a football trip.

The Sloane School was fifty yards from Chelsea football ground and the management had taken a real interest in the school's unusually high standard of football, enough to supply one of their players as a coach. I was never more than an average player. Kit, however, was of a quite different standard and had been asked by Harry Little to join the Sloane team going out to play in France, even though he was only just a month or two past his fifteenth birthday. Harry had promised to arrange a match for the team.

Harry's Commando Trips were as unlike today's school trips as you can imagine. Kit and his friends were housed in a 'dosshouse' hotel on the rue du Bac. They had been given instructions on the goods they were each to bring. Kit was detailed to bring sugar and tins of Nescafé. On the evening they arrived, Harry called all the boys together with their luggage into his room and repacked the sugar, coffee, soap and other goods into the two biggest suitcases. He then selected two older boys as porters. 'Foller me, boys, and I'll show you something of French culture you won't forget.'

He set off with the two boys struggling behind with the suitcases. His destination was a basement brothel on the Place Pigalle. There the goods were displayed. The two 'porters' understood nothing of the rapid bargaining that followed with a figure out of a George Raft gangster movie. Music played and half-dressed girls floated through the basement. None of this deflected Harry. When he was content with the deal struck and the money handed over, he advanced a couple of thousand francs to the boys and told them to go off and spend it wisely. He himself would be staying on a while.

In fact, Kit said, they hardly saw Harry after that until the morning of the match. A closely supervised school trip to Paris it certainly wasn't.

The day before the match I went to see Kit at the rue du Bac. Harry had put in a rare appearance. 'On your toes tomorrow, boys,' he admonished. 'This match is to be played at Billancourt, a suburb of Paris. The Renault people have kindly allowed us the use of their own pitch.'

'And who are we playing?' one of the team asked.

'An excellent team, one of the best teams in the land . . .'

'A school team?'

'Perhaps more college age,' Harry conceded ruminatively, and would be drawn no further. 'Don't worry, you can handle it, my boys.'

The following day (it was to be an evening match) Kit and Mike Tomkys, our centre-forward, came to the Linquiers' at La Frette for lunch.

'You're going to have to play tonight, Dee,' Kit said. 'Jackson's down with food poisoning.'

I was appalled. I knew I wasn't anything like up to standard.

'We'll carry you,' Kit said. 'At least it'll be better than playing with ten men. Just.' My brother did not think highly of my skills as a footballer.

It was a normal Linquier Saturday lunch in the garden. We began with a home-made fish pâté, accompanied by still cider. Kit and Mike enjoyed the cider. For the main courses we moved to red wine. Lamb and vegetables served separately intrigued them both and probably made them forget how much red wine they were drinking. Monsieur Linquier poured liberally to toast the Sloane team's success against our unknown opponents.

The alarm bell rang for me when I caught a flash of sunlight on Kit's hair as he rocked back and hit his head on the tree trunk behind him. It was less than three hours to the match and the centre-half was drunk. I took a quick glance at Mike Tomkys. The centre-forward was well on the way. Madame Linquier put Kit to bed; Mike Tomkys fell asleep in an armchair.

Two hours later, on the train to Paris, both Kit and Tomkys looked as fit as fiddles. I was the only one with a knot in my stomach.

We drove out to Billancourt in a team bus supplied by our opponents. There was still daunting evidence of the big RAF raid on the Renault factory in 1944. But, past the factory, lay the undamaged sports ground.

We changed into our white shorts and blue shirts in the visitors' changing room. Harry strode up and down giving pre-match tips. But even when pressed, the name of the opposing team seemed to escape him. 'They're a good quality local team,' he said.

Outside the dressing room we assembled in a broad hallway to have a team photograph taken. I looked around. The walls were covered with pictures of the trophy-winning Renault Works team. In those days companies recruited talented footballers and gave them virtually work-free employment to train and practise their football. In the French Works League, Renault with its 60,000 men to choose from was a regular winner. The captain in all the photographs was a black-haired, hard-faced man with a sardonic and triumphant smile. An unsettling thought crossed my mind.

We were first out onto the floodlit pitch. Only when we heard the roar of voices did we realise there were several hundred spectators. I looked round. The roar was for our opponents being led out on to the pitch by the same black-haired, hard-faced man I had seen in the photographs. Harry Little had fixed us up with the Renault Works Team, professionals in all but name.

They were a notably hard-elbowed team with a hostile, aggrieved manner of playing. Kit, Mike Tomkys, and others played their hearts out. By half-time we were 0–1 down.

We went in to examine our bruises and suck on our slices of orange.

Harry Little was complimentary. To himself. 'A well-chosen opponent for you, boys,' he pronounced. 'I knew you could do it.'

Somebody reminded him that we were losing 1–0.

Harry shook his head. 'I've been having a word with the French coach. He's a worried man. Now go out there and worry him a great deal more.'

In the second half there was a glut of goals.

Renault were left reeling, beaten by an English schoolboy team, 4–1.

AT SLOANE, as we entered the sixth form, we all watched American films, we listened to Glenn Miller, Frank Sinatra, we read American novels . . . Strangely my more left-leaning friends were the most admiring of American popular culture. Strange, because it wasn't difficult to see, as the Cold War polarised the world, that a very distinct left-leaning anti-Americanism had become a reality.

National Service hung over us. We became more and more divided by the prospect. There were those inclined to pacifism; there were some who welcomed the thought of the two years to come; then there were others like Ted Simon who genuinely wished to avoid military service because he did not believe in the cause for which we were to be conscripted. Others were quite simply unable to conceive the possibility of a Stalinist threat and spoke scornfully of the undecided as believers in 'Reds under the Beds'.

For those like me, the majority, in the uncertain middle, among all our doubts about Soviet intentions there still existed a parallel inclination to consider the possibility that many Soviet actions were reactions to what they saw as the menace of American power.

But if Kravchenko were recounting the truth, then all who felt any sympathy for the Soviet system had been victims of a grotesque deception. It meant that Soviet government was backed by a huge string of concentration camps. That millions of Soviet citizens had been murdered in the deliberately created Ukraine famine. That, in the workers' paradise endlessly depicted in Soviet propaganda, and Western pro-Soviet articles, thousands of innocents were dying every year in the camps.

At Sloane argument raged. To some the duplicity of the CIA was to be seen in every sentence of *I Chose Freedom*; to others it was the duplicity of the Soviet Union.

So, sometimes stormy, sometimes well argued, it became a central issue among us: was Kravchenko telling the truth?

THE SATURDAY MORNING two men knocked on the door of our house at White City and showed Metropolitan Police warrant cards was a bad shock for all of us.

My mother was white-faced as she hurried from the front door to fetch my father. Moments later she returned, suddenly composed, and smilingly invited the two policemen in.

'You gave me quite a fright,' she said. 'I thought it was bad news.'

'Just a few questions for your husband, love. I'm sure he can clear it up.'

'He'll be with you in a moment. Cup of tea while you wait?'

She chatted to them for a few minutes until my father came downstairs. Through the open kitchen door Kit and I heard one of the CID men: 'A drunk and disorderly charge was laid last night against someone named George Robert Simpson. You know him?'

My father: 'George? Known him for years on and off. Why?'

'Stack of betting slips on him when he was arrested. All neat with a rubber band round them. The top one had your telephone number on it, Mr Wheal. Quite unusual to have your own phone. Simpson wasn't phoning those bets over to you, I suppose?'

The kitchen door closed. Kit, my mother and I looked at each other in alarm.

'If they go upstairs,' my mother said, 'your father's ledgers are all over the bedroom table. There's a pack of slips too.'

We held our breath. Five minutes later we heard the front door close and my father came into the kitchen. He hugged my mother.

'What did they say?'

'They said what a nice, sensible woman your wife is. Gave one of them some advice about his daughter, apparently.'

'He was a bit worried about her boyfriend. So . . . George got picked up with a pocketful of slips?'

My father nodded. 'Our number on the top one.'

'What did you tell them?'

'I said that top one was mine. Put my number on in case I had a big win. Knew nothing about the other slips. It's not illegal to *place* a bet. Only to accept one. I'll pay George's fine for possessing betting slips. It won't go any further.'

'Thank God they didn't search the house,' she said. 'The bedroom's full of slips. And the ledgers.'

'Was. I got rid of them while I was upstairs.' He opened the back door. A pillow case was hanging on a string out of Kit's bedroom window. You could see, from the sharp angles, the outline of the weekly ledgers.

THE SUCCESS of the bookmaking, both legal and illegal, was moving my father up the income scale. This had consequences for all of us. I remember he was always urging my mother to spend her clothing coupons on a more expensive outfit, and Kit and I gradually lost our drab wartime look. Our new comparative prosperity meant that my father actively encouraged me to visit France. He saw it as part of the concept of escape which, I believe, dominated his own life, and has probably gone a good way to dominating mine and Kit's. To learn a foreign language, to become familiar with another country, was, he knew, not for him. But for his sons it was another means of distancing themselves from the life he had grown up in.

The exchange element between Daniel and myself had been quietly dropped and I was paying board and keep in sterling. This was much appreciated by the Linquiers.

I found France excitingly different from the greyness of Britain. There were so many public crises, with one premier following another with dizzying speed. Staring angrily at the morning's headline, a deeply humiliated Monsieur Linquier could stand it no longer. 'Go to the window, Daniel,' he cried to his son one morning. 'Watch for the special messenger. They've been through everybody else. They'll be calling for me next!' He got up and left the room, wiping tears from his cheeks. In Britain, politics was not played out before your very eyes in the same way.

I was full of admiration for this short, good-humoured, volatile Frenchman. When he talked about the defeat of 1940, he never once tried to lay the blame on British perfidy or any of those theories of London's betrayal of France that still swirl around French dinner tables today. In May 1940 he had been serving just behind the front in eastern France. It seemed to him as if every second soldier in his company was a defeatist, a pacifist or a Communist.

Then one morning after six months of waiting, of playing football and writing letters home, a motorcyclist came round the bend in the road, waving. 'Run for it,' he shouted. 'The Panzers are coming.'

'We were the French Army,' Monsieur Linquier said. 'We should have been prepared to fight. Instead we ran. Forward troops, French infantry, were throwing away their weapons. It seemed true, what the Communist agitators had been telling them—the old France was finished. That was the day I understood we could be defeated by whispers as effectively as by machine-guns.'

Monsieur Linquier played a large part in my teenage education, not least because, with Daniel spending much of his time at Monique's house, his father and I would stay up talking and sharing a further litre of wine when the rest of the family had gone to bed. Drunk almost every night, I struggled with my inadequate French to follow the labyrinths of French politics. Finally, I would make my way to my bedroom, reeling, or sometimes crawling up the narrow staircase.

Each time I returned to England my mother would be aghast as she hugged the pale, drawn-featured son who got off the train. 'My God,' she'd say. 'Is French food that bad? Those poor French people.'

POSTERS AND GRAFFITI covered the walls as my train steamed into the Gare Saint Lazare for the Easter holiday of 1949. Paris was in tumult. Victor Kravchenko, author of *I Chose Freedom*, had arrived in the city.

'He is here to fight for the truth,' Monsieur Linquier announced, waving his arms in excitement. 'Have you heard of Kravchenko, Donal?'

I told him I'd even read the book.

He let out a shout of delight. 'You've read it. This is wonderful!' Madame Linquier sent us out into the garden where we would not get in her way. Outside, we sat with a glass of Normandy cider as Monsieur Linquier opened the newspaper.

Kravchenko had come to Paris to fight a court case against one of the most respected magazines in France, *Les Lettres Françaises*. The magazine had published an article condemning *I Chose Freedom*. The author was Sim Thomas, a recently retired CIA man who had, he said, seen the light. He denounced Kravchenko as an illiterate, a drunk, seriously unbalanced, a defector who had sold out to American Intelligence in order to pay debts. He had written no word of *I Chose Freedom*—and no word of the book was true. The CIA refused to comment.

'What do we know about this Sim Thomas, Donal?' Monsieur Linquier cried. 'You don't know. I don't know. And *Les Lettres Françaises* won't tell us. Why? Because he doesn't exist!'

My session in the garden with Monsieur Linquier was the first of many.

The case received thousands of column inches throughout France. Kravchenko's book had appeared in French some time before. Communist newspapers condemned the book automatically. Had not many a Trade Union delegation visited Russia before the war and since, without seeing a sign of a concentration camp? Nevertheless, 500,000 copies were sold within a year.

The case immediately developed into a wide-ranging trial of the Soviet system. Soviet and American governments both recognised this as a key moment in the struggle for hearts and minds.

The days would pass quietly, but each evening Monsieur Linquier would bring in the newspapers. In the small kitchen it would be chaos. Madame Linquier would be trying to cook with the help of her ancient Italianate mother. Cooking in France requires much banging of pots and discussion *à haute voix*. The piping voice of Marie-France, aged seven or eight, would join the culinary debate. Before dinner, Monsieur Linquier and I would drink Normandy cider and discuss the course of the trial.

Monsieur Linquier saw it as a chance for democratic France to demonstrate that it was governed by the rule of law. The United States and the Soviet Union had thrown their prestige into the ring. What had fallen to France was the opportunity to hold its head high and to pronounce an impartial verdict in a Paris court.

Banished by Madame Linquier to the garden after dinner with a litre of red wine and a thick fold of newspapers, sometimes joined by Daniel, we studied the day's court report by one small light set in the apple tree and rehearsed refutations of the claims of the Communist Party witnesses. When the wind chased pages of newsprint into the dark corners of the garden Monsieur Linquier pursued them, returning triumphantly from the darkness with the papers crushed and torn. '*Voilà!*' he'd say. 'See how the Communists try to steal the truth from under our noses!'

BITTERNESS REACHED new heights, even for French politics. There were daily demonstrations in Paris and in the small towns around. In the city there was both chaos and elation. It was, I have since realised, the sort of show Paris loves. Fashion, outrage, politics and an intellectual gloss on the whole. Film stars and intellectuals came to the trial, members of the Paris bar, leaders of the Communist Party and ministers of the government. The arrival of Zinaida Gorlova, Kravchenko's first wife, created intense interest. Nobody doubted her evidence would be crucial.

Zinaida was a round-faced, attractive blonde, thirty-six years old with a full figure taken advantage of by photographers as she entered and left the courtroom. 'She's a very beautiful woman,' Monsieur Linquier said glumly.

But the evidence she gave was harsh. Kravchenko had beaten her during their married life. She confirmed what Sim Thomas had said in his article: her husband was a liar, a womaniser and a drunk. The anti-Soviet incidents Kravchenko described in the book, Zinaida insisted, had never happened. Monsieur Linquier was cast down by her evidence but sympathetic to her nonetheless. 'The poor woman,' he said. 'With her father and daughter in Russia, what choice does she have but to blacken her ex-husband's name?'

But the retaliation by Kravchenko's lawyer matched her evidence for harshness. She denied she was lying because her father was being held hostage in a Soviet prison camp. She denied she feared for the life of her daughter, held by the authorities in Moscow. The cross-examination was chaos. Kravchenko was shouting across the court at her. Was there really a Gulag awaiting her if she didn't perform? Or was that simply another of Kravchenko's lies?

Then, suddenly, under strain we can't conceive, she broke down in court. Uncontrollable in his pity as he had been in his anger, Kravchenko cried out to the court: 'The world knows she did not come here voluntarily!' Zinaida stood there distraught as he made promises across the courtroom that he would look after her if she defected, but first she must tell the whole truth. The judge and the ushers were unable to control him.

When Kravchenko finally sat back, the court went silent. This very ordinary woman, impossibly torn by the two great political systems that ruled the world, stared at the judge in wordless reply to Kravchenko's questions.

That night she was hurried off to a Russian aircraft waiting at Orly Airport and from there back to Moscow.

'*Voilà!*' Monsieur Linquier said grimly, with a wave of the back of his hand across the newspaper headline.

The last days of the trial were as sensational, as moving, and as deeply significant as the opening had been. Kravchenko's task was to prove that the appalling Soviet cruelty he claimed to have witnessed in the Ukrainian farmlands in the 1930s had in fact taken place, that Stalin had indeed contrived the murder by starvation of uncountable millions of people. If Kravchenko were proved a fraud, a plant by the Americans, I knew I would have to learn to march to a very different drummer.

WHEN MONSIEUR LINQUIER returned home on the day of the judgment, he could barely control his excitement. The verdict had been announced. For Kravchenko! (Years later Claude Morgan, editor of *Les Lettres Françaises*, admitted that there never was a Sim Thomas of the CIA. The article had been written by a French Communist.) From that day the Soviet Union was revealed, as Mao's China was later to be described, as a land ruled by the poet scattering rose petals before the long shadow of the executioner.

At his kitchen table Monsieur Linquier sat for a long time staring at the headline in the *Figaro*, tears in his eyes. His wife and mother-in-law watched him in silence. I think for him it was revenge at last against those political agitators he believed had destroyed and dishonoured his beloved France in 1940. Then he lifted his head. Slowly this time, deliberately, he struck the newspaper with the back of his hand. '*Voilà*,' he said. '*Enfin, la France a gagné*.' At last, France has won something.

He lifted his glass and drank to us all.

EIGHT

I asked my father one day during the war what class we were.

'We're working class', I remember him saying. 'For the moment anyway. It might not look it but we're on the move. I think this war has got a lot of people on the move.'

'Because they've been bombed out?'

'I'm talking about the way people are beginning to think now. The different classes have all rubbed shoulders because of the bombs and evacuation. The working classes have seen that upper-class people can be scared or brave, bright or dim, same as anybody else. And the upper classes are beginning to see that if the working classes *are* sometimes found keeping coal in the bath, they do it because there's nowhere else to keep it.'

'Do you have to have a lot of money to be upper class?' I asked him.

He shrugged. 'Not necessarily. It's more than just money. It's a generation or two of education that kicks it off, Dee. Then it's the way the upper classes dress, the way they talk, for instance, that people like us don't know anything about. If you don't say the right thing, in the right way, then you're not one of them. They laugh up their sleeves at you. I've seen it at Whitelands.'

'Is that how you know about all these things?'

'I don't.'

This shocked me. 'You mean, *you* make mistakes?'

'Dozens, I expect,' he said. 'But I don't know when I'm doing it.'

'I think it'd be better if we were all just one class.'

'It's never happened anywhere yet, Dee. And it's not likely to.'

IN THE TWENTIES and thirties there was no choice for people like my father but to accept the humiliations of the class system. But after the war, people, especially many young people, were much less willing to concede a natural inferiority they did not feel. Perhaps this was one of those massive silent changes made by six years of war. It was certainly one of the most positive results of Attlee's Labour government. And perhaps more than anything it was the increasingly liberating influence of the grammar schools.

But grammar school or not, for young working-class people your world was still the world of the streets. Having somewhere to go where you could sit and talk was the problem. There were pubs when you were old enough, but most London pubs were unappealing places. Spilt beer, ancient Scotch eggs and a bar dominated by the middle-aged is my memory of most pubs.

In the decade after the war, voices, clothes, social mannerisms still overwhelmed the working man. I find it immeasurably sad that my father, even when able to afford it, never felt able to take my mother to a restaurant by himself in his whole life. Exclusion, of course, even self-exclusion, was the key feature of class.

Many of us at Sloane School kept parts of our real lives hooded, even from close friends. Certainly Ted no longer proclaimed himself a Communist in so open a manner. Another good friend lived in a block of Industrial Dwellings off a narrow alley in Soho. He was intelligent and gifted, but I think ashamed of the small cramped flat that was his home.

Although working at the Dogs was by now legal, I was still anxious to draw a veil over the fact that I was a Stamford Bridge tick-tack man on Saturday evenings. I seldom mentioned that we had lived in Guinness Trust Buildings, although there were plenty of boys at Sloane who knew anyway.

Why we adopted this class-conscious attitude to each other is difficult to analyse. It might have been a form of working-class snobbery, but I think we were rejecting, not all authority, but the automatism of 'know your place', the status quo in the hymn 'All Things Bright and Beautiful': '*The rich man in his castle, the poor man at his gate . . .*'

Yet for most of us 'class' remained a marginal concern, far from a preoccupying factor. It would not become so for me until I reached the army.

BY THE END of my first year in the sixth form Guy Boas had pretty much retired to his study to write, it was said, a book on Churchill. Before this he had agreed to a request on the part of the sixth form that the prefects should have the power to elect the school captain. Of course he retained the right to veto the election of a totally unsuitable school captain. At the first election in 1949, he made his wishes clear: that we should elect a good friend of mine named Bernard Cousins. In fact the electors voted narrowly for me. Guy Boas was markedly displeased but felt, to his credit, that he could not declare null the result.

Almost simultaneously with my elevation, Kit was voted football captain. Football was God at Sloane. It meant that within a short time my brother and I ran every important activity in the school outside the teaching. My father was so puffed up with pride that the tenants of Whitelands House heard virtually nothing else from him.

IN OUR LAST YEAR at school, I had begun to spend more and more of my time with Larry Naughton. He was my age, between seventeen and eighteen, good-looking, bright, and with a sense of anecdotal humour much influenced by the Irish literary associations of his father, Bill Naughton, at that time a struggling writer.

Larry had a sister, Marie, who was in her first year at Oxford. I had no idea what Marie looked like but I absorbed from Larry a strong sense of sheer personality. Oxford, the Naughton looks, a stream of good stories, all added up to an acutely romantic picture. Unsurprisingly I made several attempts to get Larry to introduce me to her when she was back home for the vacations. But I felt some protective barrier would rise, some reluctance to connect his best friend and his much-admired sister.

We soon found that he and I shared a good many interests, interests in trying to educate ourselves. Stoically we endured Fauré recitals at the Wigmore Hall or the hideously uncomfortable cheap seats at Covent Garden. We failed, too, to fall under the spell of the Albert Hall although the Sunday afternoon concerts were exceptionally cheap for students. The problem was that we had received no musical education and neither of us had heard any music at home. With literature we had no such problem. It was, I suppose, our principal cultural interest. Books were enthusiastically puffed and lent by friends; and Larry was always a good source of enthusiasms acquired from his father.

The other interest I shared with Larry was France.

WE STUMBLED THROUGH the darkness. Somewhere, far too close, a big dog barked. We had left the main road down to Dover to find a barn that would take us out of the freezing wind. The shape faintly outlined against the dark sky might have been a barn or a house. Larry was confident it was a barn. I was for staying on the road to get a last lift into Dover where we could find some all-night café. Hitchhiking in pairs like this is all about give and take. Tonight I gave.

It was a barn. But with black-painted corrugated iron sides, big sliding doors and padlocks. We were balancing the idea of exploring another dark mass against the sky or returning to the main road when we were flooded with light from an open door. A woman stood in the doorway with a shot-gun lifted to her shoulder.

'Come forward,' she said, voice shrill with nervousness. 'Into the light.'

We walked forward very slowly. I think we might even have had our hands up. She was in her mid-thirties, dressed in a dark blue dressing gown and pink pyjamas. I started explaining about hitchhiking in France.

She stared at us then burst out laughing. 'Gipsies,' she said. 'There have been a lot around here lately, but I've never seen fair-haired Gipsies before. D'you want a cup of coffee?'

'Thank you,' I said, surprised by the rapid change in her welcome.

She put the gun up. 'Come in. This is the back of the hotel. You can only see the sign from the side road. Did you scramble in over the field?'

She took us into the kitchen and introduced herself as Eileen Taylor, the manageress. 'Make yourselves comfortable. It's cold out there tonight. Are you hungry? Fried egg on toast?'

We unslung our rucksacks and placed them by our chairs. While she bustled about frying eggs and making the toast, we talked about where we were from and what we hoped to do in France.

'You can stay here tonight,' she said casually. 'There are a couple of unoccupied rooms. We specialise in comfortable beds.' When her back was turned we exchanged glances of bafflement, eyebrows raised. Such extra-ordinary hospitality to two young men who had been strangers blundering into her back yard only five or ten minutes ago!

We were talking, finishing our eggs and coffee, when there was a roar of aircraft engines taking off nearby. She checked her watch. 'That'll be Johnny Maxwell,' she said. 'He's Flight Leader B group.'

The thunder of four engines was joined by those of a second, third and fourth plane hauling themselves into the air.

'Airlift,' she said. 'Berlin, Tempelhof. They do a week of nights, a week of days. Lucky for you they're on nights or all the rooms would be taken.'

I could see that she was intensely proud of this effort being made by the RAF and the US Air Force to keep Berlin alive.

'The whole airfield system in this part of Kent is signed up to it,' she said. 'We're providing coal. The Americans are flying rations and oil across the Atlantic to load it here for Berlin. It's an astonishing effort. A plane lands at Tempelhof, is unloaded by German handlers and has taken off again before you can say knife.'

'You know a lot about it,' I said.

'Heard it from the pilots. They're a fine lot. The best.' There were tears streaming down her cheeks. 'Here, join me in a glass of wine?' she said. She jumped up and poured three glasses without waiting for an answer.

Larry and I exchanged glances.

'It's no good,' she said, pushing tears away with the back of her hand. 'Can't keep it to myself . . . One of the planes went down at Tempelhof last week. The pilot was my . . . my lover, I suppose I shall have to call him, since he was married.' She drank, a large gulp, and took a deep breath. 'I shouldn't have allowed it to happen. No sense denying it now. Things like this happen in war. No excuse, perhaps, but it's painful when you can't go out to bring him back. When you can only go to the funeral as the manager-ess of the little hotel near the airfield where he stayed.'

'We could drink to him,' Larry said. We lifted our glasses.

'That's nice of you,' she said, and burst into tears.

SMALL ADVENTURES like this one peppered our time in France. Most, not all, were with women.

We were given a lift by an Algerian doctor somewhere outside Poitiers, a woman of about thirty-five, very tall and darkly beautiful with a mixture of

French, Greek, Jewish and Arab blood. She was on holiday. In Poitiers she bought us lunch and talked about the Arab advance into France, about the Occitan language that had preceded French in this area; and about the English victory at Poitiers in the Hundred Years War. She was formidably well read and when she left the table for a few moments I remember the movement of her very pale flowing khaki dress as she walked. We drove through the afternoon towards the Dordogne River and stopped at a café in Limeuil. Below was the confluence of the clear waters of the Vézère and the silt-bearing Dordogne, linked by a double stone bridge.

'I have a proposal,' our new friend said.

She had five days more before she had to catch the boat to Algiers. She would like to spend that time, day and night, with one of us.

It didn't matter which.

Larry and I sat staring at one another, stunned, as she stood up and left the table. I looked down at the tall and elegant Frenchwoman as she reached the middle of the bridge and stopped to peer down at the water. She was waiting for one of us to go down and join her.

'Jesus Christ,' Larry said. 'You think she's serious?'

I nodded. 'She made herself clear enough.'

I don't need to describe the plus side of the proposal. The idea of being paid for in a French hotel for five days to make love to this woman . . . It was the stuff of fantasy. Yet there was also something about the proposal that I'm not sure Larry and I ever articulated. We both knew that if one of us went ahead, it would have been the end of our friendship as we had known it.

She ceased staring down at the rivers and turned to rest her elbows on the stone balustrade. Then she arched her back, looking up at us. Men didn't turn down such offers from beautiful women. I felt it was ungracious and, I don't know why, tremendously sad. I didn't know where to look.

She waited for a few moments more, her large, dark eyes fixed on us. Then she pushed herself off the balustrade, turned a shoulder to us and walked with long strides towards her car.

WE NEVER MANAGED to get down to the Mediterranean. Money was short—we were forced to turn back to Paris. We arrived on the evening of July 14 having 'guided' a diminutive, septuagenarian Bordelais in an overloaded lorry round the *boulevard extérieur*. As every British visitor to Paris knew, even then, what was to become the *périphérique* is both a ring-road and a twenty-four-hour race track. Our tiny Bordelais insisted on stopping in the middle of the road as traffic raced by on either side, to shout for directions to a motorcycle cop. The policeman couldn't understand the Bordeaux accent; our driver couldn't understand the Paris accent. Larry and I hung off the back of the truck, shouting a rephrasal of the question at the motor-cyclist, and after a hundred sets of screeching tyres, drivers hooting like madmen, and vehicles criss-crossing in front of us as the Bordelais began a U-turn, we got our driver moving straight ahead.

As he dropped us off with the present of a bottle of still-fermenting wine, we discovered that our Bordelais had never been on a ring-road in his life. When the cop had pointed backwards as the direction we should be head-ing, our driver had seen a U-turn as natural enough.

NINE

The Labour government was debating a massive increase in the defence budget to counter growing Soviet hostility. National Service was on every young man's mind. There were those, of course, who opposed the whole idea of serious defence. They contended that defence budgets were rising in the West solely to satisfy the demands of the United States armaments industry.

NATO was coming into being while, in some sections of the electorate, anti-Americanism was growing stronger. I didn't have the answers. I only knew that I would shortly be going into the army for two whole years of my life. I now believed that it was an important thing to do; that there was a West European frontier to be defended by NATO against the Soviet Union.

I was one of those who insisted that you didn't have to be a supporter of Senator McCarthy in order to fear Stalinism. But of course moral rela-tivism, that brilliant tactic of the extreme Left, preached the opposite. If you opposed Stalin, you must, *relatively*, support McCarthy. This relativism was the most successful and dangerous dialectical element of the time.

Most of our arguments with friends were good-natured but it's undeni-able that the differences ran deep. For many people the division created then has remained throughout their lives.

THE RESULTS of our Higher School Certificate came through. I was given an A in spoken French, three Bs and a C. I had talked with my father about going to university. He was as keen for me to go as I was myself.

I suppose it was some reflection of our World's End background that for my father and me university meant either Oxford or Cambridge. I doubt if I knew that London University existed, and even Oxford and Cambridge meant no more to me than the Boat Race.

Oxford and Cambridge required further examinations, which would mean staying on another few months at school. It also meant getting the backing of my school. My History master, Leslie Berkeley, was enthusiastic but he infused the task ahead with a sense of his own modesty and caution. 'You will,' he said, 'be put up against the very cream of Winchester, Marlborough and Eton. The quality of teaching at the best public schools is very high indeed.' He was well-meaning and an excellent teacher but he did not inspire great confidence.

'Do you have any idea of the standard of entry Oxford and Cambridge demand? You don't just walk in, you know,' Guy Boas said irritably. 'You must know that the school can't afford a failure.'

I was furious. 'Then I'll have to do my best not to fail, sir.'

He glared at me. 'History,' he said, pulling out a bandanna-like handkerchief and flicking it under his nose. 'I'll think about it.'

I think he considered anyone reading English should be given preference. For a week he said neither no nor yes. Leslie Berkeley pressed him in his diffident manner. Guy Boas repeated that he was concerned about the school's reputation: Sloane should not be allowed to fall by the wayside with the first candidate it had sent up for Cambridge entrance since the war. Berkeley loyally pressed him some more. A verdict was finally promised.

Together Leslie Berkeley and I went to the headmaster's study. Berkeley made a cautious but effective case for my taking the Cambridge entrance but Guy Boas had already decided. He cut Berkeley short with a grumbled, 'Very well, then. If you must.'

There was one final decision. Oxford or Cambridge? As children in the World's End we'd always pledged ourselves to Oxford or Cambridge and worn their colours on Boat Race Day. I talked to Kit about it. 'Go for Cambridge,' he said. 'You've always been Cambridge.' So on the basis of a five-year-old's boat-race decision and some pale blue ribbons tied to an orange-box cart, I chose Cambridge.

BILL NAUGHTON, soon to be author of the novel *Alfie*, on which the Michael Caine and more recent Jude Law films were based, was a little over forty at this time, not tall, already balding, but with a smile that really would affect everybody in the room. Though he had left Ireland as a child, he was markedly Irish in so many ways and particularly in his literary interests. He maintained a network of contacts with Irish writers and it seemed usual to find he had a writer over from Dublin staying with him for a few days. In those early times before *Alfie* or any of the stage plays were written, Larry's father was already recognised as a writer with a future.

At this time Bill, who was divorced, lived with Larry in a small flat in Pimlico. Larry's sister Marie stayed there during university vacations from Oxford, although I had not yet met her. Most evenings I was there Bill or Larry would cook some variant of spaghetti and the current visitor would provide a couple of bottles of Spanish Burgundy. The talk was of books, plays and paintings.

One late summer afternoon I rang the bell to the flat in St George's Square and a girl of about nineteen opened the door. 'Hi,' she said. 'I'm Marie, Larry's sister. I know who you are. I can see straight away.' Whether that was the way it was intended, I took it as the most extravagant compliment.

I was bowled over. She was not tall, but well shaped without being dramatically so. She wore a black pleated skirt and black pumps, a dark blue sweater and white shirt. Her features were unforgettable. She had her father's extraordinary illuminating smile and hooded blue eyes under dark-blonde chestnut hair. You felt you were spotlit by her glance.

'Before we go in . . .' She put her hand on my arm. 'I've something to tell you,' she said. I watched her as she pursed her lips. 'Oxford,' she said. She grinned, very even, white teeth, then grimaced. 'I've been sent down.'

'God, I'm sorry.' And after a moment. 'How's your Dad taking it?'

The hooded eyes almost closed. 'Furious,' she whispered.

'Larry said nothing about it.'

'He wouldn't. He's mortified.'

'Should I push off?'

She grabbed my hand. 'No! Please. Dad likes you. And they won't keep up the black faces while you're here. I need your help.'

We had a great evening. A young Austrian woman, Erne, a friend of Bill's, came in a little later. She had brought schnitzel and cheese from Soho. The lights were turned low. A candle or two was lit. We had *terrine de canard*, schnitzel and Camembert. Red Spanish Burgundy, and a liqueur of mixed Drambuie, Avocaat, and Scotch and Irish whiskies. We were all singing drunk by nine o'clock.

I was sitting on the sofa with Marie. Under cover of candlelight and a gingham cushion, she took my hand as we sang 'Danny Boy'.

MY FATHER'S medical emergency was a shock but no surprise. At the age of seventeen he had narrowly escaped death from peritonitis. He had been rushed to St Stephen's and operated on. The suturing of the wound had been badly bungled, knotting various layers of muscle in his groin. He had always known that these would at some time have to be separated. Despite this, he continued to do the stoking at Whitelands if the regular stoker was off for any reason. Now, nearly twenty-five years after the operation, the muscle had finally been torn. The tear quickly became infected. Treatment was necessary right away.

My father kept so many balls in the air, both at Whitelands House and in his bookmaking businesses, that to keep things going while he was confined to bed was going to be difficult.

My mother was supremely capable in a crisis. She advised all the runners and customers that the pay-in/pay-out was going to be delayed over the week my father was expected to be in hospital. My mother was also taking care of the phone bets. There would be no Mick Burns stand at Stamford Bridge that week, and Kit and I were going to handle my father's current problem at Whitelands—the absence with 'flu of the stoker.

Kit and I had helped with the process of raking out the furnaces and refilling them, but we had never carried out the whole process by ourselves. So it was with trepidation that we let ourselves into the boiler room. We knew this vast underground area well. We had spent a large part of the Blitz sleeping down here and had come to hate the coke-dust-laden atmosphere and the temperature permanently approaching 100 degrees.

There were still the same great iron pokers twelve foot long; the rakes of the same grotesque length and shovels with scoops twice the size of a normal shovel designed to keep the stoker as far as possible away from the angry heat of the furnace when the iron door was opened.

Our task was to rake the red-hot crust of coke out of two of the huge furnaces and use it to light two clean furnaces. Then to take out the remaining white-hot 'canker' and let the two clean boilers cool down. The easier part of the stoker's job, keeping the furnaces topped up, would be done by the porters.

Stripped to the waist, we approached the first boiler. Kit lifted the handle with a hook poker and swung open the iron door three foot wide by two high. Flame leapt from the mouth of the monster; the hot air hit our bare chests. Kit swung the door closed with a clang. 'God Almighty,' he said.

We realised now why stokers always wore those filthy singlets. There were two undershirts my father kept in a locker. We put them on, thick with sweat and coke dust as they were, and went back to face boiler number one.

The next hours came close to a medieval descent into hell. My father could handle the change-over of two boilers in well under two hours. Two hours into our shift and Kit and I had a huge pile of white-hot cinder in front of number one and number three had gone out. We had thrown in too much coke and extinguished the glowing base that should have given us a merrily burning boiler. This mix of dead cinder and fresh coke had to be raked out before we could start again.

Coke dust covered Kit's face and hair. His eyes seemed to stare like a maniac's. I suppose I looked the same. We were weak with effort and even weaker with laughter.

We knew the porters upstairs would be having a good laugh at the idea of the two of us struggling away in the depths. We made sure we avoided them when, exhausted, we eventually crept stealthily up from the boiler room a record five hours later.

My father was still a young man, in his late thirties. Within a week he was in bed at home. Another week and he was walking about only a little less energetically than usual. My mother smiled her pleasure. Kit and I were almost as pleased to hear from Whitelands that the stoker had recovered from his 'flu.

I WAS SEEING MARIE regularly by then. She had a part-time job with a Jewish refugee friend of her father's who was running an Austrian travel business on the corner of Shaftesbury Avenue and Macclesfield Street.

De Hems is a pub a few doors down Macclesfield Street where Larry and I used to go to meet Marie after work. Her smile and bubbling intelligence gave her a ready audience from the moment she entered the saloon bar. Even the edgy, almost violent brand of older homosexual who used to frequent the place with their 'chickens' seemed captivated by Marie.

Her future was uncertain. To her father, I believe her being sent down was an acute disappointment. Winning a place at Oxford or Cambridge was seen as an extraordinary achievement in working-class families like ours. It was a ticket into another life. I think her father felt that Marie had thoughtlessly torn up the ticket and thrown it away. He was determined that his daughter should not leave university for a London life spent flitting from party to bright party given by her Oxford friends. But he had not yet made up his mind what should be done about it.

Nothing had happened between Marie and myself since that first night. I remember being very unsure about Larry's reaction to the possibility. I felt in him some resistance to anything developing between myself and his sister. I seldom, for example, seemed to get the opportunity to spend any time alone with her. Perhaps he was just unaware that I wanted to be.

Nevertheless, Marie and I were coming closer together. We enjoyed the same sense of humour, and when she mentioned them I rapidly read poets I had only heard of before—Auden, Spender, Louis MacNeice. We were by now cautiously becoming more open with each other about wanting to spend some time alone together. Mostly left unexpressed, it was clear to both of us all the same. The fact was that, intentionally or not, Larry was always there. I felt snared: I couldn't tell Larry what Marie and I wanted before I'd talked to Marie—but then I had no opportunity to talk to her.

Even worse was an impending sense of disaster that I had. Perhaps it had something to do with the way Larry and his father both seemed *not* to recognise that Marie and I were drawing together. Only Erne, Bill Naughton's wife-to-be, seemed to be aware of what was going on. I called round one day when Larry was taking a shower. Marie, she told me, was at the corner shop buying vegetables for soup. 'The soup can wait,' she said with a quiet smile. 'Go and meet her.'

I had just discovered seventeenth-century love lyrics and as we walked back to St George's Square we talked about Sir John Suckling. She knew of him but had never read his poetry. 'I'll get you a copy,' I said.

'And will you write something in it?'

'If you want.' I thought of one of his poems. 'How about:

> "Out upon it, I have lov'd
> Three whole days together
> And am like to love three more–
> If it prove fair weather."'

She laughed. 'Not entirely reassuring to a girl.'

'A pretty clumsy choice. But I have this feeling,' I said, taking my courage in both hands, 'that we don't have months. We have to take it a few days, or maybe just a few weeks, at a time.'

She looked at me, her smile fading. 'Perhaps you're right,' she said. We had reached her door.

'Let's walk on a bit,' I said. 'We can talk.'

'Uh—no.' She shook her head. 'Erne's waiting for the vegetables.'

Erne had said the vegetables could wait but she fumbled her key in the lock all the same.

ONE DAY WE WENT to the Tate Gallery. With Larry.

'We're not going to all stand gawking at the same picture, are we?' Marie said. She was slightly behind Larry and raised her eyebrows at me.

'No,' I said. 'Let's split up and meet downstairs in the entrance hall in about fifteen minutes.'

Marie and I met up almost straight away on the floor above. There were no more than half a dozen people in the gallery. We came together in the middle of this huge ornate room and kissed.

'That . . . was wonderful,' she said. 'Do it again.'

A few people turned and smiled indulgently.

We met Larry downstairs a few minutes later. We didn't say a word about the exhibition. The truth was I couldn't stop looking at Marie.

I'm sure Larry knew the dam had broken. Within no time, I think Marie's father knew too.

FINDING TIME to be alone together absorbed us both. We spent an hour here, an hour or two there. Once we managed the darkness of a film together (*Annie Get Your Gun*), and we met a couple of times by ourselves in a corner seat in De Hems. It was very little.

It seemed to me Marie's father was less his smiling self than usual but he still treated me with great friendliness. As indeed did Larry. It was difficult nevertheless not to feel that I had committed some serious *res non grata*. And there was something else too. My feeling of vague foreboding had metamorphosed into a growing certainty that Marie had not told me something which affected us both.

Once or twice I asked her directly if she was holding something back but she shook her head in reply. I spent a lot of time thinking about that shake of the head. I was sure there was something.

There was a moment when Erne was going back to Austria. Bill and Larry left with her to carry her bags to the bus stop.

I waited for the front door to bang and turned to Marie. 'Tell me,' I said. 'Tell you what?'

'I don't know,' I said to Marie. I put my hands round her waist. 'But there's something, isn't there? Do you want me to stop coming round?'

'No.' She pulled away, but she said it with so much vehemence I couldn't doubt it.

'OK. So what is it? There is something, isn't there?'

She looked at me. 'Don't ask,' she said. 'Not yet.'

I TOOK MY ARMY medical examination in Hammersmith and was duly passed fit. Afterwards I was interviewed by a selection officer.

'What do you want to do in the army?' He was looking at my school record. 'Apply for officer training? Or languages? You've the qualifications to apply to do a Russian course at Cambridge.'

Two years learning Russian, three years reading History (if I was successful). I wondered if the delights of Cambridge would sustain me through a whole five years. 'No,' I said to the interviewing officer. 'I was thinking of the infantry.'

'Were you?' He lifted his eyebrows in surprise. Cannon fodder, he seemed to be saying. If that's what you want . . .

ON ONE OF THOSE few occasions when Marie and I were alone we'd dreamed of going away somewhere together. It was desert island stuff. We had neither the money nor the time to do anything as exotic as hitchhike to Paris and our preferred destination was very much more distant than that: the virtually undiscovered paradise of Ibiza. We played with the idea, it was something to share—but we both recognised a complete fantasy.

Then something happened, I no longer remember the background. Marie and I were to be able to spend a weekend together. We would have to be back late Sunday afternoon, but it was enough. Paris or Ibiza were reshaped as Brighton. Our shortage of money meant we'd be camping.

We spent an afternoon wandering round the Pavilion, then took a bus. For that one night we stayed on the cliff top at Rottingdean. Sex was out of the question. Fear of pregnancy was acute then. So, wrapped near-naked in a double sleeping-bag, we made less than love until the dawn came.

It was a cold early-September morning. The sea was bucking white patternless waves and the wind came hard off it, scouring the cliff top. On our Primus stove we brewed up a cup of tea and drank it with the sleeping-bag round our shoulders. Our eyes locked. It was the first time in my life I had consciously thought: *I am really in love with this girl.* After a few moments Marie looked away and smiled a disconcerting, rueful sort of smile. The last hour we had spent together in the sleeping-bag had carried a pressage of this. 'I must tell you,' she said. 'It can't wait any longer.'

I blew on the tea. 'It's bad news, isn't it?'

'Yes.' She drank some tea. She was looking past me to the line of the cliff top. 'Dad wants me to go to Vienna to stay with a friend of Erne's. Apparently I can get a job with the Control Commission there.'

It was a body blow.

'Is it because of us? Is that why he's sending you away?'

She shrugged. 'Partly because I made such a mess of things at Oxford. He knows you've got the army then Cambridge—'

'If I get in.'

'I think he doesn't want me to ruin your life as well as my own.' She spoke without bitterness.

'When?' I asked her.

She turned back towards me. 'This week,' she said. 'Wednesday.'

MY LAST MONTHS at Sloane were a time of missing Marie badly, of counting the days until I would see her again when she came back for Christmas. Meantime the dark blue airmail letters arriving regularly from Austria kept my spirits at a tolerable level. At the end of the autumn term I was to take the entrance examination for Pembroke College, Cambridge.

The letter with the Pembroke College crest laid out the format of the week-long examination. You arrived at the college on Monday evening and left late Friday afternoon. There was to be a three-hour essay on the first morning. The General Paper on politics, arts and public affairs took up the first afternoon. Wednesday afternoon the Language Paper: compulsory Latin with one other language, in my case French. Thursday there were the two crucial History papers, British and European. On Friday there were interviews. It was a rigorous test of nerve and stamina.

IT WAS GROWING DARK as I left Liverpool Street Station on the train for Cambridge. I carried my Gladstone and a still-unopened letter from Marie that had arrived that morning. In a compartment by myself, I opened it.

I remember nothing of what she said but for the first sentences: her father had decided he and Larry should go out to spend a few days with her in Vienna. Marie would not be coming back to London for Christmas. What it really meant went much deeper. With my army service coming up in a matter of weeks there was every chance we would not see each other for another two years. I wasn't a fool. I was a bookmaker's son. I knew how the odds stacked up. It was the end of the road.

PEMBROKE COLLEGE is an ancient stone-fronted building with an arched doorway onto Trumpington Street. At the porters' lodge was a list of the rooms that candidates had been allocated. In the screens, the area outside the darkened dining hall, there was a list of times and places for examinations and interviews. I had an interview at 10.30 on the free morning, Wednesday, with Anthony Camps, the senior tutor. There would be two further interviews on Friday evening at six o'clock, after which I would be free to leave.

I walked forward through the screens and stood in a part-Tudor, part-seventeenth-century, ivy-covered court. I remembered from the handbook in Hammersmith Library that the rooms on the first floor of J staircase had belonged to William Pitt. Gray, writer of the 'Elegy in a Country Churchyard', had lived on the same staircase. That night, light from the ivy-fringed windows was filmed with droplets of mist. A few young men carrying cases walked through, stopping at each staircase to check the room numbers. One or two raised voices to greet another candidate. They actually knew someone else here! The Eton, Winchester, Marlborough connection that Leslie Berkeley had warned me about, no doubt.

The court emptied. Behind me chandeliers suddenly came on. I turned. Gothic windows ran the length of a nave-like hall. Above two lines of heavy oak tables running towards a raised high table, the walls were hung with portraits of college notables. A medieval master here, Elizabethans like the poet Edmund Spenser and a dozen nineteenth-century figures. Places were being set at the long tables.

I was overwhelmed. Most of all horrified at the possibility of unknowingly making some appalling social blunder. Should I eat that night in hall?

I didn't want to add this to the barriers I would have to begin hurdling tomorrow. Instead I walked down to the pub on the millrace of the River Cam and bought a Scotch egg and a pint of beer.

I walked slowly back to college. But I was also thinking how badly I wanted to be part of this as I retreated to the rooms I had been allocated beside the Wren Chapel.

Old Court, the original extent of the college, was empty. I stopped under a yellow lamp and leaned against the stonework. I recovered my balance as I often have throughout my life by summoning up an image of my grandmother Eliza, in moth-eaten coat and Eliza Doolittle hat, dancing irreverently across the central lawn singing her favourite soldier's song of the First World War: '*Mademoiselle from Armenteers, parlez-voo . . .*'

It almost worked.

THE THREE-HOUR EXAMINATION next morning was a disaster. The night before I had looked at the bookshelves in the rooms I was allocated with the idea that I should read something to take my mind off the morrow. I had hit upon Damon Runyon.

I don't have to remind anybody that the two significant characteristics of Runyon's style are the first-person singular and his favourite present tense. 'I am taking my usual mid-morning stroll down Broadway when I spot Bulldog Bagshaw standing outside Mindy's in a black snap-brim fedora, and a faultless tuxedo with the trouser legs rolled to the mid-calf over bare, wet, very cold feet.' That sort of thing.

Thirty or forty pages of Damon Runyon is relaxing but can make a big impression on a susceptible young mind. It can even carry over its neuro-imprint until the next morning. In the examination rooms I opened the paper in front of me. Six essay titles. I chose one—'Melodrama'—and set to work with a stylistic vigour Damon Runyon would have approved. Very much approved, I'm afraid, since it was a dead ringer for his own.

I wrote for the full three hours, fighting Damon Runyon all the way. I was the last to leave, a wet rag, with the rhythms of Runyon still unexorcised.

Nothing that followed was so bad. I was comfortable with the General Paper, more or less taking it in my stride, I thought. I had dinner in hall that night and, locked in common adversity, found I got on well enough with my neighbours from Marlborough and Winchester.

Wednesday morning at 10.30 was my first interview. It was a dark

December morning as I climbed the staircase to the senior tutor's rooms. He opened the door to my knock, a tall, thin-shouldered man with an enormous head. His smile was genuinely welcoming. I introduced myself and with extreme courtesy he gestured to a chair.

For the next hour we talked, I about the Russian novels I was reading at the time. He prompted me by affecting to know little about Russian literature but declared his interest in it. Since he seemed interested in everything, I also talked about Auden and Isherwood, Spender and MacNeice. Pouring me a glass of sherry, he seemed to be quite happy to let me run on into the time I had spent in France. I had been there an hour, but he had given no sign that the interview was over so I ploughed on.

Finally he stood. It was clearly time for me to go. 'I have someone to see before lunch,' he said. 'Very good of you to call. I really have enjoyed our talk. Now let me look at my list. I shall be seeing you, I see, at ten thirty tonight, will I not? Awfully late, I'm afraid.'

The Turkish carpet could have swallowed me up. The terrible social gaffe I had feared had been committed.

I felt deeply angry with myself. Perhaps if I'd realised that he actually lived in those rooms, I might have studied the times of interview with more care. But I still imagined that all senior members of college lived in their own homes with wives and children. I didn't understand what a bachelor society Cambridge was.

Yet, when I went back to the senior tutor's rooms that evening, he asked me no 'interview' questions at all and we sat there like old friends, comfortably talking about college history, with a glass of port.

A strange place.

On Friday I had lunch in hall. My neighbour said he'd seen me in the History examination room and suggested a glass of wine to celebrate the end of the inquisition. He ordered a half-bottle of Burgundy.

The Burgundy arrived and was poured. We finished the first glass and he took the bottle to top us up.

'We still have this afternoon's interviews,' I said warily.

'Not for me,' he said cheerfully. 'I have a party on tonight. I told Tony Camps I had to catch the two-thirty train and he squeezed me in before lunch yesterday. I was out in five minutes. Cheers! Army first?'

'Yes,' I said. 'Best of luck.' I raised my glass.

'Where are you posted?'

'Winchester,' I told him.

'Ah, the Green Jackets. Good friend of mine at Eton's just been commissioned in the King's Royal Rifle Corps. Adam Butler. Son of Rab, the former Education Minister. He's a training officer. You'll like him.'

I passed into New Court to my interview with David Joslin, supervisor of History candidates, still bemused by the easy manner of my lunch companion. The Eton connections—Green Jackets, R. A. Butler . . . And he had risked putting forward his interview because he had had to get back to London for a party! I never saw him again.

David Joslin was small, rounded, with an air of intimidating intelligence. I remember a few of his opening questions.

'What do you think happened to the sales of domestic coal and margarine in the depression of the early 1930s?'

Coal? I thought of the coke we used to collect from the gas works to sell in the World's End. Coal cost twice as much. 'Coal sales down,' I said, 'in favour of coke.' My grandmother used to say a dab of butter was better for you than a thick smear of margarine. 'Margarine down,' I guessed wildly. 'Butter up.'

'Would you like a glass of sherry?'

Here we go again. 'Thank you,' I said.

'You upset John Dickinson with your paper on Cromwell, you know.'

'John Dickinson?' I said.

'He teaches History here. Devoted to the memory of Charles I. Member of the Society of Charles the Martyr.' He smiled broadly. 'I thought you'd done it on purpose.' He handed me the glass of sherry.

On purpose? I had argued that the Protectorate had been necessary to resolve the pressing issues of sovereignty that Charles I had raised, and had made impossible a reversion to the claims of the earlier part of the century by any restored monarchy. How could I have done something like that on purpose?

I couldn't grasp the relationship he seemed to be offering. I'd expected it to be that of schoolmaster and pupil. This was adult to adult. It was all something of a shock.

A brief knock and the door was flung open by a tall, grinning man in a gown. He grasped my hand. 'You don't leave anyone in doubt about what you think of Oliver Cromwell, do you?'

'If I offended you . . .'

'Much the best thing,' he said. 'Strong views. We'll fight it out.'

We talked about Cromwell for the next twenty minutes.

When I was leaving, John Dickinson held open the door. We shook hands. 'See you in two years' time,' he said.

I walked slowly down the staircase. Two years' time? Did he *really* say that? That's what I *think* he said.

I tortured myself with that sentence all the way back to London.

I GUESSED, of course, that waiting for the Cambridge results was going to be hard, at least as hard on my father as on me. Kit and my mother took things more calmly, Kit reminding me (his idea of humour) that if I failed, I could always make a career in football. I had made arrangements to do a short hitchhike to Oxford with Larry Naughton, just to kill the time before the results arrived.

We enjoyed Oxford. I thought it was magnificent, but it didn't blend with the mists of December as Cambridge did.

I arrived back at White City. I was still reaching for the handle when my father dragged open the door. 'The results came yesterday,' he said, before I could speak. 'A telegram. I had to open it, Dee. I wouldn't have slept a wink.'

I could see by his face, red with excitement, and my mother's just visible by his shoulder, that it wasn't bad news. 'Have I got a place?'

'A place? Stiffen the Prussian Guards!' he exploded. 'They've given you a scholarship!'

TEN

The train arrived at Winchester on a dark, sleeting afternoon in January. I had seen one or two men of about my age wandering the corridor in the short journey from Waterloo, but had made no contact with them. I thought that could wait an hour or two. I knew that for the next two years I would be living together with them, or young men very like them. I didn't object. But I was going to take a few more minutes to myself before it all started.

I spent my last half an hour of freedom wondering whether I would ever see Marie again, wondering where in the world I would spend the next two years. It was a reverie balanced equally between nostalgia and a not unpleasant sense of anticipation. A reverie shattered by the sound of the army in full cry: 'Look in, there! Move, move, move! At the double . . . Move, you idle man!' Six corporals and a sergeant ran along the platform, banging with the flat of their hand on the side of the carriages.

I knew it was a calculated pantomime. But I was still out of that train, jogging along the platform, scrambling onto the back of an army truck, and on the road to Bushfield Camp, before I was even sure what was happening.

The first few hours after arrival at Bushfield Green Jacket Training Brigade had the atmosphere of entering a prison camp. By the fading light we were hustled into the stores. There was a brief moment of reverence when we were issued with our green berets and black Cross of Malta cap badges. Then in short order we had thrown at us khaki denim trousers and jackets ('Don't fit? Don't fit? Listen to me, with this kit, if it fits good, you're deformed!'), boots, gaiters, mug, knife, fork, spoon, two blankets and a mattress. Struggling to hold all this in our arms, we were ordered uphill to wooden huts furnished only with pairs of iron cots one above the other and rough timber hanging-cupboards, the huts arranged spider-legged to meet washrooms at a central entrance point.

We were introduced to our new routine. At the double to the cookhouse. A terrible meal which might have been fish. Back at the double. Put to polishing the boots and the impossible brasswork on belts and packs by our two corporals. We sat on the lower level of our double bunks with the corporals making clear the standards they expected to be achieved. I don't think any of us got to bed before one or two o'clock.

At 5.30 next morning we were quick-marched (at 127 paces a minute) to the cookhouse, along a path glittering with frost and with the moon still high in a clear black sky. We were exhausted, dark-eyed and apprehensive. The short, strongly built cockney next to me whispered something I couldn't catch. But the corporal in charge had heard. He brought us to a halt.

'What was that, Rifleman Snelling?' he barked. 'Did I hear you say you'd sooner be dead?'

'Not before breakfast, Corporal,' Snelling replied, straight-faced.

There was a long pause. 'Very wise, lad. Though most clever lads find they don't have time for breakfast by their second day here. You're not a clever lad, are you, Snelling?'

'Dumb as they come, Corporal.'

I thought the skies were about to fall in on Ron Snelling but he had the measure of our new life far quicker than I. The corporal grinned. 'I tell you what I like about you, Snelling . . . that's your air of quiet resignation. I'll spread the word.'

I decided I'd probably survive the army after all.

THERE WERE TWO PARTS to the draft which arrived at Bushfield Camp. There were the mainly short, stocky, highly motivated Londoners from the Green Jacket main recruiting boroughs of Deptford, Shoreditch and Bow. Totally different in background, education and very often physically (taller but usually less well-muscled), there were also those from Eton, Winchester, Marlborough, Harrow, Haileybury and Ampleforth, who hoped to obtain a commission. As the only grammar school member of the intake, I stood somewhere in the middle.

You'd think this division between cockney east London and the country's best-known public schools was the simplest cook's recipe for trouble. All in the same barrack room, glottal stops and strangulated vowels criss-crossing the bed spaces after 'lights out', how could a clash be avoided? Yet somehow it produced no problems. Public schoolboys made bad Hollywood imitations of East End accents, cockneys responded with equally poor simulacra of the fashionable upper-class drawl. Perhaps because our real enemy was the system which enveloped us, it was all done in good humour.

In that first six weeks at Bushfield we were truly run off our feet. Sixty young men were to be de-civilianised, taught that if the army says do it, you do it. Only afterwards could personal initiative be allowed. I can't imagine there's any more effective way of breaking in young men than an induction of the sort we suffered at Winchester.

During the first morning of our service we were taken out onto the parade ground to be introduced to Green Jacket drill. This requires a speed of coordination, which it took our drill sergeants less than three minutes to discover I somewhat lacked.

'Like bloody Beethoven,' his voice swelled indignantly. 'Slow in all his movements.' Insults flowed my way, but never insults you could take seriously. Frustration, mock despair and simulated rage were the training NCOs' stock-in-trade. All the same, it wasn't comforting to discover I was a nanosecond slower than my fellow recruits.

Everything depended on your attitude. If you snivelled, you had a very bad time indeed. If you saw the deadly seriousness and the mad humour of those days, you still longed for them to end but you took the opportunity to enjoy this unique sense of force-fed comradeship.

Regimental indoctrination was high on the list of the days' activities. From day one we were told that the two Green Jacket regiments, The King's Royal Rifle Corps and its sister regiment, The Rifle Brigade, were incomparably the best in the British Army. The Guards, while similarly elite, were stiff, slow and inflexible. At the time we were the only fully motorised infantry in the British Army. We would be trained to operate in small units, carried in our own armoured vehicles ahead of advancing tank formations.

My platoon instructor in all this was, incidentally, Second Lieutenant Adam Butler, KRRC.

AFTER SIX WEEKS together our intake was split into two groups, one for immediate dispatch to Germany for continuation training, the other to go before the three-day War Office Selection Board, WOSB (pronounced Wosbee) for selection as officers. I applied and was accepted as one of those to be sent before the selection board. I was confident of passing. I wasn't the best parade-ground soldier, but I was good in the classroom, and my hitchhiking days meant I took to every sort of infantry field training they'd subjected us to.

The four weeks of our training in the Potential Officer platoon was of a slightly different order. It moved from a heavy emphasis on drilling, weapon training and physical exercise, to slightly more cerebral studies such as map reading, leadership and military knowledge.

WOSB now beckoned. A pass there meant four months' training at Eaton Hall Infantry Officer Cadet School in Cheshire and a posting to a battalion. Most prized, of course, was a recommendation for a commission in the Green Jackets.

At the beginning of the 1950s class distinctions were, on the surface at least, still as strong as they had been before the war. All my companions in the Potential Officer platoon were from major public schools. Battalion officers bristled with names like Lieutenant Lord Lennox and Captain Lord St Aubyn. But somehow I still thought there was some chance of my being selected for the Green Jackets—until we were asked to hand in our birth certificates. I had never seen mine before. I sent for it from home. Under

'Father's profession', mine read: 'Journeyman plumber'. I thought ruefully that this wasn't going to crack the ice.

But I wasn't inclined to back down. Perhaps the Green Jackets *were* now taking an occasional plumber's son. I doubted it, but it was true that I had not so far in the army come up against issues of class. At the end of most days at Bushfield we were an indistinguishable huddle of mud-covered, exhausted young men. I spent as much time with the boys from Shoreditch and Bow whose resilience echoed my own World's End past, as I did with the Marlburians and Etonians who were indeed from a different world but far from the daunting strangers that Leslie Berkeley had pictured. The two groups supported each other with a sense of humour. There were almost no superior airs exhibited by the public-school group.

Yet the next stage, Potential Officer training, was paradoxically to open up that class gap again. Certainly the British Army at this time united officers and non-commissioned ranks by a sense of self-esteem rooted in a shared regimental identity. At the same time it consciously manipulated its recruits to achieve a structure of discipline and authority based on class differences.

I might have opted for a commission in one of the corps, the Army Ordnance Corps or the Service Corps. Most of their officers were from grammar school. But that seemed what my father would have called dodging the column. I applied for a Green Jacket Commission.

I CAN'T THINK of anybody I seriously disliked in my intake. But there was one man whose manner seemed impossibly aloof. He was, I think, the only member of the intake with whom I hadn't sat around the pot-bellied stove chatting and cleaning boots and rifles. He spent all his spare time lying on his bed with a book of Latin verse. Rifleman Richard Rougier was from Marlborough, as indeed were several others in the intake. I knew little or nothing about him except that he had a sharp tongue. And somebody had told me that his mother was the novelist Georgette Heyer.

I had decided early on that I'd get on a lot better with someone like Reggie Bosanquet, later the high-living ITN newsreader, or even languid, sleepy-eyed Mark Tennant, than I ever would with Richard Rougier.

Some time after midnight one night, not long before we were due to complete basic training, I found myself crammed in the back of a canvas-sided three-ton truck, legs tangled with rifles, as we left the frosted hillsides of Winchester where we had been practising night attacks. The man next to me, hands in a priestly fold across his chest, was Richard Rougier. As we turned off the hillside tracks he began to sing. In Latin!

I couldn't imagine anything so pompous or irrelevant, given our cramped, noisy travelling conditions. And then I realised he was singing a Horace Ode: 'I hate the vulgar crowd—and ward them off. Grant me your silence . . .' Not so inappropriate. I laughed.

'I thought you would like it,' he said. 'We who are destined for Pembroke must stick together.'

I looked at him in surprise. 'You're going to Pembroke too?'

'If I survive.'

'I expect you will. How did you know I was going?'

'You're a Scholar,' he said.

'And you?'

'A mere Exhibitioner.'

Exhibitioner. At the time I thought that was pretty appropriate too.

'Shall I ask the Dean to get us rooms on the same staircase? When we get there we'll need someone who knew what we went through in this Vale of Tears. We'll celebrate with a glass of excellent port and a Bath Oliver.'

I had to laugh. More port and biscuits. He obviously knew the ropes. 'It's a date,' I said, as we slowed to enter Bushfield Camp. 'A glass of port and a Bath Oliver in two years' time.'

I WAS BY THIS TIME slowly working my way through the eliminating bouts for the Green Jacket Training Brigade Boxing Championship. My semifinal match was against the amiable Reginald Bosanquet. He had boxed at Winchester College and was at that time a fit, heavily muscled young man an inch or two shorter than me. It was a close match but I passed on to the final, to be held before the training brigade the following weekend.

The championship was staged at the Green Jacket headquarters in Winchester. My opponent in the Light-heavyweight Division was a Rifle Brigade training corporal, roughly my height but with an unusually long reach. He went down just before the final bell.

I phoned home that night. My father was jubilant, my mother merely relieved it was all over. Kit was due to be called up in six months. For her it would be another three years before both sons had passed the last milestones in their long trek to safety at the end of National Service.

WE LINED UP NERVOUSLY outside Company Office. Now we would discover who among our platoon of twenty would be selected.

Alphabetically we were called into Company Office and handed an envelope. On the card inside the envelope there was simply the result: 'G-J' or 'Not G-J'. Of the twenty or so in the platoon, perhaps six or eight were recommended for the regiment if they passed WOSB. The rest would receive a card marked 'Not G-J' and, after WOSB and officer training, be assigned to county infantry regiments.

I think Adam Butler, my platoon officer, chose my result with care. My card was marked ambiguously, 'Not yet G-J'. He was well aware of things I had hardly thought about—that I would never be able to afford the mess bills or the dress uniform a Green Jacket officer had to pay for himself. It was still a blow.

WOSB came and I failed. The intelligence test left me baffled. Much of it seemed crossword-based. I had never done an anagram in my life.

A quite sympathetic colonel said I had done well on the practical and leadership tests but my intelligence test . . . he looked down at the papers on his desk and pulled a face. My intelligence tests, he began again, had recorded 'educationally subnormal', which he was happy to accept was unlikely to be the case. Was I playing the fool?

'No, sir,' I said, aghast.

'And your lecture on Plato's *Republic*.' He grimaced. 'Bad choice.'

There was nothing I could say. I suppose I had taken it for granted I'd passed. It was a far worse blow than not getting the Green Jacket recommendation, the reasons for which I think I understood.

The colonel looked at me. 'Come back in four months' time. In the meantime, do the *Times* crossword,' he advised. 'Put Plato aside until you get to Cambridge. Give your lecture on the Battle of Waterloo, Collecting Militaria, Dan Dare if you want. But "Beware the Greeks . . ."'

WITHIN TWO DAYS of returning to Bushfield I was given my posting. I was to be sent to the 1st Battalion, King's Royal Rifle Corps, in Germany and given two weeks' embarkation leave. My father was deeply disappointed by the WOSB result. He couldn't understand how I could have failed the intelligence test so badly. I gave him one of the questions in the test. It simply read: 'Question 14: Trocune-catkat.' Apparently the crossword devotee would have seen that immediately as an anagram for 'counter-attack'. I had looked at it in deep bafflement. No less my father. He was outraged. The Plato lecture, he conceded, was a poor move. But 'Trocune catkat? Stiffen the Prussian Guards! What does that tell anybody about the sort of man you are?' I was touched when he bought himself a book of crosswords.

'Not the end of the world,' was my mother's comforting reaction. 'Perhaps if you're not an officer they'll send you somewhere not so dangerous.' But I was deeply disappointed with myself.

THE MILITARY TRAIN from the Hook of Holland passed through Eindhoven and I could see the machine-gun bullet holes criss-crossing the corrugated iron engine shed. Ours, I wondered, or theirs?

Once in Germany the signs of bombing were visible in every town and city we passed through . . . Krefeld, Duisburg, Essen, Dortmund. There were frequent stops for no discernible purpose. At one I leaned out of the window to talk to two red-capped British military police. I wanted to know if they'd ever been to our destination, Sennelager. One of them had. 'Know it well,' he said. 'Small town, village almost, not exactly the bright lights but a few nice quiet *gasthauses* where you can get a drink and a meal. And some very pretty girls.'

I thanked him, feeling considerably cheered. Not immediately by the thought of the very pretty German girls. Marie was still very much on my mind. But I made a serious effort to tell myself it was over.

We continued our long slow journey, lightened by occasional visits to the bar in the end carriage. Slowly most of the units, Royal Signals, Service Corps, Catering Corps, Infantry and Armoured Corps units, were dropped off at unrecognisably named stations along the route. After several hours of travel, Ron Snelling and I left our equipment in the care of the rest of our draft and set off down the train for another visit to the bar. Once there we ordered a half-litre of the excellent German beer and bought a sort of frankfurter heating in a tin of hot water.

Ron Snelling and I speculated about what life in Sennelager would be like. I imagined a small German village, a bar on the corner. Music, dancing perhaps on Saturday nights. Learn German, get to know some of the locals, a friendly greeting from Gretchen or Traudi or whatever the name of the innkeeper's daughter was going to turn out to be.

The train had stopped in a town of some size and we ordered another beer to while away the time.

We finished our beer and started back, only a little unsteady on our feet. Ron reached the end of the bar carriage, opened the door into the next one and turned back to me, frowning. ''S funny thing,' he said, a deeply puzzled look on his face. 'Somebody's nicked our train.'

He opened the communicating door wider. No train.

I lifted my eyes to follow the line of the track. Our train was steaming round a bend about half a mile ahead.

Behind us the barman lifted both hands in an apologetic shrug but his crooked grin said he wasn't sorry not to have warned us we were being uncoupled. I just about restrained Ron. I didn't want assault on a German barman added to whatever other offence we had committed by missing the main train.

As we crossed the tracks it occurred to me that Ron and I were technically AWOL, absent without leave. This is a serious military offence. But I thought we'd be given Brownie points for initiative if with fewer than a dozen words of German, and without a single German mark in our pockets, we somehow made our way to our destination, which may have been five or 500 miles away for all we knew.

Our journey was a nightmare. Unaware that British occupation personnel were allowed to travel free on German trains and buses, I tried to negotiate our fare with station masters in the most inadequate of pidgin German. When they showed us on to trains without asking for money, I tried to press a written IOU on them. They thought I was out of my mind. Travelling on small branch lines, sometimes waiting an hour or two for a train but receiving a great deal of friendliness from Germans we met on the way, we arrived at Paderborn long after nightfall.

More friendliness from an amused station master and I was on the phone to 1st Battalion, King's Royal Rifle Corps, Dempsey Barracks, Sennelager. I asked the Regimental Police sergeant, in a fashion I didn't think too lordly, to send a car to pick us up. 'Yes, sir,' he said. I thanked him and put down the phone. I looked at Ron and we grinned triumphantly at each other.

Fifteen minutes later a green-painted battalion Volkswagen pulled into the station forecourt. The driver got out and opened the back door. We climbed into the back seat. I tried to ask him what the village (*dorf*, wasn't that the word?) of Sennelager was like.

'*Dorf?*' A long pause. His shoulders began to lift. He was chuckling.

We were driven through darkened countryside with increasing numbers of regimental signboards to different barracks. We were, I slowly realised, headed for no chintzy little German township. Sennelager was obviously the name of a huge ex-German Army barrack area. Bleak military buildings lined the road.

'Is this Sennelager?' Ron said, unbelieving.

'*Ja. Hier ist Sennelager*,' the driver said.

THE GATES OF DEMPSEY Barracks were opened by two members of the guard. Our car pulled up. A tall sergeant with a Regimental Police armband came clattering down the guardroom steps. He was lifting his arm in a salute when Ron and I, dishevelled, capless and beltless, clambered exhausted from the Volkswagen.

Sergeant Johnson's scream of rage was real. The tic above his left eye was real. The shuddering fury as he got the words out was more than real. 'Absent without leave,' he screamed. 'Impersonating an officer, improperly dressed, misappropriating battalion transport . . .'

I tried to speak but his incomprehensible scream silenced me. I heard, 'Under arrest. Before the colonel tomorrow morning . . .' I was doubling up the steps before I knew it. The heavy steel-barred doors of the guardroom jail crashed closed behind me.

AT 5.30 THE NEXT MORNING we were set to scrub floors. No floors were ever cleaner than this guardroom's even before we started, but when a Regimental Police corporal arrived at 6.30 he cursorily inspected my work, kicked my bucket of soapy water over and ordered me to start again. 'Both hands on the brush, lad—both knees on the floor!' Half an hour of that and knees, shoulders and back were telling me I'd never recover.

It was the beginning of five days' hard pounding, running, parading, polishing, scrubbing, digging, cleaning burnt soup cauldrons, from five in the morning to midnight. And it only stopped because the colonel accepted that there was no intention to go absent without leave. The five days were for abandoning valuable military equipment—to wit our belts and berets.

I WAS IN GERMANY not for four months but for twice that. I found the in-barracks routine tedious, with its emphasis on drill and equipment cleaning. I made serious efforts but must admit I was not a natural in-barracks soldier. My first five days 'confined to barracks', as the punishment was euphemistically called (and known as 'jankers' to everyone) was therefore not my last spell of this particular torture.

Life outside the barracks on manoeuvres suited me much better. We rode half-track armoured vehicles and learned to cooperate with our tank regiment, the 9th Lancers. The war of movement for which we were preparing meant that we were constantly, day and night, on the move. Later that summer we joined other national contingents in vast manoeuvres, 'schemes' we called them, with up to 100,000 NATO troops involved. We would roam the woods and hills of Westphalia, living rough, fighting to stay awake on guard, digging trenches, and learning the soldier's art of making himself comfortable whatever the conditions. It was a way of life I took to with ease.

There were times when the only roof we slept under for two or three weeks on end would be the roof of an occasional German barn. Most times we were filthy but always well-shaven and with newly cleaned boots. We would come across an army mobile shower unit from time to time, but often not for several weeks. There was no such thing as leave—I had just one weekend's leave in Germany in the whole eight months I was there. International tensions were still high. We didn't talk much about it but amid all the jokes, the lack of sleep, the aches and pains and the freezing conditions as the German winter approached, we were all well aware what we were preparing for. We were anticipating a sudden Russian attack (like the North Korean assault of the previous year) across the dividing line between East and West Germany.

Once in barracks it was a different story. One that, for me, very often ended in another spell on jankers.

Then one evening, shortly before the whole battalion was scheduled to depart on an Anglo-American-French scheme in southern Germany, I was just leaving our barrack block when the company sergeant-major stopped me. 'Rifleman.' He held out some sheets of paper. 'List of the new draft arriving Sennelager tomorrow night. Got a Rifleman Wheal, K. 22458791 here. I hope to God there's not two of you.'

I felt a surge of pleasure. 'My brother, sir.'

'You've got a brother, have you?' He shook his head. 'I only hope he's quicker on the parade ground than you are. Well, he volunteered to be in this hole. Why was that?'

'We've always looked out for each other.'

He grimaced. 'Be able to keep you out of trouble then, will he?'

'We can only hope, sir.'

I had of course known Kit was finishing his training at Bushfield but had lost track of exactly when.

The next night I was loading, under arc lights, our section half-track on the main barrack square. There were forty other half-tracks, a dozen Jeeps and a Bren gun carrier platoon all loading at the same time so it was not difficult to slip away now and again. I crossed to C company barrack block four or five times that evening. On the last visit the noise on the top training floor made me sure they'd arrived.

It was nearly six months since I'd seen Kit. I couldn't quite believe my eyes. I'd expected a raw-looking young recruit. Far from it. His kit was already laid out on his bed in the regulation manner, ready for inspection later. He looked totally at home, for someone who was straight out of basic training. He had grown in six months and we were now almost the same size.

He had taken to heart my descriptions of life in the Green Jackets. He had, for instance, remembered that on your first day at Bushfield you were handed two pairs of oiled boots and expected to make them gleam like stars in the blackest night. To relieve the first week's pressure he had therefore bought two pairs of regulation ammunition boots at an army surplus shop. He and my father had then 'hot-spooned' them to draw out the oils in the leather and polished them to a glittering finish.

It was pure pleasure to see him. For me this was nothing but good fortune. Every morning he would wake and listen for the clack-clack of my patented Wilkinson Sword razor, our B company bathroom windows being opposite his C company barrack room. If it was before 5.30 he would know I had collected another spell of 'confined to barracks' the day before and come racing over to my block.

Help was a serious necessity. The jankers principle was that you were run off your feet. Every minute of the day was filled with near-impossible orders. Nobody could live through five days of jankers without friends dressing you, getting food for you, waking you as you catnapped to recover lost sleep.

WE WERE DISPATCHED in the autumn to southern Germany, to join a scheme on the borders of the French and the American zones. The opening move was to rendezvous with a French brigade who would take our company of

150 men under command to do a night retreat across a river. The name of the river now escapes me. The village where the French and British units were to meet was small and picturesque. Gabled roofs were adorned with storks' nests. We waited for the French unit to arrive.

Two hours later the French Army drifted down the village street in small groups, wrapped in rain capes, hungry, miserable and lost. I spoke to some of the conscripts and they complained bitterly about their cigarette ration having arrived damp and their wine ration having turned up late. A cigarette ration! A wine ration! They were the saddest sacks I had ever seen in uniform. Later I spoke to a French intelligence officer. He said the morale of the French forces in Germany was dangerously low. Politics at home, he saw as the reason. A constant Communist Party propaganda barrage against NATO. Was it the same in the British Army?

This was not the view of most of the National Servicemen I served with. Out on manoeuvres, being helped by a German householder as you dug a slit trench in the middle of his lawn, or sitting in a farm kitchen chatting with a *hausfrau* as she cooked, and shared, your rations, the sense of raw fear of a Russian advance across the dividing line between East and West, went a long way towards providing us with our raison d'être.

The British Army of the Rhine operated under a system of alerts. During my time in the 11th Armoured Division we were called out several times, most on Amber but one full Red Alert. Listening posts had detected a huge movement of Soviet armour up to the line about 100 miles from our position. Perhaps three hours away at an armoured rate of advance. After a few hours the Soviet a+rmour had slowly pulled back. These were not games. The danger of an incident unwanted by either side, or of a planned attack across the line, was real.

I RETURNED TO ENGLAND in the winter to retake the WOSB. This time my father briefed me on crosswords and my ten-minute lecture covered the militarily unimpeachable subject of this year's NATO manoeuvre in Germany. I don't know if the colonel remembered me, but he smiled as he read the report on my lecture. 'Good stuff,' he said. An hour later I learned that I had passed.

EATON HALL OFFICER CADET SCHOOL was no place to be in winter. The hall itself was a lowering Victorian Gothic mass, leased from the Duke of Westminster. Most cadets lived in wooden barrack huts that nestled at the hall's base like a medieval village round a cathedral. The regime was non-stop drill, military knowledge and manoeuvres. On the drill square I achieved the all-time Eaton Hall record of being charged fourteen times by a Welsh Guards sergeant-major who couldn't believe that my slow right and left turns were anything but dumb insolence. The fourteenth charge saw me escorted to the Guardroom cells where I spent the night contemplating my future.

I was, I think, saved by the fact that I had come top in three of the four military knowledge tests. The morning of my appearance on fourteen separate charges I was faced by the colonel commanding, a formidable red-haired Guards officer named Colonel Basil Eugster. Had he (and I) possessed the ability to look into the future he would have known that his niece Diana Eugster would sometime become my wife and the mother of my twin daughters, Caroline and Elizabeth-Anne. He simply told me to try harder on the drill square in future.

I APPLIED FOR THE Parachute Regiment. It was a regiment with the same prestige as the most elite formations in the British Army but there was no class discrimination there. Officers were plumbers' sons as often as they were Peers of the Realm.

I had in fact been encouraged to apply by my company commander at Eaton Hall Officer Cadet School, himself in the Parachute Regiment. With his favourable report I was accepted. He had called me into his office to tell me this but, a grim-faced man at the best of times, remained as grim-faced as ever. A minimum period of remaining service was required for transfer to the Parachute Regiment and, with my two-month early release for university, I lacked the necessary time. I would therefore be assigned to an infantry regiment somewhere in the world, do my parachute training before release and be posted to a reserve parachute battalion if I passed.

The day our postings were handed out, Captain Fletcher came forward on the drill square and began reading out the postings. My surname, as so often, took me to the bottom of the list. I had plenty of time to speculate about where I might be sent.

The company commander finally came to my name: Second Lieutenant Donald Wheal . . . to the 1st Battalion, The Loyal Regiment—currently stationed in Trieste. I had been assigned what some thought of as one of the very best of postings, a spectacularly beautiful, Italian-speaking port on the sun-drenched coast of the Adriatic.

ELEVEN

Trieste as a city played a unique and largely unknown part in the Cold War. Tucked high in the corner of the Adriatic, bordering Yugoslavia, it was the object of territorial claims by both Tito and the new Italian Republic. In the middle, in the port itself and in the mountains around, sat three battalions of British infantry and a regiment of American troops. We had no supporting tanks, no heavy artillery. We would have been swept into the sea by a Soviet advance from Austria or Hungary, a fact acknowledged by the presence of a secret underground lorry park, the trucks kept filled with petrol and all engines tested twice a week. In other words we were ready for anything—but only as long as it was a moonlight flit.

The Italian claim to Trieste was stated by the Sunday demonstrations (sometimes turning to fairly minor riots) in the Piazza Unità, the main square. The Yugoslav demands on what was then called the Free Territory of Trieste were even less subtly pursued by guerrilla attacks on ammunition dumps and aggressive patrolling of the border. This unique Cold War situation was presided over by a British general and it was therefore the British who were considered, by Italians and Yugoslavs alike, the villains of the piece. In Trieste itself if, during the more violent incidents in the Piazza Unità, a British unit was to be relieved by an American company, there would be missiles and catcalls for us as we left and corresponding cheers for the arriving Americans.

But mostly, as spring brought a Mediterranean warmth, Trieste justified its reputation as one of the more agreeable postings. Demonstrations in the Piazza Unità seldom resulted in people being hurt, although there was some shooting and a number of deaths before the situation was finally resolved.

In the heights behind Trieste it was different. Yugoslav soldiers would risk their lives to come down the British side of the mountain and desert to the West. The Loyals, along with the two other regiments, regularly patrolled this rough, rocky mountain region.

The first patrol I was to lead along the mountain border was to have, as was usual practice, a local guide, an Italian policeman who knew the mountains.

He was nervous, very nervous, of a kidnap attempt. There had been two by the Yugoslavs, he told me, just a week earlier.

It was not a border along which you could string barbed wire. There was some soft earth where mines could be planted but it was mostly bare, inhospitable, sun-drenched yellow rock. Long before we reached the high point we were slick with sweat.

The Italian policeman asked me if he could stop on one side of a massive outcrop of rock while the patrol continued on climbing round the mountain. He would wait next to one of the Demarcation Boards saying on one side in English and Serbo-Croat: *Warning. You are now entering the British Zone*, and on the other side: *Warning. You are now entering the Yugoslav Zone.*

I was green. I knew the kidnap attempts were real. The Yugoslavs would claim the Italian policeman had infringed the border and try to barter him for three or four of their own deserters. I looked at the great rock rising sixty feet. The policeman was probably in his fifties. Old, to my eyes. I agreed.

My patrol consisted of twenty-five armed men. We set off to follow the border, which the guide had told me was a straightforward path round the massive outcrop. Within five minutes I discovered he had said nothing about the point at which the path appeared to split into three separate directions. I took the route closest to the rock, checking my compass.

We scrambled across scattered rocks, lost and refound the path, slid down screes and climbed slopes for about twenty minutes. The sun reflected white off the rocks. The temperature was in the nineties. I put out sentries while the rest of the patrol broke for a smoke, weapons handy, in the shade.

I was still fairly sure we were in more or less the right position, although I could feel alarm mounting in my chest. I knew that if we strayed across the Demarcation Line, we would have to submit to being taken prisoner or fight our way back to our zone. Either course could lead to casualties and an international incident at the very least.

'Don't look much like the country walk our Eyetalian promised us, sir,' the patrol corporal said.

'I'm thinking the same thing,' I said. 'Main thing now is that we stay on the right side of the line. I'm going to check the board.'

I climbed to the top of a mass of rock and tried to see where we were to meet up with the guide. No sign of him. No sign of the end of the outcrop either, although there was a Demarcation Board about half a mile ahead; fortunately we were well within the British Zone.

When I got back I called on the corporal to get the patrol moving, and with the usual groans they adjusted their ammunition belts and started off down the broken path, which I hoped would curve round the rock back to the point where we were to meet the guide.

Maintaining direction in such broken terrain is difficult. I tried to keep the big board in my sights. I seemed to lose and re-find it constantly until, after five minutes or so, during which time it had totally disappeared, we rounded a rock and there it was, 150 yards in front of me. It read *Warning. You are now entering the British Zone*!

It meant we were well inside Yugoslav territory. Not only was there the possibility of being shot at from the heights around us, but the existence of mines on this track was also a real possibility.

We got off the earth path and onto the hard rock of the steep mountain-side where mines were unlikely to be planted. Slipping, sliding, feeling the strain on the ankles every step of the way, I cursed the guide. And myself. It was the longest 150 yards any of us had ever walked.

The boys in the patrol reacted well to what was obviously my error. Pouring with sweat, we reached the last outcrop and had begun to round it when I stopped dead.

Six Yugoslav soldiers were sitting in the shade of an overhanging rock drinking from their water bottles, smoking cigarettes. I could see the shock on their faces. We were a patrol twenty-five strong, carrying rifles and Sten guns at the ready. I looked at the Yugoslav I took to be the sergeant in charge, the only man standing. He was now looking me in the eyes. We were only ten yards apart. I carried a loaded Sten gun. His rifle, like most of his men's weapons, was leaning against the rock. He knew he could never have got to it in time.

I lifted my hand to him and he nodded with infinite slowness. One of his men moved towards the stacked weapons. The sergeant said something and the man stayed half kneeling, ready to jump towards the rifles. The sergeant nodded again to me and I signalled for the patrol to pass, my corporal and myself walking slowly backwards, watching the Yugoslavs for any move-ment towards their rifles. Within a few minutes we had crossed under the Demarcation Board. This time the Yugoslav sergeant lifted *his* hand, as relieved as I was.

There was no Italian policeman waiting on the other side.

When we got back to barracks, I reported that we had 'lost contact' with our Italian police guide for several minutes and had observed a Yugoslav patrol at rest. I was well aware I had risked the lives of twenty-four of my own men by my willingness to accommodate the Italian policeman.

These were heavy responsibilities, and hard lessons, for a twenty-year-old.

FOR SOME OF THE HOTTEST DAYS of summer we were camped on a rocky plateau high up above Trieste. Just before sunset one evening, after a day of exercises around the mountain villages, I had carried out all the necessary junior officer's duties—checked that a meal was being prepared for the platoon, checked their rifles, checked the condition of their feet, checked that any who had suffered bad cuts or falls during the day reported to the medical tent—and I was looking forward to a cold beer and a shower, when a fellow subaltern said there was someone to see me at the guard tent of the encampment. A woman.

We were several miles up above Trieste. The roads were narrow dust tracks with screes and drops on either side. 'You serious? What sort of woman?'

My friend had only received the message from the guard tent. He hadn't seen her.

'Is she alone?'

'Apparently.'

I couldn't imagine my former Italian girlfriend, Marghareta, elegant and impeccably dressed, tottering her way alone up through these dust-covered Slovenian-speaking mountain villages. But I couldn't guess what other woman would have made it up here either.

As I approached I could hear a woman's voice speaking in English. As I reached the entrance she turned from the guard sergeant she was talking to. It was Marie.

Of course. Who else would have been able to sweet-talk her way up here to a militarised zone forbidden to civilians? She jumped up. That smile. Those hooded eyes. She was tanned and certainly not dressed for these rough hills, in a white shirt, blue summer skirt and sandals. The contrast between Marie, a visitor from my other world, and the roughness of army life took my breath away. I stared at her, for the moment stunned, only slowly breaking into a smile.

'A young lady to see you, sir,' the Regimental Police sergeant was saying. *You lucky devil* was threaded rather obviously through his words. 'If the young lady was calling on other than an officer, sir, I would have had the pleasure of putting her under arrest.'

I barely heard him.

SHE WAS THINKING of going to live in America. I was sure that meant she was going to get married. Had she come to Trieste to tell me that? It was nearly two years since we had seen each other, well over a year since we had ceased writing. Yet she was her normal, extraordinary self.

I got changed out of my uniform and we went down to Trieste. Darkness fell as we had dinner at a trattoria overlooking the Adriatic. She asked me what I had been doing in my spare time. Perhaps I told her of my brief fling with Marghareta, whose target was an officer who would marry her and take her back to England, I don't remember. What else was I to tell her? There was no spare time, or very little; there was no wider experience than what we did every day. So we talked mostly about Vienna.

We left the restaurant late. Trieste looked spectacular. We walked, right through the few hours of darkness, the length and breadth of the old city, through its cool narrow alleys and across its grand open squares, past groups of uniformed Triestino policemen in cafés singing opera. We walked with our arms round each other until dawn broke over Hungary and Austria and the Yugoslav mountains.

At 4.30 we sat on a step near the train station. The sun was already warm. I wanted to talk about her plans to live in America or about really why she had come to Trieste but I found I couldn't. I had convinced myself that she had come to tell me that she was going to America to get married. But why would she come to tell me after two years apart?

We drank one final coffee in the station while her train was huffing and spitting steam. We stood silently facing each other, glancing up with every sip, smiling at each other a brief smile. Whistles and shouts surrounded us. The guard waved his green flag and Marie climbed aboard. I caught sight of her once or twice as she threaded her way to her seat. Should I have said something? Had she wanted me to say anything?

Moments later the train was pulling away. I stood on the platform, still speechless, not even waving her goodbye.

I believe now that she came on a spur-of-the-moment decision, not to say anything, not to have anything said by me—but simply for the trip. But army life is harsh and romance is notably lacking. I think I needed

Marie's presence in Trieste to mean more than just a visit from Vienna.

I've often thought of that night. It has come to take time and space in my memory, and with it a distant, fadeless charm. A fantasy that happened.

MY NATIONAL SERVICE and parachute training completed, I was demobilised from Preston and travelled down to London to spend two days with my parents at White City.

My father kept nodding and smiling. My mother struggled to hold back the tears of relief that she had recovered at least one of her sons. Kit, of course, was still in Sennelager. He had just been selected for promotion to weapon-training full corporal. It's difficult to make it clear how significant, and indeed rare, that was in the Green Jackets.

IT WAS A MIST-LADEN October late afternoon when I reached Pembroke College. A carbon copy of the afternoon I had first arrived at the porters' lodge two years ago. This time I was an undergraduate.

I stood on the pavement opposite and watched young men unloading ancient trunks from taxis. Most of them had their names painted on the sides: 2nd/Lt. John Smith, 4th Hussars . . . 2nd/Lt. John Smythe, Royal Marines. I thanked my lucky stars that I had decided to do my National Service before coming up. I couldn't guess what it would be like for an eighteen-year-old, straight from grammar school, among the overwhelming majority of the college, all of whom were two to three years older, and bound together by military service.

I didn't go into the college immediately. I'm not sure why. It was probably the knowledge that I was about to start a new life, one that would continue what the army had started, one that would take me away from all I had previously known.

I walked on a few minutes. I had just one bag, the pigskin Gladstone of earlier days. There were lights in the shops along King's Parade. The pale stone pinnacles of King Henry's great chapel rose sharp against the receding grey background of evening. One simple question—would I have friends?—dominated my mind. I remember reminding myself that I had thought the same at Bushfield, in Germany, at Eaton Hall and in Trieste, and on each occasion it had worked out well. I thought of people I had met in the Green Jackets. My platoon commander Adam Butler, I imagined, would be beginning his second year here. I thought of Richard Rougier who had offered to write to the Dean to get us adjoining sets of rooms. But it was all a long time ago. I remember, as I passed the corner of Pembroke Street, promising myself that whatever happened I would not lose contact with my mother and father, with Kit, and with everything I thought of as World's End.

The porter had told me where to find my room and I passed through the screens to the lighted windows of Ivy Court. New Court had been built 250 years later in a Victorian classical style. I turned into it and saw my staircase ahead. Painted white on a glossy black square beside the double doorway was a list of names. I saw my own—D. J. Wheal—and stood looking at it with a tingle creeping up my spine. Somehow, with no communication between the college and myself for two years, it had all come to pass this evening in October 1952.

THE WORLD'S END never really left me. Late at night in Old Court I often summoned up the image of my madcap grandmother Eliza, dancing, large hat askew, past the medieval Old Library and through the screens into Ivy Court, trailing as she disappeared the musky odour of a twist of snuff and the last strains of '*Mademoiselle from Armenteers parlay-voo*'.

I never lost the sense of privilege I had from growing up in the World's End. Most of all I retained and still retain a strong sense of my good fortune in having had the parents I did. My brother Kit feels the same. He returned to England a man given self-confidence and experience by the promotions and responsibilities the Green Jackets had heaped on him. The World's End and the army set him on his way to the chairmanship of Hallmark Cards and the several other companies he led in Britain and Europe.

There would be tragedies to come: for the whole family, the early death of my father; for me, the break-up of my first marriage, and the death of my French second wife. But there were triumphs too, such as the birth of my daughters and the long, astonishingly contented widowhood of my mother.

But for the moment, as that first Cambridge summer arrived, the present was a punt on the Cam, a book, a girl for company (if you were lucky), a trailing bottle of white Mâcon cooling on a string, a wind-up gramophone playing Sidney Bechet or Humphrey Lyttelton, the sun-warmed brick of Queens' College above the shadows of Isaac Newton's Mathematical Bridge . . . And that sense that the world did, after all, belong to me.

For the moment.

DONALD JAMES WHEAL

Born: London, August 22, 1931
Published work: fiction, nonfiction, scripts
Interests: Victorian London, politics

RD: In 1944 you moved with your family to White City. Did you ever feel at home there?

DJW: No, I didn't. Until I was twelve, I grew up in a close community in World's End, Chelsea, but then the area was badly bombed during the war. Suddenly we were living in a rather bleak suburb, where there were no shops and virtually no pubs. It was the difference between being somewhere where generations of families knew one another and looked out for one another, and living in an area typical of the kind of planning problems that continued into the Sixties and Seventies with high-rises.

RD: But you did have your own bedroom, and the house had a bathroom?

DJW: Yes, and I don't want to criticise White City too much, because there were some very good things about it. I can still remember, deep inside, exactly how I felt walking into that bathroom for the first time, saying to my brother, 'What do you think of this?'

RD: What prompted you to write your autobiography?

DJW: I started my writing career in television and the book actually began as an idea for a television documentary about the wartime bombing of London. It proved too costly to produce, so the idea became a book. After *World's End* was published, I had a mass of letters from people who'd lived there at that time. I was amazed.

RD: Did you enjoy the experience more or less than writing fiction?

DJW: More. I particularly enjoyed the fact that through the two books I came to appreciate the part my father had played in my life. My mother had always been the significant figure. She'd left school at thirteen but she was an impressive personality.

RD: Your parents seem to have been very happy together.

DJW: They certainly were. There were never any fights or rows at home. They each had very clear roles and there was a total understanding between them.

RD: You write very sensitively about your feelings for your first girlfriend, Marie. Would you call yourself a romantic?

DJW: I'm a romantic as far as people in general are concerned. I prefer to like rather than dislike, to trust rather than distrust.

RD: You met Marie's father, the author and playwright Bill Naughton, of *Alfie* fame, through your friendship with her brother Larry. Did the time you spent with the Naughton family spur you on at school?

DJW: Bill Naughton ran a very literary household and it was my friendship with his family that gave me a much broader view. I met Larry at the Sloane School in Chelsea, which was an ordinary postwar grammar school, but a great deal was expected of us. The masters were vying for our time in their subjects, eager to see us succeed. It was disciplined and hard but we understood what they were trying to do for us.

RD: You also write about having an enlightened headmaster at that time.

DJW: Yes, Guy Boas. He was a quality headmaster, and very good at getting a lot of boys involved in acting. He produced some exceptional plays. I didn't realise, till some years later, that he was quite a famous chap. I was climbing the stairs at the Garrick Club—much frequented by theatrical types—when I happened to look up and see his framed portrait hanging, among a number of famous actors, on the wall.

RD: In the book, you describe lots of escapades in France. Do you consider yourself to be a Francophile?

DJW: Well, my second wife was French and in the eighties we lived in the Lot for about five years, so I consider myself a very well-qualified Francophile. I admire many things about the French, such as their food and wine, but I don't admire their politics.

RD: Was it tough to be a working-class scholar at Cambridge?

DJW: Not really, because I'd had the enormous advantage of two years' service in the army, and we all enjoyed a shared vocabulary. Of course I didn't have the family money that many of my Cambridge friends had, but I had a grant, which actually gave me just as much to live on as anyone else.

RD: What did you do when you left university?

DJW: I'd started to write a novel in my last year, but when I graduated I had to get a job and find a place to live. I had a wife and two small daughters to support, so I went to teach in a prep school, which was quite funny because of course I'd never been near a prep school before. Then I taught in a secondary modern for a couple of years and worked at the *Daily Telegraph* library in the evenings.

RD: What are you writing at the moment?

DJW: I'm currently writing a book on Paris and the 2005 riots and recently visited the area where they began, in the enormous and oppressive suburban tower blocks.

RD: Do you have plans to write another volume of autobiography?

DJW: It would be tricky. Many of the people I would want to refer to are still alive. My daughters are keen that I should, though. They are both writers, and they've said that if I don't do another book, they'll write one from their own perspective!

THUNDER BAY

WILLIAM KENT KRUEGER

Within the Native American community of the Ojibwe, Henry Meloux is a medicine man who has spent his life advising others on the path to spiritual contentment.

Now, though, he is seriously ill and his own heart is in need of healing. He confides in his old friend Cork O'Connor that he has one burning wish to fulfil before the end of his days: to find the son he fathered many years ago and has never yet met.

PART 1
Manitou Island

One

The promise, as I remember it, happened this way:

A warm August morning, early. Wally Schanno's already waiting at the landing. His truck's parked in the lot; his boat's in the water. He's drinking coffee from a red Thermos big as a fireplug. Iron Lake is glass. East, it mirrors the peach-coloured dawn. The dock's old, weathered.

The boards sag under my weight, groan a little.

'Coffee?' Schanno offers.

I shake my head, toss my gear into his boat. 'Let's fish.'

We're far north of Aurora, Minnesota. Among the tall pines on the shoreline, an occasional light glimmers from one of the cabins hidden there. Schanno motors slowly towards a spot off a rocky point where the bottom falls away quickly. Cuts the engine.

August isn't the best time to fish. For one thing, the bugs are awful. Also, the water near the surface is often too warm. The big fish—walleye and bass—dive deep, seeking cooler currents. But I've already guessed that fishing isn't what's on Schanno's mind.

The afternoon before, he'd come to Sam's Place, the burger joint I own on Iron Lake. His wife, Arletta, had died a few months before. A victim of Alzheimer's, she'd succumbed to a massive stroke. She'd been a fine woman, a teacher. Both my daughters, Jenny and Anne, had passed through her third-grade classroom years before. Loved her. Everybody did. Schanno's children had moved far away, to Bethesda, Maryland, and Seattle, Washington. Arletta's death left Wally alone in the house he'd shared with her for over forty years. He'd begun to hang around Johnny's

Pinewood Broiler for hours, drinking coffee, talking with the regulars. He was well into his sixties, a big man with a strong build, hands like an orangutan. A couple of years earlier, because of Arletta's illness, he'd retired as sheriff of Tamarack County, which was a job I'd held twice myself. Some men, idle time suits them. Others, it's a death sentence. Wally Schanno looked like a man condemned.

When he suggested we go fishing in the morning, I'd said sure.

Now we're alone on the lake—me, Schanno and a couple of loons fifty yards to our right diving for breakfast. Half an hour, and we haven't said a word. The only sounds are the sizzle of line as we cast and the plop of the lures hitting water.

'Heard you got yourself a PI licence,' Schanno says finally.

I wind my reel smoothly, jerking the rod back occasionally to make the lure dart in the water like a little fish. 'Yep,' I reply.

'Not happy running Sam's Place?'

'I like it fine. But I'm closed all winter. Need something to keep me occupied and out of mischief.'

'What's Jo think?' Talking about my wife.

'So long as I don't put on a badge again, she's happy.'

Schanno says, 'I feel like I'm dying, Cork.'

'Are you sick?'

'No, no.' He's quick to wave off my concern. 'I'm bored. Bored to death. I'm too young for a rocking chair.'

'They're always hiring security at the casino.'

Shakes his head. 'Sit-on-your-ass kind of job. Not for me.'

'What exactly are you asking, Wally?'

'Just that if something, you know, comes your way that you need help with, well, maybe you'll think about giving me a call.'

'You don't have a licence.'

'I could get one. Or just make me a consultant. Hell, I'll do it for free.'

The sun's shooting fire at us across the water. Another boat has appeared half a mile south. The loons take off, flapping north.

'Tell you what, Wally. Anything comes my way I think you could help me with, I promise I'll let you know.'

He looks satisfied. In fact, he looks happy.

Another boat appears. 'The lake's getting crowded,' I say. 'How 'bout we call it and have some breakfast at the Broiler.'

'On me,' Schanno offers, beaming.

Nights when I cannot sleep and the demons of my past come to torment me, the promise I made to Wally Schanno that fine August morning is always among them.

SAM'S PLACE is an old prefab hut on the shore of Iron Lake just north of Aurora. It's divided by an interior wall. The back has a small living area. The front is set up for preparing food and serving it through a couple of windows to customers outside. I've got a griddle for burgers and hot dogs and such, a hot-oil well for deep fry, a shake machine, a carbonated-drink dispenser, a large freezer. Pretty simple fare. In season, I do a fine business.

It's called Sam's Place after the man who made it what it is—Sam Winter Moon. When my father died, Sam gave me a hand in a lot of unselfish ways. I grew up working summers at Sam's Place, advised and gently guided by Sam as I stumbled my way into manhood. When Sam died, he passed the place to me.

I've been sheriff of Tamarack County twice. The first time was for seven years, at the end of which the constituency removed me in a recall election that resulted both from my own inadequacies and from things beyond my control. The second time it was for thirteen weeks, and I stepped down of my own accord. People who don't know me well wonder that I'd give up my badge for an apron. If they asked me, which they don't, I would tell them that when a man stumbles onto happiness, he'd be a fool to pass it by. It's as simple as that. Sam's Place makes me happy.

In season, from early May, when tourists begin to flock north, until the end of October, when the fall colour is gone, I arrive for work at 10 a.m. I spend an hour getting ready for business. Turn on the griddle, heat the fry oil, get the ice-milk machine churning, put cash in the register drawer. A few minutes before eleven, help arrives. In summer, it's one of my daughters, either Jenny or Anne.

That morning after I fished with Schanno, as I was getting ready to slide open the serving windows, I saw Anne jogging up the road to Sam's Place. She was sixteen, very Irish with her wild red hair. She was an athlete hoping for a scholarship to Notre Dame.

'Where's Jenny?' I asked when she came in. 'She's on the schedule this morning.'

'She had kind of a hard night.' She reached into the closet for a serving apron. 'We traded shifts. She's coming in this afternoon.'

The night before, Jenny had been out on a date with her boyfriend, Sean. I'd heard her come in. Sean had finished his first year at Macalester, a small, elite college in St Paul, and was home for the summer, working in his father's drugstore. Jenny had graduated from high school in June. Most of the past year, their relationship had been long distance. Sean was a bright kid. Like Jenny, he wanted to be a writer. They'd been out a lot together that summer.

'A hard night?' I pressed her. 'Something happen between her and Sean?'

She concentrated on tying her apron. 'What do I know?'

'You're answering a question with a question. What's going on, Annie?'

She gave me the look of a runner caught in a squeeze between third base and home.

'Is it bad?' I asked.

'Talk to Mom.'

'Does *she* know?'

'You know Mom and Jenny. They talk about everything.'

She turned away and watched a car raising dust on the road to the hut. 'We have customers,' she said, sounding relieved.

Later, when the lunch rush was over, I slipped away to call my wife, Jo. It was Saturday, so she was home. When she answered, I could tell by the shuffle of papers on her end that she was working in her office. She's an attorney. 'How's it going?' I asked.

'Quiet. Getting lots done.'

I could see her, black reading glasses perched on her nose, ice-blonde hair, her blue eyes sharp and focused. On weekends, she usually works at home, overseeing the rights of her clients. She often represents the Iron Lake Ojibwe.

'What's Stevie up to?' I said, asking about our young son.

'Playing with Dumbarton in the back yard.'

Dumbarton was a big sheepdog that belonged to a couple on our block. Sometimes he'd wander down to our yard, much to Stevie's delight. At our house, the only pet was a turtle named Clyde.

'Jo, is Jenny there?'

'Upstairs getting ready for work,' she said.

'Is there something I should know about Sean and her?'

'What makes you think that?'

There it was again. I was being answered with a question.

'Just tell me, Jo.' I hesitated before asking about the concern that came most readily to mind. 'She's not pregnant, is she?'

Jo laughed. 'Heavens no. Look, we'll talk this evening. But promise me you won't say anything to Jenny.'

'All right. I'll talk to you first.'

I put the phone down as Anne stepped into the back of Sam's Place. 'Dad. George LeDuc is outside. He says it's important.'

George was waiting in the parking lot. A big grey bear of a man, seventy years old, he was the Iron Lake Ojibwe tribal chairman. He was wearing a short-sleeved white shirt with a bootlace tie, jeans, boots.

'*Boozhoo,* George,' I greeted him. 'What's up?'

In the Ojibwe fashion, his face betrayed nothing, though the news he brought was troubling. 'It's Henry, Cork. He's dying.'

HENRY MELOUX was the oldest man I knew. He'd had white hair ever since I could remember, which was well over four decades. His face was heavily lined. His eyes were brown and soft and deep, and you couldn't look into them without feeling Henry saw all the way down to some dark room in your soul where you kept your worst secrets locked away. Henry was a Mide, one of the Midewiwin, a member of the Grand Medicine Society. He'd spent his life following the path of Ojibwe healing.

When Sam Winter Moon died, Meloux filled the void in my life left by Sam's passing. I'm part Anishinaabe—what most people know as Ojibwe—on my mother's side. Not only had Meloux's good advice guided me during a lot of confusing times, but also, on several occasions, his intervention had actually saved my life.

Now he was dying.

And the Iron Lake Reservation had gathered to keep vigil.

LeDuc and I made our way through the lobby of the Aurora Community Hospital, greeting everyone we knew as we went. On the way there, George had explained what happened.

LeDuc owned a general store in Allouette, the larger of the two communities on the reservation. That morning Henry had walked into the store to buy groceries. Meloux lived on Crow Point, an isolated finger of land on Iron Lake far north on the reservation. There was no road to his cabin, and no matter the season, he hiked to town, a good five miles. LeDuc and Meloux passed some time talking; then the old man paid, put his things in a knapsack, and went outside. A few minutes later, LeDuc heard a commotion in the street. He rushed out to find Meloux collapsed on the pavement and people crowding round. LeDuc called 911, and the paramedics took Meloux to the hospital. The old man had been conscious when he arrived, weak, barely able to speak, but he'd asked for me.

Meloux was now in intensive care. They weren't going to let me see him. Relatives only. But Ernie Champoux, Meloux's great-nephew, put up a stink, and the doctor in charge, a young resident named Wrigley, finally relented.

'Do you know what's wrong?' I asked.

'His heart,' Wrigley said. 'I suspect an occlusion, but we need to run tests to be sure.'

Meloux lay on the bed, tubes and wires running from him every which way. I'd never seen him looking so frail, so vulnerable.

His brown eyes tracked me as I came to the bedside.

'Corcoran O'Connor,' he whispered. 'I knew you would come.'

I pulled up a chair and sat beside him. 'I'm sorry, Henry.'

'My heart.' He shook his head faintly. 'My heart is in pain.'

'The doctor suspects a blockage.'

Again he shook his head. 'It is sadness, Corcoran O'Connor.'

'What sadness, Henry?'

'I will tell you, but you must promise to help me.'

'I'll do what I can, Henry. What's the sadness?'

Meloux hesitated a moment, gathering strength. 'My son.'

Son? In the forty-something years I'd known him, I'd never heard Meloux speak of a son. As far as I knew, no one had.

'You have a son? Where?'

'I do not know. Help me find him, Corcoran O'Connor.'

'What's his name, Henry?'

Meloux stared up at me. He looked lost.

'You don't know his name?' I didn't hide my surprise. 'Do you know anything about him?'

'His mother's name. Maria Lima.'

'How long ago, Henry?'

He closed his eyes and thought a moment. 'A lifetime.'

'Thirty years? Forty? Fifty?'

'Seventy-three winters.'

Seventy-three years. My God.

'It's a big world, Henry. Can you tell me where to begin?'

'Canada,' he whispered. 'Ontario.'

I could tell our conversation, spare though it was, was draining him. I had three pieces of information. A mother's name. An approximate year. And a place to start looking.

'Have you ever seen your son, Henry?'

'In visions,' Meloux replied. 'I have only seen his spirit, not his face.' A faint smile touched his lips. 'He will look like his father.'

'He'll look like his mother, too, Henry. It would be nice to know what she looked like.'

He motioned me nearer. 'A box under my bed. A gold watch.'

'All right.'

'And Walleye. He will be alone and hungry.'

'I'll take care of Walleye, Henry.'

Meloux seemed comforted. '*Migwech*,' he said. Thank you.

Outside the room, LeDuc was waiting.

'What did he want, Cork?'

'He's worried about Walleye,' I said. 'He wanted me to take care of the dog.' The rest had been told in confidence, and I couldn't repeat it. Nor could I say what I really thought—that what Meloux was asking was nothing short of a miracle.

GEORGE LEDUC dropped me back at Sam's Place. Jenny was there, looking pale, but she seemed to be doing fine. I pulled her aside for a moment and asked how she was feeling.

'OK now.' She offered me a brief smile.

I filled the girls in on Meloux, what I could tell them anyway, and asked if they'd hold down the fort while I took care of what the old man needed. Then I hopped in the Bronco and headed home.

My house is on Gooseberry Lane, a quiet street of old homes. I grew up on Gooseberry Lane, a child in the house where I've raised my own children. Until his death—the result of a gun battle in the line of duty—my father was sheriff of Tamarack County. He'd come from Chicago, married my mother, who was half Ojibwe, half Irish. Her mother, Grandma Dilsey, was a true-blood Iron Lake Ojibwe, though she preferred to call herself

Anishinaabe—or Shinnob—as do many on the rez. That makes me one quarter Ojibwe.

Until I was elected sheriff, my heritage was never much of an issue. After I put on the badge, whenever conflicts arose between the two cultures, red and white, I found that I was never Ojibwe enough for the Ojibwe or white enough for the whites. That wasn't the reason I resigned my office. I turned in my badge when it became clear to me that my responsibility as a lawman was often at odds with my duty as a husband and father.

My son was playing by himself in the front yard. Stevie was eight, then, small for his age. With his straight black hair and hard almond eyes, he was, of all my children, the one who showed most clearly his Anishinaabe heritage. He'd recently discovered golf, and that afternoon he stood in the shade of our big elm, a driver in his hand, swinging at a ball. When he saw me pull into the driveway, he dropped the club and came running.

'What are you doing home, Dad?' He looked hopeful. He was the youngest kid on the block, and with Jenny and Anne often working at Sam's Place, I knew he was sometimes lonely.

I ruffled his hair. 'Work to do, buddy. Mom's inside?'

'In her office.'

I went in the house. It was cool inside and quiet. I walked to the kitchen, ran some tap water into a glass, and took a long drink.

'Stevie?' Jo called from her office.

'No. Me.'

A moment later, she came in wearing her reading glasses, blue eyes big behind the lenses. She's a beautiful woman, Jo. A few years younger than me, but looks even more. One of the smartest women I've ever known. 'What are you doing home?' she asked.

'Meloux's in the hospital.'

'Henry? Why?'

'He collapsed this morning in Allouette. The doctor thinks it's his heart. Meloux thinks so, too, but in a different way.'

'What way?'

'He has a son, Jo.'

Surprise showed in her eyes. 'He's never said a word.'

'He has now. But only to me, so you can't say anything to anyone.' I'd told her because she's my wife and a lawyer and understands about client privilege. 'He asked me to find this son of his.'

'Did he tell you where to look?'

'Ontario, Canada.'

'Did he give you a name?'

'The mother's name.'

'Anything else?'

'Yeah. He fathered the child over seventy years ago. And he's only seen him in visions.'

'Then how can he be sure?'

'He's Meloux.'

'What are you going to do?'

'First, head to his cabin. There's something I'm supposed to find. A watch. Also, he asked me to take care of Walleye while he's in the hospital.'

'Do you have any idea how you're going to do this?'

'I'm waiting for inspiration to strike. OK if I take Stevie with me? He's looking a little bored.'

'Thanks. I'm kind of overwhelmed with paperwork.'

Outside, Stevie was using the driver as a rifle, kneeling behind the railing of the front porch, firing off imaginary rounds.

'OK, Davy Crockett,' I said. 'Time to desert the Alamo. I'm going up to Henry Meloux's cabin. Want to come?'

He jumped at the prospect. 'Is Henry there?'

Meloux and my son had a special bond.

'Henry's in the hospital, Stevie.'

'Is he sick?'

'Yes. And Walleye's at the cabin. We need to take care of him.'

Walleye and Stevie. Another special bond.

He dropped the golf club on the porch and ran to my Bronco.

I PULLED up at the side of a dusty county road a few miles north of Aurora. Far behind me were the last of the resorts on Iron Lake, hidden in the deep cover of pines and spruce. All around me was national-forest land. I parked near a double-trunk birch that marked the beginning of the trail to Meloux's cabin on Crow Point.

Stevie leapt from the Bronco. He was already on the trail before I locked up, skipping far ahead. I followed more slowly. It was a hot after-noon, typical of early August. We were in the middle of a grasshopper infestation, and the woods were full of their buzz. Thirty yards in front of me, Stevie danced through caverns of shadow and into moments of radiant light. I loved him deeply, my son. Every day I counted him—and my daughters—a blessing.

Meloux had never seen his own son. Never carried him on his shoulders or held him when he cried. I didn't doubt Meloux, didn't doubt that he had a son he'd seen only in visions. Over time, I'd experienced too many inexplicable moments with the old Mide to be sceptical about something like this. It did make me wonder, though, about the circumstances.

We crossed Wine Creek and a few minutes later broke from the trees. Fifty yards ahead stood Meloux's cabin, an ancient structure but sturdy, made of cedar logs with a timber roof covered by birch bark. Meloux had built the cabin himself, and as long as I'd known him, he had lived there year-round.

The door was open. As we approached, something inside the cabin moved. A long, yellow face appeared, big brown eyes patiently watching us come.

'Walleye!' Stevie called, and raced towards the dog.

The mutt padded out, tail wagging. Stevie threw his arms round him and buried his face in Walleye's fur.

'Hey, boy, how you been?' he said. 'Missed me?'

I gave the dog's head a good patting and stepped through the doorway into the cabin. The structure was a single room. Meloux's bunk was against one wall. In the centre, near the pot-belly stove, stood a table with a few chairs.

Meloux had told me to look under the bunk for the watch. I crossed the floorboards, knelt and peered into the dark beneath the bed frame. Shoved into a far corner against the wall was a wooden box. I lay down on my belly, stretched out my arm, snagged the box and pulled it into the light. It was cedar, ten inches long, six inches wide and deep. I opened the lid. Inside, on top of a stack of folded papers, lay a gold pocket watch. I picked up the watch and snapped it open. Opposite the watch face was a tiny photograph of a handsome young woman with long black hair.

Stevie looked over my shoulder. 'What's that?'

'Not what, Stevie. Who. Her name is Maria Lima.'

'That picture looks old.'

'It is. More than seventy years old.'

I put the watch in my shirt pocket, closed the box and slid it back into the corner where I'd found it.

'If Henry is in the hospital, maybe we should stay out here,' Stevie suggested. 'So Walleye won't get lonely.'

'I have a better idea,' I said. 'Why don't we take him home?'

'Really?' A huge, eager smile bloomed on his face.

'Just until Henry's better.' Though I didn't know if that was going to happen.

Walleye had padded into the cabin behind us and sat on his haunches, watching. Stevie turned to him. 'You want to come home with us, boy? Come on, Walleye.' Stevie slapped the side of his leg and headed out with the dog at his heels.

I closed the door behind us. There was no lock.

Walleye paused beside me, looked back at the closed door, then followed my son, who danced ahead of us down the trail as if he were the Pied Piper.

THAT NIGHT when I walked in from closing up Sam's Place, Jo was sitting on the living-room sofa, reading a book. She looked up and smiled. 'Good night at Sam's?'

'We made a buck or two.' I kissed the top of her head and sat down beside her. 'Where's Walleye?'

'Sleeping with Stevie.'

I was surprised. That afternoon when she saw the dog follow Stevie through the front door, she hadn't been happy. I'd explained my dilemma, and she reluctantly relented. She wouldn't allow the dog in the house, however. Jenny was allergic to dogs. And cats, too. Our pets had always been turtles and fish.

'We put up a tent in the back yard,' Jo said. 'They're both out there. Is Jenny with Sean?'

'Yeah. She promised to be home by midnight. So now do I finally get to hear what the big secret is?'

Jo closed her book and set it on the end table.

'Sean's not going back to Macalester this fall,' she began calmly. 'He's taking the money in his bank account and using it to go to Paris to live for a year.'

'Do his folks know that?'

'As I understand it, not yet.'

'Can't imagine that's going to please Lane. He's been counting on Sean to finish his degree and take over the pharmacy. What's this got to do with Jenny?'

'Sean wants her to go with him.'

'That's it?' I laughed with relief. 'Jenny's too sensible for that.'

Jo didn't laugh. 'She's thinking about it, Cork.'

'Running off to Europe instead of college? And what? She and Sean'll live together?'

'She thinks Sean's going to ask her to marry him first.'

I couldn't sit still. I got up and began pacing. Jenny's the academic in the family, takes after her mother. That June, she'd graduated from high school, valedictorian. She'd chosen to go to the University of Iowa, hoping eventually to be accepted into the writing workshop, which she said had a terrific reputation.

Like Jo, she was willowy and had ice-blonde hair and smart blue eyes. She was lovely. And intelligent. I always knew she would leave Aurora, go out into the world to make her mark.

It had never occurred to me that she might marry at eighteen.

'How long have you known?' I asked.

'A couple of weeks.'

'Great. I just love being on the outside of things.'

'She asked me not to say anything because she was afraid you'd get upset and overreact.'

'Me? Why would I overreact? Just because they're kids and Jenny's got her whole future ahead of her and Sean can't see beyond some crazy dream of being Hemingway? Why are you taking all this so calmly?'

'Because Sean hasn't proposed, and if he does, she'll talk to us before she decides anything. We need to give her room, Cork, and trust her. Jenny's nothing if not levelheaded.'

I stopped pacing for a moment. I rubbed my temples. 'God, I don't know if I'm ready for this.'

'Any word on Meloux?' Jo said, changing the subject.

'No. I called George LeDuc, but he couldn't tell me anything.'

'What are you going to do about your promise to find his son?'

'What every self-respecting detective does these days. Get on the Internet. Mind if I use your computer?'

'Be my guest.'

I left Jo to her reading and went into her office. It took me an hour of Googling before I had what I believed was a decent lead.

I found Maria Lima referenced on a site named Ontario Past. When I clicked on the site, I discovered there was a school in the town of Flame Lake called the Wellington School, which had been built in 1932 with funds donated by Maria Lima Wellington. The town had been constructed by Northern Mining and Manufacturing, a large company founded by Leonard Wellington, in order to house workers from the nearby gold mine he owned. Using Google again, I found that Maria Lima Wellington was the daughter of Carlos Lima and was the first wife of Leonard Wellington. She'd died young, leaving a son. The son's name was Henry.

According to the Internet information, Henry Wellington was the man responsible for making Northern Mining and Manufacturing (NMM) a major corporation. He had an interesting history. After receiving his engineering degree from McMaster University in Hamilton, Ontario, he joined the Canadian Air Force. Although no Canadian fighter squadrons were involved in the Korean War, as part of an exchange programme Wellington served with a US squadron of Sabre-equipped fighter interceptors. He was the only Canadian to achieve the coveted rating of Ace. After the war, he became a test pilot. When his father died, he took over NMM.

As a result of what one of his contemporaries characterised as his 'brilliant, restless and iconoclastic' mind, he developed innovative techniques for refining minerals. Under his direction, NMM had expanded. He invested in diverse enterprises, among them the fledgling Canadian film industry. He was often referred to as the Howard Hughes of Canada. I searched until I found a date of birth and, after a calculation, realised Henry Wellington was seventy-two years old. Seventy-three winters, Meloux had said, dating his relationship with Maria Lima. Given the normal gestation period of nine months, Henry Wellington would be right on the money.

Henry Wellington was still alive and living in Thunder Bay, Canada, where NMM was headquartered. He was a widower with two grown children. And that, according to the Web information, was part of the problem. His wife had died six years earlier, and in the time since, Wellington had become a notorious recluse. Although he was still on the board of NMM, he no longer ran the company, nor did he appear in public. I couldn't find any recent close-up photographs of him, but I did find several taken earlier in his life. His hair was black, his face angular and high cheeked, his eyes dark and penetrating. Did he look like Meloux? Or like the photograph in Meloux's gold watch? I honestly couldn't say.

By the time I clicked off the computer, Annie had come home and both she and Jo had gone to bed. It was after midnight. Jenny was still out with Sean. I went to the kitchen and fished a couple of chocolate-chip cookies out of the cookie jar on the counter. I poured some milk and sat down at the table.

The front door opened. Half a minute later, Jenny stood in the kitchen doorway. 'Still up, Dad?'

'Couldn't sleep. Have a good time with Sean?'

'OK.'

'You're still on target for Iowa, right?'

She looked at me warily. 'Mom said something, didn't she?'

'We talked.'

I offered her one of the cookies. She accepted and took a bite.

'Did he pop the question?' I asked.

'No.'

'Would you go with him to Paris anyway?'

'Dad, I don't know.' A strong note of irritation.

'And if he does pop the question?'

'See, this is why I didn't want you to know. I knew you'd interrogate me.'

'Interrogate? Jenny, I'm your father. I ought to be allowed to question your thinking and your actions. It's what I've done for eighteen years, and it's served us both pretty well.'

'It has.' Her face was intense. Beautiful and serious. 'It's helped make me who I am, a woman capable of making her own decisions.' Each word had the feel of cold steel.

'I never suggested you weren't.'

'I love him, Dad. He loves me.'

Love? I wanted to say. Oh, Jenny. There's so much you don't know. What I said was, 'Will you talk to us before you make a decision?'

'Yes, all right?' she snapped. She turned away without saying good night and started upstairs, but she stopped. 'Dad?'

'Yeah?'

'I'd like to go with Sean for a drive along the North Shore tomorrow. I asked Jodi to fill in for me. Is it OK?'

'Go,' I said.

I listened to her feet hammer up the stairs.

I turned out the kitchen light and trudged up to bed.

Two

Early the next morning I went to the hospital to see Meloux. He was still in the ICU, still looking like he had a toehold in the next world. I thought he was sleeping and turned to go.

His eyelids lifted wearily. 'You have news?'

'Maybe,' I said. I walked to his bedside. 'I found a woman, Henry. Maria Lima. Her father was a man named Carlos Lima.'

'Carlos Lima,' Meloux said. The name meant something to him.

'She passed away many years ago.'

He didn't seem surprised. A man as old as Henry probably expected everyone from his youth to be dead by now.

'She was married, Henry. To a man named Wellington.'

From the way his face went rigid, I might as well have hit him with my fist. 'Wellington,' he repeated.

'Maria Lima Wellington had a son. She named him Henry.'

His eyes changed, a spark there.

'And he was born seventy-two years ago. In June.'

'Is he . . . ?'

'Alive? Yeah, Henry, he is. He lives in Thunder Bay, Canada. Just across the border.'

Meloux nodded. 'I want to see him,' he said.

'Henry, you're not getting out of here until you're better.'

'Bring him to me.'

'It was a miracle just finding him. Bringing him here? I don't know, Henry.'

'You will find a way,' he said.

'Look, I can't promise anything. Honestly, I'm not sure how I can make any of this sound believable.'

'The watch, you found it?'

'Yes.'

'Show him the watch.'

'I'll see what I can do.'

Meloux seemed comforted. He smiled, satisfied.

'You will bring me my son,' he said. His eyes drifted closed.

I started out.

'Walleye?' the old man said.

I turned back. 'We're taking good care of him, Henry.'

He nodded and once again closed his eyes.

I SPOKE with Ernie Champoux, Meloux's great-nephew, who was in the waiting room. He told me the doctors were puzzled by the old man's symptoms and were still running tests.

I'd dressed for church, suit and tie, and when I was finished at the hospital I met Jo and the kids at St Agnes for Mass. I didn't pay much attention to the service. I was thinking about Thunder Bay and how to go about keeping my second promise to Meloux.

During the day, whenever I had a break from customers, I slipped into the back of Sam's Place and made telephone calls. I tried the headquarters of Northern Mining and Manufacturing. Because it was Sunday, all I got was a recording, pretty much what I'd expected. I'd been unable to find a listing on the Internet for Henry Wellington and had no better luck with directory assistance. Among the information I'd gathered the night before, however, was the name of Wellington's younger half-brother, Rupert Wellington, president and CEO of NMM, and also a resident of Thunder Bay.

At home that night, I told Jo what I'd learned, then said: 'I'm driving to Thunder Bay in the morning.'

She was sitting up in bed, propped against the headboard, reading a file in a manila folder, something from work. 'What about Sam's Place?' She took off her glasses and laid them at her side.

I slipped into a pair of gym shorts and a clean T-shirt, my usual sleep attire. 'Jenny and Annie can handle it. Is Jenny here?'

'She came in a while ago.'

'Did she have a good time driving the North Shore with Sean?'

'She didn't talk much.'

I sat down on the bed. 'Is that good or bad?'

'It's neither, I'd say. She's just thinking, I imagine. Weighing everything.'

'Weighing an offer of marriage?'

'I don't know that there's been one. What do you hope to accomplish in Thunder Bay?'

'A face-to-face meeting with Henry Wellington.'

'And how do you intend to go about that?'

'As far as I can tell, his brother—half-brother—Rupert runs the company now, so he's probably accessible. I'm hoping to use him to get to Wellington.'

'And you'll get an audience with the brother how?'

'The watch. I'm banking on it opening the door.'

'Four-hour drive up, four hours back. Could be all for nothing.'

'Not for nothing. It's for Henry. And you have a better idea?'

She put the manila folder on the nightstand, leaned over and kissed me. 'You'll be leaving early. Get some sleep.'

I STOPPED BY the hospital on my way out of town.

Meloux was awake. He smiled weakly when I entered his room.

'How you doing, Henry?'

'I don't sleep so good. Mostly my heart is heavy. Like a bear on my chest.'

'I'm going up to Thunder Bay today, try to talk to the man who may be your son.'

'The watch?'

'I have it.'

I'd put it in a small jewellery box Jo had given me. I opened the box, took out the watch, and handed it to Meloux. His fingers handled it gently. He opened it and studied the photograph inside.

'She was beautiful,' I said.

The old Mide looked up.

'Her beauty was a knife, Corcoran O'Connor.'

He handed the watch back.

'You will bring me my son,' he said.

I TOOK Highway 61 north along Lake Superior. It was a beautiful August day. The lake looked hard as blue concrete.

I crossed the border at the Pigeon River, and less than an hour later I entered the unimpressive outskirts of Thunder Bay.

Thunder Bay is really the modern merging of two rival municipalities: Fort William and Port Arthur. As I understand it, the French fur traders started things rolling with a settlement protected by a rustic fort near the mouth of the Kaministikwia River, which emptied into a bay on Lake Superior the French called Baie de Tonnerre. The city's an old port.

The bay is created by a long, southerly sweeping peninsula dominated by an impressive geological formation called Sleeping Giant, so named because that's what the formation resembles.

From what I'd gathered on the Internet, Henry Wellington lived on a remote island called Manitou, which was just off Thunder Cape, the tip of Sleeping Giant. Manitou is an Ojibwe word that means spirit. That's exactly what Wellington seemed to be. More spirit than flesh, more spoken about than seen.

I made my way to the Thunder Bay Marina, which was at the eastern edge of the downtown area, just off Water Street. The city's old railroad station had been remodelled into shops and a little restaurant-cum-bar. There were three main docks. Most of the slips were filled with modest sailboats and large motor launches. I walked to the end of the first dock and stared out across the bay.

'Interested in a tour?'

I glanced back. A woman stood on the deck of a sailboat docked not far away, a can of Labatt Blue in her hand. She wore white shorts, a yellow tank top, a red visor. She looked maybe sixty—a healthy, tanned, fit sixty.

'Nope. Just one island. Manitou.'

'Hunting Henry Wellington,' she said. 'Where's your camera?'

'I don't want a picture. I just want to talk to the man.'

She laughed. 'Hell, that's harder than an audience with the Pope.'

'Where's Manitou Island?'

She pointed towards the enormous landform on the far side of the bay. 'At the base of Sleeping Giant. Too far to see from here.'

'I understand the only way to get there is by boat.'

'There's a helipad. You're not a reporter, eh?'

'Private investigator.' I walked to her boat and gave her my card. 'Hired by a family member to deliver a piece of information. You seem to know a lot about Wellington.'

'Mostly what everyone in Thunder Bay knows. But with my slip right here, I pretty much see who comes and goes to the island.'

'Could you get me out there?'

'Wouldn't do you any good. Wellington's got men with guns.'

'Ever seen him?'

'Every once in a while if I'm passing near the island at sundown, I see a wisp of white moving among the trees. More like a ghost than a man. I figure that's got to be Wellington.'

'Thanks.'

'No problem. You decide you want a tour, you know where to find me.'

'What do you charge?'

'A six-pack and conversation, sweetheart.' She winked and went back to her beer.

NORTHERN MINING and Manufacturing headquarters were on a campus just north of the city. There was a tall central structure of modern design surrounded by several smaller buildings. I parked in the visitors' lot, put on a tie and sports coat and went inside. At the reception desk in the lobby, I was directed to the fifteenth floor, the top.

The waiting area was large enough that if the floor had been ice, I could have played hockey. There was a plush sofa of nice chocolate brown leather and an easy chair of the same colour and material. There was a large aquarium with darting fish. And there was a desk with a secretary who turned from her computer and watched me cross the room. 'I'd like to see Mr Wellington,' I told her.

She was young—twenty-seven, maybe thirty—nicely made up. The nameplate on the desk read MS HELPRIN. She looked up at me.

'Do you have an appointment?'

'I don't. Could I make one?'

'What's the nature of your business?'

'It concerns a family heirloom that's come into my possession.'

I took out the watch, opened it and handed it to her. 'That's a photograph of his father's first wife, Maria. I'd like to tell him a story that goes along with it, and to ask him something.'

'Ask him what?'

'That's between him and me, Ms Helprin,' I said. 'If you could just show him the watch, I'm betting he'll see me.'

'If you'd care to wait, I'll see what I can do.'

I sat in the easy chair and stared at the exotic fish as Ms Helprin disappeared through a door. A couple of minutes later, she returned. 'Mr Wellington will see you now.'

The man at the big glass desk in the inner office stood up to shake my hand. From what I'd learned on the Internet, I knew he was sixty-two years old, though he looked a decade younger. He was small and fit, with a crown of silver hair round a balding centre. He wore an expensive grey suit, white shirt, red tie. His eyes were earth brown and sharp in their appraisal.

'I appreciate your time, Mr Wellington,' I said.

'I can only spare a minute, Mr O'Connor. Have a seat.'

I sat in a chair with a curved grey metal back and a soft leather cushion. The wall behind Wellington was all glass, with a beautiful view of the bay and Sleeping Giant in the distance.

'The watch, of course, intrigued me. You have a story that goes with it.' He folded his hands on his desk and leaned forward.

'The photograph is of Maria Wellington, yes?'

He nodded. 'My father's first wife.'

'She wasn't your mother, correct?'

'That's right. After her death, my father remarried. Do I get to hear the story?'

'Only if your brother chooses to tell it to you. The man who gave me that watch and its story asked me to share it only with Henry Wellington.'

'Ah.' He sat back and looked disappointed. 'So it's really my brother you're trying to see.' His eyes narrowed. 'Mr O'Connor, my brother wants to be left in peace. A simple request. Yet he's hounded mercilessly by people like you. Exactly what tabloid do you work for?'

'I'm not a journalist. I'm a private investigator.' I hauled out my wallet and handed him a business card. 'I've been retained by the man who gave me that watch to deliver it and its history personally to Henry Wellington. This is important. My client is dying.'

'The man's name?'

'That's for the ears of Henry Wellington.' It was my turn to lean forward. 'Look, for a lot of years I was the sheriff of Tamarack County, down in Minnesota. If you need a character reference, I'd urge you to call the sheriff's office. I'm not trying to scam you. It's simply an unusual and pressing situation. Keep the watch for the time being. All I'm asking is fifteen minutes of your brother's time. I guarantee that what I have to tell him, he'll want to hear.'

A man in his position, I figured, had to be able to size people up quickly. Wellington considered for all of ten seconds, staring at the watch in his hand. 'I can't guarantee anything, Mr O'Connor. Henry has the final say as to whether he sees you or not.'

'I can't ask any more than that. Thank you.'

'How can you be reached?'

'My cellphone. The number's on my card.'

He stood up and offered his hand in parting. A gracious gesture, I thought. 'Again,' he cautioned, 'I make no promises.'

'I understand. And the watch?'

'It will be returned to you before you see my brother.'

IT WAS two thirty in the afternoon. I needed lunch. I went back to the marina, to the little restaurant-cum-bar in the remodelled depot. I got a table on the deck overlooking the docks, ordered a Reuben sandwich and a beer, and stared out at the sailboats cutting across the bay.

I ate the sandwich, a pretty good one, and was working on my second beer when my cellphone rang. No information on caller ID.

'O'Connor here.'

'This is Henry Wellington.'

'Mr Wellington—' I began.

'Be at Thunder Bay Marina at three thirty, the end of dock number one. You'll be met by a man named Edward Morrissey, my personal assistant. He'll bring you to Manitou Island.'

'Thank you. What about the watch?'

'It will be in Mr Morrissey's possession.'

Without so much as a goodbye, he was gone.

I STROLLED DOWN to the dock a few minutes early. Edward Morrissey was already there.

He wasn't an imposing man at first glance. Not tall—just under six feet. Dark curly hair. I put him in his mid-thirties. When I got closer, I saw that he was hard all over, well muscled, with a broad chest, thick arms and a neck like a section of concrete pillar.

'You O'Connor?' He'd been leaning against the railing of the dock but stood up when I neared him. He wore jeans, tight over buffed-up thighs, white sneakers, a black windcheater.

'That's me.'

'Morrissey,' he said, stepping close to me. 'Lift your arms. I need to pat you down.'

'I'm not carrying.'

'I need to be sure. Also, I'll be checking for any camera you might have hidden.'

'This is ridiculous.'

'You want to see Mr Wellington?'

I lifted my arms. While Morrissey went over me with his big hands, I noticed the woman on her sailboat a few slips down who'd talked with me that morning. She was sitting on a canvas deck chair, drinking from a beer bottle, watching the proceedings with amusement. She lifted her beer in a toast to me.

'All right,' Morrissey said. 'Let's go.'

'You're supposed to give me something.'

Morrissey reached into the pocket of his windcheater and brought out the little box that contained the watch. 'This?'

'Yes.'

I held out my hand, but Morrissey slipped the box back into his pocket. 'Mr Wellington instructed me to deliver it directly to him.'

'The other Mr Wellington promised me—'

'I don't work for the other Mr Wellington.'

He turned and walked towards the end of the pier, where a launch was waiting with a pilot at the wheel.

WE CROSSED the bay at a good clip. As we drew nearer Sleeping Giant, an island emerged, taking shape against the rugged backdrop of the peninsula. It lay, I guessed, a quarter of a mile off the mainland. It was relatively level and heavily covered with boreal forest, tall pines mostly. Finally I made out the white outline of a dock jutting into the lake. A few minutes later, the pilot at the wheel cut the engine and began to manoeuvre us in.

From a kiosk at the far end of the dock, a man emerged and walked out to meet us. He wore white shorts, a white shirt, boat shoes. As we came nearer, I saw that he also wore a gun belt with a filled holster.

The launch nosed up to the dock. Morrissey stood up and tossed a line to the man. When we were tied off, Morrissey said, 'After you, O'Connor.'

I disembarked. Morrissey was right behind me. The man on the dock returned to the kiosk. We met him there. He wrote something on a sheet attached to a clipboard. 'Stick with him,' he advised, pointing towards Morrissey, 'and there won't be any trouble.'

'This way, O'Connor,' Morrissey said.

He stepped off the dock onto a path of crushed limestone that disappeared into the trees cloaking the island.

THE TREES grew close together, tall and, in this place, forbidding. They formed a dark roof over us and a wall around us. I heard dogs barking somewhere. The only other sounds were the crunch of limestone under our feet and the sizzle of Morrissey's windcheater as he swung his heavy arms. He kept me in front of him.

'Just stick with the path,' he said.

The path didn't follow a straight line but wound through the trees. After a few minutes, we walked into a large clearing. At the centre stood a mansion built of stone. It was two storeys with a couple of wings off the large centre section. Half a dozen chimneys pushed through the roof.

I'd learned from my Internet research that Manitou Island had been the family retreat. After his wife's death, Wellington had sold his home in Thunder Bay and retired to the island permanently.

The few relatively recent photos that I'd found on the Internet were of a robed, druidlike figure among the trees of Manitou Island. The white wisp the woman at the marina had spoken of.

Morrissey's hand on my back urged me forward.

'I don't know what's in that box,' he said as we mounted the steps to the lodge. 'But it must be something. Mr W. sees nobody, I mean nobody, from the outside any more.'

He stepped ahead and opened the door, beckoning me to enter.

The moment I was inside, I caught the smell of disinfectant. It pervaded the place. The common area we entered was a maze of newspapers stacked hip high, with a couple of narrow corridors running through it. Sheets covered the furniture. Morrissey pointed towards the stairs beyond the clutter, and we manoeuvred our way there. Upstairs, he directed me down a dark hallway to a door near the end of one of the wings. We entered a kind of anteroom. Morrissey went to another door and knocked.

'Who is it?'

'Morrissey, Mr Wellington. I've got your visitor.'

'Show him in.'

Before we entered, Morrissey reached to a table beside the door and pulled a surgical mask from a small box there. He handed it to me. 'You want to see Mr W., you put this on.'

I took it, and as I tied it round my face, Morrissey did the same with another. In addition, he took a pair of latex examination gloves from another box on the table and put them on.

'Should I put on gloves?' I asked.

'You planning on touching anything?'

'Not intentionally.'

'See that you don't.'

He opened the door and stepped in ahead of me.

The gloom of the hallway, of the whole place, hadn't prepared me for what lay beyond that door. The room was claustrophobic, tiny for such a great house. Jammed into it were a bed neatly made and covered with a snow-white comforter, an easy chair of smooth white leather, an enormous television, a rolling garment hanger hung with nothing but white robes, and, lining the walls, stack upon stack of unopened Kleenex tissue boxes. The room was dark except for a single standing lamp. The chair faced the television, so all I could see was its smooth, white back. The television was on.

'Did you close the door?'

The voice came from the chair. It was thin and a little peevish.

'It's closed,' Morrissey said.

The screen went black. The chair swivelled slowly, bringing me face to face with Henry Wellington. His hair was long and white, very much like Meloux's. Although he wore a white robe, it was clear the fabric hung on a slender frame. His face, like mine and Morrissey's, was half covered by a surgical mask. I tried to look into his eyes, to see if there was something of Meloux there, but his face was deep in shadow.

'Bring me the box,' he said to Morrissey.

Morrissey stepped forward, took the little jewellery box from the pocket of his windcheater, and, with his latex-covered hands, delivered it to Wellington. Then he retreated to the place where he'd stood before, just at my back.

Wellington fumbled with the watch. Finally he succeeded in freeing the catch. For a minute, he studied the photograph inside.

'You have some story about the item and my mother?'

'It's for your ears only,' I said.

'Leave us, Mr Morrissey.'

I heard the door open and close at my back.

'The story,' Wellington said, holding up the watch.

'That watch was given to me by an old man. He was given it by your mother. His name is Henry Meloux. He's dying.'

'A rather short story,' he said.

'He gave me that watch and asked me to give it to the man who may be his son.'

The corners of his eyes crinkled. 'He believes I'm his son?'

'He didn't reveal the whole story to me, but it's clear he was involved with your mother in a way that could have produced a son. Apparently, the timing of your birth is right. And you're named Henry, like him.'

'What does he want?'

'To see you, that's all.'

'You said he's dying. Where is he?'

'In a hospital in Minnesota.'

'He wants me to go there?'

'Yes.'

He picked up an atomiser that had been tucked beside him in the chair, and he sprayed the air between us.

'Tell me more about this Meloux,' he said.

'He's Ojibwe. He's what we call a Mide, a member of the Grand Medicine Society. He heals.'

He leaned forward. 'An Indian?'

'Yes.'

He stood up, tall and brittle-looking. A ghost of a man.

'Do you realise what you're saying about my mother? What kind of woman would take up with an Indian buck?' He pointed a curling nail at me. 'If I were ten years younger, I'd knock you down.'

I tried again to speak reasonably. 'Think about it, Mr Wellington. You were born two months after your parents married. You were conceived out of—'

'Edward!' Wellington called angrily. 'Edward!'

The door burst open. 'Yes, Mr Wellington?'

'Show this man out.'

'Sure thing, Mr Wellington.'

I could hear the pleasure in Morrissey's voice.

'The watch,' I said. 'I'd like the watch back.'

'I'd say it belongs to my family.'

'I'd say not.'

'Edward,' Wellington commanded.

'Come on, O'Connor.'

I shook off his hand. 'I'm not leaving without that watch.'

Morrissey gripped my shoulder hard. I turned and swung, catching him full on his jaw. He went down, looking stunned. I spun back and sprang towards Wellington.

'Stay back,' he cried. He cringed a moment, then threw the watch at me like a spoilt child and spat, 'All right then, *here*.'

I heard Morrissey struggling up at my back. I turned to him.

'Enough, Edward,' Wellington ordered. 'Get him out of here.'

Morrissey was breathing hard, and I could see he wanted a piece of me. But Wellington once more said, 'Enough.'

Though Morrissey relaxed his body, his eyes were still tight. 'Yes, sir.' He nodded towards the door. 'After you, O'Connor.'

HE JUMPED ME on the limestone path.

We were out of sight of the mansion, winding our way through the pines towards the dock when he hit me in my left kidney.

A blow like a cannonball.

I arched against the impact and the pain. My knees buckled, and I went down, kneeling in the crushed limestone. Morrissey danced to the side and kicked me below the ribs. I toppled and went foetal, my arms wrapped round my head to protect myself.

But Morrissey had done all the damage he intended. Except to bend down and deliver this: 'You ever swing on me again, I'll kill your sorry ass.' I heard the crunch of limestone as he stepped back.

To be on the safe side, I waited several seconds, then carefully uncurled. Morrissey stood a dozen feet away, arms crossed, watching me get to my feet.

Some days you eat the bear; some days the bear eats you.

I turned and headed to the dock with Morrissey behind me at a safe distance. He handed me over to the guy in the kiosk with the clipboard, who signed me out. Morrissey spoke quietly to the pilot of the launch, who eyed me and nodded. Morrissey cast us off and stayed on the island, while the pilot manoeuvred to open water, then hit the throttle, and we sped towards Thunder Bay.

At the marina I disembarked. The pilot immediately swung the launch round to return to Manitou Island.

'Beer?'

I turned in the direction of the voice and saw the woman standing on the deck of her sailboat, a bottle lifted in offering.

'Thanks.'

I walked to her sailboat and climbed aboard.

She handed me a Labatt Blue. 'You actually got on the island?'

'Yeah.' I unscrewed the cap and took a long drink. It was ice cold. Perfect.

'What was it like?'

'Not a place I'd choose for a vacation,' I said.

'I saw them frisk you before you left. Careful people.'

'I didn't catch your name,' I said.

'Trinky Pollard. Royal Canadian Mounted Police. Retired.'

'Cork O'Connor. Former sheriff of Tamarack County, Minnesota.'

'You told me earlier that you're a PI now.'

'Part-time. Mostly I'm trying to do a friend a favour.'

We shook hands. Hers was impressively strong.

'You look too young to be a retired cop,' she said.

'Not retired. I quit.'

'What do you do when you're not investigating privately?'

'Mostly I make hamburgers.'

She smiled at that, then glanced towards the island. 'So you delivered a cheeseburger and fries to Wellington, eh.' She laughed. 'Accomplish whatever it was you were after?'

'I guess you could say I got my man.'

I lifted my bottle, and we toasted.

I looked at my watch. 'Thanks for the beer, Trinky. If I'm going to make it home tonight, I'd best be on my way.'

She saw me off her boat, still sipping her beer. When I looked back, she was staring towards Sleeping Giant.

Before I left the marina, I used my cell to call Jo.

'Hello, sweetheart,' she said. 'Where are you?'

'Still in Thunder Bay. How are things there?'

She hesitated a moment, which worried me.

'How's Meloux?' I asked, expecting the worst.

'Ernie Champoux called. Meloux's left the hospital,' she said.

'Left?'

'Walked out. Against all advice. According to Ernie, he just sat up, told the doctor he was well and ready to leave. Ernie convinced him to let them run a few tests. It was amazing, Cork. They couldn't find anything wrong. All the signs, everything, perfectly normal.'

'Did Meloux say anything?'

'He told them the weight was off his heart, that he was at peace.'

'He believes he's going to see his son. Damn.'

'Damn? What does that mean?'

I told her about Meloux's son, a man I wasn't certain any father would want to claim as the fruit of his loins.

'When will you be home?' she asked.

'Well after dark. How're the kids?'

Once again, she was quiet. And I realised that what I'd picked up in her voice earlier had nothing to do with Meloux.

'What is it, Jo? Is it Jenny? Did Sean finally pop the question?'

'It's more complicated than that.'

'Oh. How so?'

I heard her take a deep breath. 'Cork, you were right to be worried. She's pregnant.'

It was nearly midnight when I pulled onto Gooseberry Lane and turned into my driveway. Jo was waiting up. The kids had gone to bed. She kissed me and settled on the sofa beside me.

'You look tired,' she said.

'And sore.' I told her about the kidney punch and the kick.

'Let me see.'

I lifted my shirt, and she checked my back.

'Oh, Cork, there's an ugly bruise forming. These men, they sound perfectly awful.'

'How do I tell Henry?'

'Be straight with him. Anything else, and he'll know you're not being truthful.'

I looked round the living room. 'Where's Walleye?'

'In the back yard, sleeping in the tent with Stevie.'

'Stevie knows Walleye will be going home tomorrow?'

She nodded. 'He took it pretty hard, poor little guy.'

Everywhere I looked, nothing but disappointment.

'So,' I said. 'Jenny.'

'She's confused, Cork.'

'How long has she known?'

'A few days.'

'Does Sean know?'

'Yes.'

'What does Jenny want to do?'

'Go back in time and make different decisions would be my first guess.'

'Don't we all.' I felt exhausted and empty. I laid my head against Jo's shoulder. 'I have to talk to her.'

'She knows that.'

'And we have to talk to Sean. His folks, too. Do they know?'

'He was going to tell them tonight. We'll probably be calling them tomorrow about the same time they call us.'

'Guess this is the end of Paris.'

'It doesn't mean their dreams will end, Cork.'

'No, but it's one hell of a detour off the yellow brick road. What do we do?'

'What can we do? We tell her how we feel, we listen, we pray, we hope, and whatever she decides, we're there for her.' She kissed the top of my head. 'Ready for bed?'

'Let me check on Stevie and Walleye; then I'll be up.'

I wandered out to the tent in the back yard. My son was in his sleeping-bag, snoring softly. Walleye lay beside him. The old dog lifted his head when I peeked through the flap, and his tail brushed the tent floor.

A boy and his dog. Only, the dog belonged to someone else and would be going back when the sun came up.

I wasn't looking forward to morning. To wresting from my son his very good friend. To telling Meloux the truth about his own son. To listening while my daughter and the father of her baby tried to sort out what the hell their future might be.

I stood there in the dark of my back yard thinking that sometimes life sucks and that's all there is to it.

Three

Stevie was quiet in the Bronco. He kept his arm round Walleye, who sat between us. We drove north along Iron Lake past cabins and small resorts nestled among pines. At the north end of the lake, we turned off the paved highway onto the gravel county road that serviced the last of the resorts before the reservation began. It had been a dry summer, and the Bronco kicked up a thick tail of dust. A quarter of a mile along, I glanced into my rearview mirror and saw an SUV swing off the highway and plough into the cloud I'd raised.

Another mile, and I pulled to the side of the road and parked near the double-trunk birch that marked the trail to Meloux's cabin. Stevie opened his door and Walleye leapt across him eagerly. I opened my door just as the SUV behind us shot past. It was silver-grey. I yanked the door shut, glad I'd pulled far off to the side. Whoever was driving the SUV couldn't have seen the Bronco in time to avoid hitting it. As it was, I almost lost the driver's door. The SUV sped past and kept heading northeast.

Stevie and Walleye trotted ahead. I trailed behind, noting my son's slumped little shoulders.

We broke from the trees amid the buzz of the grasshoppers still infesting the woods. On Crow Point smoke drifted up from the stovepipe on Meloux's cabin. Walleye loped ahead, barking. Meloux opened the door and stepped into view. He smiled at the sight of his old friend, bent down and caressed the dog.

Looking up at us as we approached, he said in formal greeting, '*Anin*, Corcoran O'Connor. *Anin*, Stephen.' He stood up. '*Migwech*,' he finished, thanking us.

He had on a pair of worn khakis held up with new blue braces. The sleeves of his denim shirt were rolled above his elbows. He wore much-scuffed hiking boots. He looked healthy.

'I have made coffee,' he said, inviting us in.

We stepped out of the sunshine into the cool shade of his cabin. There were three chairs round his table. Stevie and I sat down. Meloux went to his black potbelly stove, where coffee sat perking in a dented aluminum pot.

He poured dark brew into three cups already placed round the table, as if we'd been expected. Stevie looked at the coffee, then at me. I nodded OK.

Walleye had padded quietly back and forth with Meloux. When the old man finally sat down, Walleye settled at his feet.

I sipped the coffee, which was hot and strong. 'Henry, I was more than a little surprised to hear that you'd left the hospital.'

The old man shook his head. 'The surprise for me was finding myself there. I did not realise the weight I carried on my heart, it had been there so long. Tell me about my son.'

'He's a sick man, Henry.'

I explained as simply as I could what I had observed.

When I finished, the old man said, 'He would not come?'

'No, Henry.'

Meloux nodded and stared for a little while out of the small window at the sunlit meadow beside his cabin. 'It may be that the weight I felt on my heart was not mine alone. It may be that I felt his, too.' He touched his chest. '*Miziweyaa*'—which meant wholeness—'is here. The way is always here. But sometimes a man needs help in understanding the way.'

The coffee had cooled. Stevie took a polite sip and squeezed his eyes against the bitter taste.

'We will return to Manitou,' Meloux declared. 'We will see my son together, and I will show him the way towards *miziweyaa*.'

I started to object, but Meloux cut me off.

'If my son is ill in the way you say, we need to leave today.'

'Tomorrow, Henry,' I offered. 'I have things to do first.'

'What things?'

'I have a business to put in order. I have a wife to explain this to.' I didn't mention Jenny. 'We'll go first thing in the morning.'

I reached into my shirt pocket and drew out the watch. I handed it to Henry. He opened it and stared at the photograph inside.

'Come on, Stevie,' I said, standing.

Stevie leaned over and patted Walleye. 'Goodbye, boy.'

Meloux got up, and the dog with him, and they saw us to the door. The meadow was full of grasshoppers.

'Tomorrow, Corcoran O'Connor,' he said. 'When the sun comes up, I will be ready.'

We crossed the meadow and entered the woods. Stevie kept in step beside me without a word. The walk back to the road felt long.

We found the Bronco covered with grasshoppers. They flew off the doors as we reached for the handles. When we were inside, Stevie asked, 'Are there grasshoppers everywhere?'

'I think so,' I said. I put the key in the ignition.

'There were grasshoppers smashed all over the Canada car,' Stevie said.

'What Canada car?'

'The one that went by when we stopped.'

'It was from Canada? How do you know?'

'The licence plate on the back. I saw it.'

Instead of turning round I drove straight ahead. Not far from the double-trunk birch, I came to one of the old logging trails. Parked just far enough off the road so that it couldn't easily be seen was the SUV. I reached across to the glove box, where I kept my cellphone, intending to call the sheriff, but I was too far north of town to get a signal. I swung the Bronco round quickly.

'What are you doing, Dad?'

'Henry's in trouble.'

I drove past the trail to Henry's cabin. A quarter of a mile further on I came to a lane that headed towards some resort cabins owned by Melissa and Joe Krick. I'd known them all my life.

I said to Stevie, 'I want you to run as fast as you can down to the Kricks'. Tell them that Henry's in trouble, that someone's trying to hurt him. Tell them to call the sheriff's office right away.'

'What are you going to do?'

'Try to help Henry.'

'I want to be with you.'

'Just do what I ask.' I reached across him and popped his door open. 'Go. As fast as you can. Go!'

I PULLED to the side of the road at the double-trunk birch. I jumped out, ran to the rear of the Bronco, and popped the tailgate. There was a locked toolbox in the back, which I opened with one of the keys on my ring. Inside was a basket-weave holster, a .38 police special wrapped in oilcloth and six cartridges. I slipped the holster on my belt, filled the cylinder of the .38 and slapped it closed. I dropped the weapon into the holster and secured the snap. Then I hit the trail at a sprint, heading for Meloux's place.

I was breathing hard by the time I reached Wine Creek, halfway to the cabin. As I danced over the stones that formed a loose bridge across the stream, I heard Walleye begin barking fiercely in the distance. A few moments later came a rifle shot and a pained yelp, and Walleye stopped barking. A second shot followed immediately.

I reached the edge of the trees. Much as I wanted to bolt for the cabin to check on Meloux, I forced myself to stop. From the shadows I surveyed the clearing, the cabin, the outhouse. Except for the grasshoppers springing up everywhere, nothing moved.

I scanned the meadow, the lakeshore and finally eyed the outcrop of rocks just beyond Meloux's cabin. A path led from the cabin through the rocks to a fire ring, where Meloux often sat and burned cedar and sage to clear his spirit. It would provide good cover if someone wanted to take out the old man.

The meadow grass stood knee high. I lay on my belly and crawled slowly across the clearing. As I neared the cabin, I heard a low wail. It came from the rocks. I paused, listened and finally understood. I got to my feet. Beyond the rocks, I found Meloux.

The old Mide sat cross-legged near the circle of stones. Next to him lay Walleye, a graze of blood along his flank. The dog licked at the wound. In front of Meloux, face down, was sprawled the body of a man. The back of his head had exploded in a gaping wound.

Meloux's eyes were closed as he sang. I recognised the chant. He was singing the dead man along the Path of Souls.

I sat down and waited. When he finished, the old man looked at me. 'Are you all right, Henry?' I asked.

'I am confused.' His dark eyes dropped to the dead man. 'He hunted me. What kind of game is an old man like me?'

'What happened?'

'You left, and Walleye sensed something. The scent he caught was not good, I could tell. I took my rifle from the wall, and I put in a cartridge. We were downwind of the rocks, which would be a good place for a bad man to hide. I was not thinking it was a man, though, but a different animal—a wolf, maybe, or a mountain lion. So he surprised me. But a man does not get old like me without luck. Just before he fired, a grasshopper flew into his face. His shot went wide. Mine did not.' Meloux reached out and gently patted Walleye. 'His bullet nicked my friend.' He shook his head. 'What satisfaction is there in hunting an old man and an old dog?'

I got to my feet and walked to the body. Although I knew I shouldn't move it, I rolled the corpse just enough to see the face. I'd never again have to worry about turning my back on Henry Wellington's bodyguard. Edward Morrissey was dead.

WHEN I resigned as sheriff of Tamarack County, one of my best deputies ran for the position and won: Marcia Dross. Now she stood just inside the doorway of Meloux's cabin, leaning against the wall with her arms crossed, listening while Captain Ed Larson, who headed up major crime investigations, sat with me at the table, taking me through the questions. Maria was tall, with hair the colour of an acorn and cut short. When I was sheriff, I wore the uniform. Dross had her own look. She generally wore jeans, a tasteful sweater or flannel shirt and a pair of chukka boots.

I'd told Ed everything I'd observed that morning. I'd also told him about my trip to Thunder Bay. He'd already interviewed Meloux, who'd been taken into town to give a full written statement. Jo was going to meet him there to make certain he had legal representation. Meloux had told Ed everything, so I didn't see any reason to hold back.

'Did Morrissey see the watch?' Dross asked.

I nodded. 'When Wellington tossed it to me.'

'Where's the watch now?'

'Meloux has it.'

'Worth much, do you think?'

'I don't know, Marcia. I suppose Morrissey could have been after the watch, but I can't imagine it's worth a man's life.'

In the cool corner of the cabin where he lay, Walleye moved and whimpered a little. The bullet had grazed a path a few inches long across the dog's left haunch. It had stopped bleeding, but stitches would be a good idea. I had told Meloux when he left for the sheriff's department not to worry. Stevie and I would get Walleye to a vet.

Dross said, 'Where were you exactly when you handed the watch back to Meloux?'

'Sitting right here at this table.'

Dross walked over and looked through the window towards the rocks where Meloux had been attacked. 'Morrissey had field glasses,' she said. 'He could easily have observed the exchange.'

'OK,' Larson said, moving us along, 'the watch is a possible motive. What else?'

'Have you got an idea, Ed?' I asked.

'How about rage directed at the father who wasn't there his whole life, then suddenly shows up out of the blue? You said Wellington's mental state was precarious. What do you think?'

'I spoke with the man for ten minutes. I honestly couldn't say.'

Dross nodded. 'Clearly, we need to interview him.'

Larson stood up. 'I'll call the provincial authorities as soon as I get back to the office, start setting things up.'

FIRST STOP after picking up Stevie was Hakala's Animal Clinic.

It was going on two o'clock when I finally pulled back into the drive on Gooseberry Lane. We'd been gone six hours, but it felt like days. I realised, as I stepped into the cool of the house, that I was hungry. I smelled something cooking, and following my nose, I found Jo and Meloux in the kitchen eating fried bologna sandwiches—the Ojibwe often call bologna 'Indian steak'— and leftover Jell-O salad. They were both drinking Diet Pepsi.

'You guys OK?' I asked.

'Good,' Meloux answered. 'We are good. And Walleye?'

'He's with Stevie in the back yard. The vet stitched him up and gave me some antibiotic pills he'll need to take to fight infection.'

'Hungry?' Jo asked, and began to get up.

I waved her back down. 'Relax. I'll fix it.'

'Henry and I have been trying to figure out why this Morrissey tried to kill him,' Jo said.

'Marcia, Ed and I have been doing the same. You come up with anything?'

Jo sipped her Pepsi. 'I think it was the watch. Henry showed it to me. It's gold, quite original, and could be valuable.'

'What do you think, Henry?'

'Just an old watch,' Meloux replied with a shrug. 'Important to me, but who am I?'

'Henry, it may be that Morrissey was sent to get the watch.'

Meloux fixed his dark, unwavering eyes on me. 'I do not believe my son would ask that man to kill me.'

'Maybe the killing wasn't part of his instructions. Morrissey may have come up with that on his own.'

Stevie stepped into the kitchen. I nodded towards the skillet. 'I've got a fried bologna sandwich coming up in a minute. Hungry?'

'Can I eat outside?'

'Sure.'

'Walleye's OK, Henry,' Stevie said to Meloux.

'I have been told. Stephen, I would like to ask a favour. I will be gone for a while. Will you take care of my friend for me?'

'Will I!' he said eagerly.

'Gone?' I asked.

'Tomorrow we will go to see my son.'

I shook my head. 'Things have changed, Henry. A man's dead. There's a police investigation in progress. Until they've had a chance to interview Henry Wellington, we need to keep out of this.'

The doorbell rang. Jo brought back Meloux's great-nephew, Ernie Champoux, who'd come for the old man. Until this business was concluded, Ernie intended to have his great-uncle stay with him.

'Sunrise tomorrow, I will be ready,' Meloux said as he went out of the front door. 'My son is not well. He needs me to heal him.'

'Henry, I won't be there,' I called after him.

Meloux turned, and his eyes hit me like a couple of rocks.

'Give the authorities a little time, Henry,' I tried.

He didn't reply. I watched, feeling lousy, as he walked to Ernie's truck. Ernie pulled away with Meloux beside him, sitting stiff as iron and staring straight ahead.

LATER THAT AFTERNOON I drove over to Sam's Place. The rush was over, and the girls were listening to the radio. Jenny wasn't there.

'Sean picked her up a little while ago,' Anne said. 'We're doing fine without her. So how's Henry?'

Kate Buker and Jodi Bollendorf, the two girls helping out that day, leaned against the serving counter and listened eagerly.

'Confused,' I said.

Anne scrunched her freckled face in bewilderment. 'Dad, why would anyone try to kill a nice old guy like Henry?'

The question of the day. I told them the police on both sides of the border were working on that one.

The rest of the afternoon turned out to be full of folks who were as interested in what happened out at Meloux's cabin as in ordering food. I deflected their questions as best I could, but it amazed me how much information was already abroad in Aurora.

Around five thirty, Wally Schanno pulled up in his red Ford pick-up. He stepped out, holding a leash. A little black-and-white puppy leapt down from the seat after him. The little dog began sniffing its way across the lot towards the hut. Eventually they both made it to the serving window.

Annie cooed, 'What a cute puppy. Is it yours, Mr Schanno?'

'Yeah,' Schanno said. 'Her name's Trixie.'

'What is she?'

'A mutt. Part border collie, part greyhound, part God-knows-what. Say, Cork,' he called past Anne. 'Talk to you a minute?'

'Meet you round back,' I said.

When I stepped outside, Trixie was all over me. She barely reached my knees, but she kept trying to jump higher. 'She's got a lot of energy, Wally.' I knelt down to pet her. 'Did you get her for security or companionship?'

'I figured I was spending too much time by myself in the house. I thought maybe a dog'd help. Cork, I heard about what went down at Henry Meloux's place. Is he doing OK?'

'He's fine, Wally.'

We stood in the sun. Trixie nosed at the gravel in the lot.

'Sounds like trouble followed you down from Thunder Bay. Is it true Meloux's got a son up there?'

'Where'd you hear that?'

He shrugged. 'So, are you going back?'

'If Meloux had his way, we'd already be on the road.'

'But?'

'There's an international investigation under way. Do you think I want to step into the middle of that?'

'Come on, Cork. Across borders, nothing moves fast.'

'Including me. Look, I'm guessing you're here thinking that there's something major in the works and maybe you can help. Well, I'm telling you that's not the case. I've done what I promised for Henry, and I'm finished. We're not cops any more, you and me. Let's let the people wearing the badges do their jobs, OK?'

'All right, then,' Schanno said curtly. He turned away and walked Trixie back to his truck.

I watched him go, feeling not at all good about how I'd treated him, but wondering, too, resentfully, why it was that everyone else seemed to have such a clear idea of what I ought to do.

SHERIFF MARCIA DROSS drove into the parking lot of Sam's Place in the brittle blue light well after sunset. She got out of her cruiser, came up to the windows, and asked to see me outside. That's never a good sign.

We walked to the picnic table under the big red pine near the shoreline. The moon wasn't up yet, and the other side of the lake was sliding into restless black. Dross got right to the point.

'Cork, you said Morrissey worked for Henry Wellington.'

'That's right.'

'According to the Canadian authorities Ed Larson spoke with, Morrissey runs a guide service, takes hunters and fishermen up into the wilderness of northern Ontario.'

'The only place he guided me was out to Manitou Island.'

'Where, according to the Ontario police, Henry Wellington is not currently in residence. They say they're trying to talk to Rupert Wellington, but he's been unavailable.'

'Unavailable? He was in Thunder Bay yesterday and quite available. And Henry Wellington was definitely on Manitou Island. Are you getting good information?'

'It's all being done by fax and phone.'

'Why doesn't Ed pay them a visit?'

'They haven't exactly invited us. Ed thinks we're being stonewalled.'

I stood up and stretched. The place where Morrissey had punched me was feeling sore. 'So what are you going to do?'

She stood up and stared out at the lake, which was almost fully black now. 'Just be patient, I guess.'

After the sheriff left, I went inside. 'Let's close up early,' I told the girls. 'You guys have had a hard day.'

I called Jo and told her I was going out to the rez to check on Meloux.

'Cork, Jenny's here. She wants to talk.'

'Can it wait until after I see Meloux?'

'Will you be long?'

'I don't think so.'

'We'll wait up,' Jo said.

As I HEADED up the eastern shoreline of Iron Lake towards the reservation, the sky still held a whisper of pale blue daylight. The road was empty, but I took it slow anyway. Twilight's when the deer and moose haunt the edges of highways.

Because he was Iron Lake Ojibwe, Ernie Champoux received a nice distribution from the casino profits, but he also liked vehicles. He had snowmobiles, motorcycles, a couple of pick-ups, an SUV, a station wagon and an old yellow VW Bug he'd spent a good deal of time restoring. He'd been employed at the Chippewa Grand Casino since it had opened several years earlier. These days he worked swing shift, heading up a maintenance crew.

So I was surprised when I approached his cabin, which was situated in a stand of poplars on the lakeshore just south of Allouette, and the old VW pulled out of his drive and swung wide, directly into the path of my Bronco. I swerved. The VW jerked back towards the proper lane and rolled on down the road. I watched the taillights in my rearview mirror. The brake lights flashed a good deal. I was concerned that whoever was driving was drunk, but I wasn't a cop any more, and chasing him down wasn't my responsibility.

Then I thought about the VW. It wasn't being driven by a drunk, I realised, but an old man who never drove.

I caught up with Henry near the south end of the lake. He'd stopped dead in the road and was standing in front of the VW, staring towards the woods. I pulled up behind the Bug, got out.

'I hit a deer,' he said sadly. 'It ran off, but it is hurt.'

'We can't follow it in this dark.'

The old man nodded.

'Where were you going, Henry?'

Meloux turned his gaze towards the road ahead, lit for fifty yards by headlights. His voice held no trace of apology. 'Canada.'

'You don't have a driver's licence, do you, Henry?'

'No.'

'Let's park the VW and pick it up tomorrow. Then we can go back to your nephew's place and talk. I'd like to know the whole story, Henry, how you came to have a son you've never seen.'

He drew himself up. In the glare of the headlights, his eyes were like fire. 'These things I will tell you, but secrets come at a price.'

'What price, Henry?'

'You will take me to my son.'

'Wait here.'

I slid into the VW, which was still running, and parked it on the gravel shoulder. 'Let's go back to Ernie's,' I said, walking to the Bronco. 'I'll think about your offer.'

I drove slowly, rolling around in my mind the deal the old Mide had laid out. It was clear he was determined, one way or another, to see his son. Also, the story Meloux had kept to himself for more than seven decades was one I wanted very much to hear. The old man had me. That was all there was to it.

I parked at the cabin, and we went inside.

'Where's Ernie?' I asked. 'He told me he'd taken a couple of days off.'

'A man is sick. They called. My nephew went.'

Considering the attack on Meloux that morning, the choice Ernie had made didn't seem a good one. On the other hand, in all this, I'd miscalculated a lot myself, so who was I to criticise?

'All right, Henry. You've got a deal,' I said. 'Tell me your story, and we'll go to Thunder Bay together.'

He looked round the cabin. 'Not here. We will sit by the lake. We will smoke. Then I will talk, and you will listen.'

I took a pack of Marlboros from a carton Ernie kept on top of his refrigerator and I found a box of wooden matches in a kitchen drawer. We left the cabin and walked across the back yard, through the poplars to the lake. The moon had just risen and its reflection cut a path across the black water solid enough to walk on. We sat on a bench Ernie had fashioned from a split log. I handed Meloux the pack of cigarettes. He took one out, tore the paper, crumbled the tobacco into his hand and made an offering. Then he tapped out a cigarette for each of us. We smoked a few minutes in silence. For Henry, as for many Shinnobs, tobacco is a sacred element, and smoking has nothing to do with habit.

'You have always thought of me as old, Corcoran O'Connor. When you were born, I was in my forty-third year.'

'That's pretty old to a kid. Besides, as long as I've known you, your hair's been white as a bleached sheet.'

'It was not always that colour. In my nineteenth year, it turned white overnight.'

'What happened?'

'It was something I saw, Corcoran O'Connor. And something I did.'

Meloux studied the moon, and I waited.

PART II
Meloux's Story

Four

He didn't keep track of years by numbers, but it was the same year President Harding died and Calvin Coolidge took his place in the White House. Sometime in the early 1920s.

That day, Henry watched the farmer's son coming across the field of corn. Under the brim of a straw hat, the kid's face was dark with shadow. He was taller than Henry and, at seventeen, older by two years. He looked like the farmer, right down to the mean little eyes. It was late June, hot in South Dakota, and Henry worked in overalls without a shirt. His shoes, supplied by the government boarding school in Flandreau, were falling apart, and dirt and pebbles always found their way inside. Periodically he stopped his work to remove the shoes and empty them. He was sitting at the edge of a dry irrigation ditch with his left shoe off when he spotted the farmer's son approaching.

'My old man don't pay you to sit on your ass,' the kid said.

'Your old man doesn't pay me at all,' Henry pointed out. He put on his left shoe and began to remove the other.

'You eat his food, sleep under his roof,' the kid threw back.

Henry could have pointed out that this choice was not his. The Flandreau school had a policy called 'outing' that placed the Indian students in jobs during the summer months. Henry knew the truth of the outing programme—cheap labour for a local family.

The other kid stood above him, arms crossed over his chest. 'You got a letter up at the house. My old man says to come get it.'

At the farmhouse, Henry let the kid go inside first while he took a few minutes to wash himself off at the water pump in the yard. He put on his shirt and went into the house through the back door.

The farmer sat at the kitchen table drinking from a glass full of cloudy liquid. He was a tense, willowy man with a head as bald as a rock. Over his glass, his small, mean eyes took in Henry.

'Lemonade, Henry?' said the wife. She was small and plump.

'Thank you.' Henry stood politely, just inside the door.

She filled the glass and took it to him, looking as if she were about to speak something comforting, but her husband cut in.

'A letter come for you. From the boarding school. Took the liberty of reading it since I wasn't sure you could.'

'I can read,' Henry said.

'The upshot is that your father's dead, boy. Logging accident.'

'Karl,' the woman said. 'Give the boy the letter.'

The farmer reached into the shirt beneath his overalls and pulled out a folded sheet of paper. 'Take it, boy,' he said.

'For heaven's sake.' The woman plucked the letter from her husband's hand and brought it to Henry. 'I'm so sorry. You take that lemonade and letter, and you find you some shade. Take all the time you need, Henry.'

He sat under a crab-apple tree near the vegetable garden. The writing was neat, the letters precisely made.

Dear Nephew,

It is sad news I tell you your father my brother die in that logging camp a white man drive here to tell me your father killed by log rolling over him he bring the body for me to bury and I have done this beside your mother's grave this news is heavy and I know will be for you great sorrow.

Woodrow Meloux

There was no date on the letter, no way of knowing when the death had occurred. It didn't matter; it was done. His mother had died three years before. His father worked as a logger and was away most of the time and could not care for his children. Henry had been sent to the Indian boarding school in Flandreau, South Dakota. His two sisters had gone to a school in Wisconsin.

Henry read the letter again, folded it and put it in his pocket.

Even in the shade the air felt thick, hot, heavy. His dark eyes followed the flat line of the horizon that circled and imprisoned him.

LONG AFTER DARK, Henry rose from his cot in his small quarters in an old tack room. He put on his white shirt, overalls and shoddy boarding-school shoes. He left the barn and walked out to the yard. The moon, nearly full, made everything around Henry silver. The farm dog barked a couple of times, then recognised him and settled near the back door of the house. Henry started towards the dirt road that ran in front of the farmhouse but stopped when he heard the hinges of the screen door creak.

She came towards him, a small, pale figure that seemed to float in her nightgown. She held out a potato sack.

'You'll be hungry, I expect. It's not much. Couple of sandwiches. And here.' She put coins in his hand. 'Fifty cents. It's all I can spare without him knowing. And take a blanket, the one on your bunk. You'll be sleeping out some, I expect.'

He looked at the coins burning in the silver light. '*Migwech*.'

She eyed him with puzzlement.

'It means thank you,' he said.

'God be with you, Henry.' She floated back to the house.

He rolled the blanket and tied it with a length of scrap rope he found in the barn. He slung the bedroll and the potato sack over his shoulder and left.

He followed roads that headed east, towards Minnesota. Whenever he spotted dust rising ahead of or behind him, he lay in the tall grass at the side of the road until the vehicle had passed. Near sunset, on the outskirts of a small town, he came across a train paused on a siding, loading from a grain elevator. The engine was pointed east. Henry climbed onto a coupling between cars and waited. Just as the sun hit the horizon, the train pulled out.

Near sunset of the third day, he reached the mission on the Iron Lake Reservation. It was a small white clapboard building in the middle of a forest clearing. Behind it lay the cemetery, enclosed by a low wrought-iron fence.

Henry eased the gate open. He knew the place where his mother was buried. Beside her marker was another: a smooth, varnished wood plank with his father's name burned across the face. Henry sat down cross-legged, weary to the bone. He felt like spilling tears, felt more empty and alone than he ever had.

He lay down in the uncut cemetery grass and went to sleep.

That night he had his first vision. It was like a dream, but it was not a dream. A huge white snake slithered among the markers of the cemetery. It swallowed Henry. Then it sprouted wings and took him on a long journey deep into the wilderness, far beyond Noopiming, the great woods of his home. It disgorged him on the shore of a lake he did not know. The lake glowed, as if a fire burned at the bottom. Fire under the water? How could this be? When he turned back, the snake had vanished.

He woke on the ground, his blanket covered with dew. Dawn was just breaking, and he was hungry. It was midsummer, blueberry season, and he knew where the patches grew. He feasted on ripe berries as the sun rose above the pines, and he continued his way north, towards the cabin his father had built.

It was nearly noon when he reached the small cabin at the edge of a pond where he'd spent the first twelve years of his life. Henry came towards it, pushed the door open, and stepped inside.

It was one room, mostly bare now, with a plank floor. The table where his family had eaten was overturned. One chair remained. The black stove on which his mother had cooked was there. The frame of the bed his father had made for himself and his wife stood against the far wall beneath a window. He checked the cupboards. Empty except for a few cans of flour and salt and baking soda and one dented pot. He also found a can of kerosene.

The floor was covered with dust, the corners hung with cobwebs. Outside, Henry used his pocketknife and cut pine branches with thick needles and bundled them together to use as a broom. He swept the floor and cleared the cobwebs.

In the late afternoon he gathered wood for the stove and built a fire. He made biscuits with what he'd found in the cans. He ate the biscuits with the last of the blueberries he'd picked. Afterwards he sat outside and watched the night come on and tried to think what he should do. He was fifteen years old. His parents were dead and buried. His sisters were far to the east. In the letters they'd sent him, his sisters told him they liked the school in Wisconsin. The people were decent to them there. Henry didn't want to go back to the boarding school in Flandreau, ever.

'WAKE UP.'

Henry felt a shove and opened his eyes.

'You sleep like a deaf old dog, nephew.'

Woodrow Meloux was not tall. He was broad across the chest and strong. He wore his black hair in a long braid. He resembled Henry's father in many ways, but harder. He had never taken a wife, never fathered children.

'Uncle.' Henry sat up. 'How did you know I was here?'

A leather pouch hung from Woodrow's belt. He reached inside and took out a strip of deer jerky, which he handed to Henry.

'Everyone on the rez knows. The smoke from the stove.'

Henry chewed on the jerky. He loved the texture and flavour, which he hadn't tasted in three years.

His uncle said, 'The whites were in Allouette yesterday. They warned there will be trouble if we do not send you back.'

'I won't go back,' Henry said.

Woodrow took a piece of jerky for himself and gave another to Henry. 'We have a long walk.'

'I'm not leaving the cabin.'

'They will look for you here.'

'I'm leaving, then. But I'm not leaving the cabin my father built.' Henry got off the bed. He put on his government shoes and walked to the corner where the can of kerosene sat. He removed the cap and began to spread fuel across the cabin floor.

Henry took the box of matches from near the stove. He stood at the door with his uncle. He struck a flame and threw it into the wet line that lay across the floor. Fire crawled through the cabin like a yellow snake. Henry waited until he was sure the logs were burning well; then he turned away with his uncle and never looked back.

They walked for several hours, keeping to the trails. Henry knew where they were headed. His uncle had a parcel of land in the northwest corner of the reservation, a small, rocky finger that jutted into Iron Lake. It was far from Allouette, far from any other dwelling. Woodrow had named it *aandeg,* or crow, because the trees were a favourite rookery for the black birds. His uncle had built a *wiigiwam,* a traditional Ojibwe dwelling. There, in the summer of his fifteenth year, Henry Meloux began to live in the old way.

HIS UNCLE trapped and fished and hunted in the vast forest to the north, which the whites called the Quetico-Superior wilderness. Through an outfitter named Aini Luukkonen, who operated on Iron Lake near the town of Aurora, Woodrow sometimes agreed to be hired as a guide. Because he knew the northern forest better than any other man, he was always in demand.

Through that summer, through the season of the wild-rice harvest that followed, through the long winter when Grandmother Earth slept and the time for storytelling came and passed, Henry Meloux watched his uncle and listened and learned. Woodrow could track an animal over stony ground.

With his rifle, he could bring down a deer at over a hundred yards with a single shot. He could take a canoe through white water and knew portages no white man had ever walked. All this knowledge he passed to Henry.

That first year, Woodrow traded furs, wild rice or syrup made from maple sap for cartridges and taught Henry how to shoot.

One morning in early May, Woodrow said, 'You will go with me to see Aini Luukkonen.'

They took Woodrow's canoe and paddled steadily the five miles to Luukkonen's. Among the trees along the shore, Henry could see that cabins were appearing in greater numbers.

They drew the canoe onto the shore near the dock behind Luukkonen's and tipped it onto the grass. The old Finn operated out of a big log structure thirty yards off the lake. When they stepped inside, a bell over the threshold jingled. The place smelled of coffee and bacon. 'Yah,' called a voice. 'Be dere in a minute.'

The outpost was full of goods a man might need in the woods. Axes and hatchets, knives, wool blankets, rope coils, fishing gear, lanterns, small stoves, hats, gloves. Henry stood silent.

A man came through a door near the rear. He was stout, bald, but with a big walrus moustache that nearly hid his mouth. 'Woodrow,' he said in hearty greeting. 'Been expecting you.' He came close and eyed Henry in a friendly way. 'Dis da boy, den?'

Luukkonen put out a hand. Reluctantly, Henry took it. He didn't like shaking hands. It was a thing white people did.

The Finn disappeared through the rear door. Henry and Woodrow waited in silence. When Luukkonen returned, he carried a rifle.

'Came in yesterday, just like I told you,' he said to Woodrow.

He handed the rifle to Henry's uncle, who inspected it and nodded his approval. Woodrow held it out to Henry. 'Yours,' he said.

For a moment, Henry couldn't move. The gift stunned him.

'Well, go on dere. Take da blasted ting.' Luukkonen smiled. 'A good piece dat. Your uncle, he knows.' Luukkonen winked.

Henry lifted his eyes briefly. '*Migwech*.'

Woodrow nodded, accepting the thanks.

'Say, I got a job for you, you want it.'

'What job?' Woodrow asked.

'Two men itching to go up near the Quetico. Prospectors, I'd guess.

Need a guide. Say they'll pay premium for someone good.'

'Gold,' Woodrow said.

Luukkonen tugged at his moustache. 'People been talking a long time about da possibility. Dey say da geology's right, but nobody's found gold yet. Tank God. So, Woodrow, what you tink?'

'Henry comes too.'

'I don't know if dey'd pay for two guides.'

'He will not be paid.'

'A free hand? Hell, what dey got to lose? Be here sunup day after tomorrow. Enjoy da rifle, Henry. You'll need cartridges. Here.' He handed over two boxes of shells. 'On da house.'

TWO DAYS LATER, in the dark before sunup, Henry set out with his uncle once again for Luukkonen's outpost.

The men were waiting, the outfitter with them. They were quiet white men but with eyes that said much. Eyes that said: Business. That said: No questions. That said: We will watch you, boy.

Like all white men, they shook hands.

'Leonard Wellington,' the tall one said. He had a big nose, deep-set eyes, light brown hair. He was older than Henry by a decade, maybe two. It was hard for Henry to judge.

The other looked to be Woodrow's age, nearing fifty. He was smaller and heavier than Wellington, with a thin black moustache. Carlos Lima, he said his name was. He spoke in a way Henry had not heard before, a strange accent that rolled melodically off his tongue. He smiled often, baring teeth white as bleached bone.

The men's gear and the packed supplies were already in the back of Luukkonen's pick-up. Henry and Woodrow threw in their own belongings and climbed into the open bed. The two white men sat up front with Luukkonen. It was a cool morning in late August, and the ride into the woods chilled Henry. They followed old logging roads for an hour through territory Henry barely knew.

The outfitter finally pulled to a stop at the edge of a long, narrow lake backed by steep hills crowned with aspen. They unloaded two canoes from the trailer and stowed the gear. In the white men's canoe was equipment whose purpose Henry didn't know, although he suspected that it was for finding gold.

'Two weeks from today,' Luukkonen said to Woodrow. 'Noon. I'll be waiting.'

'I will have them here,' Woodrow promised.

They paddled all day—six lakes, four portages, one rough passage along a swift, rocky stream. The two white men spoke mostly to each other but at every portage conferred with Woodrow. They asked about rocks and hills and ridges, and Woodrow listened and nodded and pointed this way or that. They camped that night beside a lake Woodrow called Opwagun, which meant a pipe bowl.

'Where are we going?' Henry asked in Ojibwemowin so the white men, if they heard, would not understand.

'North,' Woodrow replied. 'Three more lakes.'

'Is there gold?'

Woodrow's eyes hung heavily on the white men sitting near the lake at the edge of the firelight. They were smoking cigars and drinking from a silver flask. He stared up at the sky.

'If there is, and the white men find it, I will kill them.'

'Why?'

'When I was a boy, I travelled with my uncle to a place called the Black Hills. It belonged to the Lakota by treaty, but white men found gold there. They stole the land, ripped the earth, turned the clear streams to mud.' Woodrow's eyes went back to the men drinking by the fire. 'If there is gold here, I would die to keep it a secret. And I would kill for that, too.'

THEY SET UP CAMP the next day at noon on the lake called Ishkode. The word meant fire, and Henry thought about the vision he'd had of a lake with fire at the bottom. Was this what it had meant? The two men eagerly eyed the grey ridges along the far shore and spoke to each other in low, excited voices. They set off immediately with equipment, crossing the lake alone in their canoe. Henry took his new rifle into the woods and shot a wild turkey, which Woodrow prepared and roasted on a spit.

The men returned near sunset looking tired and grumbling in reply whenever Woodrow spoke to them.

Good, thought Henry. They have been disappointed.

For three days it went this way. On the fourth, the men returned in a different mood. They didn't say anything, but it was in their faces and in the bounce of the words they spoke to each other.

That night, lying beside his uncle after the men slept, Henry asked, 'Did they find the gold?'

Woodrow said, 'Not the gold, I think. They would be drunk. But something that makes them believe they might find gold.'

At dawn the next day, the men left. This time Woodrow followed. Henry fished and caught several walleye. He cleaned his rifle and waited, scanning the lake with uneasiness in the direction all the men had gone.

The two whites came first. Their boots and the legs of their trousers were caked with mud. Woodrow was not with them.

'Where's your uncle?' the man named Wellington asked.

Henry answered, 'I do not know.'

'I hope you have a meal ready, boy,' Lima said. 'A *big* meal.' With his accent the word came out *beeg*. 'I could eat a moose.'

Henry fed them the walleye, which he rolled in cornmeal and fried. He made drop biscuits and gave them blueberries he'd gathered, and the men were happy.

Dark came, but not Woodrow.

The men sat at the fire. They drank coffee into which they poured some of whatever was in the silver flask.

Wellington wrote in a book bound in leather. Every night they'd camped, he'd spent time after supper writing by the firelight. He looked up from his book and caught Henry staring.

'Writing my memoirs,' Wellington said with a laugh. 'I figure I'll publish them someday, get famous.'

'You read, boy?' Lima asked.

Henry was tired of being called boy, but he held his tongue. He stirred the fire with a long, sturdy maple stick. 'I read,' he said.

'Mission school or something?' Wellington asked.

'A school in South Dakota.'

'South Dakota?' Wellington laughed. 'A world traveller, eh? Ever been to Canada?'

'No,' Henry said.

'I'm from Port Arthur. Know where that is?'

'No,' Henry said.

'You're not alone.' Wellington gave a snort. 'Me, I'm going to put that burg on the map, eh.'

Lima pulled a cigar from the vest pocket of his jacket. 'You smoke, boy?'

'No,' Henry said.

Lima ran the cigar along the line of his moustache under his nose and inhaled. 'These are my own cigars. It's what I do. Manufacture good smokes. You know the island Cuba? The best cigars, they come from Cuba, from my factory. Have one, boy. On me.'

Lima held out the cigar. Henry didn't want it, but he didn't want to offend the man. He took it.

Lima pulled out a cigar for himself. 'Now, you clip the tip like this.' He pulled out his knife and deftly sliced off a small nub at the end of the cigar. Henry took his own knife and did the same.

Lima struck a match. He rolled the cigar between his index finger and thumb, near the match flame, until the tip glowed with ember. 'Now you put it in your mouth and take a gentle puff or two.' He looked at Henry expectantly. 'Well, go on, boy.'

Henry imitated Lima's actions, and soon the cigar smoke crawled down his throat like a thick snake.

'Good, good,' Lima said with a big grin. 'Enjoy.'

Henry didn't. He got sick. After he'd puffed for a while, he became dizzy. Then he stood up, stumbled out of the firelight and puked. The men roared with laughter.

Later, as Henry lay in his bedroll, he woke to the rustle of the tent flap. Woodrow entered and lay down on his bedroll.

'You fed them?' he asked.

'Yes,' Henry answered. He wanted to ask where his uncle had been, but he knew if Woodrow meant for him to know, he would say. In a few minutes, he could hear the soft susurrus of deep breathing that told him Woodrow had gone to sleep.

Next morning he watched his uncle leave to follow the two men again. Henry stayed back, dealt with the aftermath of breakfast, then took his rifle and began to circle the lake on foot. An hour later, he came to the place where the white men had drawn up their canoe. He didn't see any sign of his uncle's canoe, but he hadn't expected to. Woodrow would have hidden it.

Henry easily found a trail broken through the undergrowth. It led to the base of the ridge that ran the length of the lake. The ridge was steep, grey rock two hundred feet high. The trail followed the base. From the far side of the lake, the ridge had looked solid. After half a mile, however, Henry came to a place where a second ridge folded against the first with a narrow break between them through which a tiny creek ran. The trail left by the men led beside the creek, and Henry followed.

On the other side of the ridges, he found a great expanse of marsh and understood immediately the mud that had caked the men's boots and trousers. He lost the trail in the yellow marsh grass. He climbed the ridge to high ground and scanned the tamarack trees that grew in profusion along the edges of the wetland. He saw no sign of the men or Woodrow.

It was midmorning. The day was turning hot. Henry found a place in the shade of a cedar and waited. He sat for two hours as the sun mounted directly overhead. His rifle lay across his legs. He'd chambered a cartridge, mostly to be able to say, if he was spotted, that he'd been hunting.

The screams came to him first. Then he saw the two white men burst from the tamaracks at the northern edge of the marsh and flail their way into the black muck at a desperate run. Wellington was in the lead, Lima a few yards back. They made it halfway to the break in the ridges before an enormous bull moose crashed out of the trees, head lowered, his rack aimed at the men.

The legs of the moose lifted it high above the swamp water. It closed on the men quickly. Henry knelt and brought his rifle into position. The Winchester was meant for smaller game, deer at most. As he sighted, Henry tried to think how with a single shot of a too-small-calibre bullet he could stop the moose.

Out of the corner of his open eye, he saw Lima stumble and go down. Henry squeezed the trigger. He lost the animal for a moment in the jar of the recoil. When he found it again, he saw the moose pitch forward, coming to rest only a few feet from Lima.

Henry sat back. He began to shake. Numbly, he watched Wellington return and kneel beside his fallen companion. A moment later, the man looked up and spotted Henry on the ridge.

Henry stood, worked his way down, and waded into the swamp grass and black water. He could hear Lima's moans.

Henry went first to the moose. The animal's right eye socket was nothing but a deep, bleeding hole.

'You?' Wellington asked with disbelief. 'It was you? That was one hell of a shot, boy.'

Henry turned. 'I'm not a boy.'

Lima moaned again.

Wellington carefully lifted the other man's leg clear of the black soup. Lima shouted something in Spanish that Henry didn't understand but guessed was a curse.

'Broken,' Wellington pronounced. 'Pretty bad, I'd say. We've got to get him to a doctor.'

Woodrow was slogging towards them now across the marsh, rifle in hand. His eyes dropped to the moose as he passed.

'Can you walk?' Woodrow asked Lima.

'No!' the man yelled.

'We can carry him,' Wellington suggested.

Woodrow shook his head. 'Too far. There is another way.' He motioned to Henry. 'Come with me.' He turned away and made for the break in the ridges. Henry followed to the place where Woodrow had hidden his canoe. They paddled back to camp.

'Take the axe,' Woodrow instructed. 'Cut three saplings seven feet long. Strip the branches, then cut one of the saplings in half.'

Henry did as he'd been told. When he returned, he found Woodrow waiting with rope cut into sections of varying lengths. His uncle lashed the saplings together in a rectangle seven feet long and half that wide. He tied the sections of rope across the frame in a kind of mesh hammock. A travois, Henry realised. They were going to lay the white man on it and haul him out of the woods.

They placed Woodrow's construction across the canoe. Before they shoved off, Woodrow fixed Henry with a cold stare.

'I have never seen a better shot from a hunter.'

Henry looked down. 'Kitchimanidoo must have guided me,' he said, giving credit to the Great Spirit.

'Me,' Woodrow replied, 'I would have left them to the moose.'

IT TOOK three days of exhausting work to transport Lima and all their gear to the place where Luukkonen had dropped them.

'What now?' Wellington asked after they'd pulled the canoes onto shore. 'That outfitter won't be here for a week.'

'You and me, we will walk the logging road,' Woodrow replied. 'If we are lucky, a truck will pick us up.'

'Why both of us?'

'Because a logging truck will not stop for an Indian.'

Midmorning the next day, the men returned in Luukkonen's pick-up. They brought a doctor. While the physician examined Lima's leg, the outfitter shook his head.

'You're lucky it was Woodrow with you,' he told Wellington.

Wellington scowled at Henry and his uncle. 'I've been thinking. It strikes me as odd that you two just happened to be around when that moose charged. I'm thinking you were following us.'

Henry didn't know what to say, but Woodrow spoke immediately. 'Your safety was our responsibility. We could not keep you safe if we could not see you.'

'Forget it, Leonard,' Lima said, grimacing. 'There's nothing for us here. I hate this place. I will never come back.'

The doctor stood. 'We need to get him to my office right away.'

They put Lima in the bed of the pick-up.

Luukkonen spoke quietly to Woodrow. 'I'll come back for you and Henry directly. And I'll see to it these men pay the full two weeks. You've earned it.'

Henry stood beside his uncle and watched the pick-up disappear. Kitchimanidoo had saved the white men. Why, Henry couldn't say. It didn't matter. He would never have to see them again.

Or so he believed.

Five

For the next two years Henry continued to live with his uncle on Crow Point, growing well into his manhood, strong in his resolve to live the old ways. He saw unhappy changes creep onto the reservation. Some Shinnobs managed to purchase automobiles, and the dust they raised could be seen above the trees, like smoke from a spreading fire. In Allouette there was electricity and there were plans for a telephone line. More and more whites crowded the forests.

There was another change. In the summer he turned eighteen, and into the early fall Henry laboured with his uncle to cut and lay the logs for a one-room cabin on Crow Point. The logs were cedar, and the roof was cedar covered with birch bark.

When the first snow fell in early November, the cabin was finished. It was a blessing because, in the winter that followed, Woodrow fell ill. The winter was harsh, and life slipped further and further from his body, until all that was left one day in April were a few ragged breaths and his final words to Henry: 'My life with you has been good, Nephew. Do not be alone now.'

Henry buried Woodrow in the cemetery behind the mission. Despite his uncle's advice, he remained alone on Crow Point. There were relatives across the rez, but Henry kept away from them all. He tried to disappear into the forest, but it, too, seemed an empty place without Woodrow.

In the early fall, more than four months after Woodrow died, as Henry fished from the rocks along the shore of Iron Lake, he spotted a canoe gliding towards him from the south. In a few minutes, he could make out that it was Luukkonen, the outfitter.

He pulled up to shore. '*Anin*,' he said, greeting Henry formally.

'What do you want?' Henry replied.

The outfitter stepped from his canoe and sat down near Henry.

'A man come looking for your uncle dis morning,' he began. 'I told him Woodrow had gone to his reward, and he asked about you. Wants to hire you. He wants to go way up nort. Canada.'

Henry began to reel in his line. 'I don't want to go to Canada.'

'You ever been in a airplane, Henry? Dis man, he's going to fly you up dere. Sounds pretty good.'

'I'm not interested.'

Luukkonen leaned nearer. 'Henry, I'm tinking it would be good for you. I'm tinking you need to get away for a while.'

Away. Away hadn't occurred to Henry.

'Dere's nutting for you here right now, Henry. Go away for a while. Maybe when you come back, tings will be different.'

The outfitter was right. What was there for him here? What he loved had passed or was passing. The Finn's offer suddenly and powerfully appealed to Henry.

'All right,' he agreed.

'One ting I didn't tell you,' Luukkonen said. 'Dis man who wants you. You know him. His name is Leonard Wellington.'

WELLINGTON had changed little. He didn't seem as tall to Henry, who'd grown several inches since their last meeting. His hair was thinner. But he still had a hatchet blade for a nose and a too-proud look in his eyes.

Wellington stared at Henry with astonishment.

'You've filled out,' he said. 'Left that boy you were a good distance back, eh.' He offered his hand. It was tanned and rough. 'I was sorry to hear about your uncle but awfully glad to have you on the expedition. Luukkonen told me you understood the terms.'

They had been simple. Henry agreed to sign on for as long as necessary at five dollars a week. He was to maintain camp, provide native food to supplement the supplies and see to the safety of the expedition members, Wellington and his partner, Carlos Lima.

'Well, then.' Wellington rubbed his hands together eagerly. 'Let's get started.'

Henry had canoed past a floatplane tethered to the dock behind the outpost. He'd seen only a few such planes. Yet here he was throwing the propeller to help Wellington start the plane and then climbing afterwards into the belly of the beast. As he felt the plane glide across the surface of Iron Lake and lift free of Grandmother Earth, it seemed to Henry that he'd never been so far from who he'd thought he would become.

NEAR NOON, a great shining water appeared ahead of them. The plane began its descent.

Wellington finally spoke to Henry. 'Lake Superior.'

Kitchigami, Henry thought. He'd never seen the big water, though it was well known to him.

As they flew over the squat buildings of a town below, Wellington spoke again. 'Fort William. And up there, that's Port Arthur.'

Canada, Henry understood.

The plane landed smoothly and motored to a dock where Henry saw two people waiting. One he recognised: Carlos Lima. The other was a woman about Henry's age.

'Damn,' Wellington swore under his breath, then cut the engine.

Lima tied the plane to the dock. Wellington opened his door and stepped down. Henry followed him. Lima had changed, grown visibly older, he had put on weight and his moustache was thicker, with a dullness to it that made Henry think of a little, grey mouse. Lima looked on him with the same disdain he'd had in the summer Henry saved his life.

'Where's the other one?' Lima said to Wellington.

'Henry's uncle died last winter. Henry has agreed to work for us.'

Lima's dark, distrustful eyes did a long assessment of Henry. 'You've grown,' he finally said as if he grudgingly approved.

Wellington said, 'What's Maria doing here? I thought we agreed.'

Lima shrugged. 'You know her.'

'This isn't a trip for a girl, Carlos.'

'She's strong, Leonard. And pig-headed.'

'You're her father.'

'You've never been a father. You don't know.'

The girl was near enough to hear, but she seemed not to notice. Or maybe she simply didn't care. What she did was to look frankly at Henry, who burned under the gaze of her dark eyes.

'All right,' Wellington said, finally giving in. 'Let's get loaded. We have a long way to go.'

The plane had only two seats, so they organised the cargo area in such a way that there was a small space for Maria and Henry, who sat facing each other, seated on rolled tents. The plane was heavily loaded and seemed to struggle to rise off the lake. Once it did, it headed towards the vast green wilderness waiting to the northwest.

To keep from staring at the young woman, Henry pretended to sleep, but he kept his eyes open a slit. He watched her take a notebook bound in leather from her canvas bag and spend a long time writing. She was Lima's daughter. Henry could see traces of the father in her—the black hair, the slender nose— but Henry thought her mother must have been terribly beautiful.

It was late afternoon by the time they finally glided to rest on the shore of an immense lake contained on three sides by steep ridges. They unloaded the equipment and set up their tents. There was one for each of them. Lima and Wellington set up their own tents next to each other. Henry put up Maria's. She asked for it to be as far from her father as possible because she said he snored.

Henry erected his own tent a bit away from the others. By the time he'd finished, the sun was sinking fast. He canvassed the area for wood and built a fire. Wellington opened a big tin of soup from the supplies that Lima had brought and heated it directly on the coals. Shortly after dark they all crawled into their tents.

Henry lay awake. He had the sense that he'd embarked on a long journey, without any idea of his destination.

AT FIRST there was routine to the days. After breakfast, Wellington and Lima took off with their packs full of instruments. Sometimes they used the collapsible boat they'd brought in the plane, which they called a Folbot; sometimes they struck out on foot. Always they headed towards the ridges. Usually they were gone until late afternoon, often until almost dark.

Henry's principal job was to feed the expedition and see to the safety of the camp—and Maria. Henry didn't wonder that Lima trusted him to be alone with his daughter. He understood clearly that Lima thought of him as little better than a stock animal. Lima forbade Maria's leaving camp unless Henry accompanied her. And Henry was forbidden to leave her alone. He was eager to explore the area and to hunt game, but when she walked in the forest, Maria made more racket than a wounded moose. Henry hated taking her with him. For several days he confined himself to camp, fishing for walleye and trout from the lake. Maria spent the bulk of her time reading or writing in her journal and looking bored.

'I'm sick of fish,' she declared on the fourth day, after her father and Wellington had left. 'And I'm sick of sitting.' She squatted on a flat rock at the edge of the water, and she looked across the lake at the tallest ridge. 'I'm hiking up there today.'

'There are wolves,' Henry said.

'I don't believe you. I'm going.' She put down the book she'd been reading and stood up.

'I'm not ready to go,' he said.

'I don't care.' She stomped off, following the shoreline.

Henry sighed and waited. When she was out of sight, he took up his rifle and followed, keeping himself hidden.

HENRY EXPECTED HER to tire quickly, but he was surprised by her endurance. The lake snaked for more than two miles to the west, and Maria followed the shoreline at a steady pace.

By noon she'd reached the top of the ridge. As she stood on a jut of grey rock, smiling in the sunshine, looking at the forest scene below her, Henry found himself walking towards her. She turned and did not look happy. 'What are you doing here?' she asked.

'What I'm paid to do.'

'You followed me. I should have known.'

'I'm sorry,' he said. 'I'll wait below.' He turned away.

'No,' she said to his back. Then more gently, 'Stay.'

They stood together, for a long time silent, drinking in the magnificence of what lay before them.

'Why don't you want me with you when you go into the woods?' Maria asked.

'You make too much noise. You scare the game.'

'I don't mean to. You could teach me how to be quiet.'

He liked the sound of her voice.

'Why did you come?' he asked.

Instead of answering, she said, 'Do you have family?'

'My parents are gone. Two sisters are in school in Wisconsin.'

'I've heard my father talk about someone named Woodrow.'

'My uncle. He is gone, too.'

She nodded, and her eyes rested on the deep green that reached to the horizon. 'My mother died when I was a little girl. Since then, I've lived in boarding schools, mostly in the States.'

'I know about boarding schools,' Henry said.

She sat down on the rock and hugged her knees. Henry sat down and laid his rifle on the ground.

She said, 'They're hunting gold, you know.'

'I know.'

'Leonard is a geologist. He knows where to look, but he doesn't have the money to prospect. My father foots the bill. They met in a casino in Havana. My father was probably throwing away money, as usual. He loves to gamble. They've found gold twice already. First in Australia, but it turned out not to be a very rich strike. Then again in South America, but they lost that claim somehow. They won't talk about it. Anyway, I thought maybe if I came with him this time, it might be a chance to get to know him.'

Henry didn't like her father and couldn't imagine why anyone would want to know him better.

'I should be in college, a place called Bennington in Vermont. My second year there. But I have no interest in it right now.'

'Would you like to hunt with me?' Henry asked.

'Yes.'

'To your eyes it might not be pretty.'

'I can take it.'

THEY RETURNED to camp in the early afternoon with a fat snowshoe rabbit in hand. Henry set about the skinning and cleaning and quartering. When he'd finished, he made a fire, settled a pot of water at the edge, and put the cut-up rabbit in to stew.

Maria said, 'I'm going for a swim. Come with me?'

Henry laughed, thinking she was joking. The nights were cold and the lake would be like ice.

'All right then.' She disappeared into her tent and came out a few minutes later dressed in shorts and a man's white undershirt. Henry saw that her toes were painted red. 'Last chance,' she said.

Henry shook his head. 'You'll be out fast enough.'

'Think so?'

She dashed towards the lake and dived in. She disappeared for a long time. Henry left the fire and was about to go in after her when she burst through the surface and began stroking evenly away.

Henry went back to the fire and cut onions and carrots and potatoes to add to the stew. All the while he kept an eye on Maria. She stayed a long time in the water.

Finally she returned to shore and climbed from the lake. Beneath the thin wet cotton of her undershirt her skin was visible and pink. Henry looked away, but not before she caught him looking and not before she smiled.

HENRY COULDN'T SLEEP. He lay in his tent staring up at canvas that was drenched in silver moonlight. It wasn't the canvas he was seeing. It was Maria. He didn't understand what was happening to him or the way he felt. Strong, but also very weak. Full of fire and at the same time ice. He threw back his blanket and stepped into the night. He longed to see Maria, even a glimpse. But he was afraid.

Instead, he walked to the lake. The water was silver fire. Henry glanced back at the camp, then quietly undressed. He stepped into the lake. The cold hammered his legs, but he pushed on, further and deeper. He wanted the icy water to kill the fire that wouldn't stop burning in him. He let out his breath and sank towards a place where the moonlight didn't reach.

He felt a disturbance of the water and came up quickly. He looked towards shore and saw her slender figure slipping into the lake. He wasn't certain, but he thought she was naked. She swam towards him, her face a pale, beautiful bubble. Henry stared at her, amazed. He felt the loop of her arms around him and the press of her warm body. She kissed him.

'You're freezing,' she said. 'Come with me.'

Out of the water and in the moonlight, her naked skin was jewelled with shining droplets. She stooped and gathered her clothing and his and led him to her tent.

LONG BEFORE DAWN, long before the white men would be stirring, he rose and returned to his own tent, but he couldn't sleep. He was too full of Maria.

She didn't appear at breakfast. Wellington and Lima ate the biscuits and the oatmeal Henry had prepared. As sunlight began to climb the distant ridges, they set off across the lake. When they were out of sight, Henry went to Maria's tent. He reached out but held back from opening the flap, suddenly unsure.

'I'm awake,' she said from inside.

He found her still in her sleeping-bag, looking at him with a tired smile on her face. He lay down beside her.

Henry heard the sound of music, a muffled chime.

'What's that?' he said.

Maria reached into her canvas bag and pulled out a small box. Inside was a gold watch. 'It's a present for my father,' she said.

She snapped it open and handed it to Henry. Opposite the face of the watch was Maria's face, a small photograph behind glass.

'His birthday is next week. On the front, see the writing? It's Spanish. It says, 'To my beloved papa.' I wish it said, 'To my beloved Henry.' I wish I had something to give you. A present.'

'You already gave me a present, the best I ever had.'

He handed the watch back, and she put it away.

That afternoon she swam again while Henry plucked the feathers from a grouse he'd killed. He could barely take his eyes off her.

Out of the corner of his eye, he caught a flash of reflected sunlight among the trees a quarter of a mile to the west. It was a prolonged and brilliant glinting, the kind that came from glass or metal. Henry grabbed his rifle and slipped into the woods.

He arrived at the place along the shoreline where he'd spotted the reflection. There was nothing to be seen. Henry widened his search. Twenty yards away he found a trail of broken ground cover leading west. In soft earth a hundred yards further on, he found the imprint of a moccasin. Henry was certain now that he hadn't been the only one enjoying the sight of Maria swimming.

His inclination was to begin tracking immediately, but he had no idea how far that would take him. When he returned to camp, Maria had finished swimming and was dressed.

'Where did you go?' she asked, and kissed him.

'I saw something.'

She looked at his rifle. 'What?'

He told her. She didn't seem frightened.

'What should we do?' she asked.

'We will find him,' Henry said. 'Tomorrow.'

That night clouds blocked the moon, but Henry knew Maria's beauty without light. They were one skin, one breath, one heart. She was like nothing he'd ever known. That they shared their bodies so quickly, so easily, so completely didn't surprise him. He had the deep sense that being together this way had always been meant for them.

THE NEXT MORNING, when Wellington and Lima were out of sight, Henry slipped back into Maria's tent. He kissed her. 'Wake up.'

Her eyes, brown like acorns, fluttered open. 'What is it?'

'Time to go hunting.'

She dressed. They ate and made their way to the place where Henry had found the moccasin tracks.

The trail led them along the bank of a creek that edged the base of the ridge. After an hour, the tracks joined a deer trail that angled up another ridge. When they reached the far side of that ridge, Henry paused and pointed to a patch of haze in a hollow below.

Maria whispered, 'Smoke?'

Henry nodded. The next mile they moved at a crawl. Henry paused frequently to listen. Eventually he heard the chunk of an axe biting into wood. They came to a path along a small brook. The path led in the direction of the chopping. Henry chambered a cartridge and moved ahead.

He glimpsed the cabin fifty yards through the trees. He signalled Maria to drop into a crouch. They crept forward this way, low to the ground. The chopping stopped. Henry stopped. He spotted movement, then saw a figure carrying a load of split wood in his arms. The figure was dressed in buckskin britches. Long grey hair flowed over a buckskin tunic. Henry also saw moccasins on the feet. The figure stepped through the cabin door and disappeared. Henry signalled to Maria, and they slipped into brush that edged the small clearing where the cabin stood.

The brook flowed behind the structure, which was a log construction similar to the cabin Henry and Woodrow had built on Crow Point. A winter supply of wood lay stacked against the west wall. Fifteen yards away was another, smaller structure which Henry recognised as a smokehouse.

They waited patiently. In ten minutes, the figure emerged. This time Henry could see the face clearly, and he was surprised. The skin was very dark brown. The man gathered an armload of wood. Henry made his move. He strode forward and said, 'Stop.'

The man dropped the wood, spun towards Henry, saw the rifle, and looked poised to run. 'Don't move,' Henry said.

The man held himself tense, ready, but he didn't move.

'Maria,' Henry called.

She came from the underbrush and stood beside him. Something changed in the man's eyes, but Henry couldn't tell why.

'Who are you?' Henry demanded.

The man didn't respond.

'Maybe he doesn't understand English,' Maria suggested. '*Bonjour*,' she said.

The man waited, then nodded tentatively to her. '*Bonjour*.'

'*Votre nom?*' she asked.

'Maurice,' he replied.

'*Je m'appelle* Maria Lima,' she said. She touched Henry. 'Henry Meloux.'

For the next couple of minutes, Maria carried on a conversation with him. At the end, she said to Henry, 'He didn't mean any disrespect. He was just curious about who'd come to his land.'

'His land?'

'That's what he called it. I told him you were my husband.'

Henry looked at her.

'He saw me swimming naked and you watching. I thought it was best. He's apologised. I think you can put the rifle down, Henry.'

Henry and the man locked gazes. Henry indicated that he was going to lower the rifle. The man nodded. Henry pointed the rifle barrel towards the ground and shifted the weapon to his left hand.

Maurice spoke to Maria, who translated for Henry. 'He's asked if we would eat with him.'

Henry said, 'We should accept.'

She smiled. 'I already have.'

Inside, the cabin was spare but neat. It was a single room. They shared a meal of venison stew, and while they ate, Maria and Maurice talked.

'He has been here twenty winters,' Maria told Henry. 'He came with his wife, whose name was Hummingbird. She was Odawa.'

'Odawa?' said Henry; he then addressed Maurice. '*Anin*,' he said, in formal greeting.

'*Anin*,' Maurice replied. In the language of the Odawa, which was very nearly the language of Henry's people, Maurice and Henry talked.

'I am of the Iron Lake Anishinaabeg,' Henry told him.

'I am from Quebec,' Maurice replied. 'I married an Odawa woman and lived with her happily for twenty years here.'

'Where is she?'

'She died five winters ago.'

'Your children?'

'We had none. Only each other.'

'Why did you come here?' Henry asked.

'Because I was a black man in a white world. Here, the colour of my skin doesn't matter.'

That was something Henry understood well.

'We need to go back,' Henry finally said.

'You will come again?' Maurice asked eagerly.

'He would like us to return,' Henry told Maria.

She smiled at Maurice and said, '*Mais oui.*'

THE DAYS PASSED QUICKLY. Henry and Maria often visited Maurice, who proved to be a wonderful and grateful host. Over time, they learned his story.

His father had come from Haiti to Quebec, where a small colony of black Haitians was already established. His mother was white, and Maurice grew up with the names *half-breed*, *mule* and *mongrel* thrown at him like stones. All his life he dreamed of rising to a place where he could look down on those who'd taunted him. Money, he'd believed, would be the way. He'd grown up with stories of wealth waiting to be discovered in the great, unexplored wilderness to the northwest. As soon as he was able—when he was seventeen—he left home and set out to find that wealth.

For the next fifteen years, he spent summers exploring rivers and streams he suspected no man had ever followed. Winters, he worked in a mill in Fort William owned by a French-speaking Quebecois.

One summer day he came across a village of Odawa where a young woman named Hummingbird lived. Love, he told Henry and Maria, struck him with the force of a bullet in his heart. All his loneliness leaked out and what filled its place was happiness.

'I came here looking for gold,' Maurice told them. 'I found something better. These hills, this forest, the lakes and streams, all these are worth more to me than gold.'

LIMA AND WELLINGTON continued to return at day's end tired and discouraged. In the evening, they drank and discussed the next day's plan. One evening, Maria asked why they'd even bothered to come to this place anyway.

Wellington, whose tongue was loosened by drink, said, 'We heard a story.'

'Leonard,' Lima cautioned, and gave him a dark, warning look.

Wellington ignored him. 'We heard a story from a man named Goodkin, who canoed up here two years ago. He spent a night in an Ottawa village. While he was there, he heard a story about a Negro who dressed in buckskin and came a couple of times a year to trade for goods. The Indians said the Negro always traded gold.

'A few months ago, Carlos and I flew up to the village. The Ottawa people didn't know exactly where the Negro lived, but they told us it was generally up this way. We flew over the region, and I liked the look of this lake. I did a brief preliminary survey, and the results were extremely promising.'

'Promising? Hell, you said you were certain,' Lima snarled at Wellington. 'So far we have found nothing.'

'It's here, Carlos.'

Maria spoke up. 'But if you're right, it is, as you said, the Negro's gold.'

'Not if he hasn't filed a claim,' Wellington said.

'And if he has?'

'Then we'll strike a deal. It's just a question of figuring out what a man like this Negro would want.'

'What if there's nothing he wants?'

Wellington looked at her as if she were hopelessly naive. 'There's always something, Maria.'

THAT NIGHT, Henry lay with Maria in his arms. They no longer made love at night; it was too difficult to be quiet, and Henry was afraid of what would happen if the white men knew.

'They know about Maurice,' Maria whispered.

'They've found nothing. Maybe they will give up.' He kissed her hair. 'Sleep,' he told her. 'Just sleep.'

He woke in the morning later than he'd intended. The tent canvas already glowed with dawn. He slid away from Maria, who was still deep in sleep, crouched at the tent entrance, and reached out to open the flap. From outside came the cough and spit with which Carlos Lima greeted most mornings. Henry heard the crackle of fallen leaves as Lima made his way to his toilet. Henry waited a minute before leaving the tent. He eased the flap aside just a slit and peeked out to check the campsite. It looked clear. Quickly, he slipped from Maria's tent. As he stood and turned towards his own tent, he spied Leonard Wellington standing ten yards away. Wellington spotted Henry at the same time. The white man's eyes slid to Maria's tent, then crawled back to Henry.

'Carlos!' he called. 'Carlos, get over here.'

Lima appeared and walked towards them. 'There you are, Henry. Where's the fire, damn it? And hell, boy, where's the coffee?'

'Henry's been busy with other things, Carlos. I just caught him sneaking from your daughter's tent.'

When he heard Wellington's words, Lima stopped. Rage flared on his face. 'You savage,' he spat. 'I will kill you.'

He ran at Henry. Lima wasn't a big man, but he was powerfully built, especially in his upper body. Henry dropped low, caught Lima in the gut with his shoulder, and used the man's momentum to lift him off his feet. Lima tumbled over and landed on his back, the wind knocked out of him.

'Henry?' The canvas flap rustled at his back. Maria touched his shoulder. 'Oh, no.' She rushed past him and knelt at her father's side. 'Papa?' She looked at Henry. 'Did you hit him?'

Before Henry could reply, Wellington said, 'Your father was just trying to defend your honour. Henry nearly killed him.'

'Maria?' Lima's breath had returned. He reached out and took his daughter's hand. 'Tell me it's not the way it looks.'

'Papa, I love Henry.'

'Love?' He snatched back his hand. He rolled to his side and pushed up onto his knees. 'Love?' he bellowed. He brought himself up fully and leaned threateningly towards his daughter. 'This is not love. You are no better than a street whore!'

He slapped her hard, and she spun away. He raised his hand to hit her again. Henry lunged and grabbed Lima's arm. The man turned angrily. Henry hit him full in the face. The man went down. His head hit one of the rocks that ringed the fire, and he lay still, blood leaking from the left side of his head.

'Papa!' Maria sprang up and ran to her father's side. She knelt and put her hand to his cheek. She bent near his lips. 'He's breathing.' She tried again: 'Papa?'

Lima didn't respond.

Wellington threw a menacing look at Henry. 'Let's get him into his tent.'

They carried him in and laid him on his sleeping-bag. Maria sat down beside him.

'I'm sorry,' Henry told Maria.

'He'll be all right.' She gave him a brief smile, but Henry heard the lie in her voice.

Outside the tent, Wellington stormed about the campsite. 'Damn you, Meloux. If he dies, I'll see you hang.' Wellington waded to the floatplane and came out with a small satchel that he took into the tent.

Near noon, Wellington threw aside the flap on Lima's tent and walked to where Henry stood on the lakeshore. 'He's not getting better. He needs a doctor. Maria and I are going to fly him out of here. Give me a hand getting the plane ready.'

They laid bedding in the small cargo area, then returned for Lima. Inside the tent, Maria sat beside her father. Henry and Wellington lifted the unconscious man, carried him to the airplane and eased him inside. Maria had gathered her things, and after her father was inside, she got into the plane. Henry saw the edge of her journal jutting out from under the flap of the knapsack. Even in desperate circumstances, she couldn't bear to leave it behind.

Wellington said to Henry, 'Help me get some things from camp.'

'Maria—' Henry tried to step up to the door, but Wellington grabbed his arm.

'Now!' Wellington ordered.

When they neared the tents, he turned on Henry. 'You're staying here, you redskin son of a bitch. Make sure this equipment is safe until I come back. And you better hope to God Carlos doesn't die. Because if he does, I'm coming back with police.'

Henry wasn't afraid of the threat. He'd been threatened by white men all his life. But he'd made enough trouble already.

He said, 'I'll wait here.'

'Damn right you will. Give me a hand with the propeller.'

Wellington spun on his heel and hurried back to the plane. He pulled up the anchor, scrambled inside, and shut the door. When Wellington gave him the signal, Henry threw the propeller. The engine coughed; the propeller made a couple of lethargic turns, then caught. Henry stepped back onto the shoreline, and the plane manoeuvred towards the middle of the lake. Henry saw Maria's face at the window. Her lips moved, but he couldn't hear the words.

'Maria!' The word flew desperately from his lips. He ran towards the plane and splashed into the water to his waist.

The floatplane began its run. Henry threw himself forward, swimming wildly towards the plane. 'Maria!' he screamed.

Six

Henry sat all afternoon feeding the fire, watching the southern sky, though he knew it was useless to hope. He beat himself with the unknowns. Would Maria ever come back? Would he spend the rest of his life in prison? Should he run now instead of waiting? If he did that, how would he ever find her?

No matter how he looked at the situation, Maria was gone. Henry wanted nothing but to die. A familiar voice at his back startled him out of his reverie. 'I thought you had left.' Maurice came from the trees and sat by the fire near Henry. 'I heard the airplane,' he said. 'You look terrible, my friend. What happened?'

Henry explained the events. 'They know about you, Maurice. They will be back. I don't know what to do,' he confessed.

Maurice thought awhile. 'Come with me.'

'But if they come back—'

'They won't be back today. Come with me. There's something I want to show you, something that might help.'

They reached Maurice's cabin on the swift little stream. Maurice led him inside and blew into the embers of the fire and stoked the flame. He put water on to boil.

'Some tea will help. Hummingbird's recipe.'

Henry sat in the cabin. The hot cup was suddenly in his hands.

'Drink,' Maurice said gently. 'And listen to me.' He settled into a chair facing Henry and leaned close. 'In all my time among white people, the one thing I understood best was that for them, money forgives everything.'

'I don't have money,' Henry said miserably.

Maurice rose from his chair, went to the bunk, and pulled it away from the wall. Henry saw the outline of a trap door beneath, cut into the floorboards. A knotted rope served as a handle. Maurice grasped the rope and lifted. He beckoned Henry to look. Beneath the floor lay a dozen deerhide pouches, each larger than a man's fist. 'Take one,' Maurice said. 'Open it.'

Henry lifted one of the pouches, surprised by its weight. He undid the leather cord and looked at the yellow grains inside.

'Do you know what that is?' Maurice asked.

Henry said, 'Gold.'

'It's yours. As much as you want.'

'Why?'

Maurice smiled. 'I came looking for this. Once I had it, I realised I'd found something better here with Hummingbird. Happiness. We had each other. We had this land whose spirit is generous and beautiful. When Hummingbird died, I thought about leaving, but her spirit is here, too. I feel her with me all the time.' He put a hand on Henry's shoulder. 'What need do I have for gold?'

Henry closed up the pouch and carefully tied the cord. 'If I take the gold, they will know where it came from. They will be back.'

'They will be back anyway. It is only a matter of time.'

'I will think about it,' Henry said.

He stayed awhile with Maurice, but his mind was drawn to the campsite and the empty sky above the lake.

That night, Henry slept in Maria's tent. In the night, he heard music, the chime of the gold watch. He put the watch in his pocket.

ON THE THIRD DAY, the airplane came at noon. Henry was napping. He heard the low thrum in the sky from the eastern end of the lake. He grabbed his jacket and ran out of the tent. The plane dropped towards the water. The floats touched, the engine cut out, and the plane nosed up to solid ground. The door opened.

Leonard Wellington climbed out. He walked along the pontoon with a rope in his hand. Leaping ashore, he tethered the floatplane to a large, heavy rock. He went back to the cabin door and spoke to someone inside. Finally he looked at Henry.

'Wasn't sure you'd still be here,' he said, stepping off the pontoon. 'If I was you, I'd have taken to the woods. Vamoosed.'

Henry only half heard. He was staring at the open cabin door. His heart was a wild horse galloping in his chest.

Another man climbed from the belly of the plane. He carried a rifle. Henry's hope cracked into a thousand pieces.

Wellington saw his face. 'Expecting Maria? You'll never see her again, Henry. That's the way she wants it. You killed her father. That's right; he's dead. Yesterday.'

Henry stared at the man who'd come with Wellington. He didn't look like a policeman. He looked Indian.

'Maria told me about the Negro,' Wellington went on. 'We have a deal to offer you. Take me to him, and the police will never know it was you who killed Carlos Lima. You have my word, eh.'

Henry didn't answer. He felt dull, thick-witted.

'She hates you,' Wellington said. 'She wanted to tell you that herself, but I persuaded her to let me handle this, man to man.'

'I don't believe you.'

Wellington smiled sadly. 'I understand, Henry. You love her. Love makes you blind. But if I was lying, how would I know about the Negro? She told me everything. Except she couldn't tell me how to get to his cabin. I want to make a deal with him.'

'I don't know about this Negro.'

Wellington reached behind him, under his leather jacket, to the small of his back. When his hand reappeared, it held a revolver, which he pointed at Henry. 'You've got five seconds to start telling me how to find the Negro's cabin.'

Henry eyed the Indian, who watched impassively.

'One. Two. Three. Spill it, Henry. Four. Five.'

The revolver popped. Wellington's hand jerked. The bullet struck Henry's right leg, high above the knee. It felt as if he'd been hit with a baseball bat. He went down, sprawled on the ground. He grabbed his thigh. Worms of blood crawled between his fingers.

Wellington grinned. 'I thought you might be reluctant. That's why I brought Pierre with me. Claims to be the best tracker in northern Ontario.' He spoke over his shoulder to the Indian. 'There's some rope in that far tent. Get it.'

The Indian did as he was instructed and returned with a coil of hemp rope.

'Get him over to that tree. I don't imagine he'll be able to travel on that leg, but let's make sure he's not tempted.'

The Indian tossed Wellington the rope and slung his rifle over his shoulder. He grasped Henry under the arms and dragged him to the pine tree Wellington had indicated. He lifted Henry to his feet, shoved him against the trunk, and held him there.

As Wellington bound him to the tree, Henry tried to flex all his muscles and expand his chest. Wellington cinched the rope tight and stepped away.

'I'll be back for you, Henry. Unless the wolves get you first.' Wellington turned to Pierre. 'Find the trail.'

HENRY'S THIGH was on fire. The leg of his jeans was soaked with red, but he thought the wound had stopped bleeding. He knew the bullet hadn't hit bone or an artery. Why hadn't Wellington killed him? The only thing that made sense was that if the Indian couldn't follow the trail, Henry was the fallback.

He was determined not to wait for Wellington's return.

As soon as the two men were out of sight, he began to work on his bonds. Henry found that much of the advantage he'd hoped for in tensing his muscles he'd actually achieved. Over the next half hour, by fractions of an inch, he eased his right hand free. Next was his left. Gradually, he slipped both arms out. When he was free, he collapsed and lay at the base of the tree.

Henry dragged himself up and limped to his tent. He cut two strips of the soft canvas flap. The first strip he folded and placed over the wound in his thigh. The second he wrapped round his leg and tied to hold the compress in place. From inside the tent, he took his rifle. He grabbed a tent pole to lean on as he walked. With his rifle slung over his shoulder, he followed the two men.

HENRY KNEW THE WAY to the cabin. In this he had an advantage over Wellington, who had to wait for the tracker to read the trail. He desperately hoped this would work in his favour, allowing him to catch up with the men before they reached Maurice. His leg was the problem. Even with the tent pole to lean on, walking was agony.

When he reached the final ridge, he reckoned more than two hours had passed since he'd left camp. The whole way he'd seen evidence of the passage of the two men, an X cut deep into the bark of trees. He wondered at that. Why mark a trail the Indian could obviously read?

He felt a cold tingle on his face and glanced at the sky. Small snowflakes had begun to drift down from the clouds.

When he topped the ridge, Henry could see a thread of grey wood smoke rising from the cabin, still half a mile distant. He'd hoped Pierre's prowess as a tracker might prove to be nothing but talk. It wasn't. As he neared the clearing where the cabin and outbuildings stood, he slid several rounds into his rifle. He hid and studied the cabin. The door was closed. He saw no sign of Maurice or Wellington or Pierre.

Between Henry's position and the cabin on the far side of the clearing stood the outhouse. He decided to go for that first and from there to the cabin. He limped his way painfully across ten yards of open ground and fell against the back of the little structure.

That's when he heard the men coming. Henry eased himself along the wall and peered round the corner of the outhouse.

'You go on. Don't worry about me,' Wellington boomed.

A moment later, they stepped into the clearing, Pierre first, with Wellington not far behind. No Maurice.

'You're sure you remember the way?' Wellington said to the Indian's back.

'I remember.'

'More's the pity,' Wellington said.

He produced his revolver. He pointed the barrel at the tracker. The revolver popped. The Indian's head jerked forward and he dropped. Wellington slipped the pistol into his belt, grabbed the man's legs and dragged him into the cabin.

Henry understood now the reason for the Xs carved into the trees. They were Wellington's assurance of finding his way back without the guide. Snow drifted out of the sky and coldly kissed Henry's face. He lifted his rifle, sighted on the door, and waited.

Wellington had been in the cabin for a long time when dark smoke began to roll out of the cabin door and windows. Henry lifted his head away from the rifle stock. Why was the cabin burning?

Wellington stumbled from the cabin door, smoke clinging to his back. Henry quickly sighted. The wind hit the smoke from the cabin, and for a moment, a black curtain was drawn between Henry and his target. Henry pulled off the round anyway.

The smoke cleared a moment later. Wellington had vanished.

'Henry?' Wellington called. 'Is that you, Henry?'

The voice came from the protection of the far side of the cabin.

'Your friend the Negro, he's inside, Henry. He's still alive, but he's going to burn to death. Another couple of minutes, and you'll be hearing his screams. It'll be too late by then.'

Henry had no choice. He stepped into the open.

Through the ragged veil of smoke that drifted across the clearing, Henry saw Wellington's head and shoulder appear round the corner of the cabin. His arm snaked round next, the revolver in his hand. The first shot hit the outhouse wall far to the left of Henry. Wellington fired again, this time hitting nothing. Henry kept coming. The next time the pistol popped, Henry was no more than fifteen yards away. But by now he was like the cabin, full of fire. He saw Wellington pull the trigger again and again. Nothing happened. The man's eyes grew large and afraid, and he vanished behind the cabin. Henry hobbled quickly to the corner, his rifle raised and ready to fire, but Wellington was gone.

Henry limped along the back wall to the far corner. No sign of the man. He completed a circle of the cabin. It was clear to him that Wellington had fled into the forest. Henry would gladly have hunted him down, but Maurice was still inside the burning cabin.

Through the doorway all Henry could see was the murk of the smoke and the yellow-orange dance of flame. He slung his rifle over his shoulder and dropped to the ground. On all fours, he crawled inside. He came to the Indian first. The man lay on his back. To Henry's great astonishment, the Indian wasn't dead. Henry hesitated a moment before moving on to find Maurice.

His friend was slumped in a chair to which he'd been bound with rope. His eyes were closed. Henry pulled out his pocketknife and cut the ropes. Maurice fell into his arms. Henry scooted across the floor to the door, dragging his friend outside. Twenty yards from the cabin, he collapsed and lay on the ground coughing.

He wanted to lie there, to do nothing more, but he couldn't let the Indian burn to death. He gathered his strength, crawled back to the cabin, and hauled the man back out. Exhausted, he lay between Maurice and Pierre while the cabin burned.

'Henry.' Maurice's voice was a low, choking rattle.

Henry propped himself up. Next to him, Maurice's face was a mass of blood and swelling. His right eye was completely closed.

'South,' he whispered to Henry. 'Go south. The river. Village.'

'I'll take you with me.'

Maurice gave his head a faint shake. 'Legs. They broke them both.' He coughed again, hard, and groaned painfully.

Henry studied the bruises on his friend's body. He didn't know what Wellington and the Indian had used—their fists or clubs of some kind— but they'd made a mess of Maurice. He was probably bleeding badly inside.

'They did this for the gold?' Henry asked.

'I tried not to tell them. I knew what they would do to this place once they found it.'

Henry shrugged off his coat, slipped it under his friend's bare back, and wrapped it round him for warmth.

Maurice shook his head again, faint but insistent. 'South,' he whispered urgently. '*Now.*'

The west wall of the cabin collapsed in an explosion of spark and cinder. The south wall followed a few minutes later. When the cabin was reduced to a smouldering ruin, Henry gathered logs from the winter store and built a fire near where the two men lay. He figured Wellington had made his way back to camp and the floatplane and had lifted off before the snow could prevent him.

The snow fell into the night. Maurice drifted in and out of consciousness. Henry fed the fire and waited for Pierre and his good friend to die.

IN THE GREY of the next morning, Henry struggled to limp his way south. Three days to the village on the river, Maurice had told him. Three days for a man with two good legs. Snow fell throughout the day. There was no sun, nothing to navigate by, so he used a trick Woodrow had taught him early on. He picked a distant tree in the line he was travelling and made straight for it. Tree by tree, he made his way towards the river and the village Maurice had promised.

The first night, he camped at the edge of a small lake. In the lee of a fallen spruce, he built a fire. He cut pine boughs and laid them on the snow near the flames and sat down to eat some of the jerky he'd taken from Maurice's smokehouse.

Then he undid the canvas wrapping on his leg and took a look at his wound. There was only one hole, the entry wound.

He held the blade of the hunting knife in the fire to sterilise it, then laid it on the snow to cool before he cut. He didn't have to go deep to find the bullet, which he pulled out with his fingers. That was the easy part. He put the knife in the fire again. When the blade glowed red, he grasped the handle and laid the searing steel against the cut. He cried out and fell back, gasping.

FOR TWO MORE DAYS, he limped and stumbled on. The third day the sun finally appeared, and Henry realised his heading was off. He'd been travelling southwest. He was exhausted. His leg hurt constantly. His fever raged. He'd begun to see things among the trees, movement out of the corner of his eye, but when he looked, nothing was there. He heard things, too, sounds in the wind.

On the fourth day—or maybe it was the fifth, he'd lost track—he saw Wellington. The man stood on a hill directly ahead of him. Wellington hadn't left in his airplane. He'd followed, waiting for his chance to attack. Henry ripped the rifle off his shoulder, shoved his cheek against the stock, and fired. Wellington disappeared in a sparkling spray of powdery snow. When Henry reached the spot, he found tracks that looked like deer.

'Wellington!' he screamed. 'I will eat your heart!'

He didn't sleep that night. Nor did he build a fire that would give him away. By moonlight, he kept watch, his rifle on his lap.

Wellington didn't come that night. In the morning, clouds swept in again, bringing more snow. All day as he struggled ahead, Henry could feel Wellington in the storm. Henry lost interest in the river, in the village there. He only wanted Wellington dead. He wanted to feed on Wellington's heart.

The storm brought an early night. Henry didn't look for a sheltered place. He simply stopped walking and sat down in the snow. Dark settled over him. Time passed.

His eyes snapped open. He realised he'd fallen asleep. The storm had ended. A half-moon had risen. The forest around him was bone-white snow and tar-black shadow, and the silence was stone solid.

He knew Wellington was near. A cracking of branches came from his left. His eyes swung towards a gap in the pines.

Henry was surprised. The silhouette that appeared was much larger than a man. He stood to meet his enemy. He reached to his belt for his knife but touched only matted hair. He looked down, surprised to find that his belt was gone; in fact, all his clothing was gone. His body no longer looked human. He'd become a hairy beast, massive as a bear. He felt empty inside, except for an icy ball where his heart should have been. He was ravenous, and he could not wait to rip out Wellington's heart and feast on it.

He opened his mouth to spit out a taunt. What came instead was an inhuman roar. It was answered in kind by Wellington, who was no longer Wellington but the Windigo, the mythic beast out of the horror stories of his childhood, a cannibal giant with a heart of ice. In the moonlight, they charged at each other.

They met like mountains colliding. Henry sank his teeth into the neck of the other and tasted icy blood. The bellow of the Windigo shook the snow from the trees.

They battled savagely. Hunger drove Henry to a frenzy, and at last he plunged his hand into the other's chest, grasped its heart in his claws, and ripped it out. The Windigo let fly a death cry that was as appetising to Henry as the heart on which he began to feed.

Henry stood over the lifeless form of the Windigo that had once been

Wellington. He lifted his face to the black sky and gave an angry howl. He'd thought that eating the man's heart would fill him, but it didn't. He was hungrier than ever.

HENRY WOKE to the smell of sage and cedar burning. He opened his eyes and found himself in a *wiigiwam,* wrapped in a bearskin. A few feet away a woman sat tending a small fire. She had long grey hair woven into a single thick braid that hung over the shoulder of the plaid wool shirt she wore. When Henry stirred, she looked up.

'Where am I?' Without thinking, he'd spoken in the language of his people.

'Some men from the village found you. They brought you here.'

'Are you Ojibwe?' Henry asked.

She shook her head. 'Odawa.'

The deerskin flap that hung across the doorway was drawn aside, and an old man entered. Bright sunlight slipped into the *wiigiwam.*

'Finally awake.' He sat next to Henry. 'Who are you?'

Henry said, 'Niibaa-waabii.' His Ojibwe name. It meant Sees At Night.

'I am Ziibi-aawi. This is my daughter, Maanaajii-ngamo. You have been sick a long time.'

'How long?'

'Seven days ago you were brought here. You were lucky the men stumbled onto you. They thought at first you were an old man gone out into the woods to die alone.'

'Old man?' Henry said.

Ziibi-aawi waved towards Henry's head. 'Your hair.'

Henry reached up and grasped a handful of the fine black hair he'd let grow long since he left the boarding school. When he looked at what he held, he didn't understand. His hand was full of strands white as spider's silk.

'My hair,' he said. 'It was black as crow feathers.'

Ziibi-aawi gazed at him with deep interest. 'What a thing it must have been that turned it white. It is a story I would like to hear.'

Henry told him about his battle with the Windigo. The old man listened, and his daughter, too.

'It was a vision,' the old man explained. 'The Windigo is a beast of the spirit. It feeds on hate, and it is never full. There is only one way to kill a

Windigo. You must become a Windigo too. But when the beast is dead, there is a danger that you will stay a Windigo forever. You must be fed something warm to melt the ice inside you.'

Henry looked towards Maanaajii-ngamo, who fed cleansing sage and cedar to the fire.

'I am Mide,' Ziibi-aawi said. 'Maanaajii-ngamo is also Mide. You know the Grand Medicine Society?'

Henry knew of it. Healers of the body and spirit.

'This is an important vision. You have had visions before?'

Henry thought about the dream in which he was flown north by a snake with wings to a lake where fire burned under the water.

'Yes,' he said.

'Kitchimanidoo has guided you here,' the old man said. 'You have been given the gift of visions. You are welcome to stay with us as long as you need in order to understand this gift.'

Henry felt as if he'd already travelled to the end of the earth, but he realised he still had a very long way to go.

'*Migwech*,' he said, and closed his eyes to rest.

PART III
The Lake of Fire

Seven

By the time Meloux finished his story, it was well after midnight. We sat beside the lake, and I could see Henry clearly in the bright moon glow. 'How long were you away for?' I asked.

'Almost ten years. I became one of the Midewiwin, too.'

'You never talked to the police about what Wellington had done?'

'I have never told anyone these things until now.'

'And you never tried to find Maria?'

'For half a moon I knew Maria. I loved her. I have never loved another woman. My life, Corcoran O'Connor, has been about something different from that kind of love. For many years, I did not think about her.'

'But you knew you had a son. How?'

'From visions. They began soon after Maria left me.' Meloux paused. 'And now visions have told me that my son needs me.'

'Henry, there's no way this man is going to talk to you. He tried to have you killed.'

'I do not believe my son would do that.'

'You can be exasperating, you know that, Henry?'

'Which is stronger,' the old man said, 'the rock or the water? In the end, the rock always washes away.'

'Stow it, Henry. You've won. I'll take you, OK?'

'*Migwech*,' the old man said.

'We both need rest, Henry. We'll leave in the morning.'

WHEN I PULLED onto Gooseberry Lane, I could see lights on inside my house. I parked in the driveway and went in through the side door. The house was quiet. I walked to the living room and found Jo asleep on the sofa. Jenny wasn't there.

'Jo.' I spoke softly.

Her eyes fluttered open. 'Cork?' She sat up. 'What time is it?'

'A little after one. Jenny gone to bed?'

She nodded. 'You said you'd be home so we could all talk.'

'Sorry. Henry had a lot to tell me.'

Despite her irritation, it was clear she was curious about Meloux's story. I told her a brief version.

'So all this might be about keeping an old crime from coming to light?' she said.

'It could be much larger than that. I've been thinking about the mining claim. From what I gathered on the Internet, the wealth of Northern Mining and Manufacturing is based on what came out of that first mine in northwestern Ontario. Could be that a lot of the wealth rightfully belongs to someone else.'

'What are you going to do?'

I wasn't looking forward to this part. With all that was going on with Jenny, I knew I needed to be home.

I said, 'In the morning, I'm taking Meloux to Thunder Bay.'

She weighed the information and nodded. 'Before you go, though, we need to sit down and talk with Jenny.'

'How's she doing?'

'Struggling. Trying to figure this thing out. It's huge.'

'Oh God, Jo, I don't want it to crush her.'

'She's strong, Cork.'

I got up and began to turn out the lights. When I'd switched off the last of them, I put my arm round Jo, and we started up the stairs to bed.

'Cork, I don't think you and Henry should go alone.'

'Don't worry. I plan on taking back-up.'

She didn't ask who. It may have been because she was too tired. It was more likely that she already knew.

EXCEPT FOR SUNDAYS, Johnny Papp opens the door of his Pinewood Broiler in the morning at six sharp.

At 5.50 a.m., I found Wally Schanno waiting out front in the cool blue of that summer morning. Those days he was always at the Broiler first thing, waiting for the doors to swing wide and offer him the company of the regulars. His back was to me. He was staring down Oak Street past the dark, locked shops as if he was waiting for something to arrive. For better or worse, I was it.

I startled him with a tap on his shoulder. He spun round.

'Sorry, Wally. I didn't mean to sneak up on you.'

'I was just thinking it's a pretty town. I'll miss it.'

'Miss it? You're leaving?'

His huge right hand went to rubbing the back of his neck. 'I tossed and turned most of last night. My daughter's been trying to convince me to move to Maryland to be closer to my grandkids. 'Bout three a.m., I decided she was right. Nothing for me here.'

Inside the Broiler, the lights went on. I saw Johnny Papp chalking the breakfast special on the blackboard behind the till.

'Not leaving right away, are you?' I asked.

Schanno picked up on something in my voice and squinted at me. 'What's up?'

'I'm taking Henry Meloux to Thunder Bay today. I could use your help, if you're willing.'

Johnny Papp unlocked the door and poked his head out. 'Get in here,' he ordered, 'before you scare the good customers away.'

I said to Schanno, 'Let me buy you a cup of coffee. I've got a story to tell.'

THE MOMENT I walked into the house, I smelled coffee brewing, and I saw that the dining-room table was set. Jo came from the kitchen with a small pitcher of half-and-half in her hand.

'Lane and Virginia are on their way over with Sean,' she said. 'We're going to talk.'

'At seven thirty in the morning?'

'Lane found out about everything late last night. He'd have come over then, but Virginia convinced him to wait.'

'What's with the table settings?'

'Virginia's bringing coffee cake. I've got juice and coffee.'

'Very civilised,' I said. 'Should I shave?'

'Just sit quietly and listen.'

Jenny came downstairs, her face drained of colour. She'd brushed her hair and put on a little make-up. She wore jeans and a powder-blue top.

'How're you doing, kiddo?' I asked.

'OK, Dad.' She stood away from me a bit and stuffed her hands in the back pockets of her Levi's. 'How's Henry Meloux?'

'I'm still working on that. Right now let's focus on you.' I went to her and took her in my arms. I laid my cheek against her hair.

'I'm sorry about all this,' she said.

'Me too. But we'll figure it out, OK?'

'You're not mad?'

'I'm not exactly ecstatic.' I pulled a chair from the table. 'Sit down and tell me what you're thinking.'

Jo had come back from the kitchen, and she sat down too.

Jenny began in a calm, rational voice, but before long she was crying, and it was clear she didn't know at all what she was going to do. When I was a cop, people cried in front of me all the time. It almost never bothered me. Jenny's tears were like drops of acid on my heart. She slid into her mother's arms and sobbed.

The doorbell rang. Oh, joy.

I opened the door. Lane Pflugleman was there, with Virginia and Sean at his back. I'm not tall—just under six feet—and Lane Pflugleman is a head shorter. He's slender, congenial, and he wears a moustache, mouse brown going grey. I've known him all my life.

'Come in,' I said, and stood aside.

Sean walked behind his father. He was a tall kid, taller than his father, lean and strong, with thick black hair and a handsome, studious face. It was easy to understand why Jenny had been drawn to him. As he passed, he avoided looking at me directly.

'I brought coffee cake,' Virginia said, and handed Jo a platter covered with aluminium foil.

Jenny had dried her tears, but it was obvious she'd been crying. She sat between Jo and me. Sean and his folks took places along the other side of the table.

'I apologise for the hour,' Lane said. 'I know it's early.'

'We were all up anyway,' I said.

Things went quiet while Jo brought coffee and juice from the kitchen. She sat down and cut and served the coffee cake in that awful stillness that often precedes uncomfortable discussions.

'I'm glad we're together this morning,' Jo began. 'Sean and Jenny have some difficult decisions ahead of them. The truth is, it's a tough situation for us all.' She looked at her daughter with great compassion. 'You know that Jenny had planned to leave for the University of Iowa in a couple of weeks.'

'Sean was supposed to go back to Macalester,' Virginia said.

'I'm not going.' Sean's voice was quiet but definite.

'What do you intend to do instead?' his father asked. 'Go to Paris? That's ridiculous, especially now.'

'Is it? People in Paris have babies, too.'

'Is that what you want, Jenny?' Jo said. 'To have this baby and take it to Paris?'

'I don't know,' she said.

'It seems to me the obvious choice here is marriage,' Lane said.

That was answered with silence all round the table.

'You can go back to Macalester as a married student,' Lane continued, 'finish up there, and come back here to a partnership in the pharmacy. From what I understand, you were thinking of asking Jenny to marry you anyhow.'

'That was for Paris,' Sean snapped. Then he seemed to realise how that sounded. 'I mean . . .' He looked cornered. 'I don't want to be a pharmacist, OK? I never wanted to be a pharmacist. I want to be a writer. I want to see the world. I don't want—'

'A baby holding you back,' Jenny finished for him.

'I didn't say that.'

'It's what you haven't been saying since I found out I was pregnant.' There wasn't any accusation in her words, just a kind of dull, sad truth.

He faced her across the table, his soulful eyes full of pain. 'Look, if you want to have this baby, I'll be there for you.'

'You're a liar, Sean.' She said it quietly, as tears rolled down her cheeks. 'For you, this baby will always be something that trapped you and killed your dreams.' She got up and rushed from the table.

'Jenny!' he called hopelessly after her.

The hinges on the screen door squealed, and the door slapped shut as Jenny left the house. Sean jumped up to follow her, but his father reached out to restrain him.

'Let her go. She doesn't want to talk to you right now.'

'What do you know?' Sean eyed us all. 'What do any of you know?' He turned and stomped his way out of the front door.

'I'd hoped that would go better,' Jo said.

Virginia laid a comforting hand on her husband's arm. 'He doesn't mean all that, Lane. He's just upset.'

Lane stared down at the coffee cake, untouched, on his plate. Then he lifted his face. 'I'm sorry,' he said to us.

I PICKED Meloux up first. He had an old gym bag full of clothes and a few things for overnight. I didn't know if Ernie Champoux had gone back to the old man's cabin or simply loaned Henry what he might need. Meloux sat up front. Walleye hopped in the back.

'Get some sleep, Henry?'

'I rested,' the old man said.

'Stevie's looking forward to taking care of Walleye again.'

'The boy needs a dog.'

'Don't go there, Henry. I've already been through this with Jo.'

We left Ernie's place, and Meloux stared out of the window as we drove down the shoreline of Iron Lake.

Schanno was waiting for us on his front porch. He had a black nylon carry-on. He also had a zippered vinyl rifle bag.

'I brought my Marlin and scope,' he said as I opened the tailgate. He put the rifle inside, next to mine. 'Are you carrying?'

'Brought my rifle, that's all. You can't take a handgun into Canada.' I watched him toss in his bag. 'You're not carrying, are you?'

'Of course not.'

Schanno opened the back door. 'Well, hey there, fella.' He ruffled Walleye's fur and slid in beside the dog. 'Morning, Henry. Walleye going with us?'

'We're dropping him off at my place. Stevie's going to take care of him for Henry.'

'Good. A boy needs a dog, Cork.'

Out of the corner of my eye, I caught Meloux's smile.

'Where's that dog of yours? Trixie?' I asked.

'Boarding her with a neighbour until I get back.'

Stevie was sitting on the sidewalk in front of the house. When he saw me coming down Gooseberry Lane, he jumped up. I pulled into the drive, and he ran to greet us. He opened the door in the back. Walleye popped out. Stevie hugged him and buried his face in the old dog's soft fur. Meloux and Schanno both gave me pointed looks.

Stevie and Walleye trotted off together towards the back yard. I backed out of the drive and then took us north towards Canada.

CANADIANS are sensible about firearms. They don't like them. So I understood the scrutiny the customs people put us through in order to get our rifles across their border. It was black-bear season in Ontario, however, and customs officials at the entry point north of the Pigeon River were used to hunters.

We hit the outskirts of Thunder Bay at half-past three. It was hot and humid, and a mean-looking bank of black clouds was bullying its way into the western sky. I drove to the marina where I'd met Morrissey and parked in the lot near the renovated train depot. We walked to a small observation area overlooking the bay.

'Where's the island?' Schanno asked.

I pointed beyond the breakwater towards the great ridge on the peninsula in the distance. 'It's nestled up against Sleeping Giant.'

'How do we get across the bay?'

'In a boat. One we rent, probably.'

I led them to the slip where Trinky Pollard docked her sailboat. The boat was tied up, but I didn't see Pollard on deck.

'Ahoy, Trinky!' I called.

'Ahoy?' Schanno said.

'I saw it in a movie.' I tried again: 'Trinky!'

We headed back towards the depot and the shops. As we approached, I heard a voice call out, 'O'Connor?'

Trinky Pollard stood in the doorway of the Waterfront Restaurant, the little bar and grill at the end of the complex.

'Trinky, it's a pleasure to see you again,' I said as we approached.

She shook my hand and eyed my companions.

'This is Wally Schanno and Henry Meloux, friends from back home. Guys, this is Trinky Pollard.'

'I was just having a beer inside,' she said. 'Care to join me?'

'We'll take a rain check on that, Trinky. Right now we're in the market to rent a boat.'

She raised an eyebrow. 'Another visit to Manitou Island?'

'Yeah.'

'No official invitation this time, I take it.'

'Not exactly.'

She stood in the doorway considering things.

'I think I know a boat with a captain who'd take you—if she had a better idea of what's going on,' she said.

I glanced at Schanno and Meloux.

Wally shrugged. 'If I'm going to be out on that lake, I'd just as soon be on a boat with someone who knows what she's doing.'

I turned back to Trinky Pollard. 'If you've got the boat, Captain, I've got the crew.'

WE SAT on the deck of her sailboat drinking cold Labatts from a cooler. I told her what had happened on my last visit to the island and what had happened since. Then I gave her the salient details of Meloux's connection to the recluse across the bay.

'And your part in this?' she asked Schanno.

'I'm here as a consultant.'

She laughed, an agreeable sound. 'Now there's a word that tells people absolutely nothing.'

'Wally was a cop, too,' I explained. 'County sheriff for a while before he retired.'

'Really? You look too young to be retired,' she said, which clearly pleased Schanno. 'You're here to watch Cork's back, I'll bet.'

'That I am.'

She glanced at me. 'Your wives, they're OK with this?'

'Jo understands.'

Schanno said, 'I'm a widower. My wife passed away six months ago.'

'I'm sorry.'

While we sat, the wind had risen and the bay had filled with whitecaps. Thunderheads were tumbling out of the west.

Trinky Pollard appraised the sky. 'If we're going to make it today, we need to cast off soon.'

I put my beer down. 'I wasn't thinking we'd sail in daylight.'

She nodded at the clouds pouring in from the west. 'Unless you want to wait until tomorrow night, we need to beat this storm. We'll anchor on the lee side of the island. It's not unusual for a sailboat to use Manitou as a windbreak.'

WE SWUNG ROUND Manitou Island from the south. Pollard ordered us to pull in the sails, and she kicked in the engine. She manoeuvred us to a place fifty yards offshore, in the lee of the island, headed us into the wind, and dropped anchor just as the heavy rain engulfed Manitou and then us. 'Nothing to do now but wait,' she said, tying off the wheel. 'Might as well go below.'

The cabin was small, with padded benches. We shed our life vests in order to fit inside. We sat down, except for Pollard, who threw open the ice chest and hauled out several Labatts. She tossed one to Schanno, one to me and held out one to Meloux, who declined with a wave of his hand.

'Any idea how long this storm will last?' I asked.

'The worst'll blow over pretty quick,' Pollard said. 'Once the leading edge is past, the wind should die down, and then it'll be just rain for a while. Last radio report I heard said it's supposed to go on till near midnight. Seems to me rain would provide decent cover for someone wanting to get onto Manitou without an invitation.'

'They have security on the landing,' I pointed out.

'The official landing,' she said, 'is the one where invited guests arrive. I've anchored us near an inlet on the other side of the island. On occasion I've observed motor launches coming and going, so I assume there's another landing back there somewhere.'

'You seem to have more than a passing interest in this place,' Schanno said.

'Retired RCMP investigator,' she replied. 'These days, I take my mysteries where I can find them. And there's a lot about Manitou that's never added up.'

The boat bucked like a restless pony. Pollard opened the door and eyed the sky. 'Dark'll come early because of the rain. Another hour maybe.'

'How do we get to the inlet?' Schanno asked.

'When the wind dies and the lake calms a bit, I'll see about taking the boat in,' Pollard said as she closed the door.

'Dogs patrol the island,' I said. 'Guard dogs.'

'You saw them?' She seemed surprised.

'I heard them. Didn't sound like animals I'd want to run into.'

Pollard said, 'I've never heard them except when I can tell from a docked boat that someone is visiting the island. Dogs are dogs. They like to bark, guests or no. They also like to run. I've sailed round this island dozens of times and I've never seen the dogs. So far as I know, nobody has.'

'You're saying what? That they're virtual guard dogs?'

'Cheap security.'

'I ran into the expensive kind,' I told her. 'Guys with guns.'

'How many?'

'There was Morrissey.' I thought about it. 'Then there was the guy who piloted the launch and the security guy at the dock.'

'Benning and Dougherty,' she said.

'You know them?'

'Everybody at the marina knows them. They bring the launch in two, three times a week. Did you see anybody else out there?'

'No.'

'Nor have I.'

'But you've seen Wellington, right?' Schanno said.

'Every so often around twilight, I catch a glimpse of him walking alone along the shoreline. He's like a ghost, all in white.'

SHORTLY BEFORE EIGHT, Pollard declared, 'Time to get ready.'

The heavy rain persisted and, along with it, a stiff wind that kept the lake churning. Pollard lifted one of the seats and, from the storage compartment beneath, hauled out a large canvas duffle bag.

'What's that?' Schanno said.

'An inflatable dinghy.'

'I thought you said you were going to take the sailboat in.'

'If the wind and the lake calmed. They haven't. I don't want to take a chance on running aground. The dinghy will be safer.'

'In these waves?' Schanno said.

'We're less than a hundred yards from shore. Once you're in the shelter of the inlet, it should be easy.'

On deck the wind pushed the rain into our faces. I could see the island, charcoal-coloured in the false twilight of the storm. While Schanno and Pollard inflated the dinghy with an electric pump, I went below decks and retrieved the knapsack I'd filled with items from my Bronco—a sheathed hunting knife, a couple of flashlights and binoculars. I slung the pack on my back. By the time I got up on deck, the dinghy was ready to go. We eased it over the side and tossed in the oars; then Pollard and I held on to ropes tied to the inflatable's bow and stern while Schanno climbed in. He grasped the railing and held on to the sailboat as we helped Meloux into the dinghy. Finally I slid over the side and settled in the bow. Pollard released her rope, and we shoved into a wind that was doing its best to drive us into the open lake. Schanno and I got the oars into the locks and began to row for all we were worth to Manitou Island.

We finally made the inlet. As soon as we rounded the tip of the peninsula, we escaped the waves and the worst of the wind.

'There's a dock,' I said.

'I see it,' Schanno said.

'How're you doing, Henry?' I asked.

He looked at me over his shoulder and smiled enormously. 'Corcoran O'Connor,' he replied, 'I have never been better.'

Unlike the more public landing on the other side of the island, the dock in the inlet had no security kiosk and no lighting. We tied up and climbed out of the dinghy. The lake water had been freezing cold, but the rain and the summer air felt warm against my skin. There was a trail of crushed rock leading into the trees. We could see the lights of the great house glimmering through the sway of branches. We walked carefully.

As we approached the clearing before the mansion, I took the binoculars from my knapsack. Lights were on inside, on both the first and second floors, but in different wings. Curtains blocked any view of the interior. On the far side of the clearing was what looked like a guesthouse. Lights were on there, too, but the shades were up and the curtains open. Through the windows of the guesthouse I saw movement. To someone, it was home. I studied the big windows of the mansion. As I watched, the light went out in one of the first-floor rooms, and a few moments later the curtain of another flared as the light behind it came on. A minute later, a light flipped on in another room. Upstairs, someone was pacing restlessly.

'The police were wrong,' I said. He's home.'

'What now?' Schanno asked.

'I want to get round to the other side,' I said, 'to see who's in the guesthouse. You stay here with Henry, OK?'

Schanno shook his head. 'Better if I do the reconnaissance and you stay with Henry. You've been inside Wellington's place. If you have to move quickly, you have a better idea of the layout.'

I handed him the binoculars.

Henry and I stood in the steady rain watching Schanno vanish among the shifting pines. Water dripped from the end of my nose. My clothes were soaked.

Schanno returned in less than fifteen minutes. 'Two men,' he said. 'One tall, blond; the other stocky, dark. Both mid-thirties.'

'Benning and Dougherty,' I said. 'What were they doing?'

'Watching television, eating popcorn.'

'See any surveillance monitors?'

'Nothing.'

I wiped rainwater from my eyes. 'For a man fanatical about his privacy, Wellington's awfully slack with security.'

'He's been hiding out here for six years,' Schanno said. 'Maybe at some point, rigorous security no longer became necessary.'

I shook my head.

'You don't like the feel of it?'

'Do you?'

'Why don't we get inside and ask the man himself? Got a plan for how to do that?'

As a matter of fact, I did.

SEVERAL RED MAPLES had been planted in the clearing long ago, probably to provide shade for the mansion. They were thick with summer leaves, and their wet branches flailed in the wind.

Schanno and Meloux followed me to the nearest tree.

'I need to cut a limb,' I said. 'Give me a boost, Wally.'

'Give you a boost?'

'You know.' I intertwined my fingers and made a stirrup.

'How about you do the boosting for me?' he suggested.

Meloux said, 'You could both lift me. A sparrow weighs more.'

'You sure you'd be OK climbing this tree, Henry?'

He looked at me as if I was a hopeless idiot. 'You treat me like thin ice that will break. I will not break, Corcoran O'Connor.'

'All right, Henry.' I took the sheathed knife from the knapsack and handed it to him. 'We need a branch strong enough to break a window. And it needs to look like the wind tore it loose.'

'I understand,' the old man said.

We stirruped our hands, Schanno and I, and lifted Meloux so that he could grasp the lower branches and pull himself into the maple. He spent a few minutes lost in the foliage; then a good stout branch, thick as my wrist, dropped to the ground.

'Will that do?' he called.

'Great, Henry. Come on down.'

We helped him from the tree. He handed me the knife. I put it in the knapsack and gave it to Schanno.

'You two get back to the cover of the pines,' I told them. 'I'll join you in a minute.'

They slipped out of the clearing, and I turned to the house. I knew the window I wanted: ground floor, above the patio at the back, out of sight of the guesthouse. I still couldn't believe there wouldn't be some sort of security system for the house itself. We'd see.

The patio was large and edged with a knee-high stone wall. I stepped over the wall and came at the window quickly with the end of the branch aimed at the centre of the frame. The glass shattered, and an alarm sounded inside. I left the branch stuck in the window among the shards of glass that jutted out from the frame, then leaped over the wall. As I hightailed it to the pines, floodlights kicked on, illuminating the outside of the house. From the direction of the guesthouse came the vicious barking of a pack of dogs.

I stood in the trees with Meloux and Schanno. I hoped the speculation about the virtual nature of the guard dogs was right.

In a couple of minutes Benning and Dougherty appeared, nosing round the house. Each held a handgun and a flashlight, whose feeble beams were consumed by the blaze of the floodlights. They were alone. No dogs. They found the offending branch and stood a few minutes in discussion. Benning looked around. His gaze settled on the nearest maple. He pointed towards it and said something to his partner. They studied the window some more. Finally Dougherty pulled the branch out of the window frame. Some of the remaining glass must have come with it because they both danced back. Dougherty stayed while Benning went back to the guesthouse.

After his partner had gone, Dougherty studied the patio under the window, crossed the wall, and walked to the maple tree. He shined his flashlight up among the branches, then dropped the beam and shot the light towards the woods. Schanno, Meloux and I each cosied up to the nearest tree trunk.

'Hey!' Benning called. 'Get back here—give me a hand with this window. I'm getting soaked, damn it.'

The light swung away. A few moments later I risked a peek. Dougherty was walking back to the patio, where Benning waited now with a roll of opaque sheet plastic, a red toolbox and an aluminium stepladder. The men spent a few minutes cutting a piece of the plastic and fitting it over the window. They used a staple gun to affix it to the frame. When they were finished, they gathered up their tools and hurried back towards the guesthouse.

Schanno, Meloux and I joined forces and waited a bit before approaching the house again.

A moment later, the floodlights died. The dogs fell silent. The dark and the quiet that followed were a great relief. Inside the house, the lights that had blazed on with the alarm shut off. On the first floor, the slow progression of lights resumed.

'Ready, Henry?' I said.

The old man nodded, and the three of us left the woods. On the patio, I took the knife from my knapsack and handed it to Henry.

'We're going to boost you up again, and I want you to cut the plastic over the window so we can get inside. When that's done, clear the glass that's still in the frame so we don't cut ourselves.'

We lifted Meloux, and he cut through the plastic, which began to flap in the wind. I looked up from where I provided one of the stirrups for his feet and saw him begin carefully to remove the fragments of glass remaining in the frame.

'It is done,' he said.

'Crawl inside, Henry. We'll join you,' I told him.

Schanno went next, with a little help from me. Once inside, he reached down and gave me a hand up.

We found ourselves in a small, dark study that smelled musty even with the air drafting in from outside. I went to the door and opened it. The hallway beyond was dimly lit at the far end. I signalled, and the others followed me. We crept towards the light, which turned out to be from the chandelier in the dining room. We turned left and went through a large room and entered the area with the stacks of newspapers. We followed the maze of corridors that ran through them until we reached the staircase, where we paused. Upstairs, a light blinked out in the hallway. We waited. Another came on, dimmer, farther away.

I started up. Schanno and Meloux came after me. I looked for security cameras but didn't see any. I listened for some sound—a cough, a grumble, the squeak of a floorboard as he paced—but the man was like a ghost.

Upstairs, I stepped carefully into the hallway and looked in the direction the hall lights had indicated Wellington was moving. The hallway was empty.

'He's been wandering round upstairs all evening,' Schanno whispered. 'Why don't we just slip into a room and wait for him to pass? Then we corner him before he can slip away.'

That sounded good. We went to the nearest door and slipped inside a large bedroom with a canopy four-poster. We closed the door, leaving it open just a crack, and waited.

The light at the end of the hallway went out. I leaned to the crack. The hallway was dark now. When the light directly outside the room came on, I opened the door. The hallway was deserted.

Meloux said, 'I do not understand.'

'A timer, Henry,' Schanno guessed. 'The lights go on and off automatically. It's a way of making it appear that someone is here when they really aren't.'

'My son is not here?' Meloux looked confused.

Schanno said, 'When you saw him before, where was he, Cork?'

I led them to the other end of the hallway, to the anteroom where I'd been given my mask; then I opened the door to Wellington's sanitised inner sanctum. The bedroom was still glaring white, but Wellington wasn't there. I opened one of the doors leading off the bedroom to a bathroom with a sunken tub, a shower and a pedestal sink, all tastefully done in white and sea green marble tiles with modern stainless-steel fixtures. There was a vanity as well, the mirror outlined with bright bulbs, the sort of thing I associated with wealthy women who spent a lot of time on their make-up.

Behind me, Schanno came into the bathroom. He looked around. 'Very nice. Anything interesting?'

'Check out the vanity.'

'Whoa,' Schanno said.

He was probably responding to the wig of long white hair draped over a wooden head-shaped stand on the vanity. I checked the drawers: make-up, theatrical stuff, gum spirit, liquid latex, a contact-lens case with brown-tinted lenses inside.

Meloux stood in the doorway. 'What does it mean?'

'I'm not entirely sure, Henry. Let's check the bedroom.'

In the closet hung several white robes, but also dress shirts and slacks. In a shoe rack were casual shoes and three pairs of athletic shoes. In the drawer of the nightstand was a wire-bound notebook. The notebook contained exchanges like those between characters in a play. I read a couple of pages. Behind the last page of the notebook was a flier, folded in half. I opened it and discovered an advertisement for a production at the Loghouse Theatre, a melodrama titled *The Nightcap,* written and directed by Preston Ellsworth and starring the same. The production ran from June 1 until August 31, at 8 p.m. every night except Monday.

Henry breathed deeply, a sigh of relief. 'It was not my son you saw here.'

'That's a good guess, Henry.'

'But why this pretending?'

'The question of the day.'

'What now?' Schanno asked.

I looked at my watch—a few minutes before nine.

'If we hurry, we might have a shot at catching Ellsworth before he leaves the Loghouse Theatre.'

Eight

Trinky Pollard used the engine to take us back. It was faster, she explained, than lifting the sails and tacking against the wind. The dinghy trailed behind at the end of its line. As we rode the black swells of the bay, I filled her in on what we'd discovered.

'A stand-in? Why? And why so eccentric?'

'If Ellsworth really is our man and we can get to him, maybe we'll have the answers.'

'In the meantime,' Pollard said, 'why don't you three go below and get out of the rain? I don't have dry clothes to offer, but I've got a bottle of Glenlivet in the cupboard. It'll brace you some.'

The lake surface was relatively smooth when we finally entered the marina and docked. We tied up and hauled in the dinghy.

'I'll deflate it later,' Pollard said. 'Let's get you to the Loghouse Theatre.'

'You know where it is?'

'In Thunder Bay, I know where everything is.'

'Lucky for us,' Schanno said, and gave her a goofy grin.

WE TOOK my Bronco. Pollard sat up front with me and navigated. The Loghouse Theatre was in the old Fort William section of town. It took us fifteen minutes to get there. When we arrived, the parking lot was almost empty.

'Too late?' Schanno said.

'Lights are still on in the lobby. Let's give it a try.'

The doors were locked, but we could see two kids inside, early twenties. The young man wore an old-fashioned white shirt with a black string tie. The young woman wore a calico dress and had long gold curls with a fringe. They were straightening up the lobby. I knocked on the glass of the front door.

The woman turned towards us and mouthed the word *closed*.

'Please,' I called. 'It's important.'

She unlocked and opened up the door. 'I'm sorry, folks,' she said. 'The performance is finished. We're done for the night.'

'We've come a long way,' I told her. 'We'd like to see Preston Ellsworth. Please. Could we at least get an autograph?'

'You want Preston Ellsworth's autograph?' She glanced at the young man, who studiously avoided looking at her. 'Well, OK, I'll tell him,' she said. 'Wait here.'

The kid who remained grabbed a sweeper and began to push it back and forth over the carpet. I turned away from the door where the young woman had gone. I wanted my back to Ellsworth when he walked in so I could see his face when he recognised me.

'Here we are,' said a cheery voice a minute later. 'I understand you've come a long way.'

It didn't sound like the same man who'd spoken to me at the mansion, but I supposed a good actor ought to be able to disguise his voice. I turned to him. He was fiftyish, with a thin, handsome face and pleasant grey eyes. He'd thrown on a tan sports coat over his white T-shirt, and he wore jeans. His face was still heavily made up for performance. He appeared fit, not at all like the sickly, mad man in the mansion. If he recognised me, he hid it well.

'Yes,' I said. 'From the States.'

'Gloria said you were fans. Is that right?'

'Of one performance in particular,' I said. 'I think you know which one, Mr Wellington.'

He looked puzzled. Then puzzlement morphed into confusion laced with a hint of annoyance. 'Look,' he said, 'is this a joke?'

'No joke. Although it might be a little funny if murder weren't involved.'

Hands on his hips. Perturbation now. 'What's this all about?'

The kid with the sweeper kept at his work, but he wasn't missing a word.

'Me, you've already met,' I said. 'We almost did battle over a pocket watch, on Manitou Island. These are my colleagues. Wally Schanno, former sheriff of Tamarack County, Minnesota. Trinky Pollard, formerly with the Royal Canadian Mounted Police. And this is Henry Meloux, the real father of the real Henry Wellington. As for what this is about, Mr Ellsworth, it's about the attempt made on Henry's life the day after I spoke with you in the Wellington mansion on Manitou Island.'

His brow furrowed. 'I have no relationship whatsoever with Henry Wellington. All I know about the man is what I read in the papers. Good night.' He turned away.

'Does this mean we don't get an autograph?' I said.

He slammed the door behind him.

'Is it him?' Schanno asked.

'I don't know, Wally. Either he's telling the truth, or he's a very good actor.'

The kid with the sweeper snorted.

Pollard turned his way. 'You know him?'

The kid watched her approach and thought about it. 'Oh yeah, I know him,' he said with a smirk.

'Was he lying?'

The kid leaned on the handle of his sweeper. 'What you just witnessed was a performance.'

'Thank you,' she said.

'Here's something else for you. He does seasonal melodrama for a living, but he drives a Ferrari. How do you figure that?'

'Yes,' Pollard agreed. 'How do you figure that? I think we'll go back and talk to Mr Ellsworth further.'

The kid shrugged—no big deal to him—and said, 'Through that doorway. His dressing room's on the right.'

The dressing-room door was unlocked, and we went in without knocking. Ellsworth was at his dressing table. He'd removed his sports coat. He was in the process of wiping cold cream off his face when he saw us in the mirror. He was clearly startled, then angry.

He swung towards us. 'What do you think you're doing here?'

'We came to get the truth from you,' I said.

'If you don't get out of here, I'm calling the police.'

'Fine,' Pollard said. 'And when you do, maybe you can explain to them how an actor in local theatre gets the kind of money it takes to buy a Ferrari. And if the police aren't interested, I have friends with the Canada Revenue Agency who'd love to follow up on that.'

'I pay my taxes.'

By that time, I'd had enough. I was on him in two long strides. I grabbed a handful of his T-shirt, bunched it at his throat, and shoved him against the back of his chair.

'That goon Morrissey followed me to Minnesota and tried to kill my friend Henry. You want that face to be in shape for the stage tomorrow, you'll answer my questions now. Who hired you?'

Ellsworth gave me no answer. I lifted him out of the chair and crunched him against the wall.

'Who hired you?'

'Wellington,' he said. 'Henry Wellington.'

I eased up a bit, let him off the wall. 'Tell me about it.'

'Six years ago. He called me to the island and laid out what he wanted.'

'Which was?'

'Somebody to be him. He offered me a deal I'd have been a fool to turn down.'

'His idea to be so eccentric?'

'More or less. He said he'd been compared to Howard Hughes all his life. No reason to stop now. He thought it would be a good way to keep people at a distance. So I studied Hughes.'

Meloux walked forward. 'What was he like?' he asked.

Ellsworth thought a moment. 'Rather cold. Unhappy.'

'Who pays you?' I asked.

'I get a monthly amount deposited into my bank account. A retainer. And for each performance, I get something additional.'

'Wellington's never on the island?'

'As far as I know, he hasn't set foot there in six years.'

'Where is he?'

'I haven't the foggiest.'

'You know his brother, Rupert?'

'I know who he is. I've never met him.'

'The money that's deposited, where does it come from?'

'On my bank statement, the notation reads Entertaintec, Inc.'

'Who contacted you for my performance?'

'I have a cellphone dedicated to gigs on Manitou. Whenever they want me, they call me on it.'

'Who's they?'

'I don't know. At first it was Wellington himself. That lasted a couple of years. Then it was a different voice.'

'No name?'

'No. And so no face to go with it, either.'

'What if you decide to contact your contact? Can you call him?'

'Yes. There's a number. I leave a message. I don't do it often. They don't like it.'

'If I had the number, I could have it traced,' Pollard said to me.

'Give it to her,' I told Ellsworth.

He went to his sports coat and took a pen from the inside pocket. He wrote the number on the back of a programme lying on the dressing table and handed the programme to Pollard.

'What can you tell me about Morrissey?' I said.

'Nothing. Look, I've told you everything I know. I've probably screwed myself good.'

'I think you can count on an end to the engagement,' Pollard said. 'When the police understand the nature of your involvement with the dead man, they'll want to talk to you, and as soon as they do, you're headline news, Mr Ellsworth.'

I thought it would hit him hard, facing the end of the luxurious ride he'd managed to get out of Wellington. But he brightened.

'Hey, I could get great publicity out of this. "The man who was Wellington." The media will love it.'

'I'll contact the police,' Pollard told him. 'Where can you be reached?'

He gave her his home address and phone number.

'Stay available,' she cautioned him.

'I'm all theirs,' he said, and opened his arms magnanimously.

WE HEADED BACK to the marina to take Pollard to her boat.

'What are you going to do now?' she asked along the way.

'Get rooms for the night,' I said.

'You're welcome to stay at my place,' she offered. 'I've got a guest room, a sofa, a cot.'

'We've already imposed enough,' I said.

'Nonsense. This is the most fun I've had since I retired.'

'Guys?' I said.

'I'm game,' Schanno replied.

Meloux said, '*Migwech.*'

Pollard said, 'Eh?'

'Ojibwe,' I told her. 'Means thank you.'

Instead of returning to the marina, we went directly to her little bungalow on a tree-shaded street northwest of the downtown district. I parked in the drive; we grabbed our bags and headed towards the front door. We climbed four steps up to a small, covered porch with a swing. When we stepped inside the house, everything looked simple, neat and clean.

'Nice woodwork,' Schanno noted.

'That's what sold me on the place,' she said. 'I'd be happy to make coffee. And I've probably got frozen pizza. I don't know about you guys, but I'm starved.'

She gave Meloux the guest room. From a hallway closet she pulled out a cot, which I set up in the living room. She brought in linen for it and for the sofa. Schanno offered to take the cot, but as big as he was, his feet would hang over the end, and I argued him out of it.

By the time we'd changed into dry clothing, Pollard had the coffee ready. She pulled the pizza from the oven, and we sat round her table, feeding our faces and talking about plans for the next day.

'We still haven't located Henry Wellington,' I said. 'I think we should talk to Rupert. He probably knows where his brother is. Or at least how to contact him.'

Meloux suddenly looked very tired.

Pollard saw it. 'We should all get some sleep,' she suggested, rising from her chair. 'Tomorrow'll be another busy day.'

I WOKE in the night. I wasn't sure if I'd heard something or dreamed it. I lifted my head from the pillow and saw that the front door stood ajar. Through the open window overlooking the front porch, I heard the gentle *scree* of the chains as the swing went slowly back and forth.

I was about to check it out when Schanno sat up and shifted himself so that he could look through the porch window, which was directly behind the sofa. He stared awhile as the swing kept up its quiet rhythm. He glanced my way, and I pretended to sleep. He slipped from the sofa and padded to the front door. After a minute, he pushed the screen door open and stepped outside.

The regular beat of the porch swing ceased. I heard their voices, hushed. I heard rain dripping from the eaves. I heard a car drive past, its tyres sighing on wet tarmac.

Then the swing began again.

Wally Schanno did not return to the sofa that night.

IN THE MORNING I found Schanno and Pollard in the kitchen. Crisp bacon lay on a plate on the table, eggs were frying in a pan on the stove, coffee was fresh and hot in the brew pot, and bread was ready to be dropped into the toaster. The rain had long ago ended, and the sun was rising in the sky. Pollard wore a white terry-cloth robe. Her feet were bare, her hair brushed, her eyes happy. Schanno had on a T-shirt, plaid sleep bottoms and a big grin.

'Morning, sleepyhead,' Pollard said. 'Coffee?'

'Thanks.'

'Sit down.' Schanno wielded a spatula, which he aimed at the small kitchen table.

I sat. Pollard poured coffee while Schanno tended the eggs.

'Hungry?' she asked.

'Give me a minute. But probably.'

'How's that toast coming, Trinky?'

'Going down,' she said.

Then she laughed, as if it was the funniest thing she'd heard in forever. Schanno laughed, too.

'You guys sleep OK?' I asked.

'Marvellously well,' Pollard said.

Marvellously was drawn out and affected, the way Tallulah Bankhead might have said it. They both laughed some more.

'Henry up yet?' I asked.

'Gone for a walk,' Schanno replied. 'He said he'd be back for breakfast.'

I heard the front door open, and at the same time the toast popped up. Meloux came in looking refreshed. He was beaming just as brightly as the other two. 'It is a good day,' Henry pronounced. 'On this day, I will see my son.'

Schanno lifted the coffee cup that sat near him on the counter. 'To this day,' he toasted.

Trinky Pollard did the same.

Despite the sunny morning and dispositions, I'd awakened with a sense of doom. Why, I didn't know. But I didn't want my concern to infect the others. I raised my cup. 'To this day, Henry.'

Over breakfast, we talked specifics. I proposed that Meloux and I go together to see Rupert Wellington. 'I've spoken with him before,' I said, 'so he knows me. Henry will tell his story, and we'll see what Wellington does.'

'What if he refuses to see you?' Schanno's elbows were on the table, and his coffee cup was lost in the grip of his big hands.

'When I trot out Preston Ellsworth's name, I'm betting he'll want to talk,' I said.

RUPERT WELLINGTON saw us immediately. He was standing in front of his glass-topped desk, which seemed like a postcard compared to the size of the window behind it that overlooked the bay. He got down to business the moment his secretary closed the door behind us. 'What do you want?'

'First, to introduce my friend here, Henry Meloux. Henry, Rupert Wellington.'

Wellington refused to offer his hand.

'What are you here for? Money?'

'No. I'd like to talk to your brother.'

'The whole point of hiring Preston Ellsworth was to keep people from bothering my brother. Look, Hank's a man who can have anything in this world, and all he wants is privacy, Mr O'Connor.'

'Who arranged for Morrissey to escort me to the island?'

'I don't know. I simply passed along your request to Hank. What goes on with Manitou Island is completely in his hands.'

'And you have no idea why your brother might want Henry Meloux dead?' I went on.

Wellington paused a moment, and understanding entered his eyes. 'You're the one who shot this Morrissey fellow.'

'He was going to shoot me,' Henry said simply.

I tried again. 'Do you know why your brother might want Henry dead?'

Wellington looked at me. 'That question presupposes that he does. Look, my brother's brilliant, Mr O'Connor. But when Roslyn died—that was his wife—he had a bit of a crack-up. It was a rough time for him. He wanted to step back from everything. He concocted this scheme, having an actor step in for him, to divert the eye of the media, and he slipped away to solitude.'

'Where is he?'

'I won't tell you that. It's Hank's decision.'

'You'll let him know I want to see him?'

'I'll do that.'

'One attempt was already made on Henry Meloux's life. I want answers before anybody else gets hurt. You still have my cellphone number?'

He looked pained. 'Yes.'

'Then I'll expect to hear from your brother.'

He looked at me, unhappy and probably angry and he looked at Meloux. We turned away and left his office.

In the elevator, Meloux said, 'That is a man at war.'

'With us?'

'It spills out at us, but it is something else, I think.'

'He's going to have his hands full when the truth of all this comes out. Northern Mining and Manufacturing will have to perform some pretty amazing magic to give any of it a good spin.'

Pollard and Schanno were drinking coffee in the porch swing when I pulled into the driveway. They looked comfortable together.

As we mounted the steps, Schanno asked, 'How'd it go?'

'Wellington promised to talk to his brother, but he couldn't guarantee anything. Hank Wellington makes his own decisions.'

'Hank?'

'What his brother called him.'

'I need a drink of water,' Meloux said, and went inside.

'How's he doing?' Trinky asked, her voice full of concern.

'OK, I guess. We learned a little more about his son.' I explained what Rupert had told me about his brother. 'What did you find out about the number Ellsworth gave you?'

'An answering service,' Pollard said. 'I'd need a court order to go any deeper. But I did find out that Entertaintec, which pays for Ellsworth's services, is a subsidiary of Larchmont Productions, which is owned by Henry Wellington.'

'All roads continue to lead to Rome,' I said.

'Wherever that is in Canada,' Schanno said. 'What now?'

'Nothing to do but wait,' I said.

We didn't have to wait long. In twenty minutes, my cellphone chirped. I answered and recognised the voice, the same one that, on my first visit to Thunder Bay, had given me the instructions that got me to Manitou Island. 'I'll see you, Mr O'Connor. Go to the marina, the south end of the parking lot,' Henry Wellington said. 'Mr Benning will be waiting for you. He'll bring you to me.'

'I'm not coming alone.'

'The old man, the one called Meloux? You'll bring him?'

'Yes. And a colleague. Wally Schanno.'

'All right. Leave immediately. It's a long trip.'

He hung up. The others looked at me.

'The great and powerful Oz will see us,' I said.

WE TOOK Trinky Pollard to the marina and let her off near the dock, where, she'd told us, her car was still parked.

She stood in the sunlight, blinking at us, clearly disappointed. 'Sure you won't let me go?'

I leaned out my window. 'He only agreed to Henry and Wally. I don't want to blow this chance.'

'He also tried to have Henry killed. You might need the back-up.'

'We'll be fine, Trinky,' I said.

She came round to Schanno's side. 'You'll be careful?'

'Always have been,' he said.

She kissed him on the cheek. 'When you get back, give me a call.'

'Promise.'

We headed towards the south end of the marina. In the rearview mirror, I watched her watching us. Then she turned towards her boat.

Benning was standing beside a black Ford Explorer, leaning against the driver's-side front door. He wore a T-shirt with the sleeves rolled up over impressive biceps. He had on a baseball cap and sunglasses. As we drove up, he looked our way. When I stopped, he pushed away from his vehicle and walked to my side of the Bronco.

'I have instructions to take you to Mr Wellington.'

'Lead the way.'

He nodded and turned back to the Explorer.

We followed him northwest out of Thunder Bay, keeping to Highway 17, part of the Trans-Canada Highway system. The highway cut through flat country with a lot of timber and not many towns. A little over two hours later, we came to Ignace and turned north. We stopped at a gas station with a small restaurant. Benning pulled up to a pump and signalled us to do the same.

'Last chance for gas for quite a while,' he said.

Meloux used the men's room while I filled the tank. Schanno went inside to get us some bottled water. Within ten minutes we were off again, following a hundred yards behind the Explorer.

In a while, Meloux was napping in the back seat. Schanno and I talked. 'You and Trinky seemed to hit it off,' I said.

Schanno thought about that, then nodded. 'Trinky's thinking of sailing up the Saint Lawrence to the Atlantic in a few weeks, then heading south to the Caribbean. Needs a good deck hand, she says.'

'You interested in the job?'

He swung his gaze my way. 'Is it too soon, you think?'

'Wally, I don't know that there's any blueprint for the affairs of the human heart.' I studied my side-view mirror.

He nodded. 'Funny, you know, that I've got a dog named Trixie. Almost like Trinky. I called her Trixie last night.'

'She hit you?'

'When I explained, she thought it was cute. Say, what's so interesting in that mirror of yours?'

'We're being followed.'

He craned his neck to look back. It took a minute before the vehicle behind us came into view as it rounded a curve.

Schanno unbuckled his seat belt and crawled into the back. He dug in his bag, then came back up front. He was holding a handgun and a box of cartridges.

'What the hell is that?' I said.

'A Colt Python.'

'You brought that over the border? We could have been arrested.'

'My dad always told me to hedge my bets.' He began feeding cartridges into the Colt, then put it in the glove box.

The vehicle trailing us—a dark green SUV—kept its distance.

'If Benning slows down and that SUV behind us speeds up, I'll probably be glad you have that Colt,' I said.

AFTER FIVE HOURS on the road, we came to the outskirts of a small town called Flame Lake. We passed through it quickly and followed Benning north, out of town.

A couple of miles farther on we came to a turnoff onto another road that curved along the shoreline of Flame Lake. A large sign was posted at the intersection: PRIVATE ROAD. NO TRESPASSING.

We took the turnoff and headed west on the private road. I tried to stay far enough back from the Explorer that we weren't eating the dust it kicked up. The cloud my Bronco left behind us kept me from seeing if the green SUV was still following.

After eight miles of this, the road ended. Benning pulled up before an expansive, two-storey log house built on the lakeshore. The logs were pine. There were green shutters on the windows. A small apron of grass separated the house from the surrounding trees. We parked behind Benning, who got out and walked to the Bronco.

'Wait here. I'll let Mr Wellington know you've arrived.' He left us, jogged up the steps to the front porch, and went in through the door.

Meloux slid from the Bronco and headed round the side of the house, towards the lake.

'Henry?' I called.

He didn't pay any attention. Schanno and I followed him. Meloux crossed the back yard and stood at the edge of the lake, staring across the water towards the ridges on the far side.

With his back to us, he said, 'I stood here and watched Maria swim. She was like an otter, sleek and beautiful.'

'Hey!'

We turned towards the house. Benning had come out onto the large rear deck. 'Inside,' he called. 'Mr Wellington is waiting.'

WE MOUNTED the steps of the back deck and trailed Benning into the house. It was furnished sparely, but what was there was beautifully made. Benning led us to a room at the southwest end of the house. It was full of books and sunlight and Henry Wellington.

He stood six feet at most, taut, slender. His hair was white and thick. For a man of seventy, he had skin that was remarkably smooth. His dark eyes regarded us calmly. He was dressed in white drawstring trousers and a loose shirt of white cotton. He wore sandals. He didn't offer to shake hands, but he did invite us to sit.

He said, 'You've come a long way to talk to me. I'm listening.'

'When I was a young man,' Meloux told him, 'I loved your mother, and she loved me.'

'My mother has been dead for more than sixty years.'

'You are wrong,' Meloux said. 'In you, I see that she lives still.'

Wellington studied the old Mide carefully. 'Tell me how you knew my mother.'

Meloux told his story. Wellington listened patiently.

When Meloux finished, Wellington said, 'I'm to believe that Leonard Wellington was not only not my father but he was also a man with murder in his heart?'

'That was one thing in his heart.'

'Do you have the watch?'

Meloux brought it out from his shirt pocket. Wellington crossed the room and took it from him. He walked to a window and looked at the photograph for a long time.

'This is the only proof you have?' he asked. 'I require more.'

He and Meloux locked eyes. For the next half minute, it was as if Schanno and I didn't exist.

'I will take you to Maurice's cabin,' Meloux said.

'Now?'

'Now.'

Wellington studied the sky outside the window. 'In four hours, it will be too dark to see.'

Meloux stood up. 'Then you had better keep up with me.'

Wellington smiled. 'Very well.'

He took a few minutes to change his clothes. Under Benning's watchful eye, Meloux, Schanno and I went out to my Bronco, where I put a few things into my day pack—a flashlight, three bottled waters, DEET bug repellent and my Swiss Army knife. For good measure, I took Schanno's loaded Colt from the glove box and slipped it in the pack.

'What do you think, Cork?' Schanno asked, coming round the Bronco as I shut the door. 'It's been seventy years since Henry was here. You really think he's going to be able to find his way?'

'I guess we'll see. By the way, your Colt Python is in the pack.'

'Good. I've been thinking about that SUV.'

I walked over to Meloux. 'You doing OK, Henry?'

'I'm near the end of the journey, Corcoran O'Connor.'

Wellington came from the house and spoke to Benning on the front porch; then he joined us. He'd dressed rugged: hiking boots, Levi's, a brown, long-sleeved shirt and a camouflage jungle hat. He also carried a small pack. I wondered how much our loads might resemble each other.

'After you, sir,' he said to Meloux with what seemed to be genuine respect.

Meloux crossed the yard, heading west, parallel to the lake. Where the grass met the pines, he spent a few minutes studying the ground; then he was off, leading the way.

He kept up a remarkably steady pace for a man who'd seemed ancient to me my whole life. We came to the grey, rocky slope of a long ridge, where the trail disappeared. Meloux put his hand on the stone. 'Over seventy winters, things change. Trees die; others grow. But rocks do not change so easy. The rocks, I remember. There,' he said, and pointed upwards. He began to climb up the ridge.

Soon we climbed out of the shadow of the ridge and into the sunlight of early evening. It was seven thirty. So far north, the sun would still be around for a while. Meloux led us down the other side, into shade again, and onto a trail that ran along a stream. Ten minutes later, we entered a clearing grown over with fireweed and lupine. On the far side stood an old log structure, five feet wide and twice as long. The roof had collapsed decades before, but the four walls were still solid. The smokehouse, I thought.

Meloux walked ahead slowly, parting the deep weed cover, peering carefully. Finally he stopped. He turned to his right and went a couple of dozen paces. Then he signalled for us to come.

As I neared him, I saw, deep in the tangle of undergrowth, the long black bones of burned timbers half buried in the earth.

'Dig here,' he instructed. 'It should not be deep.'

Schanno and I pulled the weeds, then got on our knees and began to dig with our hands. Three or four inches down, we hit solid wood. We scraped the dirt away, revealing rotted floorboards. Because I knew his story, I knew what Meloux expected to find, and we kept scraping at the dirt until we uncovered the thing.

'Here it is, Henry,' I said. I took the knife from my day pack and ran the blade along the slits that outlined the trap door. I poked until I located the hole where a strand of rope had once served as a handle, and I cleaned it out. I glanced up at Meloux.

'Open it,' he said.

I jabbed my index finger into the hole and lifted. The cool, earthy smell of trapped air escaped. The light in the clearing was waning, and the pit below the trap door was too dark to see into clearly.

'In the pack,' I said to Schanno. 'My flashlight.'

He dug it out and handed it over. I shot the beam through the opening of the trap door. The pit appeared to be a cube three feet wide and deep. It was filled with deerhide bags gone brittle with time, each as large as a softball. A quick count gave me a dozen.

I stood back. 'Care to take a look, Mr Wellington?'

I held the flashlight while he reached into the pit. The bag he grasped fell apart as he lifted it, and dull, yellow sand spilled out.

'I've never seen gold dust,' I said, 'but I imagine it looks pretty much like that, doesn't it?'

Wellington stood up. 'Put the trap door back.' He didn't look at Meloux, just turned and headed towards the trail along the stream.

I lowered the door back into place. Quiet as a congregation leaving a church, we abandoned the clearing.

WE DIDN'T make it back to the log home before nightfall. When we finally saw the lights of Wellington's place ahead of us, Wellington said, 'It's too late for you to return tonight. You're welcome to stay here. There are plenty of rooms upstairs. I asked Benning to prepare dinner. As soon as you're settled, we can eat.'

We brought our bags in from the Bronco, and Wellington himself showed us to our rooms.

'I'm going to wash up, and I'll see you downstairs,' he said. He went to his own room, which was at the far end of the hallway.

I shed my shirt. As I stood at the sink in my bathroom, washing off the dirt and sweat and DEET, Schanno knocked and came in.

'This guy Wellington is one cold fish,' he said. 'Meloux delivers all the evidence to back up his claims, and Wellington doesn't say a word to him. He's hard to figure.'

'I imagine it's a lot to absorb.'

'I'll take my Python back. There's still a lot we don't know, like why Morrissey went after Henry in the first place.'

'Suit yourself.' I took it from my pack and handed it over.

We left my room, and I knocked on Meloux's door but got no answer. I poked my head in the room. The old Mide lay on his bed, fully clothed. Not dead—I could tell from the slow rise and fall of his chest—but dead tired and dead to the world. I closed the door.

We found Wellington in the dining room, pouring mineral water into the glasses on the table. He'd changed back into his loose-fitting white clothing and sandals. A meat loaf sat on a platter in the middle of the table. There was a big bowl of fresh green beans, roasted red potatoes, a tossed salad, and a good-looking dark bread.

'I don't have beer,' Wellington said. 'I can offer you wine, however. I still keep some on hand for when my family visits.'

Schanno and I both settled for the water.

'And Mr Meloux?' Wellington asked.

'He's sleeping,' I said. 'It's been a long, hard day.'

We sat down to the meal, which was delicious.

'Benning usually does your cooking?' I asked.

'I live here alone most of the time, so generally I do my own.'

That was enough small talk. 'You employed Edward Morrissey, Mr Wellington, and Morrissey tried to murder Henry Meloux.'

Wellington dabbed his lips with his napkin. 'So I understand.'

'Why?'

'I really have no idea. Ed Morrissey worked for me on occasion, but he was what you might call a freelance security consultant. I arranged for him to oversee your visit to Manitou Island. After your visit, Morrissey phoned me. He indicated you were simply working a con, trying to squeeze some money out of me. He told me he'd taken care of the situation discreetly, as he had on other occasions in the past. I was surprised when Rupert called to tell me the police were investigating the incident in Minnesota.'

'Surprised but not troubled?'

'I didn't know Henry Meloux or his story.'

'Morrissey never reported that part to you?'

'No.'

'Why wouldn't he tell you everything?'

'That's a question for which I have no answer.'

'What about Rupert?'

He shook his head. 'Rupert's only part has been to pass along requests that seem to have merit. Those have been blessedly few.'

Benning came from the kitchen. 'Would you care for dessert?'

'Gentlemen?' Wellington asked. 'I have fresh strawberries.'

My stomach was full, so I said no. Schanno did the same.

'We're fine, Sandy,' Wellington said to Benning. 'It was a good meal. Why don't you call it a night? I'll clean up.'

'Very good, sir.' Benning vanished the way he'd come.

It felt as if the evening had been drawn to a close, but there were still many questions unanswered.

I WAS TIRED, but I tossed and turned in a restless sleep. I wasn't thinking only about Meloux, however. Jenny was heavy on my mind.

Sure, we would help her make a life for herself and her baby, but it wouldn't be the life we'd dreamed of for her or that she'd dreamed of for herself. That made me sad.

I slept off and on. Three a.m., I got up and went to check on Meloux. His room was empty. I slipped my trousers on and went downstairs. The house was dark, except for a light under the door of the study where, earlier that day, Wellington had greeted us. I listened at the door and heard the rustle of a page being turned. I considered knocking but decided against it. I didn't think Meloux would be reading.

I had another idea. I went out onto the rear deck where I could see the lake, a great pool of silver poured out from the moon. I also saw what I thought I might see—the silhouette of Meloux standing alone on the dock. I walked across the yard.

'Mind if I join you, Henry?'

His head half-turned. 'Your company is always welcome, Corcoran O'Connor,' he said.

I put my hands in my pockets and stared up at the stars the moonlight hadn't swallowed. 'I'm sorry, Henry. I hoped, I don't know, that Wellington would be the son you wanted.'

'How do you know he is not?'

'He hasn't been what I would call enthusiastic about seeing you.'

Meloux didn't reply.

'What do you want to do now?' I said.

'I want you to smoke with me,' he said.

He took a pouch from his shirt pocket and sprinkled a bit of tobacco to the four points of the compass, acknowledging the spirits that governed each; then he sprinkled some in the centre. We sat down on the dock. He took papers, and in the moonlight he expertly rolled a cigarette. He lit it with a wood match. For the next few minutes we smoked in silence.

I heard the deck door open and close. I saw Meloux cock his head slightly, as if he'd heard too, but he didn't turn. Half a minute later, I felt the dock shiver under an added weight.

'I have seen you,' Wellington said at our backs. 'In visions. I've had them all my life. I never understood them or understood why they came to me.'

Meloux spoke towards the lake. 'You are my son. You have a gift.'

'I isolated myself here years ago to try finally to understand that gift. It's been lonely and difficult. I was about to give up.'

'Perhaps that is why I'm here.'

'Mother never told me about you. She believed you were dead.'

'Why?'

'She came back with Leonard the next spring and went to Maurice's cabin. She found the remains of two bodies, which the scavengers had cleaned to mostly bone. She thought one was Maurice and the other was you.'

'She married Leonard Wellington.'

'That was part of the bargain she struck with him. When her father died, she agreed to marry Leonard and give him access to her father's money. In return, he promised not to tell the police about your part in the death. She had no idea what he'd done.'

'How do you know these things? Did she tell you?'

'She wrote them in her journals.'

Wellington walked to where we sat. He held out a book bound in soft leather. Meloux took it and opened it. I saw that it was written in thin, precise script that would be difficult to read by moonlight.

'There are more than a dozen like it,' Wellington said. 'She left them to me, in the care of her attorney, not to be read until I turned twenty-one. I was a fighter pilot in Korea when I turned twenty-one and had no interest in reading them. I didn't get round to it until after Leonard died.'

'He was a good father?' Meloux asked.

'We fought all the time. I could never please him. He was a man too absorbed in his own affairs. Finally I gave up trying. Poor Rupert, though, he worked so hard to be noticed. My brother was truly his son, and Leonard still treated him like a dog.'

In front of us, a small fish jumped, creating a circle of ripples.

'I used to come here with her, just the two of us, and she would tell me stories about an Ojibwe hunter, very brave and handsome and noble. She called him Niibaa-waabii. She said it meant Sees At Night. She died when I was ten. After that, whenever I felt alone, whenever I felt that Leonard was a dense, unfathomable fog, I would imagine that the hunter was my father and that he was pleased with me.'

Meloux said, 'I am pleased.'

He sat beside the old Mide. 'After all these years, why did you come looking for me now?'

'My heart told me it was time.' The old man went quiet again, then asked a question that must have been heavy on his mind for seventy years.

'Leonard Wellington said it was your mother who told him about Maurice. I never wanted to believe it.' He turned his head and looked to his son. 'Do you know the truth?'

'No,' Wellington said. 'I'm sorry.'

I stood up. 'I think I'll call it a night.'

I left them on the dock. Inside, I looked back through the clear glass of the sliding deck door, towards the lake. Against the reflection of moonlight off the water, the two men sat talking. It had taken seven decades for this to happen. I went up to bed and lay there thinking that sometimes stories did have happy endings.

The problem was that this story wasn't over.

Nine

I woke to Schanno pounding at my door. The sun was up, already high. A cool breeze lifted the curtains on the window. I figured I'd opened my eyes to a good day.

'We're waiting for you downstairs,' Schanno said when I swung the door wide. He was dressed in clean khakis and a white short-sleeved shirt with a button-down collar.

'We? Meloux's up, too?'

'He says he never went back to sleep after you left him with Wellington. He spent the night talking with his son, then reading Maria's journals.' Schanno's face held a look of affection. 'He's something, that guy. Wellington's brother is here, by the way, and Benning's fixing breakfast, so get your ass down there, son.'

I splashed my face with cold water, threw on some clothes, and joined the others downstairs. They were gathered on the rear deck, drinking coffee that smelled like it came from caffeine heaven.

'Mr Wellington,' I greeted Rupert. 'This is a surprise.'

'Mr O'Connor,' he responded cordially. He wore jeans, a light blue polo shirt and expensive Gore-Tex hiking boots.

Meloux sat next to his son.

'Sit down, Cork.' Henry Wellington indicated an empty chair. 'Would you like some coffee?' He poured me a cup from the white ceramic pot on the table. 'Breakfast should be ready soon.'

'You flew up?' I asked Rupert. I used my cup hand to wave towards the floatplane tethered to the dock.

'I did.'

Henry Wellington flicked a deerfly from the table. 'In his younger days, Rupert was quite a bush pilot.'

Rupert shrugged off the compliment. 'It didn't compare with being an honest-to-god war hero like Hank, but it had its moments.'

'Let's not get into any of that sibling stuff, all right?'

'Sibling?' Rupert's tone was one of mock surprise. 'We have different mothers. And according to your mother's journals, we have different fathers as well.'

'Come on, Rupert, we're brothers. We were raised that way.'

Rupert shot him an obviously angry look. 'You knew, what, forty years ago that my father wasn't your father? When exactly did you plan on telling me? A deathbed confession?'

Wellington took a deep breath. 'I didn't see any reason to tell you. What difference would it have made?'

'You always made decisions without talking to me. So tell me, since you've stepped back from any responsibility for the company, do I get to make the decision about what to do with the information Mr Meloux has offered us about Dad?'

'I think, at the very least, there's a lot of restitution to be made.'

'Restitution?' Rupert seemed genuinely surprised. 'To whom?'

'For starters, the families of the two men who died up there at the old cabin. And we need to check the documentation on mineral rights to be certain Leonard didn't actually jump a claim.'

'Ancient crimes, Hank. But, hell, it's easy for you to propose, considering that Leonard Wellington wasn't *your* father.'

'You're proposing what? That we go on as if nothing ever happened? Look, I understand this is going to be hard, but we don't have a choice. I mean, these men here, they know the truth. Even if I agreed with you, what would you propose to do about them?'

Rupert swung his eyes slyly across Schanno and me. 'It's my firm belief, gentlemen, that everyone has a price. Am I correct?'

Schanno broke the embarrassed silence that followed. 'You may know business, Mr Wellington, but you're no judge of men.'

Rupert settled his gaze on me. 'He speaks for you?'

'He took the words right out of my mouth,' I said.

'Very well.' He gave a little wave towards the house.

Benning stepped out, and he wasn't alone. Dougherty was with him. They carried a couple of high-calibre automatics.

'Dougherty?' Wellington said.

'He flew up with me,' Rupert said. 'I dropped him off on the other side of the point before I taxied here. He hiked in.'

Wellington addressed Benning and Dougherty. 'What's the idea with the weapons?'

'You'll have to ask the other Mr Wellington,' Benning replied.

'I'm asking you.'

'As their employer?' Rupert laughed. 'I bought these men from you a long time ago, Hank. Morrissey too. In fact, they haven't really worked for you since almost the beginning.'

Wellington again addressed the two men from Manitou Island. 'Is that true?'

Benning shrugged. 'He says shoot, we shoot. Nothing personal.'

Rupert laughed again.

'What's so funny?' Wellington asked.

'You thought all those years that you were protecting me from the truth. Hell, Hank, your mother wasn't the only one who kept a journal. My father started his as a way of recording his prospecting expeditions, but he ended up including just about everything in his life. After he died, I found them in his personal safe. All these years, I've actually known more than you because not only did I know he wasn't your father, I also knew about what happened at that cabin in the hills. Those journals your mother wrote? My father read them, or at least one of them. When Carlos Lima was in the hospital dying, Maria left the journal out and open. Leonard took a look, read about the Negro, and went back north where he did what he had to do to get what he wanted.'

I saw a look of relief cross Meloux's face. From his hospital bed, he'd told me Maria's beauty was a knife. Now he knew the truth.

'And so you sent Morrissey to take care of Meloux,' I said to Rupert Wellington.

'You can understand it's not a story I'd like people to know. It's not just that there are legal ramifications that could shake Northern Mining, but the entire legacy of my father would be sullied.' He drilled his brother with a sudden, angry look. 'You never cared for him, Hank. You made that clear. Me, I loved my old man.'

Henry Wellington shook his head. 'Enough to kill for him?'

'Love and money, Hank. What else is there of importance?'

I thought it was time for a desperation punch here. 'Other people know Meloux's story,' I said.

He dismissed it with a quick wave. 'The ramblings of an old man who had no proof. And who, by the way, won't be around to defend his claims.'

'How do you intend to work that?' Schanno asked.

'You, O'Connor and the Indian will just disappear. As for Hank, well, everyone knows how bizarre his behaviour has become. His suicide, when it's discovered, won't be a great surprise.'

'The police will look at you very hard,' I pointed out.

'At this very moment,' Rupert replied, 'I'm being seen at the wheel of my sailboat in Thunder Bay. I took a lesson from you, Hank, and found myself a man who impersonates me quite well.'

'I thought I knew you, Rupert,' Wellington said.

'You've always been too wrapped up in yourself to see anyone else clearly, Hank. I could live in your shadow. I've done it all my life. But I won't let you destroy my father.'

I'd calculated that I might be able to jump the deck rail and zigzag my way to the trees. If Benning and Dougherty were good with their weapons, they'd nail me before I was halfway there, but I figured if I didn't try something, we were all dead anyway.

Schanno beat me to it. He wrapped his enormous hands round the table and heaved it in the direction of Benning and Dougherty. Then he vaulted the rail and hit the ground running. He cut one way, then another, and the automatics opened up across the yard. I saw Schanno falter, and I knew he'd been hit.

Just as I tensed to launch myself at the two men, the pop of a rifle came from the woods beyond Schanno. The glass of the sliding deck door exploded. Benning and Dougherty dived inside the house towards safety. Rupert Wellington was right behind them.

The shots kept coming, chunking into the logs, shattering glass in the house. For a man of ninety-plus years, Meloux moved remarkably fast.

He was down the steps and hightailing it for the woods in the opposite direction Schanno had gone. Henry Wellington was at his heels. Me, I went after Schanno, who was crawling towards the cover of the pines.

Benning and Dougherty returned fire into the woods. That gave me the chance to grab Schanno, help him to his feet and both of us reached the cover of the woods. 'Where are you hit, Wally?'

'Leg,' he said, clutching his right thigh.

I took a look. The bullet had gone cleanly through his leg. I took my shirt off, tore it in half and made two compresses, one for each hole. I still had on the drab green T-shirt I'd put on underneath that morning. 'Hold those in place,' I told him.

I slipped my belt off and wrapped it round his leg so that it covered the compresses, then looped it in a knot to hold it.

'Don't move,' I said.

I worked my way north, away from the lake. The shots from Benning and Dougherty had become intermittent. The shots from the woods had ceased altogether. I wondered about that.

Thirty yards from where Schanno and I had taken cover, I spotted a booted foot sticking out from behind a fallen log. I approached carefully. What I found nearly broke my heart.

Trinky Pollard lay on a bed of brown pine needles, staring up at the canopy of branches high above us. Next to her was a carbine. The rifle butt was splashed with blood. The blood had come from a bullet hole torn through Trinky's fine, slender throat. I knelt and felt for a pulse, but I knew in my heart it was hopeless.

How she had managed to get there, I couldn't begin to guess. She'd paid an awful price for saving our lives.

Two rounds popped from the house and snipped off branches far to my right. They were firing wildly. That one of their rounds had found Trinky Pollard was pure blind luck on their part.

I grabbed Trinky's carbine. I aimed at the doorway of the deck and pulled off three rounds. I loped to Schanno and handed him the weapon. He frowned at the blood, still wet on the stock.

'Where'd you get this?' he asked.

'I'll tell you later. I want you to use it to keep them occupied.'

'What about you?'

'I'm going to get my rifle.'

Schanno propped himself against the trunk of a pine, aimed through the underbrush and fired.

I took off and circled towards the front of the house. At the edge of the yard I paused, eyeing the couple of hundred feet of open ground that lay between me and my Bronco. I finally committed to a mad dash, keeping the Bronco between me and the front porch. I pressed myself against the passenger side.

That's when I heard the front door of the house open. I ducked, but not before I saw Benning and Rupert Wellington step onto the porch. Wellington held a scoped rifle. I dropped to the ground and flattened myself on the the drive. I could see the bottom of the porch steps. I watched the feet of the two men descend and saw them separate. Benning dashed for the woods that hid Schanno. Wellington headed in the direction of his brother and Meloux.

After they left, I slipped into my Bronco and pulled my Winchester from its zippered bag. Quickly, I fed several rounds into the rifle and put a handful of cartridges in my pocket. I started for the woods, after Benning. At the back of the house, Dougherty and Schanno were still exchanging fire. Schanno thought he was keeping them busy. Dougherty knew the score better, knew that Schanno was about to be hit from the flank. I had to get to Benning fast.

I caught a glimpse of him creeping his way towards the lake. I saw him pause and study the ground. I realised he'd found Trinky's body. It confused him, delayed him and gave me an opportunity to get myself set. It wasn't a difficult shot, and I didn't hesitate to take it. My rifle cracked; Benning dropped like a boneless man. I ran to the spot. He'd fallen a few feet from Trinky, where he lay face down. I took his automatic, which turned out to be a 9mm SIG-Sauer with a full clip. I returned to the front of the house. Leaving my rifle at the door, I slipped inside with the SIG. From the back came the pop of Dougherty's automatic. I worked my way through the rooms and peered round a corner at the sliding deck door. Dougherty stood with his back to the wall. A couple of seconds later he swung through the glassless opening and pulled off a round in Schanno's direction. Before he could turn back, I put myself in a firing stance.

'Drop your weapon, Dougherty!' I shouted.

He spun round, bringing his own weapon round to fire.

He bucked forwards before either of us got off a shot, and he fell to the floor. A dark red stain bloomed low on the back of his shirt. Schanno, I thought.

Dougherty groaned. I crossed the room and took his weapon. I stuffed the SIG into my belt and retrieved my rifle.

Then I went hunting.

I ENTERED the woods where I'd seen Meloux and Henry Wellington disappear. Their trail was easy to follow, unsettlingly easy. Meloux and his son were blundering along like elephants.

I found the place where Rupert Wellington had picked up their tracks. His own were just as easy to follow.

I padded along as quickly and quietly as I could. I'd gone a quarter of a mile when I came to a little creek I remembered from the day before. Slipping into the trees was a flash of light blue. Rupert Wellington's polo shirt. He wasn't far ahead.

From my right came a low, birdlike whistle. There was Meloux, twenty yards away, with his son beside him, both of them eyeing me over a fallen log. I wove towards them through the underbrush.

'Henry, you were too easy to follow,' I whispered.

The old man actually gave me a sly wink. 'A trick the Ojibwe learned from the bear. Give the hunter an easy trail, then circle behind.' He stood up. 'We can go back now. Or'—he looked to his son for the decision—'we can become the hunters.'

Wellington turned to me. 'What's the situation at the house?'

'Benning and Dougherty have been taken care of. Wally's hit. He needs medical attention. And, Henry,' I said to Meloux, 'Trinky Pollard's dead. They killed her.'

Meloux's eyes were dark ice. His breath became fast and angry.

'If we go after Rupert,' Wellington said, 'we risk ourselves and your friend Schanno. What's the point? We should go back.'

FROM HIS HOUSE, Wellington called the provincial police station in the town of Flame Lake. Then he turned his attention to Dougherty, who'd lost a lot of blood but was still conscious.

Henry and I went to see about Schanno. He wasn't where I'd left him. We found him sitting propped against a pine tree next to the body of Trinky Pollard. He looked empty, his face pale.

'You need to lie down, Wally. You're going into shock. The wound,' I said, though I suspected it was more than that.

'I don't get it, Cork.' He stared at Trinky's body.

'She must have followed us, been watching our backs, Wally.'

Later, the police found her green SUV, the one that had tailed us from Thunder Bay, parked in the woods, not far away.

Meloux had seated himself between Trinky Pollard and Benning. He began to sing softly to help guide them onto the Path of Souls.

From far away came the cry of a siren, a sound as out of place in that quiet morning as all the death that had come before it.

SCHANNO AND DOUGHERTY were airlifted to the community medical centre in Ignace. Dougherty, devastated by Benning's death, talked to investigators and told them what he knew.

Trinky Pollard's body was taken to Thunder Bay. A stepbrother arranged for her memorial service, which was held a week later. Schanno and I drove up from Minnesota for it.

A couple of days after the shootings, Rupert Wellington walked into the police station in Flame Lake and turned himself in. The papers and television news were full of images of him, dirty, tired and hungry, trying to use his handcuffed hands to block his face from the cameras. Later, we would all learn that the sounds of the sirens had alerted him to the danger of returning to his brother's place, and he'd kept to the woods, hoping to figure a way out of the mess he'd gotten himself into. There wasn't any.

Meloux stayed in Canada. He spent ten days with his son and his grandchildren, who came from British Columbia and Toronto to be with him and their father. I had no doubt Meloux's heart was as light and healthy as it had ever been.

IMMEDIATELY after the shootings, I spent a night in Ignace making sure Schanno was OK in the hospital there. The next morning, I took off for home.

At a gas station in Grand Portage, just south of the border, I called Jo. I tried her office first, but Fran, her secretary, told me she wasn't going to be in all day. She wouldn't tell me why, and I didn't like the reservation in her voice. I called home. Jo picked up. I could tell something was wrong.

'It can wait until you get home. You've been through enough the last couple of days,' she said.

'Jo, what is it?'

She was quiet, then said, 'It's Jenny, Cork. She started bleeding last night. I took her to the hospital. She lost the baby.'

'Oh, God.' I leaned my forehead against the wall above the payphone. 'How is she?'

'A mess.'

'I'll be home as soon as I can. No more than three hours.'

'Don't push it, Cork. It's over. Just get home safely.'

I spent the rest of the drive railing at God, beating myself up for not being there for my daughter when she needed me.

I pulled into the drive in the late afternoon and parked in the shade of our elm. Stevie came running from the back yard with Walleye not far behind. My son was all bounce. Walleye ambled along with a kind of patient obedience. His tongue was hanging out, and I felt sorry for the old boy. Stevie had clearly worn him out.

'Dad!' Stevie cried. 'Watch this!' He turned to the dog. 'Come on, Walleye. Roll over, boy.' Stevie used his arms in an exaggerated roll-over gesture, but Walleye didn't get off his butt.

'We're still practising that one,' Stevie explained.

'Good work,' I said. 'Your mom inside?'

'Yeah.' Stevie's face clouded. 'She's with Jenny.'

Jo met me at the door. She gave me a long, heartfelt hug. She whispered, 'I'm glad you're back. I've been watching the news reports of what happened up there. It sounds awful.'

'I imagine what's happened here hasn't been easy either. Jenny upstairs?'

Jo nodded. 'She hasn't been out of her room since we came back from the hospital.'

'Does Sean know?'

'I called this morning. He wanted to come over right away, but I told him that wasn't a good idea. She needs some time.'

'OK if I go up and talk to her, you think?'

'She could use you right now.'

Jo went to the kitchen to make some coffee. I started up the stairs. My legs felt heavy.

I was thinking about all the things we leave behind us, or lose, or whose value we don't recognise until it's too late. Sean had been a part of something that could have been beautiful for him, if he'd let it be. The chance was gone. No matter how much he loved her, Jenny was beyond him now. A part of Jenny had been lost. Not just her baby, but also who she'd been.

I was thinking about me as well. Two days before, I'd killed a man, but it mattered so little to me compared with the question of what comfort I could be to Jenny. Somewhere along the way I'd left behind whatever it is in a human being that grieves when violence becomes the answer. If Benning stood before me again, I'd shoot him again.

I knocked, opened Jenny's door, and offered my precious daughter the only comfort I had: my arms to hold her as she wept against my chest.

Epilogue

On a Sunday morning near the end of August, after we'd all returned home from Mass, we stood outside the house, gathered round Jo's Camry, which was packed with boxes and suitcases containing all the things Jenny was taking with her to Iowa City. She and Jo were driving down together, a mother-daughter road trip. I was staying back to tend the home fires.

Anne and Jenny had already said their goodbyes. They'd been up most of the night talking in Jenny's room. Stevie suffered his big sister's parting hug. I kissed my daughter and told her how proud I was of her and that I knew she was going to set the world on fire.

'I'll just be happy if I don't flunk out, Dad.' She smiled. Like all her smiles those days, it seemed like a bird struggling to fly.

'There'll always be an apron for you at Sam's Place,' I said.

She got in the car quickly and stared straight ahead, waiting for her mother.

'Let me know you've arrived safely, OK?' I told Jo.

'You know I will.'

We waved goodbye as the Camry shot off down Gooseberry Lane, taking Jenny to a different life.

Anne and Stevie stood looking at the empty street.

'Wish Walleye was still here,' Stevie said sadly.

'Let's take a drive, too,' I said.

Ten minutes later, we pulled up at Schanno's house. He was standing in the front yard with Trixie yanking on a long leash.

Stevie had been quiet on the drive over, but when he saw the dog, he brightened and ran towards it. Trixie jumped all over him. Annie joined them while I spoke with Schanno.

'You're sure about this, Wally?'

'I'm sure. Hell, an old man shouldn't have a young dog. Besides, every time I call her name, I think of Trinky.' Using a cane, he walked to a redwood bench in his yard and sat down. 'Realtor says the house'll move fast. My daughter's looking for something for me near her in Maryland. Condo, town house, something like that.'

'Mind's made up, huh?'

'I'm tired, Cork.' He nodded towards the kids. 'Told 'em?'

'Not yet.'

'Don't you think it's time?'

'Hey, guys,' I called. 'I've got a surprise. Trixie's coming home with us.'

'We're taking care of her for Mr Schanno?' Stevie said eagerly.

'We're taking care of her for good. She's ours now.'

'Really? I love her, Dad. I love you, Trixie.' Stevie put his face to hers, and she licked him like a lollipop.

The biggest word in the human vocabulary has only four letters and no definition that's ever been adequate. We love our dogs. We love our children. We love God and chocolate cake. We fall in love and fall out of love. We die for love, and we kill for love. We can't spend it. We can't eat it when we're starving or drink it when we're dying of thirst. But ask most human beings what they value above all else in this life, and five'll get you ten, it's love.

We're a screwy species, I thought, as I watched my son and daughter roll in the grass with the puppy slobbering all over them.

'Dad,' they squealed happily, 'help us!'

And I did my best.

WILLIAM KENT KRUEGER

Born: Wyoming, November 16, 1950
Favourite book: *To Kill a Mockingbird*
Website: www.williamkentkrueger.com

RD: Native American culture is a strong theme in your Cork O'Connor novels. What do you find most interesting or inspiring about it?

WKK: I admire tremendously the courage of the Ojibwe. In the face of great hardship, they have endured. They have not lost their language, their traditions, or their sense of humour. I have a number of contacts and acquaintances within the Ojibwe community and they are amazingly generous with their time and their knowledge.

RD: And how did the main character come by his name?

WKK: Before I knew anything else about the books, I knew the protagonist would be named Cork. I imagined a character so resilient that no matter how far life pushed him down, he would always bob back to the surface.

RD: Did you have to do a great deal of research for this book?

WKK: I wouldn't say a lot. At its heart, *Thunder Bay* is a love story and that's something I've been researching all my life.

RD: Your childhood was a little unconventional in that you moved around a lot. Why was that, and what is your clearest memory of those times?

WKK: For a long time, my father worked for a large oil company and was often transferred. Rather than thinking of these moves as disruption or hardship, my family always saw them as adventure. What I remember most is our eager anticipation of a new place.

RD: You met your wife Diane quite early in life and are still happily married to her thirty years later. How did you know she was 'the one'?

WKK: I don't think anyone ever 'knows'. And love changes across thirty years. Like a garden gone wild, it grows dense and tangled and spreads far beyond its proper borders. If you're lucky—and I am—the tendrils of love invade every nook and cranny of your life and one day you realise that the beautiful wild garden has swallowed you up.

RD: You were expelled as a student for taking a stand against what you saw as the university's complicity in producing weapons for the Vietnam War. Are you still politically active?

WKK: These days I'm more spiritual in my approach to the turmoil of the world. I pray. I volunteer. On occasion, I still march. More and more, however, I simply tend my garden.

RD: You did a lot of jobs before becoming a writer. Which did you enjoy least?

WKK: When I was a young man, I spent some time logging timber in the Rockies. One day, as I ate lunch alongside my brother, we stared across a mountainside we'd helped clear of trees. It was a devastating sight. We quit then and there and walked twenty miles down off that mountain. It was one of the best days of my life.

RD: You've said that the act of creation is more important to you than the acclaim of being a published writer—what did you mean by that?

WKK: Commitment, discipline, creative accomplishment, joy in your work: these are within every writer's grasp. Acclaim is something over which no writer has control, so I do my best to let go of that concern.

RD: What advice do you have for aspiring writers?

WKK: Write because it's what you love to do, because it gives you energy, because when you've created something that pleases you, the whole day is better. If you do this, good things will come of it, I promise.

RD: Do you have a favourite quotation from your character, Henry Meloux?

WKK: 'Every falling leaf comes to rest where it was always meant to be.'

A CONNECTION TO THE PAST

The Ojibwe, the Native American tribe to which the character Henry Meloux belongs, is one of the largest in the USA, surpassed in size only by the Cherokee and Navajo. Some 170,000 Ojibwe live on reservations across North America and southern Canada, each with its own government, laws, police and public-services. Nowadays, most Ojibwe lead a modern lifestyle, but they still keep alive the traditions of their ancestors and adhere to a fundamental belief in the absolute unity of all things, including that of land and people. Pow-wows (right), provide an opportunity for Ojibwe and non-Ojibwe to meet, dance, sing and socialise.